Harry drew back the rubber sheet from the dead girl's face, closed his eyes and rocked back on his heels. She had been sweet and young and innocent—and she had been tormented. And she still was. Her eyes were closed now, but Harry knew that if they were open he'd read terror in them. He could feel those dead eyes burning through the pale lids that covered them, crying out in horror.

Harry sighed. He would comfort her. He was the only one who could. He was the Necroscope.

Praise for the Necroscope series

"[The] lively mix of action and monstrosity transmutes the basic cliché of the vampire and turns it into a wonderfully contemporary bane."

—*Fear*

"Lumley employs a master's touch of plot and character development."

—*OtherRealms*

NECROSCOPE V:
DEADSPAWN

Brian Lumley

TOR
HORROR

A TOM DOHERTY ASSOCIATES BOOK
NEW YORK

NECROSCOPE V: DEADSPAWN

Cover art by Bob Eggleton

A Tor Book
Published by Tom Doherty Associates, LLC
175 Fifth Avenue
New York, NY 10010

Tor Books on the World Wide Web:
http://www.tor.com

Tor® is a registered trademark of Tom Doherty Associates, LLC

ISBN: 0-812-50835-1

First edition: October 1991

Printed in the United States of America

0 9 8 7 6

For Melissa, Anna, and
Eleanor: they wined and dined me on many
an *exotique*, their sweet mouths conjuring strange
and obscene topics to disgust (and maybe titillate?)
my mind. Until at last—too late—I wondered:
"What are four totally monstrous creatures
like these doing in a nice Chinese
restaurant like this?"

Résumé

HARRY KEOGH INHERITED THE PSYCHIC SKILLS OF HIS mother and grandmother, which in him have evolved to unparalleled heights of parapsychological power. He is a Necroscope: he talks to the dead like other men talk to their friends and neighbors. And indeed the teeming dead are Harry's friends, for he is the one light in their eternal darkness, their only contact with the world they have left behind.

For the common perception of death is incorrect: the minds of the dead do not accompany their bodies into corruption and dust but go on to explore the myriad possibilities of their leanings which were unattainable in life. The writers continue to "write" great works that can never be published; the architects design fabulous, near-perfect cities which will never be built; the mathematicians explore pure number to exponentials whose only boundary is infinity.

As a boy Harry utilized his esoteric "talent" to help

with his studies; since he himself did not appear academically inclined, certain of his deceased specialist friends were able to show him the shortcuts around otherwise impossible classroom problems. As a result of which he discovered his own affinity for instinctive or intuitive math.

Harry Keogh was not the only one who "talked" to the dead. In the USSR the Soviet E-Branch (ESP-Branch) made use of Boris Dragosani, a necromancer, to *tear* the secrets of corpses from their violated bodies. But where Harry was beloved of the Great Majority, they feared and loathed Dragosani. The difference was this:

That where the Necroscope merely conversed with the dead, befriending and consoling them, and asking nothing in return, the Russian necromancer simply reached in and *took!* Having been instructed in his obscene talent by a long-buried but still undead vampire, whose seed had been passed on to him, nothing could be hidden from Dragosani: he would find his answers in the blood, the guts, the very marrow of his victims' bones. In all other instances the dead can't feel pain—but that was part of Dragosani's talent, too. For when he worked he *made* them feel it! They felt his hands, his knives, his tearing nails; they knew and felt everything he did to them! It was never his way to simply question the dead for their secrets, for then they might lie to him. No, his way was to rend them apart and then read the answers in torn skin and muscle, in shredded ligaments and tendons, in brain fluid and the mucus of eye and ear, and in the very texture of the dead tissue itself!

. . . While avenging the cruel death of his murdered mother, Harry Keogh became aware of the existence of the ESP-agencies of East and West. Recruited to the aid of British ESP-Intelligence in the secret war with Russia's mindspies, he pitted himself against Boris Dragosani. And now his intuitive math came into play.

With the assistance of August Ferdinand Möbius (1790-1868) Harry gained access to the Möbius Continuum, a fifth dimension running parallel not only to the mundane four but to all other material planes. He could now in effect "teleport" instantly to anywhere in the world, just as long as he had the mathematical coordinates or a dead friend in that location to act as a beacon. In addition, he had discovered his terrible power to call up the dead from their graves!

To rid the world of the vampire Dragosani, Harry used the Möbius Continuum to invade the Chateau Bronnitsy, Russia's secluded E-Branch HQ. There he called up from death an army of mummified Tartars whose bodies had been preserved by the peaty ground. Dragosani was destroyed, and along with him many of the staff and much of the apparatus of the Soviet mindspy agency.

But Harry paid the price, too, and his *body* was also destroyed. Except . . .

. . . As the Necroscope knew well enough from personal experience, death is not the end.

Incorporeal, pure mind, he escaped the Möbius Continuum and later, by involuntary metempsychosis, came to "inhabit" the brain-dead body of a British esper. By then, however, Harry had also come to realize the role he must play in the eradication of vampire spawn from the world of men. This recognition of his purpose (his destiny?) came about through the discovery of a vampire's scarlet thread among the pure blue life-threads of humanity where they permeate the past and future time-lanes of the Möbius Continuum.

Yulian Bodescu, contaminated with vampirism by Thibor Ferenczy—the same centuries-dead vampire who infected Dragosani—threatened both Harry's life and the life of his baby son. But this time it was Harry Jr. who turned the tables and made possible Bodescu's destruction; for he too was born a Necroscope, with the same (or greater?) talents as those possessed by his father.

Following the Bodescu affair, Harry Jr. vanished (apparently from the face of the Earth) and took his poor demented mother with him. Harry Sr., searching far and wide for his wife and infant son, despaired of ever finding them; in the Möbius Continuum their life-threads disappeared mysteriously into some otherworldly place where even he could not follow.

Harry quit British E-Branch and devoted himself to his search, which soon became an obsession. Years passed and the Necroscope turned recluse, living in a rambling, ramshackle house some miles outside Edinburgh.

Then . . . E-Branch contacted him again. They were badly in need of Harry's help and guessed he'd be reluctant, but there was also a carrot. The Branch had a similar case on its hands: a Secret Service agent had gone missing, *not* presumed dead. Just like Harry Jr. and his mother, so now a young spy had disappeared into thin air. The mindspies had reason to believe he was alive, but still they couldn't find him. Harry checked it out with the Great Majority, who denied that the missing man had joined their ranks. And yet E-Branch swore that he wasn't "here" on Earth. So . . . where was he?

Could it be he was in the same place as the Necroscope's wife and child?

Eventually, Harry's inquiries led him to the Perchorsk Projekt, a Russian experiment buried deep in a ravine under the Ural Mountains. In an attempt to create a force-field barrier as a counter to the USA's Star Wars scenario, the Soviets had accidentally blasted a "wormhole" out of this space-time dimension into a parallel plane of existence. And in so doing they had also discovered the ancient source of all vampiric infestation of Earth! *Things* were coming through the Perchorsk Gate into our world. Unbelievable thing—except to the Necroscope and certain members of the British and Soviet E-Branches.

Through his contacts with the dead, and especially with the assistance of August Ferdinand Möbius, Harry discovered a second Gate and used it to venture into the world of the Wamphyri, whose skyscraper aeries gloomed gaunt and nightmarish over all Starside, where the vampire Lords held sway. There he discovered his son, grown now to a young man—but alas, infected with vampirism!

Known as The Dweller in this weird parallel world, Harry Jr. had so far managed to hold his vampire metamorphosis in check; he commanded a small band of Travellers (the original Gypsies) and a regiment of "trogs," the aboriginal men of Starside. But his enemies were monstrous and far outnumbered him. Only his "magic"—his mastery of the Möbius Continuum, and of superior science—had so far kept him safe. But under the guidance of the great and sinister Lord Shaithis, the warlike Wamphyri had recently put aside all personal grievances and banded together into an awesome, alien army. Jealous of The Dweller, his garden and works, they would move in unison against him.

The two Harrys must stand alone against this force of monsters, else total Wamphyri domination of Star- and Sunside become a grim and horrific reality. But they did not stand *entirely* alone; in the bloody battle for the The Dweller's garden, the Lady Karen joined sides with them. A vampire, indeed Wamphyri, Karen was beautiful as she was clever. She could read the minds of the vampire Lords and forecast their every move. Still Shaithis and his fellow Lords, their lieutenants, and all the vast and

terrible warrior creatures they had created from the flesh
of men and trogs alike must surely win the battle . . . if
not for the awesome powers of the Necroscope and his
son.

Using the raw light of the sun itself, the garden's defenders defeated Shaithis' vampire army, and went on to
level the towering stacks of stone and bone which were
the aeries of the Wamphyri. All except Karen's, who had
been their ally . . .

Afterwards, Harry Keogh visited Karen in the grimly
foreboding aerie which was her place. She was not long
a vampire; the *thing* within her had not yet gained full
ascendancy; if the Necroscope could drive out her vampire and destroy it . . . perhaps there was yet a chance
for Harry Jr.

Harry's method was crude, cruel, even brutal—but
hideously effective. Except . . . how could he have fore-
seen the consequences? Karen had been Wamphyri! And
now? Without her vampire she was nothing but a pretty,
empty girl. Where was her *power*, her *freedom*, her raw,
unfettered Wamphyri *spirit* now? Gone.

And when Harry awoke from his exhaustion, gone too
Karen!

From on high he saw her body wrapped in the white
sheath she wore for a gown, bloody and broken on the
flanks of her aerie, where she had thrown herself down
from the uppermost levels.

The Dweller saw what his father had done, and knew
why. If Harry Sr. had found a cure for Karen, he might
well have applied the principle to Harry Jr., too. Fearing
that one day his father might return to Starside with just
such a ''cure,'' The Dweller used his superior vampire
powers to reduce Harry's skills to nothing. He took away

his deadspeak (his ability to talk to the dead) and also his numeracy. And then he returned Harry Keogh, ex-Necroscope, to his own world, the world of men . . .

Forbidden to speak to the dead—a rule he must obey else suffer terrible mental and physical agony—and denied the use of the Möbius Continuum as a result of his innumeracy, Harry Keogh was as close as he had ever been to being a "normal" man. Which, after what he had known, equated almost to a prefrontal lobotomy. He had been the Necroscope and was now powerless.

But incapable of *conscious* communication with the teeming dead, still they could speak to him in his dreams. And their message was monstrous. Another Great Vampire had come to stalk the world!

Harry had dedicated himself to the eradication of vampirism; but what could he, ex-Necroscope, do now? As the world's foremost expert on vampires, he could at least advise. He *must* do something, for unless he and E-Branch found the vampire first, then sooner or later the undead monster would surely find him! For Harry had grown into a legend: he was the vampire slayer, and locked in his "crippled" mind were all the secrets of the Great Majority and mathematical formulae governing the Möbius Continuum itself. If the born-again monster should use its necromancy to steal his forbidden metaphysical talents . . . the result would be unthinkable!

The dead, forbidden to talk to Harry except in his dreams, rallied to him. They used other methods to get their messages across: to tell him that a vampire was at work in the islands of the Aegean. Once more in league with E-Branch, Harry Keogh and the girl who loved him went out to the Mediterranean to see what could be done.

But two British espers had already been vampirized and their esoteric talents added to those of Janos Ferenczy, the

7

bloodson of Faethor and "brother" to Thibor, the old Thing In The Ground. Janos was back to reclaim his territories and dig up again certain antique treasure-hoards which he himself had long ago buried as a safeguard against the changes which centuries of immobility in undeath would bring, treasures which would lie lost in the earth until his planned "resurrection." These preparations had been made back in the fifteenth century, when Janos had known that his powerful vampire father, Faethor, was returning again to Wallachia after almost three hundred years of blood-thirsty adventuring with the Crusaders, then with Genghis Khan, and finally with the Moslems. For Faethor hated Janos and would try to "kill" him (as he had already put down his brother, Thibor, undead into the earth), for which reason Janos had made these provisions against an uncertain future.

When Harry saw what he was up against with Janos, and after the vampire had taken Harry's woman for his own, he knew he must somehow regain his deadspeak and his command over the mysterious Möbius Continuum. Without these powers . . . he just wouldn't stand a chance.

The ghost of Faethor Ferenczy, whose place was the crumbling, deserted, overgrown ruins of a house close to Ploiesti in Romania, contacted Harry and offered to help. The damage done to Harry's mind was the work of The Dweller, Harry Jr., a vampire with hugely enhanced mentalist powers. If Harry would now allow Faethor's spirit into his mind, perhaps that "father" of vampires would remove the blockage and unlock the closed-off regions. Harry did not like the idea (to allow a vampire, *this* vampire, into his mind?) and knew it was an experiment fraught with the most terrifying dangers, but beggars can't be choosers.

As to why Faethor should want to help: he could not bear the thought of his bloodson, Janos, up and about in the world while he was nothing but a fading memory, shunned even by the dead. He wanted Janos put down again, indeed desired to be the instrument of that termination. And Harry Keogh was the only one who could do it. At least, this was the explanation which Faethor offered to Harry . . .

In Romania, Harry slept overnight in the ruins of Faethor's last refuge, and while he slept the father of vampires entered his mind and reopened certain mental "doors" which Harry Jr. had closed there. Waking up, Harry discovered his deadspeak returned to him. Now he could contact the long-dead mathematician Möbius and have *him* enter his mind, hopefully to give him back his numeracy and mastery of the so-called Möbius Continuum. But Faethor had lied; once inside Harry's mind the vampire would not leave it; the Necroscope now had an unwelcome tenant.

Finally, at Janos' castle in the Zarandului Mountains of Transylvania, Harry recovered his powers in full, returned Janos to dust, and committed the spirit of Faethor to an eternity of emptiness and utter loneliness in the infinite future time-streams of the Möbius Continuum.

But his victory was not without cost.

Strange urges are part of Harry now, and stranger hungers. His life-thread unwinds as before into the unending future of Möbius time. Except . . . where once that life-thread was pure blue, as are the threads of all entirely human beings, now it is tinged with red!

Part One

I Charnel Knowledge

"HARRY." DARCY CLARKE'S VOICE WAS TWITCHY ON the phone, but he was trying hard to contain it. "There's a problem we could use some help with. Your kind of help."

Harry Keogh, Necroscope, might or might not know what was bothering the head of British E-Branch, and it might or might not have to do with him directly. "What is it, Darcy?" he said, speaking softly.

"It's murder," the other answered, and now his twitchiness came on strong, shaking his voice. "It's bloody awful murder, Harry! My God, I never saw anything like it!"

Darcy Clarke had seen a lot in his time and Harry Keogh knew it, so that this was a statement he found hard to believe. Unless of course Clarke was talking about . . . "*My* kind of help, you said?" Harry's attention was suddenly riveted to the phone. "Darcy, are you trying to tell me—that—?"

"What?" The other didn't understand him at first, but then he did. "No, no— Christ *no*—it's not the work of a vampire, Harry! But some kind of monster, certainly. Oh, human enough—but a monster, too."

Harry relaxed a little, but a very little.

He'd been expecting a call from E-Branch sooner or later. This could be it: some sort of clever trap. Except . . . Darcy had always been his friend; Harry didn't think he would act on something—not even something like that—without checking it out every which way first. And even then Harry couldn't see Darcy coming after him with a crossbow and hardwood bolt, a machete, a can of petrol. No, he'd have to talk to him first, get Harry's side of it. But in the end . . .

. . . The head of the Branch knew almost as much about vampires now as Harry did. And he'd know, too, that there was no hope. They'd been friends, fighting on the same side, so Harry guessed it wouldn't be Darcy's finger on the trigger. But someone's, certainly.

"Harry?" Clarke was anxious. "Are you still there?"

"Where are you, Darcy?" Harry inquired.

"The Military Police duties room, in the castle," the other answered at once. "They found her body under the walls. Just a kid, Harry. Eighteen or nineteen. They don't even know who she is yet. That alone would be a big help. But to know who did it would be the biggest bonus of all."

If there was one man Harry Keogh could trust, it had to be Darcy Clarke. "Give me fifteen minutes," he said, "and I'll be there."

Clarke sighed. "Thanks, Harry. We'd appreciate it."

"We?" Harry snapped. He couldn't keep the suspicion out of his voice.

"Eh?" Clarke sounded startled, taken aback. "Why, the police. And me."

14

Murder. The police. Not a Branch job at all. So what was Clarke doing on it—*if* it was real? "How did you get roped in?"

And suddenly, the other was . . . caught on the hop? Cagey, anyway. "I . . . I was up here on a 'duty run,' visiting an old Scottish auntie. Something I do once in a blue moon. She's been on her last legs for ten years now but won't lie down, keeps on tottering around! I was scheduled to go back down to HQ today, but then this came up. It's something the Branch has been trying to help the police with, a set of—God!—*gruesome* serial murders, Harry."

An old Scottish auntie? It was the first time Harry had heard of Darcy's old auntie. On the other hand, this had to be a good opportunity to find out if they knew anything about . . . about his problem. Harry knew he would have to be careful; he knew too much about E-Branch to just go walking right into something. Yes, and they knew too much about him. But maybe they didn't know everything. Not yet, anyway.

"Harry?" Clarke's voice came back again, tinny and a little distorted; probably the wires swaying in the winds that invariably blew around the castle's high walls. "Where will I see you?"

"On the esplanade, at the top of the Royal Mile," the Necroscope growled. "And Darcy . . ."

"Yes?"

". . . Nothing. We'll talk later." He replaced the telephone in its cradle, went back to his breakfast in the kitchen: an inch-thick steak, raw and bloody!

To look at, Darcy Clarke was possibly the world's most nondescript man. Nature had made up for this physical anonymity, however, by giving him an almost unique talent. Clarke was a deflector: he was the opposite of accident-prone. Only let him get close to danger and something, some parapsychological guardian angel, would intervene on his behalf. Which meant that if all of Clarke's similarly ESP-talented team of psychics were photographs, he'd be the only negative. He had no control over the thing; he was only ever aware of it on those occasions when he stared deliberately in the face of danger.

The talents of the others—telepathy, scrying, foretelling, oneiromancy, lie-detecting—were more pliable, obedient, applicable; but not Clarke's. It just did its own thing, which was to look after him. It had no other use. But because it ensured his longevity, it made him the right man for the job. The anomaly was this: that he himself didn't quite believe in it until he felt it working. He still switched off the current before he'd even change a light bulb! But maybe that was just another example of the thing at work.

To look at him, then, no one would suppose that Clarke could ever be the boss of anything, let alone head of the most secret branch of the British Secret Services. Middle-height, mousey-haired, with something of a slight stoop and a small paunch, and middle-aged to boot, he was middling in just about every way. He had sort of neutral-hazel eyes in a face not much given to laughter, and an intense mouth which you *might* remember if you remembered nothing else, but other than that there was a general facelessness about him which made him instantly forgettable. The rest of him, including the way he dressed, was . . . medium.

These were Harry Keogh's perfectly mundane thoughts in the few seconds which ticked by after he stepped out of the metaphysical Möbius Continuum onto the esplanade of Edinburgh Castle, and saw Darcy Clarke standing there with his back to him, hands thrust deep in the pockets of his overcoat, reading the legend on a brass plaque above a seventeenth-century drinking trough.

The iron fountain, picturing two heads, one ugly and the other beatific, stood:

> . . . Near the site on which
> many witches were burned at the
> stake. The wicked head and serene
> head signify that some used exceptional
> knowledge for evil purposes, while others
> were misunderstood and wished their
> kind nothing but good.

The bright May day would be warm but for the gusting wind; the esplanade was almost empty; two dozen or so tourists stood in small groups at the higher end of the broad, walled, tarmac plateau, looking down across the walls at the city, or taking photographs of the great grey fortress—the Castle on the Rock—behind its façade of battlements and courtyards. Harry had arrived in the moment after Clarke, vainly scanning the esplanade for some sign of him, had turned to the plaque.

A moment ago Clarke had been alone with his thoughts and no living person within fifty feet of him. But now a soft voice behind him said:

"Fire is an indiscriminate destroyer. Good or evil, everything burns when it's hot enough."

Clarke's heart jumped into his throat. He gave a massive start and whirled about, the color rushing from his face and leaving him pale in a moment. "Ha-Ha-Harry!" he gasped. "God, I didn't see you! Where did you spring—?" But here he paused, for of course he *knew* where Harry had sprung from . . . because the Necroscope had taken him there once, into that every-where and -when place, that within and without, which was the Möbius Continuum.

Shaken, heart hammering, Clarke clutched at the wall for support. But it wasn't terror, just shock; his talent read no sinister purpose into Keogh's presence.

Harry smiled at him and nodded, touched his arm briefly, then looked at the plaque again. And his smile at once turned sour. "Mainly, they were exorcising their own fears," he said. "For of course most if not all of these women were innocent. Indeed, we should all be so innocent."

"Eh?" Clarke hadn't quite recovered his balance yet, wasn't focusing on Keogh's meaning. "Innocent?" He too looked at the plaque.

"Completely." Harry nodded again. "Oh, they may have been talented in their way, but they were hardly evil! Witchcraft? Why, today you'd probably try to recruit them into E-Branch!"

Suddenly, truth flooded in on Clarke and he knew he wasn't dreaming; no need to pinch himself and start awake; it was just this effect which Harry always had on him. Three weeks ago in the Greek islands (was that all it had been, three weeks?) it had been the same. Except at that time Harry had been near-impotent: he didn't have his deadspeak. Then he'd got it back, and set out on his double mission: to destroy the vampire Janos Ferenczy and regain his mastery of—

Clarke snatched a breath. "You got it back!" He grabbed Harry's arm. "The Möbius Continuum!"

"You didn't get in touch with me," Harry accused, however quietly, "or you'd have known."

"I got your letter," Clarke quickly defended himself, "and I tried a dozen times to get you on the phone. But if you were home you weren't answering. Our locators couldn't find you . . . ." He threw up his hands. "Give me a chance, Harry! I've only been back from the Med a few days, and a pile of stuff to catch up with back here, too! But we'd finished the job in the islands, and we supposed you'd done the same at your end. Our espers were on it, of course; reports were coming in; Janos's place above Halmagiu, blown off the mountain like that. It could only be you. We knew you'd somehow won. But the Möbius Continuum, too? Why, that's . . . wonderful! I'm delighted for you!''

Harry wondered: *Oh, really?* But out loud he only said: "Thanks."

"How in hell did you *do* that?" Clarke was still excited. If it was all a sham he was good at it. "I mean, wreck the castle that way? If we've got it right it was devastating! Is that how Janos died, in the explosion?"

"Slow down," Harry told him, taking his arm. "We can talk while you take me to see this girl."

The other's excitement quickly ebbed. "Yes"—he nodded, his tone subdued now—"and that's something else, too. You won't like it, Harry."

"So what's new?" The Necroscope seemed as calm (resigned, soulful, sardonic?) as ever. And though he tried not to show it, Clarke suspected he was wary, too. "Did you ever show me anything I did like?"

But Clarke had an answer to that one. "If everything was the way we'd like it, Harry," he said, "then we'd all be out of work. Me, I'd gladly retire tomorrow. I keep threatening to. But when I see something like . . . like I'm going to show you, then I know that someone has to do it."

As they started up the esplanade, Harry said: "Now, *this* is a castle!" His voice was more animated now. "But as for the Castle Ferenczy: that was a heap long before I got started on it. You asked how I did it?" He sighed, then continued:

"A long time ago, toward the end of the Bodescu affair, I learned about an ammo and explosives dump in Kolomyya and used stuff from there to blow up the Chateau Bronnitsy. Well, since the easy way is often the best way, I did it again. I made two or three trips, Möbius trips, and put enough plastic explosive into the foundations of Janos's place to blow it to hell! I'm not even going to guess what was in the guts of that place, but I'm sure there was—*stuff*—there which even I didn't see and still don't want to. You know, Darcy, even a finger-end of Semtex will blow bricks right out of a wall? So you can imagine what a couple of hundredweights will do. If there was anything there that we might call 'alive' " —he shrugged and shook his head—"it wasn't when I'd finished."

While Harry talked, the head of E-Branch studied him. But not so intently that he would notice. He seemed exactly the same man Clarke had come to Edinburgh to see just a month ago, a visit which had ended for Clarke in Rhodes and the islands of the Dodecanese, and for Harry in the mountains of Transylvania. He *seemed* the same, but was he? For the fact was, Darcy Clarke knew someone who said he wasn't.

Harry Keogh was a composite. He was two men: the mind of one and the body of another. The mind was Keogh and the body was . . . it had once been Alec Kyle. And Clarke had known Kyle, too, in his time. The strangest thing was this: that as time progressed, so the Kyle face and form got to look more like the old Harry, whose body was dead. But that was something which always made Clarke's brain spin. He skipped it, put the metaphysical right out of his mind and studied the purely physical.

The Necroscope was perhaps forty-three or -four but looked five years younger. But of course that was only the body; the mind was five years younger again. Even thinking about someone like Harry Keogh was a weird business. And again Clarke forced himself to concentrate on the physical.

Harry's eyes were honey-brown, occasionally defensive and frequently puppy-soulful—or would be if one could see under those wedge-sided sunglasses he was wearing in the shade of his broad-brimmed 1930s hat. If there was one thing in all the world Clarke hated to see, it had to be Harry wearing those dark-lensed glasses and that hat. Anyone else, no problem. But not Harry, and not now. Especially the sunglasses. They were something Clarke had told himself to look out for; for while it was a common enough thing to wear such in the Greek islands in late April or early May, it was quite another to see them in Edinburgh that time of year. Unless someone had weak eyes. Or different eyes . . .

Grey streaks, so evenly spaced as to seem deliberately designed or affected, were plentiful in Harry's russet-brown, naturally wavy hair. In a few years the grey could easily take over; even now it loaned him a certain erudition, gave him the look of a scholar. A scholar, yes, but in what fabulous subjects? But in fact Keogh hadn't been like that at all. Hadn't used to be. What, Harry, a black magician? A warlock? Lord, no!

. . . Just a Necroscope: a man who talked to dead people.

Keogh's body had been well fleshed, maybe even a little overweight once. With his height, however, that ought not to have mattered a great deal. But it had mattered to Harry. After that business at the Chateau Bronnitsy—his metempsychosis—he'd trained his new body down, brought it to a peak of perfection. Or at least done what he could with it, considering its age. That's why it looked only thirty-seven or -eight years old.

And inside Harry's body and behind his face an innocent. Or someone who had used to be innocent. He hadn't asked to be the way he was, hadn't wanted to become E-Branch's most powerful weapon and do the things he'd done. But he'd been what he was and the rest had come as a matter of course. And now? Was he still an innocent? Did he still have the soul of a child? Did he have any soul at all? Or did something else have him?

Now the pair had passed under the archway of the military guardroom, where several police officers had been interviewing a group of uniformed soldiers, into the cobbled gantlet which was the approach alley to the castle proper. All of the officers in the guardroom seemed aware that Clarke was "something big"; they weren't challenged; suddenly, the bulk of the castle loomed before them.

And now Darcy said: "So I don't need to do any tidying up? You left nothing undone, right?"

"Nothing," Harry told him. "What about Janos's setup in the islands?"

"Gone!" said the other with finality. "All of it. All of them. But I still have a few men out there—just looking—just to be on the safe side."

Harry's face was pale and grim but he forced a strange, sad smile. "That's right, Darcy," he said. "Always be on the safe side. Never take chances. Not with things like that."

There was something in his voice; Clarke looked at the Necroscope out of the corner of his eye, carefully, unobtrusively examining him yet again as they entered the shade of a broad courtyard, with gaunt buildings rising on three sides. "Are you going to tell me how it was?"

"No." Harry shook his head. "Later, maybe. And maybe not." He turned and looked Clarke straight in the eye. "One vampire's pretty much like another. Hell, what can I tell you about them that you don't already know? You know how to kill them, that's a fact . . ."

Clarke stared directly into the black, enigmatic lenses of the other's glasses. "You're the one who showed us how, Harry," he said.

Harry smiled his sad smile again, and apparently casually—but Clarke suspected very deliberately—reached up a hand and took off his glasses. Not for a moment turning his face away, he folded the glasses and put them into his pocket. And:

"Well?" he said.

Clarke's jaw fell open as he backed off a stumbling pace, barely managing to contain the sigh—of relief—which he felt welling inside. Caught off balance (again), he looked into the other's perfectly normal, unwavering brown eyes and said: "Eh? What? Well?"

"Well, where are we going?" Harry answered with a shrug. "Or are we already there?"

Clarke gathered his wits. "We're there," he said, "almost."

He led the way down stone steps and under an arch, then through a heavy door into a stone-flagged corridor. As they emerged into the corridor, a Military Policeman came erect and saluted. Clarke didn't correct his error, merely nodded, led Harry past him. Halfway along the corridor a middle-aged man—unmistakably a policeman for all that he wore civilian clothing—guarded an iron-banded door of oak.

Again Clarke's nod, and the plainclothesman swung the door open for him and stepped aside.

"*Now* we're there," Harry preempted Clarke, causing him to close his mouth on those selfsame words, unspoken. Harry Keogh needed no one to tell him there was a dead person close by. And with one more glance at the

Necroscope, Clarke ushered him inside. The officer didn't follow them but closed the door quietly behind them.

The room was cool; two walls were of natural stone; a rocky outcrop of volcanic gneiss grew out of the stone-flagged floor in one corner and into the walls there. Built straight onto the rock, this place was a storeroom. Steel shelving was stacked on one side. On the other, beside the cold stone wall: a surgical trolley with a body on it, and a white rubber sheet covering the body.

The Necroscope wasted no time. The dead held no terrors for Harry Keogh. If he had as many friends among the living, then he'd be the most loved man in the world. He *was* the most loved man, but the ones who loved him couldn't tell anyone about it. Except Harry himself.

He went to the trolley, drew back the rubber sheet from the face, closed his eyes, and rocked back on his heels. She had been sweet and young and innocent—yes, another innocent—and she had been tormented. And she still was. Her eyes were closed now, but Harry knew that if they were open he'd read terror in them. He could feel those dead eyes burning through the pale lids that covered them, crying out to him in their horror.

She would need comforting. The teeming dead—the Great Majority—would have tried, but they didn't always get it right. Their voices were often mournful, ghostly, frightening, to anyone who didn't know them. In the darkness of death they could seem like night visitants, nightmares, like wailing banshees come to steal a soul. She might think she was dreaming, might even suspect that she was dying, but not that she was already dead. That took time to sink in, and the freshly dead were usually the last to know. That was because they were the least able to accept it. Especially the very young, whose young minds had not yet properly considered it.

But on the other hand, if she had actually seen death coming—if she had read it in the eyes of her destroyer, felt the numbing blow, or the hands on her throat, closing off the air, or the cutting edge of the instrument of her destruction, slicing into her flesh—then she would know. And she'd be cold and afraid and tearful. Tearful, yes, for no one knew better than Harry how the dead could cry.

He hesitated, wasn't sure how best to approach her, not even sure if he should approach her, not now. For Harry knew that she'd been pure, and that he was impure. True, her flesh was heading for corruption even now, but there's corruption and there's corruption . . .

Angrily, he thrust the thought aside. No, he wasn't a defiler. Not yet. He was a friend. He was the only friend. He was the Necroscope.

Be that as it may, when he put his hand on her clay-cold brow she recoiled as from a serpent! Not physically, for she was dead, but her *mind* cringed, shrank down, withdrew into itself like the feathery fronds of some strange sea anemone brushed by a swimmer. Harry felt his blood turn to ice and for a moment stood in horror of himself. The last thing he'd wanted was to frighten her more yet. He wrapped her in his thoughts, in what had once been the warmth of his deadspeak:

It's all right! Don't be afraid! I won't hurt you! No one can ever hurt you again! It was as easy as that. Without even trying, he'd told her that she was dead. But in the next moment he knew that she had already known:

KEEP OFF! Her deadspeak was a sobbing shriek of torment in Harry's mind. GET AWAY FROM ME, YOU FILTHY . . . *THING!*

As if someone had touched him with naked electric wires, Harry jerked where he stood beside her, jerked and shuddered as he relived, with her, the girl's last moments. Her last living, breathing moments, but not the last things she had known. For in certain mercifully rare circumstances—and at the command of certain monstrous men—even dead flesh can be made to feel again.

In a nightmarishly subliminal sequence, a series of flickering, kaleidoscopic, vividly ghastly pictures flashed on the screen of the Necroscope's metaphysical mind and then was gone. But afterimages remained, and Harry knew that these wouldn't go away so easily; indeed, that they would probably remain for a long time. He knew it as surly as he now knew what he was dealing with, because he dealt with such a thing before.

That one's name had been . . . Dragosani!

This one, this poor girl's murderer, had been like that—like Dragosani, a necromancer—but in one especially hideous respect he'd been worse than that. For not even Dragosani had raped his corpse victims!

But it's over now, he told the girl. *He can't come back. You're safe now.*

He felt the shuddering of her thoughts receding, replaced by the natural curiosity of her incorporeal mind. She wanted to know him, but for the moment felt afraid to know anything. She wanted, too, to know her *condition,* except that was probably the most frightening thing of all. But in her own small way she was brave, and she had to know for sure.

Am I . . . (her deadspeak voice was no longer a shriek but a shivery tremor). *Am I really* . . . ?

Yes, you are. Harry nodded, and knew that she'd sense the movement even as all the teeming dead sensed his every mood and motion. *But* . . . (he stumbled), *I mean . . . it could be worse!*

He'd been through all of this before, too often, and it never got any easier. How do you convince someone recently dead that it could be worse? "Your body will rot and worms will devour it, but your mind will go on. Oh, you won't see anything—it will always be dark, and you'll never touch or taste or smell anything again—but it could be worse. Your parents and loved ones will cry over your grave and plant flowers there, seeking to visualize in their blooms something of your face and form; but you won't know they're there or be able to speak to them and say, 'Here I am!' You won't be able to reassure them that 'it could be worse.' ''

This was Harry's expression of grief, meant to be private, but his thoughts were deadspeak. She heard and felt them and knew him for a friend. And:

You're the Necroscope, she said then. *They tried to tell me about you but I was afraid and wouldn't listen. When they spoke to me I turned away. I didn't want to . . . to talk to dead people.*

Harry was crying. Great tears blurred his vision, rolled down his pale, slightly hollow cheeks, splashed hot where they fell on his hand on her brow. He hadn't wanted to cry, didn't know he could, but there was that in him which worked on his feelings and amplified them, lifting them above the emotions of ordinary men. Safe—so long as it worked on an emotion such as this one, which was grief and entirely human.

Darcy Clarke had come forward; he touched the Necroscope's arm. "Harry?"

Harry shook him off, and his voice was choked but harsh, too, as he rasped: "Leave us alone! I want to talk to her in private."

Clarke backed off, his Adam's apple bobbing. It was the look on Harry's face that brought tears to his eyes, too. "Of course," he said. He turned and left the room, and closed the door after him.

Harry took a metal-framed chair from beside the

stacked shelving and sat by the dead girl. He very carefully cradled her head in his arms.

I . . . I can feel that, she said wonderingly.

"Then you can feel, too, that I'm not like him," Harry answered out loud. He preferred simply to talk to the dead, for that way it came more naturally to him.

Most of her terror had fled now. The Necroscope was a comfort; he was warm, a safe haven. It might even be her father stroking her face. Except she wouldn't be able to feel him. Only Harry Keogh could touch the dead. Only Harry, and—

Her terror welled up again—but he was quick to sense it and fend it off:

"It's over and you're safe. We won't—*I* won't—let anything hurt you again, ever." It was more than just a promise, it was his vow.

In a little while her thoughts grew calm and she was easy, or easier, again. But she was very bitter, too, when she said: *I'm dead, but he—that thing—is alive!*

"It's one of the reasons I'm here," Harry told her. "For you weren't the only one. There were others before you, and unless we stop him there'll be others after you. So you see, it's very important that we get him, for he's not just a murderer but also a necromancer; which makes him more, far worse, than the sum of his parts. A murderer destroys the living, and a necromancer torments the dead. But this one enjoys the terror of his victim both before and after they die!"

I can't talk about what he did to me, she said, shuddering.

Harry shook his head. "You don't have to. Right now I'm only interested in you. I'm sure there'll be people worrying about you. Until we know who you are, we won't be able to put their minds at rest."

Do you think their minds will ever be at rest, Harry?

It was a good question. "We don't have to tell them everything," he answered. "I might be able to fix it so that they only know, well, that someone killed you. They don't have to told how."

Can you do that?

"If that's the way you want it," he said.

Then do it! She offered a breathless sigh. *That was the worst, Harry: thinking about them, my folks, how they'd take it. But if you can make it easier for them . . . I think I'm beginning to understand why the dead love you so. My name is Penny. Penny Sanderson. And I live—lived—at . . .*

. . . And so it went. She told the Necroscope all about herself, and he remembered every smallest detail. That was what Darcy Clarke had wanted, but it wasn't everything he'd wanted. When finally Penny Sanderson was through, Harry knew he still had to take her that one step further.

"Penny, listen," he said. "I don't want you to do or say anything. Don't try to talk to me at all. But like I said before, this is important."

About him?

"Penny, when I first touched you, and you thought it was him come back for more, you remembered how it was. Parts of it, anyway. You thought about it in brief flashes of memory. That was deadspeak and I picked it up. But it was all very chaotic, kaleidoscopic."

But that's all there is, she said. *That's how it was.*

Harry nodded. "Okay, that's fine, but I need to see it again. See, the better I remember it, the more chance I have of finding him. So really you don't have to tell me anything, not as a conscious act. I just want to shoot a few words at you, at which you'll picture the bits I need. Do you understand?"

Word association?

"Something like that, yes. Except of course that in this case the association will be hell for you—but easier than just talking about it."

She understood; Harry sensed her willingness; before she could change her mind, he said:

"Knife!"

A picture hit the screen of his mind like a mixture of blood and acid! The blood incensed him and the acid burned, etching the picture there for good this time. Harry reeled before her horror—which was unbearable—and if he hadn't been seated would have fallen. The shock was that physical, even though it lasted only a fraction of a second.

When she stopped sobbing he said, "Are you okay?"

No . . . yes.

"Face!" Harry fired at her.

Face?

"His face?" he tried again.

And a face, red, leering, bloated with lust, with an open, salivating mouth and eyes insensate as frozen diamonds, went skittering across the Necroscope's mind's eye. But not so fast that he didn't catch it. And this time she wasn't sobbing. She wanted this to work. Wanted *him* brought to justice.

"Where?"

A picture of . . . a car park? A motorway restaurant? Darkness pierced with points of light. A string of cars and lorries, speeding down three lanes, with oncoming lights whose glare momentarily blinded. And windscreen wipers swinging left, right, left, right, left . . .

But there was no pain in the last and Harry guessed that wasn't where it had happened. No, it had been where it started to happen, probably where she met him.

"He picked you up in a car?"

A rain-blurred picture of an ice-blue screen with white

letters superimposed or printed there: FRID or FRIG? The screen had many wheels and puffed exhaust smoke. It was the way she remembered it. A large vehicle? A lorry? Articulated?

"Penny," Harry said, "I have to do this—only this time I don't mean where you met him:

"Where?!"

Ice! Bitter cold! Dark! The whole place softly vibrating or throbbing! And dead things everywhere, hanging from hooks! Harry tried to fix it all in his mind but nothing was clear, only her shock and disbelief that this was happening to her.

She was sobbing again, terrified, and Harry knew that he'd soon have to stop; he couldn't bring himself to hurt her any more. But at the same time he knew he mustn't weaken now.

"Death!" he snapped, hating himself.

And it was the knife scene all over again, and Harry knew he was losing her, could feel her withdrawing. Before that could happen:

"And . . . afterwards?" (God!—he didn't want to know! He didn't want to know!)

Penny Sanderson screamed, and screamed, and screamed!

But the Necroscope got his picture.

And wished he hadn't bothered . . .

II Upon Their
Backs, to Bite 'Em . . .

HARRY STAYED WITH HER FOR A FURTHER HALF HOUR:
calming, soothing, doing what he could, and in so doing
managing to get a few more personal details out of her,
enough to give the police something to go on, anyway.
But when it was time to go she wouldn't let him without
he promised he'd see her again. She hadn't been there
long, but already Penny had discovered that death was a
lonely place.

The Necroscope was jaded—or thought he was—by
life, death, everything. He believed he needed motiva-
tion. Before leaving her he asked if she'd mind if he
looked at her. She told him that if it were anyone else
she couldn't care less, because she wouldn't even know
they were looking, not any longer. But with Harry she
would know, because he was the Necroscope. She was
just a shy kid.

"Hey!" he protested, but gently, "I'm no voyeur!"

If I wasn't . . . if he hadn't . . . if I was unmarked, then I don't think I'd mind, she said.

"Penny, you're lovely," Harry told her. "And me? After all's said and done, I'm only human. But believe me I'm not putting you down when I tell you that right now I'm not interested in that side of things. It's *because* you're marked that I want to see you. I need to feel angry. And now that I know you, I know that to see what he did would make me feel angry."

Then I'll just have to pretend you're my doctor, she said.

Harry very gently took the rubber sheet off her pale, young body, looked at her, and tremblingly put the sheet back again.

Is it bad? She fought down a sob. *It's such a shame. Mum always said I could be a model.*

"So you could," he told her. "You were very beautiful."

But not now? And though she kept from actually sobbing, he could feel her despair brimming over. But in a little while she said: *Harry? Did it make you angry?*

He felt a growl rising in his throat, suppressed it, and before he left her said, "Oh, yes. Yes, it did."

Darcy Clarke was still outside the door with the plainclothesman. Looking washed out, Harry joined them and closed the door after him. "I've left the sheet off her face," he said. And then, speaking specifically to—and glaring at—the officer: "*Don't* cover her face!"

The other raised an indifferent eyebrow and shrugged. "Who, me?" he said, his accent nasal, Glaswegian, less than sympathetic. "Ah had nothing tae do wi' it, Chief. It's just that when they're dead 'uns, people usually cover them up!"

Harry turned swiftly towards him, eyes widening and

nostrils flaring in his pale, grimacing face, and Darcy Clarke's instinct took over. The Necroscope was suddenly dangerous and Clarke's weird talent knew it. There was a terrible anger in him, which he needed to take out on someone. But Clarke knew that it wasn't directed at him, wasn't directed at anyone but simply required an outlet.

Quickly forcing himself between Harry and the special-duty officer, he grabbed the Necroscope's arms. "It's okay, Harry," he said urgently. "It's okay. It's just that these people see things like this all the time. It doesn't affect them so much. They get used to it."

Harry got a grip of himself, but not without an effort of will. He looked at Clarke and growled, "They don't see things like *that* all the time! No one's ever going to 'get used' to the idea that someone—something—could do that to a girl!" And then, seeing Clarke's bewildered expression: "I'll explain later."

He turned his gaze across Clarke's shoulder, and in a tone more nearly civil now—more civilized?—asked the officer, "Do you have a notebook?"

Mystified—not knowing what was going on, just trying to do his job—the other said, "Aye," and groped in his pocket. He scribbled quickly as Harry fired Penny's name, address, and family details at him. Following which, and looking even more mystified: "You're sure about these details, sir?"

Harry nodded. "Just be sure to pass on what I said, right? I don't want anyone to cover her face over. Penny always hated having her face covered."

"You knew the young lady, then?"

"No," said Harry. "Now I know her."

They left the officer talking into his walkie-talkie and scratching his head, went up into the courtyard and the fresh air. As they moved into sunlight Harry put on his dark glasses and turned up the collar of his coat. And Clarke said to him:

"You got something else, right?"

Harry nodded, but in the next moment: "Never mind what I got—what have you got? Do you have any idea what you're dealing with?"

Clarke threw up his hands. "Only that he's a serial killer, and that he's weird."

"But you know what he does?"

Clarke nodded. "Yes. We know it's sexual. A sort of sex, anyway. A sick sort of sex."

Harry shivered. "Sicker than you think. Dragosani's kind of sickness."

That pulled Clarke up short. *"What?"*

"A necromancer," Harry told him. "A murderer and a necromancer. And in a way worse than Dragosani, because this one's a necrophiliac, too!"

Clarke somehow succeeded in grimacing and looking blank at the same time. Then: "Refresh my mind," he said. "I know I should be getting something, but I'm not."

Harry thought about it for a few moments before answering, but in the end there was no way to tell it other than the way it was. "Dragosani tore open the bodies of dead men for information," he finally said. "That was his 'talent,' just like you have yours and I have mine. Necromancy. It was his job when he worked for Gregor Borowitz and Soviet E-Branch at the Chateau Bronnitsy: to 'examine' the corpses of his country's enemies. He could read their passions in the mucus of their eyes, tear the truths of their lives right out of their steaming tripes, tune in on the whispering of their stiffening brains, and sniff their smallest secrets in the gases of their swollen guts!"

Clarke held up a hand in protest. "Christ, Harry—I *know* all that!"

The Necroscope nodded. "But you don't know what it's like to be dead, and that's why you're not getting it. It's because you can't imagine what I'm talking about. You know what I *do* and accept it because you know it for a fact, but deep inside yourself you still think it's just too way out to think about. So you don't. And I don't blame you. Now listen:

"I know I always protested I was different from Dragosani, but in certain ways he and I were alike. Even now I don't like admitting it, but it's true. I mean, you know what the bastard did to Keenan Gormley—the mess he made of him—but only *I* know what Gormley thought about it!"

And *now* Clarke got it. He snatched air in a great gasp and felt the short hairs stiffen at the back of his neck as an irrepressible shudder racked his body. And: "Jesus, you're right!" he breathed. "I just don't think about it—because I don't *want* to think about it! But in fact Keenan knew! He *felt* everything Dragosani did to him!"

"Right." Harry was relentless. "Torture is the necromancer's principal tool. The dead feel the necromancer working on them just like they hear me talking to them. Except unlike the living, there's nothing they can do about it, not even scream. Not and be heard, anyway. And Penny Sanderson?"

Clarke went pale in a moment. "She could feel—?"

"Everything," Harry growled. "And that bastard, whoever he is, knew it! So you see while rape is one thing, and bad enough when it's done to the living, and while necrophilia is something else, an outrage carried out upon the *unfeeling* dead, what he does hits new lows. He tortures his victims alive, then tortures them dead—

36

and he *knows* while he's doing it that they can feel it! He uses a knife with a curved blade, like a tool for scooping earth when you're planting bulbs. It's razor-sharp and . . . and he doesn't use it for scooping earth.''

It had been Clarke's intention to stop at the guardroom and speak to the policemen there. But now, pale as a ghost, he reeled to the castle's low wall. Clutching its masonry for support, he gulped at the gusting air and fought down the bile he felt rising from the churning of his guts.

And: "Jesus, *Jesus!*" he choked. For he could see it all now, and there was nothing he could do to cleanse the picture from his mind's eye. Weird sex? God, what an understatement!

Harry had followed Clarke to the wall. The head of E-Branch looked at him sideways from a watery eye. "He . . . he digs holes in those poor kids, then makes love to the holes!''

"Love?" the Necroscope hissed. "His flesh ruts in blood like a pig's snout ruts in soil, Darcy! Except the soil can't feel! Didn't the police tell you where he leaves his semen?''

Clarke's eyes were swimming and his brow feverish, but he felt his nausea being replaced by a cold loathing almost as strong as the Necroscope's own. No, the police hadn't told him that, but now he knew. He looked out over the blurred city and asked: "How do you know he knows they feel it?''

"Because he talks to them while he's doing it," Harry told him mercilessly. "And when they cry out in their agony and beg him to stop, he hears them. And he laughs!''

Clarke thought: *Christ, I shouldn't have asked! And you—you bastard, Harry Keogh—you shouldn't have told me!*

37

With fury in his eyes, he turned to face the Necroscope
. . . and faced thin air. A wind blew up the esplanade
and tourists leaned into it, balancing themselves. Overhead, sea gulls cried where they spiraled on a rising thermal.

But Harry was no longer there . . .

Later, with Clarke's help, Harry fixed it that Penny Sanderson would be cremated. Her parents wanted it, and it
wouldn't hurt them that it was all a show. They wouldn't
know it, anyway: that Penny was already ashes when
their tears fell on her empty box, before it slid away from
them behind swishing curtains and became woodsmoke.

Clarke hadn't wanted to do it but he owed Harry. For
a good many things. And he wanted very badly to catch
the maniac who had done this thing to Penny and too
many other innocents. Harry had told him: "If I have
her ashes—her pure ashes, not damaged or spoiled by
burned linen or charcoal—then I'll be able to talk to her
any time I want to. And maybe she'll remember something important."

It had seemed logical at the time (if anything about
the Necroscope could ever seem logical) and so Clarke
had pulled strings. As the head of E-Branch he had that
sort of power. But if he'd known the whole story of what
had happened at the castle of Janos Ferenczy, in Transylvania, maybe he would have thought twice about it.
And then not done it at all.

He certainly wouldn't have gone along with it if Zek
Föener had stood firm on her first . . . accusation? Or if
not an accusation, a premonition at least.

Zek was a telepath and as loyal to the Necroscope as
they came. In the Greek islands at the end of the Ferenczy business, she'd had occasion to try and contact
Harry with her mind, during the course of which some-

thing had shocked her rigid. But it had been a while
before she could tell Clarke what it was. They had been
on the island of Rhodes at the time, less than a month
ago, and their conversation was still fresh in his mind:

"What is it, Zek?" he'd said to her, when he could
talk to her in private. "I saw that change come over your
face when you contacted Harry. Is he in some sort of
trouble?"

"No—yes—I don't know!" she'd answered, fear and
frustration audible in her every word, visible in her every
move. Then she'd looked at him and it was that same,
strange, disbelieving look he'd seen when she tried to
contact Harry: as if she gazed on alien things, in a distant world beyond the times and places we know. And
he remembered that indeed she had once been in just
such a world, with Harry Keogh. A world of vampires!

"Zek," he'd said then, "if there's something I should
know about Harry, it's only fair that—"

"—Only fair to who?" she had cut him off. "To
whom? To . . . what? And is it fair to him?"

At which Clarke had felt an icy chill in his blood.
And: "I think you'd better explain," he said.

"I *can't* explain!" she'd snapped at him. "Or maybe
I can." And then the empty expression in her beautiful
eyes had filled itself in a little, and her tone had become
more reasonable, even pleading. "It's just that every
other mind I've touched in the last few days has seemed
to be one of them! So maybe I've started to find them
where . . . where there aren't any? Where they can't possibly be?"

And then he'd known for certain what she was trying
to tell him. "You mean that when you contacted Harry,
you sensed—?"

"Yes—*yes!*" she'd snapped again. "But I could be
mistaken. I mean, isn't that what he's doing at this very

39

moment, going up against them? He's *close* to vampires right now, even as we talk. It could be one of them I sensed. God, it *has* to be one of them . . .''

End of conversation, but it hadn't been out of Clarke's mind from that day to this. When it was time to leave the islands and come home again, he had asked Zek if she'd like to visit England, as a guest of E-Branch. Her answer had been more or less what he expected:

"You're not fooling anyone, Darcy. And anyway, I don't like the idea that you would want to fool me, not after all of this. So I'll tell you straight out: I *detest* the E-Branches, whether they're Russian, British, whoever they belong to! No, not the espers themselves but the way they're used, the fact that they need to be used at all. As for Harry: I won't go against the Necroscope.'' And she'd given her head a very definite shake. "We were on different sides once before, Harry and me, and he gave me some good advice. 'Never again go up against me or mine,' he said, and I never will. I've seen inside his mind, Darcy, and I know that when someone like Harry says something like that to you, you'd better listen to him. So if there are . . . problems, well, they're your problems, not mine.''

It had been the kind of answer to make him worry all the more.

Back in London after the Greek expedition, at E-Branch HQ, a mass of work had built up. During the first four days back at his desk Clarke had cleared or at least commenced to clear quite a lot of it, also managed to clear his mind of much of the horror of the Ferenczy job. But nightmares kept him awake most nights. One in particular was very bad and very persistent.

This was the essence of it:

They (Clarke, Zek, Jazz Simmons, Ben Trask, Manolis Papastamos: most of the Greek team, with the important exception of Harry Keogh) were in a boat that lolled gently on an absolutely flat ocean. It was so blue, that sea, that it could only be the Aegean. A small, stark, sloping island of rock floating on the blue made a gold-rimmed, black silhouette against the blinding refraction of a half-sun where it prepared to dip down beyond the slanting rock of the island into a short-lived twilight. The serenity of the scene was immaculately structured, vivid, real, with nothing in it to hint that it was prelude to nightmare. But since the thing was recurrent—indeed a nightly occurrence—Clarke always knew what was coming and where to look for the start of it.

He would look at Zek, gorgeous in a swimsuit that left little to the imagination, stetched out along a narrow sun-bathing platform attached to the upper strakes at the stern. She lay on her stomach, her face turned sideways, with one hand dangling in the water. And the sea so calm that her fingers made ripples. But then . . .

She glanced sharply at her hand in the water, snatched it out and stared at it, gave a cry of disgust, and tumbled herself inboard! Her hand was red, bleeding! No, not bleeding, but bloody—as if it had been dipped in someone else's blood! By which time the entire crew had seen that the sea itself was sullied by a great crimson swath, an elongated splotch like an oil slick (a blood slick?) which had drifted to surround the boat with its thick, red ribbons.

But drifted from where?

They looked out across the sea, followed the swath to its source. Previously unnoticed, the warty, barnacled prow of a sunken vessel stuck up in a grotesque salute from the water only fifty yards away. Its figurehead was a hideous but *recognizable* face, mouth gaping, hugely disproportionate fangs jutting, and blood spewing in an unending torrent from the silently shrieking mouth!

And the vessel's name, as she gurgled down out of sight into her own blood? Clarke didn't need to read all of those black letters daubed on her scabby hull as they disappeared, in reverse order, one by one into the crimson ocean: O . . . R . . . C . . . E . . . N.

No, for he already knew that this was the plagueship *Necroscope*, out of Edinburgh, contaminated in strange ports of call and doomed forever to oceans of gore! Or until, like now, she sank.

Aghast, he watched her go down, then jumped to his feet as Papastamos cursed and leaped to snatch up a spear gun. The swath of blood beside the boat was bubbling, fuming, as some nameless thing drifted to the surface. A body, naked, facedown, floated up and lolled like some weird jellyfish, dangling its tentacle arms and legs. And feeble as a jellyfish, it tried to swim!

Then Papastamos was at the side of the boat, aiming his gun, and Clarke was starting forward, screaming, "No!" . . . but too late! The steel spear hissed through the air and thwacked into the lone survivor's back, and he jerked in the water and rolled over. And his face was the face on the figurehead, and his scarlet eyes glared and his scarlet mouth belched blood as he sank down out of sight for the last time . . .

Which was when Clarke would start awake.

He started now as his telephone chirruped, then sighed his relief that his morbid chain of thoughts had been broken. He let the telephone chirp away to itself for a few moments, and considered his nightmare in the light of cold logic.

Clarke was no oneiromancer but the dream's interpretation seemed simple enough. Zek, to her own dismay, had pointed the finger of suspicion at Harry. As for the Aegean backdrop and the blood: these were hardly inappropriate in the circumstances and considering the occurrences of the recent past.

And the dream's conclusion? Papastamos had put an end to the horror but that wasn't significant, hadn't been the point of it. It didn't have to be Papastamos but could have been any one of them—except Clarke himself. *That* had been the point of it: that Darcy Clarke himself hadn't done it and didn't want it to happen. In fact he had tried to stop it. Just like, right now, he was less than eager to start anything . . .

The telephone was starting in on its fifth repeat performance when he reached for it, but the relief he'd felt at the first chirrup was short-lived; his nightmare was right there on the other end of the wire.

"Darcy?" The Necroscope's voice was calm, collected, about as detached as Clarke had ever heard it.

"Harry?" Clarke pressed a button on his desk, ensuring the conversation would be recorded, and another which alerted the switchboard to commence a trace. "I'd thought I might hear from you before now."

"Oh, why?"

Harry asked good questions, and this one stopped Clarke dead. For after all, E-Branch didn't own Harry Keogh. "Why"—he thought quickly—"because of your interest in the serial killer case! I mean, it's been ten days since we met in Edinburgh; we've spoken only once since then; I suppose I'd been hoping you'd come up with something pretty quick."

"And your people?" Harry returned. "Your espers: have they come up with anything? Your telepaths and hunchmen, spotters, precogs, and locators? Have the police come up with anything? No, they haven't, because if they had you wouldn't be asking me. Hey, I'm only one man, Darcy, and you have a whole gang!"

Clarke decided to play the other at his own circuitous

game. "Okay, so tell me, to what do I owe the pleasure, Harry? I can't believe it's a social call."

The Necroscope's chuckle—normal, however dry— brought a little more relief with it. "You make a good sparring partner," he said. "Except you cry uncle too quick." And before Clarke could counter, he went on: "I need some information, Darcy, that's why I'm calling."

Who am I talking to? Clarke wondered. *What am I talking to? God, if only I could be sure it was you, Harry! I mean, all you, just you. But I can't be sure, and if it's not all you . . . then sooner or later it will be my job to do something about it.* Which, of course, was what his nightmare was all about. But out loud he only said, "Information? How can I help you?"

"Two things," Harry told him. "The first one's a big one: details of the other murdered girls. Oh, I know I could get them for myself; I have friends in the right places, right? But this time I'd prefer not to put the teeming dead to the trouble."

"Oh?" Clarke was curious. Suddenly, Harry sounded cagey. Put the Great Majority to trouble? But the dead would do anything for the Necroscope—even rise from their graves!

"We've asked enough of the dead," Harry tried to explain himself, almost as if he'd read Clarke's mind. "Now it's time we did them a few favors."

Still puzzled, Clarke said, "Give me half an hour and I'll duplicate everything we have for you. I can mail it or . . . but no, that would be silly. You can simply pick it up yourself, right here."

Again Harry's chuckle. "You mean via the Möbius Continuum? What, and set off all those alarms again?" He stopped chuckling. "No, mail it," he said. "You know I'm not stuck on that place of yours. You espers give me the shivers!''

Clarke laughed out loud. It was forced laughter but he hoped the other wouldn't notice. "And what's the other thing I can do for you, Harry?''

"That's easy,'' said the Necroscope. "You can tell me about Paxton.''

It was delivered like a bolt out of the blue, and quite deliberately. "Pax—?'' The smile slid from Clarke's face, was replaced by a frown. Paxton? What about Paxton? He didn't know anything about him—only that he'd done a few months' probation as an esper, a telepath, and that the Minister Responsible had found cause to reject him: something about a couple of small kinks in his past record, apparently.

"Yes, Paxton,'' Harry said again. "Geoffrey Paxton? He's one of yours, isn't he?'' There was an edge to his voice now, an almost mechanical precision which was cold and controlled. Like a computer waiting for some vital item of information before it could commence its calculations.

"Was,'' Clarke finally answered. "Was *going* to be one of ours, yes. But it seems he had a couple of black marks against him and so missed the boat. How do you know about him, anyway? Or more to the point, *what* do you know about him?''

"Darcy.'' The edge on Harry's voice had sharpened. It wasn't menacing—there was no threat in it, no way— but still Clarke could sense its warning. "We've been friends, of sorts, for a long time. I've stuck my neck out for you. You've stuck yours out for me. I'd hate to think you were shafting me now.''

"Shafting you?'' Clarke's answer was instinctive, natural, even mildly affronted; with every right, for he wasn't hiding anything or shafting anyone. "I don't even

45

know what you're talking about! It's like I said: Geoffrey Paxton is a middling telepath, but developing rapidly. Or he was. Then we lost him. Our Minister found something he didn't like and Paxton was out. Without us he won't ever be able to develop to his full potential. We'll give him the once-over now and then, just to make sure he's not using what he has to take too much of an advantage on society, but apart from that—''

''But he's *already* taking advantage,'' the Necroscope, plainly angry now, cut in. ''Or trying to—and of me! He's on my back, Darcy, and he sticks like glue. He tries to get into my mind, but so far I've kept him out. Only that takes effort, gets tiring, and I'm getting *pissed off* exerting so much effort on something like this! On some sneaking little bastard who's doing someone else's dirty work!''

For a moment Clarke's mind was full of confusion, but he knew that to hesitate would only make him look suspect. ''What do you want me to do?'' he said.

''Find out who's running him, of course!'' Harry snapped. ''And why.''

''I'll do what I can.''

''Do better than that,'' Harry came back like a shot. ''Or I'll have to do it myself.''

Why haven't you already? Clarke wondered. *Are you afraid of Paxton, Harry? And if so, why?* ''I've told you he isn't one of mine,'' he said out loud. ''Now, that's the truth, so you can't threaten me through him. But like I said, I'll do what I can.''

There was a pause. Then: ''And you'll get the details of those girls to me?''

''That's a promise.''

''Okay.'' The Necroscope's voice had slackened a little, lost some of its tension. ''I . . . I didn't mean to come on so strong, Darcy.''

Clarke's heart at once went out to him. "Harry, I think you've a lot on your mind. Maybe we can speak sometime—in person, I mean. What I'm saying is, don't be afraid to come to me."

"Afraid?"

It had been the wrong word. "Apprehensive, then. I mean, don't worry that there might be something you can't tell me or we can't talk about. There isn't anything you can't tell me, Harry."

Again that long, perhaps indicative pause. Then: "But right now I don't have anything to tell you, Darcy. However, I'll get back to you if I ever do."

"is that a promise?"

"Yes, that's a promise, too. And Darcy—thanks."

Clarke sat and thought about it for long minutes. And while he sat there behind his desk, drumming his fingers in a continuous, monotonous tattoo, he became aware of the first small warning bells growing to an insistent clamor at the back of his mind. Harry Keogh had required him to find out who was running Paxton. But who could be running him if not E-Branch? And to what end?

The last man to occupy this desk had been Norman Harold Wellesley, a traitor. Wellesley was gone now, dead, but the fact that he'd ever existed at all—and in this of all jobs—must have caused ructions further up the line. What, a double agent? A spy among mindspies? Something which must never be allowed to happen again, obviously; but how to stop it from happening again? Could it be that someone had been appointed to watch the watchers?

It reminded Clarke of a ditty his mother used to say to him when he was small and had an itch. She would find the spot and scratch it, reciting:

47

"Big fleas have little fleas
upon their backs to bite 'em.
And little fleas have smaller fleas,
and so *ad infinitum!*"

Was Clarke himself under esper scrutiny? And if so, what had been read from *his* mind?

He go onto the switchboard, said: "Get me the Minister Responsible. If he's not available, leave a message that he's to call me back soonest. Also, I'd like someone to run me off a duplicate set of police reports on those girls in that serial killer case."

Half an hour later the reports were delivered to him, and as he was putting them in a large envelope he got his call from the MInister. "Yes, Clarke?"

"Sir," he said, "I just had Harry Keogh on the phone."

"Oh?"

"He asked for a set of reports on the girls in the serial killer case. As you'll recall, we asked for his help on that."

"I recall that *you* asked for help, Clarke, yes. But in fact I'm not so sure it was a good idea. Indeed, I think it's time to rethink our attitude towards Keogh."

"Oh?"

"Yes. I know he's been of some assistance to the Branch, and—"

"Some?" Clarke had to cut in. "Some assistance? We were all goners long ago without him. We can't ever repay him. Not just us but everyone. And I do mean everyone."

"Things change, Clarke," said that unseen, unknown other. "You people are a weird lot—no offense—and Keogh has to be the weirdest of all. Also, he's not really one of you. So as of now I want you to avoid contact with him. But we'll talk about him again, I'm sure, later.''

The warning bells rang even louder. Talking to the Minister Responsible was always like talking to a very smooth robot, but this time he was just too smooth. ''And the police reports? Does he get them?''

''I think not. Let's just for the moment keep him at arm's length, right?''

''Is there something to worry about, maybe?'' Clarke came straight out with it. ''Do you think perhaps we should watch him?''

''Why, you surprise me!'' said the other, smooth as ever. ''It was my understanding that Keogh had always been a good friend of yours.''

''He has.''

''Well, and doubtless that was of value at the time. But as I said, things change. I *will* get back to you about him—one way or the other—in good time. But until then . . . was there anything else?''

''One small thing.'' Clarke kept his tone neutral but scowled at the phone. ''About Paxton . . .'' It was a leaf straight out of Harry Keogh's book, and it worked just as well for Clarke.

''Paxton?'' (He actually heard the Minister catch his breath!) Then, more cautiously, perhaps curiously: ''Paxton? But we're no longer interested in him, are we?''

''It's just that I was reading through his records,'' Clarke lied, ''his progress reports, you know? And it seemed to me we lost a good one there. Is it possible you've been maybe a bit too thorough? A shame to lose him if there's a chance we can bring him on. We really can't afford to waste talents like his.''

''Clarke,'' the Minister sighed, ''you have your side

of the job, and I have mine. I don't question your decisions, do I?''

Don't you?

''And I really would appreciate it if you wouldn't question mine. Forget about Paxton, he's out of it.''

''As you wish—but I think I'll at least keep an eye on him. If only from a distance. After all, we're not the only ones in the mindspy game. I'd hate it if he were recruited by the other side . . .''

The Minister was getting peeved. ''For the moment you have quite enough work on your plate!'' he snapped. ''Leave Paxton be. A periodic check will suffice—when *I* say so!''

Clarke was only polite when people were polite to him. He was far too important to let himself be stepped on. ''Keep your shirt on . . . sir,'' he growled. ''Anything I say or do is in the Branch's best interest, believe me—even when I step on toes.''

''Of course, of course.'' The other was at once conciliatory. ''But we're all in the same boat, Clarke, and none of us knows everything. So for the time being let's just trust each other, all right?''

Oh, yeah, let's! Sure! ''Fine,'' Clarke said. ''I'm sorry I've taken up so much of your time.''

''That's all right. We'll be speaking again soon, I'm sure . . .''

Clarke put the phone down and continued to scowl at it awhile, then sealed the envelope containing the police reports and scrawled Harry Keogh's address on it. He erased his and Keogh's recent conversation, then asked the switchboard if they'd traced the call. They had and it was Harry's Edinburgh number. He phoned it direct but got no answer. And finally, he called a courier into his office and gave him the envelope.

''Post it, please,'' he said, but before the courier could

leave: "No, repackage the whole thing and send it off special delivery. And then forget you ever saw it, right?"

In a little while he was alone with his dark, suspicious thoughts again, and an itch between his shoulder blades which he couldn't quite get at.

And his mother's ditty about fleas, which was equally persistent.

III   Changeling

HARRY KEOGH, NECROSCOPE, DIDN'T KNOW DARCY Clarke's ditty, but he did have a flea on his back. Several, in fact. And they were biting him.

Geoffrey Paxton was only one and probably the least of them, but because he was reachable and immediate he was the most frightening. Harry wasn't frightened *of* Paxton, rather of what he might do to Paxton if he lost control. And of what losing control might conceivably do to him, to the Necroscope himself. He knew how easy it would be to betray himself and reveal that he was no longer an innocent but that some great and as yet undeveloped (but developing, certainly) Darkness had entered him.

That was what Paxton was looking for, Harry knew: proof that the Necroscope was no longer a fit citizen or habitant of Earth—no longer, indeed, a man, not entirely—but an alien creature and a monstrous threat. And when he knew it for sure, when there was no longer any doubt, then Paxton would report that fact and there would be war. Harry Keogh versus The Rest. The rest of Mankind. And that was the last thing Harry wanted, to be at odds with a world and its peoples which he had fought so long and so hard to keep safe.

Paxton, then, was a flea on Harry's back, a niggle at the edge of—attempting to dig its way deeper into—his mind, an *irritation*. And because Paxton's presence was representative of an even greater threat, which must ultimately challenge the Necroscope's very existence, it was something Harry could well do without. For to the Wamphyri the single ''honorable'' answer to any challenge may only be written in blood!

Wamphyri!

The word itself was . . . a Power.

It was a tingling in the core of his being, an awareness of passions beyond the feeble, fumbling emotions of men, a savage, explosive nucleic energy contained—but barely—in his seething blood. It was a chain reaction which was happening to him even now, whose catalyst *was* blood. And in itself, it too was a challenge. But one which he must resist, which he must not, dare not answer. Not if he desired to remain ascendant and for the most part human.

A flea, then, this Paxton. An invader who would stick his proboscis in that most private and inviolable of all human territories, the mind itself, and siphon out its thoughts. A spy, a thought-thief—a parasite come to sup on Harry's secrets—a flea. But only one flea of several, and not one which he could afford to scratch.

Another unbearable itch was the fact that the dead—the Great Majority of mankind, who yet lay apart from and unknowable to mankind, with the sole (the soul?) exception of Harry Keogh—were withdrawing from him.

He was losing his rapport; the change in him had wrought a change in them; their trust was weakening.

Oh, there were many among them who owed him beyond their means to repay, and many more who had loved him for his sake, to whom the Necroscope had always been the one glimmer of light in an otherwise everlasting darkness, but even these were wary of him now. For when he had been simply Harry—unsullied and unsullying, innocent and gentle—why, then it had been a *marvelous* thing that he could touch the dead and they touch him! But all of that was yesterday.

And now that he was more than Harry? There are certain things which even dead men fear, and limits to what even they will lie still for . . .

Since the destruction of Janos Ferenczy and his works, Harry had been busy. Other than the constant irritation of Geoffrey Paxton, the only intrusion he'd allowed—the single distraction from his purpose, because he had no control over it—was the knowledge that a necromancer lived and practiced his abominations in England. It distracted him because Penny Sanderson was now his friend (his ward, even?) and because he was privy to what she and others like her had gone through.

Of the fact that the forces of law and order would track down and apprehend Penny's torturer, murderer, and *then* violator eventually, Harry had little doubt; but they would never charge him with the full range of his offenses, because they had no yardstick by which to measure them. They neither knew nor were capable of defining a *full* range of offenses, not in this case. And certainly, there was no punishment which would fit the crime. Not in law.

But the Necroscope fully understood the nature of this beast and his crimes, and his ideas of punishment were rather more stringent. Even before his contamination he'd had that. It was a flame which had been sparked in him by the murder of his own sweet mother, and which burned just as lively to this day. An eye for an eye.

As to what Harry had been doing since removing the last of the Ferenczys forever from the world of men: his works had been weird and wonderful, and the thoughts in his Möbius mind even more so.

To begin with, he'd brought back Trevor Jordan's ashes from Rhodes. The incorporeal telepath had wished it (death might have something of meaning with Harry to talk to), but not even Jordan had suspected Harry's real purpose.

By themselves, however, the essential salts of a man were insufficient to put Harry's plan into action, not and achieve the entirely satisfactory result which he sought. Which was why, before further reducing the ruins of Janos Ferenczy's castle, the Necroscope had removed from them certain chemical substances by means of which Janos had performed his own monstrous brand of necromancy.

Not all of the dead would wish for such a resurgence, Harry knew: the Thracian warrior-king Bodrogk and his wife, Sofia, whose world had lain two thousand years in the past, had been happy to collapse in each other's arms and return to dust (a merciful release for them, who had prayed for it so often). But what of the much more recently dead?

Like Trevor Jordan, for instance.

The answer might seem easy: why not ask him? But in fact that was the hardest thing of all. "I intend to return you to life. I have the apparatus but I'm not one hundred percent sure of the system. It worked perfectly well for another, but he had the advantage of many hundreds of years of experimentation. In the event all goes well you will be as you were; except, well . . . you'll recall that you *did* put a bullet through your brain. I'm not entirely sure how that will affect you. If when I call you up from your ashes I discover that you're a complete gibbering fucking idiot, then however reluctantly, I'll be obliged to put you down again. Now, provided you're perfectly happy with all of this . . .''

Or, in Penny Sanderson's case:

''Penny, I think I can bring you back. But if I get the mixture wrong it could be that you'll not be as lovely as you were. I mean, your skin and features could be imperfect, or blemished, or pocked . . . hideously. For example, some of the things I called up in the Castle Ferenczy were quite monstrous; there were *depletions*, inconsistencies, er, anomalies? Wherefore I reserve the right to erase you if things go wrong. But of course we'll always be able to try again later, when with a bit of luck I'll get it right.''

No, he couldn't tell them what he had in mind, not yet. If he gave them the bare bones of the thing, they'd require him to flesh it out, and if he elaborated, they'd fret about every smallest detail. And from now until the actual—resurrection?—they'd mix anticipation with dread, alternating shivers of excitement with shudders of terror most extreme. They'd climb high mountains of hope, only to tumble back into black lakes of deepest despair and depression.

''I have a shot which may cure your cancer . . . but it just might give you AIDS.''

That was how it would feel to Harry if the roles were reversed; but at the same time he knew that of course it wasn't like that: when you're dead you're beyond hope, and so any hope has to be better than none. Or does it? Or was that simply the vampire in him—tenacity aspiring to immortality—doing his thinking for him?

Or . . . perhaps he hesitated for another, far more elemental reason: something which warned him that with his small talents (small, yes, in the scale of a universe or parallel multiverses) he must not, *dare* not, usurp one of the Greater Talents of that Other whom men called God. History's necromancers, among which Janos had been a latecomer, had dared it, and where were they now? Had there been avenging angels before Harry, to put right the wrongs of these wizards? And if so, would there be one after him, to chastise him in his turn?

Harry had been the Necroscope, was becoming a vampire, and now would be a necromancer in his own right. How dare he seek out Penny's murderer to punish him on the one hand, and on the other pursue the practice of that same black art? What would be *his* punishment?

Perhaps the gears were already engaged, the wheels even now turning. Perhaps the Necroscope had already gone too far, disturbing the delicate balance between Good and Evil to such an extent that it now required radical readjustment. Had he simply become too powerful, which is to say corrupt? How did the old saying go: "Absolute power corrupts absolutely"? Ridiculous! Was God Himself corrupt? No, for the maxims of men are like their laws: they apply only to men.

Such arguments were endless in the metamorphosis of the Necroscope's mind and body, until sometimes he thought he was mad. But when his thoughts were clear he knew that he was not mad; it was just the *thing* that was in him, altering his perceptions along with everything else.

And then he would remember how he used to be, determine that he must always be that way, and know that he only hesitated out of consideration for his friends among the dead. It was simply that he didn't want Trevor and Penny to suffer agonies of protracted uncertainty, only to let them down when the waiting was over. To die once is enough, as had been made perfectly plain by Janos's many Thracian thralls in the bowels of the Castle Ferenczy.

As for God: if there *was* such a One (and Harry had never been sure), then the Necroscope supposed he must consider his talents God-given and use them accordingly. While he could.

Harry had spent a good deal of his time arguing, not least with himself. If a subject took his fancy—almost any subject—he would play word games with himself to the point of distraction and delirium: a sort of mental masturbation. But it wasn't just himself he was jerking off; in conversations with the dead he was equally argumentative, even when he suspected that they were right and he was wrong.

Indeed, he seemed to argue for the sake of it, out of sheer contrariness. He thought and argued about God; also about good and evil, about science, pseudoscience, and sorcery, their similarities, discrepancies, and ambiguities. Space, time, and space-time fascinated him, and especially mathematics with its inalienable laws and pure logic. The very changelessness of math was a constant joy and relief to the Necroscope's changeling mind in its changeling body.

Within a day or two of returning from the Greek islands he had used the instantaneous medium of the Möbius Continuum to go to Leipzig and see (speak to) August Ferdinand Möbius where he lay in his grave there. Möbius had been and still was a great mathematician and astronomer; indeed he was the man whose genius had saved Harry's life on several occasions, again through the medium of his Möbius Continuum. But while Harry's primary purpose in visiting Möbius was to thank him for the return of his numeracy, instead he ended up arguing with him.

The great man had happened to mention that his next project would be to measure space, and as soon as the Necroscope heard this he threw himself headlong into an argument. This time the argument was "Space, Time, Light, and the Multiverses."

Won't "Universe" suffice? Möbius had wanted to know.

"Not at all," Harry had answered, "because we know there are parallels. I've visited one, remember?" (And East German students with their notebooks had wondered at this peculiar man who stood by a dead scientist's tomb muttering to himself.)

Möbius had been logical about it. *Very well, then, let's concentrate on the one we know best. This one.*

"You'll measure it?"

I propose to.

"But since it's constantly expanding, how will you go about it?"

I shall stand at its outermost rim, beyond which there is nothing, transfer myself instantaneously through the universe to the far rim, beyond which there is likewise nothing, and in so doing measure the distance between. Then I shall transfer myself instantaneously back here and perform the same experiment exactly one hour later, and again an hour after that.

"Good!" Harry had answered. "But . . . to what purpose?"

(A sigh.) *Why, from that time forward—and whenever I require to know it—a correct calculation of the size of the universe will be instantly available!*

Harry had stayed grudgingly silent for a moment, until: "I too have given the matter a little thought," he said. "Though purely on the theoretical level, because the physical measurement of a constantly changing quantity seems rather fruitless to me. Whereas to *understand* what is happening, how and to what degree the age of the universe is tied to its rate of expansion—a constant, incidentally—and so forth, seems so much more satisfying.''

(An astonished pause.) *Oh, indeed!* And Harry had almost been able to see Möbius's eyebrows joining in a frown across the bridge of his nose. *"You" have thought about it, have you? Theoretically, you say? And might I inquire as to "your" conclusions?*

''You want to know all about space, time, light, and the multiverses?''

If you've the time for it! Möbius had been scathing in his sarcasm.

To which the Necroscope had answered:

''Your initial measurement will suffice; no other is necessary. Knowing the size of the universe—and not only this one, incidentally, but all the parallels, too—at any given moment of time, we will automatically know their exact age and rate of expansion, which will be uniform for all of them.''

Explain.

''Now the theory,'' said Harry. ''In the beginning there was nothing. Came the Primal Light! Possibly, it shone out of the Möbius Continuum, or perhaps it came with the colossal fireball of the Big Bang. But it was the beginning of the universe of light. Before the light there was nothing, and after it there was a universe expanding *at the speed of light!*''

Eh?

''Do you disagree?''

The universe was expanding at the speed of light?

''Actually, at twice the speed of light,'' said Harry. ''That was the essence of your problem, remember, which sparked the return of my numeracy? Switch on a light in space and a pair of observers 186,000 miles away from it on opposite sides would *both* see its light one second later, because the light expands in both directions. Now, do you disagree?"

Of course not! The Primal Light, as any light, must have expanded just as you say. But . . . the universe?

"At the same speed!" said Harry. "And it still is expanding at that speed."

Explain. And make it good.

"Before the light there was nothing, no universe."

Agreed.

"Does anything travel faster than light?"

No—yes! We can, but only in the Möbius Continuum. And I suppose thought is likewise instantaneous.

"Now think!" said Harry. "The Primal Light is *still* travelling outwards, expanding on all frontiers at a constant speed of 186,000 miles per second. Tell me: does anything lie beyond those frontiers? And I do mean *any*thing?"

Of course not, because in the physical universe nothing travels faster than light.

"Exactly! Wherefore light defines the extent—the size—of the universe! That's why I called it the universe of light. A formula:

$$aU = \frac{rU}{c}$$

"Do you disagree?"

Möbius had looked at the thing scrawled on the screen of Harry's mind. *The age of the universe is equal to its radius divided by the speed of light.* And after a moment, but very quietly now: *Yes, I agree.*

"Hah!" said Harry. "It's hard to get a decent argument going these days. Everyone cries uncle."

Möbius had been angry. He had never seen Harry like this before. Certainly, the Necroscope's instinctive math was a wonderful thing, an awesome talent in its own right, but where was Harry's humility? What on earth had got into him? Perhaps Möbius should let him continue to expound and then try to pick holes, bring him down a peg or two.

And time? And the multiverses?

But Harry had been ready for him:

"The space-time universe—which has the same size and age as any and all of the parallels—is cone-shaped, the point of the cone being the Big Bang/Primal Light where time began, and the base being its current boundary or diameter. Is that feasible, logical?"

Desperately seeking errors, still Möbius had been unable to discover them. *Yes,* he was obliged to answer eventually. *Feasible, logical, but not necessarily correct.*

"Grant me feasible," said Harry. "And then tell me: what lies outside the cone?"

Nothing, since the universe is contained within it.

"Wrong! The parallels are cone-shaped, too, born at the same time and expanding from the same source!"

Möbius had pictured it. *But . . . then each cone is in contact with a number of other cones. Is there evidence of this?*

"Black holes," said Harry at once, "which juggle with matter and so perform a necessary balancing act. They suck matter out of the universes which are too heavy, into universes which are too light. White holes are, of course, the other ends of the black holes. In space-time such holes are the lines of contact between cones, but in space they are simply—" (a shrug) "—holes."

Möbius was tired, but: *Cones are circular in cross-section,* he argued. *Put three together and you get a triangular shape between them.*

And Harry had nodded his agreement. "Grey holes. There's one at the bottom of the Perchorsk ravine, and another up an underground river in Romania."

And so he'd made his point and won his argument, if there had been one to win in the first place. For the fact was he'd only argued for the sake of it and neither knew nor cared if he was right or wrong.

But Mobius *had* cared, because he didn't know if Harry was right or wrong, either . . .

Another time, the Necroscope had talked to Pythagoras. Again his principal reason for going to see him was to convey his thanks (the great Greek mystic and mathematician had been of some assistance in his quest for numeracy), but again the visit had ended in argument.

Harry had thought to find the Greek's grave at Metapontum, or if not there then at Crotona, in southern Italy. But all he found was a follower or two until, by pure chance, he stumbled upon the forgotten, 2,480-year-old tomb of a member of the Pythagorean Brotherhood on the island of Chios. There was no marker; it was a stony, ocher place where goats ate thistles not fifty yards from a rocky shore looking north on the Aegean.

Pythagoras? No, not here, that one informed in a hushed and very secretive manner, when Harry's deadspeak broke into his centuried thoughts. *He is elsewhere, waiting out his time.*

"His time?"

Until his metempsychosis, into a living, breathing man!

"But do you converse? Are you able to contact him?"

He will occasionally contact us, when a thought *has occurred to him.*

"Us?"

The Brotherhood! But I have said too much. Begone. Leave me in peace.

"As you wish," Harry had told him. "But he won't thank you that you turned away the Necroscope."

What? The Necroscope? (Astonishment and awe.) *You are that one, who taught the dead to speak out in their graves, so enabling them to talk to one another as in life?*

"The same."

And do you seek to learn from Pythagoras?

"I seek to instruct him."

That is a blasphemy!

"Blasphemy?" Harry had raised an eyebrow. "And is Pythagoras a god, then? If so, a painfully slow one! Consider this: I have already achieved my metempsychosis. Even now I embark upon a second phase, a new . . . condition."

Your soul is in process of migration?

"I may say that a change is in the offing, certainly."

And after a while: *If I speak to our master Pythagoras on your behalf, and if you have lied to me, be sure he will damn you with numbers. Aye, and possibly me with you! No, I dare not. First prove yourself.*

Harry had contained his impatience as best he could. "Perhaps I can show *you* some numbers. As a member of the Brotherhood, I'm sure you will appreciate their importance."

Do you seek to seduce me with your puny figures? What, the work of a mere lifetime? Are you suggesting that in the two thousand years and more which have passed since I was laid to rest here I've dreamed no numbers or equations or formulae of my own? Necroscope or none, you are presumptuous!

"Presumptuous?" Harry's anger had been aroused. "Equations? Formulae? Why, I have formulae such as you could *never* dream." And he'd displayed the computer screen of his mind, and covered it with the endlessly mutating algebraics of Möbius mathematics. Then he'd formed a Möbius door, and let the other gaze a moment upon the nowhere and everywhere across the threshold.

Until gaspingly: *What . . . what is that?!*

"The Big Zero," Harry had growled then, letting the door close on itself. "The place where all numbers begin. But I'm wasting my time. I came to talk to a master and ended up chatting with a mere student—and a middling one at that. Now tell me: do I get my audience with Pythagoras or don't I?"

He . . . he is in Samos.

"Where he was born?"

The same. The last place anyone would think to look for him, he thought . . . And then frantically: *Necroscope—plead with him for me! I have betrayed him! He will exclude me!*

"Rubbish!" Harry had growled, but without scorn. "Exclude you? He will elevate you—for you have gazed upon the secret mathematical door to all times and places. You don't believe me?" (And he'd shrugged.) "Well, it's your choice. My thanks anyway—and farewell." And conjuring another Möbius door he'd stepped through it—

—And out again on Samos, twenty miles away, where Pythagoras had spent his childhood two and a half millennia ago, and to which his bones had been returned in secrecy when at last he died. Pythagoras, however introvert, secretive, diffident, could hardly escape or ignore the Necroscope's deadspeak probe at such close range. That thought in itself had been deadspeak and as such the recluse (in death even more than in life) had heard it. And answered:

What is your number?

Harry had shrugged, homing in on the mystic's mental whisper. "Any you choose for me." And when he'd located him definitely, one further Möbius jump took him from a deserted, wooded shoreline straight there: to a small olive grove on a terraced hillside above a headland with a tiny white church. Down the coast a little way, scarcely glimpsed through pines and wind-warped oaks, Tigani's harbor glinted turquoise, blue, silver; music from a taverna came drifting on the bright summer air.

It was cool in the shade of the trees and the Necroscope had been grateful to take off his wide-brimmed hat, also the dark-lensed spectacles which protected his now-delicate eyes. And because Pythagoras had remained silently thoughtful:

"There are numbers galore. I'm not fussy."

Then you should be. The mystic's whisper was tremulous, fevered. *They are The All. The gods themselves are numbers, though no man knows them. When I have discovered the numbers of the gods, then my metempsychosis may commence.*

"If you truly believe that, then you've a long time to wait," Harry had answered at once. "You can know all the numbers in all their combinations from now to eternity and it won't change anything, not for you. It isn't a magical thing, Pythagoras; however many numbers you employ, your soul won't fly into a new body; there's no science or sorcery can help you now."

Hah! The other was filled with wrath and not a little scorn. *Only see who utters these blasphemies! And is this the Necroscope, who was impotent and innumerate, to whom the simplest sum was a mystery? Are you the one they pleaded for, the legions of dust, the teeming dead? Möbius came to me on his knees for you, and what are you, after all, but an ingrate?*

Harry had been needled but hid it from the Greek. Likewise he hid his thoughts: *Pompous old fart!* While out loud:

"I came to thank you, for my numeracy. Without it

I'd be like you: dust in a grave. Or perhaps not like you, for there was a man who would have called me up to torture me for my secrets."

A necromancer?

"Just so."

It is a black art!

"Not always. It has its uses. What I am doing now is a sort of necromancy, after all. For I am a living man, talking to one who is dead."

Pythagoras gave this a moment's thought, and: *I overheard your conversation with one of the Brothers,* he said. *Is blasphemy your byword? You alleged reincarnation, transmigration, metempsychosis.*

"I stated a fact," said Harry. "I was one man in his own body, and when it died I inhabited another. Don't take my word for it but ask the dead, who have nothing to gain from lying. They'll tell you it's true. Moreover, if your ashes were pure, I tell you I could even call *you* up from the dead! Not with numbers but with words. And this isn't blasphemy, Pythagoras, but simple truth. Or . . . perhaps the act itself would constitute blasphemy, I can't be sure. If so then you're right and I am a blasphemer, and plan to be again."

You could call me up from my ashes?

"Only if they were pure, unsullied. Were you buried in a jar?"

I was buried in soil, in secret, here beneath your feet, where as a boy I ran among the trees. My flesh and bones are now one with the earth. Anyway, I cannot believe you. Words and not numbers? Words are from the lips, frivolous things which are spoken and change, while numbers spring from pure mind and are immutable.

Harry had shrugged. "It's academic, after all. In two thousand years your salts have been washed into the soil.

There are no words—and certainly no numbers—which can help you now.''

Blasphemy and *sedition! Do you seek to turn my followers against me?*

Harry could contain himself no longer. ''Pythagoras, you're a charlatan! In your world you guarded your small, pointless mathematical 'secrets'—basic discoveries which any child under instruction knows today from his schoolbooks—as if they were life and death. And true death has not changed you. I gave you deadspeak, since when you could have conferred with more modern, more genuine masters, if you'd wished it. To Galileo Galilei, Isaac Newton, Albert Einstein; to Roemer, Maxwell, and—''

Enough! The other had been outraged. *I should have ignored Möbius! I should have—*

''But you couldn't ignore him!'' (Harry's turn to cut in.) ''You dared not . . .''

What do you mean?

''That I know your real secret. That you were a fraud. That you not only made fools of your precious 'Brotherhood' in life but continue to deceive them in death! There is no mysticism in numbers, Pythagoras, and you must know it. If only because you're a learned man. Why, you yourself have told me that numbers are immutable, unchanging and unchangeable. Which means that they are solid *truth*, not flights of fancy! Iron *truth*, not ethereal magic.''

Liar! Liar! Pythagoras had raged. *You twist words, change meanings!*

''Why do you hide yourself, even from the dead?''

Because they have no understanding. Because their ignorance is contagious.

''No, because they know more than you! Your followers would desert you. You told them they would migrate, return again to men, and meet with you in worlds or pure number—and now you know that this was false.''

I thought it was truth.

''But that was two and a half thousand years ago. And are you returned? How long does it take to admit you were wrong?''

I have dreamed numbers that would blast you!

''Blast me, then.''

By this time Pythagoras had been sobbing. He hurled a catalogue of numbers at Harry, which shattered against the wall of the Necroscope's metaphysical mind. But at least they shocked him into recognition of his predicament: that again the thing inside was striving to replace him, this time by use of convoluted Wamphyri ''logic.''

On this occasion it was his salvation, for it had never been Harry's desire to hurt or even alarm the dead. And:

''I . . . I'm sorry,'' he said.

Sorry? You are a friend! Pythagoras had sobbed. *But . . . you are right.*

''No, I merely argued. Perhaps I am right, perhaps not. But I was wrong to argue for the sake of it. And let's face it, I stand in contradiction of my own argument.''

How so?

''I know that numbers are not immutable.''

Ahhh! (A long-drawn-out-sigh.) *Would you . . . could you demonstrate?*

At which Harry had shown him the screen of his mind, with all of Möbius's configurations crawling on its surface, mutating and sprawling into infinity. And for a long time the old Greek had been silent. Then:

I was a clever child who thought he knew everything, he said, his voice broken. *Time has passed me by.*

''But it will never forget you,'' Harry had been quick to point out. ''We remember your theorem; books have been written about you; there are Pythagoreans even to-day.''

My theorem? My numbers? If I hadn't done it others would have.

''But it's your name we remember. And anyway, that could be said of anyone and anything.''

Except the Necroscope.

But: ''I'm not even sure about that,'' Harry had an-swered. ''I think that perhaps there were others before me. And certainly there was one after me. They dwell in other worlds now.''

And will you dwell there, too?

''Possibly. Probably. And perhaps soon.''

What's it like now? Pythagoras had asked after a while, and Harry had suspected it was the first thing he'd in-quired of anyone in a long time.

''Upon this island,'' the Necroscope had answered, ''lie many of the more recently dead. But you've shunned them. You could have asked them about Samos, the world, the living. But you were afraid to know the truth. And do you know, the last thing of any importance to the living on this island is number? Well, perhaps not entirely true. I'm sure they're interested in the quantities of drachmae to the pound, to the deutsche mark and the dollar.'' He explained his meaning.

The world is so small now!

Harry had put on his hat, his glasses, and gone out from the shade into sunlight. With his hands in his pock-ets the latter didn't bother him too much, but he must go slowly or lose his balance on the rough tracks and roads into Tigani. Pythagoras had gone with him, his dead-speak, anyway; distance wasn't too important once con-tact had been established.

I'll open up the Brotherhood, dissolve it entirely, put it aside. There's so much to learn.

"Men have landed on the moon," said Harry.

Pythagoras's mind had flown in circles.

"They have calculated the speed of light."

The old mystic's thoughts were one huge, astonished question mark.

"But you know, among the dead are those mathematicians who could benefit greatly from your knowledge."

What, mine? I am an infant!

"Not a bit of it. You stuck to pure number. Why, in two thousand and more years, by now you're a lightning calculator! May I test you?"

By all means—but please, a simple thing. Not the dizzy designs inscribed upon your secret mind.

"Then give me the sum of all the numbers between one and one hundred, inclusive."

Five thousand and fifty. Pythagoras's answer had been instantaneous.

Harry had been right. "A lightning calculator. Among the less practical mathematicians—the theoretical mathematicians—why, you'd be like a talking slide rule! I think that for a dead man you've a great future, Pythagoras."

The Greek had been flattered. *But it was such a simple thing, and known by heart. Multiplication, division, addition, and subtraction—aye, and trigonometry, too—I've done it all so often. There isn't an angle I can't calculate.*

Harry had smiled. "There you are." And, however drily: "Believe me, there aren't many today who know all the angles."

And you, Harry? Are you a lightning calculator?

Harry hadn't wished to shatter him. "Ah, but with me it's different, intuitive."

Between one and a million, then!

"500,000,500,000," the Necroscope had answered almost in the same breath. "Take ten and multiply it by itself as many times as you like, and it works every time. Half of ten is five; put the two halves together again: fifty-five. Half of a hundred is fifty, put the halves together: five thousand and fifty. And so on. 'Magic' to some, intuition to me."

Pythagoras had been downcast. *Why would they need me when they already have you?*

"Because, as I've stated, I may not be here too long. It's like you said; the world is a small place. And it's hard to find a hiding place."

On the outskirts of Tigani he'd found a small taverna and seated himself in its shade, and ordered ouzo with a dash of lemonade. English girls splashed in the warm, blue waters of a small, rocky bay. Their breasts were shiny and Harry could smell the oil of coconut from here. Pythagoras had picked the picture from Harry's mind and scowled at it. *Perhaps it's as well I'm unbodied to stay,* he'd commented darkly. *Like vampires, they deplete a man.*

For a moment the Necroscope had been caught off guard, but then: "Ah!" he'd answered. "But there are vampires and there are vampires . . ."

IV Someone Dying

THE NECROSCOPE'S VAMPIRE—AS YET A MERE TADPOLE
of alien, parasitic contamination—was immature. As such
it had no desire for conflict either internal or external but
wished only to evolve and get on with the long process
of its host's conversion; which was why its influence was
mainly enervating. Keep Harry mentally and emotion-
ally drained, and he'd be less likely to jeopardize himself. Which by definition meant that he'd be less likely
to jeopardize his horrific tenant. Hence his flashes of
Wamphyri-awareness (half-glimpsed knowledge of burgeoning, ungovernable Power) and the burning need to
argue and cross-examine, even to engage his own mind
in long spells of intense self-inquisition, despite the bouts
of inwardly directed anger and mental exhaustion which
invariably resulted.

But quite apart from the Necroscope's mind, his *blood*
was also aware that the invader was here; it seemed filled
with a weird psychic fever which kept him jumpy and

constantly on guard. He was a man with a volcano inside him, which for now merely simmered and let off a little steam. Not knowing when the volcano was set to go off, he couldn't relax but must hold the cap firmly in place, and listen with a rapt, horrified, and yet curious intentness to the rumbling within.

On the one hand Harry would like to test out his Wamphyri talents to the full (for they were part of him even now, while yet the physical side of the thing was still embryonic), but on the other he knew that to do so would be to accelerate the process. For one thing was certain: however immature his symbiont might be, it was also fast-growing and -learning. No slow starter *this* vampire.

But while the parasite like all its kind would be dogged, the Necroscope was no less tenacious in his own right. His son had managed to keep his vampire in order, hadn't he? Like son, like father: Harry would do his damnedest to follow suit.

Except that would be hard enough in itself without the current recalcitrance of the Great Majority . . . and the knowledge or at least strong suspicion that E-Branch was gearing itself for war . . . *and* the fact that despite all of this Harry had determined to bring a certain fiend to justice but first must find him.

Previously, he would have been able to work out a logical system of approach, like writing down an itinerary of priorities. But his mental confusion and the weariness it produced obfuscated, so that while he was aware of the passage of time and of forces mobilizing against him, still he felt incapable of rising above and proceeding beyond his personal miasma. Which in turn brought frustration, more anger, and the first gale warnings that his whirling, gusting emotions craved physical release.

Like an alien autism incapable of self-expression, Harry could feel his violence lying just beneath the surface. *His* violence, yes, for the vampire in him was neither violent nor emotional: it merely amplified these properties in its host.

Perhaps most frustrating of all, he knew that none of the things he was doing—or would do if he felt capable— was of the slightest importance to his own personal survival. Another in his position might seek to change his identity, find a safe place, extricate himself permanently from all dangerous sources and focuses.

Or would he? Would he even be able to? For as Harry had pointed out to Pythagoras, the world is a small place. And by definition any other in Harry's position would likewise be Wamphyri and territorial. This was *his* world; this house not far from Edinburgh was *his* house; especially his thoughts and actions were *his* territory—most of them, most of the time—at least when others weren't snooping on them.

Yesterday he had gone to the ruins of the Castle Ferenczy and spoken to Bodrogk the Thracian. Bodrogk was too recent a friend to have known Harry before the start of his transition; he accepted him for what he was now. Also, Bodrogk was fearless and in any case could not possibly fear the Necroscope, nor for that matter any other living man. His dust, and the dust of his wife, Sofia, were scattered to the winds and only their spirits remained in the Carpathians now. They were quite beyond earthly harm.

The subject of Harry's inquiry had been the composition and proportions of the chemical ingredients of Janos Ferenczy's necromantic potions. He would only retrieve Trevor Jordan and Penny Sanderson from their "essential salts" if he could bring them back perfect or as close as possible. Bodrogk, because he had been subjected to just such experiments, was an authority. Even so, he'd inquired at length into the Necroscope's purpose before passing on the necessary information.

And so today Harry had been ready to become a true necromancer in his own right, and would have proceeded . . . but at the last moment he'd felt that twinge, that covert tweaking at the corner of his mind, which had warned him that Geoffrey Paxton was close by and watching him. Knowing that Paxton was seeking to prove just such unnatural activity in him, Harry had been obliged to postpone the experiment. And then, barely able to control his rage, he'd spoken to Darcy Clarke at E-Branch HQ.

It had come as a relief to know that Paxton wasn't Darcy's man; but if not his, whose? Maybe Darcy would find out and let him know, and maybe not. And in any case, what odds? For Harry knew that sooner or later Darcy and the others must all join forces against him. The hell of it was that the boss of E-Branch had been a good friend once. The Necroscope couldn't see any way that he would ever be able to hurt Darcy. But how to explain that to the thing inside him?

At 2:00 in the afternoon Harry had sat quite still in his study and "listened." But his vampire awareness was still a fledgling thing and he'd detected nothing. Or maybe he had: the very briefest wriggle of something on the outermost rim of his perceptions. Whatever, it was suspicious enough that he'd put back his experiment more yet, then rammed his wide-brimmed hat onto his head and gone outdoors to talk to his mother.

Now, sitting on the crumbling riverbank, Harry dangled his legs and looked down into the gently swirling water which had been Mary Keogh's grave for most of his life, and let his deadspeak thoughts reach out to her. Since there was no one here to see him, he simply spoke to her, which was also deadspeak and felt far more natural:

"Ma, I'm in a mess."

If she'd answered, "So what's new?" he would understand; it seemed he was always in a mess. But Mary Keogh loved her son as all mothers do, and death had not diminished that.

Harry? Her voice seemed very faint now, very distant, as if she'd been washed away downriver along with her physical shell. *Oh, Harry, I know you are, son.*

Well, and that was only to be expected. He'd never been able to hide anything from his ma, who had warned him often enough that there are some things you daren't get too close to. This time he'd let himself get too close. "Do you know what I'm talking about?"

There's only one thing you can be talking about, son (she sounded so sad, so sorry for him). *And even if you hadn't come to speak to me, still I would know. All of us know, Harry.*

He nodded. "They're not so keen to talk to me anymore," he said, maybe a little bitterly. "And yet I never harmed a single one of them."

But you should try to understand, Harry, she was at pains to explain. *The Great Majority were once living and now are dead. They remember what life was, and they know what death is, but they don't understand and wish nothing to do with anything that lies between. They can't understand something which preys on the living to make them undead, which takes away true life and replaces it with soulless greed and lust and . . . and evil. The children and grandchildren of the teeming dead are still in the world of the living, and so are you. And that's what worries them. It makes no difference how long people are dead, Harry, they still worry about their children. But you know that, son, don't you?*

Harry sighed. Her deadspeak, however faint (and possibly even chiding?), was as warm as ever. It covered the Necroscope like a blanket, kept him safe, made it easier to think and plan and even dream. It was so alien to the nightmare thing inside him that *that* part of Harry could neither understand nor interfere with it. Namely, it was the love of his mother, soothing as nothing else could ever be.

"But the point is," he said in a little while, "that I've one more thing to do before I . . . before I'm finished here. And it's important, Ma. Important to me, and to you and the teeming dead alike. There's a monster running loose, and I have to nail him."

A monster, son? Her voice was very soft, but he knew what she meant. Who was he to talk about monsters?

"Ma, I've done nothing wrong," he answered. "And so long as I'm me, I'm not going to."

Harry, she said, *son, I'm all used up.* And she wasn't only faint but very tired, too. *We're not inexhaustible. Left alone we'd just go on thinking our thoughts, gradually fading as all things do. We do fade in the end, be it ever so long. But torn by outside influences we go that much faster. I think that's how it works, anyway. You were a light in our long night, son, and it was like we could see again. But now we have to let you go and suffer the darkness. Alive we used to wonder: is there anything on the other side? Well, there was, and then you came and joined us up, and there was a kind of life again. So now I wonder: what's next? What I'm telling you is I haven't long here. But I'd hate to leave you not knowing you were all right. What are your plans, Harry?*

And for the first time he realized that he really did need a plan. As simply as that, his mother had cut through all of his confusion.

"Well, there's a place I can go," he finally answered.

"Not much of a place, but better than dying . . . I think. And there's someone there who can teach me things, if he's willing. He had problems, too, but the last time I saw him he was coping. Maybe he still is. Maybe I can learn something from him."

She knew where, who, and what he meant, of course. *But isn't that a sinister sort of place, Harry?*

He shrugged. "It was. Maybe it still is. But at least I won't be hunted there. I *would* be hunted here eventually, if I stayed. Which means I'd be forced to hunt, too. And that's what I'm afraid of and what I'm trying to avoid. I'm a plague in a bottle, Ma, safe only so long as no one shakes or tries to break me. But in that other place the plague has already run its course. What's unthinkable here is understood there. Not acceptable, never that, but a reality all the same."

She sighed. *I'm glad you're not just giving in, son.* And with something of her old fondness: *You're a fighter, Harry. You always were*

"I suppose I was," he agreed, "but I can't fight here. That would only bring it on. And in the end I'm afraid it might be stronger than me. There are still things I have to do here, that's all, business that needs clearing up. Which is how I'll occupy myself until it's time. You asked about my plans:

"They're simple, really. When my head's on straight I can read them like words in a book. There's a girl who died horribly and didn't deserve it, because no one deserves to die like that; and there's the creature who killed her and other innocents like her, who *does* deserve it. There's a long talk—an explanation—which I owe to Darcy Clarke; and oh, there are talents I'd like to gather, which might be useful to me in the other place.

"That's all of it: a few things to do, something I have to straighten out, and one or two new things to learn.

And then it will be time I walked. I'd rather walk than be chased.''

And you'll never come back?

"I might, if I learned how to hold the thing permanently in check. But if I can't . . . no, never.''

How will you deal with this man, murderer, monster, you're looking for?

"As quick and as cleanly as he'll let me. You don't know what he does, Ma, but I can tell you I won't soil my hands on him, not if I can help it. Killing him will be like cutting out a tumor in the flesh of humanity.''

You've cut out a few of those, son.

Harry nodded. "And one more to go.''

And the girl who doesn't deserve to be dead? That was a strange way of putting it, Harry.

"It's such a recent thing for her, Ma.'' (Harry knew he'd strayed into a mine field, looked in vain for a safe landmark.) "She's not used to it yet. And . . . and she doesn't have to get used to it. I mean, I can help her.''

You've learned a new thing, Harry, she answered, but very slowly, and he sensed something different in her voice which was never there before—fear? *You learned it from Janos Ferenczy, and I can feel it. Yes, and it's what puts you apart from us now. We can* all *feel it!* And suddenly her deadspeak was racked with small shudders.

His ma, too? Had he alienated even his warm, sweet ma? Suddenly, he had the feeling that if he let her go she'd just drift away from him and keep on drifting. Perhaps into that beyond place which she sensed waiting there. But he had one trump card left, and now played it:

"Ma, am I good or bad? Was I born good or evil?''

She read the anxiety in his deadspeak and returned at once. *Oh, you were good, son. How can you doubt it? You were always so good!*

"Well, nothing's changed, Ma. Not yet, and not here. I promise you, I won't let anything change me, not here. If and when I feel it—as soon as I feel I can't hold it any longer—then I'll go."

But if you bring that girl back, what will she be?

"Beautiful, just as she was. Maybe not physically beautiful—though it's a fact she was lovely—but alive. And that's to be beautiful. You know that."

But for how long, son? I mean, will she age? Will she die? What will she be? What will she be, *Harry?!*

He had no answer. "Just a girl. I don't know."

And her children? What will they be?

"Ma, I don't know! I only know she's too much alive to be dead."

Are you doing it for . . . yourself?

"No, just for her, and for all of you."

He sensed her shaking her head. *I don't know, son. I just don't know.*

"Trust me, Ma."

Well, I suppose I'll have to. So how can I help?

Harry was eager now, except;

"Ma, I don't want to weaken you. You said you were all used up."

So I am, but if you can fight, so can I. If the dead won't talk to you, maybe they'll still talk to me. While they can.

He nodded his gratitude and in a little while said: "There were others before Penny Sanderson. I know their names from the newspapers, but I have to know where they were laid to rest and I need an introduction. See, they were badly hurt and probably won't trust someone like me, who can touch them from this side. I mean, the one who killed them, he could do that, too. While I do need to talk to them, I don't want to frighten them more than they already are. So you see, without you it would be just too difficult.''

So you want to know which graveyards they're in, right?

''Right. It probably wouldn't be too hard to find out for myself, but there are so many things on my mind that keep getting in the way. And so time goes by.''

All right, Harry, I'll do what I can. But I don't want to have to track you down anymore, so it would be better if you came to see me. That way I . . . She paused, cut off abruptly.

''Ma?''

Didn't you feel that, son? I always feel it, when they're close by like that.

''What was it?''

Someone joining us, she answered sadly. *Someone dying. Some thing, anyway.*

A medium in life, in death Mary Keogh's contact *with* death was that much sharper. But what had she meant? It wasn't clear, and Harry felt the short hairs prickle on the back of his neck. ''Some . . . thing?'' he repeated her.

A pet, a puppy, an accident, she sighed. *And some poor child's heart broken. In Bonnyrig. Just this minute.*

The Necroscope felt his own heart give a start; he'd lost so much during his life that the thought of another's loss, however small, stung him with its poignancy. Or maybe it was just the way his mother had reported the occurrence, so soulfully. Or there again it could be an effect of his heightened emotional awareness. Maybe there was someone he could comfort.

''Bonnyrig, did you say? Ma, I'll be going now. I'll come and see you tomorrow. Maybe you'll know something by then.''

Take care, son.

Harry stood up, looked up and down the river and across it to the other side. The bright sun had passed behind fluffy, drifting clouds, which was a relief.

He climbed a tottering fence and entered a small copse, and in the dappled heart of the greenery conjured a Möbius door. A moment later and he emerged in a back alley close to the high street in Bonnyrig. And letting his deadspeak sensitivity spread out around him like a fan or cobweb, he searched for a newcomer among the ranks of the dead.

And there it was, close by: a whining yelp in memory of the panic and pain of a few moments ago, and a certain astonishment that the pain was no longer here, and disbelief that the bright day could so quickly turn black and blacker than night. A dumb animal's perception of sudden death.

Harry understood it very well, for it wasn't too dissimilar to the reaction of a human being. The only difference being that dogs have neither foreknowledge of nor preoccupation with death, so that their surprise is that much greater. But strike or kick a dog unjustly or cruelly and it will draw back with just the same astonishment, the same disbelief.

Taking a chance that he wasn't observed, the Necroscope used the Möbius Continuum to follow the pup's thoughts to their source: a curbside in the main village street, at a junction where the street turned left onto the main road into Edinburgh. A workday, there weren't many people about; the handful which had gathered had their backs to Harry, anyway, where he emerged onto the pavement as if from thin air. And the first thing he saw was the long, dark skid mark burned into the road's surface.

The pup's deadspeak thoughts were more desperate now as it realized that it couldn't extricate itself from this new predicament. There was no feeling, no contact, no light. Where was its God, its young master?

Shh! Harry hushed. *It's okay, boy! It's all right! Shh!*

He moved to the forefront of the handful of onlookers, saw a young boy kneeling there in the gutter, his cheeks shiny with tears, the broken pup dead in his arms. One of the pup's shoulders was askew and its spine kinked; its right foreleg flopped like a rubber band; its crushed head oozed brain fluid from a torn right ear.

Harry got down on one knee, put an arm round the boy, and stroked the dead pet. And again: "Shh, boy!" He comforted both of them. And in his mind the pup's whines and yelps quietened to a panting whimper. It could feel again. It felt Harry.

But the boy couldn't be comforted. "He's dead!" he kept moaning. "He's dead! Paddy's dead! Why didn't the car hit me and not Paddy? Why didn't the car stop?"

"Where do you live, son?" Harry asked the boy, a towhead of maybe eight or nine.

The other glanced at him through blurred-blue eyes. "Down there." He nodded vaguely over his right shoulder. "Number seven. We live there, Paddy and me."

Harry took the dog gently into his arms and stood up. "Let's get him home, then," he said.

The crowd parted for them and Harry heard someone say, "It's a shame. What a terrible shame!"

"Paddy's dead!" The kid clutched the Necroscope's elbow as they turned the corner into a narrow, deserted street.

Dead? Yes, he was, but . . . did he really have to be? *You don't have to be, do you, Paddy?*

The deadspeak answer which came back wasn't quite a bark and it wasn't quite a word—but it was an agreement. A dog will usually agree with his friends, and rarely if ever disagree with his master. While Harry wasn't Paddy's beloved master, he certainly was a new friend.

And the decision was made as quickly as that.

Before they reached the small garden in front of number seven, Harry looked down at the lad and said: "What's your name, son?"

"Peter." The other could scarcely get it out past his tears and the lump in his throat.

"Peter, I—" Harry jerked to a halt. Playacting for all he was worth, he glanced at the pet in his arms. "I think I felt him move!"

The boy's mouth fell open. "Paddy moved? But he's so bad hurt!"

"Son, I'm a vet," Harry lied. "Maybe I can save him. You run quickly now and tell your people what's happened, and I'll take Paddy to the surgery. And whatever happens, I'll be in touch just as soon as I know how bad he is—or how good. Okay?"

"But—"

"Don't waste time, Peter," Harry urged. "It's Paddy's life, right?"

The other gulped, nodded once, flew to the gate of number seven and through it, and as he vanished pell-mell into the garden Harry conjured a Möbius door. By the time Peter's ma came out of the house wringing her hands—came flying to see the vet—Harry was at a different address entirely . . .

The Necroscope had perhaps too few friends among the living, but one of them was an old potter up in the Pentlands who fired his own kilns. Paddy was absolutely dead, no doubt about that, when Harry handed him over to Hamish McCulloch for calcination in one of his ovens. "It's worth a twenty to me, Hamish," he told the old Scot, "if you can bring him down to ashes. Well, if not to me, to his master, a young lad with a broken heart. And I'll pay you for one of your pots, too, to keep him in.''

''I reckon we can manage that, Harry,'' Hamish said, nodding.

''Only one thing,'' said the Necroscope, ''be careful how you gather him up. I mean, the young lad wants to know he has all of him, right?''

''Just as you say,'' and another nod. And Harry waited for five hours until the job was done, but stayed calm and patient and controlled throughout. For now he was the old Harry, who, while he had little enough time left of his own, nevertheless had all the time in the world for this.

And anyway, it would serve his wider purposes, too, wouldn't it? A little preview of what was to come? A chance to observe any possible . . . discrepancies? For Trevor Jordan's brain had also been shattered, and Penny's flesh had been torn.

At 10:00 P.M. Harry was down in the spacious, dusty cellar of his old house a mile or so out of Bonnyrig. He'd cleaned the place out as best he could and scrubbed an area in the center of the stone floor until it was smooth as glass. Old Hamish had told him the weight of the dead pup's body before calcination, so that even if Harry's grasp of math was meager it wouldn't be too difficult to calculate pound for pound the various amounts of chemicals required. His knowledge was anything but meager and he'd calculated it down into grams.

Finally, ashes and chemicals were poured together, making a very small mound in the scrubbed floor space, and Harry was ready. And this time there was no pausing to check if his own personal mind-flea was up and jumping, for this time he wasn't worried for himself but a little kid who wouldn't be sleeping easy tonight.

Except now that he was ready it all seemed so ridiculously easy. Was this all there was to it? Had he perhaps forgotten something? Had those weirdly esoteric words he'd uttered down in the bowels of Janos Ferenczy's ruined castle—that formula out of hideous eons—*really* sufficed to bring about . . . resurrection?

And if so, had it been an act of blasphemy?

On the other hand, where was the profit in worrying about that now? If the Necroscope was to be damned for his works, then he was already damned. And purgatory has to be something like infinity: if you're to suffer for all eternity, there's no way you can be made to suffer twice as long. Is there?

As always his arguments went in a circle, making his head spin. But suddenly he "knew" that it was the vampire in him, working to confuse him, and in that same moment he acted and so broke the threat. Directing a rigid finger *and* his thoughts at the pile of ingredients, he spoke the words of evocation:

> "Y'ai 'Ng'ngah,
> *Yog-Sothoth,*
> H'ee-L'geb,
> F'ai Throdog
> —*Uaaah!*"

It was like putting a lighted match to a pile of incendiary materials: there was phosphorescent light, colored smoke, a not-quite-sulphur stench. And there was a yelp!

Paddy, called up from his ashes, came staggering from a mushrooming smoke ring of rapidly dispersing gas or vapor. His ears and stump of a tail were down, trembling, and he wobbled on legs of jelly which seemed incapable of supporting him. He had returned from death and weightlessness—from incorporeity—to life and substantiality in a moment, but his pup's legs were already unused to it.

"Paddy," the Necroscope whispered, going down on one knee. "Paddy—here, boy!" And the little dog fell down, stood up, shook himself so as to almost fall again, and came to him.

Black and white, short in the leg, floppy-eared, a mongrel entirely—and entirely alive!

. . . Was he?

Paddy, the Necroscope spoke again, this time in deadspeak. But there was no answer.

Paddy lived. Truly.

Half an hour later Harry delivered Paddy to house number seven of a row of neat terraced houses in Bonnyrig. He didn't mean to stay, would escape immediately if he could, but there were things he needed to now. About Paddy. About Paddy's character. Was he the same dog *exactly*?

And apparently he was. Certainly Peter thought so. Paddy's master had been ready for bed for an hour, but he wouldn't go until he'd heard from his "vet." And Paddy's return was a miracle to him, though only the Necroscope knew how much a miracle.

Peter's father was a tall, thin, callused man, but a kind one. "The boy told us he thought Paddy must be dead," he said, pouring Harry a liberal whisky, after Peter and his pup had disappeared for the night. "Broken bones, blood and brains from his ear, a spine all out of joint— it had us worried. He loves that pup."

"It looked a lot worse than it was," Harry answered. "The pup was unconscious, which made his limbs flop; there was some blood from a few scratches, and that always looks bad; and he'd coughed up some slaver. Shock, mostly."

The other raised an eyebrow. "And his shoulders? Peter said they weren't working, that they were definitely broken."

"Dislocated," Harry said. "Once we fixed that, everything else came right."

"We're grateful to you."

"That's okay."

"What do we owe you?"

"Nothing."

"That's very kind of you . . ."

"I just wanted to be sure that Paddy was the same dog," said the Necroscope. "I mean, that the bump he took hasn't changed his personality. Did he seem the same to you?"

There came a yelp and a bark, and laughter from Peter's bedroom.

"Playing," the boy's mother said, and smiled understandingly. "They shouldn't be, but tonight's special. Oh, yes, Mr. . . . ?"

"Keogh," said Harry.

"Oh, yes, Paddy's just the same."

Peter's father saw Harry to the garden gate, thanked him again, and said good night. When he went back inside, his wife said: "What an uncommonly decent, *nice* person. His eyes, so soulful!"

"Hmm?" Her husband was thoughtful.

"Didn't you think so?"

"Oh, aye, certainly. But—"

"But? Didn't you like him, then? Is there something you can't trust in a man who won't accept payment for a job well done?"

"No, no, it's not that! But his eyes . . ."

"Soulful, weren't they?"

"Were they? Down at the garden gate, in the darkness, when he looked at me—"

"Yes?"

But: "Nothing," said Peter's father, shaking his head. "A trick of the light, that's all . . ."

Back home Harry felt good. Better than at any time since Greece, when he'd got his deadspeak and numeracy back. Maybe he could feel even better, and cause others to feel better, too.

In his study he sat in an easy chair and talked to an urn where it stood shadowed in one corner of the room. Or it would *appear* that he talked to an urn, but urns don't talk back:

"Trevor, you were a telepath and a good one. Which means that you still are. So I know that even when I don't speak to you, still you're listening to me. You listen to my thoughts. So . . . you know what I did tonight, right?"

I can't help what I am, Harry, Trevor Jordan answered, his deadspeak voice "breathless" with excitement. *No more than you can. Yes, I know what you did—and what you're planning to do. I can't believe it yet, and don't suppose I will for quite some little time after it has happened, if it happens. It's like a wonderful dream that I don't want to wake up from. Except there's a chance it will be even more wonderful when I do wake up. There was no hope, none, and now there is . . .*

"But surely you knew my intention all along?"

Knowing what someone wants to do doesn't make him capable of doing it, the other answered. *But now, after the dog . . .*

Harry nodded. "But a dog's a dog, and a man's a man. We still can't be sure until . . . we're sure."

Do I have anything to lose?

"I suppose not."

Harry, any time you're ready, then so am I. Boy, am I ready!

"Trevor, just a second ago you said you can't help being what you are any more than I can. Did that mean more than it sounded? You must have read quite a lot, in my mind."

And after a long pause: *I won't lie to you, Harry. I know what's happened to you, what you're becoming. You don't know how sorry I am.*

"Pretty soon," said the Necroscope, "the whole damn rat pack will be after me."

I know. And I know what you'll do then, and where you'll go.

Again Harry's nod. "But it's like my ma told me," he said: "it's a strange and sinister place. Any help I can get, I'll probably need it."

Is there something I can do? Not much, I reckon. Not from where I am right now.

"Actually, yes," said Harry. "We could do it right now. But I won't take that sort of advantage. If the thing works, that will be soon enough. And even then—especially then—the decision will still be yours."

So . . . when? (Again Jordan's breathlessness.)

"Tomorrow."

Jesus!

But: "Don't!" the Necroscope cautioned him then. "Curse all you want but be careful who you name . . ."

After that they talked generally and remembered old times. A pity there wasn't anything good to remember. Oh, good had come out of it, but it had been evil as hell at the time. And after a lull in their deadspeak conversation:

91

Harry, you know that Paxton's still watching you, don't you? It was Jordan who had first brought the mindspy to the Necroscope's attention. Harry remembered that with gratitude. But ever since the initial warning a week ago, it had been his own intuition which alerted him to the telepath's proximity.

His first instinctive reaction to the problem had been to invoke a talent he'd inherited from Harold Wellesley, the ex-boss of E-Branch who had suicided after being found out as a double agent. Wellesley's talent had been a negative sort of thing: his mind had been better than the vaults of a bank, literally impregnable. But it had seemed to make him the ideal candidate for head of the British mindspy security organization. Had *seemed* to, anyway. By way of atonement, he'd passed on his talent to Harry.

But Wellesley's talent was sometimes a two-edged sword: if you bolt your doors against your enemies, your friends get locked out, too. Also, when you blow out the candle in a deep cave, *everyone* goes blind. Harry would prefer the light, prefer to know Paxton was there and what he was about.

And in any case it was draining to have to keep his guard up like that. Power, all power, has to be generated somewhere, and with the Necroscope's constantly increasing emotional stress, his batteries were already sufficiently drained.

Now it was the business of Harry's intuition to keep tabs on the mindspy, his intuition and the expanding intelligence of the thing inside him, its waxing talents. Eventually, these would develop into a sort of telepathy in their own right—into telepathy and other forms of ESP—but it could do no harm to have Jordan's brand of the art as an "optional extra."

Jordan heard that, too.

Harry, there's no sweat on that. I know you're different. Anything I can give you, take it. Now or after you . . . try it out on me, it makes no difference. I'm not going to change my mind. You'll use it to protect yourself, of course you will, but not to hurt us, I'm sure.

"Us?"

People, Harry. I don't think you could hurt people.

"I wish I could be so sure. But the thing is, it won't be me. Or it will be, but I won't think the same anymore."

So all you have to do is stick to your plan. When you know it's coming—or when circumstances force you to take defensive or evasive action—that's when you get the hell out of it.

"Chased out of my own world!" the Necroscope growled.

That or let the genie out of its bottle, yes.

"You're a straight talker, Trevor."

Isn't that what friends are for?

"But in a way you're a kind of genie in a bottle yourself, right?" Harry's contrary Wamphyri side was surfacing, his need to argue the point. Any point. Jordan hadn't sensed it yet, but in any case he was trying to keep the conversation light.

Maybe that's where those old Moslem legends spring from, en? A man with the Power, who knows the magic words, calling up a powerful slave from dust in a bottle. What is your wish, O Master?

"My wish?" Harry's voice was gaunt as his face. "Sometimes I wish to fuck I'd never been born!"

And *now* Jordan sensed it: Harry's duality—the strange tides in his blood, eroding the coastline of his will—the horror which challenged his human ascendancy even now, whose challenge was strengthening hour by hour, day by day.

You're tired, Harry. Maybe you should take it easy for a while. Get some sleep.

"At night?" The Necroscope chuckled, but drily, darkly. "It's not my nature, Trevor."

You have to fight it.

"I've *been* fighting it!" Harry's growl was deeper. "All I do is fight it."

Jordan was silent for a moment. Then: *Maybe . . . maybe we should give it a break now.* His deadspeak was full of trembling. Harry could feel the fear, the terror of a dead man. And to his innermost self, where Jordan couldn't reach:

Oh, God! Even the dead are afraid of me now.

He stood up abruptly, starting to his feet so as to almost topple his chair. And lurching to the curtains, he looked out through an inch of space where the drapes came together, across the river and into the night. At which precise moment, on the far riverbank and under the trees there, someone struck a match to light a cigarette. Just for a second Harry saw the flare before it was cupped in the windshield of a hand. And then there was only a yellow glow, brightening when the watcher took a deep drag.

"The bastard's out there right now," Harry spoke, almost to himself.

It might as well be to himself, for Jordan was too frightened to answer . . .

V The Resurrected

AT MIDNIGHT HARRY WAS STILL SEETHING.

He invoked Wellesley's talent, crept out into his garden and down the path to where the old gate in the wall sagged on its rusting hinges. The night was his friend and like a cat he became one with the shadows, until it would seem there was no one there at all. Looking through the gapped gate, across the river, his night-sensitive eyes could plainly see the motionless figure under the trees: the mind-flea, Paxton.

"Paxton . . ."

The word was like poison on Harry's lips and in his mind . . . his mind, or that of the creature which was now a growing part of him. For Harry's vampire recognized the threat even as the Necroscope himself, except it might deal with it differently. If he would let it.

"Paxton." He breathed the name into the cool night air, and his breath was a mist that drifted to the path and swirled around his ankles. The dark essence of Wamphyri was strong in him now, almost overpowering. "You can't hear me, you bastard, can you?" He breathed mist which flowed under the gate, across the overgrown river path, down among the brambles, and onto the glassy water itself. "You can't read me; you don't know I'm here at all, do you?"

But suddenly, coming from nowhere, there was a gurgling, monstrous voice—unmistakably that of Faethor Ferenczy—in Harry's mind: *Instead of shrinking back when you sense him near, seek him out! He would enter your mind? Enter his! He will. expect you to be afraid; be bold! And when he yawns his jaws at you, go in through them, for he's softer on the inside!*

A nightmare voice, but one which Harry himself had drawn from memory. For Wellesley's talent made any other sort of intrusion impossible; Faethor was gone now where no man could ever reach him; he was lost forever in future time.

That father of vampires had been talking about his bloodson Janos, but it seemed to the Necroscope that the same techniques might well apply right here, right now. Or perhaps it didn't seem so to Harry, but to the thing inside him. Paxton was here to prove Harry was a vampire. Since he *was* a vampire, there seemed no way he could disprove it. But must he simply sit still and wait for the consequences of this flea's reports? The urge was on him to even the score a little, to give the mindspy something to think about.

Not to actually "scratch" his itch, no, for that would be conclusive proof in itself and could only drag the Necroscope further into an already unwelcome light, ultimately to the minute scrutiny of bigger fleas, whose bite might even prove fatal. Also (Harry was obliged to forcibly remind himself) it would be murder.

The thought of that evoked visions of blood, and the thought of *that* was something he must put aside entirely!

He stepped back from the gate in the old stone wall, conjured a door, and passed through it into the Möbius Continuum . . . and out again onto a second-class road where it paralleled the river on its far side. There was no one in sight; the sky was clouded over; down through the flanking trees the river was seen as a ribbon of lead carelessly let fall in the darkness.

A car, Paxton's car, a recent model and expensive, stood half on, half off the road under overhanging branches. Its paintwork gleamed in the dark; its doors were locked, windows wound up tight. It pointed slightly downhill, towards a walled bend where the access road joined the main road into Bonnyrig.

Harry stepped from the potholed tarmac, past the car, and into the cover of the trees, and where he went the mist followed. No, it didn't simply follow, for he was the source and the catalyst. It boiled up from the ground where he walked, fell from his dark clothes like weird evaporation, poured from his mouth as breath. He went silently, flowingly, unaware of his own feet unerringly seeking soft ground, stepping between the places where brittle, betraying twigs lay in wait for him. And he felt his tenant flexing its muscles and securing its hooks more deeply in his will.

It would be a fine test of the thing's power over him, to take control here and now, causing him to do that from which there could be no return.

Until now Harry's fever had been more or less controlled. His angers had been more violent, true, his depressions deeper, and his snatches of joy poignant, but on the whole he had felt no real craving or compulsion, or at least nothing he couldn't fight. But now he felt it. It was as if Paxton had become the center of all that was wrong with his life, a point he could focus upon, a large wen on the already imperfect complexion of existence.

Some surgery was required.

Harry's mist crept ahead of him. It sprang up from the bank of the river and the boles of trees where they joined the damp earth, and cast swirling tendrils about Paxton's feet. The telepath sat on a tree stump close to the river's rim, his gaze fixed firmly on the dark shape of the house across the water, where light spilled out from an upstairs window. Harry had left that light on deliberately.

But while the Necroscope was unaware of it, still there was a half-scowl, half-frown on Paxton's face; for the mindspy had lost his quarry's aura. He supposed that Harry was still in the house, but for all his mental concentration he no longer had contact with him. Not even the tenuous contact which was his minimum requirement.

It didn't mean a great deal, of course not, because Paxton was well aware of Harry's talents: the Necroscope could be literally anywhere. Or on the other hand it could mean quite a bit. It isn't everyone who will just go flitting off in the midnight hour, putting himself beyond the reach of men and mentalists alike. Keogh could be up to almost anything.

Paxton shivered as a ghost stepped on his grave. Only an old saying, that, of course; but for a moment just then he'd felt something touch him, like an unseen presence come drifting across the water to stand beside him in the silence of the mist-shrouded riverbank. Mist-shrouded? Where in hell had *that* sprung from?

He stood up, looked to left and right, and began to turn around. And Harry, not five paces away, stepped silently into darkness. Paxton turned through a full, slow circle, shivered again and shrugged uncomfortably, and continued to stare at the house across the river. He reached inside his coat and brought out a leather-jacketed flask, tilted it, and let strong liquor gurgle into his throat in a long pull.

Watching the esper empty the flask, Harry could feel something dark swelling inside him. It was big, maybe even bigger than he was. He flowed forward, came to a halt directly behind the unsuspecting telepath. What a joke it would be, to let go of Wellesley's shield right now and deliberately *aim* his thoughts into the back of Paxton's head! Why, the esper would probably leap straight into the river!

Or perhaps he'd just turn round again, very slowly, and see Harry standing there looking right at him, into him, into his quivering, quaking soul. And then, if he went to scream . . .

The dark, alien, hate-swollen *thing* was in Harry's hands now, lifting them towards the back of Paxton's neck. It was in his heart, too, and his eyes, and his face. He could feel it pulling back his lips from drooling teeth. It would be so easy to sweep Paxton up and into the Möbius Continuum, and . . . and deal with him there. There, where no one would ever find him.

Harry's hands only had to close now and he could wring the esper's neck like he was a chicken. *Ahhh!*

The thing inside sang of emotions as yet unattained, which could be his. He thrilled to its message, to the ringing cry which echoed through his innermost being even now:

Wamphyri! Wam—

—And Paxton hitched back the sleeve of his overcoat and glanced at his watch.

That was all: his movement had been such a natural thing, so mundane, so much of this world, that the spell of an alien plane of existence was broken. And Harry felt like he was a twelve-year-old-boy again, masturbating furiously over the toilet bowl and ready to come, and his uncle had just knocked on the bathroom door.

He drew back from Paxton, conjured a Möbius door, and almost toppled through it. Too late (and mercifully so), the mindspy sensed something and whirled about—

—And saw nothing there but a swirl of fog.

Drenched in his own pungent sweat, the Necroscope vacated the Möbius Continuum into the backseat of Paxton's car. And he sat there shuddering, retching and being physically ill onto the floor until he'd sicked the thing right out of himself. At last, looking at the stinking mess of his own vomit, his anger gradually returned. But now he was mainly angry with himself.

He'd set out to teach the esper a lesson and had almost killed him. It said a hell of a lot for his control over the thing inside him, which as yet was . . . what? A baby? An infant? What hope would he have later, then, when the thing was full-fledged?

And still Paxton was there under the trees by the riverbank, there with his thoughts and his cigarettes and whisky. And he'd probably be there tomorrow, too, and the day after that. Until Harry made a mistake and gave himself away. If he hadn't done so already.

"Fuck him!" Harry said out loud, bitterly.

Yes, screw him, shaft the bastard! Which had to be better than murdering him, at least.

He climbed over into the front seat of the car and took off the brake, and felt the wheels slowly turn as she began to roll. He guided the car fully onto the road and let gravity take her along. Rolling down the gentle gradient, the vehicle gained momentum.

Harry pumped at the accelerator until he could smell the heavy petrol fumes, pulled out the choke, and pumped some more. A quarter mile later he was still pumping and the car was doing maybe twenty-five, thirty. The curve was coming up fast, with its grass verge and high stone wall. Harry let go the wheel, conjured a Möbius door out of the seat beside him, and slid over into it.

And two seconds later Paxton's car mounted the verge, hit the wall, and went off like a bomb!

Just that moment returning from the river to the road, the esper stared uncomprehendingly at the spot where his car had stood—then heard the explosion farther down the road and saw a ball of fire rising into the night. And:

"What . . . ?" he said. *"What?"*

By then Harry was home again, dialing 999. He got an emergency operator in Bonnyrig who put him through to the police station.

"Police—how can we help ye?" The voice was heavily accented.

"There's a car just burst into flames on the access road to the old estate behind Bonnyrig," Harry said breathlessly, and passed on full details of the location. "And there's a man there drinking from a hip flask and warming his hands on the fire."

"Who's speaking, please?" The voice was more authoritative now, alert and very official-sounding.

"Can't stop," said Harry. "Have to see if anyone's hurt." He put the phone down.

From his upstairs bedroom window the Necroscope watched the fire steadily brightening, and ten minutes later saw the Bonnyrig fire engine arrive along with its police escort. And for a little while there was the eerie wailing of sirens where blue- and orange-flashing lights clustered around the central leap of flames. Then the fire winked out and the sirens were silenced, and a little after that the police car drove off . . . with a passenger.

Harry would have been happy to know that the passenger was Paxton, furiously swearing his innocence and breathing whisky fumes all over the hard-faced officers. But he didn't because by then he was fast asleep. Whether sleep at night was right or wrong for his character made no difference: Trevor Jordan's advice had been sound . . .

In the morning the rising sun scorched Harry from his bed. Coming up beyond the river, it crept in through his window and seared a path across a twitching left hand which he dreamed was trapped in one of Hamish Mc-Culloch's kilns. Starting awake, he saw the room flooded with glowing yellow sunlight where he'd mistakenly left the curtains open.

He breakfasted on coffee—just coffee—and immediately proceeded to the cool cellar. He didn't know how long he had left, so it might well be a case of now or never. And anyway, he'd promised Trevor Jordan it would be today. Jordan's and Penny's urns were already down below, along with the chemicals Harry had taken from the Castle Ferenczy.

"Trevor," he said as he weighed and mixed powders, "I went after Paxton last night . . . no, not seriously, but almost. All I did in the end was toss a spanner in his works, which should keep him out of our hair awhile. I certainly don't feel him near, but that could be because it's morning and the sun is up. Can you tell me if he's out there?"

The newsagent in Bonnyrig has just opened his shop and there's a milkman doing his rounds, Jordan answered. *Oh, and a lot of perfectly ordinary people in the village are having breakfast. But no sign of Paxton. It seems a pretty normal sort of morning to me.*

"Not exactly normal," Harry told him. "Not for you, anyway."

I've been trying not to hope too hard, Jordan answered, his deadspeak shivery. *Trying not to pray. I still keep thinking I'm dreaming. I mean, we actually* do *shut down and sleep sometimes. Did you know that?*

The Necroscope nodded, finished with his powders, and took up Jordan's urn. "I was incorporeal myself one time, remember? I used to get tired as hell. Mental exhaustion is far worse than physical."

For a while, as he carefully poured Jordan's ashes, there was silence. Then: *Harry, I'm too scared to talk!*

"Scared?" Harry repeated the word almost automatically, concentrated on breaking the urn with a hammer and laying its pieces with the insides uppermost around the heap of mortal remains and chemical catalysts, so that anything clinging to them would get caught up in it when he spoke the words.

Scared, excited, you name it . . . but if I had guts I'd throw them up, I'm sure!

It was time. "Trevor, you have to understand that if you're not right . . . I mean—"

I know what you mean. I know.

"Okay," Harry nodded, and moistened his dry lips. "So here we go."

The words of evocation came as easy as his mother tongue, and yet with a growl which denied his human heritage. He used his art with—pride? Certainly in the knowledge that it was a very uncommon thing, and that he was a most uncommon creature.

"Uaaah!" The final exclamation wasn't quite a snarl—and it was answered a moment later by a cry almost of agony!

The Necroscope stepped back as swirling purple smoke filled the cellar, stinging his eyes. It gouted, mushroomed, spilled from or was residue of the chemical *materia*. It was the very essence of jinni: its massive volume spilling from such a small source. And staggering forward out of it, crying out the pain of his rebirth, came

103

the naked figure of Trevor Jordan. But the Necroscope was ready, in case this birth must be aborted.

For a moment Harry could see very little in the swirl of chemical smoke, and for another only a glimpse: a wild, staring eye, a twisted, gaping mouth, head only partly visible. Only partly there?

Jordan's arms were reaching for Harry, his hands shuddering, almost vibrating. His legs gave way and he fell to one knee. Harry felt the chill of absolute horror, and the words of devolution sprang into his mind, were ready on his desiccated lips. Then—

—The smoke cleared and it was . . . Trevor Jordan kneeling there.

Perfect!

Harry sank to his knees and embraced him, both of them crying like children . . .

Then it was Penny's turn. She, too, thought she was dreaming, couldn't believe what the Necroscope told her with his deadspeak. But it was one dream from which he soon awakened her.

She fell into his arms crying, and he carried her up out of the cellar to his bedroom, laid her between the sheets, and told her to try to sleep. All useless: there was a maniac in the house, running wild, laughing and crying at the same time. Trevor Jordan came and went, slamming doors, rushing here and there—pausing to touch himself, to touch Harry, Penny—and then laughing again. Laughing like crazy, like mad. Mad to be alive!

Penny, too, once the truth sank in, once she believed. And for an hour, two hours, it was bedlam. Stay in bed? She dressed herself in Harry's pajamas and one of his shirts, and . . . danced! She pirouetted, waltzed, jived; Harry was glad he had no neighbors.

Eventually, they wore themselves out, almost wore the Necroscope out, too.

He made plenty of coffee for them. They were thirsty; .they were hungry; they invaded his kitchen. They ate . . . everything! Now and then Jordan would leap to his feet, hug Harry until he thought his ribs must crack, rush into the garden and feel the sunshine, and rush back again. And Penny would burst into a fresh bout of tears and kiss him. It made him feel good. And it disturbed him. Even now their emotions were no match for his.

Then it was afternoon, and Harry said: "Penny, I think you can go home now."

He had told her what she must say: how it couldn't have been her body the police found but someone who looked a lot like her. How she had suffered amnesia or something and didn't know where she'd been until she found herself in her own street in her own North Yorkshire village. That was all, no elaborating. And no mention, not even a whisper, of Harry Keogh, Necroscope.

He made a note of her sizes, Möbius-tripped into Edinburgh, and bought her clothes, waited while she frantically dressed herself. He had forgotten shoes: no matter, she'd go barefoot. She would go naked, if that were the only way!

He took her home—almost all the way, only breaking the jump for a final word of warning on the rolling moors—via the Möbius Continuum, which was something else for her not to believe in. And he cautioned her: "Penny, from now on things will be normal for you, and eventually you may even come to believe this story we've concocted for you. Better for you, me, everyone, if you *do* believe it. Most certainly better for me."

"But . . . I'll see you again?" (The realization of what

she had found, and what she must lose. And for the first time the question: did she have the better of the bargain?)

He shook his head. "People will come and go, Penny, through all your life. It's the way it is."

"And through death?"

"You've promised me you'll forget that. It isn't part of our story, right?"

And then the rest of the jump, to the street corner she'd known all her life. "Goodbye, Penny."

And when she looked around . . .

As a small child she'd followed the rerun adventures of the Lone Ranger. *Who was that masked man . . . ?*

Back at the house near Bonnyrig, Jordan was waiting. He was calmer now but still radiated awe and wonder, which made him look beautiful, fresh-scrubbed, newly returned from a holiday in the sun or a swim in a mountain stream. All of these things. "Harry, I'm ready any time you are. Just tell me what I must do."

"You, nothing. Just don't shut me out, that's all. I want to get into your mind and learn from it."

"Like Janos did?"

Harry shook his head. "Unlike Janos. I didn't bring you back to hurt you. I didn't even bring you back for me. It's still up to you. If you don't like the idea of me going in there, just say so. This has to be of your own free will." Very significant words.

Jordan looked at him. "You didn't just save my life," he said, "but returned it to me! Anything you want, Harry."

The Necroscope sent his developing Wamphyri thoughts directly into Jordan's head, and the other cleared the way for him, drew him in. Harry found what he wanted: it was so like deadspeak that he knew it at once. The mechanism was easy, a part of the human psyche.

Mental in action, it was purely physical in operation, a part of the mind that people—most people—haven't learned how to use. Identical twins sometimes have it, because they come from the same egg. But discovering it wasn't the same as making it work.

Harry withdrew, said: "Your turn."

For Jordan it was easy. He already was a telepath. He looked inside Harry's mind and found the trigger which the Necroscope had pictured for him. It only required releasing. After that, like a switch, Harry could throw it any time it was required.

And: "Try it," Jordan said, when he'd withdrawn.

Harry pictured Zek Föener, a powerful telepath in her own right, and reached out with his new talent.

He (no, she) was swimming in the blue warm waters of the Mediterranean, spearfishing off Zakynthos where she lived with her husband, Jazz Simmons. She was twenty feet down and had lined up a fish in her sights, a fine red mullet, where it finned on the sandy bottom and ogled her.

"Testing . . . testing . . . testing," said Harry, with more than a hint of dry humor.

She sucked in salt water down the tube of her snorkel, triggered off her spear and missed, dropped her gun, and kicked frantically for the surface. And she trod water there, coughing and spluttering, staring wildly all about. Until suddenly it came to her that the words could only have been in her head. But the mental voice had been unmistakable.

Finally, she had her breath back and got her thoughts together. *Ha—Ha—Harry?*

And from his house in Bonnyrig, fifteen hundred miles away: "The one and only," he answered.

Harry, you . . . you . . . a telepath? Her confusion was total.

"I didn't mean to startle you, Zek. Just wanted to find out how good I am."

Well, you're good! I might have . . . I might have drowned! A swimmer like Zek? There was no way she might have drowned. But suddenly she backed off, and the Necroscope knew that she'd sensed the other thing that was Harry Keogh. She tried to shut it out of her thoughts but he cut right through her confusion with:

"It's okay, Zek. I know that you know about me. I just think you should also know that it won't be like that with me. I'm not staying here. Not for long, anyway. I have a job to do, and then I'll be on my way."

Back there? She'd read it in his mind.

"To begin with. But there may be other places. You of all people know I can't stay here."

Harry, she was quick, anxious to return, *you know I won't go up against you.*

"I know that, Zek."

She was silent for a long time; then Harry had a thought. "Zek, if you'll swim back to the beach, there's someone here would like a word with you. But better if you have your feet firmly on the beach, because you won't believe who it is and what he has to say. And this time you really might drown!"

And he was right, she didn't believe it. Not for quite some time . . .

About the middle of the afternoon, when Jordan had finally accepted everything and the glow had gone off him a little, he said: "What about me, Harry? Can I just go home?"

"I may have made a mistake," the Necroscope told him then. "Darcy Clarke knows I had that girl's ashes. He might figure it out. If he does he'll know I have a couple more talents now. Which will be confirmed—and how—if you show up! And anyway, I have this feeling that everything is going to blow up soon. You can go any time you like, Trevor, but I'd appreciate it if you'd stay here and out of sight a while longer.''

"How long?''

Harry shrugged. "I have a job to do. That long. Not much more than four or five days, I should think.''

"That's okay, Harry,'' Jordan said. "I can stand that. Or four or five weeks if I have to!''

"What will you do, anyway? Back to the Branch?''

"It was a good living. It paid the bills. We got things done.''

"Then it's best that you leave it until I've gone. You have to know that they'll be coming after me?''

"After all you've done for us? For everybody?''

Again Harry's shrug. "When an old, faithful dog savages your child, you have him put down. His services in the past don't cut it. What's more, if you knew for certain he was *going* to savage the child, you'd put him down first, right? And afterwards you might even feel sorry for the old guy and cry a little. But hell, if you also knew he had rabies, why, you wouldn't even think twice! You'd do it for him as much as for anyone else.''

Jordan played it straight, face-to-face. "Does it really worry you that much? I mean, let's face it, Harry: it won't be an easy job, taking you out. Janos Ferenczy had a lot going for him, but he wasn't in the same league as you are now!''

"That's why I have to go. If I don't I'll be forced to defend myself, which can only hasten things. And then there'd be a chance for this curse to go on forever. I didn't spend all that time doing all of that—Dragosani, Thibor, Janos, Faethor, Yulian Bodescu—just to end up the same way they did.''

"In that case . . . maybe I *should* go. I mean now.''

109

"Oh?"

"I can stay out of sight, keep an eye on them for you. They have Paxton watching you, but they won't know that I'm watching them. They don't even know I'm alive. I mean, they *do* know I'm dead!"

Harry was interested. "Go on."

"Darcy will be the man to watch, not in the office but when he's home. I know where he lives, and I know how he thinks. You'll be on his mind a lot, both ways: because of what you are, and also because he's a good sort of bloke and he'll just be, well, thinking about you. So when everything looks set to go down, I'll know it, and then I'll get back to you."

"You'd do that for me?" Harry knew he would.

"Don't I owe you?"

Harry nodded slowly. "It's a good idea," he finally said. "Okay, go after nightfall. I'll drive you into Edinburgh, and then you're on your own."

And he did. And then the Necroscope was on his own, too. But not for long.

The next morning Paxton was back.

His presence turned Harry's mood sour in a moment, but he promised himself that later he would turn the tables and take a look inside Paxton's mind for a change. He relished the thought of that. But first he would go and see his ma and find out if she had anything for him.

The sky was overcast and he stood on the bank of the river with his coat collar turned up against a thin but penetrating, persistent drizzle. "Any success, Ma?"

Harry? Is that you, son? Her deadspeak was so thin, so far-off-sounding, that for a moment the Necroscope thought it was simply background "static," the whispers of the teeming dead conversing in their graves.

"It's me, Ma, yes. But . . . you're awfully faint."

I know, son, she answered from afar. *Just like you, I don't have a lot of time now. Not here, anyway. It's all fading now, everything . . . Did you want something, Harry?*

She seemed very weary and wandering. "Ma" (he was patient with her, just like in the old days), "since I've been having some difficulty with the dead, we'd decided that you would help me out and see if they'd be a bit more forthcoming with you . . . about those poor murdered girls, I mean. You said I should give you a little time, then come and see you again. So here I am. I still need that information, Ma."

Murdered girls? she repeated him, however vaguely. But then Harry sensed the sudden focusing of her attention as her deadspeak sounded sharper in his unique mind. *Of course, those poor murdered girls! Those innocents. Except . . . well, they weren't all innocents, Harry.*

"In my book they were, Ma. For my purposes, they were. But tell me, what do you mean?"

Well, most of them wouldn't speak to me, she answered. *It seemed they'd been warned off, warned about you. When it comes to vampires, the dead aren't very forgiving, Harry. The one who would speak to me, she'd been one of the first of his victims—whoever he is—but by no means an innocent. She was a prostitute, son, foulmouthed, and -minded. But she was willing to talk about it and said she wouldn't mind talking to you. In fact, she said more than that.*

"Oh?"

Yes, she said that it would make a nice change to just . . . to just talk to a man! Harry's ma tut-tutted. *And so young, so very young.*

"Ma," said Harry, "I'm going to go and see that one—soon. But you're getting so faint that I don't know

111

if we'll ever get to talk again. So I just thought I'd tell you right now that you've been the best mother anyone could ever have, and—"

—And you've been the best son, Harry, she cut him off. *But listen, don't you cry for me. And I promise I won't cry for you. I lived a good life, son, and despite a cruel death I've not been too unhappy in my grave. You were responsible for what happiness I found, Harry, just as you've been for so much of what passes for happiness in this place. That the dead no longer trust you . . . well, that's their loss.*

He blew her a kiss. "I missed a lot when you were taken from me. But of course you missed a lot more. I hope there is a place beyond death, Ma, and that you make it there."

Harry, there's something else. She was fading very quickly now, so that he must give her all of his attention or lose her deadspeak entirely. *About August Ferdinand.*

"August Ferdi—? About Möbius?" Harry remembered his last conversation with the great mathematician. "Ah!" He chewed his lip. "Well, it could be that I insulted Möbius, Ma . . . inadvertently, you understand? I mean, I wasn't quite myself that time."

He said you weren't, son, and that he wouldn't be speaking with you again.

"Oh," said Harry, a little crestfallen. Möbius had been one of his very best and closest friends. "I see."

No, you don't see, Harry, his mother contradicted him. *He won't be speaking to you because he won't be there . . . I mean here. He, too, has somewhere else to go, or believes he has. Anyway, he talked about a lot of things I didn't much understand: space and time, space-time, the cone-shaped universes of light? I think that covers everything. And he said your argument left one big question unanswered.*

112

"Oh?"

Yes. The question of the . . . ius Continuum itself. He said . . . thinks . . . knows what it is. He said . . . was . . . mind . . . She was breaking up, her deadspeak scattering, for the last time, Harry knew.

"Ma?" He was anxious.

Möbius . . . said . . . was . . . The Mind, Harry . . .

"The Mind? Ma, did you say The Mind?"

She tried to answer but couldn't quite make it. All that came back was the faintest of all far-distant, fading whispers.

Haarrry . . . Haaarrrry . . .

Then silence.

Paxton had read the Necroscope's case files and knew quite a lot about him. Most of it would seem unbelievable to people of entirely mundane persuasions. But of course Paxton wasn't one of them. On the far bank of the river, he watched Harry through a pair of binoculars and thought: *The strange sod's talking to his mother, a woman dead for a quarter of a century and long since turned to slop! Jesus! And they say telepathy is weird!*

Harry "heard" him and knew that he'd been eavesdropping on his conversation with his mother; on Harry's part of it, anyway. And suddenly he was furious, but coldly furious, not like the other night. And again Faethor's words of advice sprang to memory:

"He would enter your mind? Enter his!"

Paxton saw the Necroscope step behind a bush and waited for him to come out on the other side. But he didn't. *Taking a leak?* the esper wondered.

"Actually, no," said Harry softly, from directly behind him. "But when I do I'd like to think it's in private."

"Wha—?" The mindspy whirled about, stumbled,

113

staggered on the very rim of the river. Harry reached out easily and caught the front of his jacket, steadied him, grinned an utterly mirthless grin at him. He looked him up and down: a small, thin, withered-looking stick of a man in his middle to late twenties, with the face and eyes of a weasel. His telepathy must be Old Ma Nature's way of making up for several sorts of deficiency.

"Paxton," Harry said, his voice still dangerously soft, a hot breath squeezed out of burning bellows lungs, "you're a scum-sucking little mind-flea. I reckon that when your father made you, the best part leaked from a ruptured rubber down your ma's leg onto the floor of the brothel. You're a scumbag bastard who has invaded my territory, stepped on my toes, and is making me itch. And I have every right to do something about you. Don't you agree?"

Paxton flapped his mouth like a landed fish, finally got his breath and his nerve back. "I . . . I'm doing my job, that's all," he gasped, trying to free himself from Harry's grip. But the Necroscope just held him there at arm's length—held him that much tighter—with no real expenditure of energy at all.

"Doing your job?" he repeated Paxton's words. "Who for, scumbag?"

"That's none of your busin—" Paxton started to say.

Harry shook him, glared at him, and for the first time the esper noticed a flush of red light coloring the Necroscope's gaunt cheeks where it escaped from behind the thick lenses of his dark glasses. An angry red light—from his eyes!

"For E-Branch?" Harry's voice was lower still, a rumble, almost a growl.

"Yes—no!" Paxton blurted the words out. Soft as jelly, all he wanted now was to get away from here; to that end he'd say anything at all, the first thing that came to mind. Harry knew it, could read it in his pale face and trembling lips; but where lips may lie, the mind usually tells the truth. He went inside, scanned it all and more, and got out again like squelching from the sucking quag of a sewer. Even through the acrid odor of Paxton's fear, still he'd been able to smell the shit.

It was a relief to know that such minds were in the minority; otherwise the Necroscope might be tempted to declare war on the entire human race, right now!

But Paxton knew he'd been in: he'd *felt* Harry in there, like slivers of ice in his mind. He started imitating a fish again.

"So now you know for sure," said Harry. "And now you'll report to your boss. Well, you go and tell the Minister that his worst nightmare has come true, Paxton. Tell him that, and then quit. Get out and stay out. I know you don't warn too easily, but this time take some good advice and run while you can. I won't be warning you again."

And while that sank in he released the other, released him violently, tossed him back and over the lip of the river, and down into the gently swirling water.

It was only then that the Necroscope saw Paxton's briefcase lying open on a tree stump close by. Several white junk-mail envelopes—and one large manila envelope—were like magnets to his eyes. They were addressed to Harry Keogh, No. 3 The Riverside, etc, etc.

Harry glared once more at the floundering esper where he gagged, gurgled, and splashed in the cold river water beyond his reach—for the moment just out of harm's way—then snatched up his mail and took it home with him.

Paxton could swim, which was as well. For the Necroscope didn't much care one way or the other . . .

VI   Red Alert!

HARRY FLIPPED QUICKLY THROUGH THE MURDER FILES, discovered the young prostitute's name, home town, and place of interment, and made his way at once to her graveside in a small cemetery on the northern outskirts of Newcastle. And the Necroscope had moved so quickly that as he seated himself in the shade of a tree close by Pamela Trotter's simple headstone, Paxton was still catching his breath where he'd dragged himself up onto the riverbank a hundred miles away.

"Pamela," said the Necroscope, "I'm Harry Keogh. I believe my mother might have mentioned my name to you."

Your mother and others, she came back at once. *I've been expecting you, Harry—and I've been warned off you, too!*

Harry nodded, perhaps ruefully. "My reputation has suffered a bit lately, it's true."

She chuckled. *Mine suffered a lot. For nearly six years,*

in fact, ever since I was fourteen and a nice "uncle" showed me his little pink sprinkler and told me where it went. Actually, I seduced him, for I'd noticed that whenever he was near me he had a hard-on. But if it hadn't been him it would have been someone else, because I was just naturally like that. We played around a lot until his old lady caught us at it one day, the jealous old bat! I was going bouncy-bouncy on him when she walked in. He whipped it out but was too far gone and spurted on the carpet. I don't think she'd seen him spurt for a long time, and she'd certainly never had it like that! Come to think of it, I don't think he had, either. Not before me. But I liked it all ways. It helps when you enjoy your work.

Harry was silent for a moment, surprised, even a little taken aback. He really didn't know how to answer her.

Didn't your ma tell you I was a tart, a trollop, a whore? There was no bitterness in her, not even much of sadness, and Harry liked her for it.

"Something like that," he answered eventually. "Not that I think it matters a great deal. There have to be a hell of a lot of you down there by now!"

She laughed and Harry liked her even more. *The oldest profession,* she said.

"But one night, nearly eight weeks ago, it caught up with you, right?" He felt that with her he could get right to it.

Her assumed indifference fell away from her at once. *That wasn't why it happened,* she said. *I didn't fetch him on. And anyway he didn't want me . . . like that.*

"It was just an assumption," Harry told her quickly. "I meant no offense, and I'm not eager to bring back hurtful memories. But it's hard to see how I can track this bloke down if no one is able to tell me about him."

Oh, I'd like to see him get his, Harry, she answered.

*And I'll help you any way I can. I just hope I can re-
member enough, that's all.*

"You won't know until you try."

Where do you want me to start?

"First show me how you were, or how you thought
you were," he said. For he knew well enough that the
dead retain pictures of themselves as they were in life,
and he wanted to try and draw some sort of comparison
with Penny Sanderson. In short, he wondered if his necromancer quarry followed a pattern.

From her mind he immediately got back a picture of
a tall, dark-eyed, leggy brunette in a miniskirt, with
slightly loose breasts unsupported under a blue silk
blouse, and a shapely backside. But there was nothing
of character in the picture, *her* picture, nothing to suggest quality of mind or personality; it was all sensual or
outright sexual. Which didn't fit with his first impressions.

So? How was I?

"Very attractive," he told her. "But I think you're
selling yourself short."

Often, she agreed, but without her customary laugh.
Then she sighed, and that was something Harry was used
to in the dead. It was the realization of a time and a thing
done and finished with, which could never return. But
she brightened up at once. *And here am I actually talking
to a man, and for once not wondering what he's got in
his pants. In the front, and in the back pocket.*

"Was it always like that, for money?"

*And sometimes for fun. I've told you, I was nympho.
Do you want to get on now?*

Harry was embarrassed. She'd given him a stock answer, had obviously heard that question before, often.
"Was I prying?"

It's okay, she answered. *All men wonder about it,*

about what goes on in a pro's mind. But suddenly her deadspeak was very cold. *All men except that one, anyway. He doesn't have to wonder, for he can always find out for himself, afterwards, when they're dead.*

And with that the Necroscope was sure she'd give him all she could. "Tell me about it," he said.

And she did . . .

It was a Friday night and I went to the dance. Since I was freelance, my time was my own. I didn't need a pimp touting for me, taking my money and bringing his friends round for freebies. But the dance was in town and I lived quite a few miles out; after the midnight hour taxis are expensive; Cinders needed her coach home.

That was okay; there are always a handful of likely lads who'll buzz a girl home on the chance of a grope. And if I liked the guy and if he wasn't too pushy, maybe he could get more than a grope. A ride for a ride, as the saying goes.

On this occasion I picked the wrong one: no, not our man, but an armful all the same. Once I was in the car, his polite, concerned attitude went right out the window. He didn't know what I was, thought I was just a straight kid but easy meat. He could hardly drive for drooling and wanted to stop in every lay-by and back alley. I was wearing expensive clothes and didn't want them ripped up. And anyway, I didn't like him.

He said he knew a place just off the motorway, and before I could tell him I didn't need it he took the fly-on for Edinburgh. In a lay-by under some trees he made his move, and got my knee in his soft bits for his trouble! When he could drive again he did, but left me stranded there.

There was a service station a quarter mile up the motorway. I went there and had a coffee. I wasn't shaken

119

up or anything, just dehydrated. Too many gin-and-its at the Palace.

But sitting there in this little booth, I was joined by a driver. That was how I saw him: a driver. A long-distance man shaking off his weariness with a mug of coffee.

Don't ask me what he looked like; the place was three-quarters empty and they'd turned the lights low to keep the bills down, and there was still a lot of gin in me. I spoke to him but I didn't really *look* at him, you know? Anyway, he didn't seem a bad sort and he wasn't pushy. When he finished his coffee and made to stand up, I asked him which way he was heading.

"Where do you want to go?" he said. His voice was soft, not unfriendly.

I told him where I lived and he said he knew it. "Your luck's in," he told me. "I go past it on the motorway. About five miles from here? There's a fly-off where I can drop you. A couple of hundred yards and you'll be at your door. Can't take you any closer than that, I'm afraid, because my miles and fuel are monitored. Anyway, it's up to you. Maybe you'd feel safer calling a taxi?"

But I wasn't one to look a gift horse in the mouth.

We left the cafeteria and went out into the lorry park. He was cool and calm, in no hurry. I felt perfectly safe with him. In fact I didn't give it a thought. His vehicle was one of these big articulated jobs, which we approached from the side and the rear. The headlights of a passing car as it flashed by on the motorway lit it up in a swath of light. The lorry had ice-blue panels with white lettering saying: "Frigis Express." I remember it well because the white paint had peeled off one leg of the "x" making it look like "Eyepress."

But at the back of the lorry my driver paused and looked at me, and said: "I just have to make sure this door is secure."

I stood beside him as he unlocked and slid up this roller door across the full width of the truck. A blast of ice-cold air came out, which made me shiver as it turned to a cloud of mist. Inside . . . there seemed to be rows of things hanging in there, but it was dark and I couldn't see what they were. He reached inside with both hands and did something, then looked over his shoulder and said, "It's okay." And I think it was then I realized that I hadn't seen him smile. Not once.

He indicated we should go to the cab, and as he started to pull the door down again I turned away from him. That was when he grabbed me from behind. One arm went round my neck and the other hand held something over my face. Of course I gasped for air—and got chloroform!

I kicked and struggled, but that only makes you gasp all the more! And then I passed out . . .

When I came to I was lying—or slithering about—on a patch of ice: that's what it felt like, anyway. There was a smell but I couldn't quite make out what it was. I was much too cold; all my senses were numb from the cold. And I felt dizzy and nauseous from the chloroform.

Then I remembered everything and knew I was in the back of the truck, slipping and slithering when he applied his brakes or accelerated. And of course I also knew I was in trouble, in fact dead trouble. Whatever my driver wanted, he was going to get it. And then there was a fair chance that he'd kill me. I'd seen his truck; I could more or less describe him, if not now, certainly later; it was odds on I was a goner.

I propped myself in one corner of the dark refrigerator (I suppose that's what it was: a large mobile fridge, a freezer truck) and tried to get some warmth back into my body. I hugged myself, blew on my hands, beat my arms about. But I was weak from the cold and the after-effects of the chloroform. I didn't have the strength of a kitten.

Then, after—oh, I don't know how long—maybe fifteen minutes, there was a bumpy patch and I heard his air brakes go on. To this day I don't know where we were, for I never did see the outside again. The truck stopped; in a little while the door rolled up and it was dark outside; a dark figure clambered up, panting, into the rear of the trailer. He pulled the door shut again and put on a dim interior light, just a single bulb under a grille in the ceiling. And then he came for me.

He was wearing a long coat which was all dark-stained leather on the outside and brown fur inside; he took it off as he approached me and threw it down on me. "Get on it," he said, panting with some weird emotion. But his voice was just as cold as the place where he planned to have me, which I now saw was a meat safe. Beast carcasses, all grey, brown, and red, hung from rows of hooks. And the layer of ice on the floor was frozen beast blood.

"There . . . there doesn't have to be any rough stuff," I told him. "We can do it just as you say." And freezing cold though I was, I opened my blouse and hitched up my mini to show him my frilly panties.

He looked down on me in that unsmiling way of his, and I saw that his face was all puffy and bloated, and his eyes winking like little lumps of shiny coal in the swollen red mask of his face. "Just as I say?" he repeated me.

"Any way at all. And I swear it will be good. Only just don't hurt me. And you can trust me. Afterwards . . . I won't say a word." I lied like hell. I wanted to live.

"Take 'em off," he panted. "Everything."

God, there was no soul behind his voice, nothing behind his eyes. There was just the steam heat of his body and the pounding of his feverish blood. I could *feel* how strong he was, and how weird and different. *"Quickly!"* he said, and his voice was a croak and his gorged face was wobbling with strain and horrible excitement.

I had to do what he told me, keep him happy. But I was so cold my fingers wouldn't obey me. I couldn't get my clothes off. He got down on one knee and I could see tools glinting in the loops of his wide leather belt. One of them was a meathook, which he took out and showed me!

When I gasped and turned my face away, he tore my jacket right off my back; my blouse, too. Then he put the hook in the top of my skirt and ripped it down through the plastic belt and material, laying it open. He ripped open my panties in the same way. And all I could do was huddle there as cold as one of the dead animals on its hook. And I thought:

What if he uses that hook on me? But he didn't. Not the hook.

Then he was tearing his clothes off: not his upper clothes, just his pants. And I knew this was it. But a man as strong and as dangerous as this could hurt me badly. I had to make it as easy for him—as easy for myself—as possible. I opened my legs and stroked my bush of cold hair. And God help me, I tried to smile at him. "It's all here," I said, my words turning to snow as they came out. "All for you."

"Eh?" he grunted, looking at me, his penis huge and jerking about on its own, with a life of its own. "All for me? All for Johnny? That?" And *then* he smiled. And he took up another of his tools.

This one was like a knife, but it was hollow and had been cut from steel tubing about an inch and a half in diameter, cut at an angle, to give it a sharp point. And its edges had been sharpened to razor brightness.

"Oh, God!" I gasped then, for I couldn't hold my terror any longer. And I clutched at myself and tried to cover my nakedness. But my driver, my all-too-soon-to-be murderer, that . . . that *thing*, he only laughed. There was no emotion in it, not as I understood emotion, but he laughed, anyway.

"Yes, cover yourself," he gurgled at me, the saliva of his lust overflowing from his wobbling, grimacing mouth. "Cover it up, girlie. Johnny doesn't want your ugly little fuckie hole. *Johnny makes his own holes!*"

He moved closer and his flesh was alive and leaping, bursting for me. And then . . . and then . . .

"It's okay." It was as much as Harry could bear. *His* voice was trembling, broken. "I know what then. You've said enough. I . . . I'll go on what I have."

Pamela was crying now, spilling out her poor mutilated soul, all of her defiance and resilience crushed and drained from her by the horror of what she'd forced herself to remember for the Necroscope.

He . . . he made my body ugly! she sobbed. *He made holes in me! Before I was dead he was into me. And after I was dead I could still feel him grunting on me, hurting me. It's not right that when you're dead someone should still be able to hurt you, Harry.*

"It's okay, it's okay," was all Harry could say to comfort her. But even saying it he knew it wasn't, knew it wouldn't be until he himself had put this thing right.

She took this from his deadspeak, understood his resolve, reinforced his anger with her own. *Get him for me, Harry! Get that dog's bastard for me!*

"And for myself," he told her. "For if I don't, I know he'll always be there, clinging like slime to the walls of my mind. But, Pamela—"

Yes?

"Simply killing this one won't be enough. I mean, it's just not *enough!* But if you're willing, there's a way you can help me. You're strong, Pamela, in death just as you were in life. And what I have in mind . . . I believe it's something you would enjoy even more than you did in life." He explained his meaning, and for a little while she was silent. Then:

I think I know now why the dead are afraid of you, Harry, she said wonderingly. And: *Is it true that you're a vampire?*

"Yes . . . no!" he said. "Not like that. Not yet, anyway. And not here. But somewhere else I will be—or may be—one day."

Yes—he sensed her nod—*I think you must be—or will be—for nothing human could ever think the thought you thought just then. Nothing entirely human, anyway.*

"But you'll do it?"

Oh, yes, she answered him at last with a grim, emphatic deadspeak nod. *Who or whatever you are, I'll do anything you tell me, Harry Keogh, vampire, Necroscope. Anything, everything, and whatever it takes to get even. Whatever you ask and whenever you ask it. Anything . . .*

Harry nodded. "So be it," he said.

For the next thirty-odd hours the Necroscope was busy; not only him but E-Branch, too. And the next day, a warm evening in mid-May, the Minister Responsible caused the Branch emergency call-in system to be brought into play.

First, acting on disturbing information received from Geoffrey Paxton (concerning among other things the files Darcy Clarke had mailed to Harry Keogh), the Minister had relieved Clarke of all duties and placed him under what amounted to house arrest at Clarke's own North

London flat in Crouch End. Second, he must now attend the O-group briefing he'd called at E-Branch HQ. The espers'would know, of course, that something big was in the offing: all available agents were to be present.

Paxton was there to meet the Minister on the ground floor. Even as they exchanged curt greetings Ben Trask, just back from a job, came in from the street through the swing doors. Trask looked drawn, even haggard. The Minister took him to one side where they conversed in lowered tones for a minute or two, and for once Paxton knew enough to keep his nose out. Then they all three took the elevator upstairs and went directly to the ops room.

The called-in agents were silent, seated, waiting for the Minister. He took the podium and his eyes swept the mainly ordinary-looking faces of the espers—Britain's ESP-endowed mindspies—where they stared back at him. He knew them all from photographs in their files, but only Darcy Clarke and Ben Trask had ever met him. And Paxton, of course.

If Clarke had been here, perhaps he would have stood up as a sign of respect, and maybe the rest of them would have followed suit. Or then again maybe not. The trouble with this lot had always been that they thought they were special. But here the Minister knew he wasn't fooling anybody, least of all himself. They *were* special, bloody special!

And looking at them, he felt as several before him must surely have felt. Physics and metaphysics, robots and romantics, gadgets and ghosts. Two sides of the same coin. Were they really? Science and parapsychology? The mundane and the supernatural? And he wondered what was the difference, anyway? Isn't a telephone or radio magic? To speak with someone on the other side of the world, even on the moon? And has there ever been a more powerful, more monstrous spell or invocation than $E=mc^2$?

These were some of the Minister's thoughts as he scanned the faces of E-Branch's espers and put names to them:

Ben Trask, the human lie detector; blocky, over-weight, mousey-haired and green-eyed, slope-shouldered and lugubrious. Possibly, Trask's sad expression sprang from the knowledge that the whole world was a liar. Or if not all of it, a hell of a lot of it. It was Trask's talent: to recognize whatever was false. Show him or tell him a lie and he would know it at once. He wouldn't always know the truth of the thing, but he would always know that what was represented wasn't so. No façade, however cleverly constructed, could ever fool him. The police used him a lot, to crack stone killers; also he came in handy in respect of international negotiations, when it was good to know if the cards on the table made a full deck.

David Chung: a young Londoner, a locator and scryer of the highest quality. He was slight, wiry, slant-eyed and yellow as they come. But he was British, loyal, and his talent was amazing. He tracked Soviet nuclear "stealth" subs, IRA units in the field, drug-runners. Especially the latter. Chung's parents had been addicts, and their addiction had killed them. That's where his talent had started, and it was still growing.

Anna Marie English was something else. (But weren't they all?) Twenty-three, bespectacled, enervated, pallid, and dowdy, she was hardly an English rose! That was a direct result of her talent, for she was "as one with the Earth": her way of defining it. She felt the rain forests being eaten away; she knew the extent of the ozone holes; when the deserts expanded she felt their desiccation, and the mass erosion of mountain soil made her physically sick. She was "ecologically aware" beyond the five senses of mundane mankind. Greenpeace could base their entire campaign on her, except no one would believe. The Branch did believe, and used her like it used David Chung: as a tracker. She tracked illicit nuclear waste, monitored pollution, warned of invasions of Colorado beetle and Dutch elm disease, cried aloud the extinction of whales, elephants, dolphins, other species. And she knew that the Earth was sick and growing sicker. She only had to look in the mirror each day to know that.

Then there was Geoffrey Paxton, a telepath, one of several. An unpleasant person, the Minister thought, but his talent was useful. And it takes all sorts to make a world. Paxton was ambitious, he wanted it all. Better to employ him where he too could be watched than have him turn to high-stakes blackmail or become the mind-spy agent of some foreign power. Later . . . Paxton's would be a career worth following. And closely.

Sixteen of them gathered here, under one roof, and eleven more out in various parts of the world, guiding that world, or at least watching over it. They were paid according to their talents, handsomely! And they were worth every penny. It would cost a lot more if they ever decided to work for themselves . . .

Sixteen of them, and as the Minister's eyes roved over them, so they studied him: a man who so far had kept himself to the shadows and would prefer to stay there, except that now some affairs of the utmost moment had lured him out. He was in his mid-forties, small and dapper, dark hair brushed back and plastered down. And he had no nerves to speak of, or none that were visible, anyway. He wore patent-leather black shoes, a dark blue suit and light blue tie. His brow had a few wrinkles but other than these his face was normally unlined, and his eyes were bright, clear, and blue. Right now, though, and especially since his conversation with Ben Trask, he was looking harried.

"Ladies, gentlemen" (he wasn't one for preamble), "what I have to say would seem fantastic to almost anyone outside these walls, as would almost everything that goes on within them. But I'll try not to bore you with too many things you already know. Mainly, I've gathered you together to tell you we have one hell of a problem. First I'll tell you how it came to be, and how it came to light. Then you'll have to tell me how we're going to deal with it, in which instance I know that even the least of you—if there is such a thing—has more practical experience than I have. In fact, you're the *only* people with practical experience of these things, and so the only ones who can deal with the matter in hand." He took a deep breath, then continued:

"Some time ago we appointed a traitor as head of E-Branch. I'm talking about Wellesley, yes. Well, he can't do any more harm. But after him it was my job to make sure it couldn't happen again. In short, we needed someone who was capable of spying on the spies. Now, I know you people have an unwritten code: you don't spy on each other. So I couldn't use one of you, not *in situ*, anyway. I had to take one of you *out* of the Branch and make him responsible to myself alone. And I had to do it before he could build up too many loyalties. So I chose Geoffrey Paxton, a relative newcomer, as my watcher over the watchers."

He at once held up his hands, as if to ward off protests, though none were forthcoming—as yet. "None of you, and I do mean *none* of you, were suspect in any way. But after Wellesley I couldn't take any chances. Still, I'd like to have it understood that your personal lives are still yours, and no tampering. Paxton has always been under the strictest instructions *not* to interfere or pry into anything extraneous, but to confine himself solely to Branch business. Which is to say, Branch security.

"A few weeks ago we had some business in the Mediterranean. Two of our members, Layard and Jordan, had come up against . . . unpleasant opposition. It was the worst sort of business, but not without precedent. The head of E-Branch, Darcy Clarke, went out there with Harry Keogh and Sandra Markham to see what could be done. Later, Trask and Chung joined them, and they also had help from other quarters. As for qualifications: Clarke and Trask both had experience of that sort of thing, and Keogh . . . well, Keogh is Keogh. If he could be reactivated, get his talents back, that would be a wonderful bonus for the Branch. But initially, he went out as an observer and adviser, for no one knew more about vampirism than he did . . ." (And here he paused, perhaps significantly.)

"Now, we still don't know *exactly* what happened out there in Rhodes, the Greek islands, Romania, but we do know that we lost Trevor Jordan, Ken Layard, and Sandra Markham. I mean lost them dead! So it can be seen they had a real problem, one which Darcy Clarke would have us believe is now . . . resolved? Harry Keogh, of course, could tell us everything, but so far he's chosen to tell us very little."

By now the breathing of the Minister's audience was quite audible, perhaps even heavy, impatient; and he saw that someone had stood up. Since the light was on the podium he had to squint to see who it was on his feet back there in the shadows, but in a little while he made it out to be the very tall, skeletally thin hunchman or prognosticator Ian Goodly. "Yes, Mr. Goodly?"

"Minister," Goodly answered, his high-pitched voice shrill but not unnaturally or unusually so, "I know you won't be offended by any sort of imagined implication when I say that so far every word you've said has been spoken with absolute honesty and integrity. It came straight from the heart, was told the way you see it and with the best of intentions. I don't think anyone here doubts that, or that it takes a brave sort of man to come in here and try to tell us anything, especially in the knowledge that there are people here who could pick your mind clean in a moment.''

The Minister nodded. ''I don't know about the bravery bit, but everything else is correct. What's more, it puts any sort of subterfuge right out of the question; it can be seen—you people can *surely* see—that I have no axe to grind. So . . . are you making a point, Mr. Goodly?''

''The point is that I *do* have an axe to grind, sir,'' Goodly answered quietly. ''We all do. And the way this briefing is going, it strikes me as likely we could have several axes to grind before you're through. Not with you, you understand. That would be pointless, anyway, for my talent tells me that you're going to be our Minister Responsible for a long time to come. So . . . not with what you've said or what you think, but maybe with what you've done and plan to do. Or plan to ask us to do. Unless, of course, there are some damn good reasons.''

''Do you mind explaining?'' The Minister's confusion was mounting. ''But briefly, because I really do have to get on, and—''

''Explanations are easy.'' Someone else was on his— no, her—feet: Millicent Cleary, a pretty little telepath whose talent was as yet embryonic. She merely glanced at the Minister but scowled furiously at the back of Paxton's head where he sat in the first row of seats. ''Some explanations, anyway. I mean, it was inevitable we'd be monitored eventually, but . . . by *that*?'' And still scowling, she tossed her head to give the final word extra emphasis. She was pointing at Paxton.

"Miss, er—?" In his confusion the Minister had forgotten her name. He prided himself on not forgetting names. He looked at her, looked at Paxton.

"Cleary," she said. "Millicent . . ." And she breathlessly continued: "Paxton didn't follow your instructions. He simply ignored your orders. Branch security? Branch business? Oh, that was the handy excuse you gave him—which he scarcely needed—but *other people's* business, more like! And his nose right in it!"

The Minister was frowning. He looked harder at Paxton. "Can you be more specific, Miss Cleary?"

But she wouldn't. She could but wouldn't. What, and tell everyone here that during Paxton's first month with the Branch she'd caught the shriveled little scumbag in her mind one night playing with himself to the purr of her vibrator and the tingling of her senses?

"He looked at all of us." Someone else saved her, his voice strong and gravelly. "He looked at the juicy bits, which like it or not we each and every one of us have, and he was doing it *before* you gave him his brief! Since then, why . . . by now he's probably looked at your juicy bits, too!"

And back to the gangling Goodly again: "Minister, if you hadn't taken Paxton out of the organization, we would have. He's about as trustworthy as a defective contraceptive. If AIDS was a psychic disease, all our brains would be shrivelling to shit right now! *All* of them!" He paused to let that sink in, and after a moment:

"So it seems to us that what you've done is to take away the one man we all trust, while at the same time giving us a watchdog who snaps at his keepers. Yes, and you've chosen one hell of a time to do it." That was twice he'd cursed, and it wasn't Goodly's style to swear at all, not even mildly.

Paxton had been cleaning his fingernails, apparently

unconcerned, but now his ears reddened up a little. He stood up and turned round, glared at the others where they all stared at him in silent accusation. "My talent is . . . unruly!" he snapped. "Also it's eager, full of all the enthusiasm which you jealous bastards have lost! I'm still finding out about it, still experimenting. It isn't some bloody bonsai tree you can just force into any old shape!"

Almost as one person they shook their heads: *they* were the last people he should ever try to convince; his pallid, lame excuses wouldn't work on them. Each and every one of them, they had it in for Paxton. Finally, Ben Trask spoke up, giving their single unified thought shape and substance. "You're a liar, Paxton," he said quite simply. And because Trask was what he was, he didn't have to enlarge upon his accusation.

The Minister felt like he'd bumped into a hornet's nest and for his pains (or by them) was being driven off course, which he really couldn't afford to let happen. He held up his hands, took on a harder, more authoritative tone of voice. "For God's sake, put your feuding and personal feelings aside!" he cried. "At least for the moment, or for as long as it takes. Whatever else any one of you is or isn't, there's one thing we can at least be sure of: you're all human!"

Which hit them like a truck. Seeing that he now had their attention, and while he retained the upper hand, the Minister turned pleadingly to Ben Trask. "Mr. Trask—but level-headed, if you please—will you repeat what you told me downstairs?"

Trask looked at him grudgingly but nodded. "Only first let me finish telling them what you started. They already know most of it and have probably guessed the rest, so I'll get straight to it. And it just might come easier if they hear it from me."

"Very well," the Minister replied, sighing his relief.

And Trask began:

"Zek Föener gave us a helping hand in the Greek islands," he said. "You'll know who she is from the Keogh files, what happened at Perchorsk and on Starside, etcetera. She's a powerful telepath, one of the world's best. But like the Necroscope himself she's opted out of cloak and daggery.

"Anyway, it was dodgy out there in the Med. We were killing vampires, and plenty of times when they nearly killed us. But Harry took the brunt of it and went up against the Big One, Janos Ferenczy himself—and I know I don't have to tell you about the Ferenczys. When Harry was in Romania that last time, just before the end, Zek tried to get in touch with him to see how things were going. But telepathy over great distances isn't easy and she didn't get too much. At least that's what she told us, but we could see that what she *did* get shocked her rigid.

"I know Darcy Clarke has been worried stiff about it, for the fact is Darcy thinks the Necroscope's the best thing since sliced bread. I know several of you also think so, and hell, so do I! Or I used to . . .

"So . . . we did the job and came back, and as far as we know, Harry was successful, too. It seems he made a great job of it. Except he's been a big cagey about what actually happened up in the Carpathians. Now me, I haven't read too much into that. Nor has Darcy Clarke. For after all, Harry did lose Sandra Markham out there. So Darcy was going to let him get it off his chest in his own good time.

"For which—or so it would seem—Darcy's been sort of 'reduced to the ranks,' decommissioned, busted, et cetera. But for what, that's what I'd like to know. For inefficiency, in that he maybe didn't want to prejudice an old friend? For holding back awhile and not going off half cocked? For having—shit—just a little faith!?"

Both the Minister and Paxton opened their mouths as if to butt in, but Trask cut them out with: "The thing you have to remember about Darcy Clarke is this: that his talent doesn't go sneaking into other people's minds, eavesdropping or spying from a distance. All it does is look after Darcy. But he's kept in touch with the Necroscope and so far there's nothing to report. Darcy's talent didn't warn him of any immediate danger. If it had . . . you can bet your life he'd have been the first to yell! The last thing he'd want is for another Yulian Bodescu to be out and about!"

"But—" Paxton started.

"Shut your face!" Trask told him. "These people are still listening to someone telling the truth! *Only* the truth . . ." And he eventually continued: "Anyway, that was all yesterday and today is today. And now things seem to have changed . . ." He paused and looked at the Minister. "Did you want to take it from there, sir?"

The Minister gave him a grim look and raised an eyebrow. "But you haven't told it all, Mr. Trask."

Trask gritted his teeth but nodded. And after a moment: "I'm just back from a job," he said. "It's this serial killer thing we've been working on, these brutal, horrific murders of young women. The thing is, Darcy had approached Harry for his help on this one, because . . . you know . . . that's what the Necroscope is: the one man in the world who can talk to a victim *after* she's dead. And Darcy told me how Harry had been especially upset by the death of the latest one, a girl called Penny Sanderson.

"Well, two days ago Penny turned up—like a bad Penny, eh?" But he wasn't grinning. "Now, this girl was dead and gone forever, and yet suddenly here she is, right as rain, back home with her folks. And the point is she couldn't even convince *them* that she hadn't been murdered! They had seen her body; they'd *known* it was

135

their daughter; they regarded her return as nothing short of a miracle.

"The police weren't happy with any of this. Oh, she had a story to tell, but it rang like a cracked bell. And if she really was Penny Sanderson, then who had been cremated? So the Minister sent me up there to sit in on a 'standard police procedure interview.' Of course, I was their lie detector.

"Well, she was—is—Penny Sanderson; she wasn't lying about that. But she *was* lying about her loss of memory and what all. So knowing the Keogh connection, I just sort of thought to ask her if she knew him: had she ever heard of him or met him? And she said no, never, and just looked blank. A barefaced lie! Which led to my next question, except I didn't frame it like a question. I simply shrugged and said: 'You're a lucky girl. It might easily have been you who was dead and not your double.'

"And she looked me straight in the eye and said: 'I'm sorry for her, whoever she was, but she has nothing to do with me. I didn't die.' And again she was lying through her teeth. Well, I trust my talent. It never has let me down. She wasn't sorry for the other girl because there wasn't another girl. And her statement that she didn't die? A funny way of putting it at best, right? So the only conclusion I can come to is that Penny Sanderson *did* die, and that she's now . . . back from the dead!"

The gathered espers let their air out in a concerted sigh. All of them. And Trask finished off with: "Of course, I couldn't tell the police she'd been—what the hell—brought back, resurrected. So I simply said she was okay. Just how 'okay' she is . . . well, that's a different matter."

At which point the Minister Responsible took his best-yet opportunity to introduce a further item of damning information. "Clarke sent Keogh the files of all those murdered girls. And up in the Castle on the Mount in Edinburgh, he actually let the Necroscope talk to Penny Sanderson—er, in his own way, you understand.''

Ben Trask, despite what he himself had just related, still wasn't one hundred percent convinced. ''But at the time, wasn't that the idea? So that Harry could find out who killed her?''

The Minister nodded. ''That was the idea.'' He dabbed at his face with a handkerchief. ''But a bad one, it now seems.''

It was Paxton's turn. ''He's a telepath,'' he said, his voice hard-edged, defiant.

''Harry?'' Ben Trask stared at him.

Paxton nodded. ''He was into my mind like a ferret down a rat hole! He warned me off and told me he wouldn't be warning me again. Also, his eyes were feral: they shone behind those dark glasses he wears. And he doesn't much care for the sunlight.''

''You've really been hard at work, haven't you?'' Trask growled. But this time he couldn't accuse him of lying.

''Look,'' said the other, ''I was given a job to do. Like the Minister said, after Wellesley he couldn't take any chances. So when Clarke came back from the Greek islands I hooked into him. And I learned about his suspicion that maybe Keogh was a vampire. Another thing: Keogh told me to tell the Minister that his 'worst nightmare' had come true. Ergo: Keogh's a vampire!''

The Minister was quick to add: ''That last isn't proven yet. But it is starting to look that way. The thing is, Keogh has had a lot of contact with these creatures. Close contact. Maybe this last time there was a little too much contact.''

Paxton again: ''Look, I know I'm a relative newcomer, and you don't much like me, and in the past you've all had reason to be grateful for Harry Keogh. But have these things blinded you to the facts? Okay, so you don't want to believe me—don't even want to believe yourselves—but just *think* what we're up against if we're right:

"He can talk to the dead, who apparently know a hell of a lot. He uses the Möbius Continuum to go anywhere he wants to instantly, like we take a step into another room. He's a telepath. And now he not only speaks to the dead but calls them back, too!"

"He could do that before," said Ben Trask, not without a shudder.

"But now he calls them back to what looks like life!" Paxton was relentless. "From their ashes! *Or undeath?*"

At which David Chung gave a mighty start, reeled like someone had hit him, and choked something out in Cantonese. Most of the espers were on their feet by now, but Chung gropingly found a chair and flopped down again. Frowning, the Minister Responsible said, "Mr. Chung?"

Chung's pallor gave his face a sickly lemon tint. He wiped his shining brow and licked his lips, and again mumbled something to himself in Chinese. Then he looked up and his eyes were wide. "You all know what I do," he said, his words a little sibilant and clipped in his fashion. "I'm a locator, sympathetic. I take a model or a piece of something and use it to find the real thing. It's Branch policy that I take and keep safe from each one of you a small item of your personal belongings. This is for your own safety: if you go missing, I can find you.

"Well, I also have several items belonging to Harry Keogh, stuff he's left here from time to time . . .

"I was out in the Mediterranean with the others. I knew Zek Föener had been worried about something, and so I too have been keeping tabs on Harry. I told myself it was for his own good. But I knew what I was doing and what I was looking for.

"At first when I scried on him it was just him; there was nothing different; it felt right. I got a picture of him,

138

you know? Not doing anything, just a picture of him as I knew him, up there at his home in Edinburgh or wherever he was. But recently the picture has been dim, misty, and last night and this morning there wasn't much of Harry there at all; just a mist, a fog. I was going to submit a report on it tomorrow.''

"In the old days," Trask said, "we called that mind-smog. It's what you get when you try to scan a vampire."

"I know," Chung said. He was more nearly recovered now. "It was partly that which hit me, and partly something else. Paxton said that Harry could call dead people up from their ashes. That's what hit me the most."

"What?" The Minister was frowning again.

Chung looked at him. "I also have things which used to belong to Trevor Jordan," he said. "And this morning, just by accident, I happened to touch one of them. It was like Trevor was right here, right next door or down the street. And I thought it was something out of my memory. It was there and then it was gone. But it just struck me that he very well *could* have been here, just down the street!"

The Minister still hadn't taken it in, but Trask soon took care of that. Pale as a ghost, he whispered: "My God! Jordan was cremated out in Rhodes, burned to ashes in case he'd been infected with vampirism. But, Jesus, now that I think of it, I remember how it was Harry Keogh who insisted on it!"

139

Part Two
(Four Years Earlier)

I   The Icelands

THE GREAT WAMPHYRI LORDS BELATH, LESK THE GLUT, Menor Maimbite, Lascula Longtooth, and Tor Tornbody were no more. All of these and many lesser Wamphyri lights, their lieutenants and warrior creatures, all wiped out by The Dweller and his father in the battle for The Dweller's garden. That battle was lost, the kilometer-high aeries of the Wamphyri (all except the Lady Karen's) reduced to so much stone, bone and cartilage rubble by the massed explosions of methane-belching gas-beasts, and the Wamphyri masters of Starside themselves brought low in the aftermath of their humiliating defeat.

Now Shaithis, once leader of the vampire army, turned his hybrid flyer's head into a wind whistling out of the bitter north, and rising on its waft, set course for the Icelands. He was not the first of the Wamphyri to venture that way. Over the centuries others had gone before him, exiled or fled there, and after the battle at the garden certain survivors of his army had headed that way, too.

Better the Icelands, whatever they held in store, than the awesome weapons of The Dweller and his father. Aye, those two, father and son: mere men. But men with talents; men come out of the hell-lands beyond the sphere-Gate; who used the power of the sun itself to blow away the protoplasmic, metamorphic flesh of the Wamphyri into superheated gas and stinking evaporation!

Harry Keogh and his son, called The Dweller: they had destroyed Shaithis's army, ruined his plans, reduced him almost to nothing. But almost nothing is still something, and in all creation there does not exist anything more tenacious than a vampire. Shaithis, if it were at all possible and given even the smallest opportunity, would build on what vestigial power was left to him, to become something again. And if and when that day should come, *then* the hell-landers would pay! Yes, and all who had stood alongside them in the battle for the garden.

The Lady Karen had stood with them, treacherous Wamphyri *bitch*! Shaithis jerked hard on the leather reins, yanking the gold bit in his flyer's mouth until it tore the flesh there. The creature—once a man, a Traveller, but hideously changed now through Shaithis's mutative art—uttered a complaining grunt through pluming nostrils and flapped its manta wings more rapidly, lifting higher still in the frosty air as if to reach for the cold diamond stars.

Behind Shaithis, suddenly the mountains were split by a golden bomb-burst of searing light; a sliver of sunlight struck like a spear at him from beyond the barrier mountains, from Sunside. He felt it glance against his robe of black bat fur and cringed, and knew that he'd flown too high. Sunup! The sun's slow creep was bringing its molten yellow rim into view. Cold as he was, Shaithis could feel it burning on his back.

Mind-linked to a flying beast made in large part from a man, now Shaithis instructed his weird mount: *Glide!*

A waste of mental effort, however small, for the flyer too had felt the sun's menacing rays. Its enormous manta wings tilted upwards at their tips and stilled their pulsing; its head went down as it slid into a shallow glide; Shaithis sighed his relief and returned to his black brooding.

The Lady Karen . . .

A "mother," some said, whose vampire would one day bring forth a hundred eggs out of her body! There would be aeries again on Starside, in some unforeseen future, and all of them inhabited by Karen's black brood, and the bitch herself hive queen of all the Wamphyri! Doubtless there would be a truce between Karen and The Dweller, peace between them, even bonds of flesh. How that could ever be Shaithis was at a loss even to think. But hadn't he with his own eyes seen Harry Keogh and Karen together in her stack, her aerie on Starside, which alone stood where all the rest were tumbled into ruins?

Karen . . .

Without exception, each and every vampire Lord had lusted after her body and her blood! And if things had gone their way in the battle for The Dweller's garden, Shaithis would have been first with her. Now, *there* was a thought to savor!

Karen.

Shaithis remembered her as he had once seen her, at a meeting of all the Wamphyri Lords in Karen's aerie:

Her hair was burnished copper; seeming to burn, it bounced like fine spun gold on her shoulders, competing with the golden bangles she wore on her arms. Gold rings on a slender golden chain around her neck supported her clinging sheath of a gown, which left her jutting left breast and right buttock exposed, or very nearly, so that with no undergarments the effect had been explosive. If the Lords who saw her like that had worn war gauntlets, and if the meeting's agenda had been anything less than of the utmost importance, then certainly the lustier Lords might have fought over her. And who among the Wamphyri was not lusty?

From one pale, perfect shoulder had depended a smoky black cloak, skillfully woven from the fur of *Desmodus*, which shimmered with a weave of fine golden stitches; on her feet sandals of pale leather, similarly stitched in gold; and dangling from the lobes of her ears, golden disks fretted with her sigil, which was the head of a snarling wolf.

She had been breathtaking! Shaithis had felt the thoughts of his fellow Lords turn hot as their blood, and he'd known they all wanted to be into her. Even the thoughts of the slyest, most devious of them (Shaithis himself) had been diverted—which of course had been the witch's purpose! Aye, a clever one, Karen. He could still see her, burning on his mind's eye:

Her body had the sinuous motion of Traveller women when they danced, which yet seemed so unaffected as to be innocent. Her face, heart-shaped, with a lock of that fiery hair coiled on her brow, likewise could have been innocent—except her red eyes gave her away. Her mouth was full, curved in a perfect bow; the color of her lips, like blood, was accentuated by her pale, slightly hollow cheeks. Only her nose marred looks otherwise entirely stunning: it was a fraction tilted, stubby, with nostrils just a little too round and dark. And perhaps her ears, half hidden in her hair, showing whorls like the strange orchids of Sunside. Beautiful but . . . Wamphyri, aye!

Shaithis shivered, even Shaithis. Not from the cold but from his lust, and from his loathing. It was a tremor which coursed through him like the vibrations of a gong. And it was the sure recognition of his ambition. To destroy The Dweller had been all of it, upon a time. But now there was more.

"One day, Karen," Shaithis promised himself out loud, his voice a low rumble, "one day, if there is justice, I *shall* have you. Ah, and while I fill you to brimming on the one hand, on the other I'll empty you to the last drop! I will feed a straw of gold directly into your heart, and for every milky driblet your sex drains from me, I shall suck a spurt of scarlet from you! Thus of our *depletions*, mine will be temporary while yours . . . yours, alas, will be permanent. So shall it be!" It was his Wamphyri oath.

And scowling into the bitter wind, Shaithis flew north . . .

The sun's slow rising over Sunside could not catch Shaithis of the Wamphyri; flying however slowly around the curve of the vampire world towards its roof, still his going was faster and farther than the sun could chase him. So that in a little while he reached and passed that margin beyond which the sun's rays never fell, and after that he knew that he was in the Icelands.

Shaithis had never been much of a one for legends and histories. Of the Icelands he knew only those details which were items of gossip or matters of common knowledge:

That the sun never shone there was self-evident; but rumor also had it that if one crossed the polar cap and kept going, then he'd find more mountains and fresh territories for the conquering. No one in living memory had tested the legend, however (at least, not of his own free will), for the great stacks of Starside had been the places of the Wamphyri, their homes and aeries since time immemorial. But . . . that was yesterday. And now it appeared that the myth would be tested in full.

As for the creatures of the Icelands:

In the margins of its oceans (some said) great hot-blooded fishes spouted, vast as the mightiest warrior and with shovel mouths that scooped the sea for smaller prey. They swam there from some eastern ocean, along a warm river than ran in the sea itself! It sounded like a lie to Shaithis.

Aye, and there were bats, too, which also ate the smallest fishes. These were miniature albinos and dwelled in caverns of ice, and were attuned to Wamphyri minds as were their kith and kin in more hospitable parts. Another myth to be tested.

Other than the whales and the snow-bats, Shaithis had heard of bears like the small brown bears of Sunside, but huge and pure white, which hid indistinguishable in the snow and ice to leap out on unwary wanderers. But again, he would see what he would see. None of these things held anything of terror for him. They were life and life is blood. And conversely, as in an old Wamphyri saying, the blood is the life . . .

For the equivalent of two and a half days Earthtime Shaithis flew steadily north; until, at the end of one huge glide and when it was time for his flyer to climb again, he spied bears basking in starlight on a floe at the rim of an ice-crusted sea. Shaithis's flyer was tired, its fats, liquids, and metamorphic flesh depleted. Starside had been cold, but the Icelands were colder far. This place would be as good as any to stop and rest awhile, for Shaithis was tired, too. And hungry.

Where a cliff of ice towered over the sea he brought his flyer down, commanding it to remain there while he strode out along the frozen shore. The elevation of the place would make it a good launching platform when it was time to get under way again. A quarter mile away the bears sensed him coming; a pair of them towered to their hind feet on the tilting floe, sniffing the air suspi-

ciously and grunting their annoyance. They were females, and cubs tumbled from underfoot as they
commenced to roar their furious warnings.

Shaithis smiled grimly and came on. Their roaring was
a challenge; his Wamphyri nature reacted to it; his face
elongated and needle teeth scythed through the cartilage
of his jaws and gums like an eruption of bone daggers.
His mouth filled with the salt taste of his own blood, and
that too served to speed his monstrous metamorphosis.

The vampire Lord was only an inch or two less than
seven feet tall, but the she-bears where they rumbled and
roared on the float of ice and threatened to tip it over
were all of that and twelve inches more at least! Their
paws were three times the size of Shaithis's hands, and
tipped with claws sharp enough to spear fish dead in the
water at a thrust.

And: *Ah!* he thought. *Good strong flesh, and ferocious
fighters born! What warriors I could build from such as
you!*

Now he was only a hundred yards away, and that was
too close for the nursing mothers. Plunging into bitter,
slapping wavelets, they struck out for the shore. They'd
see this creature off or kill him. If the first, good enough.
And if the second: well, he'd make good red meat for
the cubs.

Shaithis, fifty yards away from them where they left
the water and shook themselves on all fours like huge
white shaggy dogs, took his war gauntlet from his hip
and thrust his right hand into it. *Come on then, ladies*,
he urged with his telepathic mind, not knowing if they
heard him and caring less. *For I've come a long hungry
way, and a cold hungry way yet to go!*

Still his ''hand'' was only two-thirds the size of one
of theirs, but deadlier far. He spread wide his fingers
inside the gauntlet, and the grotesque palm was a great

149

rasp of cutting edges, blades, and scythes. And clenching his hand as nearly as possible to a fist, razor spines stood up inches from the knuckles, and four sharp-filed iron punches sprang out to point forward like ramrods.

The bears were charging, the smaller one (but only inches smaller) leading the larger on. Shaithis had chosen the site of the battle: he shrugged off his cloak, stood tall and central on a flat cake of ice frozen in a field of sharp, jumbled ice boulders. The bears were disadvantaged, came slipping and sliding over the rough terrain. They roared, and the vampire Lord roared back, which served to increase their fury.

Before, Shaithis had appeared more or less human. Now he was anything but human. His skull had elongated to that of a wolf; the gape of his mouth was enormous, where white needle teeth meshed like those of a shark. His long and sloping nose had broadened and flattened to his face, growing convoluted and sensitive as the snout of a bat. Even if he were blinded, that snout and his whorl-like ears would track the movements of his opponents as surely as his scarlet eyes. His right hand inside its gauntlet had expanded to fill that fearsome weapon and give it yet more weight, while his left hand was now lizard-like and taloned, whose fingers were tipped with sharp chitin chisels. So that for all his man-like silhouette, in fact he had become a composite warrior-creature: Wamphyri!

The leading she-bear came at a shambling run, rearing upright as she entered the arena of battle. Shaithis let her come and at the last moment crouched low and hurled himself forward into her massive legs. He clung there, reached round behind, hamstrung her with one clawing rake of his gauntlet. Howling, she crashed down on him, and before he could escape the tangle, tore open his back to the spine. The moment he felt the pain he killed it, willed it away; and kicking himself free of the crippled bear, he looked for its larger companion. She was on him!

Huge paws groped for him where he skidded on his damaged back, and crushing jaws fastened in the left forearm he held up before his face for protection. But as her great head worried at his arm and her claws tore his body, so Shaithis swung his gauntlet in a deadly arc. It smacked against her head, demolishing her left ear and slicing into the eye, so that she at once reared upright and away, dragging Shaithis to his feet. His left arm had been released but was crushed, temporarily useless. If she should fasten those great jaws of hers around his neck or shoulder, he'd be finished.

Bloodied and roaring her pain and fury, she shook her red, torn head and sent pearls of blood flying in Shaithis's eyes. He ignored them and, as she lowered her jaws towards his face, thrust his gauntlet direct into her yawning cave of a mouth. Teeth like the heads of claw hammers sheared as the gauntlet crunched through them. Shaithis drove that terrible weapon in deeper yet, wrenched it to and fro, enlarging her throat, then tore downwards into her gullet. *

She staggered this way and that, her great arms beating uselessly. Shaithis opened his gauntlet in her mouth, wrenched it free, dislocated what was left of her bottom jaw. She'd not bite him now! And while still she flailed he swung his gauntlet again, this time with its iron punches extended. They slammed into her skull through the red debris of her ear and crushed the delicate bone inwards, penetrating to her brain.

She was done; she puffed and snorted and swayed, pawing uselessly at empty air. Shaithis gathered all his remaining strength to drive his gauntlet one last time through the ruin of her flapping jaw and into the back of her throat, where he gripped, crushed, and severed the spinal column. Virtually decapitated, she was dead on her feet—for a single moment. And in the next the ice shook as her great body thudded down upon it.

Shaithis leaped on her, buried his awful face in the pulp of her head, filled himself with steaming crimson. The blood is the life!

. . . In a while he stood up. A small distance away the other bear left a trail of blood where it crawled in crazy patterns on the ice, dragging its useless rear legs behind it. Shaithis fought down his own pain as he went to the crippled creature; when chance permitted, he ripped away the muscles and tendons first from one foreleg, then the other. When finally the bear was totally incapacitated, he tore open her throat and let out the remaining bulk of her life steaming onto the ice.

And again he took hot, reeking blood, and felt himself growing strong.

Some little distance away his flyer nodded its great swaying diamond-shaped head at the top of the ice cliffs. Shaithis stood up and commanded it: *Come!*

The thing came. Slipping and slithering at the rim, its many ''legs'' uncoiled like whipping snakes to thrust it into its launch; and it soared out over the sea, then dipped one huge manta wing, turned, and came back. It settled to the ice a respectful distance away, then at Shaithis's insistence came flopping to where the carcasses waited. Meanwhile the vampire Lord had cut out the great smoking hearts of the bears and put them in a pouch for later.

He backed off and sat down on a stump of ice. And: *Eat*, he commanded his flyer. *Fuel yourself.*

And in the streaming moon and starlight, the changeling beast took back much of its lost heat, fats and liquids. *Aye, eat well*, Shaithis told it. *There'll be no more strong meat like this awhile. Not until I'm healed, anyway.*

And then, gradually, he let all his pain free to creep in on him, the agony of his split back and crushed arm, and his broken ribs where they'd tested the bear's pummeling. Pain, great pain! His vampire felt it: all the more spur to that *thing* within him, to be about the healing.

Pain, aye. There were times like this, after a battle hard fought and won, when pain was warmer than the warm, succulent core of a woman. It was Shaithis's pride to let it wash over him, and to feel the scars of his body start to heal. Perhaps he would keep some of them open, or scabbed at best, as mementoes of his victory.

Except . . . who would there be to admire them?

After a flight as long again, finally Shaithis spied the ice castles where they gleamed under the serpentine writhings of polar aurora. They could only be stacks, aeries, surely? His heart beat faster in his great breast. Wamphyri, here? What manner of creatures would they be, dwelling in the subzero temperatures of the Icelands? Albinos like the mythical bats, growing their own white fur for warmth? What would be their sustenance? And perhaps more to the point, how would they react to the Lord Shaithis?

He took his flyer up to higher altitudes, the better to spy out the ice-locked land around. Farther north, possibly at the northernmost extreme, a string of dead volcanoes thrust up their crater cones through ice and drifted snow. In both directions, east and west, they dwindled away as far as Shaithis's eyes could see, marching out of view across glittering, icy horizons. Some were cased in ice, others showed their naked stone; from which Shaithis deduced that the unclad mountains must still retain a measure of their former fire.

153

To reinforce his opinion, he noted that the central and largest cone even appeared to issue a little smoke. But the effect came and went and could be an illusion of the general dazzle. Star-dazzle and aurora-dazzle: the entire roof of the world was lit as by some weird blue daylight! Not that light was especially important to the Wamphyri; no, for the night was their element; eyes such as theirs could see even in the darkest places.

As for the ice stacks: Shaithis gave them his keenest possible scrutiny. They were mere molehills compared to the once-mighty bone and stone stacks of Starside, and even the tallest would be less than half the height of the lowliest aerie. Where they were not coated with snow, it could be seen that their ice was of the purest; like vast, inverted icicles, they grew up in concentric circles away from the central volcano. Also, where the light struck through them at their peaks, he saw that they were pure ice through and through; but at their bases many seemed to have stony cores. Perhaps in its heyday the central volcano had thrown out great gobs of stuff all around, forming splashes of hot rock in these rippling rings, like a handful of mud tossed into a pool. And then, through the centuries, ice sheaths had accumulated, gradually building into these jagged, sharply pointed stacks. It seemed as likely an explanation as any.

That the ice castles were not fit habitation seemed obvious at first, and Shaithis might well have flown on. But then he saw what looked like an exhausted—indeed frozen—flyer at the base of one such castle and went down for a closer look. Again choosing an ice cliff's rim for landing site, he left his flyer and walked a half mile to that which he had seen from on high, lying crumpled in frozen snow.

A flyer, aye, much rimed, emaciated, and seemingly dead. Seemingly. But no one knew better than Shaithis of the Wamphyri how hard it was actually to kill such a creature. Like the vampire Lords who made them, they were created to endure. He sent a telepathic message to the brain of the great diamond-shaped blanket of a thing, all of fifty feet across its wingtips, that it should stir itself, rise up. It did no such thing, which hardly surprised him: their small brains were rarely attuned to any mind other than their master's. But he might have expected a small twitch of curiosity at least, if only for the fact that some strange Wamphyri Lord had issued the beast an instruction, however invalid. There had been no such twitch, wherefore its brain most be dead. Likewise, of course, the great envelope of flesh which enclosed it.

Then, clambering over the cold humped ridge of its central body to the base of its neck at the forward junction of wings, Shaithis spied its saddle and trappings, and recognized the familiar blazon of its maker/master tooled into the leather: a face in caricature, grotesque and distorted from its weight of mighty wens and warts! And then Shaithis smiled his sardonic smile and nodded. The flyer had been the Lord Pinescu's creature.

Volse Pinescu: that most ugly of all the Wamphyri, whose habit it had been to foster running sores and festoons of boils all over his face and body, in order that his aspect would be that much more terrifying. So Volse was here, eh? Shaithis was somewhat surprised, for he had seen the Lord Pinescu and Fess Ferenc crash their crippled flyers in clouds of dust on Starside's plain of boulders after the battle at The Dweller's garden, and he'd thought that must be the end of them. Either that or they'd have to travel north on foot. In Volse's case . . . obviously he'd been wrong. Patently, the wily old devil had kept a flyer in reserve, just in case.

And what of "the Ferenc," as that one liked to be known? Could he also be here? Fess Ferenc, aye: one man, or monster, of which to be exceedingly wary. Standing at a hundred inches tall, the Ference would have dwarfed even the great she-bears which Shaithis had killed for meat. And he alone of all the Wamphyri carried no gauntlet: no need, for his hands were murderous talons! Well, well! Things might yet prove interesting in these terrible Icelands . . .

Shaithis sat in Volse's saddle and chewed on bear heart, and he called to his flyer: *Come, eat!*

As his creature arrived and settled to the ice, Shaithis got down and strode the circumference of the dead beast's body, and so discovered a great hole eaten into its side, where blood vessels as fat as his thumb had been sliced through and sucked upon, then tied off with knots. At which he rightly guessed that Volse Pinescu had survived his stricken mount. Which begged the question, where was Volse now?

Shaithis extended his vampire awareness, sent out a sweeping telepathic probe. Not to speak to anyone but to listen *for* someone. He heard nothing. Or perhaps the echo of a mind's or minds' shutters swiftly slammed shut? If Volse and Fess were here, they weren't speaking. And again Shaithis smiled his sardonic smile. No one applauds a loser. It would be different if he had won the battle for The Dweller's garden. But of course it would; for if he'd won, then he wouldn't be here.

While his flyer feasted, Shaithis looked up at the ice castle. The cold, glittering sculpture was mainly Nature's work. But not all of it. The rims of crude steps cut into the ice had been rounded by time. They led up to an arched entrance under a façade of mighty icicles. Inside, the core was of stone, dark and uninviting.

Shaithis climbed the steps, entered the ice castle, was aware of crusted rime crunching under his feet where at first he strode then crept through a mazy ice labyrinth.

For as he went so he became aware that there was something dreadful here, or that something dreadful had happened here, and for the first time since The Dweller he felt himself in awe of the Unknown.

The place echoed and moaned. The echoes were mainly his, but changed by the cavities and convolutions of the ice castle into dull bass grindings and slidings like floes crushing together in a heaving sea, or great ice doors rumbling shut. And the moaning was the freezing wind echoing in the spires of the place, distorted and amplified by the ice into the agonies of dying monsters.

"Unless he were acclimatized," (Shaithis spoke to himself in a whisper, for company if for nothing else), "I cannot see how a man, even a vampire, might live here. Oh, he *could*, for a while, possibly through a span of a hundred sunups—except here it is always sundown—but finally the cold would get him. Yes, and I can see how that would be:

"The aching cold creeping into his bones, until eventually even Wamphyri flesh would freeze. His heart, beating ever more slowly, pumping thickening ice-crystal blood through shivering veins and arteries. At last he would stiffen and lose all mobility, and the ice wax upon him, until finally he sat upon an ice throne within a glassy stalactite, thinking slow, frozen thoughts from the core of his ice brain!

"Being Wamphyri—*if* he were Wamphyri—he would not die. At least, not until the ice shifted and sheared him, or ground him away. But what would that be for life? My ancestors disposed of their enemies in three ways. Those whom they scorned they buried undead, to become fossils in their graves. Those who worked mischief against them they banished to the Icelands. And those whom they feared were driven into the sphere-Gate on Starside. Who can say which penalty was the most severe? To go to hell, to turn to ice, or to stiffen into a stone? I for one would not care to be a block of ice!''

These thoughts, breathed aloud, were carried away as whispers, amplified and thrown back as gales of sound. It was like whispering in some echoing cavern or grotto, except that these caves of ice were that much more resonant. In the high vaulted ceilings, icicles tinkled, then shivered into shards and came crashing down. Some were quite large, so that Shaithis must leap aside.

At that and when things had quietened a little, he decided to vacate the place—at which precise moment there sounded in his telepathic mind a far, faint, quavery voice:

Is it you, Shaitan, come after all this time to discover and devour me? Then you should know that I welcome it! I'm here, up here. Come, get it over with. The cold centuries have chilled even my once-fierce Wamphyri passions. So come, make haste, and snuff this last low-flickering flame!

II Exiles

STARTLED, SHAITHIS FELL INTO A DEFENSIVE CROUCH, turned in a slow circle, gazed all about. He saw only ice, but knew now for certain that this place contained more than that. And at last, crimson eyes slitted, he concentrated his own thoughts into a probe:

Who speaks?

What? the infirm, quavery voice spoke again in his mind, and Shaithis sensed a derisory snort. *Don't make me laugh, Shaitan! You know well enow who speaks! Or have the long, lonely years addled your wits? Kehrl Lugoz speaks, old fiend. We were exiled together; we dwelled awhile in the caves of the cone; we were "companions," for as long as there was meat. But when the meat was finished our friendship went with it. And I fled while I could.*

Kehrl Lugoz? Shaithis frowned as he strove to remember Wamphyri legends almost as old as the race itself. And this Shaitan which the hidden speaker referred to:

159

not *the* Shaitan, surely? He frowned again, and as suspicion turned to curiosity asked: *Where are you?*

Where I've been for . . . how long? Preserved in the ice, undead, that's where I am. Dreaming in my frozen hell of endless time. And you, Shaitan? How has it been for you? Has the cone kept you warm, or are its fires returned to drive you out?

Dreaming in a frozen hell? The very scenario Shaithis had conjured only a moment or two ago! Yes, and he believed that whoever this Kehrl Lugoz was who spoke to him, indeed he spoke from a dream. Perhaps the crashing of great icicles had roused him up somewhat from his sleep.

You're wrong, he said then, relaxing a little, *for I'm not Shaitan. A son of his sons, perhaps, but my name is Shaithis, not Shaitan.*

Oh? Ha, ha, ha! The other seemed to find his words bitterly amusing. *The Lord of Liars even to the end, eh, Shaitan? Perverse as ever. Aye, you were the worst of a bad lot. Well, what does it matter now? Come for me if you will—or begone, and let me return to my dreaming.*

The voice faded as its owner sank down again into permafrost dreams; but Shaithis, concentrating all of his vampire senses to their full, believed he'd located its source. *I'm up here!* that mental voice had told him at the onset. Somewhere up above . . .

Shaithis was in the heart of the carved, wind-fretted ice castle now. There, locked in clear ice all of three feet thick, he could see a massive central core of volcanic rock thrusting raggedly up like the ossified root of a glass tooth: a "splash" of stony spittle from the ancient volcano. And there, climbing the face of the ice sheath where it covered the castle's lava foundations, carved into its cold crystal contours, glassy steps wound up out of sight into grottoes of gleaming ice.

There was nothing for it but to follow them; the vampire Lord mounted the frost-rimed stairs and climbed to the jagged peak of the core, where its last black igneous fang pointed straight up, as if threatening to break out of its sheath. And staring through ice hard as stone, finally Shaithis spied the author of the mind-messages he'd heard in the corridors below.

There in blue-gleaming heart of ice—seated upright in a lava niche, with one hand resting lightly upon a ridge of rock, as upon the arm of a favorite chair—a man ancient as time, weary, withered, and weird! Encased as surely as any fly in amber, his eyes were closed, his frozen body motionless, his mien severe as his fate. And yet he sat there proudly with his head held high upon a scrawny neck, and with that certain something in his aspect which spoke mutely but definitely of his origin: the fact that he was Wamphyri! Kehrl Lugoz, whoever he had been.

No, whoever he still was!

Shaithis put out a hand to the wall of smooth ice, pressed down hard until his palm was cold and flat. A minute went by, then another, until finally:

Thud!

It was faint—so very faint and far-seeming—but it was still there. And after a pause of two more minutes:

Thud!—and so on. Kehrl Lugoz lived. However protracted his heartbeat, however fossilized his body (and it was, very nearly, fossilized), still he lived. Except, and as Shaithis had already inquired of himself, what was this for life?

He stared hard at the shriveled thing, studying it through three feet of ice, which, however pure, nevertheless blurred the picture and shifted its focus with Shaithis's every smallest motion. And now he believed he knew the answer to that other question he'd recently asked himself: which was worse, to be buried undead, or sent into the hell-lands, or banished here? And the vampire Lord shivered at the thought of all the nameless centuries gone by since Kehrl Lugoz had come up here and sat himself down, and waited for the ice to form.

Thud! And this time, because he'd been lost in his own thoughts and was startled, Shaithis snatched back his hand.

Kehrl Lugoz was too old to even guess at his age. The Wamphyri, when they age, do not necessarily show it. Shaithis himself was more than five hundred years of age, yet looked no older than a well-preserved fifty. But in the face of privations such as this one had known, it simply couldn't be hidden. Yes, Lugoz looked almost as old as time.

The eyebrows above his closed, steeply slanted eyes were bushy, white, locked in ice like the rest of him. His hair was white as a halo of snow over a brow wrinkled and brown as a walnut, with white sideburns which frizzed out wildly to half-obscure his conch-like ears. His ancient face was not so much wrinkled as grooved, mummified, like a trog kept overlong in its cocoon until wasted. The grey cheeks were sunken in, the chin pointed, with a thin wisp of white beard fluffing there. Eyeteeth like fangs overshot the withered lower lip; they were yellow and the one on the left was broken. There'd been insufficient strength in the frozen vampire to grow another.

The nostrils in the squat, convoluted nose (more properly a bat's snout than was usual in most of the Wamphyri) showed signs of fretting: disease, Shaithis supposed. And a huge purple wen was visible bulging under the chin, like the puffed mating wattle of one of Sunside's birds.

As for Kehrl Lugoz's garb: he wore a simple black

robe, its hood thrown back, wide sleeves floppy about his scrawny wrists, and hem loose around his chicken's calves. Except of course the sleeves and hem were not loose but frozen in ice hard as stone. His hands where they protruded from his robe were extremely long-fingered, with sharp, pointed nails, and upon his right index he wore a large ring of gold. Shaithis could not make out its sigil. Veins stood out white in the backs of his hands, instead of olive or purple. Before he froze himself, this one had gone without blood for long and long.

Wake up! Shaithis sent. *I want to know your history, your secrets. Indeed, for it would seem to me that you are Wamphyri history! This Shaitan you speak of: do you mean Shaitan the Unborn? He and his disciples were banished to the Icelands in the very dawn of legends. But still here? How? No, I cannot believe it. Wake up, Kehrl Lugoz! Answer my questions.*

Nothing came back; the old thing in the ice had returned to his dreaming; his shriveled heart continued to thud, but it seemed to Shaithis more slowly yet. He was dying. Longevity, even suspended animation, is not immortality.

"Damn you!" Shaithis snarled out loud. His curse echoed back to him—along with other echoes?—from the bowels of the ice castle. He waited until the echoes had died away and only the weird moaning of ice winds remained, then sent out his vampire awareness all around. Was anyone there?

. . . Well, if there was someone, then he was adept at shielding his presence. Except—

—Suddenly, Shaithis remembered his flyer, which he'd left feeding! If someone should find it out there . . .

He reached out his mind to the creature, discovered it gorging still, cursed long and loud but this time silently and to himself. He'd never get the beast aloft now. But at least he could send it away from here.

Go! he commanded it. *Flop, waddle, squirm, slither, but go! Westward, half a mile at least, and there hide. As best you can, anyway.* And in his mind he felt the stupid creature moving instantly to obey him.

Then, satisfied that the flyer would put distance between itself, Volse's dead creature, and what or whoever else might possibly be in the vicinity, Shaithis returned to the problem at hand. Earlier, the old thing in the ice had been awakened by a fall of icicles. So be it.

Exploring an upper terrace, the vampire Lord found a vast spout of ice like a frozen waterfall, and at its fringe many lesser formations. One of these icicles, some four feet long and nine inches through its stem, he snapped off and carried back to the ice-encased husk of Kehrl Lugoz. Since the petrified old fool couldn't be roused by mental means, let him start awake at the entirely physical shattering of this great blade of ice against his sheath.

Fully absorbed in his task, Shaithis failed to detect the furtive approach of others up the ice staircase. He "shouted" telepathically at the frozen, ice-distorted figure where it sat: *Kehrl Lugoz, wake up!* Then swung back his icicle hammer to smash it against the face of Lugoz's sheath. But the great icicle refused to swing, because something was impeding it!

Hissing and spitting his shock from the red-ribbed vault of his throat out over the glistening, vibrating arch of his forked tongue—eyes bulging and crimson, and with his less than human features instinctively flowing into a fearsomely *in*human wolf-mask—Shaithis glanced back over his shoulder, then dropped the great icicle and reached for his gauntlet. But in that same instant a huge talon of a hand fell upon his wrist and trapped it, and Shaithis stared into the grim grey faces of two fellow survivors from the battle for The Dweller's garden: Fess Ferenc and Volse Pinescu!

He snatched back his hand and stumbled away from them. "Damn your hearts!" he snarled, panting. "But you've learned stealth, you two!"

"We've learned a great many things." Volse Pinescu choked the words out past a huge scab of crusted pus which half sealed his lips, impeding his speech. "Not least how the 'invincible' vampire army of Shaithis of the Wamphyri could be burned and blasted and crushed, its aeries destroyed, and its survivors banished like whipped dogs into eternal wastelands of ice!"

Volse's boil-festooned face turned purple with fury as he took a heavy, threatening step closer to Shaithis. But the Ferenc's temper was less volatile. With his great height and strength, and with his terrible hands, he didn't much need to work up a rage in himself. "We've lost a great deal, Shaithis," he rumbled. "Since coming here it's dawned on us just how much. Aye, for this is a cold and lonely place."

"Cold?" Shaithis blustered. "What is cold to the Wamphyri? You'll get used to it."

Volse strained his head forward aggressively, and a batch of boils on the left side of his neck burst and spurted their yellow pus onto the ice. "Oh?" he gurgled. "Like *he* got used to it, d'you mean?" he inclined his loathsomely decorated head sharply towards Kehrl Lugoz, seated motionless as a mountain not three impenetrable feet away. "Him and all the others we've found, encysted in their echoing fortresses of ice?"

"Others?" Shaithis looked uncertainly from Volse to the Ferenc, then back again.

"Dozens of them," Fess Ferenc finally answered, nodding his huge, acromegalic head. "All taken to the ice, clutching at straws, waiting out their time until some magical thaw shall come and free them into a land filled with life. Or until they die. For the cold of this place is not like the cold of Starside, Shaithis. Here it goes on forever! Get used to it?'' (Now he echoed Volse Pinescu.) ''Resist it? Warm ourselves? Stoke up our internal fires against it? But fires need fuel—the blood is the life! And with what do we sustain ourselves while we're 'Getting used to it'? Blood cools, Shaithis, trickle by trickle, hour by hour. Limbs stiffen, and even the stoutest heart runs slow.''

Now Volse took it up. ''You ask: what is cold to the Wamphyri? *Hah!* How often were *you* cold on Starside, Shaithis? I'll tell you: never! The heat of the hunt kept you warm, the blaze of battle, the hot salt blood of trog or Traveller. Your bed was warm and welcoming at sunup, as were the breasts and buttocks of the lusty women who sucked the sting from your tail. All of these things you had to keep you warm. We all had them! And we had a 'leader' who said to us: 'Let's band together and take The Dweller's garden.' And now what have we got?''

Shaithis looked at the Ferenc, who shrugged and said: ''We have been here longer than you. It *is* cold and we grow colder. Worse, we grow hungry . . .'' His voice was now a growl.

Volse's hand touched the ugly gauntlet at his hip . . . tentatively . . . perhaps thoughtfully . . . it could mean anything. But Shaithis backed away.

And as the threatened Lord plunged his hand into his own gauntlet and flexed it there, displaying its gleaming knives, rasps, and cutting edges, Fess Ferenc raised an eyebrow and rumbled: ''Two to one, Shaithis? Do you like such odds, then?''

''Not especially,'' Shaithis hissed, ''but I'll make sure

you lose at least as much blood as you drink! Where's the profit in that?''

Volse grunted, coughed up yellow phlegm, and spat it out. ''I—say—it—would—be *worth* it!'' He went into a crouch, and now he too wore his gauntlet.

But the Ferenc only relaxed, stepped aside, shrugged again, and said: ''Fight if you wish, you two. Myself, I'd prefer to eat. Full bellies are less fierce, and brains with blood in them more capable of clever scheming.'' His maxim might not fit men, but certainly it was applicable to the Wamphyri.

Volse, seeing he stood alone, thought twice. And: *''Hah!''* he snorted, this time at the Ferenc. ''But it seems *your* mind schemes just as well when you're hungry, Fess! For if we were to fight, Shaithis and I, why you'd sup on the loser—and so make yourself stronger than the winner!'' He nodded and removed his gauntlet. ''I'm no such fool.''

The Ferenc scratched his jutting jaw and grinned, however grimly. ''Strange, but I had always considered you *just* such a fool . . .''

Shaithis, still wary, hung his own gauntlet at his belt, finally nodded, and took out from his pouch a purple heart as big as his fist. ''Here, if you're so hungry.'' And he tossed it. Volse snatched it from the air and closed slavering jaws upon it. But the Ferenc only shook his head.

''Red and spurting for me,'' he said. ''While I can get it, anyway.''

Shaithis frowned and narrowed his eyes suspiciously as the giant started down the ice steps. ''What's your plan?'' he snapped. ''Who will you kill?''

''Not who but what,'' the Ferenc answered over his shoulder. ''And I'll not kill it but merely deplete it little by little. I should think it's obvious.''

Shaithis and Volse went skidding after him. "What?" Volse questioned round a mouthful of bear heart. "Something's obvious?"

The Ferenc glanced back at him. "What did you eat when you crashed your exhausted flyer here?" he said.

"Ah-*hah*!" Volse spat out chunks of cold dark flesh.

"What?" Shaithis grabbed the Ferenc's huge shoulder. "Are you talking about my flyer? Would you maroon me here forever?"

The Ferenc paused, turned, looked him straight in the eye. Two steps lower than Shaithis, *still* the giant looked him in the eye. "And why not?" he answered. "Since it seems to me that you're the reason we're all marooned here?"

"No!" Shaithis spat at him, and stabbed again for his gauntlet—and the Ferenc at once swept him from the stairs!

Shaithis fell. Too depleted and restricted for metamorphosis into an airfoil, he could only grit his teeth and wait for gravity to do its worst. On the way down he struck from several ice ledges but suffered no real damage, until at the last he crashed down on his shoulder and chest—in snow! Merciful snow!

Blown in through an arched ice window, the drift was three or four feet deep with a thick crust of ice. Shaithis crunched through the latter, compressed the former, wrenched his right shoulder, and broke a pair of recently healed ribs. And then he lay there in his agony and cursed Fess Ferenc from the depths of his black heart!

Curse me all you will, Shaithis—the Ferenc had heard him—*but I'm sure you'll think better of it. Of course you will, for it was you or your flyer, after all. Volse would have chosen you: for there's a vampire in you! Ah, the very essence! But personally, I think it were better if you live. A little while longer, at least.*

Shaithis stood up, staggered away, looked for a place to hide. He allowed his hurt to wash over him, deliberately conjuring all the agonies of his crash on Starside, when he'd broken his body and face, and of his fight with the she-bears, to add to the pain of this latest tumble. And these were the false impressions of severe damage which he let flood out of him, to be picked up and (hopefully) wrongly translated by the Ferenc's vampire mind. Volse might conceivably read them, too, but Shaithis doubted it. The boil-fancier was a dullard, too much obsessed with the manufacture of abscesses.

What? the Ferenc seemed surprised, however uncaring. *That much pain? Did you crash down face-first, Shaithis?* He offered a grim mental chuckle. *Well, and now you know how I've felt all this time, for your face has always been hurtful to me!*

Aye (Shaithis could not restrain himself), *laugh long and loud, Fess Ferenc! But remember: he who laughs last . . .*

The Ferenc's chuckling faded in Shaithis's mind, and: *Not too seriously hurt, then? A pity. Or perhaps you merely put a brave face on it? But in any case, I think a warning is in order: don't interfere, Shaithis. If you think to command your flyer into flight, forget it. For if we can't find your creature, then be sure we'll come back for you. Order it to attack us, still we'll triumph in the end. For as you know well enow, flyers make poor warriors and our thoughts would stab it like arrows. And then we'd come back for you! But only let it be our way and make no protest, and for some little time to come . . . well, at least you'll know where to go when you're hungry. And for as long as your flyer lasts—and provided we are not in the vicinity when you go to feed—then you shall last just precisely so long, Shaithis of the Wamphyri.*

169

Shaithis found a deep, sheltered ice niche in the castle's labyrinth and hid himself away. He wrapped himself in his cloak and toned down his vibrant vampire aura. Now must be a time of healing. Perhaps he would sleep and conserve his energy. And there was still a little bear heart left over for when he awakened. So long as he guarded his thoughts and his dreams alike, Volse Pinescu and Fess Ferenc would not find him.

But first there was something he must know. *Why, Fess?* he sent out one last telepathic question. *You could have killed me yet let me live. not out of the "goodness" of your heart, surely. So why?*

Halfway down the ice stairs, the Ferenc smiled with a mouth almost as wide as his face. *You were ever a thinker, Shaithis,* he answered. *Aye, and a clever one at that. Oh, you've made mistakes, certainly, but the man who never made a mistake never made anything. The way I see it, if there's a way out of this place you'll find it. And when you do I'll be right behind you.*

And if I don't?

(The Ferenc's mental shrug): *Blood is blood, Shaithis. And yours is good and rich. Let one thing be clearly understood: if this is as far as we go—if the ice is our destiny—then at the last I shall be the one who sits encased awaiting the Great Thaw. Fess Ferenc and none other. But I shall not go hungry to my fate . . .*

Two exiled Wamphyri Lords—one grotesque and huge, and the other hugely grotesque—left the glittering ice castle and sniffed the bitter air, then let their snouts guide them to Shaithis's doomed beast.

Meat was not the flyer's usual fare; its diet would normally consist of crushed bone, grasses from Sunside, honey and other sweet liquids, and some blood. Having metamorphic flesh, however, it was capable of consum-

ing almost anything organic. On this occasion, having
gorged itself on the frozen flesh of another flyer, it must
now rest until the food was digested and converted.
Bloated, it no longer lay where the ex-Lords had first
spied it beside the gnawed carcass of Volse's flyer, but
had found shelter slumped in the lee of a great block of
ice half a mile to the west, where Shaithis had sent it.

Forming great saucer eyes in its leathery flanks, the
dull, stupid thing gloomed on the Ferenc and Volse Pinescu and lolled its diamond head at them as they approached. Moist and heavy-lidded, its eyes "saw" but
could scarcely comprehend. Until the flyer was instructed to do something, and then by its rightful master,
Shaithis himself, it would do nothing, not even think.
Oh, it would seek to protect itself to a degree, but never
so far as to harm one of the Wamphyri. For stabs of
concentrated vampire telepathy could sting such creatures like darts, bringing them to trembling submission
in a moment. Thus, while the flyer would not fly for Fess
or Volse, it would lie still for them. Even when they
sliced into its warm underbelly to sever great pipes of
veins, which they would then suck upon.

Shaithis, in his niche in the ice castle, "heard" the
huge creature's first mental bleat of distress and was
tempted to issue orders, such as: *Roll, crush these men
who torment you! Bound up and fall upon them!* Even
now, at a distance, he could transmit such commands
and know that the flyer would instantly, instinctively obey
him. But he also knew that while the beast might injure
the Lords, it could not kill them, and he remembered
the Ferenc's warning. To set the flyer upon them (unless
it could be guaranteed to incapacitate them utterly) would
be to place himself in direst jeopardy. Which was why
he ground his teeth a little but otherwise lay still and did
nothing.

To Shaithis it seemed a great waste: his good flyer, used for food. Especially since Volse's flyer—literally two tons of excellent if not especially appetizing meat—already lay out there going to waste. Except even that was not entirely true. Frozen, the creature would not waste but remain available for long and long. But Shaithis knew that there was more than mere hunger in it; the Ferenc had a purpose other than to fill his belly.

For one, the beast would be left so depleted by this first gluttonous "visit" of Fess and Volse that any further aerial voyagings would be out of the question; which meant that Shaithis was now stuck here no less than the others. It was partly the Ferenc's way of paying him back for his failure in the battle for The Dweller's garden, but it was mainly something else.

For the fact was that indeed Shaithis had been the great thinker, with a capacity for scheming which had set him above and apart even from his own kind, the universally devious Wamphyri. If any man could find his way out of the Icelands, then Shaithis had to be the one. An escape which must likewise benefit Fess Ferenc, who would doubtless follow his lead. And as Fess had so vividly pointed out, this was the reason Shaithis's life had been spared: so that he could concentrate on survival to the benefit of all the exiles.

That "all," of course, meaning Fess Ferenc specifically; for Shaithis had no doubt but that eventually (unless there should occur some large and unforeseen reversal) the entirely loathsome Volse Pinescu must surely go the way of all flesh. As to why the Ferenc had so far suffered Volse to live: perhaps he simply couldn't abide the thought of eating him! Shaithis allowed himself a grin, however pained and bitter, before reexamining the question of Volse's survival. A much more likely explanation would be the loneliness and boredom of these

Icelands; perhaps the giant Fess craved companionship! Certainly Shaithis, in the short time he'd been here, had felt a great weight of loneliness pressing down upon him . . . or had he?

For all that this place appeared utterly dead and empty of any noteworthy intelligence, still he was not convinced. Even here in his ice niche, with his thoughts well shielded, still there was this instinctive tingle of *awareness* in his vampire being, a suspicion in his vampire mind that . . . someone observed him in his trials? Possibly. But to know or suspect it was one thing, and to prove it another entirely.

Wherefore he would now sleep and let his vampire heal him, and later turn his attention to matters of more permanent survival—

—Not to mention a small matter of revenge, of course.

Battening his mind more securely yet, Shaithis settled down and for the first time felt the cold, the physical cold, beginning to bite. And he knew that the Ferenc and Volse Pinescu had been correct: even Wamphyri flesh must eventually succumb to a chill such as that of these Icelands. There could be no denying it, not in the face of such evidence as Kehrl Lugoz.

Then, even as Shaithis made to close his right eye (for the left would remain open, even in sleep) something small, soft, and white hovered for a moment before his face, finally darting away with tiny, near-inaudible chittering cries into upper aeries of undisclosed ice. But not before Shaithis had recognized it. Pink-eyed, that tiny flutterer, with membrane wings and a wrinkled, pink-veined snout. A dwarf albino bat, it gave Shaitnis an idea.

By now Volse Pinescu and the Ferenc would be absorbed in their meal, probably numb from their gluttony. Shaithis would risk opening his mind again. He reached out and called to the ice castle's bats, which eventually came to him. Fearful at first, finally they settled to him singly, then in twos and threes, and at last almost buried him in their soft, snowy blanket. An entire colony of the creatures, they crowded into Shaithis's niche.

And with their small bodies warming him, so he slept . . .

The minion bats of Shaitan the Unborn (also called the Fallen) not only warmed Shaithis where he slept but also watched him, as they had since his arrival. They had watched Fess Ferenc and Volse Pinescu, too; also Arkis Leperson and his thralls (both of whom, within a period of just two auroral displays, Arkis had drained before secreting their bloodless corpses in cold storage in a glacier) and a pair of Menor Maimbite's lieutenants, released from thralldom by Menor's death in the battle for the garden. All of these had wended their various ways here, whose subsequent activities the miniature albinos had faithfully reported back to their immemorial master, Shaitan.

The last-mentioned duo, ex-Travellers vampirized by Menor, had been the first of this fresh crop of exiles to get here. Having exhausted their dead master's finest flyer, they had crashed its panting, desiccated carcass in the salt sea at the edge of the Icelands and covered the last thirty miles afoot. Then they'd seen the smoke which Shaitan deliberately sent up from his chimney, and dragged themselves to what might possibly be a warm place. Well, and it had proved warm enough. Now they turned slowly on bone hooks suspended from the low ceiling of an ancient lava blowhole which opened on the volcano's west-facing flank: Shaitan's ice-cavern larder.

The lieutenants had been easy meat; they had no vampires in them; their minds and flesh had been altered but they were not yet Wamphyri. Given a hundred years or more and they might have been harder to take. But time had run out for them right here and now, along with all of their rich red blood.

As for the four Wamphyri Lords: Shaitan was rather more leery of them. Let them fight among themselves first, wear themselves out. It seemed only prudent. In his youth (which Shaitan scarcely remembered), ah, it would have been different then! He'd have had the measure of all of these and four more just like them. But three and a half thousand years is a long time, and time takes its toll of more than memory. Indeed, of almost everything. Now he was . . . tired? If it must be admitted, even his vampire was tired! And his vampire was by far the greater part of him.

Not ailing, frail, or dying tired, just . . . tired. Of the unrelenting cold, which periodically would cut through the volcanic rock to the mountain's heart, even to the blowhole caverns in its roots; of the interminably dull routine of existence; quite simply, of the sameness and emptiness of *being* in these eternal, ageless Icelands.

But not yet tired of life. Not utterly.

Certainly not to the extent that Shaitan would advertise his presence to such as Fess, Volse, Shaithis, and Arkis Leperson! No, for when you came right down to it there were plenty of better ways to die. Aye, and now that the exiles were here there might be more and better reasons to stay alive, too.

Especially this "Shaithis."

Indeed, with a name like that he might even prove to be the realization—the embodiment?—of a totally new existence. This last was only a dream of Shaitan's, true, but it had not faded with time. While all else had turned grey, his dream had stayed clear and bright. And red.

A dream of youth, renewed vigor, a victorious return

to Starside and Sunside and of laying them waste, and then the invasion of worlds beyond. Shaitan's belief, his instinctive conviction that indeed such worlds existed, had sustained him through all the monotonous centuries of his exile, giving purpose to that which was otherwise untenable.

But while the dream remained young and bright, the dreamer had grown old and somewhat tarnished. Not in his mind but in his body. The human parts of Shaitan had wasted, been replaced by *in*human tissues; the metamorphism of his vampire had trancended the deterioration of the host body until the man-part had disappeared almost entirely, leaving only rudimentary or vestigial traces of the original flesh, organs, and appendages. But the fused mind of man and vampire remained, and for all that a great deal had been forgotten, still the accumulation of that mind's contents—its knowledge—was vast. And EVIL.

Shaitan's EVIL was fathomless, but he was not mad. For intelligence and evil are not incompatible. Indeed they are complementary. The murderer requires a mind to construct his clever alibi. An idiot cannot built an atomic weapon.

Evil is the perverse *rejection* of goodness, which in Shaitan was absolute. His was an EVIL which might put the universe itself to the torch, then gaze upon the cinders and find *them* good! He was Darkness, Light's opposite; he could even be said to be the Primal Darkness, which opposed the Primal Light. Which was the reason why even the Wamphyri had banished him. But he knew, without knowing how he knew, that he'd been banished long before that.

Banished . . . by GOOD? By some benevolent God? No metagnostic, still Shaitan could conceive of such a

One. For how may EVIL exist without GOOD? But for now—

—He put such thoughts aside. He'd thought them for long enough. In three and a half thousand years a mind has time to think many things, from the remotely trivial to the infinitely profound. For the moment his origin was not important, but his destiny was. And his destiny might well be part and parcel of this man, this being, called Shaithis.

In the Old Times the Wamphyri had named their "sons" after themselves. Bloodsons, egg-recipients, common vampires—all had adopted the name of their sire. The custom had changed somewhat but not entirely. Arkis Leperson was the recipient son of his leper father, Radu Arkis: "Arkis the Leper," they'd called him. Wherefore his "son"—a Traveller lieutenant who more than a century ago found favor in Radu's scarlet eyes—was now Arkis Leperson. He carried Radu's egg.

Similarly, Fess Ferenc was the bloodson (born of woman) of Ion Ferenc; his Traveller mother died giving birth to the giant, whose size was such it impressed his father to let him live. A great error, that. While yet a youth Fess had killed Ion, then opened his body to steal and devour his vampire egg whole. This way Ion could not pass it to any other, and his aerie on Starside must devolve "naturally" to Fess.

Shaitan, in his day, had sired many offspring and by various means, but his egg had gone to Shaithar Shaitanson, who in his turn had fathered vampires. And Shaitan's bloodspawned children had been named Shaithos, Shailar the Hagridden, Shaithag, and so on. While among his egg-son Shaithar's spawn had been one called Sheilar the Slut, and possibly others with similar-sounding names, derived from the One Original. And all of these before Shaitan himself was banished.

Wherefore . . . was it too much to ask, too improbable, that three thousand years later this one, this Shaithis, should now appear, banished like his forebear before him? Shaitan thought not. But a *direct* descendant? The blood is the life, and only blood would tell. Aye, blood *would* tell.

Take from him, Shaitan commanded the miniature officers of his law. *Just one of you. A nip, the merest sip. Take from him and bring it to me.* He said no more.

And in his ice-crevice hiding place Shaithis scarcely felt the fishhook-sharp needles that punctured the lobe of his ear and drew blood, and was only faintly aware of the whir of small wings making away from him into the frozen labyrinth of the ice castle, then out of that amazing sculpture and into the star-bright night of the world.

Some short time later, the albino swooped down inside the all but extinct central cone to Shaitan's sulphur-yellow apartments, and there hovered, waiting on his word. From his dark corner he commanded it: *Come, little one. I won't crush you.*

The tiny creature flew to him, folded its wings, and fastened to Shaitan's . . . hand? It coughed up spittle and mucus into what passed for a palm, and one small bright splash of ruby blood. And:

Good! said Shaitan. *Now go.* Only too pleased to obey, the bat hastened from its master and left him to his own devices.

Fascinated, for long and long Shaitan gazed at the ruby droplet. It was blood, and the blood is the life. He waited impatiently for the vampire flesh of his hand to open into a tiny mouth and sip the droplet in—an automatic thing, born of hideous instinct—from which he would know that this was just the blood of a common man. But he waited in vain, for like himself Shaithis was uncommon. Very much like himself.

And:

"Mine!" said Shaitan at last, in a croaking, shuddering, delighted whisper. "Flesh of my flesh!"

At which the droplet quivered and soaked *through* the leprous skin of his hand, and into him as if he were a sponge . . .

III The Ferenc's Story

SHAITHIS SLEPT LONG AND LONG.

The bats kept him warm (at least kept him from freezing solid in his ice niche); his wounds healed; his thoughts, like Shaithis himself, remained hidden. Until it was time to rouse himself and be up and about. Which was when his hiding place was discovered.

What!? Who!? The astonished, involuntary mental exclamations brought Shaithis starting awake, echoing in his mind. While still the echoes rang he was on his feet, his blanket of albino bats breaking up in chittering disarray, whirring away from him like a shock of sentient snow. Another moment and his hand filled his gauntlet; he let his Wamphyri senses reach out—but cautiously, tentatively—to discover who was here. Whoever, he must be near, else he wouldn't have sensed Shaithis's emergence.

While sleeping, Shaithis's thoughts had flowed inwards, an art in which he was adept; his dreams could not be "heard" by any other. But during the transition from deep, healing sleep to waking they had escaped like a yawn, and someone had been close enough to hear it. Too close by far.

Shaithis allowed his mental probe to touch that of the other, and immediately snatched it back. Contact had been brief but recognition mutual: insufficient to detail specific identities, but enough that each creature was certain of the other's presence. Shaithis glanced this way and that. There was only one way out of his niche; if he was trapped, then he was trapped; so be it.

Who is it? He sniffed the cold air with his bat's snout. *Is it you, Fess, come for your supper? Or must I soil my good gauntlet in pus to tear out the loathsome heart of the odious Volse Pinescu?*

And back came the answer, like an astonished gasp in the vampire's mind: *Hah! Shaithis! You survived The Dweller's death-beams, then?*

Arkis Leperson! Shaithis knew him at once. He breathed his relief, watched curiously for a moment while his breath fell as snow, then made for the exit. Along the way he flexed his muscles, swung his limbs, inhaled deeply and tested his ribs. All seemed in order. *Pah!* What had those minor dents and scratches been for wounds, anyway? Repairs had been minimal; his vampire flesh had scarcely been overtaxed; he was left with an ache here, a bruise there.

Arkis stood close to the foot of the ice staircase. He was squat for a Lord of the Wamphyri: scarcely more than six feet tall—ah, but a good three feet broad, too! A massive barrel of a man, his strength had been prodigious. Now it seemed he'd lost a little weight. Shaithis moved towards him, closing the distance between with the easy, flowing glide of the vampire; sinister to ordinary men, but normal by Wamphyri standards. In another moment they were face-to-face.

"Well," said Shaithis, "and is it peace? Or are you too hungry to think straight? I'll be frank: I could use a friend. And by the look of you . . . *huh!* Our circumstances are much the same. The choice is yours, but I know where there's food!"

The other's entirely instinctive reaction was a single belched word: "Food?" His eyes opened wide and his flaring, convoluted snout plumed ice-crystal breath.

Plainly, Arkis was starving. Shaithis offered him a grim smile, took from his pouch the last piece of cold bear heart and devoured half in a single bite, then tossed the rest to the leper's son—who snatched it from the air with a cry almost of pain. And without pause he crammed his mouth full.

Arkis had been sired by Morgis Griefcry out of a Traveller waif. She'd been a leper and her infection had taken him in his member, which (along with his lips, eyes, and ears) had been among the first of his parts to slough. The disease had been like a fire in him, burning him faster than his vampire could replenish. Finally, with cries of grief echoing his name to the full, Morgis had taken a firebrand and hurled himself and his Traveller odalisque into a refuse pit whose accumulation of methane gas had done the rest. His suicide had left Arkis the youthful Lord and heir to a fine aerie. Even better, Arkis had not contracted his forebears' disease! Not yet, anyway. Perhaps he never would. It had all been many sundowns agone.

While Arkis ate, Shaithis studied him.

Squat in the body, Arkis's skull was likewise squat, as if it had been crushed down a little. His face seemed pushed out in front, and his bottom jaw farther yet, with boar's teeth curving upwards over his fleshy upper lip.

And yet the overall effect wasn't so much swinish as wolfish, especially with the inordinate length of his furred, tapering ears. Aye, somewhere in his lineage there'd been a grey one for sure. Moreover, he was lean as a wolf; well, by the standards of former times, at least. Now, eyes ablaze with the lust of feeding, upon however small a morsel, he nevertheless narrowed them to gaze on Shaithis. And when he as done:

"I'll grant you it was a bite," he grunted, "but was that the food you promised?"

"I made no promises," Shaithis answered. "I stated a fact: I know where there's food—by the ton!"

"Ah!" the other grunted, and cocked his head on one side. "Volse's flyer, d'you mean? Ah, but they guard it well, Volse and the Ferenc. It's a mousetrap, Shaithis; only approach their private pantry too closely and you'll end up in it! No chivalry here, my friend. Cold, crystallized meat can never taste as good as red *juice* of meat spurting from a severed artery! But . . . beggars can't be choosers. I have tried and failed; they're never too far away; I know they lust after my blood."

"Are you reduced to this?" Shaithis raised a black, spiky eyebrow. "Scavenging after each other?" He knew of course that they were; knew that he would be, too, soon enough. The "chivalry" of the Wamphyri was at best a myth. But in any case, his insult—the word "scavenging"—was lost on Arkis Leperson.

"Shaithis," said the other, "I've been here four, going on five sundowns; five auroral displays, anyway, which I reckon amounts to much the same thing. Reduced to hunting each other? Let me tell you that if it *moves* I'll hunt it! I had bats by the handful at first: squeezed 'em to pulp so they'd drip into my mouth—then ate the pulp, too!—but now they won't come anywhere near me. They have minds of their own, these tiny albinos. Right now,

183

I'm on my way to see the shriveled old granddad frozen in the ice up top. I'd have tried to get at him before, if I was desperate enough—which now I am! So don't talk to me about being reduced to this or that. We're *all* reduced, Shaithis, and you no less than anyone else!''

So maybe Shaithis's insult had got through, after all. That came as something of a surprise; the leper's son had always seemed such a dullard. Perhaps the cold had sharpened his wits.

''Arkis,'' Shaithis said, ''there are two of us now and we've shared food. That's good, for it strikes me we'll do better as a team. While you've been here you've learned things and must know many of the pitfalls. Such knowledge has value. Also, the disgusting Volse Pinescu and gigantic Fess Ferenc will think twice before coming on the two of us together. Now, what say we leave this echoing shell of ice and find our breakfast?''

The leper's son sighed his impatience, which angered Shaithis a little: he wasn't used to dull, squat creatures playing the equal with him. ''Now, let me repeat myself,'' Arkis grunted. ''They *guard* Volse's flyer, and guard it well! They're likewise well fueled, which we're not. And as you yourself have just this minute pointed out, the Ferenc's a bloody giant!''

Shaithis flared his nostrils and for a moment thought to leave the fool to his own devices. Except that would also mean leaving him to the tender mercies of the others—eventually. And Shaithis wanted Arkis for himself—eventually. But these were thoughts he steered inwards, lest Arkis hear them. ''And can they guard *two* beasts?'' he said. ''And did you think I'd walked here, Arkis Diredeath?'' (the idiot's other name).

It stopped Arkis dead. ''Eh? Another flyer? I haven't seen it. But then, I've not dared venture too far out on the ice lest they see me! Where, then, this flyer?''

"Where I sent it," said Shaithis. "Still good and fresh and . . . wait a moment—" He sent out a beast-oriented thought: *Do you hear me?*—and in return sensed life flickering still, but burning very low. "Aye, and not yet bled to death. Not quite."

"They know it's there, that great vat of filth and the Ferenc?"

"Of course, else I'd not require assistance from you."

"Hah!" Arkis cried. "I might have known it! Something for nothing? What? Think again, Arkis my lad. This is the Grand Lord Shaithis you're talking to. Oh, let's be friends, Arkis—because I've need of you!"

Shaithis shrugged. "So be it. I merely envisaged a joint venture which would furnish joint returns, that's all. Equal shares. But something for nothing? What, and did you think this was Sunside at sundown, with plenty of sweet Traveller game afoot?" He made as if to turn away. "Starve, then."

"Wait!" The other took a pace closer. And in a more reasonable tone: "What's your plan?"

"None," said Shaithis, "except to eat."

"Eh?"

Shaithis's turn to sigh. "Listen, and I'll ask you again: can they guard two flyers, Volse and the Ferenc?"

"Certainly—a man to each."

"But we are *two* men!"

"And if they're both together?"

"Then one beast goes unguarded! Has the cold numbed your once-agile brain, Arkis?" (That last was a lie, but a little flattery wouldn't hurt.)

"Hmm!" The leper's son thought about it for a moment, then scowled and stabbed a finger at Shaithis. "Very well—but if we come upon Volse Pinescu on his own, we kill him. And *I* want his heart! Is it a deal?"

185

"Agreed," said Shaithis. "Actually, I should think it's the only part worth eating!"

"Hah!" Arkis snorted. And: "Har, har! Oh, ha-ha-*haaa!*" he laughed, in his way.

And: *Go on, laugh.* Shaithis kept his thoughts hidden. *But when Volse and Fess are done for, you're next, bone-brain!* And out loud: "Now, guard your thoughts. We go out onto the ice . . ."

Volse Pinescu's flyer was rimed with frost, stiff as a board. Still Arkis Leperson would have set to, but Shaithis cautioned him: "Let's not waste valuable time here. What? Why, you'd wear those tusks of yours to stumps on this!"

Arkis turned to him with a scowl. "It's food, isn't it?"

"Aye," Shaithis said, "and half a mile over there a lot more of it—but thick, red, and flowing in juicy pipes. Good beasts I breed, Arkis, of the finest flesh. Now listen: do you sense our enemies? No? Neither do I. So today they're not doing much guarding, right?"

Arkis sniffed the icy air. "It worries me. What are they up to, d'you suppose?"

"Time for supposing after we've filled our bellies." Shaithis had already set off across the blue fox-fire ice. And Arkis came shambling after. Shaithis glanced back once and nodded, then faced forward and grinned his sly grin as of old. Ever the leader, Shaithis, and how easy once more to take up the mantle. And behind him Arkis Leperson, like a dog to heel . . .

A wind came up.

While Shaithis and Arkis Leperson, called Diredeath, sat in a cave carved by Volse and Fess in the underbelly of Shaithis's flyer and sipped the feebly pulsing juices of that now insensate beast, the radiant stars were blotted out by dark, scudding clouds. Snow came down in a short-lived blizzard, which loaned the ice a thin, soft coating.

When the wind died down again the cannibalized flyer was dead and its arteries already stiffening. "Cold fare from this time forwards," commented Shaithis, sticking up his head to spy out the land around. He looked towards the spine of volcanic peaks. Then looked again. And frowned his concern.

"Arkis, what do you make of this?"

Arkis stood up, belched noisomely, looked where Shaithis pointed. "Eh? That? A whirlwind, a snow devil, the last flurry in the wake of the storm. What's this great fascination with Nature, Shaithis?"

"Fascination? With what's natural, none whatsoever. With what's unnatural, plenty! Especially in a place like this."

"Unnatural?"

"By Nature's mundane standards, aye, if not by those of the Wamphyri." He continued to study the phenomenon: a whirling cloud of snow forming a squat cylinder twenty feet high and the same in diameter. Something seemed to move in its heart, like a tadpole in a jelly egg, and the whole—device?—making a beeline their way. It threw off whips of snow which quickly settled to the ground without diminishing the central mass.

Shaithis nodded; he knew what it was. "Fess Ferenc," he whispered grimly.

"What, Fess?" Arkis gaped at the thing, now only a hundred yards away across the shining ice, coming at walking pace and beginning to thin out a little. "How, Fess?"

"That's a vampire mist," said Shaithis, donning his gauntlet. "On Starside it would creep, flow, drift outwards from him. Here it turns to snow! Fess was a fine mist-maker . . . his great mass. During the hunt, I've seen him cover an entire hillside.''

They both threw out their vampire senses towards the weird, earthbound cloud. Only one creature inside it: the Ferenc, aye, but weary as never before. He hadn't the strength to hide himself. "Ah-*hah!*" growled Arkis. "We have him!"

"But let's first discover what goes on," Shaithis cautioned him.

"Isn't it obvious what goes on?" The leper's son was scowling again. "Why, he's finally burst that monstrous boil Volse Pinescu, but in the fight depleted himself. So now he's at our mercy, of which I have precious little."

Twenty paces away the cloud fell as a final flurry and Fess stood there, naked! Entirely naked, and not only of his snow-cloud cover. Arkis gawped but Shaithis called out: "Well, Fess, and how fortunes change, eh?"

"It would seem so." The other's deep bass voice echoed over the ice plain. But there was a shiver in it; he was freezing. And yet under one arm he carried his clothes in a bundle. Shaithis couldn't see the sense of it. There must be a story here and he wanted to know it.

Arkis sensed Shaithis's curiosity. "Me, I'm not interested," he snarled. "I say we kill him now!"

"You say too much," Shaithis hissed. "You think only of your own survival now, without a thought for the future. Myself, I think of my *continued* survival, now and however long I may sustain it. So you bide your time or our partnership ends here."

"Am I to die?" The Ferenc stood tall, glooming on Shaithis across that short distance. "If so, then get it over with, for I've no wish to turn to a block of ice." But he threw down his clothes and hunched forward a little, and his talons were sharp as razors hanging at his sides.

"It seems I have the advantage," said Shaithis. "Also a score to settle. You caused me not a little pain." The Ferenc made no answer. "However," Shaithis continued, "we may yet come to an agreement. As you see, Arkis and I have formed a team of our own: safety in numbers, you know? But two against the Icelands? The odds are too high. Three of us might fare better."

"Some kind of trick?" Fess couldn't believe it. If their roles had been reversed Shaithis were already dead.

Shaithis shook his head. "No trick. Like Diredeath here you have knowledge of this place. And just as the blood is the life, so is knowledge. That has always been my conviction. To fight among ourselves is to die. Sharing knowledge—by pooling our resources—we might yet survive."

"Say on," said Fess, his voice more shivery than ever.

Shaithis shook his head again. "Nothing more to say. Come out of the cold and replenish yourself, and tell us what's happened that you go naked as a babe in such a place, hidden in a weird and very unsubtle mist. Aye, and then perhaps you'd advise us on the whereabouts of the unlovely Volse Pinescu, your erstwhile companion."

The Ferenc had no choice. Flee and they would catch him, for they were well fueled. Stand still and freeze, and they'd thaw him out and eat him. Go forward and talk, and . . . perhaps he could yet make his peace with Shaithis. As for Arkis, that one was something else.

He came on, got down in the lee of the stiffening flyer, tore a vein from the wall of flesh, and bit through it. Nothing was forthcoming (the creature's blood was finished or frozen in the outer regions of its bulk), so he merely stripped the pipe down with his teeth and swallowed the pulp. It was sustenance if nothing else. Between mouthfuls he commented, "Perhaps we should have stayed on Starside. At least The Dweller would have made a quick end of it."

"Still blaming me, Fess?" Shaithis stood over him, watched him fueling himself. Arkis sat well away, scowling as usual.

"I blame all of us," the Ferenc answered, perhaps bitterly. "Hotheads, we rushed in like blind men over a precipice. Fools, we went to murder and instead committed suicide. It was your plan, aye, but we all fell in with it." He stood up and went back out onto the ice to his garments, there crouching and cleaning them thoroughly with snow. At least there was that to be said for the giant: he'd always been scrupulous. When he was done he returned again to the cave of cooling flesh and lay his clothes aside to dry or freeze out.

"Some strange contamination?" Shaithis wondered out loud.

"You could say that." The other wrinkled his already much convoluted snout. "Those stinking stains were Volse!" And as he continued to eat, so, between mouthfuls, he told them about it.

"Volse and I, we'd noticed smoke from the central cone. Also some strange activity now and then in a high cave. And we thought: if that old mountain contains heat and fire, it's only reasonable that someone's settled there. But who? Common men? Exiled Wamphyri, perhaps? No way to discover, unless we went to see. Oh, we cast our probes ahead of us, of course, but who or whatever lived in the volcano, he kept his thoughts to himself.

"The way is longer than it looks: maybe five miles to the foot of the mount, then a rising climb of two more to its cone. But near the top where the way gets steep, there was this cave. And that was where we'd seen signs of activity, like mirrors glinting in the starlight. Dwellers, we'd thought. Snow trogs or the like. Meat, anyway.

"Aye, there was meat, all right." (The Ferenc's aspect was suddenly grim.) "A ton of it! but best if I tell it as it happened and not go ahead of myself . . .

"So we arrived at the mouth of this cave, all craggy and yellow with sulphur: an old lava-run, I fancied. But hardly fit habitation, and no jot warmer than any other place around here. We cast our probes ahead of us; there *was* life in there, some dull intelligence far back in the cave; we hardly felt threatened. And it seemed likely the bore hole passed right through the mountain all the way to the core. And if that's where the warmth was, that's where we'd find the life.

"So we went in. The tunnel had its twists and turns, and it was dark and smelly as a refuse pit in there. But what is darkness to the Wamphyri?

"Volse, who had fashioned the most incredible pustules to enhance his already hideous appearance, took the lead. He'd stripped off his jacket, and his upper body was entirely festooned with all manner of morbid things. 'Who or whatever,' he said, 'only let them see me or feel me near, and they'll know there's nothing for it but to faint and hope it's a bad dream!' I thought he was probably correct and had no objection to his going first.

"Then . . . *Ah—!*" Fess gave a small start as he spied a miniature albino bat hovering near, under the overhang of the dead flyer's side. In a lightning swipe he scythed it in two parts in midair. And: "Ah, yes!" he said. "And perhaps I should mention: Volse and I, we had companions all along the way. These damned bats! They get everywhere."

"Why treat them so harshly?" Shaithis cut in "On Starside they were our small familiars."

"These aren't the same." Fess shook his great head. "They lack obedience."

Shaithis frowned. They'd obeyed him—hadn't they?

Arkis growled: "Never mind the bats, but finish your story. It interests me."

Partially replenished, invigorated from his feeding, the Ferenc began to don his clothes, generating body heat to complete the job of drying them out. He was adept at this as he was at mist-making. And while he dressed so he continued with his story:

"Volse went first, then, into the heart of the riddled rock; and I'll be honest, we thought there was nothing there. Nothing to alarm or threaten us, anyway. And yet I sensed that the picture we had of that place, of its suspected dweller or dwellers, was probably a false one. It seemed to me that my mind was *watched,* even though I'd failed to detect the watcher. But the deeper we proceeded into the mountain, the more the conviction grew in me that our progress was monitored, even minutely; as if each step led us closer to some terrific confrontation, some contrived and monstrous conclusion. In short, an ambush!"

Arkis grunted and nodded his head. "The very way I felt," he remarked in a low, dark mutter, "on those several occasions when I'd approach Volse's flyer for a bite to eat."

"Just so." Fess nodded, without taking offense, and perhaps deliberately failing to find anything of accusation in Arkis's statement. "And I knew . . . fear? Well, no, not fear, for we're none of us bred that way. Shall we simply say, then, that I experienced a new sensation, which was not pleasant? Nor was this presentiment without foundation, as will be seen. And all the while those damned albinos tracking our course, until their fluttering and chittering had grown to be such an annoyance that I stayed back a little to strike out at them where they swooped overhead. Which probably saved my life.

"Ahead of me, Volse had gone striding on. But he

sensed it coming in the same instant that I sensed it, and he said one word before it struck. The word he said was: 'What?' Yes, he questioned it, and even questioning it never knew what hit him."

"Explain!" Arkis was breathless. And Shaithis was intent, rapt upon the Ferenc's story.

Fess shrugged. Fully dressed again, he sliced gobbets of flesh from the flyer's alveolate ribs, sliding them one by one down his throat. "hard to explain," he said after a while. "*Fast,* it was. Huge. Mindless. Terrible! But I saw what it did to Volse, and I determined that it would not do the same to me. I never fled from anything in my life before—well, except The Dweller and the awesome destruction he wrought in the battle for his garden—but I fled from this.

"It was white, but not a healthy white. The white of hiding in places too dark, like some cavern fungus. It had legs—a great man, I think—with clawed, webbed feet. Its body was fish-like, its head too, with jaws ferocious! But the weapon it bore—"

"A weapon?" Arkis thrust his face forward. "But you said the thing was mindless. And now . . . mind enough to carry a weapon?"

The Ferenc glanced at him scornfully, then held up his own talon hands. "And are these not weapons? This thing's weapon was *part* of it, fool, just as your own boar's tusks are part of you!"

"Yes, yes, understood," said Shaithis impatiently. "Say on."

Fess settled down again, but his eyes were uneasy, wide in his massive, malformed face. "Its weapon was a knife, a sword, a lance. But with tines like thorns all down its length, from tip to snout. A barbed rod for stabbing, and once stabbed the victim's hooked, with no way to free himself except tear his own flesh wide open!

193

And at the tip of that bone-plated ram, twin holes like nostrils. But not for breathing . . ." He paused.

". . . For what, then?" Arkis could not contain himself.

"For sucking!" said the Ferenc.

"A vampire thing." Shaithis seemed convinced. "A warrior, but uncontrolled, with no rightful master. A creature created by some exiled Wamphyri Lord, which has outlasted its maker." He *said* these things, but he did not necessarily believe them. No, he uttered them aloud to cover the nature of his true thoughts, which were different again.

Fess fell for Shaithis's ploy, anyway. "These are possibilities, aye," the giant said. "Stealthy—sly as a fox, and all unheralded—it crept out from a side tunnel; but when it struck—*ah!*—lightning moves more slowly. It slid into view and its spear stabbed at Volse three times. The first blow ripped him open through boils and all, and spattered me and the walls of the tunnel with all of his pus, whose amount was prodigious. He was like one huge blister, bursting and wetting everything with his vile liquids. I was drenched. The second thrust hit him while he was still reeling from the first; it almost sawed his head off. And the third: that sank into him—into his heart—where it commenced to suck like a great pump! And while the thing held him upright, impaled on its weapon against the wall, sucking at him, so the creature's saucer eyes fixed me in their monstrous glare. So that I knew I was next.

"That was when I fled." (And Fess actually shuddered, which amazed Shaithis.)

"You couldn't have saved him?" Arkis sneered, questioning Fess's manhood; a dangerous line of inquiry at best.

But the other took it well. "I tell you Volse was a

goner! What? And so much of his liquids used up, his head half shorn away, and the thing's great siphon in him, emptying him? Save him? And what of myself? You, Diredeath, have not *seen* this creature! Why, even Lesk the Glut—in whichever hell he now resides—would not stray near such a monster! No, I fled.

"And all the way out of that long, long tunnel, I could hear the thing's slobbering as it drained Volse's juices. Also, by the time I struck light and open air, I fancied it slobbered all the louder, perhaps hot on my trail. In something of a panic—yes, I admit it—I called a mist out of myself and hurried out onto the slopes and down to the plain of snow and ice. There I stripped off, for Volse's drench was poisonous, and without further pause hurried back here . . . and found you two waiting for me.

"The tale is told . . ."

Arkis and Shaithis sat back, narrowed their eyes, and fingered their chins. Shaithis kept his thoughts mainly to himself (though truth to tell there was nothing especially sinister or vindictive about them); but Diredeath, feeling that he still had the Ferenc at something of a disadvantage, was somewhat loath to let the giant so lightly off the hook.

"Times and fortunes change," the leper's son eventually said. "I went starving—went, indeed, in fear of my life!—when you and the great wen had the upper hand. But now . . . you are only one man against myself and the Lord Shaithis."

"These things are true," Fess answered, standing up and stretching, and flexing the mighty talons which were his hands. "But do you know, I can't help wondering what the Lord Shaithis sees in you, leper's son? For it seems to me there's about as much use in you as there was in that mighty bag of slops called Volse Pinescu!

Also, and now that I come to think of it, it strikes me I sat still for a good many hurtful slights and insults while relating my story. Of course, I was hungry and cold as death, and a man will sit still for a lot while there's a chance he can fill his belly. But now that my belly's full and I'm warm again . . . I think you'd do well to back off, Diredeath. Or come to just such an end as your name suggests."

"Aye," said Shaithis with a quick nod, coming between them. "Well, and enough of that. For let's face it, we've all we can handle in the Icelands themselves, without we're at each other's throats, too." He took their arms and sat down, drawing them down with him. "Now tell me," he said, "what are the secrets of these Icelands? For after all, I'm the newcomer here; but the two of you . . . ? Why, you've explored and adventured galore! And so the sooner I know all that you know, the sooner we'll be able to decide on our next move."

Shaithis let his gaze wander to and fro, from one to the other, finally allowing it to settle on Arkis's dark and twitching countenance, his coarse lips and the yellow ivory of his tusks. "So how about it, Arkis?" he said. "You've had a little less freedom than Fess, it's true, but still you've managed to explore a few ice castles. Well, the Ferenc has told us his tale of the horror in the cone, so now I reckon it's your turn. What of the ice aeries, eh? What of these ancient, exiled, ice-encysted Wamphyri Lords?"

Arkis scowled at him. "You want to know about the frozen ones?"

"The sooner all is known," said Shaithis, nodding, "the sooner we may proceed."

Arkis shrugged, however grudgingly. "I have no problem with that," he said. "So . . . you want to know what

I've seen, done, discovered? It won't take long in the telling, I promise you!''

"Tell us, anyway," said Shaithis, "and we'll see what we make of it."

Again Arkis's shrug. "So be it," he said.

IV The Frozen Lords

"AFTER THE MAYHEM IN THE DWELLER'S GARDEN" (Arkis commenced), "when it was seen how The Dweller and his hell-lander father had destroyed our armies, shattered our centuried stacks, and brought our aeries crashing down, there seemed no alternative but flight. The Dweller had our measure; the Wamphyri were fallen; to remain in the ruins of Starside would surely bring these Great Enemies down upon us one last time in a final venting of their furious might.

"However, it is the immemorial right of the fallen to quit Starside and forge for the Icelands. Thus, in the lull which followed on the destruction of our aeries, those survivors who had the means for flight forsook their ancient territories and headed north. Aye, and I was one such survivor.

"Along with a pair of aspiring lieutenants—ex-Traveller thralls of mine, twin brothers named Goram and Belart Largazi, who vied with each other for my egg—I cleared away the debris of my fallen stack from the deeply buried entrance to subterranean workshops, so freeing one flyer and one warrior kept aside and safe against the event of just such a calamity as The Dweller's victory. These beasts we saddled and mounted (I myself took the warrior, an ill-tempered creature personally trained to my tastes), finally fleeing on a course roughly northward from the rack and ruin of the aeries.

"Our heading was not true north—perhaps a little west of north—what odds? The roof of the world is the roof of the world; to left or right it is still the roof. We paused only once, where a shoal of great blue fishes had got themselves trapped in the formation of a shallow ice lake, and there glutted ourselves before proceeding farther.

"Not long after that the Largazi brothers' flyer, burdened as it was with two riders, became exhausted. It went down at the rim of a shallow sea and left its riders floundering. I landed on the frozen strand, sent my warrior back to the Largazis to let down its launching limbs and tow them ashore.

"And then it was that we found ourselves in a very curious place. Hot blowholes turned the snow yellow; bubbling geysers made warm pools in the ageless ice; seabirds came down to feed on the froth of small fishes where they spawned at the ocean's rim. It was the farthest reach of these selfsame volcanic mountains, which are active still in those weird western extremes.

"After the Largazis were dragged ashore and while they dried themselves out, I looked for a launching place and discovered a glacier where it sloped oceanward. There I ordered my creature down onto the ice; aye, for by now that warrior mount of mine was likewise sore weary, whose valiant efforts in saving the twins from drowning had scarcely buttressed its vitality. They need to kill and devour a deal of red meat, warriors, else rapidly fade away to nothing. And so I thought to myself: which will prove most useful to me in the Icelands? A powerful warrior, or a pair of bickering, unimportant, and ever-hungry thralls? *Hah!* No contest.

"It was my thought to slaughter one of the brothers there and then, and feed him to my warrior. Except . . . well, I'll admit it, I'd underestimated that fine pair of Wamphyri aspirants. They too had been busy weighing the odds, and their conclusions had likewise favored my fighting beast. Now they backed off to a safe distance and descended into deep, narrow crevasses from which I could neither threaten nor tempt them to come out and approach me. Mutinous dogs! Very well: let them freeze! Let them starve! Let them *both* die!

"I climbed aboard my warrior and spurred the creature slithering down the glacier's ramp, until at last it bounded aloft and spurted out over the sea. And not before time: the launching of that depleted beast had been a very close-run thing, so that I could almost taste the salt spray from the waves against the glacier. However, I was now airborne.

"I turned inland, swept high overhead where the treacherous Largazi twins had emerged from the ice to angle their faces up to me, waved them a scornful farewell, and set course for a line of distant peaks standing in silhouette against the sky's weaving auroral pulse. Those same peaks which stand behind us even now, with their central volcanic cone whose lava vents are guarded—according to the Ferenc, at least—by sword-snouted monsters. Aye, the very same.

"Nor would I, nor *could* I, call Fess a liar in that respect—in the matter of Volse's death by some strange and savage creature—for certainly my warrior came to a sad, suspicious end. And who can say but that Volse and my poor weary warrior were not victims of the selfsame bloodbeast? I will tell you how it was:

"My warrior was weary unto death . . . well, perhaps not *so* weary, for as you know well enow they don't die easily, and rarely of weariness! But the creature was depleted and panting and complaining. I scanned the land about and saw lava-runs on the higher slopes of the central cone: good, slippery launching ramps if the warrior should ever again find itself fit for flight.

"Alas, the landing was awkward and the beast threw me; it cracked its armored carapace, wrenched a vane, and tore a propulsion orifice on a jagged lava outcrop. Many gallons of fluids were lost before its metamorphic flesh webbed over the gashes and sealed them. My own injuries were slight, however, and I ignored them; but such was my anger that I cursed and kicked the warrior a good deal before its mood turned ugly and it began to bellow and spit. Then I was obliged to calm the brute, and finally I backed it up and hid it from view in the mouth of a cavern tunnel much similar—perhaps identical?—to that of the leprous white bloodbeast as described by the Ferenc. For this tunnel was likewise an ancient lava-run from the once-molten core, and perhaps I should have explored its interior a little way. But at the time there was no evidence of anything suspicious about that central cone.

"I ordered the warrior to heal itself, left it there in the cavern entrance, let my curiosity get the better of me, and came down by foot onto the plain of the shimmering ice castles, to see what they contained. For as you've seen, they looked for all the world like Wamphyri stacks or aeries formed from ice. As for what I discovered: it was a very strange, very awesome, indeed a frightening thing!

"Expatriate Lords, all frozen in suspended animation,

ice-locked in the cores of their glittering castles. A good many were dead, crushed or sheared by shifting ice; but there were some—too many, I thought—who had variously . . . succumbed? Others were preserved, however, sleeping still within impenetrable walls of ice hard as iron, their vampire metabolisms so reduced that they seemed scarcely changed over all the long centuries. Ah, this was a false impression; their dreams were fading, ephemeral things, mere memories of the lives they had known in the Old Times, when the first of the Wamphyri inhabited their stacks on Starside and waged their territorial wars there.

"All of the ex-Lords were dying; ah, slowly, so slowly, but dying nevertheless. Of course they were: the blood is the life, and for centuries without number all they had had was ice . . ."

"Some of them!" Fess Ferenc broke in. "Most of them, aye. But one at least had not gone without. This was the conclusion which Volse Pinescu and I arrived at, when we examined the ice-castle stacks."

Shaithis looked at him, then at Arkis. "Will one of you—or both—elaborate?"

Arkis shrugged. "I take it the Ferenc is talking about the matter of the breaking, and of the empty ice thrones. For it's a fact, as I've hinted, that certain of the frozen keeps and redoubts—indeed a good many—have been broken into and their helpless, refrigerated inhabitants removed. But by whom, to where . . . for what?"

The huge, hulking, slope-skulled Ferenc broke in again with: "I've reached certain conclusions about these things, too. Should I say on?"

And again Arkis Leperson's shrug. "If you can throw some light on the mystery, by all means."

And Shaithis said, "Aye, say on."

The Ferenc nodded and continued: "As you'll have

noted for yourselves, the ice castles number between fifty and sixty, forming concentric rings about the extinct volcano, which is the central cone. But is the volcano truly extinct? And if so, why is it that a little smoke still goes up from that ancient ice-crusted crater? Also, we have seen—myself far too clearly—how there is at least one monstrous warrior creature guarding the cone's access tunnels. Ah, but what or *who* else does it guard?''

When his pause threatened to go on forever, finally it was Shaithis's turn to shrug. "Pray continue," he said. "We're in the very palm of your hand, Fess, entirely fascinated.''

"Indeed?'' The Ferenc was somewhat flattered. One by one, he very deliberately, very loudly cracked the bony knuckles of his taloned hands. "Fascinated, eh? Well, and rightly so. And so you see, Shaithis, you're not the only thinker who survived The Dweller's wrath, eh?''

Shaithis hummed in his convoluted nose, perhaps a little indecisively, and swung his head this way and that. Finally, he said: "I'll give credit where credit's due—*when* I can see the whole picture.''

"Very well,'' said the Ferenc. "So here's what *I've* seen and what I reckon:

"Me and that foul festerer Volse Pinescu, we explored the innermost ice aeries and discovered each and every one looted! Following which—and especially now that Volse is no more, sucked dry by the Thing in the lava-run—I find it easy to piece together a fairly accurate picture of what's been happening here:

"The way I see it, some ancient Wamphyri Lord or Lady is master or mistress of the slumbering volcano. In ages past and whenever outcast vampires have happened this way, he or she has fought them off from taking possession of the volcano's 'comforts' . . . it would seem to have some residual warmth at least. Then, as the vampires lying in siege have succumbed to the cold and put themselves into hibernation, so the crafty master of the volcano has emerged from time to time to pillage their ice chambers and live off their deep-frozen flesh. In effect, the ice castles are his larder!"

"*Hah!*" Arkis slapped his great thigh. "It all comes clear."

The Ferenc nodded his swollen, grotesquely proportioned head. "You agree with my conclusions, then?"

"How can it be otherwise?" said Arkis. "What say you, Shaithis?"

Shaithis looked at him curiously. "I say you blow like a pennant in the wind: now this way, now that. First you wished to kill the Ferenc, and now you agree with his every word. Is your mind so easily changed, then?"

The leper's son scowled at him. "I know truth when I hear it," he said. "Also, I can see the sense in sound scheming. The Ferenc's reckoning about the state of things sounds right enough to me, and your plea that we run together for our mutual safety seems similarly wise. So what's giving *you* grief, Shaithis? I thought you wanted us to be friends?"

"So I do," Shaithis answered. "It's just that I worry when loyalties change so fast, that's all. And now would you care to finish your own story? The last we heard, you'd left your injured warrior in the mouth of a lava-run and gone down onto the plain to examine the ice castles."

"That I did," Arkis agreed. "And I found things pretty much as the Ferenc described them: the ice-locked thrones of all those unknown Wamphyri Lords out of time, all cracked open and empty, like Sunside hives raped of their honey. Aye, and in those ice castles which stood more distant from the central cone, there too I found evidence of attempted robbery, except in many an instance the ice had been too thick and the eon-shriveled Lords remained safe, unburgled, intact. Which meant that they were also safe from me.

"Finally, I wearied of my eerie explorations. I was hungry but unable to break into these ancient, permafrost pantries; the small albino bats no longer trusted me but avoided my crushing hands; if my former thralls the Largazis still lived, by now they'd be halfway here. They'd be exhausted, too, and unable to outrun me. Ah, but *that* was a thought! It was time I returned to my warrior creature to see how it was holding up. And so I climbed up to the high cavern where I'd hidden the beast away.

"Except it was not there. Several small pieces of it were there, but that was all."

"The sucking thing," the Ferenc said. "The blood-beast with the hollow, sword-like cartilage snout."

"But how so?" Shaithis wasn't so sure. "For a mindless beast to suck a man or, given time, even a warrior dry, this I can understand. But then, to cut the carcass of so huge a creature into small pieces and drag them away . . . ?"

The Ferenc only shrugged. "These are the Icelands," he said. "They harbor strange creatures with stranger habits, and food is scarce here. Now think: on Starside would we ever have dreamed of chewing on the rubbery arteries of a flyer? What, with trogs in our larders and Travellers on the hoof just across the mountains? Not likely! But here? *Hah!* It didn't take us long to learn. Oh, we lowered our sights soon enough. And what of the mainly conjectural creatures and beings which have possibly spent their entire lives here? If the loathsome, leprous bloodbeast hunts only for itself, then perhaps it has its own pantry somewhere. And if it hunts for a master?'' Yet again his shrug. ''Perhaps he's the one who butchered Arkis's warrior and dragged its bits away.''

And Shaithis, turning his private thoughts inwards to guard them, thought: *A master, aye, you're right, Fess! A master of evil—the very source of evil—in the shape of a timeless vampire Lord; indeed one of the first true Lords. The dark Lord Shaitan! Shaitan the Unborn! Shaitan the Fallen!*

''Well?'' said Arkis Leperson. ''Does the Ferenc make sense or what? And if he does, what's our next move?''

And perhaps cautiously, Shaithis answered, ''The Ferenc makes sense—possibly.'' And to himself: *Indeed he does, for a misshapen fool! But he's been here longer than I have. Perhaps this isn't the sudden burgeoning of previously unsuspected intelligence in the great freak, but simply the fact that he's had longer to feel Shaitan's influence at work . . . to feel his ancient eyes on him, staring through the pink orbits of his myriad albino minions!*

Now the Ferenc echoed Arkis: ''Well? What now, Shaithis? D'you have a plan?''

A plan? Oh, yes, a plan! To discover more about this Shaitan: to seek him out and learn why he allowed me to clothe myself in his albinos for their warmth; but mainly to know what it is, this weird affinity, which draws me to a creature I've never known except in muttered myths and legends.

And out loud: ''A plan, aye,'' he answered. And thinking with his usual, almost casual clarity, he created a plan out of thin air, literally on the spur of the moment. One which would hopefully suit his vampire companions, and one which especially suited himself. ''First we cut a good weight of meat out of this flyer,'' he said, ''as much as we can carry comfortably; and then, on our way to the central cone, you can show me some more of the frozen Lords. So far I've seen only the one,'' *(Kehrl*

Lugoz, who was banished here along with Shaitan at the dawn of Wamphyri tyranny), "upon which, due to its insufficiency, I may not base a firm opinion. Then, in the inner ice castles, you may also care to show me these shattered keeps wherefrom the bodies of certain Lords have been stolen. These several things for a start, then." *And I'll think of others as we go along.*

Arkis seemed uncertain. "Eh? What's this for a plan? We take meat with us and visit a handful of shriveled, prehistoric, ice-doomed Lords? Also the sacked, empty tombs of other ancients, whose fate we can only guess at?"

"On our way to the central cone, aye," said Shaithis.

"And then?" said the Ferenc.

"Perhaps to destroy him who dwells within," Shaithis answered, "and gain his secrets, his beasts and possessions; and who can say, possibly even discover some means of egress from these hideously boring and barren Icelands?"

The Ferenc nodded his grotesque head. "This all sounds good to me. Very well, then let's be at it." He commenced to cut strips of frozen flesh from the curve of the flyer's rib cage, cramming his pockets with them.

However grudgingly, Arkis followed suit. "Meat is meat, I know," he grumbled. "But the frozen flesh of flyers? Huh! The blood *was* the life!"

And Shaithis snapped his fingers and said: "Ah, yes! I knew there was something else. Now tell me, Diredeath: what of your twin thralls, the brothers Largazi? Did they follow you here out of the west? From the fumarole coast, the bubbling geysers and lakes of sulphur? Did they survive? Or perhaps they perished en route?"

"Perished, aye." The other nodded agreeably and smiled a fond, knowing smile, his boar's tusks glinting dully. "But not en route. Perished when they *got* here,

207

and when I found them exhausted and shivering in the hollow core of the westernmost ice castle. Ah, how they begged my forgiveness then. And do you know, I forgave them? Indeed I did. 'Goram!' I cried. 'Belart! My faithful thralls! My trusted lieutenants! Returned at last to the bosom of your mentor!' Oh, how they hugged me! And I in my turn fell upon their necks—*and tore them open!*''

Shaithis sighed, perhaps a little glumly. ''You fueled yourself on both of them? At once? With never a thought for tomorrow?''

Arkis shrugged and finished stuffing his pockets with meat. ''I had been cold and hungry for more than two auroral periods,'' he said. ''And the blood of the Largazis was hot and strong. Perhaps I should have exercised a little restraint, kept one of them in reserve . . . and then again perhaps not. For it was about then that Fess and Volse arrived. So at least I spared myself the frustration of having one of my thralls stolen away from me. As for their corpses: I stored them in the heart of a glacier. Alas, they went the same way as my warrior! Something sneaked them away while I was out exploring.''

Shaithis allowed his narrow-eyed glance to fall upon the Ferenc, who at once shook his head. ''Not me,'' he denied the unspoken charge. ''Neither me nor Volse. We knew nothing of Arkis's glaciated thralls. If we had, well, perhaps the story were different.'' He clambered out from the lee of the ravaged flyer and stood gigantically in starlight and aurora sheen. ''Well, and are we all set?''

Shaithis and Arkis joined him; all three, they turned their faces in the direction of the central cone. Directly between the monstrous trio and the ex-volcano, an ice castle had taken (how many?) centuries to crystallize about its core of volcanic rock-splash. It would make as good a starting place as any. Shaithis, taking in the bleak scene, and after glancing a moment into the scarlet eyes of each of his "companions," finally agreed: "All set. So let's go and see what the rest of these eon-frozen exiles look like, shall we?"

And united—for the *moment* united, at least—the vampires set out to cross the snowfields and scintillant ice jumbles, and the weird terraces and shimmering battlements of their target ice castle loomed larger as gradually they narrowed the distance between. And forming a frowning centerpiece to the glittering, concentrically circling aeries, every now and then the duller, darker shape of the "extinct" volcano would appear to puff a little smoke into the radiant, ever-changing sky.

Or perhaps this was just an illusion? Well, possibly. But Shaithis thought not . . .

Soon Shaithis discovered that one ice castle was much the same as the next. This one, for example, might well be the stark, shivery, tinkling cold stack of Kehrl Lugoz; *might* be; except, of course, it was not the undead Kehrl who waited out the ages in the densely protective sheath of the core, but some other Lord. Also, and whoever he had been in life, his waiting had long since come to an end and he was now entirely dead. An ice mummy—frozen, starved, desiccated to a condition way beyond life—the olden vampire was one with all past things, leaving only his shell to represent him as part of the present.

Shaithis looked at him through the wavering impurity of the ice and wondered who he'd been. Whoever, it was probably as well that he was dead. His thoughts, if there had been any, might have told Arkis and the Ferenc secrets Shaithis would prefer them not to know . . . like why he lay there on his carved ice pedestal, propped upon a skeletal elbow, one claw-like hand held up before him as if to ward off some dreadful evil. And his colorless eyes, from which time had bleached all of the scarlet but none of the nameless horror. Aye, even this member of the olden Wamphyri, horrified! By something or someone who had stood here where Shaithis stood even now.

"What do you make of this?" The sudden, echoing rumble of the Ferenc's voice caused Shaithis to start. He looked where the giant pointed a taloned hand at a hitherto unnoticed, circular borehole in the ice. Seven or eight inches in diameter, the almost invisible bore seemed to point like an arrow at the preserved Wamphyri relic upon his carved couch.

"A hole?" Shaithis frowned.

"Aye," the Ferenc said, "like that of some gross worm in the earth. "But an ice worm?" He kneeled and stuck his hand and arm into the hole, which extended almost to the depth of his shoulder. And withdrawing his arm and sighting along the channel, he added: "Directed straight at his heart, too!"

"More such holes over here," Arkis called from a little way around the curve of the core. "And it seems to me they've been drilled. See the heaped chips where they've spilled out upon the floor?"

And Shaithis thought: *Such small privations as my dullard friends have known have made them observant.* He followed the core's curve to Arkis and examined the new holes; rather, the newly *discovered* holes. For in fact they could have been made a hundred, two hundred years ago. And sighting along them just as the Ferenc had sighted, Shaithis too noted that these perfectly circular runs seemed aimed at the main mass of the ice-shrouded mummy's body.

He thought to himself: *Runs, aye,* and narrowed his eyes a little as he examined that concept more closely. For upon a time, Shaithis had visited the settlements of itinerant *Szgany* metalworkers east of the great mountain range which split Starside from Sunside. These were the "tinkers" who designed and constructed the fearsome Wamphyri war gauntlets. Shaithis had seen the way the colorful Travellers poured liquid metal down clay pipes or along earthen sluices into molds; so that there was that about these boreholes which reminded him of running liquids. Except all of these incomplete runs climbed gentle inclines *towards* the dead Lord, which seemed to indicate that they had not been designed to carry anything to him. Something away from him, then? Shaithis shivered; he was beginning to find his investigations, and more especially his conclusions, damnable.

Indeed, there was something about this entire setup which even Shaithis's vampire heart found ominous, oppressive, doom-fraught. And finally, Fess Ferenc voiced his thoughts for him:

"Me and the whelky Volse, we saw cores where the ice wasn't so thick. In them the boreholes had penetrated right to the center, and all that was left in there were small bundles of rags, skin, and bones!"

"What?" Shaithis frowned at him.

Fess nodded. "As if the onetime inhabitants or slumberers in these frozen stacks had been sucked *entire* down the bores, all except their more solid bits."

It had been Shaithis's thought exactly. "But how?" he whispered. "How, if they were frozen? I mean, how *does* one draw an entire, frozen-solid body down a hole which can't even accommodate that body's head?"

"I don't know." The Ferenc shook his own misshapen head. "But still I reckon that's what this old lad was afraid of. What's more, I reckon he died from the fear of it . . ."

Later, a mile closer to the central cone, they entered one of the inner ice castles.

"This is one I've not visited before," said the Ferenc.

211

"But as close as it is to the old volcano, I'd guess it's a safe bet what we'll find."

"Oh?" Shaithis looked at him.

"Nothing!" the Ferenc said knowingly. "Just shattered ice about a gob of black lava, and the empty hole from which some ancient Lord's been stolen away."

And he was right. When they finally found the high lava throne, it was empty, and its ice sheath shattered into a pile of fused, frosted shards. A few fragments of rag there were, but so ancient and stiff that they crumbled at a touch. And that was all.

Shaithis kneeled at the base of the shattered sheath and examined its broken surface, and found what he was looking for: the fluted rims of a good many boreholes, patterned like a scalloped fan, all joining where they converged on the empty niche at the black core. And he looked at Fess and Arkis and nodded grimly. "The author of this dreadful thing could have sucked out the unknown Lord like the yoke of an egg, but that wasn't necessary, for the sheath was only two and a half feet thick. So he drilled his holes all the way round until the ice was loosened, then wrenched it away in blocks and shards, and so finally came upon his petrified prey."

And Fess said, "Did I hear you right? Did you say 'this dreadful thing'?"

Shaithis looked at him, also at Arkis. "I'm Wamphyri," he growled, low in his throat. "You know me well. There's nothing soft about me. I take pride in my great strength, in my rages and furies, my lusts and appetites. But if this is the work of a man—even one of my own kind—still I say it is dreadful. Its terror lies in the *secrecy,* the *stealth,* the gloating, leering *malignancy* of the slayer. Ah, yes, I'm Wamphyri! And if I should be trapped in these Icelands, then doubtless I too would develop various life-support systems, including a fortress, sophisticated defenses, and a source or sources of food. And I too would be as secretive and sinister as needs be. But don't you see? Someone here has already done it! In these Icelands, we are come into the territory of one who victimizes and terrorizes the very Wamphyri themselves! That is the dreadful thing I mentioned. Why, the very atmosphere of this place seethes with its evil. And something else: it seems to me that it is evil for evil's sake!''

After that . . . Shaithis could have bitten off his forked tongue. Too late, for he fancied he'd already said or hinted far too much. But such was the crushing weight of this place upon his vampire senses—such was its psychic jangle upon his nerve endings—he felt the others would have to be totally insensitive not to have felt it for themselves.

Arkis's mouth had fallen open a little while Shaithis was speaking. Now he closed it and grunted, ''*Huh!* You were always the clever one with the speeches, Shaithis. But indeed I too have felt the threatening, doomful aura of this place. I felt it when I discovered those several bloodied scales and various small parts of my warrior's armored carapace in the high cave; also when the bloodless—but well fleshed, and hung with good meat—Largazis were stolen from the glacier pantry where I'd lodged them. And often I've thought: 'Who is it watches over me so closely and knows my every move? Is he in my very mind? Or do the ice castles themselves have eyes and ears?' ''

It was the Ferenc's turn to speak. ''I'll not deny it, I too have felt the mystery of this place. But I think it's a ghost, a relic, a revenant out of time. An echo of something which was but is no more. Look around and ask yourselves: is anything we've seen of recent origin? The answer is no. Whatever deeds were done here were done a long, long time ago.''

Arkis snorted again. ''And my warrior? And the Largazi twins?''

Fess shrugged and answered: "Stolen by some thieving ice beast. Perhaps a cousin of the pallid, cavern-dwelling sword-snout."

Shaithis had shaken off his momentary fit of depression, had dispersed the strange and ominous mood which had descended upon him tangible as a bank of fog. The Ferenc's answer suited him well enough. He did not agree with it—not entirely—but it suited him to let the others think so. Except:

"So if there's no sly intelligence involved," he said, "or no longer involved, as the case may be, then what sense is there in moving against the volcano?"

Again Fess shrugged. "Best to be sure, eh?" he said. "And if there was some 'sly intelligence' at work here, albeit a long time ago, perhaps his works will still be available to us, deep down in the heart of the volcano. One thing's sure: we'll never know unless we go see for ourselves."

"Now?" Arkis Leperson was eager.

But Shaithis cautioned: "I vote we sleep on it. I for one have tramped enough for the moment, thank you, and would prefer to tackle the cone fresh from my rest and with a hearty breakfast inside me. Anyway, I note that the auroral display is rising to a new peak of activity. That's a good sign. Let the burning sky light the way for us."

"I'm with you, Shaithis," the Ferenc rumbled. "But where to bed down?"

"Why not right here?" Shaithis answered. "Within shouting distance, but each of us secure in his own niche."

Arkis nodded. "That suits me."

They separated and climbed to precarious but private ice ledges and niches where no one could come upon them unheard or unobserved, and each in his own place settled down to sleep. Shaithis thought to call to himself a warm, living blanket of albinos, then thought better of it. If the bats came, Fess and Arkis would probably find it a suspicious circumstance. Why should Shaithis have power over the bats when they had none? Why indeed? It was a question he couldn't answer. Not yet, anyway.

He curled himself inside his cloak of black bat fur and munched on flyer flesh. It was scarcely satisfying but it was filling. And with one eye open and set to scan the ice cavern, from Fess to Arkis and back again, Shaithis thought: *Ah, but time for the good stuff later!*

The good stuff, aye: Fess and Arkis themselves. Who for certain would be thinking exactly the same thing about him.

And settling down he began to breathe more deeply, and his scarlet eye scanned the cavern, and slowly the dreams started to come . . .

V Blood Relations

SHAITHIS OF THE WAMPHYRI DREAMED A SPLENDID FANTASY. As is often the way of it with dreams, it was comprised of a great many scenes and themes with little or no explanation except perhaps as echoes of his waking ambitions. The fantasy had been developing itself for some time in the darker caverns of Shaithis's subconscious mind before suddenly firming into an ordered sequence of scenarios, which were these:

It was Shaithis's reception, his triumph, his moment of glory. The Lady Karen kneeled naked between his spread thighs, teased his great gonads, caressed and even nibbled (but *very* carefully) upon the purple, bulbous tip of his hugely swollen phallus, and now and then paused to gentle that pulsing rod between her perfect breasts. Sumptuously cushioned, Shaithis reclined upon Dramal Doombody's raised bone-throne in Karen's aerie—the last of all the great stacks of the Wamphyri, finally his by right of conquest—and looked upon all of those persons, creatures, and possessions who were likewise his to use, abuse, or destroy as, when, and how he willed it.

Above and beyond the aerie's kilometer-high buttresses, battlements, and balconies of fossilized bone, stone, membrane, and cartilage, new stars thronged to join those already dusting the darkening sky. The sun issued its last coruscating fan of golden radiation where it sank down behind Sunside, and for breathless moments the barrier mountains were thrown into massive, jagged silhouette while the glaring yellow spikes of their peaks turned purple and finally grey.

Then . . . the rapidly elongating shadows of the mountains flowed like monstrous stains across Starside's boulder plains to blot them into darkness, and at last it was that sundown which Shaithis had so long awaited: the hour of his greatest triumph, and of his revenge.

As at a signal his lieutenants threw back the heavy tapestries from the windows and cut free Karen's sigils so that they went warping and spiraling out and down into darkness; and they shook out the long, tapering pennants bearing Shaithis's new blazon—a Wamphyri gauntlet, clenched and raised threateningly above the glaring sphere which was Starside's portal to the hell-lands—to wave in the thinly gusting currents of air over the aerie's higher parapets.

And:

"So I willed it," he growled, "and so it has come to pass." And he glared all about, defying all and sundry to deny him his sovereignty—if they dared. And yet in his heart Shaithis knew that the victory wasn't his, not in its entirety. He knew he couldn't claim that he was its sole engineer, or that he alone had whelmed the strange forces and alien magic of The Dweller. No, for he'd required a deal of help with that.

Shaithis couldn't remember exactly how the fight had

been won but he did know that he'd had a powerful ally who was here with him even now. Since he seemed to be the only one in any way aware of that Other, however, and since he alone of all men was fit to command—fit to proclaim himself Warlord of the New Wamphyri—what difference did it make? A wraith may not usurp a man.

He narrowed his eyes and glanced to the right and back a little (but not so obviously that anyone would notice), and peered a moment at the Dark Hooded Thing in its black cloak where it stood close by watching all that transpired. It was a black, evil Thing, and entirely unknown and invisible to all save Shaithis; yet this was the creature which had made Starside's conquest possible. Shaithis felt nothing whatsoever of gratitude but merely scowled; for out of nowhere it had come to him that his secret, faceless ally—his invisible familiar—was the true master here and he himself a mere figurehead, which irritated him and turned his victory sour. For he was Wamphyri and territorial, and there simply wasn't space in this or any other world for two Warlords.

Galvanized by some weird frustration, suddenly Shaithis started to his feet. His prostrate thralls and their kneeling overseer lieutenants rose with him (though all of them, masters and minions alike, shrank back from the severity of his gaze), and four small warriors in dully glinting armor hissed their alarm at such a flurry of movement, but nevertheless held to their positions in the far corners of the great hall.

At Shaithis's feet, the Lady Karen shrank back from her master. Her scarlet gaze seemed partly adoring (aye, she was treacherous as ever) but mainly fearful; he kicked her sprawling out of his way and strode alone to the high-arched windows. Out there, the dizzy aerial levels were now alive with entire colonies of smoky-furred *Desmodus* bats like clouds of excited, darting midges alongside

Shaithis's gigantic, sky-spurting warriors; also rank upon rank of manta-shaped flyers in ornate, decorative trappings, with lieutenants and high-ranking thrall riders seated proud in saddles tooled with Shaithis's gauntlet sigil. It was an airborne display of his power in the wake of his greatest victory.

Shaithis stood there a moment, arms akimbo and head held high, and watched the flypast like a general inspecting his troops. Then he turned his hooded, crimson eyes westward to light upon The Dweller's garden, or rather the high saddle in the grey hills where once a garden had blossomed. Ah, but that was yesterday and now . . . flames leaped there and black smoke boiled skyward, and the underbellies of clouds where they scudded across the peaks were ruddy from the inferno blazing below them. Shaithis had vowed it and willed it into being, and now it was real! The garden was burning and its defenders were . . . dead?

No, not all of them. Not yet.

And: "Bring them to me," the dreaming vampire commanded of no one in particular. "I would deal with them—now." A half dozen lieutenants hastened to obey, and in a little while a pair of prisoners were led into Shaithis's presence. Massive, he dwarfed them. Of course he did, for he was a Lord of the Wamphyri: he hosted a vampire in his body and brain, while his captives were merely human. Or were they? For even now there was that defiant something in their bearing which in itself might almost be . . . Wamphyri? Then Shaithis saw their eyes and knew the astonishing truth.

Ah! And how was *this* for revenge? For there is nothing so delightful to a vampire than to torment, torture, and tap the life fluids of another or others of his own kind. And:

"Dweller," Shaithis said, his voice so softly threat-

219

ening it was almost a whisper. "Dweller, come, take off your golden mask. For I know you now even as I should have known you right from the start. Ah, but your 'magic' had me fooled just as it fooled us all. Magic? *Hah!* No such thing but the true art of the great vampire! For who else but a master of every Wamphyri talent—aye, and then some—would dare to wage a one-man war against all the great Lords that were? And who else but the most crafty—ah, *crafty* vampire—might ever have won such a war?"

The Dweller made no answer but simply stood there in his loosely flowing robes and golden mask, behind which his red eyes burned. And Shaithis, believing he saw terror in those half-hidden eyes, smiled a grim smile. Oh, yes, for whether or not there was terror there now, he knew that there would be soon enough.

As for the other prisoner: Shaithis would *never* forget this one! For he was not only a hell-lander but also The Dweller's father, who had stood side by side with his son in the devastating battle at the garden, when the Wamphyri had been swatted out of Starside's skies and crushed like so many gnats. What was more, when the fighting was over and all the great aeries of the Wamphyri had been leveled (all bar the bitch Karen's), Shaithis had seen this one with that selfsame "Lady" in these very chambers: Karen's "private" chambers, as they had been at that time, so that Shaithis had wondered:

Are they lovers?

Well, perhaps they had been and perhaps not. It could be that they'd simply been allies against Shaithis and his army of Wamphyri Lords, and as a reward for her part in his defeat her aerie had been spared; but only to become Shaithis's in the fullness of time, as everything else had become Shaithis's. He supposed that one way or the other it made little difference, except that for some ill-defined reason he really would like to know whether or not this hell-lander had known Karen and been in her. Well, that was a question he could resolve easily enough.

She sprawled beside the bone-throne where he had left her, and now he called out: "Karen, come to me." She made to stand up but he quickly added: "No, crawl!"

Luscious body oiled and gleaming in the light of flaring flambeaux, with only her golden bangles and rings to cover a figure which her vampire had made irresistible, she obeyed. Her great bush of pubic hair was a glistening copper tangle; the stains of her areolas and spiked nipples were dark as bruises against the pale loll of her elastic breasts; even proceeding in the undignified, animal fashion which Shaithis demanded, still her lithe loveliness could not be disguised.

When she was close to him, Shaithis quickly reached down and bunched the mass of her red hair in his hand, jerking back her head and yanking her to her feet. She made no sound, no protest, but The Dweller leaned forward a little—a strange attitude or posture, like a dog balanced on its hind legs—and Shaithis thought he heard a low growl rumbling behind the mask. Had he aroused The Dweller's passions? And if so, what about those of his hell-lander father?

Now, still holding Karen upright, so that she stood upon her crimson-nailed toes, Shaithis deliberately looked away from The Dweller and into the strange, sad eyes of his puny-looking father. He cocked his great head on one side inquiringly. "And so you're the hell-lander who caused me so much trouble in the garden, eh? Well, little man, it strikes me that you and your son were lucky that time, and that if you're the best they have going for them beyond the sphere-Gate, then it's high time the Wamphyri went through into the hell-lands and showed them what *we* can do! Except . . . I have to admit there's something I can't quite fathom. I mean, a creature like you—small, soft, puny, with the pulpy parts of a virgin boy—and you'd have me believe you've been into this?" He knotted Karen's hair that much tighter in his great fist, lifting her higher, until she was obliged to dance on the very tips of her toes. "What, and lived to brag about it?" Shaithis's derisory laughter grated like a hot iron in ashes.

The hell-lander stiffened and his scarlet eyes widened a very little; his mouth twitched in one corner; his pale flesh turned paler yet. But he found strength to suppress the cold fury which Shaithis's scorn had momentarily induced in him. And finally, in a small, quiet voice he answered: "You must believe what you will. I neither confirm nor deny anything."

Such negativity! Shaithis took it as a sign of the hell-lander's impotence. For if he and Karen had been lovers, then doubtless he'd delight in boasting how she was his castoff, which was the way of it with the Wamphyri; in payment for which insolence Shaithis would have him gutted with middling sharp instruments, and before his living eyes feed his smoking entrails to a warrior! But however impotent he may or may not be, still the vampire Lord's question went unanswered.

"Very well," Shaithis shrugged, "then I shall assume she means nothing to you. If I thought she did I would cut away your eyelids so that you couldn't close them, and hang you in silver chains from the walls of my bed-chamber where you'd have no choice but to observe each smallest intricacy and nuance of our lovemaking—before she died from it!"

At which moment, even as he said this thing:

Don't!

The warning echoed like a gong struck in Shaithis's mind, and he knew its source at once. Glaring across the hall at the Dark Hooded Thing, he saw that where before the interior of its hood had been black and impervious as granite, now the sulphur orbits and scarlet pinpricks of eyes were visible, unblinking, burning their message into his mind. *Don't drive them too far! I hold them enthralled, their powers suppressed, but goading them is like thrusting sharp staves under a warrior's scales! It makes them unstable, galvanizes them, weakens my hold upon them.*

And Shaithis sent back: *But they're whelmed, conquered, whipped like dogs! Which no one knows better than you; for you hold their minds like grapes in your hands, to peel or crush as you will. But as well as this I have warriors here, and my many lieutenants and thralls. Aye, and all of my creatures without, thronging on the night wind. Now tell me pray: what have I to fear?*

Only your greed, my son, and your pride, the other answered. *But did you say "your" warriors, lieutenants, and thralls? Yours and not ours? Have I no part in your triumph, then? There were two of us, Shaithis, remember? And yet now you talk of "I" when you can only mean "we." A slip of the tongue, obviously. Ah, but then, the tongues of all the Wamphyri are forked, are they not?*

In answer to which Shaithis hissed: *What do you want of me?*

Only that you are not prideful, the Dark Hooded Thing told him. *For I too was prideful in my time, only to discover that it goes before a fall.*

It was all too much. Tell a vampire not to be prideful? Restrict the towering, enhanced emotions of a Being such as Shaithis? But he was Wamphyri! And to the Dark Hooded Thing: *I vowed Karen's death in a certain fashion, at my hands, in my bed. My triumph will not be complete until it has come to pass, or as nearly as pos-*

sible. Also, The Dweller and his father have been my mortal enemies, which I intend to destroy.

Then destroy them! said the other, his eyes blazing up huge, as if gorged on fire. *Kill them now, but don't torture them. For it could be that if they are driven to it . . .*

Yes?

. . . I think that even they do not know their own strength, their own powers.

Shaithis was astonished. *Their strength? But can't you see that they are weaklings? Their powers? Plainly they are power*less! *Aye, and I shall prove it.*

He released Karen's hair and she collapsed at his feet. And in his dream Shaithis again turned to his captives, who throughout his conversation with the Dark Hooded Thing had stood as in a frozen tableau, held fast by vampire thralls. "There was a time," he told the pair then, "when the bitch Karen betrayed her rightful master—which is to say myself—and all of the Wamphyri at a stroke. Betrayed us? What? Her treachery almost destroyed us! There and then I vowed that when times and fortunes had changed I would slip a siphon into her living heart and drain her blood sip by sip. Also, I vowed that while I emptied her of her juices, I would fill her with my flesh. A double ecstasy for a most undeserving Lady. So I vowed it, so let it be!"

And to his lieutenants: "Go, bring me my couch of black, silken sheets, and the sharp, slender golden straw which you shall find upon my pillow."

Shaithis's couch was carried in by six powerful thralls; a fawning lieutenant proffered a small silken cushion bearing a slim wand of gold tubing, whose funnel mouthpiece reflected the flaring torchlight. Shaithis took the golden straw, threw off his robe, and beckoned Karen to the couch. But as he moved to join her there . . . again there came that rumbling growl from deep in The Dweller's throat, and again Shaithis sensed this oddly postured being leaning towards him, like some nameless threat.

The vampire Lord paused a moment, cocked his head in mocking, silent inquiry, and smiled an utterly inhuman smile before seating himself upon the couch beside the apparently enthralled Karen. She lay there in a sort of vacant paralysis, with her scarlet eyes fixed upon him; but her breathing was shallow, palpitating, and gleaming beads of perspiration were starting from her brow in morbid anticipation. Catching up her left breast, Shaithis lifted it and examined the pale rib cage beneath, then slipped the sharp tip of his golden straw between two of her ribs and eased it towards the pounding center of her body.

As a bubble of her dark red blood formed around the siphon at the point of entry, so Shaithis's vampire lust brought him to massive erection. He released his partially inserted siphon and gripped the inside of Karen's right thigh with a huge hand, squeezing the flesh there as an indication that she should open herself to him . . .

. . . Which was when he felt her first, tentative rejection of his will—and the resistance of others bolstering her resolve—and sensed the suddenly converging foci of forces previously unsuspected. The Dark Hooded Thing sensed them, too, crying out in Shaithis's mind: *I warned you!* But too late, for the vampire Lord's dream-fantasy had now turned to sheerest nightmare.

For the third time Shaithis heard The Dweller's now unmistakably *animal* growl and shot him a wide-eyed glance—in time to see him wrench himself free from the pinioning grip of his guards, then reach up and tear his own golden mask from his face. Except . . . whatever Shaithis had expected, it was not there beneath that mask; and as for the face which *was* there, that resembled nothing even remotely human. No, for bristling and flat-eared, it was the face or visage of a great grey wolf—but its blood-gorged eyes were still those of the Wamphyri!

Its wrinkled, quivering muzzle frothed and dripped saliva; teeth like the blades of small scythes gleamed where the wet, writhing muzzle revealed them; in the next moment the snarling beast (was this really The Dweller?) had turned and snapped at an astonished former guard. And even while Shaithis gaped, the thing's jaws closed like a steel trap on the lieutenant's arm and sheared it below the elbow.

From then on, all was madness.

As the huge, upright creature more nearly completed its metamorphosis into a grey-furred, lupine form, so its voluminous robes shredded like so much rotten cloth to reveal its sheer size. It was a wolf, yes, but as large as a big man! Shaithis's thralls, having already witnessed the monster's speed and savage efficiency, quickly backed off. Hastening their retreat, the great wolf fell to all fours and launched itself at another lieutenant, crunching effortlessly upon his head.

And through all of this, the vampire Lord on his couch was only too well aware that fortune's tide had turned, and that other inexplicable reversals were even now in motion. Nevertheless, he determined that *some* of his dream-fantasy at least should be made to work for him; and crushing Karen in the circle of one great arm, he gripped the golden straw where it was poised to pierce her heart and prepared to thrust it home.

He gripped it . . . and at once snatched back his trembling hand. For a *second* metamorphosis was even now taking place, in Karen, which was no less rapid and awesome than that of The Dweller into a wolf. Moreover, it was loathsome!

As if Shaithis's siphon had poisoned her and brought on some incredibly swift aging process or corruptive catabolism, Karen's flesh was collapsing before the vampire Lord's eyes. Her arms became yellow-veined sticks from which her bangles clattered loosely onto the floor; her scarlet eyes turned a sick, sunken yellow under matted eyelashes; her skin was suddenly corrugated as the skin of dried fruit.

"What?" he croaked, as her ravaged lips drew back in a travesty of a smile and showed him her leprous forked tongue, shriveled gums, and loose, decaying teeth. "What?" It wasn't a question proper, but she answered it, anyway, and her voice was a morbid cackle as she reached for Shaithis's shrinking parts and said:

"My Lord, I'm ready for you!"

Galvanized into frenzied activity, Shaithis slapped the flat of his hand to the siphon's mouthpiece and drove it home into her body—and a gurgling stream of stinking pus at once jetted out to splash against and adhere to his shuddering flesh! With an inarticulate cry he staggered to his feet, pointed at the dissolving, liquefying thing on the couch, and commanded:

"Destroy it! Remove it now! The refuse pit!" But no one seemed to be listening. Shaithis's lieutenants and other thralls were in turmoil; The Dweller's wolf facet was ravaging among them like a fox among chickens; and as for The Dweller's hell-lander father . . . the vampire Lord could scarcely believe his own eyes.

The pair of hulking Wamphyri aspirants who had dragged this small, unassuming human being in here were now slumped, smoldering shreds of blasted flesh puddling the flagged floor with their ichor; and the magician (oh, yes, for this, surely, *was* magic!) who had cindered them was at the window, gazing out on Starside's night skies and ruin-scarred plain with devastating eyes. For where and whenever his gaze alighted and lingered it brought fresh ruin; and all across the sky in the deepening gloom of sundown, Shaithis's New Wamphyri hordes were exploding into fiery tatters and raining their debris down among the shattered stacks of their olden forebears.

Raging his frustration, Shaithis discovered himself robed again, with his gauntlet at his hip. Knowing what must be done—that he alone had the measure of The Dweller and his father—he fitted his deadly weapon to his hand and, in the tradition of the olden Wamphyri, rushed at them to cut them down. And why not? For they were only flesh and blood, after all, just as the great white bears of the Icelands had been flesh and blood. And as the vampire Lord knew only too well, all flesh is weak. Even Wamphyri flesh, in the right circumstances.

In Shaithis's mind the Dark Hooded Thing heard his chaotic, bloody thoughts and said, *Fool!* But Shaithis wasn't listening.

He came upon the hell-lander first, and swung his gauntlet . . . which froze in midair, as if time itself had stopped. But then Shaithis saw that time had simply stretched itself, and that his monstrous gauntlet crept across the intervening distance in a maddening slow motion. The Dweller's father saw it coming and his strange sad eyes turned (but oh so very slowly) to burn upon Shaithis's face. And the scarlet eyes of his son, the great changeling wolf, were likewise upon Shaithis from where that slavering creature floated on the air, caught at the high point of its spring.

In the manner of the Wamphyri, the pair spoke to Shaithis in his raging, blood-drenched mind; and not only them but the Dark Hooded Thing, too, all saying the same thing:

You have destroyed us all. Your ambition, your passion, your pride.

Die! Shaithis replied, as his gauntlet collided little by little with the hell-lander's head and slowly shattered its bright core.

Aye, bright! Bright and blinding and deadly as the furnace sun itself! For there was no blood, no bone, no grey and pulpy brain in the magician's head at all—nothing but golden fire. Like the seething, searing nuclear fire of the sun.

Indeed, it *was* the sun, endlessly expanding out of the small destruction of the hell-lander to encompass and destroy . . . everything!!!

Shaithis started awake, felt the ice against his flesh, and thought for a moment that it was searing golden fire. He cried out, and a thousand fragile icicles shattered and came tinkling down from the ice castle's fantastic ceiling. In the next split second the vampire Lord saw where he was and remembered what he was doing here, and as his nightmare receded and reality closed on him, so his breathing and the pounding of his heart gradually slowed. Then—

He scanned across the frozen expanse of the ice castle and found the dark forms of Fess Ferenc and Arkis Leperson in their niches, and saw that the former had likewise come awake. And now the Ferenc's gaze met his across the glittering ice-sheathed vault.

"Dreaming, Shaithis?" that one called out to him, his words chasing themselves to and fro in the bitter, echoing air of the place. "An omen, perhaps? You cried out, and it seemed to me you were afraid."

Shaithis wondered if the dream had been self-contained, as his inward-directed thoughts, or if Fess had been "listening in" on it. He hated the idea that anyone 9hould spy on him, especially in his subconscious, where the seeds of all of his ambitions—indeed his intentions—

were stored in darkness, awaiting their germination. "An omen?" he eventually answered, but quietly, hiding what confusion lingered still. "No, I think not. Nothing portended, Fess. A pleasurable dream, that's all, of woman-flesh and sweet traveller blood." *Of the Lady Karen rotting on my couch, and the entire Wamphyri race wiped out in the sunburst of an alien mind!*

"Huh!" the other grunted. "I dreamed only of ice. I dreamed I was frozen in an ice tomb, and that some unknown thing was melting its way in to me."

"Then it's as well my cry of sweet pleasure woke you up," said Shaithis.

"Aye, but too early," the Ferenc grumbled. "Arkis sleeps on. In this he's the wise one. Let's drift a further hour or two before we're up and about."

Shaithis agreed; and grateful that the giant had not read him, he settled down again and closed an eye . . .

And again Shaithis dreamed. Except that this time, even more certainly than the last, he knew it was much more than any common dream. The setting was a meeting between himself and the being known as Shaitan the Fallen, whom he recognized at once as that selfsame Dark Hooded Thing who had been his sinister, frowning familiar—perhaps even his alter ego?—in his nightmare of frustrated revenge.

He was aware of the Thing as a shadow among lesser shadows in a cavern of black rock, unsuspected except for the red glow of its eyes where they floated in luminous yellow orbits. What he, Shaithis, was doing in such a place he could not say, except that he felt he'd been called here. Yes, that was it: he was not here entirely of his own free will but mainly because this enigmatic being had called him here. And as if to confirm that thought:

"Shaithis, my son," said the Dark Hooded Thing, whose true voice was deeper, darker, and probably more deceiving than any Shaithis ever heard before. "And so at last you've answered me. Difficult to reach you, my son, through that clever deflective screen of yours, else I had known you and called you here long before now."

Shaithis's Wamphyri eyes and awareness were accustomed now to the gloom of the place. Indeed he saw and sensed as well as ever, which is to say very well indeed: as a cat at night or *Desmodus* on the wing. The darkness made no difference; in fact, and with regard to his whereabouts, it merely served to confirm his first instinctive guess that he was in some natural chamber deep in the belly of the slumbering volcano. Which would appear to make Shaitan the Lord of these subterranean regions.

In such close proximity, the other read his thoughts as if they'd been spoken words and answered: "But of course, just as I have been since . . . oh, a long, long time."

Shaithis peered intently at the crimson-eyed shadow which was Shaitan. It was strange, but for all his vampire-enhanced awareness he saw only an outline of the other's form. No fault of his; his senses were not impaired; Shaitan must be shielding his physical self in a manner like to Shaithis guarding his thoughts. But . . . Shaitan the Fallen? Could it really be—was it *really* possible—for any creature to live so long? He made up his mind that indeed it must be, for here he stood in the presence of just such a one. And:

"This isn't just a dream," said Shaithis then, with a shake of his head. "I can feel your presence and *know* you are real: that same Shaitan of whom Kehrl Lugoz was, and is, so mortally afraid, that ancient Being out of the first annals of Wamphyri legend. You were banished here in prehistory, and you live here still."

"All true," the other answered, and darkness stirred where he stood, as if he had offered a casual shrug. "I am that same Shaitan, the so-called Unborn, who was and is your immemorial ancestor!"

"*Ah!*" said Shaithis, as truth finally dawned. "We are of one blood."

"Indeed, and obviously so. You stand out from the others like a meteor speeding through the stirless stars, much as I stood out in that distant time when I fell to earth. And our ambitions are the same, aye, and our intelligence. I am your origin, Shaithis, and your future. And you are mine."

"Our futures are bound up together?"

"Inextricably."

"Outside of these Icelands, you mean? In more civilized places?"

"In Starside, and in worlds beyond Starside."

"What?" Shaithis was taken aback, for there was something here which smacked of that earlier dream. "Worlds beyond Starside? You mean the hell-lands?"

"For a start."

"And you know of such places?"

"Upon a time, I was the inhabitant of just such a place. But that was before I fell—or was thrown—to earth."

"And you remember it?"

"I remember *nothing* of it!" The Dark Hooded Thing growled, moving marginally closer; and there was that about its motion—as if its very flux had intelligence, a sentient viscosity—which caused Shaithis to take a pace to the rear. "My memory, all memory, was robbed from me when I was cast out."

"No memory of what you did, who and how you were?"

Again the Thing moved closer, and once more Shaithis backed away, but not too far for fear he should back right out of his own dream. "Only my name, and that I was vain and proud and beautiful," said Shaitan, conjuring more echoes of that former dream. "But it was a long time ago, my son, and given time all things change. I too have changed."

"Changed?" Shaithis tried hard to understand. "You're no longer vain, no longer proud? But even the least of the Wamphyri know such vices—and enjoy them. They always will."

Shaitan slowly shook his hooded head, which Shaithis knew from the movement of his crimson eyes in their yellow orbits, the only parts of the creature which were visible through the warp of his inky, impenetrable mental shield. "No longer beautiful!" he said.

"But it's the same for all of us," Shaithis answered. "We know we are not beautiful and accept it. And anyway, what has beauty to do with power? Why, there are those of us who even foster our ugliness as a measure of our might!" Inadvertently, he thought of Volse Pinescu.

Shaitan picked the picture clean out of his mind. "Aye, that one was ugly. But he himself willed it. I did not. And physically and mentally hideous as the Wamphyri are, still by comparison they *are* beautiful." And for the third time he came closer.

Shaithis stood his ground but groped for his gauntlet. It was a dream, true, but he'd not yet relinquished all control. "Do you wish me harm?" he said.

"On the contrary," the other answered, "for we've a long way to go together. But this art I practice is wearying. It were better if you knew me as I am."

"Then show me yourself."

"I was preparing to," Shaitan answered. "Indeed, I was preparing . . . you."

"Enough!" said Shaithis. "I am prepared."

"So be it!" said his ancestor, and relaxed his hypnotic will.

What Shaithis saw then shocked him awake a second time, as if the sleeping volcano itself had erupted under his feet. He started up gasping in his ice niche, wide-eyed and astonished by the castle's luminous light after the dream-darkness of the cone's core, with a chill in his black heart spawned more—far more—of what the Dark Hooded Thing had shown him than of any mundane or merely physical condition. And because the dream had been more than a dream, in fact a visitation, it didn't fade back into some subconscious limbo of obscurity but remained sharp, etched in the eye of his mind as clear as the sigils on an aerie's fluttering banners and pennants.

Shaithis, himself a monster in every respect, was not a creature to shock easily. Where the Wamphyri were concerned, "fear" and "horror" were more or less defunct concepts, eradicated and replaced by rage. Adrenalin was rarely released into a vampire's system to encourage or enable flight, but usually to trigger his animal passions so that he would stand and fight—viciously, brutally! An awareness of their superiority had been bred into Starside's vampires through all the long centuries of their sovereignty, when it was indisputable that of all their world's creatures they were far and away the dominant species. Much as common Man was dominant in his world.

But the fact remained that Shaithis had once *been* a common man—a Traveller vampirized when Shaidar Shaigispawn renamed him, made him his chief lieutenant or "son," and gave him his egg—and as such he'd learned what fear was all about. Even now after half a millennium he still remembered, if only when he slept. For however monstrous a man may become, the things that frightened him as a youth will continue to do so in his dreams.

What had frightened Shaithis the most in those early days of his abduction from Sunside—in that time now five hundred years in the past, before the Lord Shaidar coughed his scarlet egg into his throat and changed him forever—had been the many and monstrous *anomalies* of Shaidar's lofty aerie: the cartilage creatures and gas-beasts, the entirely unthinkable siphoneers, the vast vats in the lower levels of the stack where trogs and Travellers alike became flyers or warriors or yet weirder facets of Shaidar's hybrid experimentation. For the vampire Lord had delighted in showing to Shaithis (at that time a young, as-yet-innocent Traveller) his most nightmarish creations, and in torturing his mind with the half-threat that one day he too might be a diamond-headed flyer, armor-scaled warrior, or flaccid, pulpy siphoneer.

Morbid distortions and abnormalities such as these, then, had been the harbingers of Shaithis's worst nightmares during those early days of Wamphyri apprentice-ship. But in time, as he himself ascended to the aerie's throne room, such fears had receded, been suppressed, had succumbed to the vampire in him, which bade him become a maker of monsters in his own right; an art in which finally he'd excelled. And his flyers had been the most weirdly graceful, his warriors ferocious beyond any previous ferocity, and his other creations and experiments . . . varied. So that it was only in dreams out of his youth that he remembered and took fright at such things. Except that even in the most vivid and awe-inspiring of these, *nothing* that memory had conjured had been half as monstrous as that which the Dark Hooded Thing had shown him.

"Ugly," Shaitan had called himself, but there is ugly and there is ugly. And as for hybridism . . .

235

Shaithis pictured again the *thing* which had stood there when his ancestor relaxed his hypnotic shield to let himself be seen as he really was: an abomination which not even the most perverse or insane Wamphyri mind might envisage, made all the worse through its reality. It had been . . . what? A man-sized slug or leech—corrugated, glistening black and mottled grey-green—but rearing upright like a man? A vampire, yes, such as might develop from an egg inside a man or woman but grown huge beyond all reasonable measure; so that Shaithis had wondered: *But if this grew inside a man, then what became of its host!?*

Then, as the grotesque but mainly vague picture of the thing (*made* vague, by virtue of its obscenity) scarred itself into his mind, so he'd become aware of something of its finer detail, which in the next moment had sufficed to shock him awake.

The thing (no, he must not think of it as a ''thing'' alone but also as Shaitan, his ancestor) had rubbery limbs, *some* of which ended in suckered tentacles. Others, however, did not but were equipped with vestigial human and other animal parts: mummied hands and withered, rudimentary feet, and even a gleaming bone claw. And it was these parts, and also Shaitan's flat, composite face on its spade-shaped cobra head, which repulsed Shaithis the most and brought about the resurgence of his long-forgotten phobia.

For he knew that the hybridism he saw here was not that of some Wamphyri Lord's experimental vats but of Nature; or rather of the vampire's *un*natural tenacity, its determination to cling to life in circumstances however desperate, through travails and triumphs down all the nameless ages. Aye, for the Lord Shaitan had grown simply *too ancient* for the accommodation of mortal, human flesh, and his original body had wasted away to be replaced almost in its entirety by the metamorphic organism which was his vampire. Which was, indeed, now him.

Ugly? The result was hideous; especially so to Shaithis in his dream, for there it had been the embodiment of every nightmare of his apprenticeship.

As to how he knew the fate which had befallen Shaitan in his ice-bound isolation—his evolution, no, devolution, from man-vampire or Wamphyri to pure vampire—that had been written in the vast intelligence, hatred, and sheer evil of the leech-thing's scarlet eyes, unblinking under their cobra's hood. Not the unbridled, mindless hatred so often seen in the seething eyes of a warrior, or the vacant, lidless stare of a hugely nodding flyer, and certainly not the watery, vapid gaze of a siphoneer. But such evil *intelligence* that Shaithis had known this thing was no morbid experiment but a true mutation.

He had known, too, with reinforced certainty, that indeed this was Shaitan the Unborn, called the Fallen. For of all Wamphyri legends there was one of universal prevalence: that to the innermost core of his being, Shaitan had been evil above all other men and creatures . . .

VI   Dark Liaison

SHAITHIS'S MENTAL GUARD WAS DOWN, HIS MIND ACCESsible as he emerged more fully from sleep. And there was someone there, a dark presence, to take advantage of his confusion. It was Shaitan, of course; even at a distance his gurgling, venomous "voice" was unmistakable:

Evil? Do you say I was evil? No, I was wronged. Wronged by the Wamphyri, my own kind! For I was stronger than them and they feared me. And you, son of my sons? Do you also fear me? See how you start awake from me, as if I were some DOOM come down upon you rather than your salvation.

Shaithis went to close his mind . . . and hesitated. His hideous ancestor was the master of the dead volcano, wasn't he? What harm could he do from there? This could well be the perfect opportunity to learn more about him without alerting the others to his presence.

Shaitan picked all these thoughts out of Shaithis's mind

and chuckled monstrously. *Aye*, he gurgled, *for it would never do to let them in on our secret. Not until it's too late. Or at least, too late for them.*

Shaithis lay back, narrowed his eyes, and scanned across the glittering expanse of the ice castle's hollow heart to focus upon the huddled shapes of Fess Ferenc and Arkis Leperson where they slept on. He reached out with his Wamphyri awareness to touch upon the flimsy mental barriers they'd erected about their sleeping minds, satisfying himself that they were in fact asleep. And finally, he answered that dark intelligence which had proclaimed itself his ancestor:

I think I prefer you this way, Shaitan: out in the open, as it were, and not cloaked in dreams. But it was clever of you to break in on me like that. My so-called peers among the Wamphyri were never up to it.

They were not of your blood, Shaitan at once answered. *Or should we say, they were not of mine? Our minds mesh like those of twin brothers, Shaithis. It's a sign that you're a true son of my sons, so that we're as one. We were* meant *to be as one and triumph over all adversity, and then go on to victories unimaginable.*

Aye, Shaithis said wonderingly, *in this and in other worlds, as you have stated. I think it would be interesting to know more about that. Indeed it would interest me greatly to retake Starside from the alien enemies who dwell there now, and to avenge myself upon them. Now tell me your thoughts. For you've hinted we've a way to go together. Have you planned our first steps along that way? And how do I know I can trust you, anyway? Your legends are infamous even among the Wamphyri, who themselves are not much known for straight dealing.*

Again Shaitan's loathsome chuckle. *My son, you'll trust me because you have to—because without me you're stuck here—and I shall trust you for the same reason. But if a token of my goodwill is required: have you not already seen enough of it? Who was it sent his small albino bats to you to keep your sore bones warm while you slept? And who was it disposed of one of your enemies, whose intentions were dire against you, to say the least?*

An enemy? Shaithis raised a mental eyebrow. *And who might that have been?*

What? The other seemed taken aback. *But you know well enow! I speak of the abominable whelky one, who disguised himself with pustules and was companion to the Ferenc. Why, time and again he urged that grotesque giant to seek you out and murder you!*

Shaithis nodded. *That would be Volse's way, sure enough. I was never a favorite of his. Nor he of mine. The monstrous clown: if his wens had been wits he'd outshone the lot of us! So it was your beast that killed him, eh?*

Of course, of course. Shaitan's mental voice sank deeper and darker yet. *And do you think I could not kill you, too? Ah, I could, my son, I could . . . but will not.* His tone was light again in a moment. *No, for I sense that we'll do well together. And since in various ways I've already shown my goodwill, the next stage is up to you.*

Stage? Shaithis frowned. *What stage is that?*

Of the plan, Shaitan explained. *Or would you have me do it all, and likewise claim all the credit?*

Explain.

But there's nothing to explain. Just go along with it in accordance with your own plan—exactly as planned— and that will suffice. In short, bring them to me, my son, so that I may deal with them in my way.

Fess and the leper's son? And will you kill them? And

then me, too, perhaps? Maybe I'd do better to stay joined with them against you? Better the devil you know, they say.

And after long moments: *Devil? That's a word I don't much care for*, said Shaitan. *I don't know why, but I don't like it. Be advised not to call me that again, not even obliquely.*

Shaithis shrugged. *As you will.* And before he could say or ask any more:

They are waking up, Shaitan hissed. *The squat one and the giant both. Best if I leave now and not compromise you. Only bring them to me, Shaithis! A great deal depends on it.*

And as suddenly as that, Shaithis's mind was free of outside interference. But only just in time.

"Shaithis?" The Ferenc's rumble echoed in the cold air. "I sense that you're awake. *Hah!* It's a bad conscience make a man restless as you. You'll have to mend your ways." And he laughed uproariously. The ice castle shuddered and sent down a cascade of variously sized icicles, which in turn brought Arkis more fully awake.

Scratching himself, the leper's son sat up. "What's all the noise?" he demanded.

"Time we were up," Shaithis called across to him. "No more delays. We make our breakfast—poor fare that it is—and then we're on our way. What or whoever the volcano houses, he's our meat today. And all his goods in the bargain."

"Big talk, Shaithis," the other answered. "But we've to get past the pale, cavern-dwelling bloodbeast first."

"Three of us this time," said Shaithis, "and forewarned is forearmed. Anyway, Fess knows the beast's lair. We'll give it a wide berth and seek some other way in."

The Ferenc chewed on cold meat and made his way

down to the floor of the hall. "I for one am ready for it," he said. "A man can't live forever—not even a Lord of the Wamphyri, not that we've seen, anyway—and I'm damned if I'll die of boredom or locked in the ice, terrified that something will find me there and dig me out."

Oh? Shaithis kept his thoughts guarded. *Not live forever? Well, perhaps not . . . but close enough, if Shaitan is anything to go by. And wouldn't that in itself be sufficient reason to team up with the ancient: to discover the secrets of his longevity? It surely would.*

As for Arkis and the Ferenc: Shaithis knew that sooner or later he'd be obliged to have it out with them, anyway, so why delay matters? And even better if Shaitan desired to have a hand in it.

With these thoughts and others like them in his mind (but always guarded, especially thoughts such as these), Shaithis joined the others where they prepared to leave the ice castle. And a short time later the three set out upon their long, slow climb up the frozen rise to where the central cone jutted some fifteen hundred feet higher still. Like a black, crouching giant the tower of volcanic rock waited for them, somber under its canopy of cold stars and writhing auroral fire . . .

Shaitan's miniature albino bats accompanied them, almost invisible against the snow and ice glare, forming an endless entourage whose members came and went, reporting all back to their immemorial master. In this way he was kept informed of the progress of the three and was pleased to note that they followed a most admirable route—one which would lead them directly into one of his many mantraps. An ambush, aye, except that this time there would be no killing.

No, for there were other, better things to do with men such as Fess Ferenc and Arkis Leperson than kill them,

What? Good, strong Wamphyri flesh such as theirs? And they had their vampires in them, didn't they? Just as Volse Pinescu had once had his in him . . .

Ah, but *that* had been a treat!

Volse had been monstrous on the outside, right enough, with all of his pimples, polyps, and other excrescences; but just half an inch under his whelky skin there had been a mass of fatty tissues and good, strong, long-pig meat hanging on a frame of bones like any other man. Except, because he was Wamphyri, there was a lot more to him than there was to other men, for deep inside him there was also his vampire. So that after Shaitan's ingurgitor had drained him of his blood and dragged the shattered shell of him before its master—

—What sheer delight: to tear open Volse's pallid body and seek out his leech, the living vampire whose squirming had so cleverly avoided the ingurgitor's siphon-like probe, but which could not avoid Shaitan. And finally to behead the thing and gorge on its nectar fluids, having first scooped up its skittering egg and stored it in a jar of Volse's brains mushed to a paste, as a tidbit for later. Ah, *yes*—for to the Wamphyri, such is the essence of a gourmet feast!

Even then Shaitan had not been quite finished with his victim. For extracts of Volse's flesh (which was infected with vampire metamorphism and so not entirely dead even now) would be useful to him in his experimentation, the creation of hybrid creatures such as the ingurgitor and other useful constructs, to which end the flayed, drained, gutted, decapitated, but nonetheless "living" remains of Volse had been stored with Shaitan's other materials, for use later.

Aye, even as the giant Ferenc's and the squat Arkis Leperson's remains would be stored, if all went according to plan. But as for Shaithis . . . well, there are plans and there are plans.

Shaithis was of the blood—of Shaitan's blood—and of all the Wamphyri who had been, he was also beautiful. Not by human standards, no, but certainly by Shaitan's. Beautiful, strong, vibrant with life. Ah, but then, the blood *is* the life! And when Shaitan dwelled on matters such as these, then he, no less than his wily descendant, kept his thoughts well hidden.

Meanwhile, his small albinos continued to apprise him of the trio's progress; in a little while he saw that they'd strayed from the path somewhat, so that he must needs redirect them. But in order to do that he must first contact Shaithis, who at that very moment toiled halfway up the fused volcanic slag cliffs toward the western face of the cone. The other two were within hailing distance, but their minds were concentrated on the task in hand.

Shaitan aimed a narrow, powerful beam of thoughts directly into Shaithis's mind, with which he was now a little better acquainted:

Son of my sons, he said, *you go somewhat astray. Your route requires some small adjustment.*

Shaithis was momentarily startled but quickly controlled the agitated flutter of his thoughts. Not before Fess Ferenc had sensed something, however.

''What?'' Fess called out across the precipitous, naked rock face. ''Did something alarm you just then, Shaithis?''

''My foot slipped on a patch of ice,'' Shaithis lied. ''It's a long way down. If I had fallen . . . I was gearing myself for metamorphosis.''

The Ferenc nodded across the gulf. ''Aye, we grow weak. Upon a time I'd revel in forming an air-shape, and flying from these heights. Now it would deplete me considerably. We must watch how we go.''

Now Shaithis could answer his ancestor's inquiry, but he must do so carefully, with all of his effort concentrated on keeping his telepathic sendings private. To this end he made himself secure on a small ledge before answering:

Shaitan, you almost gave me away then. Now tell me, how do we stray from the path? And how may I correct it? Also, you'd better tell me what to expect. I've no desire to end up pierced to the heart and drained off— like Volse Pinescu.

Fool! the other at once hissed. *I thought we had had that out? If I wanted you dead you would be dead. I could send a creature even now to buffet you, all three, from the face of the cliff. Perhaps you'd fly and perhaps not. Whichever, you'd be depleted. And my creatures would find you and finish it. But I need you, Shaithis— we need each other—and so you live. As for the others: I do not wish to damage them. I want them whole! Can't you see what a fine pair of warriors Arkis and the Ferenc would make?*

Shaitan's words were so ominous he could only be speaking truth. He would not dare boast of such superiority unless he could deliver. It was in effect an ultimatum, even a threat: make up your mind, join me now or suffer the consequences. In answer to which:

Very well, said Shaithis, *we work together. Tell me what to do.*

Without pause Shaitan explained: *The leper's son climbs too far towards the east, diagonally away from you. In his way lies an old unguarded lava-run which leads directly to my rooms at the volcano's core. If Arkis were to discover the mouth of this cave he could jeopardize my position; certainly my plans would require rapid and radical alteration.*

An unguarded entrance? Careless of you.

My resources are not unlimited. No more talk. You must draw the others—especially Arkis—back towards you.

Very well, said Shaithis. And to the others, out loud:

"Arkis, Fess, we're too far apart—and I sense a problem to the east."

Arkis at once secured himself in a lava niche and peered out and about. "A problem?" he blustered. "And close by, you say? *Huh!* I sense nothing." But his voice was full of nervous tension and his thoughts went this way and that.

The Ferenc, closer to Shaithis by some fifty feet, began to edge towards him. "Something has bothered me all along," he said. "I've had my suspicions, anyway. And you're right, Shaithis: spread out like this we're too easy to pick off."

"But I see and feel nothing!" Arkis again protested, like a man whistling in the dark.

With a shrug in his voice, Shaithis called out to him: "Are you saying that your Wamphyri awareness is stronger than both of ours combined? Then by all means let's test it out. Do as you will. Be the master of your own destiny. At least you were warned."

That was enough; Arkis started climbing more to the left, bringing himself back into line on a course converging with the others. And not a moment too soon; for Shaithis, from his own position, had finally spotted the dark shadow of a cave to Arkis's right and a little above him. By now the leper's son would certainly have come across it.

In Shaithis's mind the dark thoughts of his ancestor came a little easier. *Good! The problem was not insurmountable, but the easy way is usually the best.*

What now? Shaithis inquired of him.

Above you is a wide ledge formed of an earlier cone, Shaitan answered. *When you strike it, move to the left, that is westward. Soon you will come across another lava-run; ignore it and carry on. The next entrance will seem like a mere crack occasioned as the rock cooled, but this is your route into the volcano. Except you should take up a position to the rear of the others! Do I make myself plain?*

Shaithis shivered, perhaps a little from the numbing cold, which was beginning to bite even into his Wamphyri bones, but mainly at what was implied. For thoughts, like speech, often lend themselves to diverse interpretation, and certainly he'd detected the ominous "tone" of the other's slyly insinuating mental voice. Yes, and he'd known that the depth of Shaitan's thoughts did not bear plumbing. It was strange to be Wamphyri and yet feel something of awe at the implied evil in another's scheming.

Shaitan, he eventually, cautiously answered, *I'm putting my trust in you. It seems my future is now in your hands.*

And mine in yours, said the other. *Now continue to guard your thoughts and concentrate on your climbing.*

And he was gone again.

Shaithis suddenly found himself wondering at the wisdom of this dark liaison. Indeed there seemed little of wisdom in it; it was mainly a matter of instinct, and of course necessity. But any advantage was Shaitan's. This was his territory and he knew it well, and he was not without resources. Shaithis could only hope that the ancient's plans for the Ferenc and Arkis Leperson did not extend to him also. But he sensed that they did not. Not for now, anyway.

His Wamphyri instinct again, which had seldom let him down. But there's always a first time. And a last . . .

He avoided morbid conjecture and looked for brighter omens. Of course there was always his dream: that first dream of the Lady Karen's aerie, where he had been returned to power after some fabulous conquest of Starside and the destruction of The Dweller's garden. He had the feeling that as dreams go there had been an element of foretokening to it. Except there was an old Wamphyri maxim that men should never read the future too closely, for to do so is to tempt destiny. And anyway, the dream had ended in disaster and ruin—but at least it had hinted that there *was* in fact a future to look forward to. How much of a one was anyone's guess.

"A ledge," Fess Ferenc grunted, dragging himself up ahead of Shaithis. As Shaithis's face appeared level with the rim, the giant reached down a huge, taloned hand; Shaithis looked at it for several long moments, then took it. And the Ferenc hauled him easily up onto the level surface.

"Last time you had the chance you threw me down," Shaithis reminded him.

"Last time you were reaching for your gauntlet!" the giant replied.

Then Arkis came up and joined them. "You and your premonitions!" he grumbled. "I still say I sensed nothing harmful. Also, I believe I was almost into some sort of cave. It might well have been a tunnel."

But Shaithis said, "Oh? An *empty* cave, d'you think? Or did it perhaps contain one of Fess's sword-snouts?"

"Wouldn't I have sensed it?" Arkis frowned.

Fess Ferenc scowled. "Volse didn't," he said. "Nor did I, until it was too late." And turning to Shaithis, "What now?"

Shaithis narrowed his scarlet eyes and made a small show of sniffing the air with his flattened, convoluted snout. "The area to the right still feels dangerous to me," he said. "So I vote we follow this rim to the left awhile, out of the suspect region. We'll see where it leads. At least it will give us a breather from all this climbing."

The Ferenc nodded his grotesque head. "Suits me. But how we've come down in the world, eh?"

As they set off along the ledge, Arkis said, "Come down? How so?"

The Ferenc shrugged. "Just look at us. Three Lords— or ex-Lords—of the Wamphyri, stripped of most of our powers, going like frightened children in a huddled group to explore strange new regions. And afraid of what might jump out on us!"

"Afraid?" Arkis puffed himself up. "Speak for yourself!"

The Ferenc sighed and said simply, "But I saw the thing that lanced the Great Boil, remember?"

At that moment it grew darker and the three paused to glance speculatively, apprehensively at each other. A thin cloud layer had drifted in to cover the higher reaches of the cone. The first small flakes of snow began to drift down and coat the ledge.

Arkis looked at the sky all about. "One cloud?" He voiced his thoughts out loud. "Which just happened to form here? A vampire mist, d'you think?"

"Obviously," said the Ferenc. "Whoever dwells here, he's sensed us coming and seeks to make it harder for us. He makes his lair more obscure, and the way to it more difficult."

"Which means we're on the right track," Shaithis added. He set off again along the ledge, and behind him the others almost automatically followed on.

"*Huh!*" Arkis grunted. "Well, at least your premonitions were good. Perhaps too good. It seems to me this one has the edge on us. He sees and knows all while we remain in the dark, as it were." He swatted at a small white bat which flitted too close.

And the Ferenc's eyes went wide as he gave a small start and burst out, "His albinos! *His* bats! We should have known. That's how he tracks our course. The midges pursue us like fleas after a wolf cub!"

249

Shaithis nodded sagely. "I had suspected as much. They're his minions no less than *Desmodus* and his small black cousins were ours back on Starside. They scan our whereabouts and circumstances, reporting all back to . . . whoever."

Arkis gaped and grasped his arm, drawing him to a halt. "You suspected these things and said nothing?"

"A suspicion is only a suspicion until it's an established fact," Shaithis answered, angrily shrugging away the other's restraining hand. "And anyway, it makes a very important point and gives us an insight into *his* circumstances."

"Eh? Insight? Circumstances? What are you on about? What point does it make?"

"Why, that the cone's master fears us! Bats to report our movements; a snowfall to hinder us; a sword-snouted creature guarding his hive, as the soldier bees of Sunside guard their honey? Oh, yes, he fears us—which in turn means that he's vulnerable." And to himself: *Good reckoning—perhaps he really is. But still I'll take my chances with him. At least we have this much in common: our intelligence.*

And at once, gurgling in Shaithis's mind: *And our blood, my son. Don't forget our blood!*

Again, at once, the Ferenc snapped, "What?" His huge head swung round in Shaithis's direction, and his eyes glared under gathering black brows. "What was that? Did you say—or think—something just then, Shaithis?"

Shaithis hid his momentary panic behind bland innocence. "Eh?" He raised an eyebrow. "Say something? Think something? What's on your mind, Fess?" And as the Ferenc and Arkis scanned nervously all about, he sent a triple-shielded thought:

Twice you've almost given me away, Shaitan. Do you

think this is a game? If there's so much as a hint of what I'm up to, I'm a goner!

The Ferenc scowled. "On my mind? No, nothing on *my* mind, except to get finished with this, that's all." He straightened from his half-crouch. "So what say you: do we go on, or do we call it a day? *Is* he vulnerable, this master of the volcano, or are we even more so? It's a nervy business, this climbing in the snow, not knowing what's waiting for us."

Shaitan came whispering into Shaithis's mind: *Get on with it; bring them in; bring them to me! Do it quickly. For he's no fool, this giant. He's sensitive and we've both underestimated him. You'll need to watch him—and carefully.*

"I've noticed," said Shaithis to the others, almost conversationally, "how the small albinos come and go from the west. So I say we stick to the ledge and see where it goes."

"No!" the Ferenc growled. "Something's wrong, I'm sure of it."

Shaithis looked at him, then at Arkis. "Do you wish to go down again? Have we wasted all our time and effort? Has a cloaking vampire mist entirely unnerved you? But our enemy wouldn't have issued it unless we had unnerved him!"

Arkis said, "I'm with the Ferenc."

Shaithis shrugged. "Then I go on alone."

"Eh?" The Ferenc stared hard at him. "Then be sure you go to your death."

"How so? Is this the place where Volse was taken?"

"No, that was on the other side, but . . ."

"Then I'll take my chances."

Arkis said, "Alone?"

Shaithis shrugged. "Which is worse, to die now or later? Better to do it here, I think, locked in combat,

251

than locked in the ice with something drilling its way to my heart." And then, suddenly, as if he'd run out of patience, he hissed at both of them: "There are *three* of us, remember! Three 'great'—*hah!*—Wamphyri Lords against . . . what? An unknown being who quite obviously fears us almost as much as we—as *you*—fear him." And he turned away from them.

"Shaithis!" the Ferenc called after him in a tone half angry, half admiring.

"Enough," Shaithis snapped over his shoulder. "I've done with you. If I win through, all is mine. And if I lose—well, at least I'll die as I've lived, Wamphyri!" He continued along the ledge, and without looking back sensed the eyes of the two following him. Then:

"We're with you," came the Ferenc's final decision, but still Shaithis stared straight ahead. And at last he heard Arkis's voice, too, calling out:

"Shaithis, wait for us!"

He did no such thing but hurried on that much faster, so that now they must scramble to catch up. And with the pair hot on his heels so he came upon the mouth of the first cave even as Shaitan had forewarned. Here, because it would be expected of him, Shaithis paused. Breathing heavily, the others saw the dark cavern entrance into which he concentrated his gaze.

"A way in, d'you think?" said Arkis, but none too eagerly.

Shaithis stared harder yet into the cave's gloomy interior, then made a show of carefully backing away from it. "Obviously so," he said. "Perhaps too obviously . . ." And to the Ferenc: "What say you, Fess? For it's amply apparent that the cold of these climes has focused our awareness to a fault. Is this a safe way to go or not? Myself, I think not. It seems to me that far back in the cavern something stirs. I sense a thing of great bulk but limited intelligence, yet stealthy, too.'' Which was, of course, the Ferenc's own description of a sword-snout. And as Shaithis had hoped might be the case, it put a picture of just such a creature into the giant's mind.

Fess thrust forward his great head into the cave, glared into its depths, and wrinkled his snout-like nose. And, ''Aye,'' he growled in a little while, ''I sense it, too. And indeed this could well be a way in, for the cone's master has guarded it with a bloodbeast.''

Shaithis nodded. ''Or maybe with *the* bloodbeast?''

''Eh?'' said Arkis.

''Perhaps he has only the one creature,'' said Shaithis. ''For if there were a pair, then Fess here might well have been taken at the same time as Volse.''

''But what does that matter now?'' Fess shrugged. ''Even on its own, this thing is a monster. Are you suggesting we might go against it? Madness! One of us would surely die—possibly two, even all of us—or at least end up sorely wounded, before this thing succumbed. I saw it strike three times in as many seconds, unerringly, and ram Volse through and through like a fish on a Traveller's spear. Why, he didn't even know what hit him!''

But Shaithis shook his head. ''No, I'm not proposing to take it on; quite the opposite. What I'm saying is this: if there's only one such beast and it's here, then we go in by some other route.''

''What?'' Arkis scowled. ''And they come thick and fast, these entrances and exits, do they?''

Shaithis shrugged. ''So it would seem. The tunnel where Volse was taken. The cave you thought you saw back there on the lava cliff. This dark entrance here before us. Now listen: the master of the cone sent a mist to confuse us, didn't he? But not to keep us from this cave, not if this is where he's stationed his sword-snout.

So . . . perhaps there's another entrance close by.'' He gave a sharp nod. ''I say we continue to follow the ledge, a little way at least. Then, even if it comes to nothing, at least we'll have explored this part of the face to the full.''

''Fair enough,'' said the Ferenc. ''No argument here. As long as you're not asking me to go in there!''

Arkis growled, ''Then let's get on. We waste time with all this talk and conjecture.'' He started off, in the lead, and the Ferenc followed on. And now Shaithis brought up the rear.

Overhead the small cloud had snowed itself out; the aurora writhed and the stars gave the icy curve of the world's horizon a blue sheen; Shaithis sensed the vampire awareness of his two ''companions'' focused ahead, leaving him free to converse with Shaitan. And:

There, he sent a tight-guarded thought. *And how does this formation suit you? Also, what was the idea of the small snowstorm? I thought you were eager for them, yet there you go trying to frighten them off.*

The answer came back at once:

First, your formation suits both of us very well. Second, the snow served to confuse and distract them— especially the giant. Now listen and I'll describe your route from this point forward. Very soon now you'll come to a place where the rock is riven into deep crevices. One such crack has been filled in with lava which forms a floor. Follow this and it will lead you direct to my abode at the hollow core. As for your companions, alas, their time runs very short. Indeed they haven't enough of it to find their way here. Not on their feet, anyway.

There was nothing of humor in Shaitan's mental voice, only an icy resolve. Shaithis made no further comment; and anyway, Arkis, heading the column, had come to a halt. Fess joined him, then Shaithis.

Before them the surface of the ledge and the near-vertical face of the cliff were split with deep fissures a full pace in width. Arkis looked at the others. "What now?"

"We go on," said Shaithis.

Perhaps his reply had been too ready, or he had sounded too sure of himself, for the Ferenc looked at him for long moments. And at last the giant said, "But the way looks like a jumble of broken rock. Any cave we find will surely have collapsed in upon itself."

"We won't know that until we look," Shaithis answered. "It's just that I feel we're very close now."

The Ferenc narrowed his eyes. "It appears I'm not the only one whose awareness has been focused to a fault. But very well, we press on. Arkis, lead the way."

The leper's son, muttering darkly to himself, stepped out across the first crack, teetered a little on the far side, and found his balance. And so they all proceeded. Then, after negotiating a half dozen more crevasses:

"Ho!" Arkis called back. "But this next crack has a floor, formed of a frozen river of rock."

"An ancient lava-run," said Fess, joining him.

Shaithis came last and looked at the cliff, riven where in olden times the flow had forced an exit. "Lava from the secret heart of the volcano," he said. "So perhaps we've found our way in, after all."

The Ferenc stepped under the cliff's overhang, into the shadow of the cleft. "Let me scan it."

Arkis went after him, with Shaithis bringing up the rear, and they all three sniffed the air, probing the way ahead with keen vampire senses. Until at last Arkis ventured: "I sense . . . nothing!"

"Likewise," said Shaithis, relieved that the small-talented Diredeath had discovered no threat (where in fact *he* found the place menacing and uninviting to a fault). The Ferenc, however, seemed of a similar mind to Shaithis; except he was perfectly, and honestly, willing to voice it.

"I don't like it," he gave his opinion, "for it smells too much like the cave where Volse got his."

"You've let Volse's death prey on your mind,"Shaithis told him. "And anyway—and as has been said before—forewarned is forearmed. Also, there are three of us this time. Arkis and I, we have our mighty gauntlets, and you have your even mightier talons. And in any case we're already decided that the bloodbeast was hidden in that first cave. Myself," (he paused to sniff the cave's air again), "I think it likely that the cone's master has worked some beguilement here: he has gloomed on this place and left the smell of death here. But a smell is only a smell, and *I* smell success! I'm for going in." He looked from Fess to Arkis.

Arkis shrugged. "If this so-called cone's master has comforts in there, then I'm with you, Shaithis. I've had it to the tusks with hardship! I could use some rich red blood in my belly, and a woman in my bed. D'you suppose it's a harem he guards so jealously?"

Shaithis's turn to shrug. "I've never been a one for the histories," he said, "but I've heard it said that some of the banished Lords took their concubines with them. We can't say what we'll find until we find it."

"Comforts, aye," said the Ferenc, licking his lips. "I could use some of those myself. Very well, we go on."

Shaithis put on a scowl and said, "And how's this for a turn of events? Are you suddenly our leader? It seems you like having the last word, Fess Ferenc. 'Arkis, you lead the way.' And, 'Very well, we go on.' "

"*Bah!*" was Fess's retort. "If no one ever made a decision, then we'd be here forever. Here, let me lead the way . . . ."

Which was exactly what Shaithis had wanted.

The darkness of the interior was like daylight to the vampire Lords, indeed it was preferable to the auroral light and the blue sheen cast by the stars. The Ferenc strode where the way was obvious and unobstructed, inched along where it was made obscure by jumbles, or where the uneven ceiling came down low, or where blisters of lava had burst to form jagged-rimmed, circular cusps of rock like small craters in the almost corrugated texture of the floor. And where other natural fissures or blowholes radiated from the main run, he steadfastly followed the ancient lava flow.

Arkis stayed a pace or so to the Ferenc's rear, followed immediately by Shaithis. As they progressed so the oppressive sensation of ominous expectancy or foreboding lifted a little, which (to Diredeath and the Ferenc, at least) lent credence to Shaithis's "theory" that the volcano's dweller had deliberately set a fearful aura over the mouth of the run to dissuade any would-be explorers.

Shaithis stayed very much on the alert, kept his thoughts fully guarded, would like to contact Shaitan but dared not, not with Fess and Arkis probing in all directions with their minds, their Wamphyri awareness sharp for the smallest hint of mental activity. And always they moved deeper into the heart of the rock.

Eventually, the Ferenc called a halt, whispering, "We must be halfway in at least. Time to take stock."

"Of what?" Arkis grunted. His blunt query sounded like an avalanche, echoing out and back in slowly decreasing waves of sound.

"Dolt!" Fess whispered again when he could be heard. "What use to have the sense of bats, to be able to smell out the way ahead like wolves and keep our minds tuned for the thoughts of others, when at every opportunity all you can do is make great noise?! Would you alert our enemy to our presence?"

Abashed, Arkis kept his answer low: "Hell, if he's at home, surely by now he knows we're coming."

"Perhaps," Shaithis intervened, "but in any case, let's keep it quiet."

"Taking stock, yes," said the Ferenc. "Going first all this way has taken the edge off my awareness. Arkis, you can spell me."

"No problem," and the other took the lead, glad for the chance to make amends. But after moving on only a dozen or so paces:

"Now hold!" Arkis said. "Something's weird!"

They had all felt it at the same time: a sensory void, a region vacant of *all* vibrancies, whether for good or evil, a place stagnant as some stirless, sunless subterranean lake. And they likewise knew what that meant: that the place had been *made* sterile, for even darkness and cold stone have a feel to them. Someone wanted them to believe that there was nothing, absolutely nothing, here . . . because there was something here.

Shaithis's flesh tingled and he knew the others must be feeling the same sensation. Arkis, in the lead, stood rooted to the spot, gurgling inarticulately; but it was much too late for gurgling anything. Shaithis felt the heavy mental curtain deliberately ripped open—felt fear and horror springing into being behind it and rushing to burst through its tattered drapes—then saw the blur of leprous grey which was to be the end of Arkis Leperson, called Diredeath. And indeed his death *was* dire!

Where the Thing came from would be hard to say—a niche in the wall of the place, a side tunnel, a hiding place in the lee of some bulge of lava—but it came at great speed and with fell intent. And it was exactly as the Ferenc had described it. Patched white and grey, mottled like veined marble, it seemed to uncoil or erupt into being, as if some massive boulder half buried in the floor had come to life and reshaped itself. Its legs were a blur, claws scrabbling as it reared before Arkis; its fish-like head bore a bone lance tapered to a sharp point and equipped with thorns or hooks all along its length; its eyes were like saucers, fixing its victim with their emotionless glare.

Arkis's gauntlet was on his hand, ready; but as he raised his arm the Thing struck at him in a move too fast to follow. Its lance gashed his short, squat neck as it sawed past, and its needle-toothed jaws closed on his gauntlet arm. The arm was severed, swallowed at a gulp. In drawing back, the Thing sawed at Arkis's neck again and sliced into his whistling air-pipe; in the next moment its lance was rammed forward a second time, directly into him, piercing his squat body to the heart. He jerked and throbbed where he was held upright on the bone blade, and his tusks chomped on thin air, turning red as he coughed up a spray of blood.

Fess whirled away from the scene (Shaithis thought to run) and his eyes were huge and scarlet. But a lot more than simple fear lit them: there was fury, too! The giant grabbed Shaithis with one taloned hand and drew back the other like a bunch of black-gleaming scythes. "Treacherous bastard!" he snarled. "Your father's egg was rotten, and the pus is still in you!"

"What?" Shaithis forced the metamorphic flesh of his hand to expand within his gauntlet. "Are you mad?"

"In trusting you? I must be!" The Ferenc readied himself to thrust at Shaithis: to punch in through his ribs with his taloned hand, grasp his living heart, and wrench it out. But something stopped him. Something he had seen *behind* Shaithis.

Shaitan was the color and texture of black lava. Only his movement against the rock-splash wall had given him away, and only then because he wanted to be seen. Fess

259

saw him, and his jaw fell open. He took a great gulp of air and forgot to strike at Shaithis, who rewarded him by crashing his clenched gauntlet into the side of his head. Then—

—Shaithis's immemorial ancestor brushed him aside, out of the Ferenc's suddenly loose grasp, and wrapped the stunned giant in a nest of lashing tentacles. With his arms locked to his sides, Fess was helpless, but in any case Shaitan allowed no time for any sort of recovery. With a sound like tearing leather, his elastic mouth flowed over and closed upon the Ferenc's *entire* face and head!

Shaithis, stumbling blindly away, struck stony debris and tripped. And suddenly nerveless—even Shaithis, nerveless—he crashed down onto the lava floor. To one side Shaitan's nightmarish ingurgitor hissed and bubbled as it drained off the last of Arkis's fluids, and to the other Fess Ferenc's ''invincible'' body pulsed and vibrated in the primal vampire's coils where Shaitan crushed and devoured his head. And Shaithis thought: *If there's a hell, then I stand at its gate!*

Shaitan's eyes glowed red out of the darkness which was his crushing, grinding, metamorphic head. And his reply, in Shaithis's staggered mind, was this:

Aye, a hell of sorts, where we are the Lords. For it is our hell, son of my sons, which one day we'll take with us to Starside, and then to all the worlds beyond!

Part Three

I: The Hunters and the Hunted

HARRY KEOGH, NECROSCOPE AND WOULD-BE AVENGER, had thought at first that it would not be especially difficult to track down his quarry: a young driver working for Frigis Express, who also happened to be a necromancer, sex monster, and the insane serial killer of (to date) six young women. But he'd soon discovered that it wouldn't be nearly as simple as he'd thought. Frigis had a dozen branches up and down the country, with a like number of warehouses and freezer depots, and over two hundred trucks of which fifty percent were on the roads at any given hour of the day or night. The firm must therefore employ quite a few drivers who would fit the vague description in Harry's possession; (vague, yes, for he suspected that the bloated, lusting creature he'd been shown was more a figure of terrified imagination than of the real man). Also, it seemed likely that Frigis would use casual labor, and it could be that Harry's man was one of these; but somewhere there should be a list of regular employees at least. Harry hoped to find that list, and also that the John or "Johnny" he was looking for would be on it.

On the third Wednesday in May at 3:30 in the morning, he paid a visit to Frigis's main office in London to have a look at the company's books. He went there via the Möbius Continuum, making several stops at well-known exit points before finally emerging in a shop doorway in Oxford Street. At that hour the normally polluted air was almost wholly free of traffic fumes and even bracing, and the night-lighting loaned the street a certain alien luminosity. Large, lethargically flapping pages from a discarded, dismembered newspaper fluttered like strange slow birds on buffets of blustery air along the gutters.

The offices Harry was looking for were directly opposite; no lights showed within the building; he hoped there'd be no night watchman to complicate matters. And there wasn't.

Entering the building by the Möbius route, Harry let his burgeoning vampire instincts guide him to the correct floor and then to the records office. Locked doors were no trouble at all to the Necroscope, who used numbers to conjure doors of his own out of the thin air. But twice, purely out of habit, he went to switch on lights before realizing that he no longer had need of them; and once he came face-to-face with a full-length mirror, which both shocked and fascinated him with its picture of a gaunt-faced man with luminous, red-tinged eyes. He had known of course that the change was taking place in him, but only then realized how quickly it was happening. It filled him with mixed emotions and alien longings; it was the night and the mystery, and the going in strange places, as if in search of prey. Well, and so he was. Except there is prey and there is prey . . .

The records office was dirty and untidy, and smelled

of strong coffee and stale cigarette smoke. It had an an-
tiquated system of filing cabinets, all open for Harry's
inspection. He quickly turned up a list of branch and
depot managers, but no information on rank-and-file employees. There was, however, a list of addresses and telephone numbers of all Frigis Express's subsidiary offices,
which Harry pocketed. That should save him a little time,
at least. But that was all there was, which was hardly
satisfactory.

Disgruntled, Harry pondered over his next move: pre-
sumably to start at the top of the list of branches and
work down it. But then, out of nowhere, he found himself wondering if maybe Trevor Jordan was up and about.
He could use a cup of coffee, a little companionship and
friendly conversation, someone . . . to *be* with—briefly,
anyway—if only to work the weirdness out of his system.

It was unlikely Jordan would be awake, but just on the
off chance Harry reached out with his telepathic mind
and searched for him—and immediately found him.

Harry? Jordan's unmistakable "voice" sounded in
Harry's mind as clearly as if he'd whispered the words
in his ear. *Is that you?*

Harry found telepathy similar to and yet quite different
from deadspeak. He had used something like it before—
a sort of reverse deadspeak, he supposed—but that had
been quite a few years ago in his incorporeal days and
also very different. Telepathy was therefore new to him.
Even so, still it struck him as being . . . more natural?
Well, and he supposed it *was* more natural. For after all,
almost anything in the world would be. But telepathy: it
was something like a telephone conversation, even down
to the hiss and crackle of psychic "static"; whereas
deadspeak was the wind whistling eerily down a bleak
desert canyon under a full, floating moon. In short, it
was the difference between talking mind-to-mind with

265

living people, and conversing metaphysically with dead ones.

And yet Jordan had seemed wary, unsure of Harry's identity and even unwilling to reveal his own. Just why that should be the Necroscope couldn't guess. He frowned and asked, *Who else would it be, Trevor?*

And hearing his voice, Jordan knew him at once. But his mind-sigh (of relief?) warned Harry that something was very wrong. Likewise what he said next:

Harry, you know my old place in Barnet? That's where I am. But I can't say for how long. I'd like to get out of here. I don't want to explain right now—it mightn't even be safe to—but do you think you could get round here? I mean, like now?

What's the trouble? Harry was switched on now, alert to danger. And he could still sense Jordan's uncertainty.

Harry, I don't know. I came to London to see if I could maybe find something out for you, but I've been blocked all along the line, almost from the start. I came here to watch them, E-Branch, but hell . . . I didn't think there'd be anyone watching me!

Right now?

Right now, yes.

I'm on my way, said Harry.

Air made a small implosion into the empty space where he stepped through a Möbius door, its draft causing papers to rustle in a filing cabinet he'd left standing open. But before the papers had stopped rustling Harry had tracked down Jordan's thoughts to Barnet.

He emerged silently into the resurrected telepath's front room, whose first-floor bay windows overlooked a cobbled cul-de-sac, the end wall of a park, and the dark, gently mobile silhouette of trees beyond. The room was in darkness and Jordan was at the window, looking out through a crack in the curtains on a street shining dull yellow in electric lamplight. Harry reached out to a wall switch and put on the light, and Jordan hissed, fell into a crouch, and whirled to face him. There was a gun in his hand.

"It's okay," the Necroscope told him. "It's just me."

Jordan drew a deep breath and almost fell into a chair. He waved his hand to indicate Harry should also sit down. "It's just the way you come and go," he said.

"You invited me," Harry reminded him.

Jordan nodded. "Here I am a bag of nerves, looking out into the street—and then the light going on like that!"

Harry said, "It wasn't deliberate; or rather, it was. If I had spoken you'd have turned and seen me. I'm not sure which would have shocked you more: the light going on, suddenly, or seeing my eyes in the dark."

"Your eyes?"

Harry grimaced, nodded. "They're red as hell, Trevor. And there's nothing going to stop it now. What's in me is a strong one."

"But . . . you still have a little time?"

Harry shrugged. "I don't know how long. Long enough to do one last thing, I hope, and then I'll be on my way." He finally sat down. "Now, would you like to put your gun away and tell me what's on your mind?"

Jordan looked at the gun in his hand as if he'd forgotten it was there. He gave a snort and replaced it in its shoulder holster. "Nervous as a cat," he explained. "Or rather, as a mouse *watched* by a cat!"

"Are you watched?" Harry didn't know where to aim his thoughts to check. Searching for Jordan had been different, for he'd known what he was looking for; likewise Paxton. But looking for someone he wasn't used to—some unknown someone—was a trick he'd yet to master. "Are you sure?"

Jordan got up and put out the light, went to the curtains again. "I've never been so sure. He or they are out there right now, not too far away, scanning me. Or if not scanning, obscuring. They're blocking me. I can't read past them. I keep thinking it can only be E-Branch, but how the hell would they know I was back? Alive, I mean?" He looked back from the curtains, saw Harry's alien face, and said, "I . . . I see what you mean."

Harry, a tall, dark silhouette whose eyes made his face a mask from hell, nodded. But there were other things to worry about than the glare of his blood-hued eyes. "What does it feel like, to have someone watching you, blocking your mind?"

"Being watched is how it felt with Paxton; blocking is mental interference. A screen of static."

"But I wasn't even sure Paxton was there until you told me. He was just an itch. And as for mental interference . . ."

"Okay"—the other matched Harry's shrug—"I'll give you an example. Try aiming your thoughts right at me."

Harry did it and met a buzzing wall of interference. If he hadn't known it was Jordan, then he wouldn't know what it was. Jordan said, "Find something like that, and you know someone's scrambling you. Deliberately. I know because I've had practice. When the Russian espers used to cover the Chateau Bronnitsy, it was like this all the time. We used to try and break through, and they were always trying to get through to us." He looked at Harry again, penetratingly. "Incidentally, you do it all the time, Harry, except when you're wanting to read someone, or wanting someone to read you. But with you it's different. Something that's permanent and getting stronger all the time. It isn't static but something else, and it comes natural to you. So natural you didn't even know about it, did you? Or maybe 'natural' is the wrong word for it. What you have is . . . well, in E-Branch we used to call it mind-smog.''

The Necroscope nodded. "I'd wondered about that. It's a dead giveaway. By now Darcy's espers must know what I am. Or if not he should fire the lot of them! So it looks like the talent Wellesley gave me is going to be redundant . . . or maybe not.'' And after a moment's thought: "No, definitely not. Wellesley's thing is a total blanket: it doesn't just make my mind unreadable but blanks it out entirely. The vampire thing is just mind-smog, like you said. But it makes me wonder: how come Paxton didn't discover what was happening to me earlier? How was he able to get to me at all?''

"It was only just starting then," Jordan answered. "Your vampire thing wasn't fully developed. It still isn't, but sufficiently so that it stopped me. I've tried to reach you half a dozen times this last couple of days but was only able to make it when you wanted to contact me. Oh, and something else. You mentioned Darcy Clarke, right? Well—''

Suddenly he paused and held up a cautioning hand. "Wait!" And in another moment: "Did you feel that?''

Harry shook his head.

"A probe," said Jordan. "Someone trying to get into me. The moment I relax, they're there.''

Harry stepped towards Jordan and the large, curved windows, but held himself back a little in the shadows. "You said it was on your mind to get out of here. What did you mean?''

"Only that I don't know what's on *their* minds," the other told him. "I mean, I know it can only be E-Branch out there, but I don't know what they're up to or what they're planning. Do they *know* it's me? That seems unlikely: what, that I'm back from the dead? But on the other hand, and from their point of view, who else *can*

I be if I'm a telepath using Trevor Jordan's flat? And this watch they're keeping on me: it reminds me of that time we were covering Yulian Bodescu. I mean, who the hell do they think I am, Harry?''

Very slowly, Harry nodded. ''I begin to understand,'' he said. And he gripped Jordan's elbow. ''And you're right: it's *exactly* like that time they were covering Yulian Bodescu. Which means that it's not so much a case of *who* they think you are but *what* they think you are!''

Jordan gasped. ''You mean they think I'm . . . ?''

''It's possible. You're back from the dead, aren't you?''

''But I have no mind-smog.''

''Neither did I, until recently.'

Again Jordan's gasp. ''They're waiting to see how things develop before they move in! Which would explain just about everything. Certainly it would explain why I'm shit scared of them! I'm picking up something of their suspicions, their intentions. I'm sensing the hunters hot on my track. Harry, they think—they suspect—*that I'm a vampire!*''

The Necroscope tried to calm him down. ''But you're not, and it's easy to prove that you're not. Also, Darcy Clarke's in charge of E-Branch, and . . . what were you going to tell me about Darcy, anyway?''

Jordan came away from the window. Another look at Harry's face convinced him the light would be better on. He tripped the switch on the wall, then sat down heavily. ''Darcy's at home,'' he said, ''and very unhappy about something. He was the one I was supposed to be watching, remember? Because he's the boss and would know which way things are jumping. But now he seems to have been taken off the job. And while he isn't a telepath himself, still somebody is throwing up a pretty good shield around him, making it hard to get anything.''

That felt ominous. Harry said, ''Maybe we should go

and see him. Maybe we should confront him, ask him straight out what's going on. I'm pretty sure I know already—that the Branch is just waiting for me to put a foot wrong—but if we hear it from Darcy then we'll know it for sure.''

Jordan shrugged. "At least it would get me out of here. I feel that if I don't get out, I'll go nuts! God, I don't like being watched and not know what they're thinking.''

"Okay," said Harry. "And afterwards? Will you come back here or what? The thing is, I could use some help on this serial killer thing. And we can use my place in Bonnyrig as a base. For the time being, anyway. That way we'll be able to spell each other watching out for the watchers. And when this task I've set myself is done, then, before I leave—I mean before I really leave everything—we'll find a way to square it with E-Branch and put your own record straight.''

"That all sounds good to me." Jordan breathed a sigh of relief. "Just say the word, Harry, and I'm your man.''

The other nodded. "The word is we go and see Darcy. He's single, isn't he, like most of you espers? I know he used to live in Hoddesdon; is he still there? And will he be on his own, or is there a woman? Darcy isn't likely to buckle under a shock or two, I'm sure, but I don't want to go scaring any women.''

Jordan shook his head. "No woman that I know of. Darcy's been married to the job too long. But he's not in Hoddesdon anymore. He got himself a house in Crouch End, just a mile or two away. A nice place with a garden in Haslemere Road. Only been there a couple of weeks. He moved in right after the Greek job.''

Again Harry's nod. "I don't know the area but you can show it to me. Is there anything you want to take with you?''

271

"My suitcase is already packed!"

"Then we can go right now."

"At 4:20 in the morning? If you say so. I don't have a car, though, so we either walk it or I'll need to call a—" But Jordan knew his mistake at once, as soon as he saw Harry's strange wan smile.

"A taxi's not necessary," the Necroscope told him. "I have my own transport . . ."

Darcy Clarke was still up, pacing the floor as he'd paced it all night. It wasn't his talent that was bothering him— he himself wasn't in any danger—he was just worried about the Branch and the job he suspected was being planned right now, at this very moment. About that, and about Harry Keogh. But in fact the two were one and the same thing.

The ground-floor lights of Clarke's house were bright behind a façade of shrubs and trees as Harry guided Jordan out through a Möbius exit and back into the real world. "You can open your eyes now," he told the telepath as Jordan staggered under the briefly suspended, now renewed pull of gravity. It was like the feeling in the pit of your stomach when an elevator descends to the level you want and jerks to a halt there, except this elevator had no walls, floor, or ceiling and you "fell" in every direction at once. Which was why Harry had asked Jordan to close his eyes a moment.

"My God!" Jordan whispered, swaying a little as he looked all around at the night street.

Harry thought: *God? The Möbius Continuum? Well, and you could be right. August Ferdinand thinks so, anyway!* He steadied the telepath and said, "I know. It's a weird sensation, isn't it?

Jordan looked at Harry and felt himself in awe of him. He talked about the immundane, the utterly unbelievable, as if it were merely odd. But finally Jordan gathered his senses to say, "Nice shot, Harry. That's Darcy's place right there."

They let themselves in through the garden gate and walked up a path between the shrubs. The glowing white globe of a lamp drew a cloud of moths where it hung like a small moon over the front door. Harry directed Jordan to stand to one side, put on his dark glasses, and pushed the doorbell; in a little while footsteps sounded from within.

The door was equipped with a peephole lens; Clarke used it and saw Harry standing on his doorstep, staring right at him. His talent made no objection as he opened the door, which told him a lot. "Harry!" he said. "Come in, come in!"

"Darcy," Harry said, taking hold of his arm, "Listen, take it easy—but there's someone with me."

"Someone with—?" Darcy started to say as Jordan stepped into view. He saw him and said, "Trevor . . . ?" Then he started violently and took a pace to the rear. Harry, following him in, said:

"It's okay, it's okay!"

"Trevor!" Clarke breathed, his eyes bulging in his suddenly pale face. "Trevor Jordan! Oh, my God! Oh, sweet Jesus!"

Harry wished people wouldn't keep using these Names of Power so casually, but on this occasion he understood and made nothing of it.

Trevor Jordan pushed past Harry and took Clarke's other arm; Clarke at once strained back and away from both of them. But again it was a "normal" reaction, nothing to do with his talent. Jordan said, "Darcy, it really *is* me. And I'm okay."

"Okay?" Clarke's mouth opened and closed and the word came out like a croak. He tried again. "Really you? Yes, I can see that. But I know you're dead. I was with you in that Rhodes hospital, remember, when you put a bullet in your brain!''

Harry said, "Can we go inside, sit down, talk?''

"Talk?'' Clarke looked at him—at both of them—as if they were mad, or as if he was. But then he nodded. "Sure, why not? And then I might wake up!''

In the living room Clarke pointed to chairs, poured drinks like a robot, actually apologizing for the untidiness, and said he wasn't quite settled in yet. And then he very carefully sat down and tossed back his large whiskey in one . . . and at once sprang to his feet again and said, "So for fuck's sake, talk! Convince me that I haven't cracked!''

Harry calmed him down and very quickly explained everything—or almost everything—but without going into the fine details. And when he was through: "So we've come to see you to find out what's going on, what it is that you and E-Branch are up to. Actually, I'm pretty sure I already know. So I'm counting on you to keep them off my back until I get done with what I'm pledged to do.''

Finally, Clarke closed his mouth and turned to stare hard at Jordan. Jordan, yes—looking exactly as Clarke had always known him—but still he took the other's hand and squeezed it, and stared even harder just to be one hundred percent sure. But in the end there was no way round it, this could only be Trevor Jordan. The telepath suffered Clarke's astonished scrutiny and made no complaint as this old friend of so many years standing checked him out, checked every well-remembered line of his face and form.

Jordan's face was fresh, oval, and open, and with his fair, thinning hair falling forward over grey eyes, it would normally look boyish; except that now it was lined with worry and not a little astonishment of its own. His feelings were reflected in the line of his mouth: naturally crooked, it would tighten and straighten out if something was wrong. Which was how it looked now, straight and tight. Well, and Clarke would well understand that.

And Clarke thought: *Good old easygoing Trevor! Transparent as a window, readable as an open book. Such has always been your guise, anyway. As if you'd like people to be able to read you as easily as you read them, like you were trying to compensate for your metaphysical talent, or even apologize for it. Trevor Jordan: sensitive but always determined, I never met the man who didn't like you. And if there was such a one, why, you'd simply avoid him. And if you really are you, you'll know exactly what I'm thinking.*

Jordan grinned and said, "You missed out the handsome, rangy-limbed, athletic bit! But what's this about 'boyish'? Are you calling me a big kid, Darcy?"

Clarke sat back in his chair and touched his feverish brow with a trembling hand. He didn't know which one of them to look at, Harry Keogh or Trevor Jordan. Finally, he said, "What can I say? Except . . . welcome back, Trevor!"

After more drinks, it was Darcy's turn. He told them what he knew, which wasn't much, and finished up:

"So Paxton must have reported how I sent you the files on those girls, Harry, which was sufficient to get me suspended. As for them coming after you: you know how the branch works almost as well as I do. Of course they'll be coming after you, sooner or later."

Trevor said, "And me?"

"No," Darcy told him, "because tomorrow first thing, I'll go into town and put them in the picture. I could phone the Minister Responsible right now, but at this hour he wouldn't thank me for that. So I'll go in and speak to everyone who is anyone in E-Branch, and make sure they *fully* understand what's going on. It might do the trick and get them off Harry's back for a while.''

''I hope it gets them off my back,'' said the Necroscope unemotionally. ''I really do.'' And he took off his dark-lensed glasses and asked Darcy to dim the lights.

When E-Branch's suspended boss saw Harry's face in the darkened room, he quietly said, ''Harry, I hope so, too . . . for their sake, every last one of them!''

Harry supposed that Darcy was genuine, supposed he was one of only a very few men in the entire world whom he could trust; but the Necroscope's vampire weirdness was strong in him now, and looking at Darcy Clarke he saw a man who was half friend and half enemy. Harry couldn't read the future, not with any certainty—and in any case he knew that prognostication was a dangerous game, fraught with paradoxes—but he could make a damn good guess at what was coming. If he had to stay here in this world longer than he'd planned, if this task he'd set himself took longer than just a few more days, then it could well be that Darcy would be obliged to join the other team. Darcy was an expert, and as Harry's metamorphosis progressed, the Branch would need all the expert help it could get. Eventually, one way or another, even Darcy would turn against him. He'd have no choice: sooner or later the plague carrier would have to be destroyed. It was as simple as that.

''Darcy,'' Harry said, as he turned the lights up again, ''if we ever did come up against one another, why, you'd be just about the only one who could stop me! For which reason I'm half afraid of you. You know I'm a telepath now, but I wonder: would it bother you if I took a closer look into your mind?''

Darcy's talent sensed no danger. Of course not, for

Harry intended him no harm. What he did intend was to take out a sort of insurance policy, one which could be canceled later, when the danger was past. No harm at all to Darcy Clarke the man, only to his talent itself. For that was what the Necroscope feared: to come up against Clarke knowing he couldn't win, that the deflector's guardian angel would protect him. But with his talent taken away from him, Clarke would be impotent. At least for what remained of Harry's term here. Afterwards . . . he would give it back to him.

"Look into my mind?" Darcy repeated him.

Harry nodded. "With your permission. But it has to be of your own free will."

Darcy read nothing into the Necroscope's words. "But can't you read my mind, just like Trevor here?"

"This is different," said Harry. "For this you need to invite me in, as if your mind was a door which you were opening for me."

Darcy shrugged. "Anything you say." His eyes met the other's and locked on them, and in another moment Harry was into his mind.

The mechanism Harry sought wasn't difficult to find, and he saw at once that it was a freak, a mutation. It was Clarke's unique talent, which all of his life had protected him from external dangers but was impotent to save itself from the internal danger which was Harry Keogh. And even if it could save itself it did nothing, because Harry meant no harm.

There was no trigger Harry could jam, so he simply wrapped the entire mechanism in a fragment of Wellesley's blanket. The job took as long as it takes to tell and then he was out again. And he was satisfied that Clarke's guardian angel had been gagged, for the time being at least.

"Is that it?" Darcy frowned. "Are you satisfied I'll do you no harm?"

Absolutely, Harry said to himself, while outwardly he merely nodded. *Because if you try you'll have no protection, which means I'll at least be able to protect myself.*

And then he heard another voice in his head, Jordan's, saying: *Which means he's no longer protected from anything. Won't you at least tell him what you've done?*

No, Harry answered. *You know Darcy: he'd become paranoid about his safety in a moment. That was always his paradox, that despite this weird talent of his, still he looked after himself like he was accident-prone or something.*

I hope he'll be all right, that's all, said the other.

"Well?" Darcy prompted Harry.

"I'm satisfied you won't go against me," the Necroscope told him. "And now we have to be on our way."

Jordan said, "It strikes me as likely that the Branch will know we've been here. If you want to stay on their good side, Darcy, you might like to call the Duty Officer and confirm it. Let them see that you're not in collusion with us. And at the same time you might use your good offices to clear me."

Darcy pulled a wry face. "Actually, my 'offices' aren't looking any too hot right now," he said. "But certainly, I'll give it a try." He looked at Harry. "So where are you two off to now? Or shouldn't I ask?"

"You shouldn't ask—" Harry answered, "—but I'll tell you, anyway: we're tracking your serial killer. I sort of got hooked up on it. That's the job I want finished before I move on."

Darcy nodded. "That way you'll leave a clean sheet behind you, Harry, which is the way it should be. You'll always be the right sort of legend: famous instead of infamous.''

Harry said nothing. Fame, even infamy, didn't concern him. All that mattered was his obsession. What was more, he knew why it had become an obsession. He was being chased off his territory, forced to vacate his very own world, which he had fought for. Not physically driven out—not yet, anyway—but soon. And the vampire, especially one of the Wamphyri, is tenacious and territorial. Frustrated almost beyond endurance, Harry was fighting back. But if he must take it out on someone, then at least let that someone be a fiend in his own right. Namely, the serial killer, the necromancer, the torturer of Penny and those other poor innocents. Even Pamela Trotter, innocent, yes. Compared to *him*, anyway.

It was time Harry and Trevor Jordan were on their way. They said the usual farewells, very simply, and Harry told Jordan to close his eyes again. Darcy Clarke watched them go and when they were no longer there held out his trembling hand into the space where they'd passed through a Möbius door into nothing.

And that was all he found there.

Nothing . . .

II: Finding Johnny

IN EDINBURGH IT WOULD SOON BE DAWN, BUT HARRY Keogh knew that things—all sorts of things—were rapidly coming to a head and he wasn't nearly ready to ease off now. Now that he'd started this job his one thought was to get it finished. In darkness or, if needs be, in light.

Early summer sunlight would be a problem from now on in, but it was more an inconvenience than a threat proper. The sun wouldn't kill him—not yet, anyway— but taken in large doses it would sicken and weaken him. His glasses helped keep its glare out of his eyes; his floppy hat protected his head and face but was a dead giveaway; he must keep his hands in his pockets for long periods, which gave him the slovenly look of a delinquent youth or a Labour politician but was absolutely necessary. Only the British weather, almost invariably mean, was on his side. Trevor Jordan, on the other hand, suffered no such restrictions and could come and go as he pleased; and with Harry's help, go as far as he pleased and instantly.

In the Necroscope's Bonnyrig house they drank coffee (Harry would prefer good red wine but needed a resupply), and split the list of Frigis Express depots down the middle. They would work through them alphabetically until they found what they were looking for. Jordan would take the day shift with Harry supplying the transport; Harry would do nights with Jordan for lookout. The telepath had asked what was the big deal with this job and Harry had showed him a series of vivid mind-pictures taken from Penny Sanderson and Pamela Trotter, and now Jordan was as eager as he was. There was a monster loose in the world and he had to die.

"There'll be night watchmen on these places, I'm sure," Jordan said, studying his half of the list, "but at this hour of the morning they'll be kipping off: asleep in some secret corner. We could do a few of the depots right now, before the drivers or packers or whatever get in."

"The bloke we're after is a driver," Harry said. "He uses the M1 and possibly the A1 or A7. Maybe we should start with depots close to those major routes."

Jordan had been glancing through the files on the murdered girls. Penny's report seemed to interest him greatly. Ignoring what the Necroscope had just said, he asked, "Harry, did you know Penny's body was found in the gardens under the castle's walls?"

Harry frowned. "Yes. Is that significant?"

"It could be," the other answered. "There are quite a few small, specialized units housed in the castle. For all we know our man from Frigis delivered meat to the various messes and cookhouses that night, and when the coast was clear he bundled Penny over the wall."

Harry nodded. "I'll check out the exact spot where

she was found. I remember looking over the wall. There are places where it rears over grassy ledges and steep banks, where the drop is only a few feet, and if she fell—or was tossed—her body might slip and slither a bit without breaking anything or suffering any real damage. Because apart from the damage and suffering *he* had caused her, she wasn't in bad shape." His gaunt face had turned angry as he remembered Penny as she had been the first time he saw her. Shaking his head to dismiss the memory, he growled, "Anyway, I'll look at it. If it seems at all likely or even possible . . . well, it could be you've narrowed down the field a little. Thanks, Trevor." And then, ruefully: "As you can see, I'd never have made the grade as a detective, or even a common or garden policeman!"

"Listen," Jordan told him. "You drop me off in Edinburgh right now and let me follow it up. Let's face it, you've been seen up in the castle. People may remember you. But they don't know me. I'll take this file with me. I still have an old E-Branch identity card I picked up from the flat. It's as good as a policeman's uniform for getting me into places to gather information. Then, while I concentrate on this end of the job, you can get on with checking out the list of depots."

Harry saw the sense of it. "All right," he said. "And we'll meet back here tonight. Meanwhile, we can easily contact each other if anything breaks. But you have to understand that the sun hampers me. It might stop me getting through to you or you to me. On the other hand, if the day is dull, everything will be okay. The only thing is . . . ." He paused uncertainly.

"Yes?" Jordan waited.

"You'll be on your own," the Necroscope continued. "If the Branch decides to move on me, they'll be picking my friends up, too."

"But picking them *up*," Jordan repeated him. "Not picking them off! And anyway, Darcy said he'd take care of that."

Harry nodded. "But he can't take care of the fact that I'm a vampire. And you know the Branch won't be taking any chances, Trevor. In fact I'd lay you odds that my warrant has already been issued, and that right now they're busy closing off any boltholes. For now . . . they'll probably lay off this place, because it's mine and I know it better than they do. But sooner or later even this house of mine won't be safe. Hell, it would be the perfect place to settle with me! Out of the way, alone and lonely."

"Morbid's not the way to go, Harry," the other told him. "Let's for now just try to find this Johnny, right? Plenty of time then to sort the rest of it." And the Necroscope knew he was right. All except the "plenty of time" part . . .

The following morning, the Minister Responsible called Darcy Clarke into E-Branch HQ. When Clarke walked into what had once been his office, the Minister was seated at his old desk . . . and Geoffrey Paxton was standing in one corner of the room, arms folded across his chest and with his back to the reinforced-glass windows. Clarke could do without Paxton picking at his mind, but he was no longer in a position to complain about it.

After apparently casual nods of greeting or acknowledgment, the Minister remarked how ragged Clarke looked; to which he replied, "I was up late. In fact I'd just managed to snatch an hour or two when your office called to arrange this meeting. Well, that was good, for I was coming in anyway. You see, last night I had a couple of visitors. Except I'm afraid you're not much likely to believe me when I tell you who one of them was.''

Paxton spoke up at once. "We know who they were, Clarke," he said sourly. "Harry Keogh and Trevor Jordan—vampires!"

Clarke had been ready for that. He sighed and turned to the Minister. "Do we have to have this meathead in on this? I mean, if he must forever be wriggling about like a fucking great maggot in people's heads, can't it be from a distance? Say, right outside the door here?"

Unruffled, the Minister stared right back at him. "Are you saying that Paxton is wrong, Clarke?"

Clarke sighed again. "I saw Harry and Trevor last night, yes. He's right that far."

"So you're saying that Keogh and Jordan aren't vampires?" The Minister's voice was very quiet.

Clarke looked at the him, looking away, chewed his bottom lip. And the Minister prompted him: "They *are* vampires?"

Clarke faced him again and said, "Jordan . . . isn't."

"But Keogh is?"

Clarke snapped, "But you were already pretty sure of that, right? All thanks to''—he glanced fire at Paxton—"to this slimy shit! Yes, Harry's been contaminated. He picked up this bloody thing protecting us—every single one of us—doing a job out in the Greek islands which *I* had asked him to help us with. So that, in my book at least, he's not about to turn killer now! What more can I tell you?"

"We think quite a lot," Paxton answered, but softly now, his pasty face reddening from the sting of Clarke's insult.

Clarke looked at him, looked at the Minister, and felt no rapport. He wasn't getting through to them at all. "Why don't you let me tell it my way?" he pleaded.

"And why don't you try listening to me? Who knows, you may even learn something!"

But Paxton said, "Yes, and we might get thrown right off the track, too."

Clarke glared at him, looked at the Minister across his desk, and said, "Look, your pet parrot here isn't making much sense. Shit, I don't understand a word! Do you know what he's raving about?"

The Minister came to a decision, gave an abrupt nod, and said, "Clarke, I'm going to give it to you straight. E-Branch was monitoring your place last night. Yours and Jordan's both. You see, we knew even before you did that Jordan was back from the dead, which is to say undead. What? A man dead and gone, yet up and about among the living? Undead! That's how we see it, the only way we *can* see it. And not only Jordan but one of those murdered girls, too. Vampires, for there's nothing else can they be."

Clarke desperately cut in, "But if you'll only listen to me—"

But the Minister wasn't listening. "We know what time Keogh got to Jordan's flat, the time they left it together, and where they went, and the fact that however much we *don't* know—and even if you hadn't admitted as much— still we'd be absolutely sure that Harry Keogh *is* a vampire! How can we be so sure? Because he carries all the stigmata. You could say he even smells of vampire: which is to say he covers himself in mind-smog. Do you follow me so far?"

"Of course I do," Clarke answered, feeling his desperation increasing by leaps and bounds, knowing that the Minister was building a case, but what sort of case? Against whom? He had to take one last stab at getting through to him. "But can't you see that even in this you're wrong? With all due respect, you don't know anything about vampires. You've had no experience of them. You're not even talented. You only know what you've read or heard from others. And hearsay can't make up for experience. See, this mind-smog you're talking about is something Harry can't control. He doesn't 'cover himself' with it, it just is. It's a result of what he is. Like a dog has a tail, Harry has mind-smog. It isn't deliberate. In fact if he could get rid of it he would, for it's a dead giveaway!''

The Minister looked questioningly at Paxton, who nodded however grudgingly. Or perhaps it wasn't so much a grudging nod as a grim one. A nod of affirmation? And even as his apprehension went up another notch, so Clarke said, ''So you see how easy it is to make mistakes?''

Unblinking, unwavering, the Minister said, ''All vampires have this mind-smog, right?''

Clarke did blink, however, as his nerves started to jump. There was nothing to fear here, for his talent would warn him of it, but still his nerves were jumping. ''As far as we know, yes,'' he answered. ''All of them that we've dealt with, anyway. When a telepath tries to scan a vampire, he gets mind-smog.''

''Darcy Clarke''—the Minister's face was white now—''it must have taken a lot of nerve to come here. Either that or you're a madman, or you really don't know what's happened to you.''

''Happened to me?'' Clarke could feel the tension building and didn't know what it was about. ''What the hell are you talking . . . ?''

''You have mind-smog!'' Paxton spat the words out.

Clarke's jaw dropped. ''*What*? I have . . . ?''

The Minister raised his voice. ''You out there, Miss Cleary, and Ben. You can come in now.''

The door opened and Millicent Cleary stepped inside,

with Ben Trask right behind her. The girl looked at Clarke and her voice was breathless as she said, "It's true, sir. You . . . you have it." She had always called Clarke "sir." He looked at her, backed away a step, and shook his head.

But Ben Trask said, "Darcy, she's telling the truth. Even Paxton is telling the truth."

Clarke took two hesitant steps towards him . . . and Trask narrowed his eyes, backed off, and held up his arms to ward him off! Clarke saw the look in his old friend's eyes and couldn't believe it. "Ben, it's me!" he said. "I mean, with your talent you have to know that I'm telling the truth, too!"

"Darcy," Trask answered, still backing away, "you've been got at. It's the only answer."

"Got at?"

"Without you knowing it. You *believe* you're telling the truth, and on our own that would be enough to throw me. But it's two to one, Darcy. And you have been pretty close to Harry Keogh."

Clarke spun on his heel, looked at the faces surrounding him. The Minister, white as chalk behind his desk. Paxton, grim-faced, his right hand nervously playing with the lapel of his jacket. Trask, whose talent had never once let him down—until now. And Millicent Cleary, still respectful for all that she'd just accused him of being a monster!

"Crazy, every damned one of you!" Clarke shakily husked. He thrust his left hand into his pocket, brought out his Branch ID, and tossed it onto the desk. "That's it; I'm through with all of this; finished with the Branch for good. I'm walking." He reached with his right hand inside his jacket and dragged his issue 9mm pistol into view—

—And Paxton yelled, "Freeze!" and aimed the gun which he had produced just a moment earlier.

Astonished, Clarke turned towards him—turned his empty gun towards him, too—and Paxton squeezed off two shots.

Simultaneous with the deafening reports, Millicent Cleary and Ben Trask yelled, *"No!"*

Too late, for Clarke had been hurled back halfway across the room by the first bullet, then swatted from his feet and tossed against the wall by the second. His gun went flying as he crumpled to his knees against the bloodied wall, and his hand crept tremblingly to an area over his heart. There were two holes in his jacket, both turning red and dripping through his twitching fingers. "Shit!" he whispered. And: "What—?"

He fell forward onto his face, rolled over onto his side, and Trask and the Cleary girl went to their knees beside him. The Minister was on his feet, aghast, holding on to the edge of the desk to keep from falling; and Paxton had come forward, his gun still at the ready, face pale as a sheet of paper with holes punched out for eyes and mouth. "He had a gun." He gasped the words out. "He was going to use his gun!"

The Minister said, "I . . . I thought he was trying to hand it in. That's what it looked like to me."

Ben Trask cradled Clarke's head, moaning, "Jesus, Darcy! *Jesus!*" The girl had unbuttoned Clarke's jacket, torn open his crimson shirt. But the blood had almost stopped pumping.

Clarke looked down disbelievingly at his chest and the red life leaking out of him. "Not . . . not possible!" he said. And the fact was that yesterday it wouldn't have been.

"Darcy, Darcy!" Trask said again.

"Not possible!" Clarke murmured for the last time,

before his eyes filmed over and his head lolled into Trask's lap. And as yet, no one had even called for a doctor or an ambulance.

For long seconds the tableau held . . . until Paxton broke the silence with, "Get away from him! Are you crazy? Get *away* from him!"

Trask and the girl looked at him.

"His blood," Paxton told them. "You have his blood all over you! He'll contaminate you!"

Trask stood up and the horror slowly cleared from his eyes. The horror of what had happened, anyway. But his horror of Paxton was something else. "Darcy will contaminate . . . ?" he started to repeat Paxton, and took a long loping pace towards him. "His blood will contaminate us?"

Paxton backed off. "What the hell's wrong with you?"

"Darcy was right," Trask snarled. "About you." He pointed at the Minister Responsible: "And you." And he took another pace after Paxton.

"Back off!" Paxton warned him, waving his gun.

Trask caught his wrist and twisted it, and his strength was furious. The gun went clattering to the floor. "He never spoke a truer word," Trask said, holding Paxton at arm's length like a piece of stinking, rotten meat. "You don't know anything about vampires except what you've read or been told. You have no experience of them. If you did you'd know that bullets don't stop them—not for long, anyway! But poor Darcy there, if you have any talent at all you'll know that he's stone dead. And you killed him!"

"I . . . I . . ." Paxton struggled but he couldn't free himself from Trask's grip.

"Contaminate?" Trask grated through clenched teeth. He drew Paxton close and rubbed Clarke's blood into his hair, his eyes and nostrils. "You piece of shit, what could

289

contaminate you?'' He drew back a ham of a hand and bunched it into a fist, and—

"Trask!'' the Minister snapped. "Ben! Let Paxton go! Let it be! What's done is done. An accident, maybe. A mistake, possibly. But it's done. And it's only one of several things we're not going to like doing.''

Trask's fist hung in midair, shaking with its need to crash into Paxton's face. But as the Minister's words sank in, so he tossed the telepath away from him. And lurchingly, almost drunkenly, he went back to Clarke's crumpled, lifeless body.

The Minister said to Paxton, "Get a doctor . . . and an ambulance.'' Then he saw the look on Paxton's face.

The telepath had recovered both his wits and his nerve; he was cleaning his face with a large pocket handkerchief and shaking his head. His look said, *Think what you're saying, what you're doing.* And out loud he said, "We don't need a doctor or an ambulance, just an incinerator. Clarke's for burning, by us, right now. Right or wrong, we can't take any chances with him. He's for the fire just as soon as possible. And me, I'm for bathing. Trask, Cleary, I know how you must feel, but if I were you—''

"No, you don't know how we feel.'' Ben Trask looked up at him, all emotion gone now from his face.

"Anyway,' Paxton continued, 'I'd bathe if I were you. And right now.''

The Minister indicated the door. "Go on, then,'' he told Paxton. "Go and arrange . . . disposal. Do it now— and take shower, too, if you feel it's necessary—then report back to me.''

And after the telepath left the room, past the gaping espers where they crowded the corridor: "Ben,'' said the Minister, "the killing has started. Right or wrong, like Paxton said, it's started. And we both know it has to go on. So from now on I want you in charge of this thing.

I want you to run the entire show, until it's sorted out one way or the other.''

Trask stood up, leaned against the all, looked at the Minister, and thought: *One way or the other? No, it can only be one way, for the other is unthinkable. Well, someone has to do it, and I'm as experienced as any of them. More than most. And at least if I'm running it I'll know that that idiot Paxton won't be doing any more damage.*

In the old days it would have been Darcy, Ken Layard, Trevor Jordan, and a handful of others. And Harry, of course. But this time they'd be hunting Harry himself, and that was different. And despite what Clarke had said, it looked like they'd be hunting Jordan, too. And the girl, Penny Sanderson? Jesus, according to the file she was just a kid! But an undead kid.

"All right?" said the Minister.

And Trask sighed and answered with an almost imperceptible nod. Yes, it was all right. And Paxton could well have been right, too. If there had been something—anything at all—wrong with Darcy . . .

Trask looked at the girl, her bloodied hands and blouse. "Shower," he said simply. "And make a good job of it." Then, when he and the Minister were alone, he said, "When Darcy's been . . . burned, we have to scatter the ashes. Scatter them far and wide." He gave a small shudder. "For the fact is, Harry Keogh does things with ashes. And I really don't think I ever want to see Darcy again. Not on his feet, anyway."

9:40 A.M.

Harry Keogh had just finished examining the personnel files at Frigis Express's Darlington depot when three things happened simultaneously. One: the depot clerk, whom Harry had lured from his tiny box of an office

291

with a bogus telephone call, returned unexpectedly. Two: Harry felt a pang—almost a pain—of a sort he'd never experienced before, within his chest, as if someone had doused his heart with ice water. And three: the fading echo of an unrecognized cry bounced off his mind to ricochet into an unreachable metaphysical limbo of its own. And it seemed to the Necroscope that whatever its source, it was intended specifically for him: as if his name had been called from the gulf between life and death.

Deadspeak? But this had been different. Telepathy? Well, maybe. Or a cross between the two? That seemed more likely, and Harry remembered how his mother had described the feeling in her own incorporeal heart when a pup called Paddy had been killed by a car on a Bonnyrig road.

So . . . had someone died? But who? And why had he cried out to Harry?

"Who the fuck are you?" demanded the burly, shirtsleeved, redheaded clerk, as he herded Harry into the shadows of a dusty corner where the metal filing cabinet met the wall. He gaped at the former contents of the cabinet, now spilling across the floor.

Harry barely glanced at the man's suspicious, mottled face and said, *"Shh!"*

"Shh!?" the other repeated him, disbelievingly. "You'll get shh!, brother, breaking in here! Now, what's the score?"

Harry was trying desperately to hang on to the diminishing, ethereal echo of . . . a cry for help? Was that what it had been? "Look," he told the very untypical clerk, "be quiet a minute, will you?" He tried to push by him.

"Why you—!" Blotches of angry red appeared on the man's jowly cheeks. "A con man and thief, right? I recognize your voice. It was you on the phone—*right*? Well, you picked the wrong man this time, thief!'' He grabbed Harry by the lapels and looked like he was going to butt him in the face.

The Necroscope continued to concentrate on the cry, and at the same time reached out and caught his assailant by the throat. With one huge hand he held him at bay, choking, and with the other he reached up and took off his dark spectacles. The clerk saw his eyes and choked all the more, and commenced windmilling his arms as Harry shoved him effortlessly backwards, driving him across the floor. Finally, the clerk's legs hit the edge of his desk and he sat down in a plastic paper tray, shattering it with his fat backside.

Still Harry held him, and still he listened for a repeat performance of the cry. But it was gone now, probably disappeared forever.

Harry felt anger expanding inside him—felt frustrated, cheated—and his hand on the clerk's windpipe was like iron. His nails bit into the man's flesh like it was putty, and Harry knew that if he wanted to he could crush his Adam's apple and tear his throat out all in one. What's more, the thing inside was urging him to do it, *do it!* But he didn't. Instead he swept the clerk from the desktop and sent him crashing down among the debris of his shattering chair and a wooden wastepaper basket.

"My-my . . . G-*God!*" the clerk coughed and spat and massaged his throat, and crawled dazedly into a corner where he turned and looked back fearfully at the spot where the blood-eyed, fanged, furious stranger had been standing. But of course the Necroscope was no longer there. No one was there.

And again the clerk gurgled, "My God! My g-good G-*God!*"

* * *

Working from his list, alphabetically, Harry had already investigated three Frigis depots and installations: the vehicle depot at Alnwick, the slaughterhouse and meat dressing station in Bishop Auckland, and lastly the freezer complex in Darlington. So far he had copied the addresses of four possibles, all of them "Johns" or "Johnnys" and all drivers for the firm. Now, however, with the morning only halfway through, the weird mind-cry out of nowhere had disturbed him, damaged his resolve and destroyed his concentration; to such an extent that he took the Möbius route home to Bonnyrig, and from there contacted Trevor Jordan at the Castle on the Mount in Edinburgh.

Harry? Jordan came back at once, his telepathic "voice" full of his relief that the Necroscope was in touch again. *I tried to reach you but your mind-smog was too dense, and getting thicker all the time. Can you come and get me? I think I may have a lead.*

Harry nodded, just as if he was speaking to someone directly in front of him and not ten miles away, and said, *Do you know the Laird's Larder? It's a coffee shop up there just off the Royal Mile. Ask anyone and they'll direct you. I'll be there in five minutes. But Trevor, tell me: has anything peculiar happened? Have you felt anything strange? Do I need to be, well, more than usually careful how I move?*

Watchers, you mean? The Branch? (A mental shake of the other's head.) *Not that I've detected. Maybe a tentative touch now and then, but nothing you could nail down. Nothing concentrated, anyway. If they have people up here, then they're too good for me. And I'm pretty damn good!*

No static? Paxton, maybe?

I don't feel any static. Distantly, maybe, but nothing

local. As for Paxton: I'm sure I'd be able to pick him up twenty miles away. And you?

Just an . . . *experience*, Harry answered. *In Darlington.*

Darlington? (The Necroscope could almost see the other's eyebrows going up.) *Now, there's a coincidence! And did you find any Johnnys in Darlington?*

Harry was intrigued. *Two*, he replied. *And one of them a real-life 'Johnny.' That's how he spells his name, anyway: Johnny Courtney. The other is called John Found.*

And now he pictured Jordan's grim nod as the telepath said: *Yes, and Dragosani was a foundling, too, wasn't he?*

Harry said, *Is that supposed to mean something?* He knew it was.

Better believe it! Jordan confirmed.

See you outside the Laird's Larder, Harry told him. *Five minutes . . .*

He waited out the five minutes in a fever of anticipation, then made it six to be sure Jordan had got there, and finally Möbius-tripped to the steep, cobbled road just off the Royal Mile. He emerged from the Continuum on a crowded, bustling pavement where tourists and locals alike were clustered like bees in a hive, jostling and filled with purpose as they went about their various businesses. No one noticed that Harry was suddenly there; people loomed everywhere, from every direction, side-stepping each other; the Necroscope was just another face in the crowd.

Jordan was in the doorway of the Laird's Larder. He spotted Harry, grabbed his elbow, and guided him off the street into the shade. Harry was glad of that, for the sun was out and it had grown to be more than a mere irritation. He now actively hated it. "Buy three sandwiches," he told the telepath. "Steak for me and rare as

295

they've got it, whatever you like for yourself, and anything with plenty of bread around it for the third. Okay?''

Mystified, Jordan nodded and went to the busy counter. He ordered, was served, and came back to Harry where he waited. Harry took his arm, said, ''Close your eyes,'' and ushered him through a Möbius door. To anyone watching it would look like they just stepped out of the coffee shop into the street. Except they didn't arrive in the street. Instead, a moment later, they emerged two miles away by the lake on the crest of the vast volcanic outcrop called Arthur's Seat. There was an empty bench where they sat down and ate awhile in silence, and Harry tore up the third sandwich into small pieces which he fed to the ducks and a lone swan that came paddling to the feast.

And eventually, the Necroscope said, ''Tell me about it.''

But Jordan answered, ''You first. What's all this about an 'experience' in Darlington? You sounded like something had worried you, Harry. Something other than finding a couple of suspect Johnnys, that is. I mean, tracking this maniac down is important—no one would deny that—but there's such a thing as personal safety, too. So you'd better tell me, are there going to be problems?''

''Oh, yes,'' Harry answered. ''And soon. Something inside tells me that not even Darcy Clarke can do anything about that. But that's not what this was about.'' And as best he could he explained what he had felt, and told Jordan how his mother had reacted to the death of a small dog.

''You think someone died this morning? Any idea who?''

Harry shook his head. ''Someone cried out to me, that's all. I think so, anyway.''

"And your deadspeak? Can't you . . . make inquiries?"

Harry gave a wry snort. "The Great Majority don't want to know me," he answered. "Not now. Not any longer. I can't say I blame them." He shrugged, then brightened a little. "On the other hand, if someone did die and still wants to contact me, then pretty soon he'll be able to do just that."

"Oh?"

"Through deadspeak," Harry explained. "Except he'll have to contact me in person, for I wouldn't know where to start looking. And it will have to be by night. During the daylight hours the sun interferes too much. If not for this hat of mine I'd be in trouble. Even *with* the hat I feel tired, sick, unable to think straight. There were a few clouds earlier but they're clearing. And the brighter it gets the duller I get!" He stood up and threw the last handful of crumbs onto the surface of the lake between the crags. "Let's get out of here. I could use some shade."

They took the Möbius route to the gloomy old house on the outskirts of Bonnyrig, then telepathically probed the countryside all around. "Nothing," Jordan declared, and Harry agreed.

And finally: "All right"—the Necroscope threw off his hat and sprawled gratefully in an easy chair—"now it's your turn. Just what *did* you discover up there at the castle? I can tell that something's excited you."

"You're right." Jordan grinned. "It was my chance to pay you back, Harry, for what you've done for me. For my life, my resurrection. My God, I'm alive, and I know how wonderful it is! So I wanted things to work out. You could say I almost willed it to happen, and it did."

"You think you've found our man, or monster?" Harry leaned forward eagerly in his chair.

"I'm pretty sure I have," the telepath answered. "Yes, I'm pretty damn sure!"

III Johnny . . . Found

"I SHOWED MY E-BRANCH ID AT THE GUARDROOM,"
Jordan commenced his story, "and told them I was in-
vestigating the death of the girl who was found under the
walls. I said we'd had our wires crossed the first time,
because she wasn't who we'd thought she was, which was
why we were looking into it again from square one.

"The squaddies on duty had read all about it in the
newspapers, and anyway, I wasn't the first investigator
they'd seen. Not even the first today. They told me that
in fact there were already two plainclothesmen in the
castle, down in the Sergeant's mess. That piece of information stopped me dead for a second or two while I
considered it, but then I thought what the hell? For after
all, I was E-Branch . . . wasn't I? Well, I had been until
very recently. Anyway, I never had any problem dealing
with the law. In fact the police had always shown me,
and E-Branch in general, a lot of respect. And vice versa.

"So I asked directions to the Warrant Officer's and Sergeant's mess and made my way there.

"Edinburgh Castle is a massive place, the greater part of which is never even glimpsed by the tourists and general public. Your average tourist knows that the Castle Esplanade is where they hold the Edinburgh Tattoo—with room to build a stadium of eight thousand seats, royal boxes and all, and a hardstanding that takes the military's massed bands, motorcycle and other vehicular displays, shows from all around the world, you name it—but the vast stone complex *beyond* Mons Meg, the One O'Clock Gun, and Ye Olde Tea Shoppe (or whatever it is they've named that café in the crag) remains a mystery to most people. And where the way is roped off, that's where the real castle begins. But you've been there, Harry, and know what it's like: a maze of alleys and gantlets and courtyards . . . a fantastic place! And one that's easy to lose your way in.

"Eventually, I found the Sergeant's mess and the two Jock plainclothes officers, who were talking to a Sergeant Cook and his civilian assistants and jotting down a few notes. I showed my ID and asked if I could sit in on their questioning, and they didn't bat an eyelid between them. They knew how the Branch—in the shape of Darcy Clarke and yourself, Harry—had been helping out with the job.

"Anyway, I'd arrived right on cue, because they were asking about the night of the murder, especially about any deliveries of refrigerated meat which had been made to the cookhouse that night. Apparently, forensic had alerted them to beast blood on Penny's clothes, do you see?

"Well, you can imagine how it felt, Harry, to be right there when the Cook Sergeant got out his register of deliveries to check details of the beast carcasses that had

300

come in . . . yes, from Frigis Express! Naturally, I said nothing, just kept my ears wide open and my mouth tight shut, and took in as much as I could get. Which was quite a bit; because this overweight, red-faced, hot-and-bothered Sergeant's mess cook was efficient to a fault. He not only kept a record of dates and times of all deliveries of foodstuffs—and copies of his own countersigned receipts, which bore the signatures of his suppliers—but he even had the registration numbers of delivery vehicles, too! And naturally, I made a mental note of the number of the truck which had made the deliveries that night.

"This is how the delivery system works:

"During the day the esplanade gets crowded, and anyway, Edinburgh's streets are no place for big articulated trucks during daylight hours. So Frigis Express delivers at night. Of course, big vehicles can't make it under the arch of the guardroom and up the narrow gantlet, so they park down on the esplanade and the cookhouse sends down a driver in a military Land-Rover to collect the carcasses. The Frigis driver passes the meat straight out from the back of his truck into the back of the Land-Rover, which then conveys it up to the main cookhouse. And the Frigis driver goes up as a passenger in the Land-Rover to get his docket signed. And sometimes he'll have a beer with the Cook Sergeant in his little office, before walking back down to his truck on the dark esplanade. By night, of course, the esplanade is empty and he has plenty of room to turn the big vehicle round and get out of there.

"So . . . the plainclothes officers wanted to know if this had been the routine on the night of the murder, and it had. In fact the Cook Sergeant knew this delivery man quite well; he worked for Frigis out of Darlington (yes, Darlington, Harry) and made deliveries to the castle every three or four weeks. And when the Sergeant was around they'd usually have a pint together in his office.

"As for his name: well, his signature was a scrawl, quite unreadable, possibly even disguised . . . all except for the 'F' which started his surname. But the fat Sergeant was willing to swear that he referred to himself as—that's right—'Johnny'!

"Well, that was about it. When the officers were satisfied with what they'd got I came out with them. Along the way I made mention of how they seemed to be doing okay without E-Branch on this one. It was pretty obvious they weren't exactly sure what the Branch is all about—hell, who is, except Branch members?—but that they guessed we were some sort of higher echelon intelligence organization which 'fools about,' however successfully, with psychic stuff: table-rapping and divining and such. And I suppose in a way they were right at that.

"Then we spent a little time looking over the wall in various places and down on the gardens towards Princes Street, and sure enough there are places you could dump a body without breaking its bones. The Jocks seemed especially interested in looking down on one spot, and I guessed that's where Penny had been found. A peep inside their minds told me I was right.

"Finally, as I parted company with them on the esplanade, I said, 'We'll be in touch, and if this Johnny bloke doesn't work out the way you—'

"But one of them broke in on me: 'Oh, we're pretty sure he's the one. And we can wait a few days longer. Actually, we'd like to catch this bastard in the act of picking up some girl before we move on him. He's been doing these jobs of his thick and fast, so we think he'll try it on again the next time out. Another day or two at most. And you'd better believe we'll be right behind him . . .' Then he shrugged and let it go at that.

"So I told them good luck, and that was it. I felt great—great to be alive, and even better that I'd made a dent in the case—and so had a beer on the Royal Mile. Following which I just waited around for you to contact me. End of story . . ."

The Necroscope seemed a little disappointed. "You didn't get a general description of this man, or discover when he's driving for Frigis again?"

"These things weren't in their thoughts," Jordan answered, shaking his head. "And anyway, if I'd had to concentrate on scanning their minds I might have slipped up, done something stupid, given myself away. Remember, you and I are both telepaths. When we read each other and it comes over strong and true, that's because we're doing it deliberately. But reading the mind of an ordinary person is different. They're cluttered things, minds, and rarely concentrate on anything for more than a moment or two."

Harry nodded. "I didn't mean to put you down. What you've done is wonderful. It's worked out perfectly—so far. But now I want to find out something about this man's background, like *why* he's the way he is. Such knowledge might be of use, that's all. If not to me, to E-Branch after I've gone. Also, I'm curious about his name. You said something about Dragosani also being a foundling? Well, maybe there's more to that than you thought or intended. So . . . I have one or two things to learn about this Johnny Found. And of course, I want to get to him before the police. He'd be charged with murder, I know, but what he's done and would still do is worth a lot more than that. He came on very cruel. And that's how he should go out."

The Necroscope's voice as he finished speaking was a deep growl sinking deeper all the time. Jordan was happy to keep out of his mind, but he couldn't help thinking to himself: *Mr. Johnny Found—who or whatever, or whyever, you are—I wouldn't be in your shoes for all the gold in Fort Knox!*

Ben Trask had called his briefing for 2:00 P.M. and all available E-Branch operatives were present. The Minister Responsible was there, too, accompanied by Geoffrey Paxton, who Trask really hadn't expected to see. But he made no fuss about it; it had dawned on him that the job was too important to let personalities interfere. It just struck him as incongruous that while a low-life specimen such as Paxton was safe and legitimate, the good stuff such as Harry Keogh had crashed foul of fate and was about to become a victim of his own methods.

Sure, for it had been Harry who showed the Branch how to do this sort of thing. How to set it up, what weapons to use—the stake, the sword, the fire—and how to strike. In order to kill vampires.

When everyone was present Trask wasted no time but got right down to it:

"By now all of you know what Harry Keogh has become," he began. "Which is to say, he's the most dangerous creature who ever lived . . . *partly* because he carries this plague of vampirism, which could consume all of us and for which there's no cure. Well, there have been others before Harry and they all succumbed—usually to the Necroscope himself! And that's the rest of what makes him so dangerous: he knows all about it, about us, about . . . just about everything. Now, don't get me wrong: he isn't a superman and never has been, but he is the next best thing. Which was great when he was on our side but isn't quite so hot right now. Oh, yes, and unlike the other vampires the Branch has dealt with, Harry will know we're after him.'' He let that sink in, then continued:

"Some other things that make him dangerous. He's become a telepath, so from now on all you thought-thieves keep a close watch on your minds. If not, Harry will be in there. And if he knows what we're doing as we're doing it, then he won't be waiting around for it to happen, right? He's a teleport, too, and uses something called the Möbius Continuum to come and go as he pleases. He can be literally *anywhere* he wants to be, instantaneously! Think about that . . .

"Last but not least—that we know of, anyway—Harry is now a necromancer no less than Dragosani was; no, more than Dragosani was. Because Dragosani only *examined* his victims. Harry on the other hand can bring them back from the dead, even from their ashes, we think as vampires. And as such, obviously they'd be working for him. So, what I'm saying is that everything he's previously achieved has now been totally reversed: *he* is our target! Harry, and anyone who works with him.

"A lot of you will be wondering about Darcy Clarke, so let me put you in the picture. Darcy died . . . by accident.'' Trask at once held up a restraining hand, because he'd seen faces beginning to tighten and mouths opening questioningly. "It *was* an accident of sorts,'' he repeated, "and in its way understandable if not entirely acceptable. Now, I've had to do a lot of soul-searching myself in order to come to terms with this, and so I can readily understand your confusion. But Darcy had been changed. He must have been, else we couldn't have killed him. That's right, I said, 'we,' the Branch. If he'd lived he would have been our weakest link, and sooner or later we'd be obliged to deal with him, anyway. But he isn't alive and can't be brought back or . . . interfered with, not where he is now. For we've had him cremated—already, yes—and even now his ashes are being scattered. If he was one of Harry's people, which it has to be said seems likely, then he isn't anymore.

"Okay, I've said it was an accident. But the real accident—or more properly, the tragedy—was that Darcy Clarke and Harry Keogh were friends, and that they'd had a lot of contact with one another. It's as simple as that. Harry's own 'accident' happened to him out in the Greek islands, or more likely in Romania, just a few weeks ago. Since when it's taken him over completely. And conceivably unknown to Darcy—and *just* conceivably unknown or unrealized even by the Necroscope himself—the thing, disease, contagion, whatever and however you think of it, somehow passed between them. That's the way we see it, anyway.

"But the fact is that Darcy had a very bad case of mind-smog, and he'd lost his guardian angel, the talent which had kept him secure through everything the Branch has thrown at him all these years. As for Darcy working with Harry: well, we knew that he'd been passing him information, even before we knew for sure that he'd been changed. Just when these changes occurred isn't easy to tell. They might have been in the wind for some time, but they came to light just last night. For that was when Harry visited Darcy at home. He didn't stay long but after he left . . . then Darcy had mind-smog.

"So that's what I meant when I said Darcy had been changed. When he died . . . he just wasn't Darcy Clarke anymore, not the one we all knew. And now he isn't anyone. But more important, he isn't, and can never be, a threat to the Branch or to the world.

"Harry Keogh very definitely *is*, however, and so are the people we believe he's already contaminated. There are at least two of these: a young girl called Penny Sanderson, and . . . the telepath we knew as Trevor Jordan.'' Again he held up his hand. ''Yes, I know, Trevor was my friend, too. And hell, he was also dead! But he isn't anymore. Harry Keogh has resurrected both of these people from their ashes—which in itself must surely confirm what they've become. Undead!

''So where does all of this leave us? Plainly, it leaves us with a fight on our hands, and one which will take all the skills and efforts of every last one of us. Because if we don't win this one, then there won't *be* a last one of us! Now here's how we go about it:

''As of tonight the Sanderson girl goes under covert surveillance. We're going to leave that to Special Branch. *No* espers to be involved at this stage. Why? Because Keogh or Jordan would pick up on our·people like they were radioactive. So it's the dear old British bobby who covers for us, but without really knowing what it's all about. Just another stakeout as far as they're concerned. Which should be safe enough, for as far as we know the girl's had no contact with Jordan or the Necroscope since Harry . . . well, since he did whatever he did to bring her back. So we just let the common or garden Law keep an eye on her until it's time, then call them off, and finally move in. By which time we'll know how we're going to deal with her.

''Incidentally, if I seem cold-blooded about this, it's because that's how it has to be. I'm the only one who's left of the old crowd, which means I'm the only one who knows what hell is like. I saw it during the Bodescu case, and out in the Greek islands. Anyone who thinks I'm exaggerating hasn't read the Keogh files or Darcy Clarke's report on the Greek thing. And if any one of you really *hasn't* read those items, then he bloody well better had, and now!

''Okay, so as of tonight we'll have the girl covered, and she'll stay that way until we're all set. But she's small fry, and the big fish—the sharks—are still cruising. They're the ones we have to worry about. But how *much* do we have to worry about them? Let's talk about Jordan.

"This morning he was at Edinburgh, in the Castle on the Mount, taking an interest in the serial killer case. Darcy Clarke had asked for the Necroscope's help on this one, and it looks like Harry got hooked on it. Now he and Jordan seem to be working together on it; don't ask me why, except that Penny Sanderson was one of the killer's victims. Revenge? It could well be, for vampires are like that. If so, then sooner or later Harry and Co. may be having a go at this sex freak.

"As to how we know Jordan was in the castle: he just casually latched onto a couple of plainclothesmen during their investigations up there! He was able to do it because he still has his Branch ID. Later, when one of the investigators mentioned Jordan to a superior—the fact that E-Branch still had a man on this thing—his boss got straight on the phone to us saying thanks but no thanks, they don't need our help anymore, they think they've already got their man. Well, at least we managed to obtain the suspect's name and address, which might come in very handy. Apparently, he's called John or Johnny Found and has a flat in Darlington. So there'll be some common or garden Law watching Mr. Found, too, and I'll be detailing someone to watch *them*—with a warning to stay well out of the picture, for the moment, unless or until Keogh and Jordan decide to move on him.

"What else about Jordan? Well, as you know, Trevor was—I mean is—a pretty good telepath. It could be that that's where Harry got his new talent. For Harry's also a necromancer, remember? And as such he might be able to accumulate talents as he goes, much as Dragosani did. That's speculation, however, and still to be proven. Another thing about Jordan is this: he was always one hell of a nice bloke. Oh, I know, there's no such thing as a nice vampire. You don't have to tell *me* that! But what I'm saying is I don't think evil will come naturally to him. It will probably be a gradual process. I hope so, anyway, because of course his vampirism will quickly enhance his already powerful telepathy. Following which . . . well, put it this way: there won't be any sneaking up on him!

"All right, I'm almost through. You'll all be detailed to your new tasks within the hour, as soon as I can get them worked out. Anything else you're busy with, drop it until you're told otherwise.

"So to sum up on how we're going to work this thing:

"We know that Harry Keogh's favorite haunt—the place he rightly considers his 'territory,' because it's been his home for most of his life—is an old house near Bonnyrig not far out of Edinburgh. We think he must be working out of there, with Jordan assisting him in whatever he's doing. Probably tracking down Johnny Found, or, if they've already located him, gearing themselves up to bring him to some kind of justice. So as well as watching the Sanderson girl and Mr. Found, we're also, obviously, going to keep a covert eye on Harry's old house. But—and I can't stress this too strongly—a *very* surreptitious eye, right?

"If we can get the girl, Harry, and Jordan all at the same time—especially if we can get them on their own, as individuals—that's when we'll move on them. Which might possibly be precipitated if or when Harry and Jordan decide to take out Found. Ideally, we'll wait until we can move on all three of them simultaneously. That way they don't get any warning. What we *mustn't* do is try to pick them off one by one, which would alert the others. Are we straight on that?

"Lastly—or rather before we go on to examine the

tools of our trade—I have something to tell you that I know won't go down at all well: namely that the Minister here has confided in Soviet E-Branch on this thing.'' Trask stared into the small sea of astonished faces, but no one spoke.

"The point is," he went on, "that even if we find a way to trap the Necroscope, which won't be easy, still he'll have a bolthole into a place he could conceivably come back from—bringing God only knows what back with him! Yes, I'm talking about the Gate at the Perchorsk Projekt under the Urals. We've kept tabs on *that* nightmare ever since we found out about it, and we know that the Russians are managing to contain it while they decide on a more satisfactory solution. If we make life intolerable, hopefully impossible, for Harry here, he might just try heading for Starside. So that's why we've confided in the Russians, because we daren't let him go back there. Fine if he wanted to stay there, but monstrous if he ever decided to bring anything back here with him.

"What makes us think he might hide out in another world? A notebook we found an hour ago at Clarke's flat, that's what. Darcy had been jotting down a few thoughts, but that must have been before Harry got to him. It may even be why he got to him. The notes are only a mess of scribble but they make it plain that Darcy thought Harry would skip to Starside. Well, now the Soviets know about Harry, as much as we could tell them, anyway, and they'll be looking out for him. So it looks like the Perchorsk Gate is closed.

"Okay, so now let's consider our . . . equipment. And how to use it. Then we'll get round to breaking you all down into balanced teams and doing a preliminary itemization of your tasks."

Trask removed a blanket from various pieces of equipment laid out on a stout folding table. "It's important you learn how to use this stuff," he said. "The machetes speak for themselves. But be careful with them—they're razor-sharp! As for this: I suppose you all recognize a crossbow when you see one? This third item, however, might not be quite so familiar. It's a lightweight flame-thrower, a new model. So I think maybe we'll take a look at that first.

"This is the fuel tank, which sits on your back like so . . ."

And so it went. The briefing lasted another hour.

Right after sunset Harry made his way to Darlington via the Möbius Continuum. He left Trevor Jordan sleeping (not surprisingly exhausted; his return from Beyond was still like the very strangest dream to him, from which he still feared he might suddenly awaken) in a secret room under the eaves of the house on the river. From the attic room there was a way into the deserted, crumbling old place next door, so that if anything should happen Jordan might use this route to effect something of an escape. But both espers had checked out the psychic "atmosphere" of the locality and there didn't seem to be anything happening; and in any case Jordan had been busy rationalizing his fears in that respect and really couldn't see E-Branch doing a Yulian Bodescu on him. He was satisfied, at least, that they wouldn't do anything rash.

Johnny Found's address in Darlington was the ground-floor flat in an old, four-storied, Victorian terraced house on the outer edge of the town center. The old red bricks were black from being too close to the mainline railway; the windows were bleary; three steps led up from a path in the tiny, overgrown front garden to a communal porch. And behind the façade of that porch—behind the fly-

specked, dingy windows, there in those very rooms—
that was where Found lived.

In the twilight Harry's skin tingled at the thought and
he felt his eager vampire senses intensifying as he walked
the street first one way, then the other, past this gloomy
street-corner residence of a twentieth-century necromancer. The murderer of sweet young Penny Sanderson.

Simple confrontation would be the easy way, of course,
but that wasn't part of the Necroscope's plan. No, for
then the result could only be precipitate: the accused
would either "come quietly," in the parlance of the Law,
or he would react violently. And Harry would kill him.
Which would be far *too* easy.

Found's way, on the other hand, his *modus operandi*,
was cruel, creeping, designed to terrify even before the
terrible act—the monstrous crime itself—was committed.
And Harry was concerned that in his case the punishment should fit the crime. Except . . . there should be
something of a trial, too. But trial as in ordeal, not as in
examination as a precursor to judgment. For if Johnny
Found was in fact the man, then the sentence had already
been passed.

The working day was over; traffic was thinning in the
darkening streets; people wended their ways home. And
some of them entered the house of the necromancer. A
middle-aged woman with a bulging plastic carrier-bag,
letting herself in fumblingly through the front door; a
young woman with straggly hair and a whining child
pulling on her arm, calling out after the woman with the
bag to wait for her and hold the door; an older man in
coveralls, weary and slump-shouldered, carrying a
leather bag of tools.

A light came on in a garret room under steeply sloping
eaves. Another winked into being on the second floor,

and one on the third. Harry looked away for a moment, up and down the street, then looked back—

—In time to see a fourth, much dimmer light come on in an angled corner window in the ground-floor flat. But he hadn't seen Found go in.

The house stood on a corner; there must be a side door; Harry waited for traffic to clear, then crossed to the other side of the road and turned the corner. And there it was: a recessed doorway at the side, Johnny Found's private access to his lair. And Johnny himself was in there.

Harry crossed the cobbled street away from the house and merged with the shadows of the building on the far side. He turned and leaned back a little against the wall, and looked at the light where it shone out on this side, too, from a tiny window in Found's ground-floor flat. And he wondered what his quarry was doing in there, what he was thinking . . . until it dawned on him that he didn't have to just wonder. For Trevor Jordan had given him the power to find out for himself.

He let his vampire-enhanced telepathy flow outwards on the night air, out and away into the dark and across the road, and through the old brickwork into the smoke-grimed, stagnant house of evil. But the probe was aimless, unpracticed, and lacking authority, spreading out like ripples on a dark pond in all directions. Until suddenly—the Necroscope found more than he'd bargained for!

His telepathy touched upon a mind—no, two minds— and he knew at once that neither one of them belonged to Johnny Found. They weren't in the house, for one thing, and for another . . . they were already intent upon him! Upon Harry Keogh!

Harry drew breath in a sharp *hiss* of apprehension— fought hard against the urge to crouch down, which would only serve to illustrate his awareness—and looked this way and that along the dark alley. E-Branch? No, for there was no strength there, no talent, no metaphysical power. So who and what were they? And where?

Along the alley a cigarette glowed in the dark as someone took a drag, someone keeping to the shadows no less than the Necroscope himself. And across the main road under a lamppost, there stood a figure in a dark, lightweight overcoat with his hands stuffed forlornly in his pockets, turning first this way and then that, for all the world like a man stood up who still hopes that his date will show: a decoy, to distract attention from the one in the shadows.

And both of them wondering about Harry, so that he picked up their thoughts in snatches right out of their unsuspecting minds. The one under the lamppost:

Found's home, but who's this bugger? . . . Up and down the street, prowling like a cat . . . The one we were told to watch out for? . . . Said if he showed up we shouldn't touch him, but . . . feather in the old cap . . . Promotion to Inspector?

And the one in the shadows, who was now stepping *out* of the shadows and heading Harry's way:

Dangerous, they said . . . Well, let him try it on. If I'm obliged to protect myself . . . blow his fucking head off! (And Harry could actually feel the man's hand tightening nervously about the rubber grips on the butt of a pistol in his pocket.)

As the one with the gun came almost jauntily on, so the other straightened up and took his hands out of his pockets, then headed across the road towards Harry. And quite casually, patiently (but with their hearts pounding in their chests and their eyes sharp as daggers), so they converged on him.

Harry glared at them and was surprised to hear himself

snarl. A river of fire raced in his veins, setting light to something inside which blazed up and sang to him of slaughter and spurting, crimson blood; of life, and of death! *Wamphyri!*

But the human side said: "No! These are not your enemies! Upon a time, before you were a law unto yourself, they might even have been your friends. Why hurt them when you can evade them so easily?"

Because it isn't my nature to flee but stand and fight!

"Fight? Not much of a fight! They're like children . . ."

Oh? Well, at least one of these children has a gun!

The man crossing the road waited for a stream of cars to go by in the nearside lane; he was ten to fifteen paces away, no more. The other one was maybe twenty paces away. But both of them were definitely homing in on Harry. His vampire knew the danger no less than he did, and worked to protect him. The Necroscope sweated a strange, cold sweat and breathed a weird mist, which clung to him like an ever-thickening cloak. And as the two policemen came on, so Harry's mist spilled out of the shadows where he waited and poured itself into view like the exhalations of a basement boiler room.

Their guns are useless now. They can't see me in this. But I can see, smell, sense, even reach out and touch them, if I wish it. Reach out and snuff them!

"Damn you!" Harry cursed himself—or the thing inside him—out loud. "*Damn* you—you slimy black bastard thing!"

"Yeah, well, never mind all that, pal," one of the policemen answered him, crouching down and aiming his gun two-handed into the fog. "We've been damned and cursed before, right? So just come on out of there, okay? I mean, all of that steam has to be bad for you.

Do you want to ruin your lungs? Or do you want me to do it for you, eh? Now, I said come on *out* of there!''

There was no answer, only a sudden swirling as the fog seemed to fold inwards upon itself, as if someone had shaken a blanket or slammed a door right in its heart. And in a few seconds more the mist thinned out, fell to earth, turned to a film of liquid which made the cobbles damp and shiny. And the wall was high, black, and blank, with no alley and no basement boiler room.

And there was no one there at all . . .

Back in Bonnyrig, Trevor Jordan was awake; some immediately forgotten night terror had drenched him in his own sweat and snatched him panting out of his bed in the attic room; now he prowled the rooms and corridors of the old house where it stood by the river, putting on all the lights, his every nerve jumping as he looked out from curtained windows into the night. Just what his apprehensions were he couldn't say, but he felt something looming, hovering, waiting. Some terrible Thing for the moment conserving its energy, but full of monstrous intent.

Was it Harry? Jordan wondered. The thing that Harry was far too rapidly becoming? Possibly. Could it be concern over Harry's fate if—when—E-Branch finally moved on him? Well, yes, that too. Or was he worried about his *own* fate, if he was still with the Necroscope at that time? Was this how Yulian Bodescu had felt at Harkley House in Devon, that evening when the Branch had closed in on him to destroy him? Something like this, Jordan was sure.

It was time for Jordan to leave Harry, and he knew it. To leave him for good and merge back into the mundane world of ordinary men. Oh, the telepath knew he could never more be truly mundane, for he had seen the other side and returned from it. But he could try. He could work at it, work *into* it, gradually forget that he had been (God, he couldn't bear the thought of it even now!), that he had *not* been alive, and eventually become just another man again, albeit one with a talent. And when Harry was well out of it and fled into that other world which Jordan could scarcely imagine, then he might even return to the Branch. If they would take him back. But of course they would want to be sure about him first. They would want to check that he was who and what he was supposed to be.

But the trouble was (and Jordan knew now that this must be the source of his nightmare) that he couldn't be sure he would be the same person. For if Harry's awful metamorphosis continued to accelerate . . .

Harry!

Jordan sucked air gaspingly as telepathic awareness of the Necroscope suddenly flooded his being. The sensation was like being doused with ice water, causing his whole body to shudder violently. Harry, out there somewhere, across the river. Harry, listening to Jordan, to his thoughts. But how long had he been there?

Only a minute or two in fact. And he had not been eavesdropping on Jordan but telepathically checking the vicinity of the house. He *had* detected something of Jordan's fears, however, which did precious little to calm the beast which raged within him, denied expression when he'd fled from the two policemen watching Johnny Found's flat.

The reason Harry chose to emerge from the Möbius Continuum into the bushes on the far side of the river and not directly into the house was simple: when he'd read the minds of those plainclothes policemen in Darlington, he'd plainly seen that they were expecting him. Indeed, someone had told the man with the gun that

Harry might be dangerous. Obviously, E-Branch must have alerted them to the possibility of him showing up. So . . . whatever Darcy Clarke had told the Branch about him, it hadn't cut any ice. They weren't having any.

And if they were looking out for him in Darlington, plainly it wouldn't take long before they were doing it here, too. He'd scared off Paxton (for the moment, anyway) but Paxton was only one of them and untypical of the species. So from now on he would have to check locations very carefully before venturing into what were previously "safe" places. It all went to reinforce the Necroscope's feeling of claustrophobia, a doom-laden sensation of space—Möbius space included—narrowing down for him. To say nothing of time.

And now, to discover that Trevor Jordan was also afraid of him, of what Harry might do to him . . . it was too much.

The dead—even Möbius himself—had turned against him; his mother had become worn out and left him; there was no one in the world, neither alive nor dead, who had anything good to say on his behalf. And this was the world, and the race, which he had fought so long and so hard for. Not even his own race. Not any longer.

Harry stepped through a Möbius door into a dark corridor of the house across the river and silently commenced to climb the stairs to his own bedroom. Suddenly, he was tired; his cares seemed too great; sleep would be curative, and . . . to *hell* with everything! Let the future care for itself.

But Jordan's voice stopped him when he was only half-way up the first flight:

"Harry?" The telepath looked up at him from the foot of the stairs. Trevor Jordan, who could read the Necroscope's mind as easily as Harry read his. "I . . . shouldn't have been thinking those things."

Harry nodded. "And I shouldn't have overheard you. Anyway, don't worry about it. You did your bit for me and did it well, and I'm grateful. And it won't be so bad being alone, for I've been alone before. So if you want to go, then go—go now! For let's face it, I'm losing more and more control to this thing, and leaving now might be the safest thing to do."

Jordan shook his head. "Not while the whole world's against you, Harry. I won't leave you yet."

Harry shrugged and turned away, and continued to climb the stairs. "As you wish, but don't leave it too long . . ."

IV Dreams . . .

THE NIGHT WAS STILL YOUNG WHEN HARRY LAID HIS head on the pillow, but the moon was up and the stars were bright, and it was his time. His senses were no longer strong in daylight, but in the dark of the night they were sensitive as never before. Even those which governed or were governed by his subconscious mind. And his dreams were stronger, too.

He dreamed first about Möbius and sensed that it was more than an ordinary dream. The long-dead mathematician came and sat on his bed, and while his face and form were indistinct, his deadspeak voice was as sharp and no-nonsense as ever:

The last time we can talk, Harry—in this world, anyway.

Are you sure you want to? the Necroscope answered. *It seems I can't help giving people a bad time lately.*

The vague, weightless figure of Möbius nodded. *Yes, but we both know that's not you. That's why I've chosen to come to you now, while your dreams are still your own.*

Are they?

I think so. Certainly, you sound more like the Harry I used to know.

Harry relaxed a little, sighed, and sank down in his bed. *So what is it you want to talk about?*

The other places, Harry. The other worlds.

My cone-shaped parallel dimensions? The Necroscope gave a wry, apologetic shrug. *They were mainly bluff; I argued for argument's sake; we were practicing, my vampire and I.*

That's as it may be, Möbius answered, *but bluff or none you were right, anyway. Your intuition, Harry. The only thing your vision didn't take into account was how.*

How?

More rightly, who, said Möbius.

How? Who? Are we talking about God again?

The Big Bang, said Möbius. *The Primal Light, back at the dawn of space and time. All of this couldn't have come out of nothing, Harry. And yet we've already decided that before The Beginning there was nothing. Which was foolish of us, because we both know that you don't need flesh to have mind!*

God, Harry said. *The Ultimate Incorporeal Being. He made it all, right? But to what end?*

Möbius's turn to shrug. *To find out what would happen, maybe?*

You mean He didn't already know? What's that for omniscience?

Unfair, said Möbius. *No one can know before the fact. And it's dangerous to try. But He's known everything since.*

Tell me about the other places, said Harry, fascinated despite himself.

The world of Starside and Sunside is one, Möbius told
him. *But it was . . . a failure. There were unforeseen
paradoxes and things went disastrously wrong. Starside,
the vampire swamps, and the Wamphyri themselves: they
were cause and effect both! But that's for the future, and
for the past! To tell it now might be to change it, which
would be presumptuous.*

Space and time are relative, Harry argued. *Haven't I
always said so? And in their own way they're fixed. You
can't damage them by talking about them.*

Möbius chuckled, however sadly. *Clever, Harry, I'll
grant you that. But you can't work your vampire wiles
on me, my boy! And anyway, Starside isn't the place I'm
talking about.*

Well, I'm listening, the Necroscope answered, just a
little disgruntled.

Once when we talked, Möbius reminded him, *you
mentioned the balance of the multiverse, with black and
white holes shifting matter around between all the different layers of existence and delaying or even reversing
entropy. Like the weights governing the swing of an old
clock's pendulum. But that's only one sort of balance,
the physical sort. Then there's the metaphysical, the mystical, the spiritual.*

God again?

The balance between Good and Evil.

Which all had origin in the same source? Your argument, August Ferdinand! Remember, "before The Beginning there was nothing." Right?

Möbius shook his head. *We're not in dispute. On the
contrary, we're in complete agreement!*

Harry was astonished. *God had a dark side?*

Oh, yes, which he cast out!

The mathematician's words and their delivery had riveted Harry. *And I can do the same? Is that what you're saying?*

I'm saying that the other places are like levels, some of which are higher and some lower. And what we do here determines the next step. We go up or down.

Heaven or hell?

Möbius shrugged. *If it helps you to think of it like that.*

You mean that when I move on, I can leave my dark side—maybe even my vampire—behind me?

While there's a difference, yes.

A difference?

While we may still distinguish between you.

You mean if I don't succumb?

I have to go now, said Möbius.

But I have to know more! Harry was desperate.

I was allowed to come back, Möbius said simply. *But I am not allowed to stay. My new place is higher, Harry. I really can't afford to lose it.*

Wait! Harry tried to stir himself, sit up, and take hold of Möbius's wrist. But he couldn't move and anyway, it would be like trying to grasp smoke. And like a set of his own esoteric formulae, the great man mutated into nothingness and was gone . . .

If anything, Möbius's visit had wearied Harry even more than before. He drifted deeper into sleep. But his vampire-influenced mind was full of a certain name, which tormented him and wouldn't let him be. And the name was Johnny Found.

Harry was a telepath; he had a quest, a task which he must finish; and he had a vampire in him. When he had gone to face Faethor Ferenczy's bloodson Janos in the mountains of Transylvania, the Ferenczy had warned him that only one of them would come out of it alive, and that the winner would be a creature of incredible power.

323

Janos had read the future, seen the same thing, known he couldn't lose. Except . . . one should never try to understand the future. Read it if you must, but don't try to understand it. Harry had been the one who came down out of the mountains. And though he didn't yet have the measure of his powers—especially his most recent acquisition, telepathy—still they were incredible. They had been incredible before, but now, with the booster which was his vampire . . .

Dreaming, he no longer had control over his talents, which were active nevertheless. Dreams are the clearinghouses of the mind, where the balance is kept, the cutting room where all the junk and trivia of life are discarded and the meaningful set in order. That is the function of men's dreams. That and wish fulfillment. And also, for anyone with a conscience, the elevation of suppressed guilt. Which is why men sometimes have nightmares.

Harry had his share of guilt, and more than sufficient of desires requiring fulfillment. And what he himself had failed to put in order during his waking hours, his subconscious self—and the vampire which was part of it— would try to put in order while he slept.

His enhanced awareness spread outwards from him to form a telepathic probe which, in a moment, unerringly leaped all the miles to its target in Darlington. For that target was the sleeping mind of Johnny Found, a mind with a talent as weird as it was warped. Which Harry desired to know about.

And with the sinister guile of the vampire, he need only hint, suggest, propose, strike this chord or maybe that, and with any luck at all Johnny Found would tell him.

All of it . . .

Johnny was dreaming, too, of his childhood. This wasn't something he would do voluntarily, but a night specter kept rapping on the door of childhood memories and demanding that he open it.

Childhood memories? Oh, he had them, but he wouldn't say they were worth remembering or dreaming about. Which was why he didn't. Usually.

He tossed a little in his bed; his subconscious mind moaned and went to take up a hammer to nail shut the door to his past; something pushed the hammer aside, beyond his reach, and Johnny could only watch helplessly as the door creaked open. Inside, all the Bad Things of yesterday were waiting for him: the many small crimes he had committed, and the range of punishments and penalties he'd been made to pay for them. But he'd been a child then and innocent (so they said) and would soon grow out of it, and only Johnny himself had known he wouldn't ever grow out of it, and that they'd never be able to find punishments severe enough to fit his crimes.

They'd tried to convince him that the things he did were bad, and had almost succeeded, but by then he was old enough to know that they lied to him, because they didn't understand. And *because* they didn't understand, they would never know how *good* the things were which he did. How *good* they made him feel.

Yes, it had been a lonely place, childhood, where no one understood him or wanted to know about . . . the things he did. Because they didn't want to even think of such things, let alone know about them.

Lonely, yes, the place beyond that beckoning door. And how much more lonely if he hadn't had the dead things to talk to? And to play with. And to torment.

But because he'd had that—his secret thing, his clever way with creatures which were no more—being an orphan hadn't been nearly so bad. Because he'd known there were others worse off than him, whose plight was far worse. And that if it wasn't, then Johnny could soon make it worse.

The open door both repelled and attracted him. Beyond it, the mists of memory swirled, eddied, and hypnotized him; until—against his will?—Johnny found himself drifting in through the door. Where all his childhoood was waiting for him . . .

They'd called him "Found" because he had been, in a church. And the pews had vibrated with his screams, and the rafters had echoed with them, that Sunday morning when the verger had come to see what all the to-do was about. He was still bloody from birth, the foundling, and wrapped in a Sunday newspaper; and the placenta which had following him into the world still warm in a plastic bag, stuffed under the bench in one of the pews.

But lusty? Johnny had screamed to wreck his lungs, howled to break the stained-glass windows and bring down the ceiling, almost as if he'd known he had no right to be in that church. Perhaps his poor mother had known it, too, and this had been her attempt at saving him. Which had failed. And not only was Johnny lost, but so was she.

In any case, he'd yelled like that until they took him out of the church to the intensive-care unit of a local hospital's maternity ward. And only then, away from God's house, had he fallen silent.

The ambulance which whirled him to the hospital carried his mother, too, found seated against a headstone in the churchyard in a pool of her own blood, head lolling on her swollen breasts. Except unlike Johnny she didn't survive the journey. Or perhaps she did, for a little while . . .

A strange start to a strange life, but the strangeness was only just beginning.

In the intensive-care ward Johnny had been washed,

cared for, given a cot and, for the moment—and indeed for all his life—a name. Someone had scribbled "Found" on the plastic tag which circled his little wrist, to identify him from all the other babies. And Found he'd stayed.

But when a nurse had looked in on him to see why he'd stopped sobbing and gone quiet so suddenly . . . that had been the weirdest thing of all. Or perhaps not, depending on one's perspective. For after all, the mortuary was only a little way away. Perhaps his young mother hadn't been *quite* dead. And perhaps she'd heard the babies crying and had known that one of them was hers. That must be the answer, surely? For what other explanation could there be?

There Johnny's unnamed, unknown mother had sat, beside his empty cot; and Johnny in her dead arms, sucking a dribble of cold milk from a dead, cold nipple.

Johnny was at an infant orphanage until he was five, then fostered for three more years until the couple who had taken him split up in tragic circumstances. After that he went to a junior orphanage in York.

About his foster parents:

The Prescotts had kept a large house on the very outskirts of Darlington, where the town met the countryside. At the time they adopted Johnny in 1967, they already had a small daughter of four years; but there had been problems and Mrs. Prescott was unable to have more children. A pity, for the couple had always planned to be the "perfect" family unit: the pair of them, plus one boy and one girl. Johnny would seem to fit the bill nicely and make up the deficiency.

And yet David Prescott had been uneasy about the boy from the very first time he saw him. It was nothing solid, just—something he could never quite put his finger on—

a *feeling*; but because of it things were just a little less
perfect than they should be.

Johnny was given the family name and became a Prescott—for the time being, anyway. But right from the start
he didn't get along with his sister. They couldn't be left
alone together for five minutes without fighting, and the
glances they literally stabbed at each other were poisonous even for mismatched children. Alice Prescott blamed
her small daughter for being spoiled (which is to say she
blamed herself for spoiling her), and her husband blamed
Johnny for being . . . odd. There was just something,
well, *odd* about the boy.

"Well, of course there is!" his wife would round on
him. "Johnny's been a waif, without home and family
except in the shape of the orphanage. Yes, and *that* wasn't
the best sort of place, either! Love? Suffer the little children? They seemed altogether too eager to be *rid* of him,
if you ask me! Precious little of love there!"

And David Prescott had wondered: *With reason,
maybe? But what possible reason? Johnny isn't even six
yet. How can anyone turn against a child that small?
And certainly not an orphanage, charged with the care
of such unfortunates.*

The Prescotts had a corner shop which did very nicely,
a general store that sold just about everything. It was
less than a mile from their home, on the main road into
Darlington from the north, and served a recently matured estate of some three hundred homes. Working nine
till five, four days a week, and Wednesday and Saturday
mornings, they made a good living out of it. With the
help of a part-time "nanny," a young girl who lived
locally, they were not overstretched.

David kept pigeons in a loft at the bottom of their
large, secluded garden; Alice liked to be out digging,
planting, and growing things when the day's work was

done; they took turns seeing to the kids on those occasions when their nanny took time off. So that apart from the friction between Johnny and his sister, Carol, the lives of the Prescotts could be said to be normal, pleasant, and fairly average. Which was how things stood until the summer when Johnny turned eight. Indeed until then, their lives might even be described as idyllic.

But that was when David Prescott started having problems with his birds; and the family cat—a placid, neutered tom called Moggit, who slept with Carol and was the apple of her eye—went out one morning and never came back in; and there were long periods of that hot, sultry weather which irritates, exacerbates, and occasionally causes eruptions. And it was the same summer when David built a pool for the kids, and roofed it over with polythene on an aluminum frame.

Johnny had thought it would be great fun, swimming and fooling around in his own pool, but he soon became bored with it. Carol loved it, however, which annoyed her adopted brother: he didn't care for people enjoying things which he didn't enjoy, and in any case he didn't much care for Carol at all.

Then, one morning three or four days after Moggit had gone missing, Johnny got up early. He didn't know it, but Carol was awake and throwing her clothes on as soon as she heard his door gently opening and closing. Her *brother* (she always put a heavy sneering accent on the word) had been getting up early a lot recently—hours before the rest of the household—and she wanted to know what he was doing. It wasn't especially malicious of her, but the fact was she was a little jealous and more than a little curious. Even if Johnny *was* a pig, still she'd rather have him playing with her in the pool than off on his own playing his stupid, mysterious, lonely games.

As for Johnny: his time was all his own now and no

one to make demands on it. School was out for the summer holidays; he had "things" to do; he could usually be found beyond the garden wall, in the hedgerows where they blended into meadow and farmland that stretched out and away to the north and northwest. But he would always come when he was wanted (a loud call would usually bring him home directly), and he was sensible about getting back for mealtimes.

Just what he did out there all the hours of the day was something else. If his foster parents asked him, he would say, "Playing," and that was all. But Carol wanted to know what it was he played *at*. It was beyond her that he could find anything more interesting than the pool. So she went out after him, tiptoeing past her parents' door, into the early morning light where dawn hadn't long cracked the horizon with its golden smile.

Johnny went down past the pool under its polythene blister to the garden wall. He climbed the high wall at a well-known spot, jumped down the last few feet on the other side. And he started out along the overgrown hedgerow into the maze of fields shimmering in the morning light. And Carol right after him.

Half a mile into the fields, at a junction of ancient, rutted, overgrown tracks, the jumbles of a ruined farm lay humped and green with flowering brambles and clumps of nettles, where sections of broken, grey-lichened wall and the buttressed mass of an old chimney poked up in teetering stacks of stone. Johnny cut diagonally through a meadow and only his dark head, shiny with sweat, could be seen above the tall, swaying grass.

From where she balanced precariously on top of a disused stile, Carol saw where he was heading and resolved to follow him. The old ruin was obviously Johnny's secret place, where he played his secret games. But they wouldn't be secret much longer.

Johnny had disappeared somewhere into the tumble of fallen, weed-grown walls by the time his sister came panting out of the meadow. She paused awhile and looked this way and that, along the tracks which had once serviced the farm, then made to cross them to the ruins . . . and paused again!

What was that? A cry? The cry of a cat? Moggit?
Moggit!

Carol's hand flew to her mouth. She drew a gasping breath and held it. What, poor little Moggit, lost somewhere in the shell of this crumbling old pile? Maybe that was what had drawn Johnny here: the sound of Moggit, jammed in some hole, trapped and starving in this tottering ruin.

Carol thought to call out in answer to Moggit's strange, choking cries and maybe bring him a little hope; but then she thought no, for that would only make him struggle the harder and perhaps get himself in more of a fix. Maybe he was only crying like that, so urgently and piteously, because Johnny was already trying to rescue him.

Holding her breath, Carol crossed the hard-packed, dusty tracks to what once would have been a wide entrance through high farmyard walls to the cluster of buildings within. Now the gap was a mass of collapsed stone choked by brambles and bolting ivy, with a few hazelnuts and straggly elders crushed under the weight of parasitic green. Broken bricks and rubble shifted underfoot where a well-marked trail had been worn through the undergrowth, Carol supposed by Johnny.

Dusty and cobwebbed, the trail in through the foliage was almost a tunnel; the light was shut out; seven-year-old Carol felt stifled as she forced her way through. But when she might have faltered, Moggit's howls (she was sure it must be Moggit, while at the same time praying it was not) drove her on. Until finally she broke cover into yellow sunlight, and blinking the grit out of her eyes saw Johnny where he sat in the central clearing. And saw the . . .

. . . The things he had there; but without really *seeing* them at first, because her child's mind couldn't conceive, couldn't believe. And finally she saw . . . but no, no, there was no way that this could be Moggit.

What, Moggit of the snow-white belly and paws, the bushy tail and Lone Ranger masked face, the sleek, gleaming black back and neck and ears? This tortured, dangling thing, Moggit? Carol almost fainted; she slumped down behind a broken wall and knocked loose a brick, and Johnny heard the clatter. When his head snapped round on his neck to look Carol's way, he didn't see her at first, only the ruins in the clearing as he'd always known them. But Carol still saw him: his bloated face, bulging, emotionless eyes, and bloody, claw-like hands. His penknife lying open beside him on the wall where he sat, and the sharpened stick with its red point clutched tight in one hand.

And she still saw Moggit, too. Moggit with his hind paws just touching the ground, feebly dancing to stay upright and keep his weight off his neck, which was encircled by a thin wire noose that hung down from the branch of an elder! And one yellow eye hanging out on a thread, dribbling wetly and dancing on his wet furry cheek even as Moggit danced; and his fat white belly thin and crimson now where it had been slit open to let a bulge of shiny black, red, and yellow entrails dangle!

And Moggit wasn't all. There were two of Carol's father's favorite pigeons, too, hanging limp from other branches with their wings twisted all askew. And a hedgehog still alive but with a rusty iron spike through its side, pinning it to the ground, so that it staggered dizzily round and around on its own axis in unending agony, snuffling horribly. Yes, and there were other things, too, but Carol didn't want to see any more.

Johnny, satisfied that no one was there, had returned to his "game." Through eyes that were brimming tears, Carol saw him stand up, catch a dead pigeon in one hand, and thrust his stick right through its clay-cold body. And he worked the stick in its unfeeling flesh almost as if . . . as if it *wasn't* unfeeling at all! As if he really believed that the bedraggled, stiff, broken thing could feel it. And all the while he laughed and talked and muttered to these poor, tortured, alive or dead or soon to be dead creatures, caring nothing for their waking or sleeping agonies. Indeed, his sister now understood something of the nature of his game: that having harried a living thing to its death, Johnny couldn't bear that it had escaped him and so *continued* to torture it in the lightless world beyond!

And at that she was the first to know the truth about her adopted brother, without even knowing she knew it. For a child herself, she recognized a child's fancy when she saw one, knew also that Johnny was simply a cruel and hateful boy, and that what she'd imagined just couldn't be.

But Moggit, poor Moggit! Finally, it got through to Carol that it was indeed her battered, half-eviscerated cat which Johnny was slowly hanging. And she could bear it no longer.

"Mogg*iiiit!*" she screamed at the top of her voice. And: "Johnny, I hate you—*oh, how I hate you!*"

She stood up, stumbled and regained her balance, flew at him, clutching the jagged half of a brick. Johnny finally saw her and his red-blotched face rapidly turned pale. He snatched up his penknife—not to use on her but with an entirely different, perhaps even worse purpose in mind—and went to slice through a length of tough kite string which held down Moggit's branch. Strands parted but the string didn't; in a sudden rage Johnny jerked the string this way and that, and Moggit was lifted and whirled like a rag, his hoarse cat cries cut off as the wire bit into his rubbed-raw throat.

Then Johnny gave a gasp of triumph as his knife cut through the string, and Moggit was jerked aloft, choking and spitting for a second or two as the noose tightened to finish the job. But Johnny was so *intent* on the murder of the cat that Carol was on him. Blindly, whirling her arms, she came at him with the sharp nails of one hand and the half-brick grasped tight in the other. He avoided her raking nails, but a sharp, broken corner of the brick struck him on the forehead and knocked him down. In a moment he was sitting up, shaking his head, looking around for his knife. And his eyes blazed as he glared at his sister and threatened, "First Moggit, and now you!"

He got unsteadily to his feet, his forehead grazed and bleeding, then spotted his penknife and pounced on it. And in that same moment Carol knew she was in deadly danger. Johnny couldn't let her tell her parents what she had seen, what he had done. And there was only one way he could be sure to stop her.

With a backwards glance that took in the whole scene one last time—poor Moggit hanged and bobbing with the motion of the elder branch, the hedgehog finally exhausted, gasping its life out where it lay, and the dead, mutilated birds strung up in a row—she turned away and fled for home. And bursting through the tunnel of undergrowth out of the ruins, she knew that Johnny was right behind her.

And he would have been; except he knew that if she got home first, she would bring someone to see. And he mustn't let anyone see.

Quickly, he cut down Moggit and the birds and yanked

the hedgehog's stake from the ground. Panting from the furious pace of his exertions, and from his fury in general, he tossed the lot into a deep, stagnant well which he'd discovered on the site, whose battened cover had long since rotted away in one corner. He hated to see his dead and dying things go down into the dark like that, making splashes in the deep, black, unseen water below. Wasted, all of them, and so much ''life'' still left in them! It was all Carol's fault. Yes, and there'd be a lot more to blame her for if she got home first.

He set out after her, following her wailing and the wild, zigzag trail she left through the long grass.

A half mile across rough, open countryside is a long way when you're a heartbroken child with your eyes full of tears. Carol's heart hammered in her breast and her breath was ragged and panting; but to drive her on there was always that picture burning on her mind's eye, of Moggit dangling and jerking in the wire noose, with his guts hanging out like a small bag of crushed fruits when her mother made jam in the kitchen. And to drive her even faster was Johnny's voice crying after her: ''Caaarol! Carol—wait for me!''

She did no such thing; the garden wall was just ahead, at the end of the hedgerow; behind her, panting—and yet growling, too, like some savage dog—Johnny was catching up. His groping hand missed her ankle by inches as she half climbed, half fell over the wall. But on the garden side she just lay there, too terrified, tearful, too exhausted to go on.

And Johnny jumping down after her, his eyes mad and glaring, small fists tightening and slackening where he held them to his sides. She looked towards the house but it was hidden behind fruit trees and the misted dome of the pool. Would her parents be up yet? She didn't even have the wind for yelling.

Johnny snarled as he bunched her hair in a strong fist and commenced dragging her towards the pool. "Swimming!" he said, the word bursting from his lips like a bubble of slime. "You're going swimming, Carol. You're going to like it, I know. And so am I. Especially afterwards!"

For the last week or so, David Prescott had also taken to getting up early. Alice didn't complain or ask why, because he was always so quiet and considerate and invariably brought her a cup of coffee. It must be the summer, the light mornings, the old "early bird" syndrome. But in fact it was the mail.

Out this way the mail deliveries were always early, the very crack of dawn, and David was expecting a letter. From the orphanage. Not that it would contain anything of any significance—he was sure it wouldn't—but still he'd like to get to it before Alice. If she saw it first . . . well, she'd only say he was paranoid. About Johnny. And certainly it would look as though he was, else why would he write to the orphanage about him?

The thing was, David was desperate that things should work out all right; he really *did* want to love the poor kid. But at the same time he'd always been more receptive of mood than Alice—more aware of the aura of people, especially kids—and he knew that Johnny's aura just wasn't right. If it was something out of his past (but what past? He was just a child), something the orphanage would know about, then David believed that he and his wife should be told. For he suspected Alice was right to complain about the attitude of the orphanage; they *had* seemed too eager to wash their hands of Johnny, or rather: "To place him in the care of a normal, loving family, where he can grow into a healthy person. Healthy in mind, as well as in body . . ."

That's what the orphanage director had said the day they went to pick up their new son, and the words had always stuck in David's memory. "Healthy in mind, as well as in body."

Something wrong with Johnny's mind? Something a little sick? Or a lot sick? For that was the nature of the aura which David sometimes felt washing out from the boy: a sick one, and clammy as an old man on his deathbed. Johnny *felt* sick as death. But not *his* death.

And this morning, sure enough the letter was there. David tore it open and read it, and for a little while the words made no sense. Budgerigars in the kids' rooms, and Johnny stealing, killing, and collecting them? A collection of dead things: mice, beetles, the budgies, even a kitten?

A dead kitten under his bed, crawling with maggots, and Johnny twisting its legs until they came off in his hands? That was how the orphanage people had found out about it, when the other kids came screaming.

But a kitten?

Moggit . . . ?

Screaming?

And David could hear the horrified screams of those kids from here. Except it wasn't *those* kids but one of his own—no, *his* own—Carol, from the bottom of the garden!

What . . . ?

And Alice's sleepy, mumbling voice from upstairs, calling down, "Where's the coffee? The kids are up early."

And another scream from the garden, cut off gurglingly at its zenith.

David had ever been the one to leap to conclusions, often incorrectly. He did so now, and this time was right.

Down the garden path with his dressing gown flapping, yelling for Carol, hoarsely, like crazy. But no answer. And a small blurred figure inside the polythene dome, kneeling at the side of the pool. David burst in, it was Johnny kneeling there; he looked like he was trying to drag Carol out of the water. And she was floating there, facedown, arms limply outstretched, crucified on the blue, gently lapping water.

Johnny had been playing in the fields; he'd heard Carol's screams and seen a man—dirty, bearded, dressed in rags—climbing the wall out of the garden. The man ran away across the fields and Johnny went to see what he'd been doing. Carol was in the pool and he'd tried to drag her out.

He told the story to David, to Alice, the police, anyone who wanted to hear it. And most of them believed him; even David half believed him, though he didn't want him near anymore. And Alice probably believed him, though that would be hard to say for she wasn't much good for anything from that time forward.

The police found a camp site in the ruins of the old farm and brought up a lot of rubbish from the well. Someone, person or persons, must have been living rough there, stealing from gardens and properties (David's pigeons) in order to eat. It could be Gypsies (the hedgehog), or maybe a tramp. Hard to say. Chances were they'd get him or them eventually.

But they never did get anyone.

And Johnny went back to the orphanage . . .

Harry slept on and for a little while longer experienced Johnny Found's dreams. Of course, he saw Found's past only from the necromancer's own point of view, which if anything was worse than the whole picture and more than sufficient to guarantee he had the right man. But eventually, Found's excesses became too much—his dreaming memories of his own evil deeds a lurid litany of his inhumanity—by which time Harry's hatred of him had grown into a rage.

Johnny Found had lived all his young life a monster and murderer and so far had got away with it, but until recently his stepsister Carol had remained his single human victim. Between times he'd made do and played his unthinkable ''games'' with creatures dead of causes other than murder.

But as men and monsters alike mature, so their tastes also mature, and Johnny was no exception. Except . . . what grotesque form does maturity take in something rotten from the start?

Once, for entirely unthinkable reasons which even Harry Keogh couldn't bear to contemplate, Found had taken a job in a morgue; only to be fired when his boss became suspicious. It was his dream about another job he'd had, however, this time in a slaughterhouse, which did the trick and, like the last straw, broke the Necroscope's back.

That was when Harry had drawn back his shuddering telepathic probe, pulled out of Johnny's mind, and let the man get on with his nightmaring. Except of course in Found's case the nightmares could barely match up to the reality . . .

V . . . And Fancies

AND THEN THE NECROSCOPE HAD DREAMED OF DARCY Clarke, which was also a form of nightmare, for in it Darcy was dead and his voice came to Harry as deadspeak.

Even so it didn't come clearly but was distorted, drifting, a thousand echoes coming together from all directions and combining to form a strange, out-of-sync sighing.

I couldn't believe you would have done that to me, Harry, said Darcy when he'd established his identity. *I mean, I knew the moment they killed me—when I saw that they actually* could *kill me, despite my guardian angel—that you were responsible. It could only have been something you did inside my head when you were in there. You killed off the thing that watched out for me, and so left me vulnerable. But I still can't believe you would, and I still don't know why. I thought I knew you, but I didn't know you a damn!*

This is just a dream, Harry answered him then. *This*

is my conscience—while I still have one—giving me trouble because I protected myself at someone else's expense. This is a nightmare, Darcy, and you're not really dead. It's just me blaming myself that I had to interfere inside your head. As for why I did it: to be sure that if you came up against me before I was out of here, then that you would be vulnerable. Because of all the talents in E-Branch, yours is the one that scares me most. It gives you the edge, makes you invincible. I could try to stop you again and again, and fail, but you would only have to pull the trigger once and I'd be a goner. And it wouldn't be new to you—you could do it—for you've done it before.

Darcy's deadspeak presence was gathering itself now, coming together almost as an act of sheer will, so that his fragmented voice lost its echoing sigh and took on authority as he said:

It's no dream, Harry. I'm dead as can be. And even though I've come to you while you're asleep, still you should be able to see that. But if you doubt me, why not ask your thousands of friends, the Great Majority? The teeming dead will tell you I don't lie. I'm one of them now.

A cop-out! Harry answered, smiling and shaking his head. *I can't ask the dead anything, because they don't want to know me anymore. Hey, I'm a vampire, remember? I'm not one of you living guys, and I'm not one of those dead ones. I'm somewhere in the middle, Darcy. Undead. Wamphyri!*

Harry, said Darcy bitterly, *there's no need for all this subterfuge. You don't have to try out your Wamphyri word games on me. I'm admitting it: you won. I don't know why you wished me dead, but anyway, you got your wish. I am dead! I really am.*

Harry tossed and turned in his bed and began to sweat.

Sometimes, like any other man, his dreams were just so much junk; or again they might be erotic or esoteric fancies and fantasies; or they could be, well, just dreams. But at *other* times they were a lot more than that. And this was beginning to feel like one of those times.

Okay, he finally said, still unconvinced and wanting desperately to stay that way, *so you're dead. So who killed you? And why?*

The Branch, Darcy answered, with a typical dead-speak shrug. *Who else? Whatever you did to my mind, the mere fact that you'd been in there gave me mind-smog. You interfered inside my head, canceled something, took something away from me. And in its place I got your taint: No, I'm not saying you vampirized me, just that you . . . spoiled me. They could smell you on me—in the heart of my being—and they daren't take any chances with me. Which was surely the way you planned it . . . ?*

Harry thought about it a moment, then said: *Darcy, if you really are dead, if this isn't just my conscience acting up—because you're right and I did interfere with your mind, which I know was wrong—then I'll be able to find you when I'm awake. I mean, we'll be able to talk to each other again, through deadspeak. Right?*

He sensed the other's nod. *I'll be waiting for you, Harry. Except . . . it isn't easy. I'm still learning how to get it all together.*

Eh? Will you explain?

They burned me and scattered my ashes, Darcy told him. *I'm sure I don't have to tell you why . . . But it means I have no focal point. I don't belong in any special place. I'm blowing on the winds, drifting on the tides, flushed away down the city's sewers.*

And suddenly, the Necroscope suspected it was true, and he began to toss and churn in his bed that much more violently. It seemed that Darcy picked up his torment, for when he spoke again, his words were less harsh, even conciliatory. *If I wrong you with accusations, Harry, it's only because you've wronged me.*

This has to be a nightmare, Harry gasped. *Darcy, it has to be! I didn't mean to harm you. Of all the men I've known, you are the one I* couldn't *harm! Not under any circumstances. Not because of your talent but because . . . because you're you. And so you see, this has to be a bloody awful nightmare.*

And now Darcy knew that indeed Harry was just as innocent as ever, and that if anyone—anything—were to blame, then it was the creature inside him, which was rapidly becoming one with him. He would have comforted him then, if there was a way, but he felt himself drifting again, coming apart, and he knew he didn't have the strength or the know-how to keep it together. He was only recently dead, after all.

I'll be . . . around when you're awake, Harry. Try contacting me then. It will be . . . easier . . . if you . . . come looking . . . for me . . .

And with that Harry was alone again. For a while, at least. Gratefully, he relaxed and sank down deep in his bed, and even deeper into sleep. As is the way of dreams, he quickly forgot the last one and prepared to move on to the next—

Which was when the Necroscope dreamed of someone else. Except that this time he knew for sure it was more than just a dream and that his visitor was or had been more than merely human. For his parasite responded to *this* visitor—this *other* vampire—in typical Wamphyri fashion, prompting Harry to inquire:

Who are you, that you dare come creeping into my

sleeping thoughts? Answer quickly . . . there are doors in my mind which would swallow you whole!

Ahhh! came back the answer at once. *So it's true. You won your fight with Janos, but you also lost. I'm so sorry, Harry. So sorry.*

And now Harry knew him. *Ken Layard!* he said. *We took your head and burned your body in the mountains over Halmagiu. And you went willingly to your death.*

Layard answered with a deadspeak nod. *Death was nothing compared to the prospect of being undead, in thrall to Janos Ferenczy. He would have put me down into ashes, too . . . but only to have me at his beck and call, and bring me up again whenever he had need of my talent! Anyway, and as you said, I went willingly. For I knew it would be harder for me if I tried it the other way. And Bodrogk and his Thracians were quick about it. I didn't feel a thing.*

Harry's deadspeak thoughts turned sour. *But you owe me one, right? The worst one you can give me? Because whichever way you look at it, I was the one who tracked you down. And now they're about to track me down, and so you've come to gloat.*

Layard was taken aback. *How wrong can you be, Harry?* he said. *Listen, I know you've been getting a hard time from the teeming dead, but you still have a few friends left!*

You came in friendship?

I came to say thanks! For Trevor Jordan.

Harry shook his head. *I don't follow you.*

To thank you for what you did for him. And to offer my help if there's anything I can do for you.

The Necroscope began to make sense of it. *Trevor was your friend and colleague, right? You and he were one of the best teams—one of the best partnerships—E-Branch ever had.*

The best! said Layard. *So when I died it was only natural I'd want to keep tabs on him, see how he made out. What I did best in life came even easier in death, and in life I'd been one hell of a locator. Which was pretty fortunate for me, else I'd have had a really dreary time of it. What, me? A vampire? The dead didn't want to know me, Harry.*

So locating people you'd known in life occupied a little of your time, eh?

A little of it? All of it! I mean, once you get over your fear of death—of being dead—it can pretty soon get boring! So I traced Trevor, and discovered that he was dead, too, and I would have spoken to him except the Great Majority did a job on me and blocked me out. There are some fine talents among the dead, Harry, and not a lot they can't do if they've a mind. So they'd throw up a lot of deadspeak flak every time I tried to talk to anyone. Anyone, that is, except . . .

. . . Me?

Exactly! They'll do their damnedest to mess us around, but they don't mess with us! We want to talk to each other, that's fine—just as long as we're not trying to pervert one of them.

I see, Harry said. *So the only way you could get to speak to Trevor was through me.*

That's right.

Except you're too late and your deadspeak won't work, anyway—because Trevor is alive again. Which means you still can't communicate direct but must use me as a go-between.

Complicated but, in a nutshell, correct.

Well, you picked the wrong time. Harry was half apologetic. *Try me when I'm awake.*

I'll do that. But in the meantime—maybe I can do you a favor, too.

Oh?

Harry, Layard said, *I was one of the good guys a long time before I copped it. And even at the end I was still pretty much my own man. I was a creature of Janos's making, "in thrall" to him, yes, but given even the smallest chance I'd have taken him out if that were at all possible. It wasn't possible—not for me, anyway—and so I died. But you'll never know how glad I am that he got his, too. So as you said, I owe you one. Not one of the worst but a good one. Like . . . the talent of locating? How would you like to be a locator, Harry?*

It would come in handy, certainly, the Necroscope answered. *I already have deadspeak, telepathy, one or two other things. Being able to find someone or -thing in a hurry would be a big bonus.*

That's what I thought. So maybe we can trade. You get my talent, and I get to talk to you now and then, plus a reintroduction to Trevor Jordan. I mean, you act as our go-between. Trevor would like that, I'm sure.

Harry became cautious. *What will it entail?*

Well—Layard offered a deadspeak shrug—*I'm already in your mind—in contact, anyway—so I suppose you'll just have to open up and let me look deeper inside. I mean, I know my own trick, the mechanism which makes me a locator, and if I can find a similar thing in you . . .*

. . . And activate it?

Something like that.

And you want me to open up to you of my own free will, right?

Layard chuckled, albeit drily. *You've played this game before, Harry.*

Harry nodded. *Yes, I have, occasionally with disastrous consequences.*

Layard was serious at once. *Harry, there's none of that*

shit in me. I was still myself when I went out. I don't have anything up my sleeve.

The Necroscope considered it. But what did he have to lose? *Very well,* he finally said, *except . . . I've already warned you that my mind's a weird place. Don't try to mess with me, Ken. You don't have much, I know, but I swear if you fool around in there I won't leave you with anything.*

Hey, you don't have to convince me!

Okay, Harry said. And, after a moment: *One last thing. You said you came to thank me, for what I did for Jordan? I take it you mean his resurrection? So how did you know I'd brought him back?*

Layard shrugged. *Just because the Great Majority don't speak to me doesn't mean I can't eavesdrop now and then. Also, the dead don't move around too much, you know? But Trevor does. So I knew that what I'd heard was true. You have a heap of rare talents there, Harry. A pity you didn't get Darcy's, too, before they got him!*

That focused the Necroscope's attention to a pinpoint. He fastened on it in a moment. *Darcy, dead? I thought that was just a nightmare. I hoped it was, anyway. Which means I have to hope this is, too.*

You have my sympathy, Harry, Layard told him. *But it's all real.*

No one brings me any good news anymore . . . Lost for words, Harry shook his head, then deliberately returned to the former subject. *All right, Ken, my mind's all yours.*

The locator went in—and was out again almost as quickly. And: *You're right and that's a strange place, Harry,* he said. *It's as if it was radioactive in there: hot and cold at the same time! But I found what I wanted; or rather, I didn't find it. You don't have the equipment. There's nothing there for me to switch on.*

Harry shrugged. *You tried, anyway.*

But you do have David Chung's kind of mind.

Chung? The sympathetic locator?

That's right. So I tripped that switch instead. Now all you need is something belonging to the one you need to locate. You focus on it, and bingo! Except being what you are—everything you are—you'll probably be better at it than Chung is.

Harry nodded, said: *Well, I suppose it's my turn to owe you again. Thanks, Ken.*

Oh, I'll be back later to collect, Layard told him. *I mean, Trevor was like my kid brother, you know? And now I'll go and let you get some sleeping done. You're tired, Harry, in mind and body both.*

As Layard backed off and faded into nothing, the Necroscope's mind cleared itself for whatever else, whoever else, was waiting. And she didn't take long in coming.

He dreamed of Penny. But was she a dream . . . or just a fancy? Even dreaming, he wondered about it: was she an adjustment of psyche—part of the pigeonholing of mundane occurrences into all the subconscious slots between "forget it," through trivial, to highly important—or just a remnant left over from a moment or two of waking lust?

He'd known of course that the dead girl had a crush on him. It had been obvious even from their first meeting. For after all, how many men get to see their ladies naked on a first date? In Harry's day, damn few! Maybe this was simply the extrapolation of something his subconscious mind had been working on, and should be titled: "How Things Might Have Been if Harry Keogh Could Spare the Time and if He Wasn't a Bloody Vampire."

Whichever, it was a soothing and blessed relief to his tormented mind after the nightmare of association with

Johnny Found, the delirium of Darcy Clarke's accusations, and the revelations of Ken Layard; and it brought physical relief, too, as he answered Penny's caresses and loved her with his body as any ordinary man loves a girl. The initiative, however, was all hers—had to be—else his exhaustion must drag him down even deeper into dreamless sleep.

And Harry wondered about that, too: how come she knew how to do it all? For after all, he knew she was an innocent . . . his little innocent, whose death he would soon avenge.

"Isn't bringing me back enough?" she whispered, guiding his rubbery fingers to her stiffening nipples. "Do you have to go after him, too? You know, Harry, I've been doing a lot of thinking since all of this happened. And, I mean, I've got so much to be glad for. I was dead, and now I'm alive! It would be sort of ungrateful of me to want revenge, too. Oh, I wanted it at first, I know, but now I'm not so sure. But I'd settle for you, certainly."

He lay back and listened to her, and felt her small, gentle fingers tight on his flesh where it throbbed, but lazily as yet like a motor waiting for the throttle. And in the darkness she sat up beside him, crouched over him, and patted him with her hands so that he swayed from side to side, jerking and snatching at the darkness.

Are the sexual arts instinctive in some people? Harry couldn't remember who had shown him. Or had he just known? Maybe he would remember when he woke up. But for the moment he didn't want to wake up. Here, now, asleep, he was just a man. No more the Necroscope, no more the vampire, just a man being loved and making love, and waiting for the sweet sucking thing which was the heart of Penny's womanhood to descend onto his silently singing flesh. And hoping against hope that the dream wouldn't fade or change its course, and that he would get to come. The last time he'd made love had been . . . just weeks ago, but already it felt like forever. He felt full to bursting. Maybe it was just *being* with this girl, Penny, just being human, which from now on he could never be again.

And the poignancy of that was so great that when at last, gasping, she actually slid her sweet young body down onto him, he came almost at once, like an urgent youth stroking his first love's breasts. And feeling him shuddering within her—the hot spurt of his juices—she clenched him that much tighter, until the jerking of his flesh had spent him to the last drop.

Following which . . . the gradual resurgence of his need was slow but sure, and her guidance unwavering, until he was in her again.

This time they lay on their sides, and while his left hand stroked, squeezed, and compressed the pillow of her right buttock, so the tight tube of her vagina sucked on him for the milk of love and life. And Harry thought: *If this were real I wouldn't dare, for fear of making her pregnant with my damned "milk of life"! Or in my case, my tainted Wamphyri sperm!*

And deep inside, his vampire laughed at him. Milk of life? Frothing spume of lust, more like. For as everyone knows, only the blood is the true life.

"Harry!" She clawed at his shoulders, rubbed his chest furiously with her flattened, elastic breasts. And, "Harry!" she panted again. "I'm coming . . . coming . . . *coming!*"

It brought him to climax, too, the thought of her orgasm and the feel of its wet, wrenching tremors. But more than that, it brought him to his senses. Suddenly, he was awake. Wide awake in their sweat and their fluids and the pungent smell of their love—which wasn't fading back into the depths of his subconscious mind! Which wasn't the ephemeral stuff of dreams! Which was in fact totally, terribly real! *Because Penny was there in his bed with him!*

Harry gasped and opened his eyes, and shot bolt upright in the tumbled bed.

"It's all right, it's okay!" Penny said, grasping his wrists in the moment before she saw his eyes. Then: "Oh!" she said as her hand flew to her mouth.

Harry's mind whirled. What the hell was happening here? How had Penny got into the house? Where was Jordan? "Oh?" he finally repeated her. "Bloody oh!? Penny, you don't realize what you've done!"

He tossed back the covers and pulled on his clothes; naked, she came after him, drew him to a standstill, and reached tremblingly to touch his redly illumined face in the darkness of the room.

"When I was dead," she said in a whisper, "they tried to tell me you were a monster. I wouldn't listen to them, because I didn't want to talk to dead people. But I remember they said there was life, and death, and a place between the two. People have existence in the first two places but not in the third, which is reserved for . . ."

". . . For vampires," Harry cut in harshly. "Yes, and for their victims, people they turn into vampires. And for foolish girls who through their thoughtless actions change *themselves* into vampires!"

She shook her head. "But you didn't take my blood, Harry. You didn't even make me bleed!" She was defiant. "I'm almost nineteen and anyway, I wasn't a virgin. I . . . I knew a man for a whole year, once."

"Knew a man!" he snorted. "You're a child!"

"And you're out of touch!" she hit back. "It's 1989! Plenty of girls—British girls—get married at sixteen and seventeen these days. Yes, and plenty more prefer not to

351

get married but simply live with their lovers. I'm no child. Are you saying my body felt like a child's?''

"Yes!" he snapped, then gritted his teeth, folded her in his arms, and groaned, ''No. You felt—you feel—like a woman. But still a foolish one. Penny, you don't understand. I didn't need to make you bleed. You see, there's something of me in you now. It's not much but it doesn't need to be, for even a little is enough to change you.''

"Then let it, as long as I'm with you." She clutched him to her. "You brought me back, Harry, gave me my life. For what it's worth, I owe it to you. All of it. And I want you to have it.''

"You've run away from home?" He put her away from him, to arm's length.

"I've *left* home," she sighed. "1989, remember?''

He wanted to hit her and couldn't. He thought: *Dear God, she's in thrall to me!* And then thought, *But she was, even before this. Except we'd call it a crush. Please* don't *let anything of me—of that—be in her!*

His head cleared; sleep and all that had accompanied it receded; the implications came home to him fully. "What time is it?" He glanced at his watch. Only 10:30 P.M. "How did you find me? More important, how did you get in?''

She sensed his urgency and reacted to it. ''What's wrong, Harry?" And now her eyes were frightened.

As he put on the lights and his face took on a more normal aspect, she said, "When I was here before, I saw the address on some of your mail. I remembered it, remembered everything about you. In fact you haven't been out of my mind for a minute. And I knew I would have to come to you. No matter what!''

"And Trevor Jordan let you in? Without waking me?" Harry hurled open his bedroom door. "Trevor!" he shouted. "Will you come—the—hell—*up* here?!''

There was no answer, just Penny shaking her head.

Harry looked at her; long-legged, yellow-haired, blue-eyed. His gaze took in her firm breasts, thighs, and backside, all of her beautiful young body. And the uneven slant of her mouth, which was quite unintentioned but still made her look sexy and somehow provocative. When he'd first seen her like this, naked, there had been ugly black holes in her flesh. But now she was whole again. Whole, but probably unholy.

"Better get dressed," he said. And: "Jordan?"

"Gone," she said, slipping easily into her clothing. "I told him I had to be with you; he made me promise to look after you; he told me to tell you goodbye."

"That's all?"

"No, he also said I shouldn't stay. But when he couldn't convince me, then he went. And he said you would understand. Oh, and I remember he said he only hoped that—er, E-Branch?—that they would understand, too. For his sake."

"E-Branch," Harry echoed her. And then, remembering his dream, *"Darcy!"*

"Who?" She was dressed. She stared at him.

"Go downstairs," he said. "Make some coffee. For yourself. There's red wine in the fridge for me. Pour me a glass."

"Harry, I—"

"Do it now!"

She went.

And when he was alone, Harry sent out his deadspeak thoughts to search for Darcy Clarke, and prayed he wouldn't find him . . . but found him, anyway. Found him blowing on the wind, drifting with the tides, flushed away like so much flotsam. Or maybe jetsam? Jetsam, yes: materials hurled from the deck of a ship in peril. Sacrificed for the greater good.

The Necroscope sat on the edge of his bed and shed several hot, slow tears. It was his humanity, amplified by the overpowering emotions of the Wamphyri. Even if he were only human he would have cried, except then his tears wouldn't burn like the overflow of the volcano rumbling within.

"Darcy," he said, "who was it?"

It was you, Harry. Darcy's deadspeak was faint as the wind over the sea, heard in the whorl of a small shell.

"God, I know!" Harry felt stabbed to the heart. "But who was it physically? Who took your life? And . . . *how* did you die? Not the old way?"

The stake, the sword, the fire? No, just a bullet. Well, two bullets. The fire wasn't until later.

"And your executioner?"

Why? So you can go after him? Oh, no, Harry. For after all he was only doing his job—and he obviously suspected that I was a deadly threat. Also . . . well, it's a fact my own actions could have been more prudent. So maybe it was as much my fault as it was yours. But on the other hand, maybe if I'd known I was no longer protected, then I would *have been more careful.*

"You won't tell me who killed you?"

I have told you. You did.

"Then I'll have to find out some other time, from someone else."

Why don't you just steal it out of my deadspeak mind?

"I don't just take. Not from my friends. If you won't tell me of your own free will, then I'll just have to find out some other way."

But you did take—and not just information—and it most certainly was not *of my own free will! So that now I'm a dead friend. Just one of the Great Majority.*

A third party asked, "Find out what some other way?" And Harry gave a small start. But it was only Penny, standing in the doorway with a glass of red wine in her hand. She'd heard the Necroscope apparently talking to himself.

Harry's concentration slipped; Darcy Clarke's deadspeak disintegrated; contact was lost. But Harry wasn't angry. Not with Penny. If he and Darcy had continued, they probably would have parted on even worse terms. "Let's go downstairs," he said. "Out into the garden. It's a warm night. Are the stars out? I'd like to look at the stars. And think."

He would like to look at *his* stars, yes: the familiar constellations. For who could say, maybe it would be his last opportunity. And the stars over Starside were very different. And he would like to think. About what Penny had said, for one thing: did he really need to even the score with Johnny Found? And why the hell should he want to know who had killed Darcy Clarke? Darcy wasn't himself vengeful, was he?

And then there was Ken Layard and his gift. Harry was now a locator. Well, and he always had been, to an extent. Telepathically, he could readily seek and discover others of his acquaintance, such as Zek Foener and Trevor Jordan. And given an introduction to a dead person, from then on he'd always been able to find his way to that person's graveside. And no matter the distance, he'd rarely had difficulty conversing with such dead friends. But now . . . the teeming dead didn't much want to speak to him anymore.

Some do, said another voice in his metaphysical mind, one which laved him like a shower on a sweltering hot day. It was Pamela Trotter, and she was a breath of fresh air.

Penny had come into the garden with the Necroscope, but of course she hadn't heard Pamela's deadspeak. Harry sent her indoors; if not, she would only talk to him, question and distract him. But turning away toward the house she looked like she might cry, and so he said: "I'm not putting you away from me, but I need to be alone for a couple of minutes. After that we'll have lots of time for being together." *Because I'll have to watch you until I'm sure you're just you. Or if it comes to the worst, until I'm sure that you're something else.*

His thoughts were deadspeak, or good as, and Pamela picked them up. As Penny went back indoors, so the ex-whore said: *A vampire lover, Harry? I'm jealous!*

"Well, you shouldn't be." He shook his head and explained what had happened, the trouble Penny had probably landed herself in.

Hey, I could use that sort of trouble! Pamela retorted. *I mean, I really wouldn't mind being undead with someone like you! But . . . too late for that. I'm not much up to fun and games anymore. Maybe just one last time, eh? For the right man, you know?*

She went quiet and waited for his answer; a long, pregnant pause which defied him to cry off now. Not that he intended to. Eventually, he said, "You think we should go ahead with it?"

She sighed. *Well, no question which one of you is in charge right now.*

"Oh?"

You have the upper hand, Harry—the human you. For if your vampire was ascendant you'd have no such doubts. You would know *what was right!*

Harry gave a snort. "My vampire would know what to do for the best? The best for my vampire, maybe!"

So what's your problem? (She was becoming impatient with him.) *You're one and the same, or will be.*

"My problem is simple," the Necroscope answered. "If the dark side of me gets its way, the human side loses—perhaps permanently. So maybe I should just let the police have Johnny Found. I know that left to their own devices they'll get him soon enough anyway, because they're right on his tail even now. But—"

—*But we had a deal!* she cut in. *I can't believe you'd want to cry off. I mean, you were so* hot *for this! Did I let you into my mind—to read what you read there—for nothing? And the other girls? Are they dead for nothing, with no chance to square it?* You *were the only chance we ever had, Harry. And now you say let the police have him? I mean, fuck the police! Why, they wouldn't even know what to* do *with him! What, lock him up in a lunatic asylum for a couple of years, then turn him loose to do it again? No! You were right the first time around: he has to pay now. The full price.*

He held up his hands. "Pamela, wait—"

Wait, nothing! You . . . *chickenshit vampire! Have me and the others been digging our way out all this time for nothing?*

That took Harry by surprise. "Others?"

I've made a few friends. And they want to help.

"So," he said, "let them help . . ."

And after long, wondering moments: *Then* . . . *you haven't changed your mind?*

He shook his head. "Not for a minute. I was just thinking my way round it, that's all. You're the one who's coming on all excited and changeable."

She was silent for a count of three, then said, *I think that just now, just a minute ago, you deliberately let me run on—or off—at the mouth!*

"It's possible," he admitted, nodding. "We chickenshit vampires are like that: argumentative just for the sake of it."

I'm sorry, Harry (she felt an utter fool), *but it's just that we're all set now. And when I homed in on you, it seemed to me you might be reconsidering things.*

"No," he said again, "just thinking things through—

or maybe arguing with myself—for the sake of it. What did you want, anyway?''

He could almost hear her sigh of relief. *I was hoping you'd have some idea when we can expect . . . ?*

"Soon," he cut her off. "It has to be very soon now." And to himself: *Because if I'm going to get Johnny Found, it has to be before E-Branch gets after me. If they're not already after me.*

In fact he strongly suspected that they were—no, he knew that they must be—and the night would yet prove him right . . .

Harry finished his drink and went back inside.

Penny was waiting for him, pale and lovely, and the look on her face begged the question: what's going to become of us? The Necroscope wasn't sure yet, so gave her a kiss instead. Which was when she asked him how it had happened to him. That was something he'd asked himself time and again, until he now believed he had the answer.

Wasting few words, he quickly told her about old Faethor Ferenczy's place in Ploieşti, Romania: the once-ruins where an ancient father of vampires had lain, where surely by now the bulldozers had leveled everything and a concrete mausoleum was mushrooming to the grey skies. Except the vast hive would not be intended as a memorial to the evil of Faethor (for he had been secretive to the end, so that no one living today remembered him) but to that of the madman Ceaucescu's agro-industrial obsession. Anyway, there was nothing of Faethor left there now; or if anything, only a memory; and even then not in the people, only in the earth which the Great Vampire had poisoned.

"I'd lost my talents," Harry explained. "I had no deadspeak and was locked out of the Möbius Continuum. But Faethor told me he could fix all that if I would only go to see him. I was over a barrel and had to do it; but in fact he *did* give me back my deadspeak, and he assisted in my rediscovery of the Möbius Continuum. But all of that was incidental to his plan, which was to come back, to return as a Power and a Plague into the world of men.

"As to how he would do it:

"I still don't know if it was an act of evil will or the automatic action of alien nature. I don't know whether Faethor caused it to come about, or if he knew it would happen of its own accord. I can't be sure it wasn't something he himself set in motion, 'with malice aforethought,' or simply the last gasp of his own vampire's incredible urge for survival. All I know for sure is that there's *nothing* more tenacious than a vampire.

"The mechanics of the thing were simple:

"Faethor had died when his home was bombed during the war. Staked through by a fallen ceiling beam, and decapitated out of mercy by a man who happened upon the scene, his body had been burned. Nothing of him escaped the fire . . . or did it?

"What of his fats—vampire fats—rendered down from his flesh, dripping into cracks in the floorboards, seeping into the earth while the rest of the house and Faethor's flesh went up in flames? The Greek Christian priests of old had known how to deal with vampires: how *every piece* of the Vrykoulakas must be burned, because each smallest part has the power of regeneration!

"Anyway, that's how I see it: Faethor's spirit—and not only that but something of the monster's *physical* essence, too—had remained there in the atmosphere of the place, and in the earth, waiting. But waiting for what? To be triggered? By what? By Faethor, when he found himself a suitable vessel or vehicle into the future? I believe so. And also that I was to have been that vehicle.

"Something of him—call it his essential fluids, if you like—had gone down into the earth under his ruins to escape the furnace heat, and when I went to see him and laid myself down to sleep upon that selfsame spot (God, I did, I really did!) then that something surfaced to enter into me. But what was it? I had seen nothing there but a few bats flitting on the night air, which came nowhere near me.

"No, I had seen . . . something."

At this point the Necroscope directed Penny's fascinated gaze to a shelf of books on the wall by the fireplace. There were a dozen of them, all with the same subject: fungi. She stared hard at the books, then at Harry. "Mushrooms?"

He shrugged. "Mushrooms, toadstools, fungi—as you can see, I've made something of a study of them. In fact they've occupied quite a bit of my time in the last few weeks." He got her one of the books, titled, *The Handbook Guide to Mushrooms and Other Fungi*, and turned to a well-thumbed page near the back. "That's not the one"—he tapped a fingernail on the illustrated page—"but it's the closest I've found. My fungus was more nearly black—and rightly so."

She looked at the page. "The common earthball?"

Harry gave a grunt. "Not so common!" he answered. "Not the variety I saw, anyway. They weren't there when I settled down to sleep, but they were there when I woke up: a ring of morbid fruiting bodies—small black mushrooms or puffballs—already rotting and bursting open at the slightest movement, releasing their scarlet spores. I remember I sneezed when their dust got up my nose.

"Later, when they'd rotted right down, their stench was . . . well, it was like death. No, it *was* death. I remember how the sun seemed to steam them away. Shortly after that, Faethor wished me well—which should have been a warning in itself—and advised me not to waste any time but complete the task I'd set myself with dispatch. I thought it a queer thing to say, that the *way* he'd said it had been queer, but he didn't elaborate.''

She shook her head. ''You *breathed* the spores of a toadstool and became . . . ?''

''A vampire, yes,'' Harry finished it for her. ''But they weren't the spores of just any toadstool. These things were spawned of Faethor's slime, of his rottenness. They were his deadspawn. But . . . well, that wasn't all there was to it. For I'd had a lot of truck with vampires, too, over the years, and I'd learned their ways—perhaps learned too much. Maybe that's also part of it, I'm not sure. But at least you can see now why you shouldn't have gone to bed with me. A few spores was enough for me. So . . . what about you?''

''But as long as I'm with you . . .'' she began.

''Penny,'' he cut in, ''I'm not staying here. I'm not even staying in this world.''

She flew into his arms. ''I don't care which world! Take me wherever you go, whenever you go, and I'll always be there to care for you.''

Well, he thought, *and I will need someone. And you are a lovely creature.* And out loud:

''But I can't go anywhere until Found is finished. It's not just for you but all the others he murdered, too. And one in particular. I made her a promise.''

''Found?''

''Johnny Found, that's his name. And I have to get after him. He has to die because he's . . . he's like me and all the others I've had to deal with: not meant to be. Not in any clean world. I mean, Found hurts the very dead! Isn't dying enough without him, too? And what if he ever fathers children? What will they be, eh? And will their mother leave them on a doorstep like Johnny was left? No, he has to be stopped here, now.''

Just thinking about the necromancer had worked Harry into a fury, or if not Harry, his vampire certainly. He wondered what Found was doing right now, this very moment.

He *more* than wondered—he had to know.

Harry freed himself from Penny's arms, put out the light, stood dark in the darkened room, and reached out with his metaphysical mind. He knew Found's address, knew the way there. He sent a probe there, to Darlington, the street, the house, into the ground-floor flat . . . and found it empty.

This was his chance to take something belonging to the necromancer. Would there be watchers in the street? Probably. But with any luck he wouldn't be there long enough that they'd see him. "Penny, I have to go somewhere now," he said. "But I'll be right back. A few minutes at most. You're to lock the doors and stay right here, in the house." His red eyes glowed. "This is my place! Only let them *dare* to . . . to . . . and . . ."

"Let who dare?" she whispered. "E-Branch? Let them dare to what, Harry?"

"A few minutes," he growled. "I'll be back before you know it."

VI Countdown to Hell

THERE WERE WATCHERS.

Harry chose to exit from the Möbius Continuum at his entry point the last time he'd been there, in the shadow of the wall across the alley from Found's place. And one of the watchers was right there!

Even in the moment he stepped from the Continuum into the "real," physical world, Harry heard the plainclothesman's gasp and knew someone was there in the shadows with him; knew, too, that even now this unknown someone would be reaching for his gun. One big difference between them was that Harry could see perfectly well in the dark, and another was that his adversary was only a man.

Reacting in a lightning-fast movement, Harry reached out to slap the man's weapon out of his hand . . . and saw what kind of a "gun" it was which the other had produced from under his coat. A crossbow! He knocked it away, anyway, sent it clattering on the cobbles, and held the esper by his throat against the wall.

The man was terrified. A prognosticator—a reader of future times—he had known that Harry would come here. That had been as far as he could see; but he'd also known that his own life-thread went on beyond this point. Which had seemed to mean that if there was trouble, Harry would be on the receiving end.

The Necroscope read these things right out of the esper's gibbering mind, and his voice was a clotted gurgle as he told him: "Reading the future's a dangerous game. So you're going to live, are you? Well, maybe. But what as? A man—or a vampire?" He tilted his head a little on one side and smiled at the other through eyes burning like coals under a bellows' blast, and in the next moment stopped smiling and showed him his teeth.

The esper saw the gape—the impossible gape—of Harry's jaws, and gagged as the vampire's steel fingers tightened on his windpipe. In his mind he was screaming, *Oh, Jesus! I'm dead—dead!*

"You could be," Harry told him. "You could oh so easily be. It rather depends on how well we get on. Now tell me: who killed Darcy Clarke?"

The man, short and sturdy, balding and narrow-eyed, used both hands to try to loosen Harry's grip on his throat. It was useless. Turning purple, still he managed to shake his head, refusing to answer the Necroscope's question with anything but a gurgle. But Harry read it in his mind, anyway.

Paxton! *That* vicious, slimy . . .

At that, Harry's fury filled him to bursting. It would be so easy to just tighten his grip until this staggering shit's Adam's apple turned to mush in his hand . . . but that would be to punish him for what someone else had done. Also, it would be to pander to the monster raging inside him.

Instead he tossed the man away from him, took a deep breath, and breathed a vampire mist. By the time the esper was able to prop himself on one elbow against the wall, choking and massaging his throat, the mist lay over the alley like a shroud and Harry had disappeared into it—

—Or rather through it, and through the Möbius Continuum into Johnny Found's flat.

He knew he didn't have a lot of time; it depended how many men the Branch had up here; they could be coming through the main door of the building right now. And they'd be equipped with all the right gear, too. A crossbow is a hellishly ugly weapon, but a flamethrower is far worse!

Found's flat was grimy as a pigsty and smelled just as bad. Harry moved through it without touching, thinking: *Even my shoes will feel unclean.*

First he checked the door. It was sturdy as hell, made of heavy old-fashioned oak hung on massive hinges, fitted with three locks and, on the inside, two large bolts. Obviously, Johnny hadn't intended that anyone should break in; which sufficed to make Harry feel a little safer, too. He quickly moved on.

In the front room, before a small, grimy window overlooking the now quiet road, he paused beside a cheap writing desk. One drawer of the desk was half open; Harry glimpsed a metallic sheen from inside but was distracted by the items on top of the desk: a creased, stained, huge-breasted Samantha Fox calendar, with today's date ringed in biro alongside some scribbled marginalia, and a hand-scrawled message on a sheet of A4 bearing the Frigis Express logo. The calendar didn't seem especially important . . . at least, not until Harry had read the message on the A4:

Johnny—
  Tonight. A London run. Your "lucky charm" truck, which I'll have loaded for you. Pick her up at the depot 11:40. It's for Parkinson's in Slough. They'll be dressing it for Heathrow Suppliers starting first thing in the morning, so we can't be late with this. Sorry for late notice. If you can't make it, let me know soonest.

The note was signed in some indecipherable scrawl, but Harry didn't need to know who had signed it. The date at the top was today's. Johnny had a London run tonight, leaving the Darlington depot at 11:40.

Now Harry looked at the calendar again. In the margin opposite the ringed date, Found had scribbled: "London run! Good, cos I feel lucky and this could be my night. And I need to fuck inside a tit . . ."

Glancing at his watch, Harry saw that it was 11:30. Johnny was at the depot right now.

The Necroscope came to a decision there and then. His mad quarry used a Frigis Express truck (his "lucky charm" truck) as a prop in his crazed games of sex, murder, and necromancy; and so the truck should likewise feature in his punishment. Very well, tonight would be Johnny's last run. And now all Harry needed was an item from the lunatic's personal belongings.

He yanked the desk drawer open the rest of the way, and a half dozen heavy metal tubes jumped in their velvet-lined compartments. Harry looked at them and thought, *What the . . . ?* But as he carefully lifted one of the tubes out of the drawer he knew well enough what the.

The thing was a weapon, which Found himself must have made or had manufactured, for use on his victims. Or for use on one of them, anyway. A name had been painted with a small brush in black enamel on the shining metal: Penny. And Harry thought, *This was what went into Penny, before Found went into her*.

The weapon fitted Pamela Trotter's description perfectly. A section of steel tubing about an inch and a half internal diameter, one end was cut square and had a rubber sheath or handgrip, and the other end was cut diagonally to a point. That was the cutting edge of the tool, and its rim had been filed from the inside out to a razor's sharpness. The Necroscope already knew how—and why—such a hideous knife would be used. The very thought of it was sickening.

As a kid Harry had played in the deep snows of England's northeast coast. When he was quite small he'd love to just sit there in the piled snow with an old tin can, driving the open end *plop* into the cold, soft white bank. When you pulled the can out again it would be full of snow; short fat cylinders of snow, from which you could build castles like on the beach. Except unlike sand castles, which melted away when the tide came in, these castles would last for days until the weather warmed up. But it wasn't the castles he pictured now but the perfectly circular holes which the can had used to leave in the snow. In his mind's eye he could see those holes even now . . . and they were crimson. And they weren't cut in snow.

Harry looked at the other steel-tubing knives. There were five more of them. Four were called after girls whose names he knew from the police files but didn't know personally, and the fifth carried the name Pamela. This bastard kept them like *mementoes*, like photographs of old flames! Harry could imagine him masturbating over them.

Six weapons in all, yes, but there were seven velvet-lined trays in the drawer. Found must have the seventh tube with him, except it wouldn't have a name yet.

Suddenly, Harry's vampire awareness warned him of someone—in fact more than one—entering the main door of the house to creep in the communal corridor outside Found's door. E-Branch? The police? Both? He sent out his thoughts to touch upon their minds. Another mind stared back at him for a moment, then withdrew in shock and horror. It had been a middling telepath; E-Branch again; but the others out there were police. Armed, of course. Heavily.

The Necroscope snarled a silent snarl and felt his face twisting out of its familiar contours. For a mad moment he considered standing and fighting; why, he would even win! But then he remembered his purpose in coming here—the job still to be finished—and conjured a Möbius door.

He went to the Frigis Express depot.

Emerging from the Möbius Continuum onto the grass verge where the Frigis works exit turned onto an A1 South access road, he was in time to feel the blast of a big articulated truck as it sped by. The man at the wheel was just a shadow behind the glassy night sheen of his windscreen, but despite the fact that the legend on the side of the truck said only "Frigis Express," still it spoke volumes. For one leg of the "x" was missing where the paint had peeled away, making it look like "Eypress."

Johnny Found's "lucky charm" truck.

Harry came forward to the edge of the road, was trapped for a moment in sweeping headlight beams where a large, powerful car followed not too far behind the truck. Intense faces merely glanced at him as the car swept by.

But there was something about those faces. Harry reached out and touched their minds. Police! They were after Found; they still wanted to catch him red-handed, or if not that, at least on the point of picking up some poor unsuspecting girl. Fools! There was evidence enough in his flat to put him away for . . . not for long enough. Pamela was right: he'd probably go into a madhouse and be out again in short order.

That other party back at Johnny's flat in Darlington: maybe they had broken in by now. Maybe they knew. So if Harry wanted the necromancer for himself, he was going to have to work fast.

But then he remembered Penny, alone in the house in Bonnyrig. He didn't know how long this was going to take. He could simply kill Found out of hand, of course, or cause him to be killed in any number of ways. Except he'd made a deal with Pamela Trotter, and he still wouldn't cheat on the dead. Also, Found's punishment should fit the crime. But Penny shouldn't be left on her own . . . not for too long . . . They'd killed Darcy Clarke, hadn't they? . . . *Why the fuck was everything so complicated?*

Harry felt the tension building . . . felt it swelling until the pressure inside was enormous . . . then gulpingly filled his lungs with the cool night air and took a firm, deliberate grip on himself. Penny had put him first; he must put her first; he took the Möbius route to Edinburgh.

She wasn't in the house!

Harry couldn't believe it. He'd told her to stay here, to wait for him. So where had she gone? He reached out with his telepathic mind—

—But which direction? At this hour of the night,

where *could* she have gone? Why? For what reason? Or had she simply taken Trevor Jordan's advice and walked out on him?

He let his vampire awareness guide him, sent probes into the night, spreading outwards like ripples on the surface of a sentient mind-pool, seeking for Penny . . . and found others! Espers! Again!

He snarled at them, in their minds, and felt the shutters slam into place as they clamped down tight as limpets to rocks when the tide goes out. They'd been close but not too close, probably in Bonnyrig, some house they'd made their HQ. Harry passed them by, attempted to search farther afield, came up against mental static that sizzled like bacon frying in his mind. It was E-Branch scrambling his sendings.

Damn all you mindspies! he cursed. *I should get out and let you all find your own paths to hell. But I should leave something behind me to make sure you get there, something to give you nightmares forever!*

He could do it, too, if he so desired, for he had the plague in him. This could be his legacy to a world and race which had forsaken him: a plague of vampires.

Physically, his own vampire was undeveloped, immature as yet; but its blood was his blood, and his bite must surely be virulent. And at his command, the infinite vastness of the metaphysical Möbius Continuum. Why, he could plant vampires in every continent in the world—right now, tonight—if he wished it. And maybe then they would wish they'd left him the fuck alone!

He rushed out into his garden under the stars and the risen moon. It was night, his time. *Ahhh, his time!* But maybe in more ways than one. They were here for a reason, these espers. They could be coming for him right now, invisible under their shield of static.

"Come then, come!" he taunted them. "And only *see* what's waiting for you!"

At the bottom of the garden, someone pushed the gate creakingly open. "Harry?" Penny stepped into view and started up the path towards him.

"Penny?" The Necroscope reached out to her with his arms and with his mind, but *her* mind was a blur—or rather a mist—in which her psyche hid without even knowing it. Mind-smog!

Harry felt devastated, but he must hide it. Now she was a vampire, or would be, and now she *was* his thrall. It wasn't a crush any longer. And he wondered if it ever had been. After all, he had brought her back from the dead.

"What were you doing out in the night? I told you to wait."

"But the night was so beautiful, and just like you I needed to think." She let him fold her in his arms.

"What did you think about?" *The night lured you. You felt the first fires racing in your veins. And tomorrow the sun will hurt your eyes, irritate your skin.*

"I thought . . . maybe you didn't want to take me with you. Maybe you wouldn't."

"You thought wrong. I will." *I have to, for to leave you in this world would be to sign your death warrant.*

"But you don't love me."

"Oh, but I do," he lied. *But it won't matter one way or the other, for you won't love me, either. Still, we'll have our lust.*

"Harry, I'm frightened!"

Too late, too late! "I don't want to leave you here now," he told her. "You'd better come with me."

"But where?"

He took her into the house, ran through the rooms turning on all the lights, quickly returned to her. And

371

he showed her Johnny's knife, with her name on it. She gasped and drew back from him. "Can you imagine him?" he asked her, his voice dark as a winter night. "Can you picture him looking at this and remembering your pain and his pleasure?"

She shuddered. "I . . . I thought I'd forgotten. I've tried to forget."

"You will forget," he said, "and so will I—when it's over. But I can't leave you here, and I have to finish it with him."

"Will I see him?" She turned pale at the thought.

Harry nodded. "Yes," and his scarlet eyes lit in a strange smile. "Yes—and he will see you!"

"But you won't let him hurt me?"

"I promise."

"Then I'm ready . . ."

One hour earlier at Waverly station in Edinburgh, Trevor Jordan had boarded the overnight sleeper for London. He'd made no plans as such; tomorrow morning, early, he would probably give E-Branch a ring and see if he could sniff out which way the wind was blowing. And if it felt right he'd offer them his services again. They'd check him out (in the circumstances it was only to be expected) and of course they'd want to know all about his experiences with Harry Keogh. But he'd make sure that all of that took time, and by then Harry wouldn't be here anymore. In the event he *was* still here, Jordan would cry off any work that went against him.

Not out of fear but respect, and out of gratitude . . . yes, and if he was truthful, out of fear, too. Harry was Harry and a vampire. In that respect, anyone who didn't feel at least something of fear had to be an idiot.

The telepath had paid for a bed but couldn't sleep.

There was just too much on his mind. He was a man back from the dead and he couldn't get used to it, probably never would. Not even a man who makes a full recovery from a desperate illness could feel like Jordan felt. For he had gone beyond illness—beyond life itself—and returned. And it was all down to Harry.

Unknown to Jordan, unknown even to Harry himself, was the fact that there was a lot more than that down to him. For the one thing Jordan hadn't taken into account was that Harry had been in his mind: the Necroscope had *touched* upon his mind—"fingered" it, however briefly—enough that he'd left his prints there. And no way to erase them.

To E-Branch—certainly to the two espers who had followed Jordan onto the train, one a spotter and the other a telepath—those prints took the form of a reeking mental mist called mind-smog. Of course, they couldn't probe too deeply, because Jordan was himself a quality telepath and he'd know it; indeed Gareth Scanlon, one of the two men who shadowed him, had once been Jordan's pupil, brought on by him until his own talent had matured and taken shape. Jordan would know his mind (not to mention his face, his voice) immediately. Which was why the two kept well away from him, boarded a carriage far down the train, on the other side of the buffet car, and sat for the first part of their journey with their hats on, hiding behind newspapers which they'd already read four or five times.

But Jordan never once headed in their direction or sent a single thought their way; he was satisfied to just sit in his sleeper compartment, listen to the clatter of the wheels on the tracks, and watch the night world roll by beyond his window. And be glad he was once more a part of that world, without once pausing to wonder for how long.

As the train slowed down a little for a viaduct crossing between Alnwick and Morpeth, Scanlon sat up straighter in his seat and closed his eyes in sudden, half-fearful concentration. Someone was trying to get through to him. But the thoughts were sharp, clean, and entirely human, with nothing of vampire mind-smog about them. It was Millicent Cleary at the HQ in London, from where she, the Minister Responsible, and the E-Branch Duty Officer were coordinating and running the show.

She kept it short:

Gareth? Do you have a sitrep?

Scanlon relaxed his screen of static and gave a brief situation report, finishing: *He's in a sleeper, coming all the way into London.*

Maybe not, she came back. *It depends how things are going, but the Minister says we might pull the plug on all three of them very soon now.*

What? Scanlon's concern was obvious; also his horror, that at any moment he and his colleague might be called upon to kill a man; indeed, to kill a former friend.

Cleary picked that up. *A former friend, yes, but now a vampire.* And a moment later: *The Minister wants to know, is there a problem?*

There wasn't, except: *I mean, we are on a train, remember? We can't very well burn him on the bloody train!*

The train will be stopping in Darlington, and we already have agents there. So be ready for the word. You may have to get off the train there and take Trevor . . . er, Jordan, with you. That's it for now. We'll get back to you.

Scanlon passed the message on to his companion, the spotter Alan Kellway, who was one of the Branch's more recent recruits. "I didn't know Jordan all that well," Kellway answered, "and so have no problem that way. All I know is he was dead and now is alive—life of a sort—and that it isn't natural. So we'll only be restoring the natural order of things."

"But I *did* know him." Scanlon shrank down in his seat. "He was my friend. It will be like murder!"

"A Pyrrhic killing, yes." Kellway put it his way. "But is it really? You have to remember: Harry Keogh, Jordan, and their kind . . . they could murder our entire world!"

Scanlon nodded. "That's what I keep telling myself. That's what I have to keep telling myself."

In the Möbius Continuum, Johnny Found's unthinkable knife was like a lodestone: it pointed in Found's direction. Rather, Harry's locator talent pointed the knife, and he simply followed where it led.

Penny clung to him with her eyes closed; she had looked once, but that had been enough. The darkness of the Möbius Continuum was like a solid. That was because of the absence of everything material, the absence even of time. Where there is Nothing, however, even thoughts have weight.

It's a kind of magic, she whispered, as much to herself as to anyone.

No, the Necroscope answered, *but you can be forgiven for thinking it. After all, Pythagoras thought it, too*. At which point, expert in the ways of the Möbius Continuum that he was, Harry sensed a cessation of motion and knew he'd found Found.

Forming a Möbius door and looking through, he saw a hedgerow paralleling a ribbon road that stretched into the distance straight as a ruler. Vehicles thundered by on the metaled surface, their lights strobing the bushes of the hedgerow into a flickering kaleidoscope of yellow, green, and black. And even as Harry watched, so the Frigis Express truck whoofed by.

A short Möbius jump took them a mile farther down the road, where they exited inside a catwalk spanning the A1's multiple-lane system. And a minute later Harry said: "Here he comes."

They gazed down through the walkway's windows, watched the Frigis Express truck thunder by beneath them to rumble on down the road. As its lights diminished and merged with those of the rest of the night traffic, Penny asked, "What now?"

Harry shrugged and checked their location. "Boroughbridge is a mile or two farther south," he said. "Johnny might stop there or might not. In any case, I don't intend to monitor his progress mile by mile; but I do know that somewhere along the line he'll call a halt, probably at an all-night diner. That's his *modus operandi*, right? It's his venue, the hunting ground where he finds his victims: women, on their own, in the dead of night. Except . . . I don't have to tell you that, do I?"

Penny shuddered. "No, you don't have to tell me that."

They looked around. On one side of the road was a petrol station, on the other a diner. Harry said, "I'm happy now that I can find Johnny any time I want him. So let's take a break for a coffee, okay? And I can maybe explain something of how I want to play it."

She nodded and even managed a shaky smile. "Okay."

They headed along the walkway towards steps leading down to the cafeteria. People were coming up the steps, heading back to the petrol station and its car park. Before they could climb up to the walkway's level, Penny grabbed Harry's arm. "Your eyes!" she hissed.

Harry put on his dark glasses, then took her hand. "Lead me," he said. "You know, like I was a blind man?" It wasn't a bad idea. From then on, in the cafeteria where a handful of travellers were eating, people only looked at them once and quickly looked away.

It's a funny thing, Harry thought, *but people don't much look at someone with an affliction. Or if they do, they look sideways. Hah! They'd jump sideways if they knew the nature of my affliction!*

But they didn't.

Not all of them, anyway . . .

On the bank of the river some little way from Bonnyrig, Ben Trask and Geoffrey Paxton stood in the dark of the night under the moon and stars and listened to the gurgle of blackly swirling waters. They "listened" for other things, too, but heard nothing. And they watched.

They watched the old house across the water—the house of the Necroscope, with all its lights ablaze—watched it for movement behind the open, ground-floor patio doors, for shadows falling on the fabric of the curtains in the upper windows, for any sign of life . . . or absence of life, undeath. And watching it they fingered their weapons: Trask his submachine gun, with a magazine of thirty 9mm rounds seated firmly in its blued-steel housing, and Paxton his metal crossbow, loaded with a hardwood bolt under pressure sufficient to hammer through a man like a nail into softwood.

A mile away, on the road into Bonnyrig, two more E-Branch operatives sat in their car, waiting. They had small talents of their own but weren't telepaths; neither one of them had Ben Trask's experience or Paxton's "zeal." But if it became necessary, certainly they would be able to do whatever must be done. Their car was equipped with a radio, tuned in on London HQ. At the moment their job was simply to relay messages and act as backup for the men up front. If Trask or Paxton called them, they could pick them up in little more than a minute. Which at least gave the men on the riverbank a feeling of security; Paxton a little less than Trask, for he had been here before.

"Well?" Trask whispered now, taking the telepath's elbow. "Is he in there or isn't he?"

Standing close to the very spot where Harry Keogh had tossed him into the river, Paxton was nervous. The Necroscope had warned him that next time . . . that there had better not *be* a next time. And now that time was here; and Trask's hand still gripped Paxton's arm just above the elbow. The telepath shook his head. "I don't know. But the house is tainted, for sure. Can't you feel it?"

"Oh, yes." Trask nodded in the dark. "Just looking at it, I can see it's not right. What about the girl?"

"An hour ago she was here, definitely," the other answered. "Her thoughts were clouded—mind-smog, yes—but readable to a degree. She's in thrall to him, no doubt about it. I thought Keogh was here, too—in fact I was sure he was, briefly—but now . . ." He shrugged. "Telepathy with vampires is a very tricky business. To see without being seen, and to hear without being heard."

Before Trask could answer him or make further comment, a tiny red light began to flash on his pocket walkie-talkie. He extended the aerial and depressed the incoming-call button. There sounded the customary wash of background static, and then the quiet, faintly tinny voice of Guy Teale, saying: "Car here. How do you read me?"

"Okay," Trask answered him, soft and low. "What's up?"

"We've had a call from HQ," Teale came back.

"We're to move to final strike locations now, situate ourselves, from there on in maintain radio and ESP silence, and wait for the word."

Trask frowned and said: "We can ready ourselves, sure, but how will we be able to strike if our target isn't here? Ask HQ that, will you?"

Without pause Teale came back: "HQ says that in the event there's no one in the house when they give the word, we remain *in situ*, stay alert, and wait to see what happens."

Trask's frown deepened. "Ask them to repeat that, will you? With some of the blanks filled in?"

"I already did"—Teale's sigh was clearly audible—"before I even called you. As far as HQ knows, Keogh has the Sanderson girl with him, and he and she are onto the serial killer. Likewise *we* have people on Keogh and Found—within limits, that is—and also people on Trevor Jordan, on a night train bound for London. So we'll let Keogh and/or the police settle with Found, then move on the Necroscope, the girl, and Jordan simultaneously, wherever they are at that time."

Trask nodded. "So if our people don't get Harry at their end—and if he escapes back here—we'll be waiting for him, right?"

"That's how I see it," Teale answered.

"Okay, secure the car and come on in on foot. Meet us at the old bridge, ready to cross in . . . ten minutes. Then we'll reorganize, split into two pairs, and choose vantage points at the front and rear of the house. That's all for now. Be seeing you."

He pressed the off button.

Paxton, nervously scanning all about in the darkness under the trees, said, "Do you think Teale and Robinson will be okay working together? I mean, I'm sure we'll be fine together, but they don't strike me as having a hell of a lot of candlepower between them!''

"You're probably right." Trask stared hard at him in the dark of the night, disliking everything that he saw and felt; especially the fact that every now and then he'd feel Paxton's talent tugging on the covers of his mind and trying to turn them back. "So I'll team up with Teale, and you can take Robinson."

Paxton turned more fully towards him and his eyes were slightly feral in fleeting moonlight. "You don't want us to work together?"

"Paxton, let me put you right," Trask told him. "The only reason I wanted to work with you up here in the first place was to keep an eye on you. See, I think you're full of it, and it's leaking on your attitude. So you're right, I *don't* want us to work together. In fact, I'd rather work with raw shit!"

Paxton scowled and started to turn away, make tracks back up to the road. But Trask caught him by the arm and turned him around. "Oh, and there's one other thing, Mr. Hugely Talented Telepath. I've about ninety percent had it with you trying to read my mind. When I'm a hundred percent pissed you'll be the first to know it. Because after that, Harry Keogh won't be the only one who ever tossed you in a river, right?''

Paxton was wise enough to say nothing. They returned to the road in silence, made their way to the old stone bridge over the river, waited for Teale and Robinson to join them there . . .

Harry and Penny had finished their first coffees half an hour ago. Now they had seconds, which were going cold in their cups. Penny had tried a cream cake, too, from which she'd taken just one bite. She wasn't sure if it was the cake or her mood, but since nothing tasted right it was probably her mood. Every so often the Necroscope would reach into his inside pocket and take Johnny's hideous steel-tube weapon into the palm of his hand. Penny was aware each time he did it—aware that he was touching the instrument of her once-death—and she shuddered every time.

Finally, as Harry reached into his pocket yet again, she burst out: "What if he doesn't stop? What if he drives clear down to London?"

Harry shrugged. "If it looks like he will, then I'll let him get as . . . far . . . as . . ." He came to a jerky halt as his fingers touched the awful knife, and briefly closed his eyes behind their dark lenses. When he opened them again his voice had turned cold and taken on a cutting edge. "But it won't come to that. He *has* stopped, now!"

She clutched his hand. "Do you know where?"

He shook his head. "No. The only way to find out is to go there and see."

"Oh, my God!" she whispered. "I'm going to see the man who murdered me!"

"More important," Harry told her, "he's going to see you. And he's going to wonder about you. If he reads the newspapers he'll know that Penny, one of the girls he killed, had a look-alike called, by some peculiar coincidence, Penny! But he'll have a hard time believing he's actually happened across her. I mean, there are coincidences and coincidences. If he has any brain at all, he'll find it a damned suspicious thing. It will worry him. That's what I want to do: worry him. I think Johnny deserves something of a harrowing time before we even up the score more permanently."

"We?" she repeated him. "It . . . it feels like you're using me, Harry."

"I suppose I am," he answered her, allowing her to lead him out of the cafeteria into the night. "Though not as hard as he did." He quickly went on: "And don't tell me that's not fair. Fair is like beauty, it lies in the eyes of the beholder. Also, I'm not asking you to do much, just to be there. There's someone else with a much larger part to play."

"Maybe you're right," she said as he folded her in his arms, conjured a door, and carried her over the threshold into the Möbius Continuum. *About what's fair and what's beautiful, I mean. And it's a fact, I don't think there was anything of beauty in Johnny.*

No, Harry answered grimly, *and nothing fair about him, either. But me, I'm fair. I only take an eye for an eye . . .*

VII Nightmare Junction

Johnny had stopped at an all-services motorway watering hole north of Newark. He'd chosen the A1(T) rather than the larger M1 because its service stations usually had richer pickings: not only long-distance truckers and motorists used its facilities but locals, too. It was Johnny's experience that when the town and village dance halls slowed down around midnight, the young ones headed this way for a cheap motorway meal after a hard night's drinking, dancing, and whatever. He'd stopped here before, but no luck as yet. Maybe tonight.

On clutch and air brakes, he'd snorted and whoofed the big articulated truck around the tarmac until he'd found a place to park it where its nose sniffed the exit route. It was as well to be able to drive out of such places with as little trouble as possible. The place was on a major junction; the car park was busy and the lorry park half empty; people came and went in small parties to and from the brightly lit diner. Johnny's would be just one more face over a plate of chicken and chips and a pint of alcohol-free.

Inside, there'd been nothing much of a queue at the self-service bar; in a little while Johnny had settled at a table in a corner booth where he'd toyed with his food and casually looked the place over for a likely female face. There were several, but . . . they didn't fit his bill: too old, too drab, slack-faced, sharp-eyed, accompanied, or stone-cold sober. A few bright-eyed young things, yes, but all hanging on to flash boyfriends. Well, that's how it went. But there were plenty more places just like this between here and London. And you never could tell when your luck was going to change.

He remembered a time when, on a lonely stretch of road, this bird had roared by in a little red sports job. He'd bombed after her and forced her off the road into a ditch, then told her he was sorry and it was an accident— but he would be glad to give her a lift to the nearest garage. Oh, he'd given her a lift, all right, but not to a garage. And then it had been her turn to give *him* a lift, a really good one, a real high. Johnny had been in a weird mood that night: after killing her he'd chopped a channel up under her jaw and fucked her in the throat. She'd felt it, of course, and how the dead bitch had yelped! Oh, she'd had cock in her throat before, but not coming from *that* direction.

Thinking about it had got him worked up. He must have one tonight. But not from this place. Maybe he should move on.

And that was when he saw . . . he saw . . . *what the shit?*

It wasn't possible but . . . he had to fight with his eyes to keep them from looking in her direction again. She was just over there; she'd just slid her backside onto a seat in a booth close by; there was a blind guy there, too—or a guy in dark glasses, anyway—but he didn't seem to be with her. She had a coffee, just a coffee, and she was the same as last time. She was *exactly* the same. And for a moment Johnny's mind whirled, for he could swear he'd had this one before!

How can that be? he asked himself. How *can* it be? And the answer was simple: it couldn't be. Unless this girl was the other's twin sister . . . *or her double!*

And then he remembered reading something about that in the papers: how they thought the one he'd had in Edinburgh—Penny, that was her name—was someone else. But then she'd turned up alive: the spitting image of the one he'd screwed, murdered, and screwed again. Stranger still, the one who'd turned up had also been called Penny. Coincidence? *Jesus*, coincidence! But the biggest coincidence of them all: here she was, right now, right here. That is, unless he'd started seeing fucking things.

Slowly, Johnny looked up from his food, through the acid-etched, fern-patterned glass dividers which loaned the booths a little privacy, until her face was directly in his line of vision. Maybe for a moment he caught her eye, but just for a moment, and then she looked away. The half-blind guy—the guy with the eye problem, anyway, who shared her booth—had his back to Johnny; but he didn't look much, anyway, slumped over his mug of coffee like that. Her father, maybe?

No, her lover, Harry Keogh answered, but silently, speaking only to himself. *Her vampire lover, you scumbag*.

He had been into Found's mind from the moment he and Penny had entered the place, and the mental cesspool in there was as rank as anything he'd ever come up against. Together with the necromancer's recognition of Penny as a former victim, or that victim's double, it strengthened Harry's resolve, confirmed his commitment. But as yet Found's recognition of her hadn't produced the reaction Harry had expected. Curiosity, yes, but not fear. In a way, perhaps that was understandable.

For after all, Found knew that the other Penny was dead; he *knew* that this couldn't be the girl he had violated. Still, his shock had been short-lived and Harry was disappointed. Also, he knew now that he was dealing with a very cool customer. Whether Found would be able to stay cool when confronted with what was on the cards for him . . . that was something else entirely.

Leaving Johnny's mind, the Necroscope leaned across the table a little towards Penny and quietly said, "I can see how badly shaken you are. I can feel it, too. I'm sorry, Penny, but just try to stay calm. It won't be long now; when Found leaves I'll go after him; you'll stay here and wait for me. Okay?"

She nodded and said, "You seem very . . . well, cold about all of this, Harry."

He shook his head. "Just determined. But you see, Found *is* cold, which might give him an advantage if I allowed myself to get too heated."

As he spoke, Harry saw two men enter the diner from the car park. They seemed ordinary enough but there was something about them. As they moved along the self-service bar collecting cold drinks, their eyes scanned the room, found the Necroscope and Penny in their booth, moved on. Harry went to probe their minds—and his telepathic probe at once came up against a wall of mental static!

He withdrew immediately. At least one of these men was an esper, which mean E-Branch was closing in . . . on both Johnny Found *and* Harry Keogh! They probably wouldn't try anything in here—maybe not even in the darkness of the car park—but in any case Harry didn't want them on his trail. And they'd obviously figured out that if they followed Found they'd find the Necroscope, too. Now of all times he really couldn't afford this sort of complication.

Now, too, he remembered the car he'd seen tailing Found's truck out of Darlington: an unmarked police car with . . . how many men aboard? Two or three? He'd thought they were all policemen but now knew better. Suddenly, coming from nowhere, he felt a growl rising in his throat. His Wamphyri side was reacting to the threat. Aware of Penny's gaze, he stifled the growl at once.

"Harry." Her voice was concerned. "You're very pale."

Fury, my love. "There's something I must do," he told her. "It will mean leaving you here—but only for a minute. You'll be okay?"

"In here, alone, with him?" Her eyes were huge and round.

"There are fifty people in here," he answered. *And two of them at least are pretty sharp characters.* "I promise I'll be right back."

She touched his hand and nodded. "Then I'll be okay." But she avoided looking Found's way.

Harry stood up, smiled a robot's smile at her, and went out into the night.

At first, to anyone watching, it would appear that he'd been heading for the gents' toilets, but as he passed close to the swinging glass doors of the exit he turned sharply and pushed through them—

—And as soon as he was outside crouched down, breathed a mist, and moved wraith-like between the cars ranked as soldiers on the hardstanding. His Wamphyri senses guiding him, he went straight to the unmarked police car and approached it from the rear. There was a driver, a plainclothes policeman, with one elbow on the sill and a cigarette dangling from his lips where he sat silhouetted in a steel frame, looking out of his wound-down window into the darkness and breathing the mild night air.

Exuding fog, the Necroscope moved like a low-slung spider—performed a weirdly loping limbo—to draw silently alongside the car. And then he stood up.

The policeman's jaw fell open in a gasp of astonishment as a shadow, coming from nowhere, blocked out the stars and flowed over him; his cigarette flew as the Necroscope hit him once, hard enough to send him sprawling across the passenger seat.

He was out like a light, indeed like his cigarette, which Harry ground under his heel. Then he reached inside the car and snapped the key in half in the ignition. So much for that: they wouldn't be following Johnny—or Harry—anywhere in this car. But to be doubly sure he took out Found's steel-tube knife and drove it into the wall of a tire until it hissed air and sagged down onto its rim. But as he began to straighten up he glanced into the back of the car and froze.

The Necroscope's eyes were attuned to the night, which was his element. He could see into the back of the car just as clearly as in broad daylight. And there on the backseat, a bulky, ugly, dark-snouted shape which Harry knew at once: a flamethrower. And on the floor back there, the blued-steel glitter of a pair of loaded crossbows. *Loaded* crossbows!

Harry hissed and crouched down into himself. They were ready for him, all of them. It must be coming soon. Perhaps sooner than he'd anticipated. Bastards! And he was the one who'd showed them how!

He attacked a second tire and grunted his satisfaction as it collapsed into extinction, then moved round the car and did a third. Following which he paused and drew a ragged breath, and forced himself to be calm, calm . . .

He was trembling, but *only* trembling. No more hissing, snarling. Mere moments of violence, but they had acted as a safety valve on Harry's awful pressure. As his mist began to thin he sighed his relief, stood more humanly erect, put away the knife, and headed back towards the diner . . .

Mere moments—less than two, three minutes at most—but more than sufficient time that the menace of Johnny Found had got to Penny, canceling her former resolve to "be okay." For she had known from the moment Harry left the glass doors swinging behind him and disappeared into the night that she would not be okay, not in the same enclosed space as this monster, not with fifty or five hundred people around her.

Mere moments, yes, but enough time for Johnny to make up his mind that Penny would be The One. Obviously, the guy with the dark glasses hadn't been with her, after all, and now she was on her own. What was more, she was aware that Johnny was interested; he could feel her avoiding his eyes, even avoiding his thoughts, his existence. And suddenly he wondered: *does she know me*? But how could she possibly know him? What the fuck was going on here, anyway?

He put aside his plate and placed his hands on the table, palms down, as if to push himself to his feet. And all the while he stared at Penny, willing her to look his way. She *was* looking his way, however obliquely, and saw him slowly rising. All the color fled from her face as she too rose, slid out of her booth, backed away from him. She collided with a fat man with a tray and sent milk, hot food, bread rolls flying.

Johnny paced after her, smiling a deliberately feigned,

surprised smile. It was as if he were saying, "What's wrong? Did I startle you?" Anyone watching would think: What on earth is wrong with that girl? Is she drunk, on drugs? So pale! And that nice young man looking so surprised, so astonished.

And that was the whole thing of it: Johnny Found did look like a "nice young man." When Harry Keogh had seen him, he'd been surprised that he didn't more nearly fit the bill. Medium height and blocky build; blond, shoulder-length hair; good, square teeth in a full mouth with a droopy, almost innocent smile . . . only his slightly sallow complexion marred the boy-next-door image. That and his eyes, which were dark and deep-sunken. And the fact that he lived in a pigsty. And that he was a cold-blooded ravager of both living and dead flesh.

Penny blurted an apology to the gaping, spluttering fat man where he fingered his milk-soaked jacket, looked up and saw Johnny closing with her, turned and fled for the swing doors. Johnny glanced around at the dozen or so nearby patrons in their booths, shrugged and pulled a wry face, as if to say: "A weirdo . . . nothing to do with me, folks!" and calmly walked after her.

But he was so intent on his act, and on following the girl into the night, that as he caught the still-swinging door on the in-swing and passed out through it he didn't see the two sharp-eyed men starting to their feet and coming after him.

Outside, Penny turned frantically this way and that. A thin mist lay on the tarmac of the sprawling, tree-bordered car park; the headlights of vehicles on the nearby trunk road blinded her where they went scything by; she couldn't see Harry anywhere. But Johnny Found could see Penny, and he was right behind her.

She heard the crunch of gravel on the path leading

back to the diner's door but didn't dare turn round. Of
course, it could be anyone . . . but it could also be him.
She felt rooted to the spot, all of her senses straining to
identify what if anything was going on behind her, but
utterly incapable of turning round and using the most
obvious sense of all. And: *God!* she prayed. *Please let it
not be him!*

But it was.

"Penny?" he said, sly and yet somehow wonderingly.

Now she turned, but with a sort of slow-motion jerk-
iness, like a puppet controlled by a spastic puppeteer.
And there he was, bearing down on her, wearing a
painted-on smile under eyes that were jet-black and flint-
hard.

Her heart very nearly stopped; she wanted to cry out
but could only choke; she almost fainted into his arms.
He caught her up, looked quickly all around and saw no
one. And: "Mine!" he gurgled, glaring into her half-
glazed, sideways-sliding eyes behind their fluttering lids.
"All Johnny's now, Penny!"

He wanted to ask her questions, right now, right here,
but knew she wouldn't hear them. She was sliding away
from him—away from the horror of him—into another
world. Escaping into unconsciousness. That was a laugh.
Why, no way she could escape from Johnny! Not even
into death!

Here, in front of the diner, was the car park; behind
it was the lorry park, and dividing the two a belt of trees
with paths between. Johnny picked Penny up, hurried
with her into the cover of the trees, carried her through
them light as a child. Behind him the E-Branch agent
and a Special Branch Detective Inspector erupted from
the diner, glanced this way and that, saw him hurrying
into darkness.

They came running after him—and the Necroscope came loping after them.

Harry had heard her cry out. Not aloud, for she'd been too terrified to make any sound whatsoever. He'd heard her in his mind. She was his thrall, and she'd called to him. The call had come just as he was leaving the disabled police car, and at first he hadn't known what it was. But the vampire in him had known. He had seen Found carrying Penny into the screening trees, towards the lorry park, and he'd seen the two men from the diner running after him. All of them were moving quickly, but not as quick as Harry.

His lope was more wolf—more alien—than human, and he covered ground like the shadow of a fast-fleeting cloud under the moon. But as he entered the trees on a diagonal course calculated to intercept Johnny Found and his captive, he knew he'd made a mistake. The trees and the shrubs beneath them were an ornamental screen designed to separate the two car parks, and as such they were protected by high wire-mesh fences. Precious seconds were lost as Harry came up against a fence, cursed, and conjured a Möbius door. In another moment he cleared the belt of trees and emerged on the perimeter of the hardstanding . . .

. . . Where a reeling, gagging figure collided with him and brought him to a halt! It was the esper. He knew Harry at once—sensed the awesome power of his metaphysical mind, that and the vampire in him—and threw up a hand to ward him off. The hand was bloody as the gaping wound in his cheek, where Johnny Found had torn a third of his face away.

Harry held him upright, snarled at him, then thrust him towards one of the paths through the trees. "Go and get help, quickly, before you bleed to death!"

And as the esper choked out something inarticulate

and staggered away, the Necroscope reached out with his vampire awareness to cover the entire park. He found three people at once: Penny, unconscious; Johnny Found, furious and bloody; and the policeman, dead where Found's weapon had crashed through his ear to gouge into his brain.

Harry pinpointed their location, conjured a door, and ran through it . . . and out again at the rear of the Frigis Express truck, where even now Johnny was slamming home the bolt on the roller door. At his feet, the policeman lay crumpled in a pool of his own blood, the left side of his face a raw red pulp.

The necromancer had taken the policeman's gun; he sensed Harry's presence, whirled, aimed, and fired! Harry was coming head-on; he felt a colossal blow as the bullet smashed into his collarbone on the right side, spun him round, and hurled him down on the tarmac.

Then, startled by the explosion and the flash, Johnny was fumbling the gun and dropping it. Stumbling across Harry, he kicked at him where he lay curled up in his pain; and running past the trailer towards his truck's cab, the madman raved, cursed, and laughed all in one.

The pain in Harry's shoulder was a living thing that took hold of his flesh with white-hot pincers and twisted it, causing him to moan his agony. And he thought: *Bastard thing in my blood, my mind! Your fault, you berserk, headlong idiot! Very well, you've caused me to be hurt—now heal me!*

Found was in his cab, starting up and revving the engine. Air brakes hissed and the reversing lights blazed crimson to match Harry's eyes or the jelly coagulating on the side of the dead policeman's head. Racked by pain, the Necroscope saw the huge bulk of the truck jerk, shudder, and start backing up; in another moment a pair of its twinned wheels skidded viciously, then gripped and dragged the policeman's body under. Blood and guts gushed as the wheels lifted up barely an inch and the weight of the truck crushed the corpse like toothpaste from a tube.

He's lucky he's dead! Harry dazedly, *un*thinkingly thought. *It's something he wouldn't want to happen while he was still alive!* They were instinctive thoughts, shocked out of him by the squelching eruption of brains and shit and flailing guts, but they were also deadspeak and the policeman heard him.

Exhaust gases belched in Harry's face where he rolled desperately from the path of the reversing truck; the scarlet-dripping wheels missed him by inches; but through all the roar and the stink and the mess on the tarmac he heard and was riveted by the policeman's answer:

But I did feel it! And God, it was like dying twice! And Harry's blood—even *his* blood—froze as he remembered who was driving the truck: Johnny Found, necromancer, whose actions his victims could feel even as the teeming dead had once felt Dragosani's!

Then the air brakes hissed again and the truck jerked to a halt, shuddered, started forward, turned, and rumbled away towards the exit. Johnny Found was making his escape, with Penny aboard. But:

No, you fucking don't! Harry fixed the truck's location in his mind, got to his knees, toppled through a Möbius door and out again into the refrigerated trailer. It was dark in there but that was nothing to the Necroscope. He saw Penny, crawled to her, put his left hand under her head, and drew it into his lap. She opened her eyes and looked into his where they blazed.

"Harry, I . . . I didn't stay in the diner," she whispered.

"I know," he growled. "Did he hurt you?"

"No." She shook her head, but weakly. "I . . . I think I just fainted."

Harry had no time to waste. Not now, for his blood was up. Literally! "Cling to me," he said.

She did as she was told and Harry let the Möbius equations roll across the computer screen of his mind. One moment later and Penny felt the awesome immensity of the Möbius Continuum, and in the next gravity returned where they fell prone onto Harry's bed in the house outside Bonnyrig. "This time stay here!" he told her. And before she could even sit up he was gone again . . .

In the operations room at E-Branch HQ, Millicent Cleary and the Minister Responsible sat with David Chung, who was also the Duty Officer, at one end of a large desk. The desk was equipped with a radio receiver, a radio telephone, standard telephones, blown-up ordnance survey maps of England under illuminated plastic, and a tray containing various small items of property belonging to Branch agents in the field. Spotlights in the ceiling were concentrated on the desk, turning it and its immediate surroundings into an island of light in the large room's comparative darkness.

Millicent Cleary had just a moment ago received a brief telepathic message from Paxton at the house near Bonnyrig, stating that the assault team was in position. Keogh and the girl had been back briefly, but Paxton was sure that the Necroscope was no longer in the house. Similarly, Frank Robinson, the spotter who was Paxton's partner on the job, believed one of the two was still there; since there was no noticeable disturbance of the psychic "ether," he would guess it was the girl. Keogh must have used the Möbius Continuum to drop her off at the house before moving on. If there'd been any indication that the Necroscope himself was still in there, then the team would have maintained ESP silence. But since he wasn't . . . Paxton was eager to learn what was happening.

Cleary passed the mind-message on and the Minister Responsible gave a snort. "I've come to the conclusion that you're right about Paxton," he said. "All of you. I get the feeling he won't be satisfied until he's running the world!"

Cleary frowned however prettily, and nodded. "Ruining it, you mean!" she said sourly; then quickly added, "Er . . . sir! But we *are* right, and you don't have to be psychic to know it. He's a menace. We're lucky Ben Trask is up there keeping an eye on him. Do you want me to tell him anything?"

The Minister looked at her—also at Chung where he busied himself touching and concentrating on his many contact sigils in their tray, fathoming the whereabouts, mood, and feelings of the agents in the field—and mentally reviewed the situation:

The telepath Trevor Jordan (who by all rights and natural laws should be a small heap of ashes in a vase) was on a night train heading for London via Darlington. Two E-Branch agents were on the same train and didn't anticipate too much trouble, even though it was a pretty safe bet that Jordan was a vampire. They were equipped with powerful automatic weapons, and one of them had a small but deadly crossbow. Another man was on his way to the mainline station in Darlington to give them a hand. He had a car, and in its boot a flamethrower.

Penny Sanderson, also a resurrected vampire, was probably in Keogh's house outside Bonnyrig. The agents up there were (again probably) as strong a team of espers as E-Branch could throw together, which they would need to be if or when Keogh rejoined the party. For the odds were that sooner or later he'd go back there for the girl.

As for the Necroscope himself: he could be quite literally anywhere, but he was probably tracking Johnny Found. His reasons for doing so were all his own, but the Sanderson girl had been one of Found's victims. Vengeance? Why not? It seemed the Wamphyri had always been big on revenge.

So if E-Branch moved now, two of the three targets were good as dead (the Minister recoiled for a moment, shocked by the necessarily cold efficiency of his own thoughts) but Keogh would still remain the big question mark, the pivot on which everything else turned. And it would be to everyone's advantage—literally everyone's, everywhere—if the Necroscope could be taken out at the same time as the others.

"Sir?" The girl was still waiting for an answer.

The Minister opened his mouth to speak, but at that moment David Chung held up a hand and said, "Hold it!" Cleary and the Minister looked at the locator; his other hand was resting on a Zippo cigarette lighter, the longtime property of Paul Garvey, a telepath working with the police out of Darlington. That hand was steady, the tips of Chung's long fingers motionless where they touched the cold metal. But the hand he held up was trembling violently.

Suddenly, he snatched back his hand from the tray, stepped back a little from the desk. In another moment he'd recovered himself, came forward again, and said: "Garvey has been hurt! I don't know how, but it's serious . . ." He closed his eyes and his hand hovered a moment over the maps beneath their clear-plastic laminate.

As the small Asian's hand came down to cover a section of the A1 north of Newark, the Minister turned to Cleary. "Can you get hold of Garvey?"

"I've worked with him, lots." She was breathless. "Let me try."

She closed her eyes and concentrated on mental pictures of her fellow esper, and got him at once. Garvey was in fact sending at that very moment. But his signal and message were weak, garbled, distorted by his pain . . . which Clearly immediately became heir to! She gasped and staggered, and for a second lost him. Then she picked him up again, but barely in time before he blacked out and his telepathic thoughts flew into shards in her mind. The rush of psychic sendings had not been without images, however, which she'd received even as he was going under.

She turned to the Minister and her features were drawn, bloodless. "Paul's face," she said. "It's ruined! His cheek is hanging in tatters. But there's a doctor with him. They're in some sort of . . . motorway café? I think he was attacked by Johnny Found—but the Necroscope was also there. And a policeman is dead!"

The Minister grabbed her wrist, steadied her. "A policeman dead? And Keogh was there? You're sure?"

She nodded, gulped. "It was in Paul's mind: a picture of a . . . bloody hole in a policeman's head. And another of Harry, with eyes like red lamps burning in his face!"

Chung said, "Garvey's somewhere here," and he pointed at the map. "On the A1."

The Minister took a deep breath, nodded, and said, "This is it; it's all coming to a head, right now. Keogh might have guessed it all along but by now he must *know* we're after him. So while all three of these . . . these *creatures* are in different locations—from which two of them at least can't escape—now has to be the best time to move on them." He turned to the girl. "Miss Cleary, er, Millicent? Is Paxton still waiting? Get back onto him and tell him to move in now, at once. Then speak to Scanlon and tell him the same thing.'' He turned to Chung. ''And David—''

But the locator was already busy on the radio, speaking to people in Darlington . . .

Meanwhile:

By the time Johnny Found's thundering Frigis Express truck took the curves on the roundabout at the junction of the A1 and A46 outside Newark, he was much calmer and showing a lot of skill and driving discipline. Had there been a police patrol car stationed at the roundabout, its officers probably wouldn't look twice at him.

There was no patrol car, however, just Harry Keogh.

Using Found's knife, the Necroscope had followed the truck's progress in a series of short Möbius jumps, waiting for his quarry to slow down a little before attempting what must be an extremely accurate jump on a moving object; which was to say, directly into Found's cab! Also, it must be accomplished as smoothly as possible, so as not to jar his badly shattered collarbone. The pain of that alone would have left any other man writhing on his back or entirely unconscious. But Harry wasn't any other man. Indeed, with every passing moment he was a little less a man and more a monster, albeit one with a human soul.

And as the necromancer straightened up his truck off the roundabout and back onto the A1, that was when Harry emerged from the eternal darkness of the Möbius Continuum into the empty seat on his left. At first Found didn't see him, or if he did he considered him a shadow in the corner of his eye. And Harry sat still and quiet in the very corner of the cab, pressed against the door with his face and upper body turned towards the driver. He kept his eyes three-quarters shuttered, studying Johnny's face, which had seemed previously scarcely to match up with any of the descriptions given him by the girls, but which he now saw to be very terrible indeed.

As for Johnny himself: he knew that it was all over. Too many people had seen him tonight, in the diner, the car park, with or close to the girl. Indeed, it seemed to him that he'd been set up. They had traced him, then trapped him with a girl who was the image of one of his victims. And he had fallen for it. Well, two of the bastards at least had paid for it, and the girl would pay, too, when he climbed into the trailer with her, chopped a passage through the orbit of her left eye, and fucked her brain!

These were his thoughts, which Harry, looking directly at him, read as clearly as—more clearly than—the pages of a book. And if before there had been any doubt at all in the Necroscope's mind that his course of action was the right one, these were also the thoughts which dispelled it. Now, as Johnny dwelled more intimately on the pleasures he intended taking with or from the girl, Harry very quietly spoke up and said:

"None of those things will happen, for the girl isn't in the trailer. I freed her. As I intend freeing all of the dead. From their terror, Johnny. From your tyranny."

Found's jaw had fallen open at the first word. There was a trickle of saliva, slime, froth, in the left-hand corner of his mouth, which now ran down under his lip and into the dimple of his chin. He said, "Wha—?" and his coal-black eyes slowly slid to the left in their deep sockets . . . then stood out like inkblots on the gaunt parchment which until a moment ago had been the flushed, bloated flesh of his face.

"You're a goner, Johnny," Harry told him, and opened

his furnace eyes to reflect ruddily on the other's paralyzed, astonished features.

But Found's paralysis was short-lived, and the rest of it—his almost immediate response—was all instinct, so that not even the Necroscope could have seen it coming. "What?" he gurgled, taking his left hand from the wheel and reaching up behind his head for a meat hook where it hung from the cab's frame. "A goner? Well, *one* of us is, that's for sure!"

Harry's plan had been simple: as Found attacked him, he'd conjure a Möbius door and wrestle him through it. But it was difficult enough just to take hold of a man in the cab of a truck, let alone when he was wielding a meat hook.

Johnny had seen the huge bloodstain on Harry's jacket and recognized him as the one he'd shot back in the diner's vehicle park. How he came to be in the cab was something else, but he surely wouldn't be much good for anything with a gaping hole in his shoulder. And even less good when Johnny was finished with him. "Whoever you are," he grunted, swinging the hook, "you're dead fucking meat!"

The blow was awkward and left-handed, but still Harry couldn't avoid it. He ducked down a little and the question mark of shining metal passed over his right shoulder, swooped down on him, and caught in the hole which the bullet had torn out of his back. He gasped his renewed agony as Found yanked him towards him and glared into his face. Then—

—Using Harry as a counterweight, the necromancer lifted his left leg, reached it across Harry's knees, and kicked open the cab door. And as the truck careened down the twin lanes he kicked again, this time at Harry himself, and simultaneously released his hold on the meat hook.

Sliding free of his seat into the rush of night air, the Necroscope made a desperate grab for the wildly swinging door. Luckily, the window was down; as he looped his arms through the frame, so his feet slammed down onto the running board. Johnny could no longer reach him without letting go of the wheel, but he could at least try to shake him loose.

Heedless of other vehicles, the maniac threw his huge truck this way and that across the lanes, and Harry hung on like grim death until the thought suddenly occurred, *Why not a big door? Why not the biggest bloody door you could ever imagine?*

On his left and almost directly under his skidding, skittering feet, a car was sideswiped and sent spinning, crashing through the roadside barrier in a shriek of ruptured metal. It smashed onto the embankment nose-first and exploded like a bomb. But the big truck rushed on and left people frying and dying in its wake, and in the cab Johnny fueled himself with their pain and knew that even dead they would hear his crazy laughter.

Enough! Harry thought, and conjured his giant door— on the road directly in front of the truck.

The rumble and thunder and rocking violence of the vehicle died away in a moment as it plunged through the Möbius door into darkness absolute; likewise the mad laughter of Johnny Found, shut off as he delivered a single gonging thought into the awesome Möbius Continuum: WHAT?

What indeed!

The beam of his headlights went on forever, cutting a tunnel through infinity. But apart from the headlight beams and the truck where its mass surrounded him, there was nothing whatsoever. No road, no sound, no sensation of motion, nothing.

402

WHAAAAT!? Johnny screamed again, deafeningly, in both his and the Necroscope's mind.

But: *No good shouting now, Johnny*, Harry told him, hanging on the door and guiding the truck, aiming it like a missile to its final destination. *Like I said, you're a goner. And we're very nearly there. Welcome to hell!*

Johnny let go the wheel and sprawled across the wide seat, reaching for the Necroscope where he clung to the door of the cab. But too late; they were there; Harry conjured another door in front of the truck and pushed himself free, slowing his motion to an abrupt halt. And the truck went rushing on—

—Out of the Möbius Continuum to emerge inches over the surface of a narrow road. It crashed down, bounced, rocked, and roared; and as its free-spinning tires found purchase on the tarmac, so it rocketed forward. Johnny screamed as he saw the sharp bend coming up where the road skirted a long, high wall of ivy-clad stone. He made a desperate grab for the steering wheel, but the truck had already mounted the curb. It shot across a narrow strip of grass, tore through a mass of night-black shrubbery, slammed into the wall . . . and stopped.

Stopped dead.

. . . But not Johnny!

As the truck and its trailer concertinaed—as the wall cracked and sent stone debris flying—as massive petrol tanks shattered and showered fuel onto hot, tortured metal, turning the truck into a blazing inferno—so Johnny was ripped out of his driver's seat and hurled through the windscreen. Bones in his left arm and shoulder broke where, pinwheeling, he hit the top of the wall before crashing down onto something hard far on the other side.

There was pain, more pain than he'd ever known; and then, apart from flickering firelight from beyond the wall, and a booming, *whooshing* explosion as the emergency tank blew, there was a deafening silence. The silence of mental concentration, of *knowing* even through waves of agony that someone—several pitiless someones—were watching him.

He cranked his neck up an inch from where sharp gravel chips stuck to the tattered mess of his face, and saw Harry Keogh standing there, looking down on him. And behind the red-eyed Necroscope there were other—people? *Things*, anyway—which Johnny knew should never be. They came (crawled, staggered, crumbled) forward, and one of them was or had once been a girl. Johnny backed off, pushing with his raw hands, sliding on his belly and his knees, skidding in the bloodied gravel until he collided with something hard, which brought him up short. He somehow turned his head and looked back, and saw what had stopped him: a headstone.

"A . . . a . . . a fucking graveyard!" he gasped.

And Harry Keogh said, "End of the road, Johnny."

Pamela Trotter said, *You kept your promise, Harry.* And he nodded.

And Johnny Found, Necromancer, knew what had passed between them. "No!" he gasped. Then screamed: *"Noooooooo!"*

He would get to his feet. Even broken, shattered, cut to ribbons, he *would* flee from the hell of it. But Pamela's dead friends fell or flopped on him and bore him down, and a hand that shed rotting flesh and maggots stoppered his mouth. Then *she* came to him and searched among his rags, until she found his new knife. And close up like that—badly gone into corruption though she was, even with the flesh beginning to slough from her face—still he knew her.

You remember that good time we had? she said. *You didn't even say thanks, Johnny, and you didn't leave me anything to remember you by. Well, now I think it's time*

I had me a small memento. Or even a big one, eh? Something I can take back down into the earth with me, right? She showed him his own knife and smiled at him, and her teeth were long where the blackened gums had shriveled back from them.

Harry turned away and shut out the sight; shut out Found's silent, frenzied shrieking, too, from his mind. But to Pamela he said, "Make sure you kill him."

Except: *Too late!* She was weeping her frustration. *Or rather, too soon! Damn the bastard, Harry, but he's already died on me!*

Harry sighed his relief and thought, *Just as well.* She heard him and a moment later agreed:

Yes, I suppose it is. Shit, I didn't want to dirty my hands on this filth, anyway!

And now Found's deadspeak reached out to both of them, to Harry and to Pamela. *What . . . is this? Where . . . am I? Who . . . is it out there?*

Neither one of them answered him, but the sheer weight of Harry's presence impressed itself on Found's mind like a light shining in through the stretched membrane of shuttered eyelids. He knew that Harry was there, and that he was special. *It's you, right?* he said. *The guy with the dark glasses, with some kind of magic? You brought me here with your magic, right?*

Harry knew that Pamela would probably never speak to Johnny Found, neither Pamela nor any other of the outraged Great Majority. Instead of taunting the necromancer, they'd merely shun him, lock him up or out, like a leper. So maybe Harry shouldn't speak to him either but simply go away. And perhaps that would be the most merciful thing to do.

Except . . . Harry had a less than merciful thing inside him, which now caused him to speak up:

You had the same magic, Johnny, he said. *Or you could*

have had. You could speak to the dead—could have trained yourself, as I did, to converse with them and befriend them—but no, you chose to torture them instead.

Found was quick to catch on. *So now I'm one of them, right? I'm dead and you did it to me. But just answer me this: Why?*

Harry could have explained: that he'd needed to focus his Wamphyri passions on something—to have something to let them loose on—rather than on people who were previously his friends; which was to say E-Branch and the world in general. He *could* have explained, but didn't. For his vampire wouldn't let him. Found had been the cold, cruel, uncaring one in life; death should be a cold, cruel place, too. And just as uncaring. An eye for an eye.

Why did I kill you? Harry shrugged, began to turn away.

Hey, fuckface! Found shouted after him, defiant, furious even in death. *That doesn't cut it. You had your reasons, sure enough. Because of the dead? Shit! Who gives a fuck for the dead? So come on, tell me . . . why?*

And so—coldly, cruelly, and uncaringly—Harry told him. *You're right*, he said. *No one gives a fuck for the dead. And you, Johnny, you're dead. You want to know why?* And again he shrugged. *Well, why the fuck not?*

VIII   The Vampire Killers

EVEN THOUGH THE GREAT MAJORITY NO LONGER trusted him, Harry had always respected them. He thanked Pamela and those of her friends who had assisted in bringing Johnny Found to justice; and as they commenced their arduous return to what would now be their *final* resting places, so the Necroscope employed his metaphysical mind's fantastic equations and materialized a Möbius door. But in the moment before he stepped through it . . .

. . . An agonized voice—not deadspeak but telepathy, which even as he received it *changed* to deadspeak—reached out to him from a deserted stockyard not far from the mainline station in Darlington. It was Trevor Jordan: alive at first, then dead, turning to fused flesh, bubbling blood, and charred, blackened bone as a squad of former E-Branch colleagues torched him to sticky, steaming cinders!

Trevor! Harry gasped, his own agony almost as great

as the telepath's as he received the full, searing impact of his final seconds. *Trevor, I'm coming—right now—just keep talking and I'll find—*

No! Jordan cut him off, as all the pain of a life at its termination faded away and death's cool darkness crashed over him, laving him like an ocean wave. *No, Harry, don't . . . don't come here. They're expecting you, and believe me they have the right gear. And anyway, you have no time. The girl, Harry, the girl!*

The Necroscope understood. Of course: Penny.

The Branch had been closing in on him; they *had* closed in on Jordan; they *would* close in on Penny—and they'd be doing it even now!

Trevor! Harry was torn—felt himself riven—two ways: a secondary agony, of frustration and indecision. But Jordan was right. No one should be put to such an agonizing death, and certainly not an innocent. Jordan had been just such a one, and so was she. No matter what name anyone gave her now, or what she would be tomorrow, tonight she was an innocent.

You can't help me, Harry, Jordan told him, trying to make it easier for him. *Not this time. You can only jeopardize your own safety—and Penny's. But it's okay, it's okay. I lived twice, which was enough. And dying twice was . . . that was too much. I don't need any more.*

In the Möbius Continuum, Harry still felt himself dragged apart, pulled two ways. He moaned his horror—and his anger—as he deliberately shut Jordan's deadspeak thoughts out of his mind. Later, maybe later, he'd have time to thank him for the warning. But as for now—

—Bonnyrig.

He emerged along the riverbank, well away from the house, emerged to a darkness shot with the crimson of his fury. Wamphyri fury! The thing within held sway; its awareness washed out from the Necroscope like human-

—like *in*human—radar; it scanned the house standing in darkness. Except . . . when Harry left here the lights were ablaze!

Harry's telepathy was carried on his vampire probe. In the house, five people—five warm beings full of blood—five clever, thinking creatures, and four of them possessed of wild, weird talents. But nothing so weird as Harry's. His metaphysical mind touched upon their minds, but guardedly, so that they wouldn't suspect:

Penny first, terrified for her life, but as yet unharmed. Then Guy Teale, an as yet undeveloped seer, given on occasion to glimpsing the future, which Harry well knew was an unwieldy, unforgiving talent at best. And Frank Robinson, a spotter with the ability to recognize another esper on sight, or even in close proximity (*his* mind flinched a little when Harry touched it, but not enough that the Necroscope's presence was revealed; Robinson's talent too was as yet embryonic). But then . . . ah, then there was Ben Trask. A sad thing: Harry had hoped there'd be no old friends here, but here was Ben. And finally—

—Paxton!

Paxton the mind-flea, the previously unreachable itch, a vampire no less than Harry himself, who scorned the blood of others for the secret juices of their minds, their very thoughts. And indeed Paxton *was* something else: keen beyond the call of duty, zealous to a fault, vicious as the crossbow he even now held on Penny Sanderson in the Necroscope's bedroom. So that quick as Harry was to withdraw his probe, still he wasn't quick enough and Paxton knew he was there.

The telepath at once narrowed his eyes and quietly, with a shiver in his voice, called downstairs: "He's close! He's coming!"

In the spacious front room of the house, which had

served mainly as Harry's study—whose French windows looked out over a garden decending in shallow terraces to a high wall and the riverbank beyond—Ben Trask and Guy Teale received Paxton's hushed warning and acknowledged it with tight-lipped glances and cramped, edgy movements. Moon and starlight were their only sources of illumination, which in itself was a mistake on their part. Their eyes had required to adjust to the darkness, and even now worked inefficiently in the room's gloom. But the Necroscope's every sense was already adjusted; the night was his element.

It was the same for those upstairs as for Trask and Teale: their only light was that of the moon, creeping into Harry's bedroom through a window with the curtains thrown back. But downstairs: Teale felt Harry's presence, touched Ben Trask's elbow, and husked, "Paxton's right. He's close. And my God, I suddenly realize what we're doing here! Ben, what if he comes here, right to this room?"

"You do nothing," Trask answered gruffly. "You hold that crossbow on him and do nothing. You give me a chance to talk to him, is all. But if I don't get that chance, or if you yourself are threatened, then you shoot—and you shoot for real! The heart. Is that understood?"

It was.

"Now be quiet. Watch. And listen."

Outside in the garden, mist crawled through the gate in the wall where it hung on rusted hinges. Milky tendrils covered the lower terraces and lapped along the paths. And Trask knew well enough what that meant.

Harry made a Möbius jump from the riverbank beyond the gate and emerged with his back to the wall of the house, just to one side of the open French windows. He listened and could hear the breathing of the two men in the room, could feel their very heartbeats. One of them was Ben Trask, but Penny wasn't with them. She was upstairs . . . and so was Paxton.

"Jesus!" Teale panted, the short hairs rising at the back of his neck. "He's here! I know he is! And I've just seen a lot of trouble, a whole load of pain, for one of us."

Trask cocked his SMG. He took two paces out through the French windows and stood ankle-deep in mist, looking this way and that about the night garden. But he failed to look up. He backed into the room and said, "Trouble? Pain? For me? You? Who for, for fuck's sake?"

"Paxton!" Teale hissed. "For Paxton!"

Trask turned horrified eyes to the ceiling. Paxton, Robinson, and the girl were upstairs; Harry owed Paxton one, maybe several, and that vicious little bastard was holding his woman up there. Trask had worked out, with entirely human logic, that like any ordinary adversary the Necroscope would enter the downstairs rooms first; which was the main reason he'd sent Paxton upstairs: to keep Harry safe, for a little while, anyway. Long enough that Trask could maybe talk to him and make sure he got whatever breaks were due him. But Harry wasn't any ordinary adversary and Trask might have guessed he wouldn't work that way. He'd work *his* way, which was unique. But Paxton was in charge up there, and Robinson had a bloody flamethrower!

"Upstairs!" Trask gasped. "Let's go—now!"

Harry too had decided that it was time. Upside down above the high window of his bedroom, he used the great webbed sucker disks of his hands to cling to the pitted wall of the house and lowered his head to look in. A cloud scudding over the moon obscured the small shadow which his head cast. He glanced inside for a moment only, then withdrew. But adding together what he saw and the thoughts of those inside, he now had a complete picture. And before anyone or -thing could move or do anything to change that picture, he acted.

He relaxed his hold on the wall, conjured a door, and fell through it—

—Into the bedroom.

Robinson knew it at once. *"He's here!"* the spotter yelped, spinning on his heel, jumping and gyrating, trying to aim the hot nozzle of his flamethrower in every direction at the same time but seeing and aiming at nothing.

Paxton knew it was true; he could actually *feel* the Necroscope's mind touching his own like an oozing slug—as close as that—but inside the room nothing seemed to have changed. And from downstairs the voices of Trask and Teale were hoarse where the two came running, thundering through the house and up the stairs, shouting their warnings.

"Where?" Paxton's voice was a screech of terror. "Where *is* the bastard?"

He and Robinson faced each other. Paxton looked down the glowing muzzle of Robinson's flamethrower into the flicker of its pilot light, and Robinson stared at the business end of Paxton's crossbow. They both reached for the light switch.

Penny was in the bed, naked, a sheet pulled up under her chin, around her neck . . . and Harry was under the sheet with her where he'd materialized. Not knowing what was happening, she felt his arms go around her— felt his huge webbed disks restructuring themselves into hands once more—and screamed!

Paxton read her mind; Robinson finally pinpointed Harry's vast ESP talent; as the room came alive with electric light, both men turned towards the bed and triggered their weapons. But Harry had already conjured a door—directly *under* himself and the girl, so that they tumbled through it and apparently through the bed itself. As they went he dragged the bed sheet after them. In the Möbius Continuum Penny opened her eyes, then gasped and screwed them shut again. But now that she knew who had her it was okay.

Harry took her to a safe place, wrapped the sheet around her, grated, "Stay here, be quiet, wait!" And as she sat down with a breathless bump in the shade of a wind-carved tree on a deserted, midday, Australian beach, so he returned to the house.

He had to go back, for he'd been challenged.

Paxton had challenged him—ignored his warning and *challenged* him—and Harry's vampire was furious!

in an upstairs room in the house outside Bonnyrig, the Necroscope's bed roared up in fire and smoke, with Paxton and Robinson dancing like maniacs around it, trying to damp down the flames. But already they knew that Harry and the girl had escaped. Trask and Teale came crashing through the door, and the latter took one look, turned white, and backed right out of the room again. Trask went after him and grasped his arm. "What did you see?"

Teale's mouth opened and closed like a fish out of water. "He . . . he's coming back again!" he finally gasped. "And he's mad as hell!"

Trask stuck his head back inside the smoke-filled bedroom. "Paxton, Robinson—out of there, now!"

"But the house is burning!" Robinson yelled.

"That's right," Trask shouted back, "and all the way to the ground! We'll torch it downstairs—heavily, every room—raze the place. It's one refuge he won't be able to use again." And to himself: *Sorry, Harry, but that's the way of it.*

Except it wasn't entirely to himself, for the Necroscope was listening, too. Listening with his mind—and watching with his scarlet eyes—from across the river, where a minute later he heard the gouting roar of the flamethrower and saw the fires spreading through all the downstairs rooms. And:

My place, Harry thought, *and there it goes in flames. This is the end of it. There's nothing to keep me here now.*

In Harry's downstairs study Paxton turned on Trask and his face was livid. "Just what is it you're trying to do?" he demanded. "You know he won't come into a burning house. Teale says Keogh wants me, and Robinson reckons he's close—but you, you're holding him off. He has to *come* to us before we can kill the bastard! Or maybe that's it. Maybe you don't want him killed, right?"

Trask grabbed him by the front of his jacket and almost lifted him off his feet. "You shithead!" He dragged him into the garden, out of the blazing room. "You scumbag! No, I don't want Harry killed, for he was my friend. Still, I'd do it if I had to. But that's okay, for in fact I don't think we *can* kill him. Not you and me nor an army like us. You ask why I'm warning him off? For you, Paxton, for you!"

"For me?" The other struggled free, loaded his crossbow.

"Damned right," Trask snarled. "For while you can't kill Harry Keogh, you'd better fucking believe he can kill you!"

The downstairs rooms of Harry's house were a red and yellow inferno now, and smoke had started to pour from the upper windows and ancient gables. In the garden, as the glass in the French windows surrendered to the heat and began to shatter, the four E-Branch agents backed away. Paxton, suddenly anxious, stared this way and that in the glare and flicker of firelight and held his crossbow close to his chest. The high garden walls seemed to frown on him, and he stumbled as his shuffling feet missed a step to send him reeling down a path into the knee-deep mist of the lower terraces—

—That eerily sentient mist, out of which Harry Keogh rose up like a ghost from its tomb, with his hellish orbs more than reflecting the destruction of his house.

"Nuh-uh-urgh!" Paxton's eyes stood out in the parchment of his face as the Necroscope towered over him, and his inarticulate gurgle of a cry caused the other agents to turn from watching the burning house towards him in his extremity of terror. What they saw was this:

Paxton in the grip of something which was only half or less than half human. They *saw* Paxton, but only as a detail of the main scene, whose utter horror seemed to sear itself onto their retinas. And in the minds of the three, one thought was universally uppermost: that they were here as volunteers, come to kill *this*, an act which must surely qualify them as the bravest or most lunatic heroes of all time!

The lower half of Harry's figure was mist-shrouded, visible only as a vague outline in the opaque, milky swirl . . . but the rest of him was all too visible. He was wearing an entirely ordinary suit of dark, ill-fitting clothes which seemed two sizes too small for him, so that his upper torso sprouted from the trousers to form a blunt wedge. Framed by his jacket, which was held together at the front (barely) by one straining button, the wedge-shaped bulk of Harry's rib cage was massively muscular.

His white, open-necked shirt had burst open down the front, revealing the ripple of his muscle-sheathed ribs and the deep, powerful throb of his chest; the shirt's collar stuck up now from Harry's jacket like a crumpled frill, made insubstantial by the corded bulk of his leaden neck. His flesh was a sullen grey, dappled lurid orange and sick yellow by leaping fire and gleaming moonlight. But there was scarlet there, too, leaking from the hole in his jacket and splashed diagonally across his straining shirt. He towered all of fifteen inches taller than Paxton, whose cringing form he quite literally dwarfed. And his face—

—That was the absolute embodiment of a waking nightmare!

Ben Trask gawped at him in utter disbelief and thought: *Oh, my good God! And I thought I could maybe talk to that!*

Oh, but you can still talk to me, Ben, the Necroscope told him, Trask's first personal experience in the use of telepathy, made possible through the sheer power of Harry's probe. *It's just that where Paxton's concerned, I may not be willing to listen, that's all.*

Teale was gibbering, trying desperately to find strength to lift and aim his crossbow, and failing. His talent, a generally untrustworthy ability to read something of the future, was conjuring all sorts of monstrous events in his mind's eye, piling them up so thick and fast that he was utterly unnerved. It was his proximity to Harry, of course. Robinson was similarly stricken. This close to a true metaphysical Power, his own small talent was reacting like an iron filing whirled in a strong magnetic field. But in any case he couldn't use his terrible weapon, not without burning Paxton, too.

Trask was on his own, the only capable one among them, and now he raised and aimed his SMG at Harry where he held Paxton up before him like a rag doll. Paxton, dangling there in midair, staring gape-jawed and bulge-eyed into the Necroscope's unbelievable face, knowing he was only inches from the gates of hell. That close, yes, for he was the mind-flea; he was the unbearable, unscratchable itch. Or he had been—until now.

Harry looked at him through halogen Halloween eyes which seemed to drip sulphur, looked at him and . . . grinned? A grin, was that what it was? In an alien, vampire world called Starside on the other side of the Möbius Continuum, there at least it might be called a grin. But here it was the rabid, slavering grimace of a great wolf; here it was teeth visibly elongating, curving up and out of gleaming gristle jaw-ridges to shear through gums which spurted splashes of hot ruby blood; here it was the gradual inclination of a monstrous head through several degrees to an almost curiously inquiring angle, the way you might look at a mischievous pet. And having looked it was a writhing of scarlet lips, a flattening of convoluted snout, the beginning of a slow yawning of mantrap jaws to tut-tut and even chastise that disobedient lapdog.

And perhaps to punish it?

That face . . . that mouth . . . that crimson cavern of stalactite, stalagmite teeth, jagged as shards of white, broken glass. What? The gates of hell? All of that and worse.

When Harry had grabbed Paxton and lifted him off his feet, he'd knocked the telepath's crossbow from his grasp and thrown it down. Unarmed, Paxton was a piece of candy, a sweetmeat, a Coconut Flake. He was something to munch on. Why, Harry could bite his face off if he wished it! And suddenly, Trask thought: *Maybe he does! Maybe he will!*

"Harry!" Trask shouted. "Don't!"

The Necroscope slowly closed his jaws, looked up. He glared at Trask across the misted garden, in the ruddy illumination of the burning house. At Ben Trask, once a friend, with whom he'd stood side by side against . . . against just such a creature as he had now become.

417

And Trask, whey-faced, staring back, thinking: *For fuck's sake don't, Harry!*

Would you shoot me, Ben?

You know I would. I wouldn't want to, even now, but I'd have to. It's you or the world, don't you see? I don't want to see my world die screaming . . . then laugh and crawl right back out of its grave! But if you let him go— Paxton, I mean—If you let him live, then I'd be ready to believe you'd let us all live.

Your world is safe, Ben. I'm not staying here.

Starside?

Harry's mental shrug. *There's nowhere else.*

Trask looked down the sights of his SMG. He could shoot at Harry's mist-wreathed legs and maybe chop him down, or he could aim at the Necroscope's head and upper body and try not to hit Paxton in the bargain. But he was a good shot and unlikely to miss his target. Or he could simply take Harry's word for it, that he was going away from here and the world had nothing to fear from him. Except, looking at him now, who could believe that?

Harry read these things in Trask's mind and tried to make it easier for him: he put Paxton down. Which was anything but easy for the Necroscope; he had to fight the Thing inside him, and fight hard; but he did it. And speaking out loud, or rather grunting in the deep bass monotone of the Wamphyri, he asked, "How's this, Ben?"

Trask gasped his relief. "It's good, Harry. It's good." But even answering he was aware, out of the corner of his eye, of Teale and Robinson unfreezing and lining up their weapons. "Hold it, you two!" he shouted.

Harry shot a blood-tinged glance at Teale, which sufficed to send him staggering back, and tuned into Robinson's mind to advise him: *Better listen to Trask, son. Try to fry me on Earth and I'll fry you in hell!*

Trask put his SMG on safe and tossed it aside. "The war's over, Harry," he said.

But Paxton, lying in the mist where Harry had dropped him, squeezed the trigger of his regained crossbow and cried, "Oh, no, it fucking isn't!"

Moments earlier the Necroscope had picked up the message from Paxton's mind: that a deadly hardwood bolt was about to come winging his way. Almost instinctively, he had conjured a Möbius door; and now, with the deceptively .sinuous grace of the Wamphyri, he stepped or flowed backwards into it. To the four espers it seemed that he had simply ceased to be. Paxton's bolt shot forward into the misty swirl of Harry's vacuum and was eaten up by it, leaving the telepath panting:

"I got him! I . . . I'm sure I *got* the bastard! I couldn't miss!" Laughing however shakily, he got to his feet . . .

. . . And the mist where it had closed on the Necroscope opened up again, and his clotted, gurgling, disembodied voice came out of it, saying, "How sorry I am to have to disappoint you."

Shit! Trask thought, snatching a breath of hot, smoky air as a huge grey hand with nails like rust-scabbed fishhooks reached out of empty space, closed over Paxton's head, and dragged him shrieking out of the garden and right out of this universe. And Harry Keogh's monstrous voice left hanging on the air, saying:

"Ben, I'm afraid I just have to do this . . ."

In the Möbius Continuum Harry hurled Paxton away from him and heard his scream dwindling into conjectural distances. He should leave him there, let him spin on his own axis, flailing across parallel infinities forever, shrieking and sobbing and, if his heart should burst, finally dying a raving madman. But that would be to pol-

lute this mystical place. There had to be a better way—
a more reasonable punishment—than that.

He sped after him, caught and steadied him, and drew
him close. And there in the Möbius Continuum—whose
nature even Harry was only just beginning to suspect or
understand, where even the smallest thought has weight—
he said to him:

Paxton, you're a miserable creature.

"Get away from me! Get the f-f-fuck away from me!"

Tsk, tsk! Harry sucked his teeth, which as his blood
began to cool were halfway to normal again. *And you a
telepath! You don't need to shout in the Möbius Continuum, mind-flea. Just thinking it is enough.* And in that
selfsame moment Harry knew what he must do.

Of course. Paxton the mind-flea, the mental vampire
who lived on the thoughts of others rather than their
blood; the thought-thief; the unscratchable itch. How
many victims had felt his bite? E-Branch was full of
them. And how many more didn't even know—weren't
equipped to know—that he'd ever been into their minds
in the first place?

Or maybe not a flea. Maybe . . . a mosquito? But in
any case, a harmful parasite with a painful, irritating
sting. It was high time someone drew that sting. And the
Necroscope knew just exactly how to do it.

He entered Paxton's dazed, terrified mind to search
for and discover the telepathic mechanism which was the
source of the man's talent. It was something Paxton had
been born with and there was no switching it off; but it
could be shielded, buried in psychic "lead" like a rogue
reactor, until it melted down or burned itself out trying
to break free. Which was precisely what the Necroscope
did. He wrapped Paxton's talent in essence of Wamphyri
mind-smog, smothered it in a blanket of ESP opaque-
ness, mothballed it in ephemeral and yet almost unbreak-

able threads of what ordinary people term "the privacy of their own minds." Except that in Paxton's case, that privacy would be his prison.

And when Harry was done with him, he delivered Paxton back to the garden of the burning house, where the men from E-Branch had moved down to the river wall away from the heat of the conflagration. Against a backdrop of roaring, gouting gold and crimson fire, Harry emerged from the Möbius Continuum and tossed a sniveling Paxton into Ben Trask's arms.

The telepath at once collapsed in tears, sank raggedly to his knees, and hugged Trask's legs. Looking down at him, Trask was aghast. "What have you done to him?"

"Neutered him," said Harry.

"What?"

Harry shook his head. "Not his balls, his telepathy. Mental emasculation. He's raped his last mind. And where the Branch is concerned, I've done you my last favor."

"Harry?"

"Look after yourself, Ben."

"Harry, wait!"

But the Necroscope was no longer there.

He stood off for long moments along the river and watched the old house burn. What was it Faethor Ferenczy had called his castle in the Khorvaty, when finally that morbid pile had been reduced to rubble? His last vestige on Earth? Well, and this obsolete old house had been Harry's last vestige.

In this world, anyway . . .

On a beach of gleaming white sand on the other side of the world, Penny had fashioned a bikini for herself from strips of Harry's bed sheet. Now, walking at the rim of the ocean, she picked up and examined exotic shells where they littered the tide's reach. Strangely (because she usually tanned without difficulty, and also because her as yet innocent mind hadn't recognized the significance of it), she found the sun spiteful; her exposed skin was already blotched and rapidly turning red. To cool herself, she kneeled in the shallows of a tidal pool and let the sea lave her. Which was when Harry returned and called out to her from the shade of the wind-blasted tree.

She looked up and saw him, and felt the power of his magnetism stronger than ever before. It was love and it was much more than love; he need only command it and there was nothing she wouldn't do for him; she was entirely enthralled. Taking a magnificent conch with her, she ran to him and saw how different he looked. Different and yet the same. Before returning to her, the Necroscope had stopped off somewhere to pick up a wide-brimmed black hat and a long black overcoat; weird gear, Penny thought, for a beach in the heat of the midday sun! Now he reminded her of the grim-faced bounty hunter or undertaker in . . . how many of those old spaghetti westerns? Except they hadn't worn dark-tinted glasses.

Where the tree gave its maximum shade, Harry eased off his coat and displayed evidence of his wounds: great mats of blood congealed into rusty scabs which crusted his tatters and glued them to him. Feeling his hurt—indeed, feeling more of it than he felt—Penny unwrapped the strip of soaked cotton sheet from her breasts and dampened the Necroscope's bloodied areas with brine. And then she was able to peel the soiled rags from his now entirely human body. His human-*looking* body, anyway.

From the front, the bullet hole in Harry's right shoulder didn't look too bad, but from the back it was awful. A chunk of flesh the size of a child's clenched fist had been blown right out of him, and its rim at the top had been ripped by Johnny Found's hook. But amazingly (to Penny, if not to the Necroscope himself), the wound was already healing. New skin was forming around the crater where flesh and bone had been blasted away, and while the pulp within gleamed red as meat on a butcher's block, still it had almost stopped bleeding.

"It's healing now," Harry grunted. "If you just sat there and watched it, you'd see it closing up. Another day, two at most, and there'll be only a scar. Another week and even the restructured bone will have stopped aching."

Fascinated, drawn to him irresistibly, she clutched his shoulders and turned her lithe, lovely body this way and that, brushing her breasts against the gaping hole in his back. Done on impulse, her eroticism caused the Necroscope a little pain and gave him a lot of pleasure. Looking over his shoulder, he saw the brown of her nipples stained red by blood fresh from his body. But in the next moment, astonished by the strength of her own sensuality, Penny said, "I . . . I don't quite know why I did that!"

"I do," he growled, taking her there on the sand—and in turn being taken—again and again through the long hot afternoon.

It was love and lust and what lovers have done since the beginning of time; but it was other than that, more than that. It was an initiation of sorts, for Harry as much as for Penny. And it proved beyond a doubt how utterly inexhaustible are the Wamphyri and their thralls.

Later . . . she woke up feeling chilly, saw Harry sitting there with her shell in his lap. His face was gaunt, almost pained. The sun, setting over the rolling ocean, highlighted the rims of hollows in his face like shallow craters in a moonscape. Squinting her eyes until he was little more than a dark silhouette, Penny tried to make this newly perceived Harry less stark. The too-distinct lines melted a little and softened his face, but the pain was still there. Then, when he felt her eyes on him, the mood was broken. And when she sat up shivering, he draped her with his coat.

Picking the shell up, she said, "It's beautiful, isn't it?"

He gave her a strange look. "It's a dead thing, Penny."

"Is that all you see, death?"

He shook his head. "No. I feel it, too. I'm the Necroscope."

"You feel that the shell is dead?"

He nodded. "And how the creature it housed died. Well, not *feel* it, exactly. I . . . experience it? No, not that, either." He shrugged and sighed. "I just know."

She looked at the conch again, and the sun struck mother-of-pearl from its iridescent rim. "It isn't pretty?"

He shook his head. "It's ugly. Do you see that tiny hole towards the pointed end?"

She nodded.

"That's what killed it. Another snail, smaller but deadly—deadly to it—bored into it and sucked out its life. A vampire, yes. There are millions of us." And she saw him give a shudder.

She put the shell aside. "That's a horrid story, Harry!"

"It's also a true one."

"How can you know that?"

His voice was harsher now. "Because I'm the Necroscope! Because dead things talk to me. All dead things. And if they haven't the mind for it, then they . . . *convey* to me. And your 'pretty' bloody shell? It conveys the slow grind of its killer eating into its whorl, the penetration of its probe, and the dully burning seep of its fluids being drained off. Pretty? It's a corpse, Penny, a cadaver!''

He stood up and scuffed listlessly at the sand, and she said, ''Has it always been like that? For you, I mean?''

''No,'' he shook his head, ''but it is now. My vampire is growing. As he grows sharper, so he hones my talents. There was a time when I could only talk to dead people, or rather to creatures I could understand. Dogs go on after death just like we do, did you know that? But now,'' again his shrug, ''if they were alive once but now are dead, I can feel them. And I feel more and more of them all the time.'' He kicked at the sand again. ''You see this beach? The very sand sighs and whispers and moans. A million billion corpses broken up by time and the tides. All of that life wasted, and none of it ready or willing to lie quiet and still. And every dead thing wanting to know, 'Why did I die? Why did I die?' ''

''But it has to be that way,'' she gasped, frightened by his tone. ''It always has been. Without death, what would be the point of life? If we had forever, we wouldn't strive to do anything—because *every*thing would be possible!''

''In this world,'' he took her shoulders, ''there's life and there's death. But I know another world where there's a state between the two . . .'' And as it grew dark he told her all about Starside.

When he was done she shivered to the inevitability of it and asked, ''When shall we go there?''

''Soon,'' he told her.

''We can't stay here? I know that place is bound to frighten me.''

''Do my eyes frighten you?'' They were like small lamps in his face.

She smiled. ''No, because I know they're *your* eyes.''

''But they frighten others.''

425

"Because they don't know you."

"On Starside I'll build an aerie," Harry told her, "where your eyes will be as red as mine."

"Will they?" She seemed almost eager.

"Oh, yes!" Harry told her. And to himself: *You may be sure of it, you poor darling child*. For even here and now, as early and unanticipated as this, he could detect the faintest scarlet flush in them . . .

While she slept in his arms, Harry sat and made plans. They weren't much, just something to do. They kept him from thinking too deeply about his and Penny's imminent departure, its possible perils. About its inevitability.

For it *was* inevitable—as was the drone of the helicopter whose searchlights came sweeping along the beach from the east. Harry had thought they'd be safe here for . . . oh, a long time. But as he reached out and touched the minds of the people in the droning dragonfly airplane he saw that he'd been wrong. They were espers.

"The Branch," he said, perhaps bitterly, waking Penny up and forming Möbius equations in his mind.

"What, even here?" she mumbled as he shifted her across the continent to a clothing store in Sydney.

"Even here . . . there . . . yes," he said. "Indeed, anywhere. Their locators will find me no matter where I go; they'll alert their contacts worldwide; espers and bounty hunters will track and trap and eventually burn us. We can't fight a whole world. And even if I could, I don't want to. Because to fight is to surrender—to the thing inside me. And I'd prefer to be just me. For as long as possible, anyway. But tonight we'll lead them all a dance, right? For tomorrow we die."

"Die?"

"We'll be dead to this world, anyway," he said.

They chose expensive clothes willy-nilly, and an expensive leather suitcase in which to pack them. Then, as the store's alarms began to clamor, they moved on.

It had been 9:00 P.M. local time when they left the beach; it was 11:30 in the store they robbed; moving east they got dressed on another beach (Long Beach) at 5:00 A.M. in the first light of dawn, and started a champagne breakfast in New York a little after 8:00 A.M.—and all in the space of thirty or so minutes!

Penny ate her steak barbecued, medium rare; Harry's was *so* rare it dripped blood, just the way he'd ordered it. They drank three bottles of champagne. When presented with the bill the Necroscope laughed, snatched Penny into his lap, and tilted his chair over backwards . . . and the pair of them out of this world into the Möbius Continuum.

Minutes later (at 10:30 P.M. local time) and some three and a half thousand miles north of where they'd started out, they robbed the innermost security vaults of the Bank of Hong Kong; and by midnight they'd lost a million Hong Kong dollars on the gaming tables in Macau. A few minutes later (at 6:30 in the evening, local), still ordering and drinking champagne, Harry bundled an entirely tipsy Penny into a hotel bed in Nicosia, and left her there to sleep it off. She dripped pearls and diamonds and her skin smelled of a fine haze of alcohol. Most women (were they truthful) would give an entire world for the things she had seen and done and experienced in the last half-day of her life. So had Penny given a world. That's why Harry had arranged and executed it.

Their binge had taken a little over three hours; the locators at E-Branch HQ in London—and others in Moscow—were quite dizzy. But the Necroscope knew that Penny was as yet too weak a source for them to track as a single entity. On her own, they probably wouldn't be able to find her. Even if they could, he doubted if they'd have a man in Cyprus. She'd be safe there. For a little while, anyway.

And now it was time he made their Starside reservations . . .

Part Four

I Faethor—Zek—Perchorsk

IN THE MÖBIUS CONTINUUM, HARRY OPENED A FUTURE-time door and went looking for Faethor Ferenczy. Faethor was long dead and gone, and had been incorporeal—which is to say bodiless—for a very long time; so long that by now he was probably mindless, too. But there were things of great importance which the Necroscope wanted to ask him. About his "disease" and how he'd come by it; maybe even about how he could cure it, though that possibility seemed almost as remote as Faethor himself.

Möbius time was awesome as ever. Before launching himself down the ever-expanding time-stream, Harry paused framed in the doorway and looked out on humanity as few flesh-and-blood men had ever seen it, and only then on his authority. He saw it as blue light—the near-neon blue of all human life—rushing out and away with an interminable sigh, an orchestrated angelic *Ahhhhhhhhh*, into forever and ever. But the sigh was all

431

in his mind (indeed he knew that it *was* his mind sighing), for time is quite silent. Which was just as well. For if all the sound in all the years of all the LIFE he witnessed had been present, then it would have been an utterly unbearable cacophony.

He stood or floated in the metaphysical doorway and gazed on all those lines of blue light streaming out and away—the myriad life-lines of the human race—and thought: *It's like a blue star gone nova, and these are its atoms fleeing for their lives!* And he knew that indeed every dazzling line was a life, which he could trace from birth to death across the trackless heavens of Möbius time; for even now his own life-line unwound out of him, like a thread unwinding from a bobbin, to cross the threshold and shoot away into the future. Except where the rest were pure blue, his thread carried a strong crimson taint.

As for Faethor's line: if it existed at all, it would be pure (impure?) scarlet. But it didn't, for Faethor's life was over. No life now for that ancient, once-undead thing, but true death, where he sped on and on beyond the bounds of being . . . all thanks, or whatever, to Harry Keogh. Bodiless, yes, the old vampire, but still the Necroscope knew how to track him. For in the Möbius Continuum thoughts have weight and like time itself go on forever.

Faethor, Harry called out, sending a probe lancing ahead as he launched himself down the time-stream, *I'd like to pay you a visit. If you're in the mood for it.*

Oh? The answer came back at once, and then, astonishingly, a chuckle; one of Faethor's most dark, most devious chuckles. *A meeting of two old fiends, eh? And is it visiting day? Well, and why not? But truth to tell, I've been expecting you.*

You have? Harry caught up with Faethor's spirit: with

the memory, the mind which was all that remained of him.

Oh, yes! For who else would know the answer if not me, eh?

The answer? But Harry knew well enough what he meant. The answer—the solution—to his problem, assuming such a solution existed.

Come, come! Faethor tut-tutted. *Am I naive? Call me what you will, Harry, but never that!* And now he gave a deadspeak nod and looked the Necroscope over. *Well, well! But you know, you never fail to amaze me? I mean, so many talents! And now this: faster-than-life travel! Why, look—you've even outstripped yourself!*

Even as Faethor spoke, Harry's life-line gave a wriggle, a shudder, and split down the middle. Half of the line bent back a little on itself and shot off at right angles to the Necroscope's line of travel, shortly to disappear in a brilliant burst of red and blue fire. But the other half, like a comet with Harry himself for its nucleus, sped on as before and kept pace with Faethor.

Harry had been expecting some such. The phenomenon he'd just witnessed (which in fact had been his departure point for Starside) was in the probable future. But this was Möbius time, which is to say speculative time, and nothing was for certain. It was the reason why reading the future was so very hit-and-miss. For if in the real world anything contrary should happen to him between now and then, his departure simply wouldn't happen. Or possibly not. In other words—and despite the fact that he'd seen it—it was only something which *might* happen.

But probably, said Faethor. And again he chuckled. *So . . . they're driving you out, eh?*

Harry shrugged. *No, I'm going of my own free will.*

433

Because if you stay they'll hunt you down and destroy you.

Because I will it, Harry repeated.

You brought yourself into prominence, said Faethor, *and they looked at you—closely! Now they know you for what you are. All of these years you've been their hero, and now you're their worst nightmare come true. And so it's back to Starside. Well, good luck to you. But mind you look out for that son of yours. Why, the last time you were there he crippled you!*

Before continuing their conversation, Harry very carefully shielded his mind. Only show Faethor the tiniest crack in the door and he'd be in. Not only to spy on the Necroscope's most secret thoughts, but to lodge himself in his mind as a permanent tenant. It was the ancient vampire's one chance—his very *last* chance—for any sort of continuity other than this empty, endless speeding into the future. And so, when Harry was satisfied that he'd made himself impregnable:

Yes, my son crippled me, he agreed. *Robbed me of my deadspeak, denied me access to the Möbius Continuum. It was easy for him then, because I was only a man. But now . . . as you see, I'm Wamphyri!*

You go back to do battle with him? Faethor hissed. *Your own son?*

If that's the only way. Harry shrugged again, mainly to disguise his lie. *But it doesn't have to be a fight. Starside is a big place. Even bigger, now that the Wamphyri are dead or fled.*

Hmmm! Faethor mused. *So you'll return to Starside, build yourself an aerie there, and if necessary do battle with your son for a piece of his territory. Is that it?*

Possibly.

So why have you come to see me? What have I to do with it? If this is your plan, then go to it.

For long moments Harry was silent; finally, he answered: *But it was my thought that . . . you might like to come with me?*

Faethor's gasp—and the ensuing silence—was of stunned disbelief. Until, eventually: *That I might like . . . ?*

To come with me, Harry said again.

But: *No*, said Faethor in a while, and Harry sensed the unbodied shake of his head. *I can't credit this. It is— can only be—a trick! You who once fought so long and hard to keep me out, now invite me in? To be one with you in your new Wamphyri mind, body, and—*

Don't say soul! said Harry. *Also, you have it wrong.*

Eh? Faethor was at once on his guard. *But how can I have it wrong? To go with you from this . . . this hellish no-place into Starside is out of the question, unless it is as part of you. Here I am nothing, but if of your own free will you're now inviting my mind into yours . . . ?*

Initially, yes, said Harry. *But this time you must agree to move out when I desire it. And without a struggle, without that I must use trickery, as last time.*

Faethor was flabbergasted. *Move out to where?*

Into the mind and body of some lesser man, some Traveller king or such, in Starside.

And finally, Faethor understood, or thought he did, and his deadspeak thoughts turned sour as vinegar. *And so you are unworthy, after all*, he said then. *And have been from the start. I used to lie in the earth in my place in Ploiesti and think: 'The Necroscope can have it all, everything, the world! Thibor was a ruffian, unworthy, but not so Harry. Janos was the scummy froth of my loins, beside which Harry has the consistency, the purity—or if not that, then at least the homogeneity—of cream. I shall make Harry my third and last son!' Yes, these were my thoughts, of which you were unworthy.*

How come? said Harry. *I mean, why do you insult me?*

What? (astonishment, disbelief). *Surely you mean why do I sorrow! But you could have been—could still be—the most powerful creature of all time: The Master Vampire! The Great Plague Bearer! Because I, Faethor Ferenczy, willed it, you are Wamphyri! You have admitted as much yourself. And yet now you would throw it all away. Does it mean nothing to you, to be Wamphyri? What of the passion, the power, the glory?*

What of me? Harry answered. *The real me, before my adulteration?*

The new you is greater!

Harry shook his head. *I don't resent the greatness. Only that it was not on my terms. But now I'm offering you terms, and no more time to waste. Can you help me . . . or can't you?*

Cards on the table, then, said Faethor. *You will take me into your mind, transfer or transport me to Starside—which after all is or should have been my natural place—and there pass me on to some other to guide him as I would have guided you. In return for which, you desire to know if there's a way you may rid yourself of the thing growing within you. Now, do I have it right?*

And if there is a way, Harry qualified the deal, *you'll describe it in detail, a fool's guide, so that I may be my own man again.*

Following which, you'll return to your own world, leaving me, embodied once more, on Starside?

That's the plan.

And if there is no way to free you?

Harry shrugged. *A deal is a deal. You'll be a power on Starside, anyway, as stated.*

Eventually to become your rival? And your son's rival?

Yet again the Necroscope's shrug. *Like I said, with the old Wamphyri dead or fled, Starside is a big place.*

Faethor was cautious. *It seems to me that whichever way it goes, still I get the best of this bargain. Now, why should you be so good to me?*

Maybe it's like you said, Harry told him, *a meeting of two old friends.*

Fiends, Faethor corrected him.

As you will, except I'm an unwilling fiend. And despite the fact that you're the engineer of my current fix, still I can't forget that in the past you've put yourself out to do me one or two favors; even though all of them (a little sourly), *as I've since come to realize, were to your ultimate benefit. Still, it seems I've grown accustomed to you; I understand you now; you played the game according to your own rules, that's all. Wamphyri rules. Also, I'm full of human compassion—I can't help it—and I have to admit my conscience has been bothering me. About you, stuck here in Möbius time. About my leaving you here. And finally . . . well, you said it yourself: if there is a cure for my complaint, who'd know it better than you? Which is the number one reason I'm here and doesn't leave me with much choice.* He was very convincing.

Very well, said Faethor (as Harry had supposed he would), *you have a deal. Now take me into your mind.*

When you have told me what I want to know.

Whether or not you may rid yourself of your vampire?

A little more than that.

Oh?

Where it came from. How it got into me in the first place.

You haven't thought it out for yourself?

It was the toadstools, right?

Faethor's deadspeak nod. *Yes.*

And the toadstools were you?

Yes. They were spawned of my fats festering in the

earth where I'd burned and melted down, an ichor, an essence, simmering there, waiting. Then, when the brew was ripe, I willed the fungi up into the light—but not until I knew you'd be there to receive them.

And you were in them?

As you well know, for through them I came to you. But you cast me out.

And these fungi: are they a natural part of the Wamphyri chain? Part of the overall life cycle?

I don't know. Faethor seemed at a genuine loss. *There was no one to instruct me in such mysteries. Old Belos Pheropzis might have known—might even have passed such knowledge down to my father—but if so, then Waldemar Ferrenzig never told me. I only knew that the spores were in me, in the fats of my body, and that I could will them into growth; but don't ask me how I knew. How does a dog know how to bark?*

And the spores were your very last vestiges?

Yes.

Could it be that such toadstools grow in the vampire swamps on Starside? It seems logical to me, since those swamps are the source of Wamphyri infestation.

Faethor sighed his impatience. *But I've never even seen the vampire swamps on Starside, though I hope to—and soon! Now then, let me into your mind.*

Can I be rid of my vampire?

Do we still have a deal, however I may answer?

So long as you answer true.

No, you are stuck with your vampire forever!

Harry wasn't hard hit; he had supposed it would be so; even with regard to the very question or idea or thought of ''curing'' himself, his will was already weakening, probably had been for some time. For he was learning what it is to be Wamphyri. And if his right hand didn't like it, then his left hand did. The dark side of men has always been their stronger side. And what of women? The Lady Karen's cure had been her destruction.

In his mind, like an echo, the Necroscope heard once more Faethor's answer: *You are stuck with your vampire forever!* And he thought: *So be it!* And to Faethor said:

Then farewell.

He began to decelerate, leaving the astonished vampire to speed on ahead as before. As the gap rapidly widened, Faethor despairingly called back, *What? But you said—*

I lied, Harry cut him off.

What? You, a liar? Faethor couldn't accept it. *But . . . but that's not like you at all!*

No, Harry answered grimly, *but it is like the thing inside me. It is like my vampire. For it's part of you, Faethor, it's part of you.*

Wait! Faethor cried out in his extremity. *You can be rid of it . . . It's true . . . You really can!*

And that *is the part!* said Harry, transferring out of time and back into the Möbius Continuum. "The lying part."

And in Möbius time Faethor was left to shriek and gibber, but faintly now and fading, like the slithering whispers of winter's crumbling leaves, whirled forever on the winds of eternity . . .

Harry went to see Jazz and Zek on the island of Zakynthos in the Ionian. They had a villa in the trees, overlooking the sea and hidden well away from the holidaymakers, in Porto Zoro on the northeast coast.

It was eight in the evening when he materialized close to the house; he put out a probe and saw that Zek was on her own, but guessed that Jazz wouldn't mind his wife speaking for both of them. First he reached out to her telepathically; and the way she answered him, unafraid, it was as if she'd expected him.

"For a day or two?" she said, after inviting him in, when he'd explained what he was doing. "But of course she'll be okay here, the poor girl!"

"Not so poor," he was prompted to answer, almost defensively. "Because she doesn't really understand it, she won't fight it as hard as I have. And before she knows it, she'll be Wamphyri."

"But Starside? How will you live there? I mean, do you intend . . . intend to . . . ?" Zek gave up. She was after all talking to a vampire. She knew that behind those dark lenses his eyes were fire; knew, too, how easily she could be burned by them. But if she feared him it didn't show, and Harry liked her for that. He always had liked her.

"We'll do what we have to do," he answered. "My son found ways to survive."

"The way I see it," she said with an almost unnoticeable shudder, "blood is a powerful addiction."

"The *most* powerful!" he told her. "It's why we have to go."

Zek didn't want to push it, but felt she must: her female curiosity. "Because you love your fellowman and can't trust yourself?"

He shrugged and offered her a wry smile. "Because E-Branch can't trust me!" But his half-smile swiftly faded. "Who knows? Maybe they're right not to." And after long moments of silence he asked, "What about Jazz?"

She looked at him and lifted an eyebrow, as if to say, do you really need to ask? "Jazz doesn't forget his friends, Harry. But for you, we were long since dead on Starside. And in this world? But for you, the Ferenczy's son, Janos, would still be alive and festering. Anyway, Jazz is in Athens seeking dual nationality.''

"When can I bring Penny here?"

"That's up to you. Now, if you wish.''

Harry gathered Penny up from her bed in the Nicosia hotel without even waking her, and moments later Zek saw how gently he laid her between cool sheets in the guest bedroom of this, her new, temporary refuge. And she nodded to herself, certain now that if anyone was able to look after this girl—on Starside or anywhere else—then it would be the Necroscope.

"And what now, Harry?" she queried, serving coffee sweetened with Metaxa brandy, on her balcony where it jutted over the cliffs and the moonlit sea.

"Now Perchorsk," he answered simply.

But halfway down his cup, he fell asleep in his chair . . .

It was a measure of his trust that he felt he could rest here. And it was a measure of Zek Föener's that she didn't go and fetch her spear gun and silver harpoon and try to kill him there and then, and Penny after him. She didn't; but even Zek couldn't feel *that* safe.

Before retiring she called for Wolf (a real wolf, born on Starside), and when he came from the dark, scented cover of the Mediterranean pines, stationed him at her door. And: *Wake me if they should move,* she told him . . .

At midnight Harry woke up and went to Perchorsk in the USSR's Ural'skiy Khrebet. Zek watched him go and wished him luck.

In the Urals it was 3:30 in the morning, and in the depths of the Perchorsk Projekt Viktor Luchov was asleep and nightmaring. He always would nightmare, as long as they kept him here. But now, since British E-Branch's warning, the nightmares were that much worse.

"What exactly did that warning consist of?" a vague, shadowy Harry Keogh inquired of him in his dream. "No, don't tell me—let me take a shot at it, have a go at guessing it. It had to do with me, right?"

Luchov, the Projekt Direktor, didn't know where Harry had come from but suddenly he was there, pacing the disk's bolted metal plates with him in the glare of the sphere-Gate, arm in arm like old friends in the harrowing heart of Perchorsk, in the very roots of the mountains. And finally, he answered, "What's that you ask? Did it have to do with you? But you sell yourself short, Harry. Why, you were *all* of it!"

"They told you about me?"

"Your E-Branch, yes. I mean, not me specifically. They didn't tell me. But they did warn the new man in charge of our own ESPionage Group, who of course passed it on to me. Except, I'm not sure I should be repeating it to you."

"Not even in a dream?"

"Dream?" Luchov shuddered, his subconscious mind briefly, however unwillingly, returning to the horror of what had gone before. He considered *that* for a moment . . . and in the next recoiled from it as if scalded. "My God—but the whole monstrous business was a *nightmare!* In fact, and for all that you scared me witless, you were one of the few human things about it."

"Human, yes," said Harry, nodding. "But that was then and this is now."

Luchov disengaged his arm and moved a little apart, then turned and looked at the Necroscope—stared hard, curiously, even fearfully at him—as if to bring him into definition. But Harry's outline was fuzzy; he wouldn't come into focus; against the glare of the Gate where its dome came up through the disk, he was a silhouette whose rim was punctuated and perforated with brilliant lances of white light. "They say that you . . . that you're . . ."

"That I'm a vampire?"

"Are you?" Luchov lay still a minute in his bed and stopped breathing, waiting for the other's answer.

"Are you asking: Do I kill men for their blood? Has my bite turned men into monsters? Have I *myself* been turned into a monster by a vampire's bite? Then I can only tell you . . . no." His answer wasn't entirely a lie. Not yet.

Luchov breathed again, began tossing in his bed as before; and he and Harry continued their tour of inspection around the rim of the glaring sphere-Gate. As they went so the Necroscope used a basic form of ESPionage, telepathy, to study the Projekt's secret core, its awesome nucleus where it was mirrored in the Russian scientist's subconscious mind. He saw it, that great spherical cavity carved in the mountain's solid rock, eaten out by unimaginable forces; and in Luchov's mind the enigmatic Gate was the gravity-defying maggot at its center, coiled into a perfect ball of matterless white light, motionless, still glutted on energy absorbed in the first moments of its creation. The Gate, floating there like an alien chrysalis, with everything it contained waiting to break loose, to break out.

But Harry also saw that certain things had changed. Some things, anyway. The last time he was here (or rather there, *physically* there, at the core) it had been like this:

A spidery web of scaffolding had been built halfway up the curving wall at its perimeter, supporting a platform of timber flooring which surrounded the glaring Gate or portal floating on thin air at the cavern's center. The effect had been to make the sphere look like the planet Saturn, with a ring system composed of the encircling timber floor. The cavern was a little more than forty meters in diameter, and the central sphere a little less than a quarter of that. There had been a gap of a few inches between the innermost timbers and the event horizon which was the sphere's ''skin.''

Backed up against the black, wormhole-riddled wall at the perimeter of the cavern, where the supporting scaffolding and stanchions were most firmly seated, three evenly spaced, twin-mounted Katushev cannons had pointed their ugly muzzles almost point-blank at the blinding center, ready at a moment's notice to discharge hot, sleeting steel at anything which might emerge from the glare. Closer to the center, an electrified fence with a gate had been an additional precaution.

But precautions against what?

The answer to that was simple: against what appeared to be the denizens of hell.

As to what the Perchorsk Projekt had been originally, and how it mutated into what it was now:

When the USA started work on its SDI program, the USSR thought to answer with Perchorsk. If America's aim was to knock out ninety percent of incoming Russian missiles, then the Reds must discover a way to terminate—or otherwise render ineffective—one hundred percent of missiles having origin in the USA. The answer was to have been a screen of energy (several, in fact) which would enclose the Soviet heartland or large, vital parts of it under an impenetrable umbrella.

A team of top-rank scientists was quickly assembled, and in the depths of the Perchorsk ravine an amazing subterranean complex was blasted and hewn out of the mountain itself. A dam was constructed in the ravine; its turbines would supply sufficient hydroelectric power to drive the complex and supplement the energy of its atomic pile. Working furiously, the Soviet task force completed the Perchorsk Projekt in short order and with nothing to spare in what had been a very tight schedule. Except that perhaps the schedule had been just a little *too* tight.

And then the device had been tested.

It was tested just once, and went disastrously wrong . . . mechanical failure . . . energies which should have fanned out and been dispersed across a great arc of the sky were turned back in their tracks, deflected downwards into the core of the Projekt. Into the pile. And the Perchorsk Projekt ate its own heart!

It ate flesh and blood and bone, plastic and rock and steel, nuclear fuel and the atomic pile itself. For a second—maybe two seconds, three—it was ultimately voracious, so much so that finally it ate itself. And when it was over the shining sphere-Gate hung in thin air where the pile had been, and the laboratories and levels all around had been reduced to so much magmass.

That was what Direktor Luchov had termed those monstrous regions in the vicinity of the central cavity and Gate, "the magmass levels": *made* monstrous by what had occurred in them at the time of the blowback, when flesh and rock and whatever else had been gathered together and fused or molded into this or that incredible, unthinkable shape like so much plasticine. Men, reversed so that their innards hung outwards, had become one with the rock walls. And closer to the center, where they had been incinerated by the heat of the blowback, there they'd left their twisted, alien impressions scorched into the blackened rock. Pompeii, in a fashion, is similar to look upon; but there in the ashes and lava, at least the figures are still recognizably human.

After that, it had soon become apparent just what the sphere was: the fact that the failed experiment had blown a hole through the wall of this universe into another, which lay parallel. And the sphere was the doorway, the portal . . . the Gate. But it was a weird kind of gate; anything going through it couldn't come back; likewise for anything that came through from the other side, from the parallel world of Sunside and Starside. And the trouble with Starside, of course, was that it was the source of vampirism, the "home" of the Wamphyri.

Things *had* come through from the other side, which by the grace of God—or by chance, good fortune—had been destroyed before they could carry their lethal taint, the plague of vampirism, into the outside world. But such had been their horror that men just couldn't face up to them. Hence the Katushevs. Hence the flamethrowers everywhere evident, where in other secret establishments one might expect to find fire extinguishers. Hence the FEAR which had lived and breathed and occasionally held its breath in Perchorsk. The FEAR which lived here even now.

Even now, yes . . .

It was different, Harry observed, but not that different. For one thing the wooden floorboards of the Saturn's rings platform had been replaced by these steel plates, radiating outwards from the sphere like giant fish scales. The Katushevs had gone, too, leaving the Gate surrounded at its own height by a system of ominous-looking sprinklers. And higher up the curving wall of the cavern, on platforms of their own, were the great glass carboys which contained the liquid agent for this sprinkler system: many gallons of highly corrosive acid. The steel plates of the rings sloped slightly downwards towards the center, so that any spilled acid would run that way; below the sphere-Gate, central on the magmass floor, a huge glass tank served as a catchment area for the acid when its work was done.

Its "work," of course, would be to blind, incapacitate, and rapidly reduce to fumes anything that should come through from the other side; for after the last grotesque emergence—of a Wamphyri warrior creature—Viktor Luchov had known that exploding steel or a team of men with conventional flamethrowers just wouldn't be enough. Not for *that* sort of thing.

What *had* been enough was the fail-safe system which was in use at that time, which poured thousands of gallons of explosive fuel into the core and then ignited it. Except it had also reduced the complex to a shell. Since when—

"Why didn't you get out, then?" Harry inquired, when he'd seen everything he needed to see. "Why didn't you just quit the place, close it up?"

"Oh, we did—briefly," Luchov answered, blinking rapidly where he peered at his dream visitor in the glare of the Gate. "We got out, sealed off the tunnels, filled all the horizontal ventilation and service shafts into the ravine with concrete, built a gigantic steel door onto the old entrance like a door on a bank vault. Why, we did as good a job on the Perchorsk Projekt as they'd later do on the reactor at Chernobyl! And then we had people sitting out there in the ravine with their sensors, listening to it . . . until we realized that we just couldn't stand the silence!"

Harry knew what he meant. The horror at Chernobyl couldn't reactivate itself; it wasn't likely to become sentient. But if sentient minds could plug the holes at Perchorsk, others—however alien—might always unplug them.

"We had to know, to be able to see for ourselves, that all was well down here," Luchov continued. "At least until we could deal with it on a more permanent basis."

"Oh?" Harry was keenly interested. "Deal with it permanently? Will you explain?"

And Luchov might have done just that, except Harry had allowed himself to become just a fraction too intense, too real. And suddenly, the Projekt Direktor had known that this was more than any ordinary dream.

Starting awake in his austere, cell-like room, the Russian jerked upright in his bed and saw Harry sitting there, staring at him with eyes like clots of fluorescent blood in the room's darkness. Then, remembering his dream, and panting his shock where he pressed himself to the bare steel wall, Luchov gasped, "Harry Keogh! It *is* you! You . . . you *liar!*"

Again Harry knew what he meant. But he shook his head. "I told you no lie, Viktor. I haven't killed men for their blood, I've created no vampires, and I wasn't myself infected that way."

"That's as may be," the other gasped, "but you *are* a vampire!"

Harry smiled, however terribly. "Look at me," he said, his voice very soft, almost warm, even reasonable. "I mean, I can hardly deny it, can I?" And he leaned himself a little closer to Luchov.

The Russian was as Harry remembered him; his skin might be a shade more sallow, his eyes more feverish, but basically he was the same man. Small and thin, he was badly scarred and the hair was absent from the left half of his face and yellow-veined skull. But however vulnerable Luchov might seem, Harry knew that in fact he was a survivor. He had survived the awful accident which created the Gate, survived all the Things which subsequently came through it, even survived the final holocaust. Yes, survived everything. So far, anyway.

Luchov blanched under the Necroscope's scrutiny and panted that much faster. He prayed that the steel wall would absorb him safely within itself, maybe to expel him in the cell next door, away from this . . . man? For Luchov had faced a vampire before, and even the thought of it was terrifying! Finally, he forced out words. "Why are you here?"

Harry's gaze was unwavering. He watched the yellow veins pulsing rapidly under the scar-tissue skin of Luchov's seared skull, and answered, "Oh, you know why well enough, Viktor. I'm here because of what E-Branch told you or caused you to be told: that I'm obliged to abandon this world, and in order to do so must use the Perchorsk Gate. But no big deal. Why, I should have thought you'd all be glad to see the last of me!"

"Oh, we would! We would!" Luchov eagerly agreed, nodding until droplets of sweat flew. "It's just that . . . that . . ."

Harry inclined his head a little on one side and smiled his awful smile again. "Go on."

But Luchov had already said too much. "If what you say is true," he babbled, trying to change the subject, "that as yet you've . . . harmed no one . . . I mean . . ."

"Are you asking me not to harm you?" Harry deliberately yawned, politely hiding the indelicate gape behind his hand—but not before he'd let the Russian glimpse the *length* and serrated *edges* of his teeth, and not without displaying the hand's talons. "What, for the sake of my reputation? Every esper in Europe and possibly even farther afield baying for my blood, but I have to be a good boy? Fair's fair, Viktor. Now, why don't you just tell me what E-Branch told your lot, and what they've asked you to do? Oh, yes, and what measure—what permanent solution—there could possibly be to this Frankenstein monster you've created here at Perchorsk?"

"But I can't . . . daren't tell you any of those things," Luchov whined, cringing against the steel wall.

"So despite all you've been through, you're still a true, brainwashed son of Mother Russia, eh?" Harry grimaced and gave a mocking snort.

Luchov shook his head. "No, just a man, a member of the human race."

"But one who believes everything people tell him, right?"

"What my eyes tell me, certainly."

The Necroscope's patience was at an end. He leaned closer still, grabbed Luchov's wrist in a steel claw, and hissed, "You argue well, Viktor. Perhaps you really should have been one of the Wamphyri!"

And at last the Projekt Direktor could see his worst nightmare taking shape before his eyes, the metamorphosis of a man into a potential plague, and knew that he might all too easily become the next carrier. But he still had a card left to play. "You . . . you defy every scientific principle," he babbled. "You come and go in that weird way of yours. But did you think I had forgotten? Did you think I wouldn't remember and take precautions? Better go now, Harry, before they burst in through that door there and burn you to a crisp!"

"What?" Harry let go of him, jerked himself away from him.

Luchov snatched back the covers of his bed and showed the Necroscope the button attached to the steel frame. The button which he had pressed—how long ago?—and whose tiny red light was flashing even now. And Harry knew that however unwittingly, still he'd been betrayed by his own vampire.

For this was a failure of his dark side. The Thing within him had wanted to be seen, to take ascendancy, to do this thing its own way and *frighten* the answers out of Luchov. Yes, and then possibly to kill him! If Harry had fought it down, then he might simply have plucked the answers right out of the scientist's mind. But too late for that now.

Not too late to fight back, however, and drive the hidden Thing to ground, beat it back into subservience. He did so, and Luchov saw that he was just a man again. Sobbing, the Russian said, "I thought . . . I thought . . . that you would kill me!"

"Not me," Harry answered as running footsteps sounded from outside. "Not me—it! And yes, it just might have killed you. But damn you, you trusted me once, Viktor. And did I let you down? All right, so the flesh-and-blood me has changed; but the *real* me, I'm still the same."

"But it's different now, Harry," Luchov answered, suddenly aware that he'd averted . . . whatever. "Surely you can see that? I'm not doing anything for myself anymore. Not even for Mother Russia. It's for the human race—for all of us."

They were banging on the door now, voices shouting.

"Listen." Harry's face was as earnest and as human as the Russian had ever seen it; or it would be, but for those hellish eyes. "By now E-Branch—and your Russian organization, too, if they're worth their salt—must know I only want out. So—why can't—they—just—let—me—*go?*"

Shots sounded from the corridor, ten or more in rapid succession, hammerblows of hot lead that slammed into the lock on the steel-paneled door and shattered its works to scrap metal. "But . . . are you telling me you don't know?" Luchov saw only Harry now, only the man. "Are you saying you don't understand?"

"Maybe I do," Harry answered, "I'm not sure. But right now you're the only one who can confirm it."

And so Luchov confirmed it. "But they're not worried about you going, Harry," he said as the door was slammed back on its hinges and light flooded in. "They're only worried that one day you might come back, *and about what you might try to bring with you!*"

Scared men crowded the doorway; one cradled a flamethrower, its flickering muzzle pointing directly at Luchov. *"Don't!"* the Direktor screamed, ramming himself into the corner and covering his face with frail, fluttering hands. "For Christ's sake, don't! He's gone! He's gone!"

They stood there in the doorway, smokily silhouetted in cordite stench, looking round the stark cubicle. And finally, one of them asked: "Who has gone, Direktor?"

And another said, "Has the Direktor been . . . dreaming?"

Luchov collapsed on his bed, sobbing. Oh, how he wished he'd only been dreaming. But no, he hadn't. Not all of it, anyway. For he could still feel the pressure on his wrist where the Necroscope had gripped him, and he could still feel those terrible eyes burning on his face and in his mind.

Oh, yes, Harry Keogh had been here, and pretty soon he'd be back. But the Direktor also knew that unless he was hugely mistaken, Harry had only learned part of what he came to learn. The *next* time he came, the rest of it would be waiting for him.

But the next time could be any time as of right now!

"Switch it on!" he gasped.

"Eh?" A scientist hastily, unceremoniously pushed by the rest and squeezed himself into the gap beside Luchov's bed. "The disk? Did you say we're to switch it on?"

"Yes." Luchov grasped his arm. "And do it now, Dmitri. Do it right now!" Then Luchov lay back gasping and clutched at his throat. "I can't breathe. I can't . . . breathe."

"Out!" Dmitri Kolchov ordered at once, with a wave of his arm. "Out, all of you. Let's have some air in here."

But as the men filed out: "Wait!" Luchov held out a claw-like hand after them. "You, with the flamethrower. Wait right outside. And you, with the shotgun. Is it loaded? Silver shot?"

"Of course, Direktor." The man looked puzzled. What use to have it if it wasn't loaded?"

"And is there a grenadier with you, with grenades?" Luchov was quieter now, steadier.

"Yes, Direktor," came the answer from outside.

Luchov nodded and his Adam's apple wobbled a little as he gulped down air. "Then you three—all of you— wait for me outside. And from now on don't let me out of your sight." He swung his legs wearily to the floor, then noticed Dmitri Kolchov standing there, staring at him.

"Direktor, I—" Kolchov started to speak.

'Now!' Luchov screamed at him. "Man, are you fucking deaf? Didn't you hear me? I said switch on the disk right now. Then report to the Duty Room and get me Moscow on the hot line."

"Moscow?" Pallid now and shrinking a little, Kolchov backed out of the small room.

"Gorbachev," Luchov rasped. "Gorbachev and none other. For there's no one else who can order what comes next!"

II A Thing Alone—
Starside—The Dweller

THE NECROSCOPE KNEW THAT THERE WAS VERY LITTLE time left and certainly none to waste. The Soviets had worked out some "final solution" to the Perchorsk problem, which meant that he had to be through the Gate before they could put it into effect.

He went to Detroit and just after 6:20 P.M. found a bike garage and showroom on the point of closing. The last, tired employee was locking up; the next to last, a black forecourt attendant, had just this minute put away his broom, washed his hands, and was sauntering away from the garage down the evening street; marvelous chrome-plated machines stood in a glittering chorus line behind the semi-reflective plate glass.

The Necroscope, right? said a deadspeak voice in Harry's mind, after he'd used a Möbius door to get into the showroom. It surprised him, for the dead weren't much for talking to him these days. *I mean, you'd have to be the boogyman* (whoever it was continued), *'cos I kin hear you thinkin'!*

"You have me at a disadvantage," Harry answered, polite as ever, at the same time examining the chain which passed through the spoked front wheels of the parade of gleaming motorcycles, securing them.

I have your what? Oh, yeah! You don't know me, right? Well, I was an Angel.

Deadspeak occasionally conveys more than is said. With regard to Angels: Harry would no longer be surprised to learn that there really were such creatures, and especially in the Möbius Continuum. But on this occasion he saw that the Angel in question wore no such halo. "A Hell's Angel?" Harry stood on the chain and hauled with both arms, exerting furious Wamphyri strength until a link came apart with a sound like a pistol shot. "But didn't you have a name?"

Hey! Whooooah, man! And the Angel whistled appreciatively. *Like, I bet you leap tall buildings, too, right? Is it a bird? Is it a plane? Shit, no—it's the ever-lovin', chain-breakin', dead-wakin' Necroscope!* He grew quieter. *My name? It was Pete. Pretty shitty handle, right? Here, Petey, Petey, Petey! Sounds like a fuckin' budgie! So I used my chapter name: the Vampire! Er, but I see you have your own problems.*

Harry took a Harley-Davidson off its stand and backed it out of the line of bikes, towards the rear of the showroom. But the last employee had heard the "gunshot" of the snapped chain and was working his way back through a series of locked doors.

"Pete seems a good enough name to me," said Harry. "So what are you doing here?"

It's where I hung out, the Angel told him. *I never could afford one of these really big babies. But I'd come down and look 'em over all the time. This place was a shrine, a church, and these Harleys were its High-powered Priests.*

"How did you die?" Harry turned the key in the ignition and the big bike thundered into life, each pulse of each fat piston almost individually audible.

One night, me and my Pillion Pussy had a fight, the Angel answered. *Randy Mandy split. So later, me and the Machine . . . we were both full of high octane! The booze caught up with us about the same time as we clocked the big One Zero Zero. Ran out of road on a bend, piled into a filling station, crunched a pump. We burned, me and the bike both, in a white-hot geyser! What was left of my body blew away on the wind. But* me, *I gravitated here.*

"Pete," said Harry, "I always wanted to ride one of these things but never seemed to find the time."

You don't know how?

"In one." Harry nodded. "I mean, I can learn the hard way, or take a little expert advice, right? So . . . fancy a ride?"

Me?

"Who else?"

Hooo-haaa! And Harry could almost feel him right there on the saddle where it ass-hooked at the back; indeed, their minds were one as Harry revved her up and up and up, then let her rip in smoking tires and shrieking gears straight at the wall of glass!

Meanwhile the last employee had reopened the final door and entered the showroom, and was now backed up against the giant display windows right in Harry's way. Spread-eagled, the man mouthed a silent gaping scream as the big bike snaked towards him. He knew he'd be cut to ribbons, he and this maniac rider both, and didn't know which way to jump. Closing his eyes and saying his prayers, he slid down the glass even as the bellowing monster bore down on him . . .

. . . And passed through him, and was gone!

As the noise subsided he opened his eyes first a crack, then all the way. The Harley-Davidson and rider were no longer there. There were skid marks, blue exhaust smoke, even the roar of the engine, slowly echoing into silence. But no bike and no rider. And the plate glass was still in one piece.

Haunted! the man thought, before he passed out. *Christ, I've always known it! This place is haunted to hell!*

He was right and he was wrong. The place had been haunted, but no longer. For Pete the Vampire Biker was now with Harry Keogh, and like Harry he wouldn't be back . . .

Harry coasted through the Möbius Continuum to Zakynthos, conjured a door, and blazed out through it at forty onto the uneven surface of a starlit Greek island "road." An inexperienced rider, he might have come to grief right there and then, but Pete the biker was in his mind and his hands, and the huge machine stayed upright and steady on the potholed tarmac.

Zek met the Necroscope on the white steps which wound to her door, but she had spoken to him moments earlier: *Penny's awake. She's been drinking coffee—a lot!*

My fault, Harry had answered. *We did a little celebrating. A moving-out party.* And he thought of his place near Bonnyrig, Edinburgh. Housewarming with a difference, yes.

Wow! said the Vampire, seeing Zek mirrored in Harry's mind. *Is this your Pillion Pussy?* But of course his exclamation and question were deadspeak and Zek couldn't hear them or even know he was here at all.

No, it isn't. Harry spoke only to Pete. *She's just a good friend. Anyway, mind your business—and your mouth!*

Penny joined Zek and Harry even as they touched hands. She came ghosting to the door and smiled (however tiredly, however . . . eerily?) when she saw that the Necroscope had returned. And there in the Greek night Zek saw the cores of Penny's eyes glowing red as a moth's where they reflected the light of the lamp over the door. As for Harry's eyes: Zek avoided looking at them. In any case there was no need, and no need to say anything out loud, not when their minds were touching.

Zek, he said, *I owe you.*

We all owe you, she answered. *Every one of us.*

Not anymore. You've squared it for the rest.

"Goodbye, Harry." She leaned forward and kissed his lips; just a man's lips for the moment, but cold.

He led Penny through the trees to the big bike, and mounting up looked back. Zek stood in lamplight and starlight and waved. The Harley-Davidson's lights cut a swath under the trees, picking out the track back to the road.

Zek heard the roar of the engine pick up to a howl, saw the headlights cutting the night, held her breath. Then—

—The engine noise was only a receding echo doing a drumroll along the hills, and the headlight beam was gone like it had never existed . . .

Are your eyes closed? Harry asked over his shoulder.

Yes. Her answering thought was a whisper.

Then keep them that way—tight-closed—until I tell you to open them.

Hurling the big bike through the Möbius Continuum, with Penny and Pete the Vampire riding pillion, Harry headed for the Perchorsk Gate. He knew exactly—indeed *precisely*—where the Gate was. Möbius equations flickered across the screens of his metaphysical mind, opening and closing an endless curve of doors as he went. But when the doors began to warp and waver he knew he was almost there. It was an effect of the Gate: to bend the Möbius Continuum like a black hole bends light. A moment later, Harry guided the bike through the last fluxing, disintegrating door, and hurtled out of the Möbius Continuum onto the perimeter of the steel disk surrounding the Gate.

And Viktor Luchov saw it all even as it happened.

At the very rim, where the plates of the disk were covered in rubber three inches thick, the Projekt Direktor was conversing with a group of scientists; the perimeter had been made safe, roped off with nonconductive, plastic-coated nylon; the disk not only carried a lethal voltage but was now linked to the sprinkler system. Fat white and blue sparks danced as Harry's huge, powerful machine came roaring off the Möbius strip to erupt into this space-time.

The Screaming Eagle's Dunlops were wide, heavy, and of the very best rubber, but the sudden shock of the bike's 570-plus pounds jarred fish-scale plates together in a crackle and hum of electrical discharge. Blue energies skittered across the disk like snakes of lightning, adding to the throaty chaos of snarling pistons in the cathedral acoustics of the spherical cavern. And overhead, the acid floodgates were opened!

The Necroscope's intuitive, Möbius math was in top form; he had calculated well; and after all, what could possibly go wrong in something slightly less than the space of a single second? Walking round that central cavern with Luchov (*in* the Direktor's mind), he'd seen no guns there. The acid sprinkler outlets had been maybe twenty feet above the disk; they'd take a little time to activate and fill before they could commence spraying; he should be into the sphere-Gate and gone before the first droplets smoked murderously down onto the steel plates.

And yet even as he'd emerged into the glare of the cavern and his tires had shrieked on the plates where they tried to find purchase, even then he'd known that something was wrong. Not with his figures but with the plan itself, with what he already knew of that plan, with what he'd already *seen* of it in action. For he *had* seen something of it, yes . . . when he'd visited Faethor in future time:

His scarlet-tinged, neon line of life turning aside from its futureward thrust, shooting off at right angles and disappearing in a brilliant burst of red and blue fire as it left this dimension of space and time and raced for Starside.

But only as *it*—that solitary life-line, *one* life-line— departed. Harry *himself*, Harry alone . . . without Penny!

Slowing from forty to thirty miles per hour while the bike yawed and his tires found purchase, Harry remembered a vastly important rule: never try to read the future, for that can be a devious thing. But he had taken even this temporary deceleration into account, and even so the timing was still only a second, one tick of a clock. So what was wrong?

The answer was simple: Penny was wrong.

Had she *once* obeyed him? Had she *once* obeyed his instructions to the letter? No, never! She might be in thrall to him, in love with him, fascinated by him, but she didn't go in fear of him. He was her lover, not her master. And in her innocence, Penny had been inquisitive and vulnerable.

"Don't open your eyes," he'd said, but being Penny

she had; opened them as they shot through the Möbius door into Perchorsk, opened them in time to see the glaring Cyclops-eye Gate looming where the bike skidded, fishtailed, and rocketed towards it. And seeing, ''knowing,'' they were going to crash, she'd reacted. Of course they were going to crash—crash right through—which was the whole plan and shouldn't be her concern. If time wasn't of the essence, he might have explained all of that to her.

All of which flashed across the Necroscope's mind in the split second that Penny screamed and let go his waist to cover her eyes . . . and his rear suspension bucking like a bronco to absorb the shuddering of the steel plates . . . and just *exactly* like a bronco ass-hooking the gasping girl into an aerial somersault! In the next split second he ruptured the Gate's skin and shot through . . . but on his own, a thing alone. Or at best, with only Pete the Vampire Biker hanging on behind.

Shit! Pete's deadspeak howled in Harry's mind. *Necroscope, you've lost your Pillion Pussy!*

Harry saw it in his mirrors, looked out through the Gate's skin and watched Penny come down in dreadful slow motion onto the plates of the disk. He saw the languid flash of lightning that stiffened her limbs to a crucifix, laced her hair and clothes with webs of blue fire, and spun her body like a giant, coruscating Catherine wheel. He saw the acid rain come down and the curtain of hissing vapor which at once went up; saw Penny turn wet and black and red, skittering like a flounder on her back where her skin peeled open or was eaten away; saw her rhumba, roller-skated this way and that across the steel plates on vibrating molecules of her own boiling blood, like droplets of water flicked into a greasy, smoking-hot pan.

She'd been dead, of course, from the first flash of blue

fire, and so felt nothing of it. But Harry did. He felt the
absolute horror of it. And he sucked in his breath as at
last the current glued her to the steel fish scales, where
acid and fire both worked on her, turning her to ashes,
tar, smoke, and stink.

And . . . there was nothing he could do.

Not even Harry Keogh.

For he was through the Gate and no way back.

But there are certain mercies. Her single, silent, telepathic shriek had failed to reach him, for he'd already
been over the threshold and into another world. Likewise, her deadspeak; if she was using it now, it was shut
out by the Gate . . .

The Necroscope wanted to die. Right here, right now,
he could happily (unhappily?) die. But that wasn't the
way of the Thing inside him. And Pete the Angel wasn't
about to let it happen, either. Between them, they closed
Harry down, turned him to ice, froze him out.

Lolling there emotionless, mindless, vacant in the saddle of the Screaming Eagle, he wasn't riding the bike
anymore but they were.

And they rode it all the way to Starside . . .

When Harry recovered he was a full mile out on the
boulder plain, seated on a rock beside the now silent
Harley-Davidson. The big machine stood there, silvered
by full moon and ghostly starlight. It had seemed awesome enough in a showroom on Earth, but here on Starside it was utterly (and literally) alien. The bike was
alien, but Harry wasn't. Wamphyri, he belonged here.

A picture of Penny surfaced out of memory's scarlet
swirl; he remembered, drew breath to howl and choked
on it, then clenched his fists and closed his red eyes for

long moments, until he'd driven her out of his mind forever.

The effort left him limp as a wet rag, but it had to be done. Everything Penny had been—everything anyone had been—was a dimension away and entirely irretrievable. There was no going back, and no bringing her back.

Bad vibes, man, said Pete the biker, but quietly. *What now, Harry? We done riding?*

Harry stood up, straightened up, and looked around. It was sundown, and in the south there was no gold on the jagged peaks of the mountains. East lay the low, tumbled tumuli of shattered aeries, the fallen stacks of the Wamphyri. Only one remained intact: an ugly column of dark stone and grey bone more than a kilometer high. It was or had been the Lady Karen's, but that was a long time ago and Karen was dead now.

Southwest, up in the mountains, that was where the Dweller had his garden. The Dweller, yes: Harry Jr. with his Travellers and trogs, all secure in the haven he'd built for them. Except . . . The Dweller was a vampire. And the battle with the Wamphyri lay four long years in Starside's past, so that Harry wondered: *Is my son still ascendant, or has the vampire in him finally taken control?*

His thoughts were deadspeak, of course. And Pete the Angel answered them:

Whyn't we just go and see, man?

"The last time I was here," Harry told him, "we argued, my son and I, and he gave me a hard time. But—" and he shrugged, "—I suppose he has to know sooner or later that I'm back, if he doesn't know it already."

So let's go! Pete was eager to ride. *Just climb aboard the old Screamin' Eagle and start 'er up, man.*

But the Necroscope shook his head. "I don't need the bike, Pete. Not anymore."

The ex-Angel was cast down. *Hey, that's right. You got your own form of transport. But what about me?*

Harry thought about it awhile, then gave a wan smile. And it was a measure of his strength that he still had it in him to smile. Pete the biker read his deadspeak thoughts, of course, and whooped wildly. *Necroscope, do you mean it?* He was breathless with excitement.

"Sure," said Harry. "Why not?" And they got aboard the big bike.

They turned her around, found a good straight stretch of hard-packed, boulder-free earth, and took her up to a ton. And it was as if a primal beast bellowed in the starlit silence of Starside. Then, still howling a hundred and waving a tail of dust half a mile long, Harry conjured a Möbius door and they shot through, followed by a future-time door which they likewise crashed. And now they rode into the future with a great many blue and green and (Harry noted) even a few red life-lines. The blues were Travellers, the greens would be trogs, and the reds . . .

. . . *Vampires?* Pete picked the thought out of his mind.

Looks like it, said Harry, sighing.

But Pete only laughed like a crazy man. *My kind of people!* he yelled.

And on they rode, for a little while.

Until Harry said, *Pete, here's where I get off.*

You mean . . . she's all mine?

Forever and ever. And you needn't ever stop.

Pete didn't know how to thank him, so didn't try. Harry opened a past-time door, then paused awhile before crossing the threshold and watched the big Harley rocketing away from him into the future. Eventually, he heard the Angel's whooping cry come echoing back:

Heee-haaaaaaaaaa! Well, at least Pete was happy now.

And then Harry went back to Starside and the garden . . .

The Necroscope stood at the forward edge of the garden, his hands resting on the low stone wall there, and looked down on Starside. Somewhere between here and the old territories of the Wamphyri, where the broken remains of their aeries now lay in shattered disarray, the sphere-Gate—this end of the space-time "handle," the dimensional warp, whose alternate extension lay in Perchorsk—would be lighting up the stony plain in its painful white glare. Harry fancied he could see something of its light even from here, a ghostly shimmer way down there in the far grey foothills.

He and the incorporeal Pete had come out of the Starside Gate on the big bike—come through the aching dazzle of the "grey hole" from Perchorsk and out of it onto the boulder plain—but Harry remembered very little of that. He did remember the last time he was here, however, which strangely felt more real to him than all that had gone between. Probably because he now desired to forget all that had gone between.

He turned his head more directly northward and gazed out across all the leagues of Starside's vast unknown to the curve of the horizon lying dark blue and emerald green under fleeting moon, glittering stars, and the writhing allure of aurora borealis. That way lay the Icelands where the sun never shone and into which the doomed, forsaken, and forgotten of the Wamphyri had been banished since time immemorial. Shaithis too, after the defeat of the Wamphyri and the destruction of their aeries in the battle for The Dweller's garden. And he remembered how Shaithis had sped north aboard a huge manta flyer in the peace and the silence of the aftermath.

Harry and the Lady Karen had spoken to Shaithis before he exiled himself; unrepentant even then, the vampire Lord had openly lusted after Karen's body, and even more so after The Dweller's and his father's hearts. But he'd lusted in vain. At that time, anyway.

As for the Necroscope: he'd had his own use for the Lady Karen. For just like his son, she had a vampire in her. If he could exorcise Karen's nightmare creature, perhaps he could also cure The Dweller.

He starved Karen in her aerie, used the blood of a piglet to lure her vampire out of her, then burned the thing before it could escape back into her body. But after that, things had not gone according to plan. And the rest of it was still seared on the screen of his memory:

She came to him in a dream, stood over him in her most revealing white gown, and turned his triumph to ashes. "Can't you see what you've done to me?" she said. "I who was Wamphyri am now a shell! For when one has known the power, *the* freedom, *the magnified emotions of the vampire . . . what is there after that? I pity you, for I know why you did what you've done, and also that you've failed!" And then she was gone.*

He woke up and searched for her in all the rooms on all the many levels of the aerie, and could not find her. Eventually, he went out onto a high bone balcony and looked down, and saw Karen's white dress lying crumpled on the scree more than a kilometer below, no longer entirely white but red, too. And Karen had been inside it.

Harry shook himself, came out of his reverie, deliberately turned his back on Starside and the scars it had given him, and looked at the garden—which now he saw was not entirely as he remembered it. A garden? Well, yes, but not the well-tended garden he had known. And the greenhouses? The hillside dwelling places of the Travellers? The hot springs and speckled-trout pools?

There was green algae on the pools; the polythene panels in many of the greenhouses were torn and flapping in cold-air eddies out of Starside; the dwelling houses, especially Harry Jr.'s, showed signs of disrepair where tiles were missing from the roofs, windows broken, and central-heating pipes from the thermal pools cracked and spilling their contents out upon the open ground, so that the radiators went without.

"Not the same, Harry Hell-lander, is it?" said a deep, sad, growling voice from close at hand, if not in those words exactly. But the Necroscope's telepathy had filled in the bits which his ears had failed to recognize; it's easy to be a linguist when you're also a telepath. Harry turned to face the man approaching him jinglingly along the lee of the wall; as he did so the other noted his gaunt grey flesh and crimson eyes, and paused.

"Hello there, Lardis." The Necroscope nodded, his own voice as deep and deeper than the other's. "I hope that shotgun's not for me!" He wasn't joking; if anything he might be threatening.

"For The Dweller's father?" Lardis looked at the weapon in his hands as if seeing it for the first time, in something of surprise. He shuffled a little, awkwardly, like a boy caught in contemplation of some small crime, and said, "Hardly that! But"—and again the Traveller chief looked at Harry's eyes, and this time narrowed his own—"wherever you've been and whatever you've done since last you were here, Harry Hell-lander, I see you've known hard times." Finally, he averted his gaze, glanced here and there all about the garden, then down onto Starside. "Aye, and hard times here, too. And more still to come, I fear."

Harry studied the man and asked, "Hard times? Won't you explain?"

Lardis Lidesci was Romany; in this world, on Earth, anywhere, there would be no mistaking the Gypsy in him. He was maybe five eight tall, built like a crag, and looked of one age with the Necroscope. (In fact he was a lot younger, but Starside and the Wamphyri had taken their toll.) In contrast to his squat design he was very agile, and not alone in body; his intelligence was patent in every brown wrinkle of his expressive face. Open and frank, Lardis's round face was framed in dark flowing hair in which streaks of grey were now plainly visible; he had slanted, bushy eyebrows, a flattened nose, and a wide mouth full of strong if uneven teeth. His brown eyes held nothing of malice but were careful, thoughtful, penetrating.

"Explain?" said Lardis, coming no closer. "But isn't all of this explanation enough?" He opened his arms expansively, as if to enclose the entire garden.

"I've been away four years, Lardis," Harry reminded him, but not in exactly those words. He made automatic conversions; time on Sunside and Starside was not measured in years but in those periods between sunup, when the barrier peaks turn gold, and sundown, when auroras dance in the northern skies. "When I left this place and returned to the hell-lands" (he did not say, "after my son had crippled and banished me," for he'd read in Lardis's mind that he knew nothing of that), "we'd just won a resounding victory over the Wamphyri. The sun had burned The Dweller, very badly, but he was well on the road to a complete recovery. The futures of you and your Traveller tribe, and The Dweller's trogs, too, seemed secure. So what happened? Where is everyone? And where's The Dweller?"

"In good time." Lardis nodded slowly. "All in good time." And in a little while, frowning:

"When I saw you come here," (he seemed to have changed the subject), "—when you appeared here in that way of yours, as once The Dweller was wont to appear—" (past tense? Harry contrived to hide a small start), "well, I knew it was you, obviously. I remembered how you looked—you, Zek, Jazz—as if all of that were yesterday. Yes, and I remembered the good times, in the days immediately after the battle here in the garden. Then, approaching you, I saw your eyes and knew you were a victim no less than The Dweller in that earlier time. And because you are Harry Wolfson's father, his *natural* father—and I suppose also because I carry this shotgun, loaded with silver from your son's armory—I wasn't afraid of you. For after all, I am Lardis Lidesci, whom even the Wamphyri respected in some small part."

"In some *large* part!" Harry said at once. "Don't sell yourself short. So what are you trying to say, Lardis?"

"I am wondering . . ." the other began to answer, paused, and sighed. "The Dweller, when lucid, has mentioned . . ."

When "lucid"? Now, what the hell was this? Harry would look inside Lardis's head, but something warned him not to take on too much. "Yes?" he prompted.

"Is it possible"—Lardis jerked the shotgun shut across his arm, thus loading it, its twin barrels pointing straight at Harry's heart—"that you are their advance guard?"

The Necroscope conjured a Möbius door directly under his own feet and fell through it—and in the next moment rose up out of another door behind the Traveller chief. The echoes of the double blast were still bouncing between the higher crags; a whiff of cordite stench drifted on the air; Lardis was cursing very vividly and swinging the double barrels of his weapon left and right through a 180-degree arc.

Harry touched him on the shoulder, and as Lardis crouched down and spun on his heels took the gun from him. He propped the weapon against the wall, narrowed his eyes and tilted his head on one side a little—perhaps warningly—and growled, "Let's walk and talk, Lardis. But this time let's try to be a little more forthcoming."

The Gypsy was built like a bull; for a moment he remained in his half-crouch, eyes slitted, arms reaching. But finally he changed his mind. Harry was Wamphyri. Go up against him? One might as well hurl oneself from a high place, which would be a much quicker, far less painful death.

But this time, no longer distracted by the gun, Harry read his thoughts. "No need to die, Lardis," he said as softly as possible. "And no need to kill. I'm no one's vanguard. Now, will you tell me what has happened— what *is* happening—here? And take the shortest route about it?"

"Many things have happened," Lardis grunted, catching his breath. "And many more will happen. That is, if The Dweller's premonitions—his dreams of doom— should come to pass."

"Where is The Dweller now?" Harry demanded. He glanced sharply at Lardis. "Wolfson, did you call him? And where's his mother?"

"His mother?" Lardis raised his slanted eyebrows, quickly lowered them again. "Ah, his mother! Your wife, the most gentle Lady Brenda."

Harry nodded. "She was my wife, once."

"Come this way," said Lardis.

He led the Necroscope across the garden, and Harry saw for himself how great were the changes. For it was plain now that the place had been left untended. The pools were stagnating; the greenhouses were empty and cold; a bitter wind blew, bouncing wiry balls of tumbleweed across the flat, once fertile saddle. And to one side, where the level ground began to climb again like foothills to the higher peaks, there lay Brenda's simple cairn.

Harry felt the poignancy of the moment and reached out with his deadspeak. It was instinct . . . like the beat of his heart . . . like breathing . . . but in another moment, remembering how she'd been, he withdrew. She wouldn't know him, and even if she did remember it would only disturb her. To Lardis he said, "She died peacefully?"

"Aye," the Gypsy answered. "Sunup and gentle rains, and all the flowers in bloom. A good time to go."

"She wasn't ill?"

Lardis shook his head. "Merely frail. It was her time."

Harry turned away. "But alone, here . . ."

"She wasn't alone!" Lardis protested. "The trogs loved her. My Travellers, too. And her son. He stayed with her to the end. It helped keep his own trouble at bay."

"His trouble?" Harry repeated him. "You mean when he's not himself, not lucid? And you've called him Harry Wolfson. I ask you one more time: where is The Dweller, Lardis Lidesci?"

The Gypsy stared at him a moment, then glanced at the full moon riding the peaks and shivered. "Up there," he said, "where else? Wild as his brothers, aye, and like a king among them where they lope in the trees along the ridges. Or snug in a cave with his bitch on Sunside when the sun is up, or hunting foxes in the far west. Men see him from time to time with the pack . . . they know him from the hands he wears where the rest have paws, and from his crimson eyes, of course."

Harry need ask no more, for now he knew. It was something he'd wondered about often enough. Almost to himself, softly, he said, "With The Dweller . . . changed, and the Wamphyri defeated, no longer a threat, there was nothing to keep his people here, nothing to hold them together. Perhaps you even feared him. And so you Travellers have drifted back to Sunside, the trogs have returned to their caves, and the garden . . . will soon come to an end. Unless I put it to rights again."

"You?"

"Why not? I fought for it, upon a time."

Lardis's voice was sour, gruff now. "And will you also hunt on Sunside—hunt men, women, and children— when the nights are dark?"

"Does my son hunt the travelling folk? Did he ever?"

Lardis turned abruptly away. "I have to go. At the back of the saddle there's a track, a cleft, a pass. My route back through the mountains to Sunside."

Harry followed close behind. "Do you go alone? Why did you come here, anyway?"

"To remember what was upon a time, and to see what has become. Just this one last time."

"And now that the Wamphyri are no more: how goes it on Sunside? Have you settled, or do you journey as before?"

Lardis looked back and gave a snort. "What? The Wamphyri, no more? Well, perhaps—for now! But the swamps boil with their spawn. All is as it was in the long ago, and what has been will be again. Vampires today, Wamphyri tomorrow!"

Harry came to a halt, let the other stride away into a rising mist. "Lardis," he called after him, "remember this: don't bother me and I won't bother you and yours. That's a promise. And if you're in need, seek me out. Except . . . seek carefully."

"Hah!" the Gypsy's reply rang from the mist. "But you're Wamphyri now, Harry Hell-lander! What, and do you make promises? And should I believe them? Well, and perhaps I *would* have believed them upon a time. But believe the thing inside you? No way! Never! Oh, you'll come a-hunting soon enough, for a woman to warm your bed, or a sweet Traveller child when you've wearied of the flesh of rabbits."

"Lardis, wait!" Harry growled after him. "There are things I need to know, which you can tell me." Of course, he could always stop him instantly, and do what he would with him. But he wouldn't, for the old times. And also because *he*, the Necroscope, was still ascendant, still in command of himself.

The moon raced full and low in the sky; it silvered the peaks, turned the shadows of the crags black, made the mist luminous where it crept. And Harry saw that the mist wasn't rising but falling: down from the shadowed places, to fill the saddles and false plateaus, and tumble over the crags like glowing, slow-motion waterfalls. The howl of a wolf reverberated, echoing from one peak to the next. It was joined by another, and another. No natural mist, this. And these unseen creatures, they were strange and mournful.

Finally, Lardis's voice came back hoarse and panting. "Do you hear that, Harry Hell-lander? The grey brotherhood! Aye, and their king with them, come to sit by his mother and talk with her awhile, as is his wont. Ask *him* these things you would know, and maybe he'll talk to his father, too. But as for me, farewell."

There came a distant crunching of pebbles, the sound of scree dislodged and sliding, and Lardis was off and running, on his way to Sunside.

And the howling ceased.

Harry waited . . .

Finally, they came out of the mist: long-eared, grey-furred, tongues lolling, with eyes like molten gold. A pack of wolves. But they were *only* wolves.

Harry looked at them and they looked back. He was unafraid and they were cautious. They lined up on both sides of him and left a gantlet for him to run. Except he wouldn't run but walk it, back to The Dweller's house. And as he went the mist and the grey brotherhood closed in behind him.

Inside the house, all was darkness, which mattered not at all to the Necroscope. Mist swirled ankle-deep like something sleeping, whose dreams Harry disturbed by passing through. The Dweller sat upright at a table in what was once the living room, where moonbeams came slanting through an open window; he wore a hooded robe, with his eyes burning like triangular coals within the cowl; only his hands, long and slender, were otherwise visible.

Harry sat down opposite.

And: "I had thought you might come back one day," said the Dweller, his voice a snarl, a cough, a croak. "And I knew it was you from the moment you came howling out of the sphere-Gate. Someone who comes into a place like that—brash and full of fire—he is either fearless or very afraid, or he doesn't much care one way or the other."

"I didn't much care," said Harry. "Not then."

"Let's not waste words," said The Dweller. "Once I had all the power. But I also had a vampire in me and thought you would try to exorcise and kill it, and so kill me. Being afraid of what you might do, I put a thought into your head and used it like a knife to cut out all of your secret talents. Like me, you could come and go at will: I immobilized you. Like me, you listened to the dead and talked to them: I made you deaf and dumb.

And when all was done, then I returned you back to your own place and stranded you there. Not so terrible; at least you were in your own world, among your own kind.

"Then for a while there was peace in this world. And to a lesser extent there was also peace in me.

"But I had used the power of the sun itself to destroy the Wamphyri. You and I together, we had burned them with bright sunfire, and toppled their aeries down onto the plain! All very wonderful, but in so doing—in playing with the sun like that—I too had been burned. Well, and I would soon recover from it. So it seemed . . .

"I did not recover. What started as a healing process soon stopped, indeed reversed itself. My metamorphic vampire flesh could not replenish itself *and* the flesh of my human body, and the vampire must come first. That which was human in me gradually sloughed away, eaten out as by leprosy or some monstrous cancer. Even my mind was erased and in large part replaced, and what was instinct in my vampire gradually became instinct, inherent, in me. For the vampire must have a host, active and strong, to house its egg until it could be passed on, and it 'remembered' the shape and nature of its first host. As you know, father, my 'other' father—the source of my egg—was a wolf!

"I knew that my body was going, my mind, too, and saw that I was reverting. But still there was someone who knew my story—all of it, from the day I was conceived— and to whom I could talk in my hour of need. My mother of course. And in practicing my deadspeak so I kept at least that one last talent alive. But as for the rest: they are gone, forgotten. Ironic: I destroyed your talents and lost my own! And now, when I . . . forget things, I talk to the Gentle One Under the Stones, who reminds me of what has been; who even reminded me of you, when I might so easily have forgotten."

Harry's emotions—the gigantic emotions of the Wamphyri—had filled him to overflowing. He couldn't find words to speak, could scarcely think. In a few short hours, the smallest fraction of his life, his *entire* life had been changed forever. But that meant nothing. His pain was nothing. For others had *really* suffered and were suffering even now. And he could trace all of it back to himself.

"Son . . . !"

"I'll come here no more," The Dweller said. "Now that I've seen you—and now that you've . . . forgiven me?—I can forget what I was and be what I am. Which is something you might try for yourself, Father." He reached out a hand to touch Harry's own trembling hand, and his forearm was grey-furred where it slid from the sleeve of his robe.

Harry turned his face away. Tears are unseemly in scarlet, Wamphyri eyes. But a moment later, when he looked again . . .

. . . The Dweller's robe was still fluttering to the floor, while a shape, grey-blurred, launched itself from the window. Harry leaped to see. There in the vampire mist his son sprang away, then paused, turned, and looked back. He blinked triangular eyes, lifted his muzzle, sniffed at the cold air. His ears were pointed, alert; he tilted his head this way and that; he was . . . listening? But to what?

"Someone comes!" he barked warningly. And before the Necroscope could question his meaning: "Ah, yes! That one. Forgotten until now, like so many other things I've forgotten. It seems I'm not the only one who marked your return, Father. No, for she too knows you're back."

"She?" the Necroscope repeated his werewolf son as that one turned and loped for the higher peaks; and all the grey brotherhood with him, vanishing into the mist.

Then:

A shadow fell on The Dweller's house and Harry turned his startled eyes skyward, where even now a weird diamond shape fell towards the garden. And: "She?" he said again, his query a whisper.

He means me, hell-lander, her telepathic voice—hardly severe, nevertheless exploding in Harry's mind like a bomb—reached down to him. Telepathy, yes, and not deadspeak. But how could this be? It whirled him like a top.

You! he finally answered in her own medium, as her flyer swooped to earth.

The long-dead—the no longer dead—the undead Lady Karen!

III Harry and Karen— The Threat of the Icelands

KAREN GLIDED HER FLYER TO EARTH AT THE NORTH-facing front of the garden, just beyond the low wall there, where the ground sloped steeply away towards Starside. It was a good relaunch site and well known to her, for this was where she'd blinded the crazed Lesk the Glut, cut out his heart, and given his grotesque body to the garden's defenders for burning.

Leaving The Dweller's old house and making his way towards her through the dispersing mist, the Necroscope sent a dazed thought ahead of him: *Is it really you, Karen, or am I seeing and hearing things? I mean, how can this be real? I saw you dead and broken on the scree where you'd thrown yourself down from the roof of your aerie.*

Hah! she answered. And without malice: *But that was when you were seeing things, Harry Keogh!* She had stepped through a break in the wall and stood poised there, waiting for him, silhouetted against wall and flyer both. The latter, a nightmare dragon thing but harmless for all its prehistoric design, nodded, salivated, and blinked huge, owlish eyes. It swayed its flat, spatulate head this way and that; its damp, gleaming manta wings were of fine, flexible alveolate bone thinly sheathed in metamorphic flesh; worm legs or thrusters bunched beneath the doughy bulge of its body.

Harry looked at it and wondered why he felt no horror and very little of pity. For he knew that the thing had been fashioned from the flesh of trogs or Travellers. Perhaps there was no more horror left in him. Or perhaps there was no more human. Except, drawing closer to Karen, he knew that some of his emotions at least were still human.

She was breathtaking. In the world beyond the sphere-Gate—the world of men, now an entire universe away—her like had been quite unknown. Even her crimson eyes seemed beautiful . . . now. Harry was awed by her beauty, stricken by it no less than when he'd first seen her, that time when she came here to join the garden's defenders in defiance of the Wamphyri. She had enthralled him then and did so again now. He couldn't take his eyes off her.

He drank her in:

From the burnished copper of her hair, down through every gorgeous curve of her body (which, whether half hidden or half exposed, was always given emphasis by her sheath of soft white leather), to the pale leather sandals on her feet, open at the toes to show her toenails painted gold, she was ravishing. Over her shoulders she wore a cloak of black fur, and about her waist a wide black belt whose grey-metal buckle was shaped into a snarling wolf's head. The sigil's significance was lost in the past; Dramal Doombody's ancestors had passed it down to him, and he in his turn had passed it to Karen. And not only his crest, but Dramal had given Karen his vampire egg, too.

Riveted for long moments by her weirdness, her unearthly beauty and contrasting colors, Harry had paused; now he moved closer. Face-to-face, Karen was even more beautiful, more desirable. Countering his approach—shifting her body to mirror his every move—she displayed the sinuous motion of a Gypsy dancer which he remembered so well. But of course, for upon a time she'd been a Traveller. Why, only listen and he might hear the chime and jingle of her movements . . . yes, even when there was none to hear! He heard these things now, and then her telepathic voice, chiming in his mind:

You very nearly killed me once, Harry. And I should warn you: my first reason for coming here was to return the favor! She brought forward her right hand, until now hidden behind her back. Her battle gauntlet was in position; when she flexed her hand, a torturer's delight of blades, hooks, and small scythes gleamed silver in the starlight.

Harry conjured a Möbius door on his immediate right and fixed it there. Invisible, it was the perfect bolthole if such were needed. Let Karen take a swing at him, he'd merely feint right and disappear. But these were thoughts he must keep to himself, while out loud: "Are you saying you're here to kill me?"

To which, in a voice that trembled at the very edge of her control, she answered in kind: "And are *you* saying you don't deserve it?"

Still keeping his own mind guarded, Harry looked into hers and saw the furious passions brewing there, saw anger bordering on rage, but nothing of hatred. Also, and very important, he saw the Lady Karen's loneliness.

They were two of a kind now. "I didn't understand what it was like to be . . ." he began, and paused; and tried again: "I mean, I thought I was helping you, curing you, as of some vile disease. But I admit it, I did it for my son as much as for you. For if I could cure you . . ."

"Cure!" She spat the word out. "Why don't you try curing yourself! There is no cure, Necroscope! Surely you must know that by now?"

He nodded, took a chance and inched closer yet. And: "Yes, I do know," he answered. "But in a way I did cure you. You had a vampire in you, the sort the Wamphyri called a 'mother.' If you had spawned so many vampires, in the end it must diminish you, kill you. Am I right?"

"We'll never know, will we?" she growled.

Harry stood directly before her, less than a pace away, well within the arc of her gauntlet. "So you came to kill me," he said. "But surely you can see I've suffered my own change? And surely you know in your heart that I was never your enemy, Karen? I was merely innocent. In my way."

She stared hard at him for a moment, narrowed her eyes a little, then nodded and smiled. But it was more a sneer than a smile proper. "I've found you out!" she said. "I sense your door, Harry! You took me there once, remember? You carried me from the garden to my aerie, all in a moment. And now there's another door right here beside you. Would you dare stand so close without it? If so, then do it. Show me how 'innocent' you are."

He shook his head. "That was then," he said. "As for now: whatever I might wish to be, I can only be Wamphyri! Precious little of innocence in me now . . . about as much as there is in you? Yes, the thing within advised me to conjure a door, for my protection. Or for its protection? But the man which I still am tells me I don't need this safeguard, that it makes anything I might say to you—the things I *want* to say to you—a mockery. And while I live, the man in me has the upper hand. So be it!''

He threw caution to the wind, collapsed the Möbius door, and opened his mind wide to her. In a few moments she read or scanned all that was written there, for he kept nothing hidden. But in telepathy, to read is often to feel, and most of all she felt his pain: as great as and greater than her own. And his loss—*all* of his losses—whose total was so much more. And she saw how lonely and empty he was, which brought her own loneliness and emptiness into proper perspective.

But . . . she was a woman and remembered certain things. As his right hand closed in the curve of her waist at first gently, then possessively, so she bent her elbow at his side until her open gauntlet leaned loosely against his back and upper left arm. And she said, ''Do you recall the time I told you how I'd lusted after you? In how many *ways* I lusted after you? Like a woman, perhaps—but certainly like a vampire! And do you remember when you trapped me in my room, how I tried to lure you? I went naked, writhing, panting, thrusting at you—and you ignored me. It was as if your flesh was iron and your blood ice.''

''No,'' he husked in her ear, drinking in the natural musk of her body, drawing her to him and bending down his head to her. ''My body was flesh and my blood was fire. But I had set myself a course and must run it. Now . . . it's run.''

She felt his need swelling to match, to intensify, her own—so *much* need—and was aware of his heartbeat like a hammer against her breast. ''You . . . you're a fool, Harry Keogh!'' she whispered as he crushed her even tighter. And every nerve of her body thrilled as Wamphyri instinct demanded that she scoop her gauntlet into the flesh and bone of his back and spoon it out, then reach inside and slice his heart to a crimson-pumping geyser. Thrilled, yes, and thrilled again—in astonishment—when she relaxed her hand so that the weapon fell from her fluttering fingers, fell loose to the ground!

"Even as great a fool as I am," she moaned then, sinking red-painted razor-sharp nails through cloth and skin and shivering flesh into his back and neck, as he in turn wrenched her sheath dress apart, and clutched her bruisingly wherever his hands could reach, and bit her face and mouth until the blood flowed. "Which is to say," she panted, when finally they held each other burning at bay, "a very great fool indeed!"

They flew to her aerie.

Mounted behind her in the ornate saddle at the base of the flyer's neck where its manta wings sprouted, Harry must cling to Karen or risk falling—in which case he would conjure a door and fall through it into the Möbius Continuum. But he would not fall while he fondled her straining breasts, whose nipples were nuggets under her ruined sheath. And he would not fall while his manhood strained in the crevice of her delicious behind, surging there as if to lift her out of her seat.

"Wait!" she had told him back there in the garden, at the wall, where with his newfound Wamphyri passions he would have taken her immediately and ploughed her like a field of yielding flesh. And: "Wait!" she'd repeated twice during the flight, when he'd moaned louder than the wind in her ear and bitten the back of her neck, and she had felt his metamorphic flesh flowing to enfold her while his hands enlarged and flattened as if to touch all of her at once.

And yet again, "Wait! Oh, *wait!*" she had pleaded

with him, when the flyer set them down in a launching-landing bay some levels lower than her topmost apartments, and she had almost to flee before his lust across the cartilage causeways and up stairways of fretted bone to her rooms. But at last he caught her in her bedroom and knew that the waiting was over, for both of them.

Harry had made love so very recently, yet now it was all forgotten and perhaps not surprisingly. For if space and time are so linked as to be inextricable (to any ordinary man), just *how long ago* was it since he had known Penny? A dimension ago? An entire universe? And as a universe is huge almost to infinity, how then the time gap *between* universes? Time is relative, as the Necroscope knew only too well. But in any case, that earlier phase now seemed fuzzy as a dream, while "now" was the only reality. Penny had been a mirage, a dream-creature, a waif light as thistledown, enthralled and drawn into his dream with him, and at last destroyed by it. But Karen was . . . Woman. She was substantial, compelling, consuming; a magnet, with gravity of her own great as a small planet, so that she held him like a moon to light her flesh and lust after it. For Harry she was the embodiment of all earthly (unearthly?) desire; greater than a mere planet, she was his own personal black hole, which might suck him in in his entirety. Indeed, Karen was all of this and more. Karen was Wamphyri!

Upon her bed they twined and tangled, panted, grunted and groaned, and in all truth Harry no longer knew what was real and what was fantasy. He had not previously explored his metamorphism; he didn't know the extent of fleshly flexibility; he was "innocent" in respect of his own passion's potential. And Karen, too, innocent. Or very nearly so.

"You have kept yourself to yourself?" the Necroscope

gaspingly inquired of his vampire love while extending a hand and its fingers within her to examine and caress all of her innermost organs and places, and while she moistened with spittle the shining fist which was his glans and taunted its throbbing with the slither of her forked tongue.

"No," she groaned truthfully. "Twice I flew to Sunside at sundown to seek me out a lover. But how may one seduce a terrified man? Anyway, I brought one back here. In a little while he overcame something of his fear and crept into my bed. Ah, I was a yawning chasm, an aching gorge . . . into which he dropped a pebble! He could not fill me. I milked him dry and wanted more, but all he had left was blood. I knew that I could grind him down, turn him to pulp, murder him within the heart of my womanhood, and devour him into myself as easily as eating him. But . . . I took him back to Sunside. Since when I've kept me to myself, yes. Just as men and women are for each other, so we Wamphyri may only cleave unto Wamphyri flesh. For there's no pleasure in beasts, and when Wamphyri blood is up, humanity is frail."

"All true," gurgled the Necroscope, feeling her left nipple extend into his throat like a tongue, while his scrotum swelled to bursting from the pressure of his juices. "A woman would die in agony from what I have done to you!"

"Likewise a man from these caresses of mine," she replied, shuddering. "But of pleasure, however monstrous!" And she drew out his great, soft, spider-crab hand from her body, folded his legs at the knees, and fed them into herself; until finally he was drawn in to his navel, and she experienced the geysering of his cold semen laving her palpitating innards.

"And yet the Old Lords in their time took Traveller women for themselves," Harry panted in his delirium. She was full of him now, her pale belly round and shining, grotesquely bloated where his arms and hands encircled it; and her body had so gorged on him that he looked half born. She coiled herself forward to kiss him, and their teeth clashed as the flesh of their faces melted into one face.

A moment later she extruded him in a huge contraction; but just as quickly he entered her again, headfirst this time, so that she must speak to him telepathically to answer his query:

Those women died screaming, she said. *I've heard it said that following a raid, Lesk the Glut would take ten or more in a night, bursting them like bladders with his sex! Ah, that was violation! But the so-called Lords weren't all alike; if a girl was beautiful, then she might survive. Brought on by degrees, she would be vampirized, and as her metamorphosis progressed so her satyr Lord would instruct her. The Lord Magula fashioned himself a huge mound of a woman, and slept within her when their excesses exhausted him.*

She expanded herself convulsively to let him out, then fell on him and grasped at his slick body with exploratory hands of her own. The Wamphyri equivalent of "talking dirty" had incensed them . . . what orifices could be entered (of *each* of them) were entered; their kisses fetched blood; their juices drenched the bed and dripped from it onto the floor all around. They themselves flopped damply from the bed, slipping and sliding in their own liquids. Harry's system endlessly manufactured semen, which was endlessly sucked from him by Karen's various lips. They let their vampires run rampant. Scythe teeth nibbled (but never so deep as the bone), and nails like claws of *Tyrannosaurus* pulled and gouged (but only to bruise, never to break).

They reduced the bedclothes to drenched rags, the slate bed itself to rubble, the huge room to a shambles.

Their lovemaking (lustmaking?) grew frantic and impossible to follow in its contortions and convolutions. Their cries became primal as their bodies shared totally; they knew sex as no other human beings had *ever* known it; the Necroscope's greatest climax of many was when Karen entered him.

For fifteen hours they spent themselves, vented, tormented, and demented themselves. So that in the end they didn't merely sleep but fell unconscious in each other's coils . . .

When Harry came out of it, Karen was washing him. "Don't," he said, feebly trying to push her away. "A waste of time. I want you again, now, while you're still here."

"Still here?" She took his member in her hand to cool its bruises with water, and watched it grow there like a club.

"It's a dream, Karen, a dream!" he gasped, his hand seeking her softness. "Like everything gone before. Dreams of a madman. I know it now for sure, for I saw you lying dead. Yet here, now . . . you live! Unless . . . is there a necromancer in Starside?"

She shook her head, drawing back from him a little where his hands began to pull with some insistence at her once more entirely human breasts. And: "It were best if you listened to me, Harry," she said. "I wasn't dead that time. It wasn't me you saw lying there, broken in the bony scree."

"Not you? Then who?"

"Do you remember when you starved me?" Karen stared hard, earnestly, even accusingly at him. "Do you remember how you lured my vampire out of my body with a trail of pig's blood? Ah, but I was Wamphyri and crafty! The mother creature *inside* me was crafty! More so than any other. She—it—left an egg in me. The tenacity of the vampire, Harry.''

"You . . . you were still Wamphyri?'' His mouth had fallen half open. "Even after I burned your vampire and its eggs?''

"You burned all but one,'' she insisted, "which remained in me. The thing would grow again, yes. But I knew that if *you* suspected as much, then that you'd try again. And then that I *would* die! Oh, and the thought of that terrified me.''

"I remember how I slept." Harry licked dry, almost desiccated lips. "I was even more exhausted than now: by what I'd seen and done.''

"Yes,'' she said, "you fell asleep in a chair, which was when I was saved. For while you slept one of mine returned to the aerie.''

"One of yours? A creature?'' Harry frowned. "But they were all destroyed or sent away.''

"Sent away, yes,'' she answered. "You had set this one free out of the 'goodness' of your heart . . . sent her away to die!''

"Her?''

"A trog, a handmaiden, a creature who performed menial tasks within the aerie and in my personal chambers. But she had been born here and understood no other existence, and eventually, she returned to the only home she'd ever known. I knew it the moment she set foot on the bottom step of the nethermost stairwell; she heard my mind-call and came as fast as she could; but she was starved from her wandering in the cold wilderness of Starside, and wearied unto death by her climb through all the aerie's levels. Even unto death, aye.''

"She died?'' Harry felt Karen's small sadness, as at the death of a favorite pet.

The vampire Lady nodded. "But not before she'd removed the silver chains from my door and disposed of the potted kneblasch plants! *Then* she collapsed and died, and I saw my chance.

"While still you slept, I dressed her corpse in my best white dress and bundled it from the ramparts. She fluttered down, down, almost as if she flew! But in the end she rushed to the rocks and was broken. This was what you saw when you looked down from that high balcony, Harry. But me: I was in hiding, where I stayed until you were gone from here."

The Necroscope saw it all now. "I went back to The Dweller's garden," he said. "My son knew what I'd done. Fearing for his own existence, he took my powers from me, then transported me back to my own world where for a time I was only a man. But I discovered monsters there and they discovered me. Until, as you can see, in the end I set myself against one vampire too many."

Karen had settled down between his spread legs. Despite the seriousness of their discussion of past events, Harry's shaft pounded there like a second heart where her fingers teased the shining rim of its bell. She paused awhile to moisten its pulsing tip with her snake's tongue, and to trap its swaying trunk between her breasts. And: "How strong you are, Harry," she sighed, perhaps wonderingly. "Indeed, I do believe you're full again."

"To see your face," he answered, "to smell your body, and feel you wet in your core . . . how could I be other than full again?" He lifted her up to seat her on his rod, but instead she slipped from his grasp and stepped down from the bed.

"Not here," she panted.

"Oh?"

"There!" she said.

"There?"

"In that secret place of yours."

"The Möbius Continuum? To make love there?"

"Why not? Is it a holy place?"

Harry didn't answer. But . . . it could well be. It could well be.

"Will you take me there, Harry? And will you *take* me, fuck me there?"

"Oh, yes," he answered throatily. "And I'll show you a place you just won't believe, where we can fuck for a second or a century, as you will!"

She flew into his arms and he rolled her out of the sheets and into the Möbius Continuum. "But . . . there's no light!" she hissed, opening her legs wide and guiding him into her. "I need to see you: the way your face quakes when you come, the slackening of your mouth as the throbbing subsides and the aching starts."

"You shall have light," he grunted, nodding . . . and in the next moment felt a deadly fear. For that had been close to blasphemy. But he had not intended it. She *would* have light, yes: blue light, green, and a little red. And as she clawed at his buttocks and rode his bucking, whipping piston shaft, so he foamed within her and carried her moaning through a future-time door.

And now she saw the future racing away from her, and the scarlet light streaming from her own body, with only the faintest trace of blue. Indeed Karen's light mingled with Harry's, twining even as their bodies twined, and his was only slightly less red than hers.

Our life-lines, he told her. *We ride them into our future*. And then, quoting Faethor: *We ride there faster than life!*

We ride each other into the future, she answered, thrilling to the starburst sensation of it, and to the shock of Harry bursting inside her. And in a little while: *The blues?*

Travellers, he told her. *True human beings.*

Then the handful of reds can only be Wamphyri! Survivors in the Icelands. And the greens must be trogs. I . . . I never saw such colors, such light! Even the brightest auroras over the Icelands were never as bright as this.

Harry plied her breasts like dough in his hands and came yet again, and she felt his seed spraying her inner walls and shuddered to its gush. *Your come is cold as a waterfall.*

No, it's hot. But cool against your insides, which are a volcano.

It only feels that way, she moaned. *For in truth we're both cold, Harry. Both of us.*

We're Wamphyri, he answered, *but we aren't undead. We've never been dead, not in the way some vampirized people "die" and sleep awhile before their rebirth from the grave. I had expected to be cold, certainly—expected to feel the lust of the Wamphyri, their raw, roaring appetite for life and for all dark carnal experience—but with nothing of enduring emotion. But this is much more than that, other than that.*

For you, perhaps, she answered, *for you're not long a vampire. And yet . . . maybe you're right. This isn't as I imagined it. The Old Wamphyri were liars, as anyone knows; could it be that they lied about this, too? Incapable of love, they said. But were they? Or merely incapable of owning up to it? Is it weak to love someone, Harry? And is it strong to be cold and without love?*

He welded himself to her, all of his parts melting into hers. *Cold?* he growled. *Well, if we're that cold, then why is our blood so hot? And if we're that weak, then why do I feel so strong? No, I think you've got it in one. The last and most blatant lie of the Wamphyri: that they were without love. They weren't, they were merely afraid to admit it.*

And the Necroscope knew that at last the truth of the matter was exposed. The Wamphyri had always been capable of dark passions, desires, and deeds beyond the human range; but now, on the same far side of the spectrum, he and Karen had discovered *in themselves* genuine, equally powerful bonding emotions. And letting those emotions rule could only properly be described as an ecstasy. However sudden, weird, and alien their love, they *were* true lovers. There was lust in it, of course, but was there ever a love affair between man and woman without lust?

As a single fused mass—the first half-human couple ever to "cleave" to one another in the fullest sense of the word—they sped down the future time-stream. Until out of nowhere, suddenly:

A new light . . . golden fire . . . incredible . . . bursting . . . all-consuming! At first Harry thought it was some strange and wonderful effect of their sex, their love, but it was more than that.

The great, throbbing, one-note *Ahhhhhh* chorus of the future—which was not sound at all as such but the mind's reaction to a three-dimensional display of ever-expanding time—changed in the space of a single moment to a fiery *hissssss!* And the Necroscope brought their headlong rush to an abrupt, tumbling halt. Partly extricating themselves but still mainly fused, they spun on an axis of their own while time rushed on. And Karen, temporarily blind, sank needle claws into Harry's shoulders to gasp, *What was that?*

But the Necroscope, even Harry Keogh, had no answer. As his own eyes adjusted to the golden brilliance, and his mind to the sear and the sizzle, so he glanced back at what had been: like looking into the heart of an exploding blue star, where chemical imbalances caused red and green imperfections. Back there, all was as before. But up ahead, in future time—

—Harry's and Karen's threads of life were no longer red but bright gold where they rushed out of their bodies into the future. And the future itself was a blaze of gold tinged with the leaping orange flares of fire!

Slowly, the brazen yellow glare diminished and faded away, smoking into darkness like embers drenched in rain—and the life-lines of the two vanished with it! Beyond this point there was no future for them, not on Starside. But there was a future for some. For however dazed, the rest of the blue lines of life raced on; likewise the greens, though there were fewer of them now. But as for the reds: nowhere a sign of them. And the darkness seemed greater than the light.

A . . . disaster? Harry wondered, and Karen heard him.

But what happened—what will *happen—here?*

Baffled, he could only shake his head and shrug. *The greens seem sickly. They are dying.*

It was so: a good many trog life-lines grew dim, flickered low, and blinked out even as they watched. But the Necroscope's heart picked up again as he noted that others seemed to gain strength and brightness to speed on. And he breathed a mental sigh of relief as new lines commenced to spark into existence, signifying new births and beginnings.

Then:

He gathered his startled wits, conjured a door, and drew Karen through it into the more nearly "normal" flux of metaphysical being.

But what happened? She clung to him even tighter.

I don't know, he said, and guided her through a final door, emerging from the Möbius Continuum onto the roof of her aerie. And facing into a cold wind off Starside, he added, "But whatever it was, it will happen, be sure."

Feeling her shivering where she huddled in his arms, and sensing her despair, he stared inquiringly into her crimson eyes.

"Perhaps *I* know," she told him then. "For we've sensed their resurgence awhile now."

"We?" He allowed her to lead him below, out of the starlight and into the aerie's topmost rooms.

"Your son and I," she said. "While he was still himself."

And: "*Their* resurgence? Them?" But even asking, so Harry worked out the answer for himself. And now, too, he understood Lardis Lidesci's anxiety and animosity in The Dweller's garden.

"The Wamphyri," she said. "The Old Lords. Condemned to the Icelands, but not content with the Icelands."

They passed through massive, fiercely frescoed halls of fretted bone and carved stone, descended cartilage stairs to her chambers, where they collapsed into great chairs. And in a while: "Tell me all," Harry grunted.

It had started (on Harry's time scale) two years earlier, which was to say two years after the battle for The Dweller's garden, whose outcome had been the defeat and rout of the Old Wamphyri Lords.

"Sensing a threat from the Icelands," Karen went on, "I requested an audience with The Dweller, during the which I confided in him the substance of my fears. By that time he knew well enow that I had survived your 'cure,' but in any case there was a truce between us. After all, I'd fought alongside you and your son against the Wamphyri; he could not doubt but that I was his ally. Occasionally, I would visit him in the mountains, and there were times when he even came to see me here. We were friends, you understand, nothing more.

"But they were strange times; the change was on him; he was losing human flesh and putting on the shape and ways of a wolf. Still and all, and while he retained the mind of a man, we became true allies a second time. For he too, in his way, had felt the Icelands threat: a weird foreboding that waxed and waned with the auroras, a DOOM which crouched there like a beast on the frozen frontier, all hunched down into itself and tensed ready to spring.

"I have said he sensed it 'in his way.' Your son is a wolf now, Necroscope, with a wolf's senses and instincts. Across all the leagues he could smell them on the winds out of the north, see them riding in the auroras, hear them whispering and plotting. Plotting their return and their revenge, aye!

"Their revenge, Harry: on The Dweller and his people, on me, on any and all who had helped defeat them, destroy their aeries and banish them into the great cold. Which is to say, on you, too. Except, of course, you were not here at that time. There was only The Dweller and myself. And going the way he was . . . it would not be long before I was alone.

"I asked him what must be done.

" 'We must set guards,' he told me, 'out there in the cold waste, to look north and report back on any curious incursions from the Icelands.'

" 'Guards?'

" 'You must make them,' he said. 'Are you not Wamphyri and Dramal Doombody's rightful heir? Didn't he show you how?'

" 'Indeed, I know how to make creatures,' I told him.

" 'Then do it!' he barked. 'Make warriors, but make

them male and female. Make them so they can make themselves!'

" 'Self-reproducing?' The very idea made me gasp. 'But that is forbidden! Even the worst of the Old Wamphyri Lords would never have dared . . . would not even consider—'

" '—Which is why you must do it!' He was forceful. 'Aye, for it will save you time at the vats. Make them so they can live and breed on the ice, and feed themselves on the great fishes which live under the ice. But build them with a safety device: only three whelps to a pair, and all males. After that, they'll die out soon enough. But not until they've reported whatever it is that threatens—*and* done battle with it when it comes rumbling out of the north!' "

Karen shrugged. "Your son had great wisdom, Necroscope. He knew good from evil, and knew the source of the worst possible evil. But his humanity was failing fast; he knew that when the time came he would not be able to help me; and so he would help me now, with good advice. I thought it was good, anyway."

"And in the Icelands?" Harry queried. "Shaithis? Is it him?"

Karen shuddered. "None other. And not alone."

"Oh?"

She grasped his arm. "Do you remember that time at the garden? The fire and thunder; the gas-beasts exploding in the sky and raining their guts down on everything; the screams of trogs and Travellers when Wamphyri Lords and lieutenants came strutting with their gauntlets dripping red?"

Harry nodded. "I remember all of that: also how we seared them with The Dweller's lamps, blinded their flyers, set your warriors against theirs, and finally reduced them to vile evaporation with rays from the sun itself!"

"But not all of them," she said. "And Shaithis was only one of the survivors."

"Who else?"

"The giant Fess Ferenc and the hideous Volse Pinescu; also Arkis Leperson, plus several lieutenants and thralls. None of these were accounted for in the fighting. We must assume they fled north, after discovering their aeries shattered and tumbled down to the plain."

The Necroscope breathed a sigh of relief. "No more than a handful, then."

She shook her head. "Shaithis on his own would be more than a handful, Harry. Not then, when we had your son and his army to side with, but now, when we have only ourselves. And what of all the other Lords banished and driven into the Icelands throughout Wamphyri history? What if they have survived, too? Prior to the battle in the garden, all such went singly, slinking, never in a group. Or they might be allowed to take a woman and the odd thrall with them. Perhaps Shaithis and the others have found them and organized them into a small army. But could *any* army of the Wamphyri ever be said to be small?"

Harry gloomed at her. "It could be worse than that. If they took women with them—if they could live with the unending cold—why shouldn't they breed like your warriors? Let's face it, we don't even know what the Icelands are like. Maybe the only thing that kept Icelanders from invading all of this time was the fact that the Old Wamphyri were stronger! But now . . . there are no 'Old' Wamphyri. Only us, the 'new' Wamphyri."

"Also," she reminded him, "out there at the rim of the cold and sluggish sea, a dozen or more warriors, watchers, guards."

"You followed my son's advice and made yourself some creatures?"

"Yes . . ." But she looked away.

"Out of what? And why do you avoid my eyes?"

Karen snatched her head round to glare her defiance at him. "I avoid nothing! I found my materials in the stumps of the shattered aeries, in the workshops of the Lords. Most were ruined, crushed or buried forever, but some were intact. At first I blundered, creating flyers which could not fly, warriors which would not fight. But gradually, I perfected my art. You have seen and ridden upon my flyer: an exceptional beast. Likewise my warriors. I made three pairs which were sound and fearsome and mighty, who by now have made six or even nine more. Except . . ." And again she turned her face away.

Harry caught her chin in a hand and turned it back again. "Except?"

"For a while now they have not answered my calls. I send my thoughts out across Starside, requesting information, but they don't hear me. Or if they do, they fail—or refuse—to answer."

Harry frowned. "You've lost control over them?"

She tossed her head. "It was something the Old Wamphyri were always afraid of: to make creatures with a will of their own, which might one day bolt and run wild. Mercifully, I heeded The Dweller's warning and they are doomed genetically. There'll be no females among the offspring."

Harry gave a grunt. "So you have watchers who don't watch, and warriors which won't war. What other 'precautions' have you taken against this threat from the Icelands?"

Now she hissed at him. "Do you snigger at my works, Necroscope? And should I tell you how I had decided to meet the threat, when and if it should arise? Remember, before you came I was a woman alone; and how do you think Shaithis would deal with me—with Karen, great traitor bitch of the Wamphyri!—if he had survived the Icelands and would now return here? Should I surrender myself to his tender mercies? *Hah,* no, not while I could defy him to the last!''

"Defy him? (Lit up in the blaze of her hair and eyes, and in the gleam of her teeth, Harry was struck anew with the thought: *She's a volcano, inside and out!*) And out loud: "How, defy him?''

Again she tossed her head. "Why, rather than have Shaithis force himself upon me, I'd give myself to a more destructive, even more faithless lover. For I'd mount my flyer and head south, over the mountains and across Sunside, even into the brazen face of the sun itself. Let Shaithis chase me there if he would, into streaming gases and exploding flesh and nothingness. So be it!''

Harry drew her into his arms and she came without resistance. "It won't come to that,'' he husked, stroking her hair while her furious tremors subsided. "Not if I have anything to do with it.'' But etched on the mirror of the Necroscope's inner mind, kept hidden even from Karen's telepathy, was a scene out of future time which try as he might he could not banish:

A picture of a fiery, molten gold future. A vision of THE END, framed in the scarlet, all-consuming fires of an ultimate hell . . .

IV Again Perchorsk—
the Icelands Now

THE HIVE-LIKE CAVERNS, BURNED-OUT BURROWS, AND
haunted magmass levels of the Perchorsk Projeckt had
seen a period of intense activity. Six days since Harry
Keogh's night visit with Projeckt Direcktor Viktor Luchov, and his subsequent invasion of the core riding a
powerful American motorcycle; as a result of which, a
final, terrifying scene had now been set. The pieces were
all in place for what Luchov could only hope would be
the permanent closure of the Gate.

Down in the core, standing on the now deactivated,
recently cleaned and polished fish-scale plates where they
encircled the dimensional portal, Luchov's unblinking
gaze fell in silent awe on the would-be instruments of
that disconnection: a pair of top-secret Tokarev Mk II
short-range missiles (in more common parlance, nuclear
exorcets), mounted atop the compact, caterpillar-tracked

carriage of their grey-metal launching and guidance module. Behind the smoked lenses of his plastic eye-shields, the Projekt Direktor's eyes were mere slits, as if frozen in a wince or grimace; for it had been his responsibility, passed down from Moscow, to order the Tokarevs armed and programmed. He knew only too well what he had here: knew that obscene slugs of toxic metal had been loaded into the slender steel bellies of the missiles, where now they lay quiescent but ready on the instant to spring shrieking awake. All it required was the push of a button.

A group of military technicians in white smocks were busy in the vicinity of the Tokarevs, checking and double-checking electrical hookups, semiautomatic and computerized systems, radiation levels, other instrument readings. Their senior man, directly responsible to the Projekt Direktor, touched Luchov's arm and caused him to give a start. Vainly trying to conceal his nervous reaction, the Direktor barked, "Yes, what is it?"

The man was young, no more than twenty-six or -seven but already a Major; he wore upon his lapels the crown of his rank inside the stylized atomic nucleus insignia of the Special Artillery Arm. "Sir," he formally reported, "we're all ready here. From now on or until these weapons are required for use, there will always be two of us on duty here . . . armed, of course, as a safeguard against sabotage. We are aware that the Projekt has a history of, er, intruders?"

Luchov nodded. "Yes, very good." But he'd scarcely been paying attention. Turning jerkily away from the Tokarevs and pointing towards the glaring sphere-Gate, he said, "And do you know what you're on guard against—from that, I mean? Are you sure that if ever it's required, you'll know just *exactly* when to press the button?"

The other stiffened. He knew his duty well enough. A

pity he now found himself in a position where he must take orders from a damned civilian, that's all! He was tempted to answer Luchov in *just* such terms and from the heart, except it had been made adequately clear to him that the senior scientist was a power in his own right. And so:

"I've acquainted myself with the Projeckt's history, certainly, sir," he said coldly. "Also, we've watched all of the films. But in any case, the firing sequence may not be initiated except on your instructions."

"Listen." Luchov turned more fully towards him, fixed him with a wide-eyed glare, and grasped his arm in a trembling claw. "That's your brief, yes, but it doesn't say everything. Indeed, it says very little. You've seen the films? Good! But you can't *smell* them, can you? They can't spring out from the screen and swallow you whole, can they?" Nodding wildly, and again pointing at the glaring white upper hemisphere of the Gate, he continued hoarsely:

"In there, a curse, a plague, something to make Chernobyl seem of no consequence whatsoever! If it, they, whatever, got out into the world . . . that's the end, I mean of *everything!* Mankind joins the dinosaurs, the trilobites, the dodos—gone! So don't get snotty with me when I ask if you know what you're dealing with."

Pale with barely suppressed anger, the young officer came to attention and his thin mouth cracked open; but Luchov wasn't finished with him, hadn't yet told him the worst. "Listen," he said again. "One week ago a man, or something which was once a man, went through that Gate into whatever lies beyond. When he went, the world breathed a sigh of relief—since when it's been *holding* its breath! We were glad to see the back of him because he was tainted, a carrier. Only now we wonder: how long before he finds his way back here? And if he does, what will he bring with him? Do you follow me so far?''

Something of the color had returned to the Major's face. He sensed the importance of what the Projekt Direktor was saying, the enormous stresses playing on his mind. ''I follow you so far,'' he said.

''Very well,'' said Luchov, ''and now something which wasn't in your brief. You mentioned our previous problem with intruders. Quite right; we did have this problem; we could have it again. So now I'm going to add to your brief and issue a new order.'' He pushed his face closer. ''This one:

''If I should get taken out—if anything weird or inexplicable should happen to incapacitate me or even, yes, *exclude* me permanently from the scheme of things— then you're the next in line. Consider yourself appointed, here and now.''

''What?'' The officer looked at Luchov's pale, shining face, his hideously scarred skull, and wondered if he was entirely sane. ''You are . . . *appointing* me, Projekt Direktor?''

''Indeed I am!'' Luchov was vehement. ''As Guardian of the Earth, yes!''

''Guardian of . . . ?''

''Press it!'' Luchov whispered, cutting him short. ''If anything should happen to me, *press* the bloody thing! Don't delay—don't waste time phoning Gorbachev or those mumbling cretins who so poorly serve him—but press the button! Get it over and done with and send your exorcets on a *real* mission of exorcism, into the world beyond the Gate, before the devil himself comes spewing out of there right into your face! Have you got that?''

The Major took a pace to the rear. His eyes were very wide now, very concerned; and still Luchov held his arm in a steel grasp. ''Sir, I . . .''

Abruptly, Luchov released him, straightened up a little, and stiffened his back and shoulders, then glanced away. "Say nothing." He gave a curt, almost dismissive nod. "For the moment, don't say anything at all. But neither must you forget what I said. Don't you *dare* forget it, that's all!"

How to answer him? With a smile, which might be misinterpreted? With words? But Luchov had advised him to say nothing, and anyway, the Major had no words. Perhaps it were better if he simply forgot the whole incident. Except Luchov had warned him about that, too. And anyway, would it be a wise move: to forget that this possibly dangerous man was in charge here? And in so doing, to forget what he was in charge of . . .

Saving the Major from further embarrassment and possibly worse, a hatch in the fish-scale plates clanged back on its hinges and a maintenance engineer came up from below. Staggering a little as he stood up in the glare of the Gate, he wrenched breathing apparatus from his pale damp face and put on plastic goggles. Then he reached out a groping hand, as if seeking support, and staggered again.

Luchov recognized him, went to him at once with the Major following on behind. "Felix Szalny?" The Projekt Direktor took the man's arm, steadied him. "Is it you, Felix?" (He could be familiar when he thought the situation required it.) "But you look like you saw a ghost!"

The coveralled maintenance man, small, balding, smudged with grime, nodded. He blinked his eyes rapidly and glanced back towards the open hatch. "The next best thing, anyway, Direktor," he muttered almost to himself, wiping cold sweat from his brow with a rag.

"What is it?" Luchov felt the short hairs rising at the

back of his neck, which they were wont to do all too often in this place. "Something below?"

"Down there, in one of the sealed shafts which was part of the original complex, yes," Szalny answered. "I was checking a wormhole hotspot. Curiously, the radiation has decreased almost to background; it's no longer dangerous, anyway. So I opened up the seal and . . . and entered. Eventually, the wormhole came out into the old abandoned reactor maintenance level. In there . . . I found magmass, of course."

"Ah!" Now Luchov knew what had happened. Or thought he did. "There were bodies!"

"Bodies, yes," Szalny answered, nodding. "That was part of it, at least. They'd been roasted, inverted, transformed. Some were half in, half out of the magmass, like mummies wrapped in warped rock, rubber, and plastic. And even after all these long years of entombment, Lord, still I fancied I could hear their screams!"

Luchov was well able to picture it. He had been a scientist here in Perchorsk when the hideous accident happened; he still bore the scars, both upon his seared parchment skull and more permanently in his mind, which was why he now shuddered. "It's as well you came up out of there," he said. "Later you can go down, seal the place up again. But for now . . ."

"I . . . I tripped over something." Szalny was still dazed, still talking almost to himself, because as yet he hadn't told it all. "Something crumbled into dust where I stepped on it, so that I stumbled and crashed against a cyst—which immediately shattered!"

The young Major touched Luchov's elbow, but this time very carefully. "Did he say something about a cyst?"

The Direktor glanced at him. "Oh, and are you interested?" And without waiting for an answer, nodding grimly, he continued, "Then you must see it for your-self."

He called over a private soldier and sent him hurrying off on an errand. And while they waited: "Can we borrow a couple of these radiation tags from your staff here?" And then to Szalny: "Felix, I want you to go and sit in one of those chairs on the perimeter." And finally, to a second soldier: "You there—go and get this man a mug of hot tea. And hurry!"

Luchov and the Major clipped radiation hazard tags to their clothing; the first soldier returned with a pair of gas masks; slinging these over their shoulders, the pair descended through the steel hatch into the lower half of the chamber. Down there, the Gate glared on them from where it hung suspended, weightless in the center of spherical space.

Reaching the bottom of the steel ladder, Luchov stepped carefully down between the gaping mouths of circular shafts cutting at all angles into the giant stone bowl of the floor. These were "wormholes": energy channels which had been eaten through the solid granite in the first seconds of the Perchorsk accident, when previously rigid matter had taken on the consistency of dough. "Watch how you go," he called up to the young officer. "And give a wide berth to wormholes with their radiation seals intact. They're still a little hot. Of course, you'd know all about that sort of thing, wouldn't you?" He set out to negotiate the perfectly smooth, cold stone floor, following corrugated rubber "steps" which had been laid down to provide for a firmer tread.

And climbing away from the hub, they were soon obliged to use iron rungs where these had been grafted into a sloping "floor" which gradually curved into the vertical; which was also when Luchov drew level with a three-foot-diameter shaft whose lead-lined manhole seal had been left standing open. He'd first spotted the open hatch as he came down the ladder and guessed that this was where Szalny had been working. For corroboration, a pocket torch with the maintenance engineer's name scratched into its plastic casing lay where Szalny had left it in the wormhole's gaping mouth.

Luchov took up the torch, and lighting the way ahead he crawled into the hole. "Still interested, are you?" His almost sardonic voice echoed back to the Major, who followed on hands and knees. "Good. But if I were you I'd put on that gas mask."

Szalny had left a rope attached to the last rung; it snaked out of sight into the wormhole, which wound first to the left, then tilted into a gentle descent for maybe thirty feet before leveling out, and finally turned sharply right . . . into darkness. Into the permanent midnight of a place long abandoned.

"In the old days," Luchov breathed, where he pierced the smoky darkness with a shaft of light and lowered himself carefully to the lumpy, uneasy-feeling floor, "they used to service the pile from down here." His voice, mask-muffled, had become a susurrating echo. "But of course, that was before the pile ate itself."

The young officer was close behind; clambering awkwardly out of the wormhole, he stood up and caught hold of Luchov's smock to steady himself. But Luchov was pleased to note that the Major's hand shook and his breathing was a little panicked. Probably from unaccustomed exertion; indeed, mainly from that . . . until Luchov let the beam of the torch creep across the walls, the floor, the magmass *inhabitants* of the place.

Then the Major's breathing turned to panting and his shaking got a lot worse, until after a while he gasped, "My God!"

Luchov stepped carefully, fastidiously over anomalous

and yet homogenous debris. Over debris which had tried to be homogenous, anyway. "When the accident happened," he said, "matter became very flexible and flowing. A melting pot without the heat. Oh, there was some heat—a lot, in places—but that was mainly chemical reaction or nuclear residual. It had little to do with the way rock, rubber, plastic, metal, flesh, and bones melted together into this. This was a different sort of heat, an alien sort, the result of the forging of the Gate. As you can see, things get tangled at the crossroads of universes."

Abruptly, his slithering torch beam passed over, and immediately returned to, something in the wall. Szalny's "cyst": a fine eggshell sheath of magmass stone, like a man-sized blister clinging there, but broken open now and dripping black stuff on the nightmarish floor. Even with their masks filtering out any poisons, still they could smell it; their movements and Luchov's muffled, echoing voice had disturbed it; as they stared, so sticky black bones came lolling out of it.

After that—

—the Major didn't stop moving and mouthing, panting and gasping, until he was back through the wormhole to the white-glaring core; where finally, at the foot of the ladder, he paused, removed his mask, and threw up. Having followed him, Luchov stood off at a safe distance and watched. And as the young officer finished but continued to kneel there, hanging like a limp rag on the lower rungs, so the Projekt Direktor said:

"So now you begin to understand. You understand something of the horror this place has seen, inherent in its atmosphere, indeed in its walls! Down here, sealed in by the magmass—and in other places bricked up by men who couldn't bear to contemplate it—there is much horror. Ah, but up there," he lifted his eyes to the belly of the steel disk with its overlapping plates, "on the other side of that madly glaring Cyclops Gate, there is so much more. An entire world of horror, for all we know, which is still alive!''

The Major wiped his mouth.

''I could see it in your eyes that you thought I'd cracked,'' Luchov told him. ''Well, of course I have! Do you really think I'd be here if I was entirely sane?''

The Major coughed into his hand and mumbled, ''My God! My God!''

Luchov nodded, and without malice said, ''Nice thought . . . but what has He to do with this place, eh?'' He shook his head. ''Very little, I fear. And the longer you're here, the more godless it gets to be.''

Not even attempting to answer, the other continued to cling tightly to the ladder's rungs . . .

Below the caldera of an ancient volcano, in a place not unlike subterranean Perchorsk and yet an entire universe away—a place of wormhole lava-runs and sulphur walls, where ages ago superheated gas had expanded to form caverns like bubbles in chocolate, and the liquid guts of a planet had first forced and then made permanent a spiderweb network of channels in the permeable rock—this was where the monstrous Lord Shaitan had made his ''home'' in a time immemorial. And here, just four years ago, his descendant Shaithis of the Wamphyri had discovered him alive and plotting still.

Now, standing tall but dramatically insignificant against the dark uppermost fangs of the caldera's broken walls—like a statue there on the old cone's lava rim, under writhing auroral vaults shot through with the occasional scar of a meteorite's suicide, and gazing south upon a far, faint horizon—Shaithis selected and highlighted memories of those years: of how they'd passed, of what he'd seen and learned, and of what had been planned. By his ancestor Shaitan and by himself. Plans which purported to coincide, though not necessarily. Indeed, not at all.

And guarding such thoughts (ah, but jealously, fearfully!), Shaithis remembered his journey here from Starside on the rim, across surly iceberg oceans and vast wintry wastelands, he and the other survivors of The Dweller's wrath: the giant Fess, hideous Volse, squat Arkis, and various thralls, all fled here, self-exiled under threat of a vampire's death, which is far more terrible than that of any mere man and not alone from an entirely physical point of view. For a man knows he must die, but a vampire knows he need not.

Four years ago, aye . . .

After the whelky Volse's loathsome demise, Shaithis in his treachery had directed Arkis Leperson, called Diredeath, and the acromegalic Fess Ferenc into the clutches of Shaitan the Unborn, where, in the shrieking sulphur shadows of an ancient lava-run, that immemorial monster had *struck* out of his own mind-silence! Even now remembering how it had been, Shaithis gave an unaccustomed start:

The lightning-swift, shadow-silent attack of the siphonsnout (as Shaithis thought of such creatures now); then Arkis speared and held aloft on nimbly skipping tiptoes, jerking and throbbing on the hollow bone blade where it pierced him to the heart, eyes bulging and cheeks going in and out like a bellows, puffing out a fine damp scarlet mist. *Extremely* fine that life-mist, for Shaitan's ingurgitor had been loath to lose or spill a drop. And Fess the giant rounding on Shaithis in a fury, all intent upon tearing out his heart; but Shaitan to the rescue, flowing out of the darkness like a tide of evil, wrapping the berserker in a nest of tentacles while Shaithis swung his gauntlet to burst his head in. And the one final scene which remained fresh as steaming blood in Shaithis's mind to this day:

The great pulsing mass of the Ferenc held fast for long and long in Shaitan's many-armed embrace, until at last the giant's throbbing ceased and elastic cobra jaws released his head, leaving it wet and smoking and *apparently* whole—except it was seen how the eye sockets were empty and trickling, with similar dribbles escaping from the nostrils and slack yawning mouth. And Shaithis thinking a thought so cold it burned him still:

Oh, yes, surely Hell's gate! Where I've just witnessed a so-called ancestor of mine emptying the Ferenc's head like a rat sucking out a stolen egg.

And: "Indeed you have!" Shaitan had at once, gurglingly, agreed, while his crimson eyes in their yellow orbits glared out from the darkness beneath the black, corrugated flesh of his cobra's hood. "My creature siphoned off his blood—for safekeeping, until later, you understand—and I sucked out his brain. But you'll note how we left the best for you, eh?"

With which he'd made a small effort to propel the corpse in Shaithis's direction, so that it had appeared to take two stumbling, flopping steps towards him before crashing at his feet. And of course he'd known exactly what the other meant. For hiding in the Ferenc's huge, pale, dehydrated shell, his vampire (ah, sweetmeat of sweetmeats!) was still to be discovered and reckoned with. And:

"Won't you join me?" Shaitan had offered a clotted, gurgled invitation—before wrenching Arkis from the bubbling blade of the ingurgitor and throwing him down to the lava floor, there falling or flowing over him as he commenced to search for his frantic, cringing parasite.

To this point events had left Shathis somewhat stunned—but not for much longer. He was after all Wamphyri, and all of this had been much as anticipated. And of course, the blood *was* the life. Dining with Shaitan may even have sealed something of a bond between them.

It might have, anyway.

After that . . .

There was a lot to remember and events contrived to jumble. A good many fractured scenes and conversations overlapped their jagged edges in Shaithis's memory. As contrary breezes blew up off the cold blue star- and aurora-litten waste, bringing nodding snow devils to swirl around the bases of the glittering, plundered ice-castle tombs of anciently exiled Wamphyri, so he attempted to arrange these fragments in chronological order, or failing that to separate them at least.

Shaitan's cavernous workshop, for example, located immediately beneath the volcano's hitherto unseen north-facing scarp, where soon after Shaithis's advent the Fallen One had escorted him upon a guided tour.

Apart from the high-ceilinged, stalactite-adorned vast-ness of the place—with its near-opaque windows of ice looking out upon and lending grotesque distortion to the very roof of the world, and its deep permafrost pits where Shaitan was wont to confine in ice his more volatile, less manageable experiments—the workshop had seemed much like any other. Shaithis, too, was a master of just such creative metamorphism; or so he had always con-sidered himself, until he saw his ancestor's work.

Gazing down on one such piece through ice clear as water, he had offered his opinion: ''This alone would suffice to have you denounced and banished afresh, or destroyed outright, if this were Starside and the Old Wamphyri still held sway. Why, it has reproductive or-gans, which were forbidden!''

''A bull, aye,'' Shaitan had answered with a nod of

his cowl. "Alas but procreation, the act of copulation, its contemplation—even the possession of organs, of the means—drives creatures to rage. I made this one a mate, female, which for thanks he at once tore to pieces! But even if she'd lived and brought forth, what then? I cannot see that he'd permit offspring to survive but would surely devour them at the first opportunity. Just look at him, and as yet half grown! But so untrustworthy, at last I was obliged to freeze him here. The fault was his sex. It made him prideful and pride is a curse. It's the same with men, of course . . ."

"And therefore with the Wamphyri," Shaithis had said.

"More so!" Shaitan cried. "For in them all such urges are amplified by ten!"

"But they don't tear their odalisques in pieces. At least, not always."

"More fool them," said Shaitan. "For if you can live forever, what sense to breed that of your own flesh which may one day usurp and destroy you?"

"And yet you sought out women in which to spend yourself," Shaithis had been quick to point out, "else I'd not be here."

And at that their eyes had met and locked across Shaitan's creature frozen in its pit of ice, and after a while the Fallen One had answered: "I did, it's true—and perhaps for that very reason . . ."

It had been their first argument or discussion as such, but only one of a great many to come. And while it would soon become Shaithis's complaint that his ancestor conversed with him in terms more befitting a child, generally he accepted that the ancient, evil Being was trying to instruct him. Perhaps he considered his great age gave him the right; for after all, he was Shaithis's senior to the extent of seven spans.

* * *

. . . Another time: Shaithis had been shown a developing siphon-snout, absorbing liquids where it gradually took on shape and substance in a vat. The thing was much similar to the guardian ingurgitors (of which the volcano's master had three) but the siphon was longer, more flexible, and bedded at its roots in great walls of flesh, so that the creature's tiny, greedily glittering eyes were almost entirely hidden in bulging bands of grey, gleaming muscle. Shaithis had known immediately what the thing was, inquiring of Shaitan:

"But don't you have enough of these? It surprises me you trouble yourself to make more. By now you've surely had the best of the ice-encysted Wamphyri . . . those of them who were readily got at, anyway. So what use to persist?"

Shaitan had cocked his cobra's head on one side, coiled up his arms, and inquired: "And have you fathomed it all, my son? Do you know the *precise* use to which they're put, these things of mine?"

"Certainly. They are variations on a theme: ingurgitors not unlike that or those which stopped Volse and Arkis, but rather more specialized. Their slender, bone-tipped cartilage snouts vibrate in ice to shatter it, whereby paths are drilled to the suspended exiles in their otherwise impenetrable sheaths. Once a channel has been cut, then the beast drains off its victim's liquids through its snout, which siphoned fluids—"

"—Are then *re*gurgitated into my reservoirs!" Shaitan, perhaps peeved with Shaithis's ingenuity, had finished it for him. "Yes, yes—but aren't you curious to know how? *How* may the driller siphon off solids, eh? For of course his victims are mainly frozen, whose fluids gurgle like glue."

"Ah!" Shaithis had been fascinated.

"I will explain . . . in a moment. As to *why* I bother myself with these Old Lords, when (as you've pointed out) they're now so few in number and invariably low in sustenance, the answer to that is simple: because it pleases me to do so. The terror in the minds of those of them who can still think at all is so rare and delicious as to be exquisite. If I had not them, then whom would I terrify, eh? Could I even exist, without my measure of tyranny and terror?"

And Shaithis had understood. Evil feeds on terror; without one the other cannot exist; they are inseparable as space and time. And reading his thoughts, Shaitan had whisperingly, gurglingly, chortlingly agreed:

"Aye, it's simple as that: I *like* it, and I need the practice!"

So that was why; and the how of it was likewise simple:

The drillers squirted metamorphic acids into their victims, whose desiccated tissues then dissolved into liquids which were drawn off before they could resolidify.

"It still doesn't answer my first question," Shaithis had argued. "Which was: why do you trouble to make more of these creatures?"

(Shaitan's shrug, of sorts.) "I say again, mainly for the practice; as has been almost everything I've done these last three thousand years. Practice yes, towards the time when we shall build an army of warriors, and with them set out against Starside and all the worlds beyond!"

For a moment the scarlet eyes beneath the Fallen One's cobra's hood had burned more brightly yet, like fires stoked from within. But then he'd nodded, gradually returned from the privacy of his dark-cloaked thoughts, and said: "Ah, but now you must tell me:

"Since you seem of the opinion that I breed too many, just *how many* of my ice-drillers and kindred creatures have you seen?"

515

Shaithis had been taken aback. He'd imagined a *great* many such beasts, to be sure. But what evidence he'd seen of them in the looted ice castles had been the slow work of countless centuries, in no way the concerted effort of a handful of auroral periods, nor even entire cycles of such. And while here in the workshops at the roots of the volcano several vats steamed and bubbled where Shaitan's experiments continued to shape, still there were precious few working beasts. No flaccid siphoneers here as in Starside's aeries, for the cone's caldera contained a small lake of water; nor any great requirement for gas-beasts, where several of the volcano's caverns—especially Shaitan's living quarters—were warmed by active blowholes. So that after giving the question some little thought, Shaithis had been obliged to answer:

"Now that I think of it, I can't say I've actually seen any—except this one cooking in its vat."

"Exactly, for there are none! Not of the visible, mobile-and-eating-their-heads-off varieties, at any rate. I keep only my ingurgitors, for the protection they afford me. Now come." And Shaitan had taken his descendant down to black, lightless nether-caverns where every niche, crevice, and extinct volcanic vent served as a storage chamber for the ice-encased progeny of his experimental vats. And there he inquired of him:

"So advise me: how would *you* keep such as these both awake and full-bellied?" And answered himself, "Out of the question! What, in these almost barren Icelands? You wouldn't. Which is why, as their various purposes are served, I freeze them into immobility down here. And here they stay, inert for the moment, the raw *materiel* of tomorrow's army. And when I require another, perhaps different *sort* of creature—why, I simply design and construct one! The art of metamorphism, Shaithis. But nothing wasted, my son, never that."

Continuing to gaze down on his ancestor's preserved experiments, Shaithis had nodded. "I see you've tried a warrior or two," he'd commented. "Fearsome but . . . archaic? Perhaps I should advise you: Starside's warriors have come a long way since your day. In all truth, these things of yours would not last long against certain of *my* constructs!"

If Shaitan was offended, it hardly showed. "Then by all means instruct me in these superior metamorphic skills," he'd answered. "Indeed, and in order that you may do so, you shall have complete freedom of my work-shops, materials, and vats."

Which had been much to Shaithis's liking . . .

Another time, Shaithis had asked:

"What of your ingurgitors? Since plainly they are work-ing beasts, and since it's your habit to—separate them?—from what they take from their victims, how do you sustain them? On what do you feed them? For as you yourself have pointed out: these Icelands are very nearly barren."

Shaitan had then shown him his reservoirs of frozen blood and minced, metamorphic flesh, explaining: "I've been here a long long time, my son. And when I first came here, ah, but I quickly learned what it meant to go hungry! Since when I've made provision not only for myself but for my creatures, both now and in the dawn of our resurgence."

In blank astonishment, Shaithis had gazed upon the rims of (literally) *dozens* of potholes of black plasma. "Blood? So *much* blood? But not from the frozen Lords, surely? There were never sufficient of the Wamphyri in all Starside to fill these great bowls!"

"Beast blood," Shaitan told him. "Whale blood, too.

Yes, and even a little man blood. But you are correct, only a *very* little of the latter. The blood of beasts and great fishes is fine for my creatures; it will fuel them to war when that time is come, following which . . . why, there'll be food aplenty for all, eh? But the man blood is mine—and yours, too, now that you're here—for our sustenance.''

Shaithis had been even more astonished. "You've bled the great fishes in the cold sea?"

"Actually, while I called them fishes, they are mammals." Shaitan had shrugged in his fashion. "They're warm-blooded, those giants, and suckle their young. Soon after I came here I saw a school at play, spouting at the rim of the ocean, so that my first ingurgitor was designed with them in mind. It was a good design and I've scarcely changed it down the centuries. Doubtless you've noted the vestigial gills, fins, and other seeming anomalies in the volcano's guardian creatures; likewise in my driller.''

Shaithis had noted those things. Indeed it was his habit to note everything . . .

On another occasion, fascinated by the sheer *age* of his self-appointed "mentor," Shaithis had thought to suggest:

"But you have been here—upon the earth, in Starside and in the Icelands, mainly in these frozen wastes— almost since the beginning!" Even speaking those words he had realized how naive they must sound and how much in awe of the other he must seem, which his ancestor's dark chuckle had at once confirmed.

"The Beginning? Ah, no, for I perceive that the world is a million times older than I am. Or did you mean the beginning of the Wamphyri? In which case I can but agree, for I was the first of all.''

"Really?" Again Shaithis forgot to distance himself from his astonishment. It was hard to be inscrutable in the face of revelations such as these. Of course, the legends of Starside *said* that Shaitan the Fallen had been the first vampire, but as any fool is aware, legends are like myths: mainly untruths or at best exaggerations. "The first? The father of us all?"

"The first of the Wamphyri, aye," Shaitan had answered at last, after a long, curious silence. "But not . . . the Father, did you say? No, not the Father. Oh, I fathered my share, be sure, for I was young with a young man's appetites. I had *been* a man entire and fallen to earth here, where my vampire came to me . . . came out of . . . out of the swamps . . ." He paused, leaving his words to taper into a thoughtful silence.

And after a while: "Out of the vampire swamps?" Shaithis had pressed him. "There are great swamps to the west of Starside, and according to legend others in the east. I've heard of such but never saw them. Are these the swamps of which you speak?"

Shaitan was still distanced by strange reverie. Nevertheless he nodded. "Those are the swamps, aye. I fell to earth in the west."

Shaithis had heard him use this term—about "falling to earth"—before. Frowning and shaking his head, he'd said, "I fail to understand. How may a man fall to earth? Out of the sky, do you mean? From your mother's womb? But weren't you also called the Unborn? *Where* did you fall from, and how?"

Shaitan had snapped out of it. "You are a noisy person, and your questions are rude! Still, I'll answer them as best I may. First understand this: my memories start at the swamps, and even then they are faded and incomplete. Before the swamps, I . . . I'm not sure. But when I came naked to this world I came in great pain and great pride. I believe that I was exiled into this place, thrown down here even as the Wamphyri exiled me at last to these Icelands. The Wamphyri exiled me because I would be The One Power. Well, and perhaps I had tried to be a Power in that other place, too, wherefrom I was banished and fell to earth. It is a mystery to me. But this I do know: *compared* to the other place, this world was like a hell!''

''Someone had sent you here as a punishment, to a life of hell?''

''Or to a world which could *become* a hell, of my making. It was a question of will: anything could be, if I so willed it or allowed it to be. I repeat: it was *because* I was willful and prideful that I was here. Or at least, that is how I seem to remember it.''

''You do not actually remember falling, then? Only that you were suddenly there, in the vampire swamps?''

''Close to the swamps, yes, where my vampire came into me.''

Shaithis had been keenly interested in that last. ''In our time,'' he mused, ''we've both had occasion to kill enemies and tear their living vampires out of them to devour. Fess Ferenc and Arkis Leperson were only the most recent. We know what such parasites look like: full-formed they are barbed leeches, which hide in men to shape their thoughts and urges. And in certain hosts, over long periods, they may grow so fused as to become inseparable.''

''As in myself, yes,'' Shaitan had answered. ''Indeed, there remains precious little of the original me left at all, while my vampire is grown to what you see.''

''Just so,'' said Shaithis. ''You, or rather your vampire—as a result of prolonged metamorphism—is now gross. But how was it *then*? Did it come to you as an egg? Did the parent creature remain in the swamps? Or did the parasite come to you full grown, take you by surprise, and slither into you complete?''

"It came to me from the swamp," Shaitan had repeated. "That much I know . . . how, I do not know.''

The problem had vexed Shaithis (and his ancester no less), but on that occasion at least they'd been at a loss for further questions and answers.

A good many auroral periods later, however, when Shaithis was busy in a corner of the workshop, carefully constructing a warrior for his ancestor's approval:

"*This* is how it was!" said Shaitan, coming swiftly and in some excitement upon Shaithis where he worked, and flowing up to him like a midnight shadow. "In that earlier existence of which I apprised you, I served another or others but desired to serve only myself. As a reward for my pride—which is to say for my wit and great beauty, of which I was perhaps too much aware—and for my pains, I was thrown out and removed from my rightful place in that society. I was not destroyed, not wasted, but used! I became to *Them* . . . a tool! A seed of evil, which *They* would sow between the spheres! Do you see? I was the folly and the penance! I was the Darkness which allows for the Light!''

In the face of this outburst, Shaithis had brought his work at the vat to a halt. Unable to understand the other, he could only shake his head and throw up his hands. "Can't you explain yourself more clearly?"

"Damn you—*no!*" Shaitan had shouted then. "I dreamed it; I know it for the truth; but I cannot understand it! I've told it to you so that you also may attempt to fathom it—and likewise *fail* to fathom it, even as I have failed!''

With which and in a fury, he had rushed off and disappeared into the volcano's labyrinth.

* * *

For a long time after that Shaithis had not seen the other at all; he had merely been aware of his ancestor's shadowy presence. But a time had come when, going again to the vats, he'd found the ancient gloomily examining his various adaptations where they squirmed and hardened in their liquids; and there, following customary greetings but in answer to no specific remark or query, Shaitan had listlessly mumbled:

"I have been banished out of many spheres and thrown down from many worlds. Aye, and others like me, throughout all the myriad cone-shaped dimensions of light." That had been all.

Mad creature! (Shaithis had kept this thought, and others he was thinking, very much to himself). *But it's as well you rush around crazed while I'm about my work. The last thing I would want is for you to become interested in what I'm doing now.* For in fact he was there at that time in order to inject brain matter into his new construct, so stimulating and even directing the fetal ganglion's growth. Except . . . these were cells obtained from a rather special source, and by means of Shaitan's ice-boring ingurgitor . . .

Putting all such business aside for the nonce, however, and pandering to Shaitan's insanity, if that is what it was, he had answered: "In which case, when we go against Starside with these warriors I'm fashioning, your revenge will be so much sweeter. Nothing will stand before us; and if there are higher worlds to conquer, they too shall finally fall, even as you fell to earth."

His words had seemed to suffice to draw the other up from whatever morbid depths claimed him, even so far as to correct his temporary imbalance. And: "Indeed, these appear to be *good* warriors, my son!" he'd at once remarked. A rare compliment; at once relegated by:

"Which they should be, for in Starside you had a sufficiency of superb clay with which to practice."

And after that the ancient rambled no more . . .

Later still:

The two had constructed a slender, streamlined powerful flyer, equipped it with a sucking snout and given it the stripped-to-basic brain of one of Menor Maimbite's otherwise defunct lieutenants. Fueling the beast on quality plasma, they'd sent it on a reconnaissance flight to Starside. After that and over the space of a good many auroral displays, they'd waited on its return but in vain. Eventually, when almost all hope had faded, the flyer had returned, bringing back with it a scrawny shivering waif of a Traveller child.

The flyer had snatched him, a boy of eight or nine years, at sundown from a party of Travellers where they camped in the hills over Sunside. It appeared that the Travellers no longer went to earth when the sun sank down into night. Why should they, when the Wamphyri were no more? But the return journey from Starside had been long, and the child almost dead from exposure.

Shaitan had carried him away to his private chambers for "questioning"; shortly thereafter, the ancient's mind-call had summoned Shaithis from where he worked at the vats:

Come!

A single word, yes, but its author's excitement had spoken volumes . . .

V Sundown—
Exorcets—the Godmind

SHAITHIS STOOD TALL AND SEVERE IN THE BLACK, gapped caldera wall and looked south towards Starside. Overhead, the aurora wove in a sky which was otherwise black, but he knew that on Starside it would be sunup. The mountain peaks would be burning gold, and in Karen's aerie thick curtains and tapestries woven with her sigil would guard the uppermost windows, where lances of sunfire might otherwise strike through.

He looked south, narrowing his scarlet eyes to focus upon a far faint line of fire all along the horizon, a narrow golden haze which separated the distant curve of the world first from blue then black space, where all the stars of night hung glittering and hypnotic, seeming to beckon him. Which was a call he would answer. Soon.

Indeed he must, for when the aurora died to a flicker and the sky in the south darkened to jet, then it would be sundown; in advance of which, Shaithis and his devolved, depraved ancestor would muster their warriors, mount their flyers, and launch a small but monstrous army from the volcano's steep lava slopes. For them the realization of a dream, and for Starside the advent of a nightmare, was finally in the offing. Shaitan's dream for so many hundreds of years, now looming into being, brought into sharp relief by a lone flyer's recent return out of Starside with its burden of a stolen Traveller waif.

Shaithis remembered the event in minute detail: the way his gloating ancestor had carried off the exhausted, half-dead boy into the gloom of his sulphur-floored chambers; following which (eventually), his mental summons:

Come!

In his mind's eye Shaithis saw it all again: the Fallen One, jubilant where he paced or flowed to and fro across the black, grainy floor of his apartments in his excitement. And before Shaithis had been able to frame a question:

"This Dweller of whom you've spoken." Shaitan had turned to him. "This alien youth who used the power of the sun itself to bring down the mighty Wamphyri."

"Yes, what of him?"

"What of him?" Shaitan had gurgled darkly, delightedly, in his fashion. "Devolved, that's what! Even as I myself am devolved—but to his far greater cost. So he bathed you all in blazing sunlight, eh? By which reducing Wamphyri flesh to steam and stench? Well, and he seared himself, too! His vampire must have been injured; it could not repair itself; his metamorphic man flesh sloughed away even as a leper's. Then . . . his desperate vampire returned him to an earlier form: that of its original host and manifestation. Less bulk in that, making the wastage easier to contain, d'you see? And so your Dweller is now . . . a wolf!"

"A wolf?" Astonished, Shaithis had remembered his dream.

"A beast, aye, going on all fours. A Grey One, the leader of the pack, with nothing of powers except those of the wild. The Travellers hold him in awe, whose fore-paws are human hands. A little of his mind must be human, too, at least in its memories. And of course his vampire has survived, in however small part, for that was what saved him. But the rest is wolf."

"A wolf!" Shaithis had breathed it again. Well, it wasn't the first time he'd experienced oneiromantic dreams. It was an art of the Wamphyri, that's all. "And his father, the hell-lander Harry Keogh?"

"He is back in Starside, aye."

"Back?"

"Indeed, for following the battle at The Dweller's garden he returned to his own place. Something which you could hardly be expected to know, for by then you were in exile."

"His own place? The hell-lands?"

"Hell-lands! Hell-lands! They are *not* hell-lands! How often must I tell you: *this* place is hell, with its sulphur stenches, vampire swamps, and sun-blasted furnace lands beyond the mountains! Ah, but Harry Keogh's world . . . to the likes of us it would be a paradise!"

"How can you know that?"

"I can't—but I can suspect it."

"This Harry Keogh," Shaithis had mused: "he had powers, to be sure, but he was not Wamphyri."

"Well, now he is," Shaitan at once contradicted him, "but as yet untried. For who is there to test him, in devious argument or in battle? What's more, the Travellers don't much fear him, for he will not take the blood of men."

"What?!"

"According to the boy," Shaitan had said, "The Dweller's father eats only beast flesh. Compared to *your* vampire, my son, it seems his is a puling, unsophisticated infant of a thing."

"And the so-called *Lady* Karen?"

"Ah, yes," Shaitan had said. "The Lady Karen: last of Starside's Wamphyri. You have designs on that one, don't you? I remember you remarked on her treachery, and even now her name falls like acid from your forked tongue. Well, Karen and Harry Keogh are together. So at least he's that much of a man. They share her aerie; if she's the beauty you say she is, doubtless he's in her to the hilt and beyond, even as we speak."

It was a deliberate jibe and Shaithis knew it, but still he could not resist rising to the other's bait. "Then they should enjoy each other while they can," he had answered darkly. And finally, he had looked around for the Traveller child.

"Gone," Shaitan told him. "Man flesh, pure and simple. I've had my share of metamorphic mush these thousands of years. The boy was a tidbit, but welcome for all that."

"The entire child?"

"In Sunside there are entire tribes," Shaitan had answered, his voice a clotted gurgle. "And beyond that entire worlds!"

With which they'd commenced to ready themselves for their resurgence . . .

Now Shaithis waited on the emergence of his latest warrior creature, and his ancestor Shaitan the Fallen waited with him. When the beast's scales, grapples, and various fighting appendages had stiffened into chitin hard as iron, a matter of hours now, finally it would be time to venture forth against Starside.

As for any future "battle": would it even last long enough to qualify as such? Shaithis doubted it. For he firmly believed that on his own—single-handedly controlling a mere fistful of warriors from the back of a flyer, and without his ancestor's help—still he would have the measure of Karen and her lover, and whatever allies they might muster. And therefore the measure of Starside, too.

What, a mere female? A pack of wolves? And a vampire "Lord" who shied from man blood? No army that but a rabble! Let Keogh call up the dead if he would; fine for scaring trogs and Travellers, but Shaithis had no fear of the crumbling dead. And as for that other facet of Keogh's magic—that clever trick of his, of coming and going at will, invisibly—that wouldn't help him. Not this time. If he went, good riddance! And if he came let it be to his death!

But on the other hand . . .

Shaithis could scarcely deny his own troublesome dreams, whose patterns were strange as the auroral energies which even now wove in the sky high overhead. Perhaps he should examine those dreams yet again, as so often before, except—

—No time, not now; for he felt a familiar encroachment and knew that Shaitan was near, in mind if not in body. And:

What is it? he inquired.

How clever you are, the other purred telepathically. *And oh so sensitive! There's no sneaking up on you, my son.*

Then why do you persist in trying? Shaithis was cold.

Shaitan ignored his testiness and said: *You should come now. Our creatures are mewling in their vats and would be up and about. They must be tested. We have things to do, preparations to make.*

Indeed, it was true enough. And:

I shall be there immediately, Shaithis answered, commencing the treacherous climb down from the cone. Yes, for his ancestor wasn't alone in his eagerness to be free of this place. Except there's freedom and there's freedom, and the concept is never the same to any two creatures.

Shaitan would merely free himself from the Icelands, while his descendant . . . he had something else to be free of.

Some little time earlier, and several thousands of miles to the south:

The Necroscope had been out to inspect Karen's advance guard: her early-warning system of specialized warrior creatures (or rogue troops, as they seemed to have become) where she'd stationed them at the rim of the frozen sea against any incursion from the Icelands. He had gone there via the Möbius Continuum, in a series of hundred-mile jumps which had taken him far across consecutive northern horizons into aurora-litten wastes where the snow lay in great white drifts on the shores of a sullenly heaving, ice-crusted ocean.

Karen's creatures had been there sure enough, and Harry was soon to discover how well they'd adapted. Metamorphic, a single generation had sufficed to accelerate their evolution: they'd grown thick white fur both for protection against the cold and as a natural camouflage. When Harry had thought to detect some slight movement in a humped snowfield, and after he'd carefully moved a little closer, then he'd seen just how effective the latter device was. His first real awareness of the beasts had been when three of them reared up and charged him: in combination, a quarter acre of murder running rampant!

Then, removing himself some small distance, he'd thought: *I'd be little more than a minnow to be divided between three great cats. They'd get no more than a taste apiece.*

But note their instinctive tendency to secrecy, Karen had commented from her aerie some two thousand miles south. *Their minds may be feeble, but still they were able to hide their thoughts, and thus themselves, away from you. What's more, you are Wamphyri—a Lord, a master—but that didn't stop them, either!*

The Necroscope had detected a degree of pride in Karen's thoughts; these were her creations, and she'd made a good job of them. Alas, but then she'd allowed them to slip the leash. Still focusing on him, she had detected that thought, too.

The distance was too great, she'd said with a shrug. *I see that now. Telepathy is a special talent which we share. Our mainly human minds are large, and we focus them well, wherefore contact between us is simple. But their minds are small and mainly concerned with survival.* Again her shrug. *Quite simply, they've forgotten me.*

Time they remembered, then, Harry had answered. And as she amplified and reinforced her original orders and instructions, so he'd relayed them directly and forcefully into the group's dull minds. Following which, and when he went among them a second time, they'd behaved with more respect.

Brave of you! she'd commented, however nervously. *To examine them at such close quarters. And perhaps a little foolish, too. Come out of there, Harry, please? Come home now?*

Home . . . Did she mean back to the aerie? he wondered. And was that really his home now? Perhaps it was in keeping: that monstrous menhir rising over Starside's boulder plains, whose furnishings were fashioned from the hair and fur, gristle and bones of once-men and -monsters. What better home for a man whose lifelong friend had been the Grim Reaper himself?

Bitter thoughts. But on the other hand it had seemed to Harry that Karen pleaded with him, and that she was concerned for him. And any home was better than none.

Anyway, his job was finished here now and he was cold. But he knew that Karen would warm him . . .

A universe away, in the Urals:

Major Alexei Byzarnov was present in the Perchorsk core for the latest computer-simulated test firing of the Tokarevs. His 2 I/C, Captain Igor Klepko, was in charge of the test. Klepko was short, sharp-featured, with the dark eyes and weatherworn complexion of his steppemen ancestors. Throughout his preparations, the officer had kept up a running commentary for the benefit of the half dozen junior officers in attendance. Also in attendance and keeping a close eye on the proceedings from where he stood apart on the perimeter walkway under the inward-curving arch of the granite wall, Projekt Direktor Viktor Luchov was quietly intense, totally absorbed in Klepko's instructive monologue as it approached its climax.

"Two missiles, yes," Klepko continued. "A dual system. In the field their launching would constitute either a preemptive strike in a hitherto nonnuclear battle zone, or retaliation against an enemy's use of similar weapons. The first Tokarev would seek out enemy HQ somewhere beyond the forward edge of the battle area, and the second would home in on heavy enemy troop concentration in the battle zone.

"For our purposes, however, here in Perchorsk—" Klepko shrugged. "While our targets are somewhat more specific, they remain paradoxically conjectural. We aim to detonate the first missile in a world beyond this, er, Gate'' (with a cursory wave of his hand, he indicated the glaring white sphere behind him), "and the second Tokarev while it is still inside the 'passage' between universes. The mechanics of the thing are very simple. On-board computers are linked by radio; as the first Tokarev clears the Gate into the far world, contact will be broken; one fifth of a second later *both* devices will detonate.''

Captain Klepko sighed and nodded. "As for the purpose of this system: if and when used, it will be entirely defensive. You've all been shown films of creatures from the other side breaking through into this world. I'm sure I don't have to stress how important it is that in future, no further emergence be allowed.

"Lastly, and before the simulation, there remain the questions of command and personal security. Command:

"These weapons will only be used on the instructions of the Projekt Direktor, as *qualified* by the Officer Commanding, Major Byzarnov or, in the unlikely event of his absence, by me. Except under circumstances where a chain-of-command situation has been initiated, no other person will have that authority.

"Personal security:

"From the moment the button is pressed the warheads are armed; there will be a delay of five minutes before firing; anyone who remains in Perchorsk at that time will be alerted by continuous claxons. The claxons have only one meaning: GET OUT! Exhaust from the Tokarevs is toxic. As a safety measure against the unlikely failure of the Projekt's ventilation systems, any stragglers will need to employ breathing apparatus until they've exited the complex. It takes about four minutes for a fit man to make it out of here from the core into the ravine.

"These Tokarevs are weapons; their use will not be experimental but for effect; there is no fail-safe. After firing, the system cannot be aborted and we cannot rely on more than sixty seconds before detonation. Which makes a total of six minutes after initiation. The explosion of the device on the far side should have no effect here, but the one in the passage . . . may be different. It could be that the sheer power of the detonation will drive radioactive gases and debris back through into Perchorsk. Hopefully, all such poisons will be contained down here in the vicinity of the core, by which time the place will have been vacated and the exits sealed."

Klepko straightened up and put his hands on his hips. "Any questions?" There were none.

"Simulation is computerized." He relaxed, scratching his nose and offering an apologetic shrug. "Bit of a letdown, I'm afraid, if you were expecting a fireworks show. Instead it will all happen on the small screen there in black and white, silent and with subtitles. And no special effects!"

His audience laughed.

"Mainly,"—Klepko held up a warning hand to silence them—"this is to let you see how short a span six minutes really is." And he pressed a red button on a box seated in front of him on top of his lectern.

Major Byzarnov had seen the simulation before. He wasn't especially interested in that, but he was interested in the expression on Viktor Luchov's face. One of rapt fascination. Byzarnov took two paces backwards onto the perimeter walkway, edged up quietly on the gaunt scientist, and coughed quietly in the back of his throat.

Luchov turned his head to stare at the major. "You still think this is some kind of game, don't you?" he accused.

"No," Byzarnov answered, "and I never did."

"I note that any order I might give on the use of these weapons is to be 'qualified' by you or your 2 I/C. Do you suspect I might order their use frivolously, then?"

"Not at all." The Major shook his head, only too well aware of several close-typed, folded sheets of paper where they bulked out his pocket: Luchov's current psychological profile as supplied by the Projekt's psychiatrist. And to himself: *Insanely, yes, but not frivolously.*

Luchov's eyes were suddenly vacant. "I sometimes feel that I'm being punished," he said.

"Oh?"

"Yes, for my part in all of this. I mean, I helped build the original Perchorsk. In those days Franz Ayvaz was the Direktor, but he died in the accident and so paid for his part in it. Since when the responsibility has been mine."

"A heavy enough load for any man." Byzarnov nodded, moved apart a little, and decided to change the subject. "I saw you come up from below, before Klepko started on his demonstration. You were . . . down in the abandoned magmass levels?"

Luchov shuddered and whispered: "God, what a mess things are in, down there! So many of them were trapped, sealed in. I opened a cyst. The thing inside it was like . . . it was an alien mummy. Not rotten or liquid this time, just a grotesque mass of inverted, half-fossilized flesh. Several major organs were visible on the outside, along with a good many curious—I don't know, *appendages*?—of rubber, plastic, stone, and, and, and, et cetera . . ."

Byzarnov felt sorry for him. Luchov had been here too long. But not for much longer, not if Moscow would act quickly on the Major's recommendation. "It *is* terrible down there, Viktor," he agreed. "And it might be best if you kept out of it."

Viktor? And Byzarnov's tone of voice: what, pity? Luchov glanced at him, glared at him, abruptly turned away. And over his shoulder, stridently: "So long as I am Projekt Direktor, Major, I'll come and go as I will!" And then he made away.

Byzarnov approached Klepko. By now the twin dart shapes moving jerkily across the computer screen had popped into oblivion; the simulation was over; Klepko was finishing off:

". . . will still be filled with toxic exhaust fumes and could well be highly radioactive! But of course we shall all be well out of it." The Major waited until Klepko had given the dismiss, then took him to one side and talked to him briefly, urgently.

About Luchov.

The Necroscope dreamed.

He dreamed of a boy called Harry Keogh who talked to dead people and was their friend, their one light in otherwise universal darkness. He dreamed of the youth's loves and lives, the minds he'd visited, bodies he'd inhabited, places he had known now, in the past and future, and in two worlds. It was a very weird dream and fantastical—more so because it was true—and for all that the Necroscope dreamed about himself, his own life, still it was as if he dreamed of another.

Finally, he dreamed of his son, a wolf . . . except this part was real and not just a memory from another world. And his son came to him, tongue lolling, and said:

Father, they're coming!

Harry came awake on the instant, slid from Karen's bed, went swift and sinuous to the window embrasure, where he drew aside the drapes. He was wary, kept himself well to one side, was ready to snatch back his hand in a moment if that should be necessary. But it wasn't, for it was sundown. Shadows crept on the mountain divide, usurping the gold from the peaks. Stars, at first scarcely visible, came more glowingly alive moment by moment. The darkness was here, and more darkness was coming.

Karen cried out in her sleep, came awake, and jerked bolt upright in the tumbled bed. "Harry!" Her face was ghostly pale—a torn sheet, with a triangle of holes for eyes and mouth—where she gazed all about the room. But then she saw the Necroscope at the window, and the holes of her eyes came burning alive. "They're coming!".

Their scarlet glances met and joined, forming a two-way channel for thoughts which moments ago were sleeping. Harry saw through Karen's eyes into her mind, but he answered her out loud, anyway. "I know," he said.

She came off the bed naked and flew to him, buried herself in his arms. "But they're *coming!*" she sobbed.

"Yes, and we'll fight them," he growled, his body reacting of its own accord to the feel and smell of her flesh, which was soft, silky, pliable, ripe, musty, and wet where his member grew into her.

She trapped him there with muscles that held him fast, and groaned, "Let's make this the very best one, Harry."

"Because it might be the last?"

"Just in case," she grunted, forming barbs within herself to draw him further in. After that—

—It *was* like never before, leaving them too exhausted to be afraid . . .

Later, he said: "What if we lose?"

"Lose?" Karen stood beside him; they leaned together and gazed out through a window in a room facing north, towards the Icelands. As yet there was nothing to be seen and they hadn't expected there would be. But they could feel . . . something. It radiated from the north like ripples on a lake of pitch: slow, shuddery, and black with its evil.

Harry nodded slowly. "If we lose, they can only kill me," he said. And he thought of Johnny Found and the things he had done to his victims. Terrible things. But compared to Shaithis and any other survivors of the Old Wamphyri, Johnny Found had been a child, and his imagination sadly lacking.

Karen knew why the Necroscope closed his mind to her: for her own protection. But it was a wasted effort; she knew the Wamphyri much better than he did; nothing Harry was capable of imagining could ever plumb the true depths of Wamphyri cruelty. That was Karen's opinion; which was why she promised him, "If you die, I die."

"Oh? And they'll let you die, will they? So easily?"

"They can't stop me. On this side of the mountains it is sundown, but beyond Sunside . . . true death waits there for any vampire. It burns like molten gold in the sky. That's where I'd flee, far across the mountains into the sun. Let them follow me there if they dared, but I wouldn't be afraid. I remember when I was a child and the sun felt good on my skin. I'm sure that in the end, before I died, I could make it feel that way again. I would *will* it to feel good!"

"Morbid." Harry stood up straighter, gave himself a shake. "All of this, morbid. Keep it up and we're defeated before we even begin. There must be at least a chance we'll win. Indeed, there's more than a chance. Can they disappear at will as we can, like ghosts into the Möbius Continuum?"

"No, but . . ."

"But?"

"Wherever we go," she said, "and however many times we escape, we'll always have to return. We can't stay in that place forever." Her logic was unassailable. Before Harry could find words to answer—perhaps to comfort her or himself—she continued, "And Shaithis is a terrible foe. How devious"—she shook her head—"you could scarcely imagine."

True, a voice came startlingly from nowhere, entering the minds of both of them. *Shaithis is devious. But his ancestor, Shaitan the Fallen, is worse far.*

"The Dweller!" Karen gasped as she recognized their telepathic visitor. And then, incredulously, "But did you day . . . Shaitan?"

The Fallen One, aye, the wolf-voice rasped in their minds. *He lives, he comes, and* he, *not Shaithis, is the terror.*

Harry and Karen reached out with their own telepathy, tried to strengthen the mind-bridge between themselves and their visitor. And for a moment the aerie was filled with flowing mental pictures:

Of mountain slopes where domed boulders projected through sliding scree; of a full moon lending the crags a soft yellow mantle; of great firs standing tall. And in the shadow of the trees, silver triangle eyes blinking—a good many—where the pack rested before the hunt. Then the pictures faded and were gone, and likewise the one who lived with them and moved among them.

But his warning remained with Karen and the Necroscope. How he could know what he had told them . . . who could say? But he was, or had been, The Dweller. And that was enough.

Time passed.

Sometimes they talked and at others they simply

waited. There was nothing else to do. This time, seated before a fire in the aerie's massive great hall, they talked:

"Shaitan is part of my world's legends, too," said Harry. "There they call him Satan, the Devil, whose place is in hell."

"In Starside's histories your world *was* hell!" Karen answered. "And all of its dwellers were devils. Dramal Doombody believed it firmly."

Harry shook his head. "That the Wamphyri—monstrous as they were, and still are—should hold with beliefs in demons, devils, and such," (again the shake of his head), "it's hard to understand."

She shrugged. "How so? Isn't hell simply the Unknown, any terrible place or region of which nothing is understood? To the Traveller tribes it lay across the mountains in Starside, while to the Wamphyri it waited on the other side of the sphere-Gate. Certainly, it must be horrible and lethal beyond that Gate, for no one had ever returned to tell of it. That was how the Wamphyri saw it. I saw it that way, too, in the days before Zek and Jazz, you and your son. And don't forget, Harry, even the Wamphyri were once men. However monstrous a man may grow, still he'll remember the night fears of his childhood."

"Shaitan," Harry mused. "A mystery spanning two worlds. The legend was taken into my world by banished Wamphyri Lords and occasionally their Traveller retainers when they were sent through Starside's Gate." But in his own mind: *Oh, really? Or is the so-called legend more properly universal? The Great Evil, the Lord of Lies, of all wickedness? What of the similarity in the names . . . ? Satan, Shaitan? Are there devils in all the universes of light? And what of angels?*

"Better stop thinking of him as a legend," Karen warned, as if she'd been listening to his thoughts, which she had not. "The Dweller says he's real and coming here, which means that in order to live we have to kill him. Except, if Shaitan has already lived for—how long? two, three thousand years?—is it even reasonable to believe that we *can* kill him?"

Harry had scarcely heard her. He was still working things out. "How many of them?" he finally asked.

"Shaitan will be their leader, and Shaithis with him. But who else?"

"Survivors from the battle at the garden," Karen answered. "If they also survived the Icelands."

"I remember," Harry said. "We've considered them before: Fess Ferenc, Volse Pinescu, Arkis Leperson, and their thralls. No more than a handful. Or, if others of the Old Lords survived the ordeal of exile, a large handful." He drew himself up. "But I'm still the Necroscope. And again I say: can they come and go through the Möbius Continuum? Can they call up the dead out of their graves?" (And once more, to himself: *Can you, Harry? Can you?*)

"Shaitan may have the art," she answered. "For after all, he was the first of the Wamphyri. Since when, he's had time enough for studying. It's possible he can torment the dead for their secrets."

"But will they answer him?" Harry growled, his eyes glowing like rubies in the firelight. "No, no, I didn't mean necromancy but Necroscopy! A necromancer may 'examine' a corpse or even a long-dead mummy, but I talk to the very spirits of the dead. And they love me; indeed, they'll rise up from their dust for me . . ." *A lie. You even lie to yourself now. You are Wamphyri, Harry Keogh! Call up the dead? Ah, you used to, you used to.*

He started to his feet: "I have to try," and went down to Starside's foothills under the garden, where long ago he called up an army of mummied trogs to do battle with Wamphyri trogs. He talked to their spirits in his fashion, but only the wind out of the north answered him. He sensed that they were there and heard him, but they kept silent. They were at peace now; why should they join the Necroscope in his turmoil?

He went up into the garden. There were graves—far too many of them—but untended now: Travellers who died in the great battle, Trogs laid to rest in niches under the crags. They heard him, too, and remembered him well. But they felt something different in him which wasn't to their liking. Ah, Wamphyri! Necromancer! This man, or monster, had words which could call them to a horrid semblance of life even against their will.

"And I might!" he threatened, sensing their refusal, their terror. But from within: *What, like Janos Ferenczy? What price now your "humanity," Harry?*

He went back to the aerie, to Karen, and told her bleakly, "Once . . . I could have commanded an army of the dead. Now there are just the two of us."

Three. The Dweller's growl was in their minds, but clear as if he stood beside them. *You fought for me once. Both of you, for my cause. My turn now.*

That seemed to decide it, to state their case, set their course. Even though it was the only course they'd ever had.

Karen fetched her gauntlet and dipped it in a cleansing acid solution, then set to oiling its joints. "Me," she said, "I tore the living heart out of Lesk the Glut! Aye, and there was a lot more to fear in those days. And it dawns on me: I'm not afraid for myself but for the loss of what we have. Except that when you look at it, well, what *do* we have, after all?"

Harry jumped up, strode to and fro shaking his fists and raging inside and out. And then grew deadly calm.

It was his vampire, of course, still seeking ascendancy. He nodded knowingly and grunted, "Well, and maybe I've kept you down long enough. Perhaps it's time I let you out."

"What?" Karen looked up from working on her gauntlet.

"Nothing."

"Nothing?" She arched her eyebrows.

"I only asked . . . where shall it be?"

The garden, said The Dweller, far away in the mountains.

They heard him, and Karen agreed. "Aye, the garden has its merits. We know it well, anyway."

Finally, with a furious nod, the Necroscope surrendered to his vampire. In part, at least. "Very well," he snarled, "the garden. So *be* it!"

And so it would be.

In Starside . . .

It was the hour when all that remains of the furnace sun is a smudgy grey luminosity in a sky gnawed by jutting fangs of mountain, and the nameless stars are chunks of alien ice freezing in weird orbits. The deepest, darkest hour of sundown, and the last of the Wamphyri—Shaithis and Shaitan, Harry Keogh and Karen—were coming together to do battle in an empty place once called the garden. All four of them the last of their race, and The Dweller, too; except he was no longer Wamphyri as such, or if he was, even his vampire scarcely knew it.

Karen had known for some time now that the invaders were close and closing on Starside, ever since her creatures out on the rim of the rimy ocean called to her one last time to pass on that information—before they died. And *as* they died, so Karen had asked them: *How many are the enemy, and what are their shapes?* It was easier far to gauge strength and substance that way than from complicated descriptions; the distance was great, and the brains of warriors are never too large (unwise to invest such masses of menace with other than the most rudimentary intelligence). Nevertheless, vague pictures of flyers, warriors, and controlling beings had come back pain-etched out of the north, showing Karen how small was the army of Shaitan.

It consisted only of a pair of controlling Lords, who rode upon massive flyers with scale-plated heads and underbellies, and a half dozen warriors of generally unorthodox construction. Unorthodox, aye . . . to say the least. For the invaders (who could only be Shaithis and Shaitan the Fallen, though Karen held back from any kind of direct contact with *their* minds) had apparently seen fit to break all the olden rules of the Wamphyri in the fashioning of *these* beasts. For one they had organs of generation, much like Karen's constructs, and for another they seemed to act much of their own accord, without the guidance of their supposed controllers. Lastly, one of them was a monster even among monsters! So much so that Karen didn't even care to dwell upon it.

At first (she was informed) there had been an extra pair of flyers, weary beasts whose riders landed them in deep drifts close to the edge of the ocean. Alighting, the Wamphyri Lords had then called down their warriors and fresh flyers out of the sky, allowing them to fuel themselves on the exhausted bodies of these first mounts. And while they were busy with their food, that was when Karen's guardian creatures had attacked . . . only to discover the overwhelming ferocity and superiority of Shaitan's warriors. That was the message which the last of Karen's beasts conveyed to her, before its feeble mind-sendings were swamped by dull pain and quickly extinguished.

Harry had been asleep at that time, racked by nightmares. Karen had watched him tossing and turning, and listened to him mouthing of: "the cone-shaped universes of light," and of Möbius, a wizard he'd known in the hell-lands: "a mathematician who got religion; a madman who believes God is an equation . . . which is more or less what Pythagoras believed, but centuries before him!" And of the Möbius Continuum, that fabulous, fathomless place where he'd made metamorphic love to her, and which he now considered: "an infinite brain controlling the bodies of universes, in which simple beings such as myself are mere synapses conveying thoughts and intentions, and perhaps carrying out . . . some One's will?"

By then the Necroscope's dream had been a feverish thing, full of thoughts, conversations, and associations out of his past, even past dreams, all tangled in a kaleidoscope of the real and surreal, where his life from its onset was observed to have been metamorphic as his flesh in the way it had burst open to sprout weird discoveries and concepts. The dream contained—even as a dying man's last breath is said to contain—crucial elements of that entire life, but concertinaed into a single vision of mere moments.

When the cold sweat started out on his grey brow, Karen might have gentled him awake; except his words fascinated her; and anyway, he needed to sleep, in order to be strong for the coming battle. Perhaps he would settle down again when the nightmare was past. And so she sat by him while he sweated and raved of things quite beyond her conception:

About time's relativity and all history, that of the future as well as the past, being contemporary but occurring in some strange "elsewhere"; and about the dead—the real dead, not the undead—waiting patiently in their graves for a new beginning, *their* second coming; and about a great light, the Primal Light, "which is the ongoing, unending Bigger Bang as all the universes expand forever out of darkness!" He mumbled about numbers with the power to separate space and time, and of a metaphysical equation, "whose only justification is to extend Mind beyond the span of the merely physical."

On one level, it was the subconscious whirlpool of Harry's instinctive mathematical genius enhanced by his now ascendant vampire; while on a higher plane it was a violent confrontation between two entirely elemental powers: Darkness and Light, Good and Evil, Knowledge for its own sake (which is sin), and the total absence of knowledge, which is innocence. It was the Necroscope's subconscious battle with himself, within himself, which must be fought and won lest the final darkness fall; for Harry *himself* would be the bright guardian of worlds still to come, or their utter destruction before they were even born.

But Karen didn't know any of that, only that she mustn't wake him just yet. And Harry fevered on:

"I could give you formulae you haven't even dreamed of . . . " he sneered out of some all but forgotten past time, while the lights of his eyes burned scarlet through lowered, frantically fluttering lids. "An eye for an eye, Dragosani, and a tooth for a tooth! I was Harry Keogh . . . became my own son's sixth sense, before Alec Kyle's emptied head sucked me in and made his body mine . . . The great liar Faethor would have lived in there with me, but where's Faethor now, eh? And where's Thibor? And what of the Bodescu brat? And Janos?" Suddenly, he sobbed and great tears squeezed themselves out from under his luminous eyelids.

"And Brenda? Sandra? Penny? Am I cursed or blessed . . . ?

"I had a million friends, which would be fine except they were all dead! They 'lived' in a dimension beyond life, where I could still talk to them and they could still remember what it was to have been alive.

"There are many dimensions, planes of existence without number, worlds without end. The myriad cone-shaped universes of light. And I know how they came about. And Möbius knew it before me. Pythagoras might have guessed something of it, but Möbius and I *know!*

"Let there be . . ." (He screwed up his tightly closed eyes.) "*Let* there be . . ." (Great slugs of sweat oozed out of his shuddering lead-grey body.) "Let there *be* . . ."

Until Karen could stand his pain—for this could only be pain—no longer. And clutching him where he writhed upon her bed, she begged him: "Let there be what, Harry?"

"Light!" he growled, and his furious eyes shot open, aglow with their own heat.

"Light?" she repeated him, her voice full of wonder.

He struggled to sit up, gave in, and let himself sink down into her arms. And he looked at her, nodded, and said, "Yes, the Primal Light, which shone out of His mind."

Harry's eyes had always been weird, even before his vampire stained them with blood, but now they were changing from moment to moment. Karen saw the fury go out of them, then the fear, and watched fascinated as all alien vitality—even the very *passion* of the Wamphyri—died in them. For with only one exception the Necroscope was the first of his sort to know and believe.

"His mind?" Karen repeated him at last, wondering at the softness of his face, which was that of a child.

"The mind of . . . God?" Even now Harry couldn't

be absolutely certain. But near enough. "Of *a* God, anyway," he finally told her, smiling. "A creator!"

And inside him, instinctively aware of looming defeat, his vampire shrank down and was small, and perhaps bemoaned its fate: to be one with a man who only desired to be . . . a man.

VI: Sky Fight!

FROM THEN ON THE NECROSCOPE HAD BEEN DIFFERENT; his parasite's ascendancy had been reversed; once again his humanity had the upper hand. Karen to the contrary: she tried to insist that he accompany her on raids into Sunside to "blood" himself. Naturally, he would hear nothing of it, and she would be furious.

"But you're not blooded!" she'd growl at him as they made love. "There's a frenzy in the Wamphyri which only blood will release, for the blood is the life! Unless you take, you may not *par*take in your fullness. You must fuel yourself for the fight, can't you see that? How may I explain?"

But in fact there was no need for explanations; Harry knew well enough what she meant. He'd seen it in his own world. In boxers, the moment they draw blood: how the first sight and smell of it inspires them to greater effort, so that they go at their opponents with even more determination, and always hammering away at the same wet, red-gleaming spot. He'd seen it in cats large and small: the first splash of mouse blood which turns a kitten to a hunter, or drives the hunter to a frenzy. And as for sharks: nothing else in all the unexplored span of their lives has half so much meaning for them!

But: "I've eaten well," he would answer.

And: *Hah!* he would hear her mental snort of derision. "Of what? The flesh of pigs, and roasted? What's that for fuel?"

"It fuels me well enough."

"And your vampire not at all!"

"Then let the bastard *starve!*" But he would never allow himself the luxury of greater anger than that.

Sometimes, he would try to explain:

"What's coming is coming," he told her. "Didn't we see it in the Möbius Continuum, in future time? Of all the lessons of my life, Karen, this is the one I've learned the best: never to try to change or avoid what's written in the future, for it *is* written. All we can hope for is a better understanding of the writing, that's all."

Again her snort: *Hah!* And bitterly, "And now who is beaten, even before the fight?"

"Do you think I don't feel tempted?" he said then. "Oh, I do, believe me! But I've fought this thing inside me for such a long time now that I can't just let it win, no matter the cost. If I succumbed to rage and lust— went out and took the life of a man, and drained his blood—what then? Would it give me the strength I need to destroy Shaithis and Shaitan? Perhaps, but who would be next after them? How long before I started the Wamphyri cycle all over again, but strong this time as never before, with all the powers of a Necroscope to play with? And with my vampire's bloodlust raging, what then? Do you think I wouldn't begin to look for a way back into my own world, to return there as the greatest plague-bearer of all time?''

''Perhaps you'd be a king, there,'' she answered. ''With me to share your bone-throne.''

He nodded, but wryly. ''The Red King, aye, and eventually Emperor of a scarlet dynasty. And all of our undead lieutenants—our bloodsons, and those who got our vampire eggs, and *their* sons and daughters—all of them pouring their pus on a crumbling Mankind, building their aeries and carving kingdoms of their own; as Janos would have done from his Mediterranean island, and Thibor the warlord after he'd turned Wallachia red, or Faethor on his blood-crazed crusades. And all of our progeny Necroscopes in their own right, with neither the living nor the dead safe from them. Hell-lands? *Now* you're talking, Karen!''

Following which he wouldn't even listen to her. But even if he had it would have been too late.

For that was when Karen's *other* watchers, great *Desmodus* bats from the aerie's colony, brought news of the arrival on Starside's far northern borders of Shaitan and his small but deadly aerial forces. Inaudible except to Karen and to others of their own genus, the cries of the great vampires relayed the message back across seven hundred miles of barren boulder plains: the fact that after four years of peace, the Old Wamphyri were finally returning to Starside.

She was bringing mewling warriors out of their vats when the warning arrived, and went straight to Harry where he stood wrapped in his thoughts on a balcony facing north. ''Stand there long enough, Necroscope,'' she told him, ''and you'll be able to wave them a welcome! Nor will you have to wait too long.''

He barely glanced at her, acknowledged her presence with a nod. ''I know they're here,'' he said. ''I've felt them coming like maggots chewing on the ends of my nerves. They're not so many, but they shake the ether like an army shakes the earth. It's time we went to the garden.''

''You go,'' she told him, touching his arm as some of the sting went out of her voice. ''See if you can call down your son out of the hills. Maybe he'll bring the grey brotherhood with him, though what good they'll be is hard to say. But me, I've a trio of warriors to wean and instruct. They're built of fine, fierce stuff, right enough—good stuff, left behind by Menor Maimbite and Lesk the Glut, which I found intact under the ruins of their stacks—but when it comes to the fashioning . . . well, it's true I'm a novice compared to them.''

''Just make sure they'll own me as their master as well as yourself,'' was Harry's reply. ''That way, even if they haven't the measure of Shaitan's creatures, still I might be able to come up with a trick or two.''

Then he turned and caught her up so swiftly in his arms that she gasped aloud. And:

''Karen,'' he said, ''we've seen our futures: the red threads of our lives melting into golden fire, then fading to nothing. It didn't look too good for us, but at the same time it could mean anything. We simply don't understand it. And in any case, whatever it means, it has to be better than what we saw of our enemies' futures; for they didn't have any! No scarlet threads in Starside's tomorrows, Karen.''

''I remember,'' she said, without freeing herself, pressing more firmly to him. ''And so I stay and fight. Whatever becomes of us, it's worth it to know that they die, too.''

Harry held her very close, very tightly, and his looks were even more those of a small boy. He found himself wishing it were all a fantastic dream, and that he'd wake up a schoolboy with all of his future ahead of him, but retaining enough of the dream that he'd make no false moves. Ah, if only things worked that way! "I wish I'd known you as some ordinary girl in my own world, when I was just a man," he told her on impulse.

Karen wasn't so romantic. She had been an innocent in her time, until she was stolen. Now and then a blushing Traveller youth had wanted her, but in those days she'd kept herself (as she'd thought) for something better. *Hah!* Her answer was harsh. "We would be fumbling, giggling lovers for an hour. To hell with it . . . I prefer what we've had! Anyway, you are the Necroscope. What do you know of ordinary men?"

The fire in her was a catalyst; it burned outwards through her shell to illuminate her as she really was: Wamphyri! Harry *could* be like her, yes, but did he *need* to be? He'd gone up against Dragosani, Thibor, Yulian Bodescu, and all the others as a man, albeit a man with powers. No, never an ordinary man, but neither had he been a monster. And now there were others to set himself against. But again, as a man, or as nearly as possible.

He released her. "Is there a flyer ready?"

"In the launching bay, yes. But won't you use the Möbius route?"

He shook his head. "My son and his grey brothers wouldn't see me. He might know, in his way, and he might not. Riding a flyer I'll be visible, a curiosity. Not many flyers in Starside's skies these days."

At the launching bay, watching him take off in the saddle of the pulsing manta-shape which was his flyer, she saw that he was right: other than himself, the skies were empty. For now.

Feeling empty herself, Karen went back to her warriors . . .

* * *

Harry and Karen were together in the garden's desolation when Shaithis and Shaitan the Fallen came back into the old Wamphyri heartland. But contrary to expectations the invaders did not launch an immediate attack; instead they came gliding and squirting out of dark, aurora-flickering northern skies, and oh so warily circled the debris-littered plains where the tumbled stacks of extinct vampire Lords lay in shattered ruin. Eventually, ever cautious, they landed in the bays of Karen's aerie and explored its empty levels, finding nothing inimical, no hidden pitfalls, no hostile creatures waiting in the shadows. But neither did they find gas-beasts, siphoneers, servitors in any shape or form. No comforts whatsoever, except perhaps in the strength of the aerie's ancient walls. And even these weren't secure enough for Shaithis.

"I was witness to the destruction of greater stacks than this one," he told Shaitan. "My own included!"

"Two of them." The other chuckled, nodding his great black cowl. "It took both Harry Keogh *and* The Dweller to control the power of the sun that time. Can't you see that? But there is no more Dweller—he's gone, shriveled to a wolf. And as for his father: why, on his own this pale unblooded alien is less than a puling child!"

"Then why don't we attack, and without delay?"

"We do, but not until we've fueled our beasts and filled our own bellies. Then, after we've rested our bones a little—and perhaps seen to other needs too long denied—that will be soon enough. For we've come a long, cold, weary way, Shaithis; and not merely to dispose of this hated enemy of yours, or to let you sate yourself on the flesh of a female who spurned and betrayed you. So calm yourself and be patient, and everything you most desire shall be."

But for all Shaitan's apparent confidence, deep in his black heart he too was concerned about their opponent, the so-called hell-lander Harry Keogh, a vampire who had not yet tasted the blood of other men. Unknown to Shaithis, the great leech which was his ancestor had already employed his own superior, infinitely furtive vampire powers in a remote, partial examination of the Necroscope. Shaitan's telepathy was more advanced even than Karen's and Harry's (indeed, his was the maggot which had gnawed on Harry's nerve endings); even so, what probes he'd attempted had been perfunctory. The reason was simple: only penetrate the outermost shell of the Necroscope's psychic aura—come within miles of the core of light, the unplumbed, emerging Center of Power which he must never be allowed to become—and any sensitive being would feel it for himself. (As Shaithis might if he weren't such a dullard; but such a beautiful dullard, and all wasted . . . for now, anyway.) That pent *energy* which was so much greater than that of a mere man, possibly greater even than that of certain vampires.

But energy of what, from where? These were the questions which caused Shaitan's concern; for until he knew what Harry Keogh was, or what he might become, he couldn't really be sure how to deal with him.

Far easier, when the time was right, to deal with Shaithis the self-considered Devious—Shaithis the very beautiful, very dull, would-be Great Traitor—who would soon prove himself to be Shaithis the Great Fool. That same Shaithis who kept such a tight guard on his mind, lest its vile and treacherous thoughts fly free. Except Shaitan had long ago made himself privy to all of his descendant's thoughts, which were secret no longer!

But imprudent to fuss over all of that now; time enough when Starside's weird, alien defender was dead or otherwise disposed of. Or perhaps earlier, but only if Shaithis himself should bring it to a head.

These were Shaitan's thoughts, but all kept hidden from Shaithis, of course . . .

They left a lone warrior guarding the aerie and took the rest with them into Sunside, where soon they spied the fires of a Traveller settlement. Then for a little while the night air was filled with the screams of men, the bellowing of warriors and the sounds of their gluttony; also with the hot reek of the freshly dead, and with the shrieks of those taken alive. Of the latter: there were six, and they were all women.

Later . . . the higher windows of Karen's aerie came flickering alive with the ruddy light of fires; smoke went up from the chimneys; it was as if a great and merry party took place there. For vampires so long denied it was merry, anyway.

What battered, broken tidbits were left when Shaithis and Shaitan were done went to the warriors for sweet-meats. A small mercy that nothing of that ravaged flesh still lived . . .

In the garden, Harry and Karen slept.

The Necroscope still reckoned time in days and nights. As yet, when his mind told his body it was night, his body's response was to sleep. But in any case his weariness would be as much mental as physical, for he knew that in any battle to come he would be fighting himself no less than the enemy. The problem, which always chased itself in circles until he grew tired, never changed: how to win without calling on his vampire for its assistance, without giving it full rein over the range of its powers? For to allow his leech total ascendancy would be to signal his own submission, following which he'd no longer be his own man but Wamphyri in every sense of the word.

Karen had no such problem: she already *was* Wamphyri! But before that she'd been woman, and the Necroscope was her man. When he slept, so did she, curled in his arms. They were not totally unprepared, however: they were clothed, and Karen's gauntlet lay close to hand. And not unmindful of their position, they'd set a watch. A warrior grunted a little, shifting its hugely armored bulk for comfort where it had been positioned in the shadows beyond the crest of the saddle; likewise Karen's second beast, forward in the lee of the wall where the ground fell steeply away to Starside's foothills and the plain beyond. As for the third creature: it was situated at a higher elevation, on a ledge under an overhang in the western crags, where its many night-oriented eyes peered far out across the boulder plains, searching the skies and starlit wastes for any unwarranted movement.

But unknown to the sleepers, there was a fourth, far less conspicuous watcher. Once known as The Dweller, now he was a lean grey shape who kept himself apart, observing the unkempt garden from the cover of the ragged tree line. Sometimes, in a flash of memory, he would understand why he had come here, but at others he wasn't quite sure. Anyway, here he was.

And it was his snarled mind-call—together with a sudden bellowing and screaming of embattled beasts—which startled the Necroscope and his Lady awake when at last the invaders struck. And for all their precautions, still they were taken by surprise, for the enemy didn't strike out of Starside at all but from Sunside over the mountains, where it was still sundown!

The invaders had departed Karen's aerie in full force, crossed the peaks far to the east where there was no one to observe them, and turned west in the lee of the mountains. Under cover of the great barrier range, their Sunside flight path had followed the spine of the crags to the latitude of the garden, where, rising up over the peaks to look down on the territory of the defenders, they'd carefully noted the locations of the warriors and the fact that nothing else was stirring. Then their probes had discovered Karen's sleeping mind. As for the Necroscope's mind: even asleep it had been shielded and impenetrable. And dreaming.

Harry dreamed that he sped down Starside's future time-stream; his eyes were full of the dazzle of blue, green, and red lines of life, and his ears seemed tuned to the unending *Ahhhhhhhh!* monotone of life's expansion into all of the tomorrows of all the Universes of Light. Last time he had been with Karen, but this time he was alone, paying more attention to his surroundings, and aware of the convergence of scarlet vampire threads upon his own. And just when it seemed they must fuse together in some weird temporal collision, that was the point at which Möbius time turned golden in that furious melting pot which terminated . . . everything?

Maybe not.

But that was when his dream terminated, and Harry sprang awake in the ruined Traveller dwelling which he and Karen had made their headquarters. And Karen, too, waking up in his arms.

"The warriors!" she gasped, expanding her hand to thrust it into the coarse-lined matrix of her gauntlet.

"I'll see," Harry answered, already on his feet and conjuring a Möbius door, which coincided with the door frame of the stone-fashioned dwelling. And as he stepped through both, so he glanced at the sky. Up there, flyers! He saw them in the moment before the Möbius Continuum enveloped him: vast manta-shapes pulsing on high, from whose saddles Wamphyri riders directed the attack of their warriors. But apart from warriors already landed and joined in battle with Karen's creatures, there were several still airborne, squirting across the stars like aerial octopi, their vanes extended and propulsion orifices blasting. Three of them in a protective triangle formation around their controllers, but how many were already down?

Harry emerged from the Continuum at the back of the saddle. Karen's guardian warrior was under attack from two lesser but incredibly ferocious beasts; one was underneath, pincers and sickles working to disembowel, while the other rode its back, biting a way through to the spine. Even metamorphic flesh must soon succumb to this!

Disengage, the Necroscope ordered. *Get aloft if you can. Harass the enemy in the sky.* In order to address the warrior, he had opened his mind. Karen was in at once:

I've launched the warrior from the ledge in the crags, she immediately informed. *He's fast and fierce. If you can get that one airborne . . . Shaithis and Shaitan may well be disadvantaged. Their flyers are unconventional, heavily armored, but still no match for warriors. Maybe we can knock the bastards out of the sky!*

But now, in close proximity with the enemy, their thoughts were no longer private. *Ho, Karen!* Shaithis called down gleefully from on high. *Ever treacherous, eh? Why, I do believe you'd damn me with your last breath. And so you shall, for I shall see to it!* And to Harry, growlingly, *As for you, hell-lander: ah, but I remember you well enow! For I had an aerie, upon a time—till you and your Dweller son reduced it to so much rubble. But where's your son now, eh? A great wolf, I hear, siring pups by the light of the moon. Oh? Ha, ha, ha! And what bitch did you get him out of, eh?*

Harry heard Shaithis's sneering clearly enough; also Shaitan's abrupt interruption, which oozed in his mind like mental slime: *Taunting serves no purpose. Kill him, by all means, when the time is right—but until then let it be.*

The Necroscope's vampire raged; it wanted its way; its demands on Harry were mental as well as physical, so that he could almost hear it screaming: "Give *me* the right! Let *me* smite them! Only give your mind and body to me, and in my turn I'll give you . . . everything!" But Harry knew it was a lie and that in fact his parasite would *take* everything.

He heard a buffeting of air, adopted a defensive crouch, and glanced aloft. Karen was already airborne; Harry's flyer, which she had sent, made a tight turn and descended towards him. As the creature's fifty-foot span of membranous manta wing, spongy flesh, cartilage, and alveolate bone swooped low overhead, Harry leaped and snatched at the harness fittings under its neck. Another moment and he was hauling himself into the saddle. And on the ground the beleaguered warrior threw off its attackers and squirted aloft.

Good! Harry told it. *Now get up there with your ugly twin and help him tear those enemy flyers out of the sky.*

Let's all assist them, came Karen's mind-call, as her beast commenced climbing a spiraling wind off Starside to where the invaders seemed to sit among the stars.

And rising up towards the armored flyers of Shaithis and Shaitan within their arrowhead formation of hissing, throbbing warriors, Harry queried: *Where's our warrior number three?*

Dead on the ground, Necroscope, Karen answered grimly. *Crushed by the most terrible construct I ever saw. In the old days, even to conceive of such a beast would have meant automatic banishment. The old rule was simple: never bring to being anything which might prove difficult to put down. For even the feeblest brain will eventually learn tricks of its own. As for these things which Shaithis and Shaitan have devised—especially that one—why, can't you feel their evil intelligence? They are abominations!*

Harry looked all around in the sky, finally glanced down through a thousand feet of dark, empty air and saw what followed on behind. And: *I see what you mean*, he said.

What he saw was this:

Rising alongside Karen and himself, in the same section of the spiral, the warrior he had ordered aloft dripped fluids from an underbelly whose scaly armor had been breached. Plasma gouts gleamed red as a ruby necklace where metamorphic tissues were already at work healing deep neck wounds. For the present the warrior's propulsors blasted as before, but Harry fancied he could detect a sputtering even now.

A little higher than he and Karen and climbing that much faster, the unscathed warrior she'd launched from the crags vented propulsive gases in a fury. It snorted like a dragon where it made an all too obvious beeline for the alien flyers and their riders overhead. Responding like monstrous automata to the threat, the trio of escorting warriors turned inwards and began to converge, lost a little height, then fell like stones with their vanes angling them towards their target.

All of this registered in a moment: the fact that here in the middle air and overhead, Karen and the Necroscope were already gravely outnumbered. As for the situation below, that was worse. The enemy warriors which had given Karen's creature a mauling at the back of the garden had launched themselves into the same updraft and were gaining; and coming up even faster behind them was that destroyer of her third creature, which she'd described as the most terrible warrior she ever saw. No expert in such things, still Harry had to agree.

It had squid-like lines . . . which was where any comparison with creatures of previous knowledge must break down. Gigantic, it was flesh and blood, cartilage and bone, but it had the look and grey mottling of some weird flexible metal. Clusters of gas bladders like strange wattles bulked out its throbbing body and detracted from its maneuverability, but were necessary to carry the extra weight of its arms and armor. These were not additional to the warrior but integral; like a great thunder lizard of primal Earth, its weaponry was all built-in. Except Nature in her wildest dreams had never equipped anything like this. No, for this thing was of Shaithis's fashioning.

Well, Necroscope? Karen's telepathic voice was suddenly shrill with alarm.

Running for it will simply delay things, he answered.

So? Panic was rising in her like the wind off Starside.

So let's give it our best shot right here and now!

Overhead, a deadly arrowhead formation stooped on Karen's warrior like hawks to a pigeon. Harry ordered his flyer, *Stay with your mistress,* then rolled from his saddle through a hastily conjured Möbius door . . . and emerged in the next moment onto the scaled back of Karen's warrior, where he could almost taste the hot stench of the incoming warriors. That close!

Sideslip! he ordered his startled mount. And conjuring a massive door, he guided the monster through it. The enemy trio slammed together in a snarling knot where Harry had been, but now he came squirting out of the Möbius Continuum far above them—on a level with the armored flyers of Shaithis and Shaitan! Even as his eyes met theirs across the gulf of air, so he picked up something of Shaithis's telepathic ranting:

You and your damned magic, you ordure of the helllands!

Harry was distracted; he'd looked into the scarlet eyes

561

of Shaitan, too, and the Fallen One had looked burningly into his. No hatred in the mind of that great leech, no, not for the Necroscope; only an intense curiosity. *Save your curses,* he told Shaithis. *For this one might yet do us great harm. Then you'll have real reason to curse him.* And Harry heard that, too.

Down below, the trio of confused warriors had untangled themselves; their propulsors roared as they commenced climbing again. *Two of you,* Shaithis called to them. *To me, and hurry!* But to the third warrior: *Get after the woman. You know what to do . . .*

Slimy bastard thing! Harry hurled the thought at Shaithis before realizing it was no great insult. He looked for Karen's flyer and saw it turn out of the rising spiral to follow the mountains east. A pair of warriors—one of which was her own wounded creature—spurted in her wake; they clashed sporadically, fiercely in the sky. Karen's warrior was getting the worst of it, but her flyer was gaining time and distance. For the moment Harry seemed to have lost the giant warrior.

Chancing that Karen was in no immediate danger, he clung to the scales of his monstrous mount and sent it spurting head-on at his enemies. They turned tail and sped out over Starside's plain of boulders, heading roughly towards the broken aeries of the Wamphyri. Now it became apparent that the flyers had the advantage of speed in level flight; seeing that he couldn't hope to catch them this way, Harry conjured a door and guided his warrior through it—

—And emerged directly above the flyers where they streamlined themselves and winged east. Shaithis heard the warrior's howling propulsors, felt its shadow on his back, and looked up. The Necroscope's grin was scarlet, furious, as he slammed his mount down on Shaithis's flyer and tried to crush him in his saddle. His target at once hurled himself flat in the hollow of his mount's shoulders. Harry's warrior extended grapples, pincers, retractable jaws, began cutting the flyer to pieces in mid-air; its razor-sharp appendages came dangerously close to Shaithis where he squirmed for his life. Dripping the blood of its torn victim, Harry's warrior lifted up a little, again dashed all of its bulk down on the flyer. And slipping from his saddle to hang from its trappings in the scarlet rain, Shaithis knew his beast was a goner.

Shaitan! he cried out where he dangled.

The great leech flew slightly below and to one side. *Jump!* he advised, passing directly underneath. Shaithis made to leap for his ancestor's flyer . . . was thrown off course as for the third time Harry's warrior crashed down onto his mount's back, breaking it. And tumbling past Shaitan, Shaithis found himself in free-fall.

It was a while since Shaithis had flown in his own right, but he was in fine fettle and had more than sufficient height. His loose clothes ripped as he flattened himself into a prehistoric, pterodactyl airfoil, and gradually his plummet slowed to a glide. Far to the east he spied a glowing beacon down on the boulder plain and knew it for the Gate to the hell-lands. It made a good marker and he aimed himself in that direction.

The Necroscope had lost him. A dark speck in a darker sky, Shaithis had vanished. But Shaitan remained to be dealt with. Meanwhile, that immemorial father of vampires had drawn ahead; Harry could cover the same distance in the time it took to conjure an equation. He made to do so . . . and his warrior was hit from behind! The shock almost tore him loose from the plates of his mount's back. Behind him, that most monstrous warrior of all gripped his creature in crab claws and tore out great chunks of meat from the musculature of its sputtering propulsive vents. Shaitan's other creatures stayed

563

well back to let their far more monstrous cousin get on with its work.

In the last few seconds Karen had linked minds with Harry. She saw his problems and he saw hers: the lesser warrior which Shaithis had sent after her had dispatched her fighting creature and was now closing on her flyer. To Karen, it all seemed ended. *Necroscope, it's over!* she sent. *My mount's a weakling, already winded. There's only myself to blame, for I designed him. I'd head for the furnace lands and a golden death in the rising sun, but doubt if we'd make it. Well, at least I'll go out honorably: a gauntlet against a warrior!*

Riding Karen's last creature where its mewling, slavering attacker shredded its way to him, the Necroscope looked out through Karen's eyes:

Her flyer heaved and panted where she drove it south for the great pass, for already its altitude was insufficient to carry it over the peaks. But spurting down on her from above and behind came that monster which Shaithis had ordered: *Get after the woman. You know what to do!* And directly down below, close to where the gash of the great pass split the mountains . . . that glaring light? Starside's Gate, of course; Harry would have known it at once, except this aerial view was new to him. In the next moment, turning that view red, the torn carcass of Karen's defeated warrior crashed down and burst into pieces.

And its destroyer was falling on Karen ever faster.

Harry tumbled from his doomed creature's back through a Möbius door, stepped out into the foothills rising up from Starside's portal. The Gate was a fault in the matter of the multiverse, a huge distortion in the fabric of Möbius space-time; but the Necroscope was far enough away that it had little effect. He scanned the wide mouth of the pass where the enemy warrior was playing with Karen's exhausted flyer, forcing it down. A second

flyer, riderless, flapped uselessly close by: Harry's
mount, which he'd ordered to stay with its mistress. He
took the Möbius route into its saddle and called to Karen:
We're not done yet.

She heard him, but so did Shaithis. At the end of his
long, fast glide he landed close to the Gate and re-formed
into his man-shape. And seeing his warrior in the sky
where it menaced the flyers and their riders, he ordered
it: *Bring me the woman—in pieces, if that's the only way!*

The warrior's response was immediate: it crashed its
bulk down onto Karen's flyer and knocked her half out
of the saddle. And while she reeled there and tried to
recover her senses and balance both, it put out appendages with hooked claspers and snatched her up. Then,
with its propulsors roaring triumphantly, the monster
smashed down on the riderless flyer one last time to break
its neck. And as Karen's crippled beast spun and tumbled
down out of the sky into the pass, so the warrior turned
back towards the boulder plain.

Good! Shaithis applauded his beast. *Bring her to me.*

Harry sent his mount plummeting from on high directly into the path of the warrior; ignoring him, the
thing came straight on. He sent: *Release her to me,* directly into its small brain.

Do not! its rightful master countered his command.
Knock him aside . . . crush him if you can!

The monster was upon Harry. Karen, held fast in its
palps of chitin thorns—which pierced her flesh, holding
her like a fish on a hundred hooks—could only scream
as its neck arched to strike at him; while jaws like a
small cave, more lethally equipped than the mouth of
Tyrannosaurus rex, opened to sweep him up.

What happened next was all instinct. It was as if Faethor Ferenczy lived in the Necroscope yet, and whispered in his ear: *When he opens his great jaws at you,*

go in through them! Harry knew he could never hope to cause this creature any real physical injury, not from the outside. But somewhere within that monstrous skull was a tiny brain; and somewhere inside himself, something was or still desired to be Wamphyri!

Go in *through them!*

Harry stood up in the saddle, stepped into the stench of the warrior's mouth as it snapped shut on him. But within that door of teeth was another conjured from his metaphysical mind. He passed through that one, too, into the Möbius Continuum . . . and out again within the warrior's head. Physically *inside* its head! Among the rude materials of its cranium, the pulsing pipes and conduits, knobs and nodules, muck and mucous membrane of its living skull!

He felt the cringing of displaced mush—the shrinking of metamorphic flesh as his body materialized to rub against raw nerve endings and wet, spongy tissues, and the throb of plasma carrying oxygen to the small, agonized brain—then reached out with tearing, taloned vampire hands to find and fondle the central ganglion itself. And to crush it into so much pulp. Then—

—Gravity disappeared as the warrior's propulsors closed down and the thing went into free-fall. And inside its head, Harry desperately sought to make room for himself and conjure a Möbius door. He needed space to work in, air to breathe; he had never before attempted a door underwater or surrounded by viscous solids—namely hot blood—but now he must. Must conjure a door; get out of here; rescue Karen from this dead thing's claw before it hit the ground.

But even as Möbius math commenced mutating on the screen of the Necroscope's mind, so he saw how alien—how inescapably *wrong*—it was! The door pulsed and vibrated but wouldn't firm into being. Instead, its energies fastened upon the region of space on the perimeter of its matrix and violently reshaped it; and common matter, displaced from its natural shape and form, flowed like magmass in the moment before the aborted door exploded into nothingness!

Shaithis saw his creature tumbling to earth and for a moment thought it must fall into the Gate. Astonished, he saw its armored head warp and melt and burst open even *before* it crashed down only a few paces from the dimensional portal! And *as* it hit, he saw something manlike—but red, yellow, and slime-grey—vomited from the shattered skull and hurled out onto the boulder plain. As the dust settled and the last gobs of slime and plasma arced down to slop among the rocks and the dirt, so he went forward.

Shielding his eyes against the glare, he stepped wonderingly among the debris of his warrior and gazed on the Lady Karen, bruised and bleeding and unconscious in the thing's claspers; and upon the broken, disjointed hell-lander Harry Keogh, as bloody a sight as the vampire Lord ever saw. But not yet dead, no, not by a long shot.

Of course not, Shaithis thought, *for he is Wamphyri! And yet . . . different, and hard to understand.*

Indeed! Shaitan agreed as he glided his flyer to earth. *And yet that is what we must do: understand him. For his mind contains all the secrets of the Gate and the worlds beyond it. So do him no more harm but let him heal himself as best he can. And when he can answer me, then I shall question him . . .*

Betrayed by his own talent when he attempted to materialize a Möbius door too close to the Gate, the Necroscope's metaphysical mind had taken the brunt of the shock. His flesh was vampiric and would repair itself in time, even the core of his damaged brain, but until then he must remain largely oblivious. And to some extent, perhaps he was lucky at that.

Karen, on the other hand, was not nearly so broken and by no means so lucky. While Shaitan concerned himself with Harry, his dark descendant's only thought was for Karen. Both of them sought knowledge; in the latter's case, carnal.

Shaitan's examination was telepathic. As Harry's mind healed and shards of splintered memory slowly cemented themselves together, so the Fallen One extracted what information was of value to him. Certain concepts were difficult; where a memory had been too complicated (or too painful) for detailed retention, Harry had kept it in outline only. For example: the underground complex at Perchorsk, which he'd always considered a dark, brooding fortress. His mental images of the Perchorsk Projekt were starkly monochrome; what memories he retained of the place—their mood and texture—were not unlike those of some menacing aerie; he shied from filling in details. Penny was the reason, of course, for even in his damaged condition Harry couldn't bring Perchorsk to mind without her intrusion.

But of Harry's life prior to Perchorsk, and of the world of men in general, Shaitan had gauged much. Sufficient to be sure that when he went through the Gate and invaded first the underground complex—disarming its defenses and making it his impregnable fortress—and then the rest of the Necroscope's world, little would stand before him. His army of vampire servitors would spread out insidiously through all the Earth, and his dark disciples would carry his plague into every part until he reigned supreme. Even as he had sought to reign in that far dim dawn which he was not permitted to remember.

And each time Shaitan thought of that, then he would

go to where Harry lay upon a Traveller blanket close to their fire, gaze on him anew, and wonder where he'd seen that vaguely familiar face before. In what far land, in what dim and unremembered time, in what previous existence?

He wondered, too, about the Necroscope's strange powers, amazing powers which he alone possessed, brought with him out of an alien world. With his own ancient but trustworthy eyes, Shaitan had seen him move instantaneously from place to place—but without crossing the distance between! Yes, he had come through the Gate from the world beyond almost as if . . . as if he had *fallen* from the one into the next. As Shaitan had once fallen? And from the same world? Possibly. Except . . . except Shaitan had forgotten; for they (but *who?*) had robbed him of all such memories.

The Necroscope's fellowmen had cast him out (even as Shaitan was cast out in that time *before* the Wamphyri exiled him), causing him to flee here for his differences. So that in a way the father of vampires even felt a weird kinship with the Necroscope. And when Harry's mind was repaired a little, Shaitan entered it again to ask him:

Do I know you? Where have I seen you before? Are you of their order, who expelled me from my rightful place?

Harry's mind was frequently coherent in its limbo; he knew he was addressed; even knew something of the one who addressed him, and the meaning of his questions. And: *No,* he answered to all three.

Shaitan tried again. *I have heard your thoughts. In them, you wonder about strange worlds beyond common ken. Not in the spaces between the stars, but in the spaces between the spaces! Indeed, you have access to just such an invisible space, where you move more surely and speedily than a fish in water. I too would move there, in the darkness which is not of the world. Show me how.*

It had been the Necroscope's best-kept secret, but damaged in mind and body, he could no longer keep it. And if he should try, the Fallen One's mental hypnosis would unlock the mystery, anyway. And so he showed Shaitan the computer screen of his mind, where Möbius equations at once commenced mounting to a crescendo. Shaitan saw, felt warned, was afraid.

Stop! he commanded, when the faintest pulse of a tortured Möbius door began to form out of nothing in his mind. And as the screen was wiped clean and the unformed door imploded into itself, so the great leech sighed his relief and was pleased to remove himself from Harry. For having felt the energies emanating from those equations and surrounding that door, he suspected that indeed he had known them before in a world beyond, where they'd been part and parcel of his downfall.

But now . . . Shaitan knew that Harry's secret place was forever beyond him, and the knowledge angered him. What, kinship? With this puling babe, this infant in dark arts, this bruised and bloodied, *un*blooded innocent? He must be mad even to have dreamed it. Anyway, what did it matter that there were forbidden, invisible places? The *visible* ones would do for starters, and one at a time would suffice. Now that Starside had fallen, the world beyond the Gate—the Necroscope's own world—would be next. And entry into that place would be soon, before sunup.

Between times . . .

Shaitan knew all he needed to know from the Necroscope; Shaithis could have him now; let the so-called hell-lander suffer a vampire's agonies and death, and him and all of his mystery go up in fire and smoke and so be at an end.

Such were the Fallen One's thoughts, which he allowed to go out from himself. But inside him there were deeper currents. Fit and well, this Harry Keogh had been a force. If he should live he could well become a force again—even a Power! Which was why Shaithis, if he had any vision at all, would be wise to deal with him with dispatch.

Aye, before Shaitan dealt with him in his turn.

From the Necroscope's point of view—or rather, to his traumatized perceptions—events revolved in an endless round of nausea and drifting confusion, semiconscious agony, and a waking hell of blurred vision, haunting flashes of incomplete memories, and vivid but all too frequently meaningless bursts of input. Sometimes, while his metamorphic flesh worked hard to heal both body and brain, his mind seemed part of a morbid merry-go-round, turning on its own axis and reviewing the same scenes over and over. At others it was trapped in the mirrors of a kaleidoscope, where each scrap of colored tinsel was a disjointed fragment of his past life or current existence.

In his more lucid moments, Harry knew that given even the best of conditions his injuries would take time in the healing; he had neither the conditions nor the time. After Shaitan gave him to Shaithis, the latter had had him crucified close to the Gate. Silver nails held him to the green timbers, and a silver spike passed through him, through his vampire and the trunk of the cross, and out the back where it was bent to one side. As fast as his Wamphyri flesh worked to repair him, so the silver poisoned him. And he guessed—no, he knew—that he wouldn't come down off this cross alive. At his feet, a bonfire of dry, broken branches confirmed it.

A second cross had been erected for Karen. Sometimes she hung there, which impaired her healing processes and kept her servile, and at others she was absent. Harry felt for her most when her cross was empty, for that was when Shaithis used and abused her. If he had the strength, the Necroscope would talk to her telepathically; except he suspected she would not let him in. No, for she would keep her torments to herself and not add to his despair. But from time to time, when Karen's cross was empty, Harry would look down on Shaithis's tent of skins and the hatred would burn in him like a fire. And then—but far too late—he would wish he'd given his vampire free rein. Perhaps mercifully, such moments of mental clarity, understanding, and remorse were few and far between.

He didn't remember the arrival of the Travellers, called through the pass by Shaithis. "Loyal" in their way to the Wamphyri, they were of a fearful, much despised supplicant tribe of gauntlet-makers. En route here from Sunside and obedient to Shaithis's commands, they'd stolen away the women and younger men from a party of less subjugated Travellers. Also, they had been employed to build the shelters of the vampire Lords, and to cut and gather the wood for fires and crosses. Little good any of this did them; Shaithis and his monstrous ancestor served all of them alike; they brutalized and impregnated the women, vampirized the pick of the men to be their thralls and lieutenants, and fed the rest to the warriors preparatory to the invasion of the Gate.

That last was something which the Necroscope *did* remember: the butchery as the last of the Travellers tried to flee, and the gluttony of the warriors. Especially he remembered how Shaithis, for his amusement, had given a Traveller woman to a warrior with the parts of a man. When it was over (and apparently aroused), Shaithis had taken Karen down from her cross and into his tent. And when *that* was over and she was nailed up again, then he had come to gloat at the foot of Harry's cross.

"I've had my fill of your bitch, wizard," he said with a shrug, as if in casual conversation. "It was even my thought to lie with her in the open and let you watch, except, as you've seen, these beasts of mine are frisky. I had no desire to give them ideas. But the next time she comes down off her cross . . . ah, that will be the last time. And while you are burning—or at least until the skin of your eyes turns black and peels away—you shall see it all. Only a shame that your own agonies must detract from your enjoyment of hers!"

Then . . . Harry's hatred had been a greater torture than the nails and the spike together, so great that he was driven back into the darkness of oblivion. But not before he had heard the Fallen One's mind-warning to his descendant:

'Ware, Shaithis! Be advised not to drive this one too far. I fancy there's that in him which even he fails to appreciate. Something beyond his control—some weird instinctive mechanism—which works through him. Don't trigger it, my son. Even the Travellers, when they hunt and kill wild pigs, are wise enough not to taunt their prey.

But in Shaithis's secret mind was nothing but scorn. He'd lived through too many auroras just dreaming of these moments of triumph. Taunt this tame pig of a Necroscope? Oh, yes! Right to the bitter end . . .

VII Fusion—Fission—Finale

THE WAMPHYRI LORDS STOLE MORE WOMEN OUT OF Sunside; with their lust and their bellies satisfied, they slept; likewise their beasts and thralls. Sunup gradually approached and the sky began to lighten over Sunside. When the first soft rains awakened them, before the sun's first deadly rays could shoot between the peaks into Starside and the north, then they would pass in through the Gate to invade the world beyond.

But while they slept:

Harry Wolfson—once Harry Jr., then The Dweller, and now the leader of the grey brotherhood—padded down from the mountains and through the foothills, and stood off in the shadows to gaze upon the forces of evil where they slept in the Gate's glare. He gazed on them, and upon the naked human figures crucified in their midst. And while the great grey wolf had no way of knowing it, he, his father, and Shaitan the Fallen, all three of them, shared a common problem: their memories were impaired. But where in Shaitan the deficiency had localized itself and was stable, and where in Harry Sr. it gradually improved, in Harry Wolfson it grew worse from moment to moment, and would not improve until he was a wolf entire.

But for now faint memories stirred: of the woman in the hard ground who had suckled him, of a man on a cross who was his father, and of a girl likewise crucified who had been an ally. Also of a battle long, long ago, in a place called the garden, which had been the end of one life and the beginning of another; and of a second, more recent battle in the same place, in which he and his grey brothers had no part but were only observers. He remembered now how he had *planned* to fight in that battle, on the side of the two who were crucified, but . . . he didn't remember his reasons. In any case, it would have made no difference; they'd done their fighting in the air and their warriors were huge, and he and the pack were only wolves. Yet still he felt that he'd somehow failed these poor, crucified creatures: the man unconscious on his cross, and the woman, awake, inured and even resigned now to pain, but not immune to her own black hatred.

Back in the foothills, one of the brothers laid back his head and howled at the moon rising over the mountains. In its lower quarter, the moon was golden with reflected light; soon it would be sunup. Another howl, echoing up to accompany the first, caused Harry Wolfson to issue an instinctive thought: *Hush! Be quiet! Let the sleepers sleep on.*

His brothers heard him, and so did the Lady Karen.

Dweller? Her thoughts were faint, shielded from the minds of sleeping vampires. But they evoked a flood of memories, however blurred. Harry Wolfson knew she spoke to him.

I am that one, he finally answered. And again, *I . . . was that one.* But now he must know the truth and asked her: *Did I . . . betray you?*

The fight? (A shake of her head, telepathically sensed.) *No, that was doomed from the start. Your father and I, we had already seen our futures: golden fire burning in the Möbius Continuum! As for our enemies: we thought we'd seen the end of them, too, but we were mistaken. For it appears that their futures don't lie here in Starside but in the world beyond the Gate.* Pictures accompanied her words—a scenario straight out of the Necroscope's and her own trip in future time—and she wondered if he would understand them.

He did, and: *I'm sorry.* But his memories were sharper now and coming faster. *My father should have known better: to read the future is a devious thing.*

Aye, she agreed. *I thought the golden fire might be that of the sun. But no, it was only . . . fire. They both burn, it's true, but Shaithis's will burn the worst, because it is his. I hate the black bastard!*

He saw the logs and branches heaped beneath her. *Shaithis will burn you?*

What's left, when his warriors are through with me. And even in a wolf's mind, she read horror.

Is there anything I can do? Harry Wolfson came closer, on his belly, creeping between thralls where they lay in an open circle around the two central black tents.

Go away, she answered. *Back into the mountains. Save yourself. Become a wolf entire. Eat what you kill and never bite a man or woman, lest they suffer your fate!*

But . . . we were together at the garden, he said. And in his mind she saw again the fire and death and destruction.

Yes, but you were a power then. You and your weapons. But no sooner that last thought than suddenly there was another in her head. One of revenge. *Does anything remain of your armory?*

His mind was wandering again; he looked this way and that and wondered what he was doing here; his recently pregnant bitch would be hungry where she waited for him. *Armory?*

He couldn't remember, so she showed him a picture. *Can you bring me one of these?*

Some two hundred yards away out on the boulder plain, a sated warrior snorted in its sleep. Harry Wolfson snaked back into the shadows, loped for the foothills to rejoin the pack. A single thought came back to Karen before the connection was broken. *Farewell!*

And hanging there in her pain, in the night and the chill of Starside, she thought: *He won't remember.*

But she was wrong.

He came again, but barely in time; came with the clouds from the south, with the first warm rain, with the grey light glowing in the sky beyond the mountains; he came with the false dawn, before the true dawn of sunup, and braved the circle of thralls where now they scratched and muttered in their sleep.

And climbing the logs and branches of Karen's pyre, he stood upon his hind legs, face-to-face, as if to kiss her. But her mouth gaped like a gash in her metamorphic face, and what passed between the two was not a kiss.

Wizard, Necroscope, wake up!

Harry gave a start as Shaithis's thoughts lashed him like a whip; his thoughts, and then his spoken words: "Your torment will soon be over, Necroscope. So open your eyes and say good-bye to all of this. To your Lady, your life . . . to everything."

Harry's thoughts had something of form and order; his

mind was almost healed; his body, not nearly so. Silver was present in his vampire blood like grains of arsenic, so that his broken flesh and bones couldn't mend. But he heard Shaithis taunting him and felt a splash of rain, and opened his soulful eyes in the dark grey predawn light. Then he almost wished he was blind.

Lieutenants of Shaithis were up on ladders, bringing Karen down from her cross. Her head rolled this way and that and her limbs flopped loosely as they tossed her down on a blanket upon the stony ground. Shaithis turned from Harry's cross, went to his tent, and slashed through its ropes, collapsing it like a deflated balloon.

"And so you see, Necroscope," he crowed, "how I intend to honor my promise. For perceiving that you now see, hear, and understand all, this time—for the *last* time—I shall take her in the open. No thrill in it for me, not any more; this time my labors are all for you. And when I'm done, then you shall witness how my warriors deal with her! As well to keep one's creatures happy, eh? For after all, they too were men, upon a time."

The rain came on harder and Shaithis issued commands. His thralls ripped the collapsed tent into two halves, then used its torn skins to cover the faggots of the torture pyres. It would not do for them to get too wet. Shaithis had meanwhile returned to the foot of the cross; Shaitan too, from his own tent. More leech than man, the Fallen One's eyes were glowing embers in the shadow of a black, corrugated cowl of flesh.

"It's time," he said, his voice a phlegmy cough, "and the Gate awaits. I say have done with all this. Put the woman on her pyre and burn them."

Shaithis paused. He was reminded, however briefly, of his old dream. But dreams are for dreamers, and he was weary now of all dark omens—especially his ancestor's warnings. "This man was the cause of my exile in the

Icelands," he answered. "I vowed revenge, and now I take it."

They glared at each other, Shaitan and Shaithis. There in the Gate's white dazzle, their eyes blazed where they measured one another. But finally, the Fallen One turned away. "As you will," he said, but quietly. "So be it."

The clouds were flown and the rain had stopped. Shaithis called his thralls to light torches. He took a torch and held it up to Harry on his cross. "Well, Necroscope, and why don't you call up the dead? My ancestor has told me that in your own world you were their champion, and I saw you call up crumbling trogs in the battle for The Dweller's garden. So why not now?"

Harry hadn't the strength for it (which his tormentor knew well enough), but even if he were strong he knew that the dead wouldn't answer him. No, for he was a vampire and they had forsaken him. But in the foothills behind the Gate, a grey shape fretted and whined, prowling to and fro, to and fro; and the pack watching him intently through feral eyes, where they lay with their tongues lolling and ears erect. The great wolf's memory was imperfect and his nature devolving, but for now he understood the Necroscope's every thought. In a bygone time, as a human infant, Harry Wolfson's mind had been one with his father's.

The Necroscope sensed his son there, felt his concern, and at once closed his mind to external scrying. It was an effort, but he did it. Shaitan knew it at once, flowed forward, and said to Shaithis, "Get on with it. This one's not finished, I tell you! Now he has closed his mind, so that we don't know what's brewing in there."

"In just a little while," the other snarled, "his *brains* will be brewing in there! But for now, leave . . . me . . . *be!*"

And again Shaitan backed off.

"Well, Harry Keogh?" Shaithis called up to the crucified man. He waved his torch and tugged aside the skins from the dry branches of the balefires. "And did you think to shut me out from your delicious agonies? And can you ignore the pain itself? Ah, we Wamphyri have our arts, it's true: we steel ourselves to the throb of torn flesh and the ache of broken bones; aye, even as they're healing. But the vampire never lived who was insensitive to fire. And you'll feel it, too, Necroscope, when your flesh begins to melt!" He reached down with his torch to the base of the pile. "So what do you say? Should I light it now? Are you ready to burn?"

And at last Harry answered him. "*You* burn, you . . . ordure of trogs and stench of gas-beasts! Burn in hell!"

Shaithis slapped his thigh and laughed like a madman. "Oh? Hah, ha, ha! A taunt for a taunt, eh? What, and do you think to insult your executioner?" He touched his torch to tufts of kindling and a wisp of smoke at once curled up, then a small tongue of flame.

And in the shadowy foothills Harry Wolfson issued an ululating howl, then turned and at a fast lope headed downhill for the tableau set in the light of the Gate. The grey brotherhood made to accompany him, but he stopped them:

No! Return to your mountains. What befalls me befalls.

Flames licked up from Harry's pyre, small bright tongues but gaining rapidly. Shaithis went to Karen, where his thralls held her down. She was conscious now, would throw them off but had no strength for it. "Necroscope," the vampire Lord continued to taunt, "wanderer in strange worlds and stranger spaces between the worlds. Now say, why don't you conjure one of your mysterious boltholes and come down from your cross? Step down and challenge me face-to-face, and champion this bitch whose flesh we've both known. Come, Necroscope, save her from my embrace."

Instinctively, Harry's metaphysical mind began to conjure Möbius math. Invisible to all other men, the shimmering frame of a door commenced to form in the eye of his mind. Except, of course, it was warped and highly volatile. Only let it develop fully and all of this would be over: so close to the Gate, Harry would probably be shredded and his atoms diffused through the myriad universes of light. Maybe that was the answer, the way to go. At least he would be spared the agony of the fire. But what of the agony of others? What of the *future* agony of the entire world which lay beyond the Gate?

Too late to worry about that: Earth was already doomed. Or was it? For Harry knew that miracles *can* happen, and also that they occasionally happen when all seems lost. But in any case, he could always conjure another door—a bigger, more powerful door—when things became unbearable. But:

No! said Harry Wolfson in the Necroscope's inner mind, even as he thought to collapse what he'd made. *Hold it there, Father. Just for a moment.* And Harry felt his son looking at the Möbius equations where they mutated in his mind, and at the flickering, warping configuration of the part-formed door. Looking, trying hard to understand . . . and finally remembering!

In another moment the great wolf conjured equations which even Harry in the fullness of his powers could never have identified, symbols revenant of a time when the Necroscope's son had been far more powerful than his father. For a few seconds certain of Harry Wolfson's lost talents were recalled, and with the effortless skill of all but forgotten times he used one of them to diffuse *through* his father's ill-formed door a picture of their here and now, and a warning of possible tomorrows. It sped out from him at the instantaneous speed of thought, into all the innumerable universes of light.

The Necroscope canceled his own numbers and let go of the now highly dangerous door, which drifted away from him towards the magnet of the Gate. But his son's message—and his warning—had been transmitted. Harry Wolfson had completed the mental part of his self-imposed mission; all that remained now was the physical. But where the first had been merely improbable, the rest was impossible. That made no difference, not to the great grey wolf, who remembered now that he had been a man. As well, then, to die like a man.

In through the encircling thralls he loped, like a wraith appearing from the smoke of Harry's fire. And snarling he made for Shaithis where the vampire Lord kneeled beside Karen. But he didn't make it; lieutenants got in his way; one of them hurled a spear and brought him down. Slavering and snarling, with the spear transfixing his breast and emerging bloody through his hackles, still his slender human hands reached spastically for Lord Shaithis—until a sword flashed silver and took his head.

From his cross, through billowing smoke (though the flames had not yet reached him), Harry had seen it all. "No!" he cried out loud. And in his mind cried out again: *No . . . no . . . no!!!* And something of his agony, not merely of the flesh but of the soul, went out through the disintegrating Möbius door, which on the instant imploded into the Gate. Then—

—A single, brilliant, prolonged flash of lightning illuminating the peaks, followed by a long, low, ominous drumroll of thunder, and finally a silence broken only by the crackle of the bonfire and the sputtering of fresh raindrops striking the flames.

Until, for the third time, Shaitan came forward.

"You cannot feel it, can you?" He stood over his descendant, glared at him awhile, then lifted his head to sniff like some great hound. "The Necroscope has released something into the air, and into his secret places. But you feel only your own lust. You've neither thought nor vision for the future, only for what you can take today. And so I warn you one last time: beware, son of my sons, lest you lose us a world!"

Shaithis's face was twisted in its madness; he was first and foremost Wamphyri, and now allowed his vampire full sway. A beast, his hands were transformed into talons. Blood slopped from his great jaws where his teeth elongated into fangs and tore the flesh of his mouth. With Karen's once crowning, now lusterless hair bunched in his fist, he looked up at Shaitan and beyond him to the man on the cross. And his eyes blazed scarlet as he answered.

"I should feel something? Some weird, mystical thing? All I desire to feel is the Necroscope's agony, and the flight of his and his vampire's spirit as he dies. But if I can hurt him a little more *before* he dies, so be it!"

"Fool!" And a heavy, grey-mottled appendage of Shaitan's—a thing half-hand, half-claw—fell on Shaithis's shoulder. He shrugged it off and came easily to his feet. And:

"Ancestor mine," he ground the words out, "you have pushed me too far. And I sense that I shall never be free of your interference in my affairs. We'll talk more about that—shortly. But until then . . ." With a mind-call, he brought forward his warrior out of the shadows, placing the creature between himself and Shaitan the Fallen.

Shaitan backed off and gloomed on the warrior— which, in the Icelands, had been Shaithis's most recent construct prior to their departure—and inquired of his descendant, "Are you threatening my life?"

Shaithis knew that sunup was nigh and time of the

essence; he had none of the latter to waste right now; he would confront his ancestor later, possibly after the fortress beyond the Gate had been taken. And so: ''Threatening your life?'' he answered. ''Of course not. We are allies, the last of the Wamphyri! But we are also individuals, with our individual needs.''

For which reason Shaitan in his turn let Shaithis live. For the moment.

And as the fire smoked and blazed up brighter, despite a renewed downpour, and as Harry Keogh felt the first breath of heat where flames closed in towards his lower limbs, Shaithis again turned his attentions to the Lady Karen.

While in another world.

. . . It was midnight in the Urals.

Deep under the Perchorsk ravine, in the confines of his small room, Viktor Luchov snatched himself awake from a monstrous nightmare. Panting and trembling, still only half awake, he stood up on jelly legs and gazed all about at the grey-metal walls, and leaned on one for its support. His dream had been so real—it had impressed him so badly—that his first thought had been to press his alarm button and call out to the men he kept stationed in the corridor outside. Even now he would do so, except (and as he'd learned only too well the last time) such an action could well be fraught with a terror of its own. Especially in the claustrophobic, nerve-racking confines of the Perchorsk Projekt. He had no desire to have anyone come bursting in here with the smoking, red-glowing muzzle of a flamethrower at the ready.

As his heartbeat slowed a little and while he fumblingly dressed, he examined his nightmare: a strange, even ominous thing. In it, he had heard an awful, tortured cry go out from the Gate at Perchorsk's core, and he'd known its author: Harry Keogh! The Necroscope had cried out his telepathic anguish to any and all who could hear him, but mainly to the teeming dead in their myriad resting places across the world. And in their turn they had answered him as best they could—with a massed moaning and groaning, even with their soft and crumbling *movements*—from the airless environs of their innumerable graves. For the dead knew how they had misjudged the Necroscope, how they'd denied and finally forsaken him, and it was as if they were grief-stricken and preparing for a new Golgotha.

And the departed spirit of Paul Savinkov—a man who had worked for KGB Major Chingiz Khuv right here at Perchorsk, worked and died here, horribly—had materialized and spoken to the Projekt Direktor in his dream, telling him about the warning which Harry Keogh's son had sent out through the Gate. For in life Savinkov had been a telepath, and his talent had stayed with him, continuing into the afterlife.

And seeing in Luchov's mind the nuclear solution to the threat from beyond the Gate, Savinkov had told him: *Then you know what to do, Viktor.*

"Do?"

Yes, for they are coming, through the Gate, and you know how to stop them!

"Coming? Who is coming?"

You know who.

Luchov had understood, and answered: "But those weapons may not be used until we are sure. Then, when we can see the threat—"

—It will be too late! Savinkov cried. *If not for us, too late for Harry Keogh. We've all wronged him and now must make amends, for he suffers needless agonies. Wake up, Viktor. It's in your hands now.*

"My God!" Luchov had tossed and turned, but Savinkov had seen that he wouldn't wake. Not yet. But . . . there were others sleeping here who would. And then, when Luchov heard the telepath talking again—*to whom, and what he asked, begged them to do!*—that was when he'd started awake.

Now he was dressed and almost in control of himself, but still breathless, still alert and listening, tuned into the Projekt's heartbeat. The dull throb of an engine somewhere, reverberating softly through the floor; the clang of a hatch, echoing distantly; the hum and rattle of the ventilation system. In the old days the Direktor had been accommodated on an upper level, much closer to the exit shaft. Up there, it had seemed quieter, less oppressive. But down here, with the magmass caverns and the core almost directly underfoot, it could be that he felt the entire mountain weighing on his shoulders.

Still listening intently, Luchov's breathing and heartbeat gradually slowed as it became apparent that all was in order and it really had been a dream. Only a terrible dream. Or had it?

That sudden clatter of running footsteps, coming closer in the corridor outside. And voices shouting hoarse warnings! *Now, what in the world . . . ?*

He went to open the door to the corridor and heard in the back of his mind, like an echo from his dream: *But Viktor, you already know "what in the world"!* Paul Savinkov's telepathic voice, and clear as a bell. Except this time it was no dream!

A hammering at his door, which Luchov opened with hands which were trembling again. He saw his guards, astonishment written in their drawn, tired faces, and a pair of gaunt technicians just this moment arrived here from the core. "Comrade Direktor!" one of the latter gasped, clawing at his arm. "Direktor Luchov! I . . . I would have telephoned, but the lines are under repair."

Luchov could see that the technician was stalling; the man was terrified to report what must be reported, because he knew it was unbelievable. And now for the first time there sounded the sharp *crack! crack! crack!* of distant gunshots. At that, galvanized, Luchov found strength to croak, "It's not . . . something from the Gate?"

"No, no! But there are . . . things!"

Luchov's flesh crawled. "Things?"

"From *under* the Gate! From the abandoned magmass regions. And oh God, they are dead things, Comrade Direktor!"

Dead things. The sort of things Harry Keogh would understand, and which understood him only too well. And according to the warnings of a dead man, the worst of it still to come. But hadn't Luchov tried to warn Byzarnov what could happen? And hadn't he advised him to press that damned button right there and then? Of course he had, even knowing at the time that the Major didn't fully understand, and that in any case circumstances didn't warrant it. Also, Byzarnov was a military man and had his orders. Well, circumstances had changed; maybe now he would put his orders aside and take matters into his own hands.

Luchov had experienced and lived through similar disasters before. Now he felt torn two ways: should he make his escape to the upper levels and abandon the Projekt entirely, or should he see what could be done down below? His conscience won. There were men down there, after all—just following bloody orders! He headed for the core.

As he ran along the angled, split-level steel ramp through the upper magmass cavern to the steep stairwell leading down to the Gate, the Projekt Direktor heard the first shouts, screams, and more gunshots from the core. The technicians were right behind him; his own men, too, armed with SMGs and a flamethrower. But as he approached the actual shaft where it spilled light from the Gate up into the cavern, so Major Alexei Byzarnov's voice echoed from behind, calling for him to wait. In a moment the Major had caught up.

"I was alerted," he gasped. "The messenger was incoherent. A gibbering idiot! Can't you tell me what's going on, Viktor?"

Though Luchov hadn't seen it yet—not with his own eyes—still he had a fair idea what was "going on"; but there was no way he could explain it to Byzarnov. Far better to let him see it for himself. So that when he answered, "I don't know what's happening," his simple lie was in fact a half-truth.

In any case, there was no time for further conversation. For as a renewed burst of screams and gunshots rang out, so the Major grasped Luchov's arm and shouted, "Then we'd damn well better find out!"

A box of plastic eye shields lay at the head of the ramp just inside the shaft. Byzarnov, Luchov, and his guards each paused to snatch up a pair of tinted lenses before continuing down to the core. There they emerged in a group, spreading out onto a railed platform high in the inward-curving wall. From that vantage point, looking down on the glaring Gate with its reflective perimeter of steel plates, they could take in the entire, unbelievable tableau in all its horror.

Dead men—once-men who had become hideous mag-mass *composites*, whose stench was overpowering even up here—were active in the core, coming up through hatches in the fish-scale plates, invading the safety perimeter and the rubber-floored area of the missile launcher. There were nine of them all told, six of whom had already emerged and moved clear of the currently inactive electrical and acid spray hazard area. But such was their nature that Byzarnov could scarcely take in what he was seeing. Again clutching Luchov's arm, he reeled like a drunkard at the rail of the platform. "For Christ's sake . . . *what*?" he mouthed, his eyes bugging as they swept over the madness down below.

Luchov knew he need not say anything. The Major could see for himself what these things were. Indeed he had seen several of them before, down there in the magmass, when they had been *part* of the magmass! Some were rotting; others were mummified; none was composed of flesh alone. They were part stone, rubber, metal, plastic, even paper. Some were inverted, with material folded-in which had tried to become homogeneous *with* them. They were magmass, neither pure nor simple but highly complex: magmass at its nightmarish worst.

One of them, guarding the perimeter walkway, had an open book for a hand. He had been reading a repair manual when the original Perchorsk Incident happened, and the book had become a permanent part of him. Now . . . his left forearm mutated into a stiff paper spine at the wrist, with pages fluttering and detaching themselves as he moved. This wasn't the worst of it: the lower half of his trunk had been reversed, so that his feet pointed backwards. Even the plastic frames of his spectacles had warped into his face and bubbled up in crusts of brittle blisters there, while their lenses lay upon his cheeks where first they'd melted, then solidified into tears of optical glass.

And yet he had been one of the . . . luckier ones? Shut in by magmass, crushed in the grip of convulsive forces and confined away from the air, he had died instantly and his fleshy parts had later undergone a process of mummification. But when the Perchorsk Incident was over and space-time righted itself, others had been left dead and twisted and isolated out in the open, and their condition had been such that ordinary men just could not bring themselves to tend to them. Fully or partly exposed—occasionally joined to the greater magmass whole or partly encysted within it—they had simply been left to . . . *degrade*, in areas of the Projekt which were then sealed and abandoned. Eventually, their human parts had rotted down to deformed skeletons, for even bone had been subject to change, in those awful moments when matter had devolved to its inchoate origins.

Byzarnov saw men who were part machine. He saw a creature with a face composed of a welding torch jutting from a crumpled oxygen-cylinder skull. Another was skeletal from the waist down but encysted around the chest and head in glassy stone, like a figure in a half space suit. Spiky magmass crystals were growing out of the fused bone of his legs, and behind the glass of his "viewplate," his unaltered face was still trapped in an endless scream. Another was legless, a half-man which the magmass warp had equipped at the hips with the wheels of a porter's trolley. He propelled himself with arms which were black where scorched flesh had shriveled into the bone. The trolley's long wooden handles projected upwards from his shoulders like weird antennae framing his head.

The twisted, mummied hybrids were bad enough; the semimechs were worse; but worst of all were those who were partly liquescent, who but for their magmass parts must simply collapse into stinking ruin.

Byzarnov had almost stopped breathing; he started again with a gasp, said, "But . . . how? And what are they doing?" He turned to one of his terrified technicians. "Why haven't we fried them, or melted them with acid?"

"The first one up made it to the defense mechanism," the man told him. "He ripped out the wiring.

No one lifted a hand to stop him, not then. No one believed . . .''

Byzarnov could understand that. "But what do they want?''

"Are you blind?'' Luchov started down the steps. "Can't you see for yourself?''

And indeed Byzarnov could see for himself. The nine once-men had isolated the exorcet module; they were closing in on it, invading it. Three of the Major's technicians, together with a handful of Perchorsk's soldiers, were trying to hold them off. An impossible task. Dead men don't feel pain. Shoot at these magmass monsters all they would, the launcher's defenders couldn't kill them a second time.

"But . . . why?'' Byzarnov came stumbling down the steps after Luchov. Behind them on the platform, the other technicians and Luchov's guards were reluctant to follow. "What's their intention?''

"To press the bloody button!'' Luchov barked. "They may be dead, warped, weird, but they're not stupid. We're the stupid ones.''

At the foot of the steps, the Major caught up and grasped Luchov's shoulder. "Press the button? Fire the missiles? But they mustn't!''

Luchov turned on him. "But they must! Don't you see? Whatever brought them up knew more than we do. The dead don't walk for just anyone or anything. No, they need a damn good reason to put themselves to torture such as this!''

"Madman!'' Byzarnov hissed. He was close to breaking. "Oh, quite obviously this is some long-term, alien effect of this totally unnatural place, but these reanimated—*things*—can't have any real purpose. They're blind, insensate, dead!''

"They want to launch those missiles,'' Luchov shouted

in the other's face, over the clamor of discharged weapons, "and we have to help them!"

At which the Major knew that the Projekt Direktor really was mad. "Help them?" He drew his pistol and pointed it at Luchov's chest. "You poor, crazy bastard! Get the hell back away from there!"

Luchov turned from him, hurried along the rubber-floored safety perimeter towards the creature with the page-shedding manual hand. "It's all right," he was gasping. "Let me pass. I'll do it for you." And to Byzarnov's amazement, the thing shuffled aside for him.

"Like hell you will!" the Major shouted, and squeezed the trigger of his automatic. The bullet hit Luchov in the right shoulder and passed right through, punching out in a scarlet spray from a hole in his chest. He was thrown forward, facedown on the walkway, where he lay still for a moment. And Byzarnov came on, aiming at him a second time.

But the magmass things knew an ally when they saw one. The thing with the book hand got in Byzarnov's way, blocking his aim, while another, whose limbs were cased in stony magmass welded to a trunk which was a jumble of fused bone, rubber, and glass, came lurching to the Direktor's assistance. The Major fired at this one point-blank, time and again, to no avail. But as the thing loomed in front of him, finally a shot cracked the magmass casing of its left arm. The brittle sheath fragmented at once, and a black, vile soup—a decomposed mush of flesh—began leaking from inside.

Almost overwhelmed by the stench, the Major fell against the curving wall. Still the rotting hybrid came on. Byzarnov lifted his pistol and pulled the trigger, and the firing mechanism made a click! He had a spare magazine in his pocket. He reached for it . . .

. . . And the magmass thing closed a bony hand on

his windpipe. Byzarnov choked. He could see Luchov getting to his feet, staggering, moving towards the launching module, where most of the defenders had either fainted or stampeded in terror. Only one technician and one soldier remained there now; their weapons were empty; they danced, gibbered, and clung together like children as decomposing nightmares closed in on them.

But Luchov: two of the magmass composites were *helping* him, supporting him where he lurched towards the firing console!

The Major made a final effort, drew the spare magazine from his pocket and tried to fit it into the housing in the pistol grip of his weapon. As he did so, the magmass sheath fell away completely from his assailant's left arm. Byzarnov opened his mouth to yell or throw up . . . and the anomalous thing stuffed its skeletal arm and envelope of jellied, rotting flesh right down his throat!

The Major gagged and vibrated where the thing pinned him. His eyes stood out in his head and his heart stopped. He died there and then, but not before he'd seen Luchov at the firing console. Not before he'd seen him slump there and crumple to the rubber floor, even as the claxons began bellowing their final warning.

In Starside, Harry Keogh burned. The rain was a drizzle which tried but couldn't damp down the flames, and the Necroscope burned. He burned inside and out: fire on the outside, and a burning, consuming hatred within. For Shaithis, who even now took the Lady Karen by force, there in front of Harry's cross. She seemed completely exhausted, resisted not at all as he tore at her. And Harry thought: *A beast, even a warrior, could do no worse.* But he hoped he'd be dead before that was put to the test.

A moment ago, he had tried to conjure a Möbius door—the biggest door of all, right there in front of the

Gate—which with any luck would implode massively and suck the vampires and their creatures and all into eternity. But the numbers wouldn't come, the computer screen of his mind had stayed blank. It was as if his skills had died with his wolf son, like a slate wiped clean. And indeed such was the case: after a lifetime of esoteric use, finally Harry's mind had given way, crumpled under the weight of one too many tragedies. Now he was a man again, just a man, and the vampire inside him too immature even to flee his melting body.

"Come down, Necroscope," Shaithis taunted. "Should I leave some of this bitch for you?"

The flames were licking higher now, and black smoke belching. Shaitan had somehow got round the obstacle of Shaithis's warrior and stood observing all across a short distance. And for all that the Fallen One was alien, unmanlike, unreadable, still there was that in his poise— the way his eyes stared out from the darkness of his cowl—which spoke of an almost human uncertainty and apprehension. As if he'd seen all this before, and now waited for some awesome termination.

Harry's lower trunk was being eaten alive by fire. Now he must sleep and escape from the agonies of life forever. Except . . . instead of blacking out, suddenly he felt the pain laved away from him, deflected, turned outwards. And he knew that this was not simply an art of the Wamphyri. His body burned, but the pain was someone else's. *Many* someones were absorbing it: all the dead of Starside who, now that it was too late, only desired to comfort him.

No, he tried to tell them, trogs and Travellers alike. *You have to let me die!* But his deadspeak wasn't working.

"Where's your power now?" Shaithis laughed. "If you're so strong, set yourself free. Call up the teeming dead. Curse me with Words of Power, Necroscope. *Hah!* Your words, like the dead themselves, are dust!''

And somehow, from somewhere, Harry found the strength to answer. ''Put yourself aside, Shaithis. The sight of you hurts worse than any fire. These flames are a blessing: they cleanse you from my sight!''

''Enough!'' Shaithis raged, foaming over Karen like a scummy wave. ''One last kiss and she's gone, and you with her!'' He fell on her; his jaws cracked open; he began to close his mouth over Karen's face, to crush her head—

—And her scarlet eyes opened into blazing life.

Perhaps she also opened her mind, to let Shaithis read his doom. At any rate, he tried to rear back from her. But no, her arms and legs were around him and their metamorphic flesh was welded into one. And coughing up The Dweller's grenade into her throat, Karen pulled the pin with her forked tongue and buried her face in her tormentor's gaping jaws!

Shaithis tried to separate from her . . . Another second and he might succeed . . . Too late!

Goodbye, Harry, she said.

And the darkness of Starside was split by a single flash of light, accompanied by a detonation only slightly muffled by the flesh and bone which it turned to grey and crimson pulp!

As the red spray settled and their headless, shuddering bodies fell apart, Shaitan flowed forward to stand over them. He ignored Karen, saw only the shell of Shaithis. And reaching a clawed tentacle into the shattered cavity of his descendant's neck, Shaitan drew out his whipping, decapitated leech; drew it out and hurled it into the heart of the bonfire—and laughed! For Shaithis had no head, no brain. And Shaitan had no body. Not the body he wanted, anyway. Not yet!

"You fool," he told the empty shell of flesh. "And would you set your warrior on me? We were of one blood, you and I, but my grip on the minds of creatures such as these was ever greater than yours! Close on three thousand years I listened to old Kehrl Lugoz moaning in his ice-encased sleep, cursing me in his dreams. Did you think I would not notice when suddenly he stopped?

"Ah, he cursed me, but he was craven, too. Did you really think to inspire your construct with *his* hatred and passions? What? Old Kehrl? He *had* no passion, not any longer! And as for 'hatred' ":

He turned and hurled a mental dart at Shaithis's warrior, which at once reared up and shrank back, mewling. "You do not know the meaning of the word! What, hatred? And how I have hated *you!* If I had let my jealousy loose . . . why, I could have killed you a hundred times! But never so sweetly as this."

He flowed up to Shaithis, picked up his loosely flopping corpse, and hugged it close. And Shaitan's black, corrugated flesh began to crack open down all its length, like a wrinkled nut displaying its soft kernel. Within the cavity of his ancient trunk, a smaller, more flexible, and yet more durable version of himself—the *original* vampire—was waiting, as it had waited these thousands of years. But Shaitan's plan, to join with flesh of his flesh and so be renewed, was not to be.

For the two Harrys had sent out word of their agony not only into Starside, Earth, and all the worlds beyond, but also into the spaces between them. Their travails were known by all the teeming dead, and their warnings had been heard by Others who were not dead and never can be.

In the same moment, Shaitan and the Necroscope sensed the One Great Truth. Harry knew, and Shaitan . . . finally, he remembered!

"Ahhhh!" the Fallen One gasped, staggered by the memory. Even as his vampire struggled to be free of the old shell and into Shaithis, so the eyes under his cowl looked up at Harry Keogh, burning on his cross. He looked at his face, framed in fire, and *knew* where he had seen it before!

But now he saw (or sensed rather than saw, it was that swift) something else. Something that flashed silver out of the Gate's white glare, and then became an even greater glare as a nuclear sun burst over Starside to briefly rival the dawn. And between the coming of the exorcet and the bursting of its all-consuming warhead, Shaitan saw something else: a sight which might have drawn one last, long sigh from that Prime Evil's throat . . . except he was no more.

It was Harry's cross, but *empty* now and pierced by the spears of a great light, where at last it was blasted to atoms . . .

Epilog

DEATH: HARRY WONDERED WHY HE'D FEARED IT. FOR of all men, the Necroscope had known it wasn't like that. Because he had been there before. Incorporeal, bodiless as any dead thing whose flesh has finally failed, he was now free of all that. Except that in his case it seemed a mundane death wasn't part of the scenario.

He had always known that death wasn't the end: that whatever a man pursues in life, he will habitually pursue in his afterlife continuation. Harry Keogh had been the master of the Möbius Continuum; so it was hardly a surprise to find himself there now, in Möbius time, hurtling back among the blue, green, and red threads of Starside into their remote past. A surprise . . . no, but strange, anyway, for in the end *he* had not conjured a door. *He* had not contrived an escape.

Which could only mean that he'd been . . . rescued?

But by Whom? And if indeed Someone or Ones had seen fit to save his incorporeal mind, what possible purpose could He or They have with his burned, vampiric body? For as Harry shot back into Starside's past, he saw his separate, smoking corpse tumbling alongside, winding back on its scarlet thread to his point of entry into Starside, and then plunging on beyond it. And he went with it, but incorporeal, apart, speeding blindly into times he'd never physically known.

As for his ruined shell's destination—and his own, for that matter—and the question of Who was their guide . . .

Harry had never in his life been one hundred percent sure, *positively* sure, about God or *a* god. But back there in Starside he'd sensed the arrival, the presence of a Power, and had known that Shaitan sensed it, too. Moreover, he had known the source of that Power, and also that Möbius and Pythagoras before him had been right.

Now . . . Harry and his exanimate shell were mere impulses in the Mind he had called the Möbius Continuum, integers in the infinite matrix of the Great Unknowable Equation. And he wasn't afraid when at long last that Mind itself spoke to him:

Things have uses, Harry, always. What use to create, if your efforts are only to be wasted? Sometimes we succeed, and sometimes we fail. But there are always uses for the best, and for the worst, of our works.

Harry couldn't tell if an answer had been invited, and in any case he didn't really have one. But he did have a question, however brief. "God?"

He sensed a vast shrug. *A creator, an advisor, an angel? God is . . . let's say He's a few steps higher up the ladder. His mind, as you know, is vast! We carry His thoughts, expedite His wishes. As best we can.*

"I've had my doubts," Harry admitted.

So do we, sometimes. So did Shaitan, when he was one of us . . . Except he would have tried to convince everyone that he was right, throughout all the Universes of Light! He would have forced their belief—in him!

Harry believed he understood. And understanding should have been enough. But because he was or had been human—and because he saw that his course was veering, angling away from his tumbling corpse—even now he was curious. So that he asked, "What now?"

Your feet are on the first few rungs. You've made your point, chosen your course and stuck to it. You are a success story. We don't believe in waste; we certainly, wouldn't waste someone as valuable as you! Like Shaitan, you won't remember, but you will know! *Except where he knew only a great darkness, you shall know light. In all of your worlds.*

"All of my . . . ?"

Wherever you manifest. For His worlds are infinite as His thoughts.

"And . . . that?" Harry indicated his blackened shell where it grew small, tumbling towards some undefined purpose.

Causes have effects, and effects causes. Nothing may come to pass which has not passed before. The world of Sunside and Starside was a failure where evil won. So maybe a second chance is in order. Also it will occupy Shaitan, who has balanced himself against light in a great many worlds. Here . . . he begins again, on the bottom rung. For as you well know, Harry Keogh, what will be has been. Time is relative.

Harry's turn to shrug. With no vampire in him, he was innocent again. The very heart of innocence. "It's all very hard to understand," he said, "but I suppose I'll learn as I go."

Oh, you will! the other promised. And: *Are you ready?*

Harry's corpse had cartwheeled out of sight into the multihued haze of past time. Pure thought, he had no body, no head to nod; but his deadspeak nodded for him. And as his incorporeal mind fragmented in a glorious bomb burst—a hundred golden splinters, breaking up and speeding into as many worlds—his thoughts and even his deadspeak were at an end.

Except each and every one of those brilliant shards, they were him . . . and they *would* know.

Starting into awareness, Shaitan cried out.

He cried out as he felt consciousness cloaking an intelligence previously bereft, will without knowledge inhabiting a mind wiped clean. He discovered himself kneeling at the edge of stagnant water and saw his image mirrored in scummy depths. And when he saw that he was naked, he was ashamed; but when he saw that he was beautiful, he was proud. For shame and pride are of the spirit, not of intelligence.

Standing upright, Shaitan saw that he could walk. And in the twilight of a dim, misty dawn he moved by the edge of the dark, rank waters, which were a swamp. And he saw how dismal and lonely was this place where he had fallen, or into which he had been cast. So that he knew himself for a sinner, and the place as his punishment.

Such knowledge defined his nature: that he instinctively *understood* such concepts as sin and punishment. And he thought his crime must be that he was beautiful, which was his pride working; which was in fact his crime! For Shaitan saw Beauty as Might, and Might as Right, and Right as he willed it to be.

Which was a will he would impose.

So thinking, he moved away from the rank waters and went to impose his will upon this strange world. But in the moment he turned away, so the mud bubbled up behind him, and he paused to look back where black bubbles came bursting to the surface.

And with the parting of the weeds, Shaitan saw a figure floating up into view. In its body it was bloated and burned, but its face was whole. He knew it for an omen, but of what? He had will: he could wait and discover what would be, or move on, according to his will. Also, he suspected that this thing in the swamp harbored evil; why else would such an unclean thing be here, in a world which was new? For a moment he stood still, as at a crossroads . . . then turned back, and knelt again beside the swamp. For he had willed it that he would know this evil.

He gazed upon a face he had never known, which he would not recall to memory for numberless years, and sensed nothing of moment except that he tempted fate, which he was proud and glad to do. And as the beasts of this dawn world came to the water to drink, and as the mists were drawn up from the swamp, so the Fallen One gazed upon his own future where the weeds anchored it in scum and slime.

In a while the scorched, bloated limbs of the corpse split open and small black mushrooms clustered there, growing out of the rotting flesh and opening their gilled caps. They released red spores into the twilight before the dawn, which of his own free will Shaitan breathed: his last act of any innocence.

The wheel had turned full circle and the cycle was closed.

And opened . . .